I0631467

THE CHESAN LEGACY SERIES BOOK TWO

CHAOS
UNLEASHED

D. E. WILLIAMS

Williams Works

This book is a work of fiction. All plots, themes, dates, events, persons, characters, and character descriptions contained in this material are completely fictional. Any resemblance to any events, persons, or characters, real or fictional, living or deceased, is entirely coincidental and unintentional. Williams Works Publishing, LLC and D.E. Williams are not responsible for any use of the character names or any resemblance of these character names to actual persons, living or deceased.

Published in the USA by
Williams Works Publishing LLC
7112 Tesuque Drive NW
Albuquerque, NM USA 87120

Printed in the U.S.A.

First Edition

Cover Design by Rick Holland at Vision Press - myvisionpress.com

Author photo: Emily Smith Photography

Copyright © 2018 by D.E. Williams. All rights reserved. No part of this publication may be reproduced, stored in a retrieval system or transmitted in any form or by any means, electronic, mechanical, photocopying, recording, or otherwise without the prior written permission of the copyright holder, except brief quotations used in a review.

ISBN-13: 978-0-9969080-2-3
Library of Congress Control Number: 2018909392

For

CLARE DAVIS

Thank you, my friend.

CONTENTS

Acknowledgments   i

1   Chapter One   1

2   Chapter Two   13

3   Chapter Three   27

4   Chapter Four   40

5   Chapter Five   48

6   Chapter Six   61

7   Chapter Seven   73

8   Chapter Eight   82

9   Chapter Nine   94

10   Chapter Ten   102

11   Chapter Eleven   107

12   Chapter Twelve   122

13   Chapter Thirteen   133

14   Chapter Fourteen   148

15   Chapter Fifteen   159

16   Chapter Sixteen   172

17   Chapter Seventeen   176

18   Chapter Eighteen   183

19   Chapter Nineteen   192

20   Chapter Twenty   200

21 Chapter Twenty-One 211

22 Chapter Twenty-Two 221

23 Chapter Twenty-Three 223

24 Chapter Twenty-Four 226

25 Chapter Twenty-Five 230

26 Chapter Twenty-Six 239

27 Chapter Twenty-Seven 247

28 Chapter Twenty-Eight 259

29 Chapter Twenty-Nine 271

30 Chapter Thirty 276

31 Chapter Thirty-One 292

32 Chapter Thirty-Two 301

33 Chapter Thirty-Three 316

34 Chapter Thirty-Four 328

35 Chapter Thirty-Five 339

36 Chapter Thirty-Six 349

37 Chapter Thirty-Seven 365

38 Chapter Thirty-Eight 375

39 Chapter Thirty-Nine 392

40 Chapter Forty 400

41 Chapter Forty-One 409

42 Chapter Forty-Two 419

43 Chapter Forty-Three 433

44	Chapter Forty-Four	443
45	Chapter Forty-Five	452
46	Chapter Forty-Six	463
47	Chapter Forty-Seven	474
48	Chapter Forty-Eight	480
49	Chapter Forty-Nine	489
50	Chapter Fifty	500
51	Chapter Fifty-One	510
52	Chapter Fifty-Two	513
53	Chapter Fifty-Three	522
54	Chapter Fifty-Four	528
55	Chapter Fifty-Five	534
56	Chapter Fifty-Six	544
57	Chapter Fifty-Seven	552
	Epilogue	558

ACKNOWLEDGMENTS

This book is an effort on the part of many friends who tirelessly – and relentlessly – encouraged me to finish. I can't thank them enough or give them enough credit for their efforts. My steadfast first readers – some of whom were also second readers and final readers – Clare Davis, Shari Holmes, Kevin Cooley, and Ted Leyerly, gave honest and invaluable feedback and shared their inspirations when I struggled to find the words. The second readers, Dana Jackson, Alex Quinlivan, Katherine Covey, and Dwight Smith, caught so many things – big and small – and helped smooth out the character flaws that I didn't see. My proofreaders, Suzy Davies and Blaine Bachman, caught the last bits with fresh of eyes. Thanks to my friend and mentor, Kirt Hickman, who reminded me that a *good* book is worth the time and effort. My amazing tech support: Kevin Cooley, who talked me down from more than one formatting ledge, and Kristie Fregia, with Texas Webworks, who keeps my beautiful website alive. Thanks to Rick Holland with Vision Press for another eye-catching cover. Amanda Zamarippa, thanks for persevering to read the manuscript while trying to corral three busy kids with your husband's at sea. I know there will be someone I've forgotten, please forgive me, you know me well enough by now, right? I wouldn't overlook you on purpose. If there are any remaining mistakes or loose ends, I claim them all for myself. Finally, and always, I give glory to God for His many blessings, which include these wonderful friends and family

CHAPTER ONE

"How do you intend to kill Commander Odana?"

Ambassador Brenden Aren paused long enough to glare at his grandmother, Empress Dojene, of the planet Kanu, before returning to his hurried packing.

The empress stood beside the bed in his private chambers waiting for a response. "Well?"

Brenden shoved two clean shirts into his duffle bag before turning to face her. "The *deathstrike* worked well enough the first time, it will suffice again. Failing that, I will have a blaster on my hip as soon as we're out of Core Alliance space."

"You cannot let her live," Dojene insisted. "You will have to ferret out the dangers threatening Prince Drayden another way. The more I think about it, the more I'm convinced she is the danger threatening him."

"I will dispatch her when I've gotten the information I need and not before," Brenden said. "The matter is closed. This mission to rescue your adopted daughter will likely get us all killed anyway."

"Commander Odana is a child matured far beyond her years." Dojene changed the subject. "I assume that's how you managed to produce the vision you saw of the skirmish in the Public Hearing Room? You thought it would be safe to kiss her?"

"Yes. Despite your low opinion of me, I was trying to protect her by leaving her on the hospital ship. The kiss was a ruse to make the doctor think she was my abused concubine. That's all it was."

"Your strategy was flawless. The question is, how did you survive the Chesan enzyme in her kiss? You should have died without further quantities of it – or consummation of your relationship."

Brenden looked away, lifted the duffle bag to his shoulder, and then returned it to the bed. "I *would* have died had not my personal medic met

1

me on the way to Zerathon station and administered drugs to keep me breathing. Afterward, my own Chesan glands developed and counteracted the enzyme."

"What?" Dojene sat heavily on the edge of the bed, her eyes wide and mouth open. "This changes everything."

"This changes nothing," Brenden said. "If I survive this farce of a rescue, you and I need to have discussions about Chesan maturity."

Dojene's stunned look almost brought a smile to his lips.

"Trust me," he said. "I'd sooner blunder through Halzar's nebula unshielded, but you're my only source of information on this matter."

Dojene stood. "This does change everything! Those glands make you vulnerable to Commander Odana. It could keep you from killing her or cloud your judgment regarding her. This discussion can't end here. Whether you feel it now or not, you'll be drawn to the girl because of the enzyme. There are repercussions from being exposed to it without bonding and mating."

Brenden hefted the duffle to his shoulder again and moved toward the door. "I can maintain control until this mission is finished. The Sentinels will separate us if necessary, but I don't have time for a lengthy discussion now. Deeca won't wait if we're late getting to her ship, and there's a lot to do before we leave."

"Just don't be alone with her if you can avoid it," Dojene commanded. "You should kill her."

"I will ask the J'Nai Sentinels to stay with you until you leave for Kanu." Brenden ignored his grandmother's words. "You're welcome to remain here at the embassy for a few days, until we have news of Princess Anza's location."

"The consequences are on your own head, grandson." Dojene said. "I will remain here with the J'Nai until my return to Kanu can be arranged. You'll wish to go directly to Hulac when you're done?"

"If I survive, I'll contact you on a secure channel."

Brenden jerked open the door and almost collided with the ebony-skinned J'Nai Sentinels waiting outside. Their slit-pupiled eyes narrowed. He slammed his mental barriers into place.

Great. Brenden nodded to the two J'Nai. The telepathic clones must have heard his words as well as his thoughts, since neither he nor the empress had bothered to keep their voices down or their minds shielded. The J'Nai would communicate all threats regarding Commander Odana to the Hariok Sentinels, who would be protecting the girl, and travelling with them in Deeca Varin's personal spacecraft. *That's all I need.*

***

Commander Tridia Odana scowled over the jumble of items on the bed in the embassy guest room. She'd emptied her pre-packed duffle bag and rummaged through the clutter of clothing, shoes, hairbands, and other necessities, with a desperate hope of finding the journals Master Aren had mentioned during her trial, or the silver memo disk containing the message from her friend, Davik Schie. Those things weren't among the jumble. Every item was new, compliments of Master Aren, except the blue jumpsuit and scuffed boots she wore. A couple of stray threads indicated the jumpsuit had once had insignia of some kind and the cloth smelled laundered. The boots, though well-worn, were also well cared for. Polish hid most of the blemishes and the linings shaped to her feet as if they had been made for her. Unfortunately, neither jumpsuit nor boots prompted even the smallest memory from the darkness in her mind. Master Aren hadn't wanted her to remember too much about her past without him present to question her. It made sense that he'd keep the journals and disk separate, but she clenched her fist at the thought.

Tridia turned away from the bed with a heavy sigh and caught her reflection in the full-length mirror near the wall. She stepped toward it, massaging her aching shoulder, then rubbing her neck. Her recent transformation from a six-foot-four-inch Felinus warrior to her own slender humanoid frame had left her body in pain and her muscles twitching. She studied her reflection. The last time she'd seen it, she'd beheld a tawny Felinus female with a golden mane of hair. Now, she saw a tall, slender wisp of a girl with a jet-black braid hanging over her shoulder almost to her knee. Her almond-shaped steel-gray eyes drooped with exhaustion, even after she'd showered and sipped huttle juice to revive her stamina. She turned away and stretched her back.

The pain that had settled into every joint and vertebra was significant, but nothing compared to the punishment her mental faculties had received. It started with the freezing mind probes from the Hariok Sentinels. Then Empress Dojene and Master Aren revealed that she *could* plunge the galaxy into chaos and holocaust – and they wanted her dead to prevent it. The mental punishment culminated with the Hariok Sentinels engulfing her in the emotions and pain of visions from a dangerous and emotionally-charged future. The exposure had left her reeling with uncertainty. In the aftermath, she'd retained a lingering mental connection to the Hariok clan's Truthsayer, Winniel, and her mate, Alanel. The Sentinel presence in her mind was a subtle reminder of the vendetta the clan harbored against her – and a constant taunt of guilt for the lives she'd taken.

Tridia struggled with knowing she was an assassin and the Child of Chaos – an unchosen survivor of the holocaust that claimed almost the entire Chesan race – and the part she might play in a horrific future. More difficult was facing the emotions she'd experience in the future. The

3

loyalty, love, and fear she'd held for the young men she'd seen, were foreign in their intensity.

She shook her head. Spending time analyzing things that hadn't happened and over which she had little control made no sense, so she scowled and examined the jumble again.

Master Aren had left her with nothing to prompt a stray memory. He wanted to be privy to every recollection, especially if it had anything to do with Drayden Anjenay. She had no real memory of Drayden. It was Davik Schie who haunted her. She remembered his face and name, but nothing more. Master Aren claimed they were good friends but Davik remained hidden in her memories. Why did she see Davik's face every time someone mentioned Drayden? Could they be the same person?

Tridia let the objects on the bed blur in her vision as she turned her thoughts inward, applying a gentle pressure to the darkness, searching for something more of Davik.

A loud knock made her spin to face the door and throw barriers around her mind. Her heart pounded as she waited for the Sentinels to burst into the room. No one entered and the knock came again.

"Come in," Tridia said, her cheeks warm. If the Sentinels wanted to get to her, they wouldn't have knocked.

A young female acolyte entered, followed closely by two tall, bronze-skinned, blonde-haired Sentinel clones. Alanel and Winniel's beautiful faces held expressions of unconcern that teetered on the edge of boredom. Tridia bristled at the intrusion of Winniel's presence in her mind.

"Commander," the acolyte said. "Ambassador Aren is waiting in the receiving room downstairs and he says you should hurry."

"To be precise," Alanel added. "He said to tell the Commander she's got five minutes to finish up or he will come get her."

A ripple of humor arced through Winniel's connection and Tridia shot a surprised glance in her direction. Sentinels weren't known to possess emotion in any degree.

"Please tell Master – Tell the ambassador I will be downstairs momentarily." Tridia turned back to the jumble on the bed and began to roll and re-pack the items.

The acolyte left, but the Sentinels remained.

Tridia took a bracelet and a pouch from under a pillow and zipped them both into a pocket on her sleeve.

"That is the bracelet and pouch the Felinus doctor gave you, is it not?" Winniel asked.

Tridia removed both items for Winniel to see. She held out the bracelet, made of a rough leather cord strung with stone beads and bone, for examination. Once the Sentinel had studied it, Tridia returned it to her pocket without comment. The pouch she opened to allow Winniel to see the contents.

"It's a stasis pack," Tridia said. "Three injection vials of my own DNA to keep me stabilized – if I can get to them in time. Two Felinus, if I'm too late with my DNA they'll ease the transformation. There's two super-nutrient boosters for a Felinus transformation. A single one isn't enough to fuel the whole process, but it should keep me conscious so I can try to obtain other nutrients. I don't know what to expect, so I want them handy."

"A wise precaution," Alanel said.

Tridia replaced the pouch in her sleeve pocket and returned to her packing.

"I'm surprised you let me have so much time on my own." Tridia didn't look up as she spoke.

"You have endured a great deal in the past few hours," Winniel stated. "Indeed, in the past few weeks from what we saw in your memories. You needed time to gather your thoughts, but you've struggled with them instead."

Tridia turned to face the Sentinels. "These darkened memories are making me crazy. And, I'm sorry, but this irritating link with you isn't helping."

"As the First Truthsayer of our clan, Winniel is a vital link between each of us and the other clans," Alanel's deep voice resonated in harsh tones. "Our existence is threatened by the void from your mind. This *irritating link* is all that keeps us connected."

"This child is not to blame." Winniel placed a calming hand on his shoulder. Her eyes took on a distant expression. "The ambassador grows uneasy at our absence."

"We'd better go." Tridia shoved a last pair of socks into the duffel with more force than necessary and slid the bag's strap over her shoulder.

She and the Sentinels walked into a room filled with all of the tension and turmoil of a command center. Master Aren stamped around, giving rapid-fire orders to a small army of assistants while speaking to someone named Mr. Tang on his comlink. Tridia caught her breath and stared at her master before he noticed her. He was only slightly taller than her, with blonde hair, electric blue eyes, and a soldier's toned physique. He rivaled Alanel in looks, and both were equally deadly.

"Finish with those backpacks first," Master Aren said to an acolyte, and then glanced in Tridia's direction. "About time. Familiarize yourself with the contents of the blue pack while he fills it. Adjust the pack's straps to suit yourself once he's done."

Tridia stepped to the center of the room and knelt beside the young man with the blue pack. She surveyed the gear displayed on the floor around him. Thin climbing ropes, an anchor launcher, reflective disks, dark lenses, flashlights, and a small medical kit lay amid other odds and ends. To her amazement, he managed to get every single piece into the bulging pack with its many pockets. Once it was sealed, she dropped her duffle and hefted the pack to her shoulders, adjusting the straps and getting used to the fit. With the duffle once more in hand, she turned to Master Aren.

"It's an odd assortment of equipment," she said.

"We don't know what we'll be facing, so we need to be eclectic with our choices." He glanced up once as he spoke. "The rest of the gear will be in the ground transport by now. Moving on the streets will be a lot slower than using a hopper, so we'd better leave now. Our ride to Cystia won't wait for us."

The herd of underlings vocalized varying levels of distress that he was leaving again so soon.

"I'll remain in touch as far as the hangars, so prioritize your questions and make good use of the time." Master Aren's words silenced their complaints.

On the sidewalk behind the embassy, two other Hariok Sentinels approached Alanel and Winniel. Tridia couldn't help but stare. The two new Sentinels were identical to the two she knew. The new pair handed small duffle bags to Alanel and Winniel, exchanged silent looks, then left without speaking.

"Doesn't that get unnerving?" Tridia asked Master Aren. "Those silent exchanges, and their just knowing about you?"

"Not anymore." He climbed into the middle section of the transport.

Tridia ended up with Winniel seated on her right and Alanel on her left. Master Aren sat across from them, using his compad non-stop to send messages and gather data. He didn't look up, making conversation only with the comlink attached to his right ear.

Tridia kept her thoughts shielded as much as possible, but the pressing awareness of Winniel's presence at the edge of her mind kept her uneasy. Apart from the link, she couldn't sense the Sentinels. She could see them and hear them, but if she closed her eyes, they disappeared from her senses. Sitting so close, Master Aren's presence remained clear. The shape of his body, the subtle emotion projected in his voice, and the slight energy that swirled around him registered in her mind, even with her eyes closed. He couldn't mask those things. But the Sentinels kept their physical presence hidden from her heightened senses. Only the ghostlike binding with Winniel whispered of the Sentinels' presence. Tridia shivered. Their nearness in the transport made it worse.

To combat the mental stress, Tridia made an effort to study the unique mixture of alien and human architecture as they passed through the streets of Dajelania. Square or rectangular-shaped human buildings with rectangular doors and windows stood side by side with edifices of curlicue design bearing round, trapezoidal, or slanted doors and windows. Colors ranged from pastels to vibrant primaries with a rainbow of shades in between. The pedestrian traffic was as mixed as the structures, and Tridia couldn't identify many of the species. Traffic ebbed and flowed in the markets and business district but got lighter in the predominantly residential areas.

When they reached the open spaces separating residences from the vast hangars that accommodated the interplanetary traffic, Tridia dropped her eyes to her well-worn boots. The fit and feel of the material suggested the boots were probably expensive. Had she been picky about such things? It made sense – if she wore them most of the time, she would have spent extra money to insure their quality. She'd obviously been meticulous in taking care of them. Even though polish hid the worst of the scuffs and scratches, each mark represented a story hidden in the darkness in her mind. Possibly stories of death and tragedy she didn't want to remember.

She wanted to think of *Somi* Robel and examine the new memories she'd gained after her hearing of their time together. With those memories no longer behind the barrier, she was free to do so. Did he know her as the Child of Chaos? Is that why he hadn't contacted her after she'd been resurrected from the *deathstrike*? The idea she alone could be responsible for a major galactic holocaust seemed unthinkable, but were there other hidden memories that would make it more believable?

"You have a dire mission ahead of you, Tridia Odana, and a strong desire to reach the planet Cystia. Would not your thoughts be better focused on these things?"

Tridia jumped at Alanel's deep voice in her ear. He was a small part of her connection with Winniel, but the sound of his voice made his presence undeniable.

"Causing trouble, Commander?" Master Aren asked. He didn't look up from the compad.

"Not with intent, I assure you." Tridia eyed Alanel as she spoke. The male Sentinel didn't return her inspection. "How is it their lack of presence doesn't disturb you?"

"The ambassador has long since disciplined his mind to ignore the incongruity caused by our shielding," Winniel said. "A discipline you should practice."

Tridia swallowed down a reply, before realizing Winniel would have heard her thoughts anyway. She studied her boots again, but in her mind, she saw a perfect white flower. The velvet details of its petals drew her focus and the memory of its fragrance filled her nostrils. She'd seen this flower before and touched it with her hands. It had meant something profound to her once. The simplicity of her thoughts lulled her into a peaceful meditation and the nearness of the Sentinels ceased to matter.

"We're here, Commander."

Master Aren's voice called Tridia from her meditation. She was the only one in the transport. The others had already gotten out and started unloading the gear from the rear of the vehicle onto a hover sled. Tridia slid from the seat, closed the vehicle's door, and froze. They had stopped in front of an arched entrance with numbers in several scripts painted beside it. The arch provided an opening into a pinkish stone building that stretched ahead of them in the distance – perhaps for miles. Ground traffic rumbled or hummed past as people – humanoid and other alien – hurried to and from other identical arches. Above the arches, spacecraft of every size and make imaginable eased to land on or to rise from their designated hangar spots. She stumbled to the back of the transport while watching an enormous luxury craft lift from its mooring.

"Careful, Commander, or you'll get your fingers smashed."

Tridia snatched her hand back. Master Aren grinned as he closed the cargo door.

"I've never – at least –"

"No, according to your mission records, you've never been to Aga, and no other planet has anything quite like the hangars of Dajelania. This is only one section for mid-sized crafts."

"The ship that just took off –"

"The personal cruiser of the oldest child of a wealthy merchant. It's the largest thing allowed in this section, and it's here by special dispensation. Our accommodations will be much more manageable and maneuverable."

Tridia shouldered her backpack and duffle. Master Aren turned away and continued using the compad. Alanel and Winniel stood beside the hover sled loaded with a trunk of equipment, three backpacks, two duffle bags, and a case of weapons which had been delivered from an off-site storage unit. They waited for Tridia to catch up before entering the hangar's arch.

"Looks like you've got enough goods there to wage a small war, Ambassador."

Without thinking, Tridia dropped her duffle and stepped between Master Aren and the speaker, a dark-skinned man with numerous long braids and a charming smile. Dark lenses perched on the bridge of his nose hid his eyes.

"The circles in which I move can be dangerous." Master Aren made no effort to step around Tridia, a sure sign the man posed a threat. "What can I do for you, Val?"

"It's more what I can do for you, actually." Val turned toward the Sentinels and took a half-step back, as if recognizing what they were for the first time. "Perhaps I'm mistaken in the purpose of your journey."

"And perhaps not. Why not share your information and if it applies, you'll get your usual fees?" Master Aren waited.

Val inclined his head toward Tridia. "This the Odean Blade, then?"

"You have information for the ambassador?" Tridia asked.

Val's smile broadened. "Word is you're headed into Hierarchy territory with that Guardian outcast, Deeca Varin."

"If I am?"

"There'll be a party waiting for you," Val replied. "There are still some pretty big bounties on the Odean Blade here. Of course, they all require proof of death or her incapacitated body before payment's made.

"Someone thinks they can escape the promise of death at the hands of the J'Nai?" Master Aren asked.

"Maybe someone doesn't care – or feels safely above the threat," Val replied.

"Who will be waiting?"

"Tezekelen and Onzai." Val used his middle finger to position the shades farther up his nose. "With fully armed ships and Nezadian shields. You understand the significance?"

"The information is sound?" Master Aren's voice took on a more serious tone.

"It is."

"Your usual is deposited. If you hear anything else, relay it to my embassy. Payment will follow if appropriate." Master Aren's steps faded in the direction of the hangar door, but Tridia continued to face Val until he grimaced and hurried away.

When she turned toward the entrance both Sentinels stood at the edge of the walkway, their bags on the ground at their feet. She looked back over her shoulder at the retreating Val. Three burly men had joined him.

"They meant to take you," Winniel said.

"Take me? Here off the street, with the two of you standing there? Are they mad?" Tridia retrieved her duffle and joined the Sentinels on the walkway.

"Large sums of money pervaded their thoughts," Alanel said. "Our presence altered their decision."

"Thank you for your presence. The Triad would likely take offense if I maimed four men on the day they granted me amnesty." Tridia tossed her duffle on the sled and pushed it through the entrance. The Sentinels followed.

They emerged on the other side into a roofless enclosure. A silver craft with gold markings, less than half the size of the luxury vessel she'd watched earlier, sat in the center of the open area. Tridia studied the sleek, spearhead-shaped ship with awe. The sheen of the silver metal swirled and its surface shifted.

"A Stellar Morph." She glanced at the Sentinels as she continued. "Impossible to track by conventional means. On the ground, in this mode, it's invisible to any known form of detection. There are only a few of them in existence. The technology to build the shell isn't quite stable." Tridia frowned. "The name is wrong. *Star Seeker.* It should be *Star Trail.*"

Pain shot through Tridia's brain. Visions of the Felinus warrior she'd seen in her mirror chased across her thoughts and a snarling voice echoed unintelligibly in her mind. Fear and desperation threatened to choke her senses. She staggered and clung to the sled for support. Alanel and Winniel came immediately to her side.

"Your exhaustion is catching up with you." Winniel clamped a hand on Tridia's arm.

"Just a random memory." Tridia inhaled, grateful for the added support. "They come out of the blue. But that one was unusual."

Master Aren walked away from an argument with Deeca Varin. The petite blonde scowled at his back, her violet-blue eyes squinting to mere slits.

"Is she alright?" Master Aren asked Alanel.

The Sentinel nodded.

"She can speak for herself," Tridia managed to stand up straight and Winniel released her arm.

"Yes, but she wouldn't necessarily tell me the truth, now would she?" Master Aren asked.

"I won't intentionally lie to you," Tridia said.

"Which is not the same as telling me the truth. What was that about?"

"I had just noticed this ship is a Stellar Morph. Somehow I knew it was a concept ship of a very limited edition. I got confused from a crossed memory about the name. I don't know how I even knew that."

"Because you've flown one just like it," Master Aren turned toward the ship as he spoke. "Only five were produced for testing. You stole one a few months ago and used it to escape back into Hierarchy space."

"Not this one?" Tridia frowned.

"No, this one has always belonged to Deeca. That one belonged to the Sentinels."

Tridia's eyes widened and she looked up at Winniel. "The *Star Trail.* I must have been desperate."

"You used it to escape after the death of one of our clan," Alanel said.

Tridia opened her mouth to speak, but no words came out.

I don't remember any of that. I don't know what to say.

Winniel's voice intruded in her mind. *Say nothing. Alanel is not rational*

CHAOS UNLEASHED

concerning that death.

The four of them stood as if petrified and looked from one to the other. Tridia's heart pounded. Was the theft of the ship what caused the vendetta? Or had she been somehow responsible for the death of one of the Hariok clan?

"Okay, people!" Deeca's voice, broadcast from an external speaker, broke the spell. "Load up or get left behind!"

Tridia glanced at each of the Sentinels and swallowed hard before pushing the sled toward the ramp. Master Aren fell in step beside her, with Alanel and Winniel walking a pace behind. Tridia stopped again.

"Before we board, what is it I'm supposed to have done?" Tridia glanced to the top of the ramp toward Deeca. "She blames me for the loss of her brother and her fiancé. One's death and the other's rejection, but I don't know what happened to them, and I don't remember her."

"The night you allegedly killed the teenaged girl, someone leaked Guardian Varin's assignment to hostile parties," Master Aren whispered.

"She thinks I betrayed her assignment?" Tridia asked.

"You'd infiltrated the children's group she was protecting. Then apparently murdered one of the girls and her father and escaped. Deeca was close on your trail when she got the call from the kidnappers to surrender or lose her fiancé."

"Lose her fiancé?"

"They kidnapped her fiancé and forced her to surrender, then made her watch as they tortured him. When she refused to disclose the location of the children she'd been guarding, they killed him. The children would have been critical hostages in the Sharian war raging between five rival families in the Genta sector." Master Aren paused. "A Guardian's gold bands make a formidable weapon. As her fiancé died, she managed to get one arm free and brought the bands together. The resulting explosion took out a large section of the city where the kidnappers held her. When the Guardians reached her, she was still chained to one of the posts in an untouched five-foot circle in the middle of the devastation. She was unconscious for days.

"No Guardian had ever caused that kind of damage and a lot of people called for her execution. The Guardian Controller refused to punish her or remove the gold bands imbedded in her forearms. The Guardians held her on their base planet for a few weeks while she recovered her senses, then released her from service as a Guardian so long as she never invoked the bands again. She was supposed to return to her home world and resume her family position, but her father and brother refused her. Now she's a Hunter, someone who finds lost people or artifacts for a fee. With her background and instincts, she's made a reputation as one of the best in a very short time, but she hates the life."

11

Tridia's stomach tightened as they started up the ramp. She stared inside the ship where Deeca stood waiting for them, arms crossed, foot tapping. "Did I do it? Kill the girl and betray a Guardian?"

"I found nothing in your journals, official or private, that gave any indication that you committed either crime."

"But I might have." The damaged bay in the hospital ship, the dead workers, and bodies sliding down the hall toward the vacuum, raced through Tridia's memories. She could have betrayed Deeca to make good her escape.

CHAPTER TWO

The Sentinels took over the sled and pushed it toward the cargo hold that Deeca pointed out. Tridia followed Master Aren to the passenger lounge where a beautiful woman with red hair and green eyes reclined on one of the sofas.

"Well, well, Ambassador Aren, how nice to see you again."

"Hello, Sonei. Deeca chose you as her second for this mission? Did she tell you it's likely a one-way trip to Cystia?"

"We've all got to go eventually, Ambassador. Even friends of Morgan Jacks end up dead from time to time. Besides, the money's good, and I get to see what your little pet is like in action."

Tridia didn't reply to Sonei's snipe, but her right fist clenched at her side.

"She looks much younger in person. Not really the type I'd pegged you for." Sonei smiled.

"This trip is dangerous enough," Master Aren said. "You don't need to make enemies before it starts."

"Touched a nerve, did I?" Sonei purred. "Alright, I'll play nice for now. You can't protect her forever."

"It's not her I'm protecting." Master Aren turned to Tridia. "Stay here. The Sentinels will join you as soon as they've secured the cargo. Try to not damage your companion in the meantime."

Sonei's eyes widened as she watched Master Aren leave.

"I don't understand the attraction for either of you," she remarked.

"Attraction isn't a factor. I'm a piece of property useful to him in ways that aren't your concern," Tridia said. "When my usefulness ends, no doubt I'll be discarded. As for my part, service to him is preferable to death at the moment. And preferable to killing others in order to survive. There's actually very little to understand when the perspective is correct."

Tridia sat in a chair opposite Sonei.

"Do you know —" Sonei popped up into a sitting position with her legs tucked under. "I like you! I didn't think I would from all I'd heard about you. But you put that silly judge in his place and held your own even after the Sentinels invaded your mind. It takes something special to do that. And here you are sitting as calmly as you please with a complete stranger who insulted you and your owner. Not showing any sign you'd like to rip my head off. You've got what it takes, kid. We're going to get along just fine."

Tridia smiled without mirth. "As long as I take nothing you say at face value?"

"You *are* a bright one," Sonei said. "Yes, we'll get along just fine."

The Sentinels entered the lounge and Sonei stood. They faced her with stoic disinterest.

"If you'll excuse me? I want to check my gear before we take off." Sonei addressed the remark to no one in particular, but her eyes remained on the Sentinels until she left the room.

Alanel and Winniel sat on the sofa Sonei had vacated. Tridia shifted into a cross-legged position, then closed her eyes and tried to recall the white flower.

"We've been cleared for take-off. Buckle up." Master Aren's clear voice came across the intercom. "We should be en route for about sixteen hours. Make yourselves comfortable after the jump."

Tridia fastened a retractable harness across her chest, but otherwise remained sitting cross-legged throughout the take-off and the sling into hyperspace. The ship handled so smoothly she hardly noticed the directional changes or increased speed. Only the mild hiccup of entering hyperspace registered with any significance.

They'd been underway to Cystia for more than three hours and the Sentinels had not spoken a word. Tridia marked the time in irritated silence. The events of the day caught up with her in the second hour. She couldn't recall the white flower with any clarity and the calm she'd reached in the ground transport had vanished. Unanswerable questions assaulted her thoughts and Winniel's presence hovered at the edges of her mind. By the third hour, it took a major effort to control the shaking in her hands.

The questions rolled through her mind again. Guilt haunted her. Master Aren had said she'd killed forty-nine people, but she couldn't remember any of them. Shouldn't she remember their faces or their names? Had she really betrayed Deeca Varin so the Hunter had suffered the death of her fiancé and been driven to destroy part of a city in her anguish? What kind of person did such things? The snarling Felinus flashed in her memories again and Tridia jerked upright. She glanced at the Sentinels and they both looked at her but made no comment. She closed her eyes against their gazes.

Tridia pinched the bridge of her nose between her index fingers. Her body trembled, but her mind refused to release the guilt. It seemed the progenitor of all headaches was forming behind her eyes. She shivered and Winniel's mental connection intensified. Unlike the everyday exposure to other people's thoughts which she could, for the most part, shut out, Winniel could read *her* mind. The fact she couldn't read Winniel's caused her chest to tighten, constricting her breathing.

The Sentinel didn't probe into her thoughts. There was no icy presence as she'd felt during the interrogation, just a defined awareness that she wasn't alone in her mind. The awareness ran over her skin like so many insects. She'd scream if she thought it would help, but it wouldn't. She'd be tied to the Sentinel as long as the darkness existed in both their memories.

As badly as she didn't want to release the memories she'd locked away, she couldn't continue with this level of exposure for long without going mad. How did the Sentinels stand such openness among themselves?

Anger flashed through Tridia's mind and her eyes flew open. Alanel's glance hardened to a glare. They stared at each other for several seconds before he released her. Something she'd thought had touched him, angered him. Had she hurt Winniel? Alanel had warned her to not cause Winniel pain. That wasn't it. He would have spoken if she had done something unintentionally. He'd be swift to punish her if she'd done anything she'd been warned against.

I've got to get myself under control.

Flailing mindlessly against the darkness in her mind could get her killed. Could she press against it systematically?

Tridia turned her concentration toward the darkness. Her outer barriers weakened as she bent her thoughts inward. Master Aren, Deeca, and Sonei materialized in her mind from their various places about the ship. She ignored them. The obsidian veil had to be the only thing in her mind's eye – and there it was. It wasn't a solid block, but a thick wall of darkness, neither fully opaque nor translucent. She'd never been able to examine it so closely without the blinding pain of the barrier block forcing her to stop. Now that the painful deterrent had been removed she could observe and touch the barrier that kept her from her memories. Objects – thoughts or memories? – moved beyond the wall. She couldn't see them, but she could sense them. Why couldn't she get through to them? The cold realization that something more than her own thoughts waited beyond the barrier swept through Tridia's mind.

Another shiver raced down her spine. Something strove to break free. How had anything other than her memories gotten beyond the block?

Winniel. Tridia couldn't keep her eyes from the woman's serene face. Winniel had pierced the veil. She'd gone into the darkness and taken it into herself. Had she also left something of herself behind? Tridia closed her eyes and reached out to touch the darkness. She pressed against its barrier with a gently increasing force. Another presence joined her, then another, and finally a third lingered at the edge of her awareness. One of them was Winniel, the other Alanel. The third had to be Master Aren, the only other telepath on the ship.

Tridia pressed harder against the darkness and the pressure of the other minds increased with hers. A dull pain emanated from the veil, but she increased the pressure. Something she needed to know beckoned her, urged her to go deeper into the darkness.

Sweat broke out on her face. The veil pressed back, protecting its secrets with an equal force. Tridia pressed again, ignoring the headache throbbing behind her eyes, ignoring the warning Alanel had given her. Tears streamed down her face as she shouldered harder against the blackness.

A vice-like hand tightened around her throat, slamming her against the bulkhead. Her feet dangled several inches above the floor. Tridia wrapped both hands around the one holding her and tried to pry it loose so she could breathe. Her fist beat at the rock-hard arm extending from the hand. Her vision blurred against the angry spark in Alanel's eyes. Through the haze, Winniel staggered to her feet to catch him by the shoulder. Master Aren ran into the lounge and spoke to him. Their shouted words were unintelligible in her ears. Over Alanel's shoulder a large beast appeared in the corridor. Just as darkness crept across her vision the hand released her. She dropped to the floor in a heap, too weak to move, and sucked in air through her aching throat. The beast disappeared as her vision cleared. *Just a hallucination?*

"What in Hielos did you think you were doing?" Master Aren demanded. He grabbed her and pulled her to her feet.

"Memories," Tridia gasped. "Something in there I need to know."

"Little fool. I should have let him choke you into unconsciousness." Master Aren helped her into her chair and Tridia sat without moving.

A glass of water appeared in front of her face, and Tridia looked up to see Sonei standing beside her.

"The show was worth at least a glass of water," Sonei said. "I've never seen a Sentinel back down from a rage. I've never seen a Sentinel *in* a rage. What did you do, kid?"

Tridia shook her head but accepted the water.

I warned you not to cause Winniel pain. Alanel's voice boomed in a loud angry tone in her aching head.

You could have stopped me before it got that far. You knew what I was trying to do. You could have said something, Tridia snapped back.

"Undisciplined child!" Alanel took a step toward Tridia with his hand raised to strike.

Tridia sprang to her feet, balanced on the chair arms, dropping the water. She raised her hands before her, in a loose defensive style. "You don't get another free strike."

Winniel stepped between them.

The Sentinels didn't speak aloud, but from the flashes in their eyes and the tense set of their shoulders, they carried on a heated conversation in the silence. At length, the tension drained from Alanel's shoulders and he took a step back. Winniel's stance relaxed, too, but Tridia's muscles tightened. Winniel hadn't tried to reach into her thoughts, but their connection had gotten stronger during the argument. Tridia flinched as Winniel turned to face her. They stood close enough for Tridia to see the gold flecks in Winniel's copper-colored eyes.

"Your training and discipline will be left to me. If I lose consciousness my mate will step in." Winniel continued in thought. *This concession to you comes at a great cost to him, child. He lives only to protect me until this darkness is lifted. Don't push him to his limit. Even I won't be able to stop him again. Do you understand?*

"Yes, Ma'am," Tridia said.

"Don't use titles with me, child. My name is Winniel, address me as such."

"Yes, Winniel. I understand."

"Do you people think you can make it to Cystia without killing each other now?" Master Aren asked.

"Return to your play-acting, Ambassador," Winniel said. "There will be no repeat of this event."

"Sonei?" Master Aren looked at the red-haired woman standing beside him.

"What did she mean by play-acting?" Sonei asked, stooping to retrieve the empty glass.

"That's between me and the Sentinels," he snapped. "Can you stay out of the way here?" He dropped his voice to a whisper. "He would have killed you if you'd tried to interfere. Even in that shape."

Sonei glared. "I'll return to my cabin. As curious as I am to witness Sentinel training and discipline, I think I'd be safer in another room."

"A wise decision," Alanel said.

Sonei wasted no time in disappearing down the corridor. Master Aren waited.

"The child will not be harmed again, Ambassador, by me or you."

Alanel's words left no doubt the J'Nai had passed on the plans to kill Tridia. "Winniel will teach her discipline in as near the Sentinel way as one of your kind can learn it."

"I'll return in a few hours. Deeca has decent provisions stored away. We'll eat before we make the next directional jump. Then we'd better discuss our plans." Master Aren returned to the bridge.

"Sit, child." Winniel indicated the chair and Tridia folded down into her cross-legged position again. "You have difficulty accepting my presence in your thoughts."

"Yes," Tridia said.

"Because you don't see it as a part of yourself." Winniel's voice once again took on the soft lilt. "You wondered how the Sentinels could bear such exposure. In truth, we cannot bear to be without it. From our first consciousness, we are a part of our clan. We know the welcoming thoughts and emotions of all who surround us. We belong in the presence of our kind."

Tridia forced her shoulders to relax. Winniel's thoughts were warm as they lingered at the edge of her consciousness. This wasn't the icy probe from the interrogation, it was a connection of the type the Sentinels shared. Winniel had never known an individual life and this link represented her only remaining outside touch. For sanity's sake Tridia had to come to terms with the connection.

"I was never separated until I entered the darkness in your mind." Winniel stated. "I fell from contact with my entire clan. Through me, they lost contact with each other. For a brief moment, we each stood in the isolation humans experience from birth. That's why we lost consciousness, why the other clans came to our rescue. While we share awareness with them, and we interact with them, they are not of the same oneness with us, but they sensed our separation and feared for us. It's never happened before. Now, because I brought your darkness into my mind, I'm distanced from my clan. My connection with them is now linked through you. Even Alanel is separated from me in a way we've never experienced since the first time I saw his face. It's why he's so easily angered with you."

"Wait," Tridia said. "You brought the whole of my darkness into your mind? Everything I've hidden from myself, you'll know when the veil comes down?"

"I expect you will have to assist me to remove it," Winniel replied. "In the same way you'll take it apart in your own mind, you'll need to take it apart in mine."

"You took an enormous chance," Tridia said.

"It was the only way to return to myself and reunite my clan. I couldn't escape, so I brought the darkness with me."

"I don't understand." Tridia's brow furrowed. "Your consciousness is still inside my mind, behind the barrier, and my barrier is in your mind?"

"A very simplistic way of putting it, but yes. You and I exist in each other's minds. That's why you sense my presence. No one, apart from the Sentinels, has ever sensed a Sentinel. Not even our creators shared such awareness with us."

I can hear you as though you were speaking your thoughts. Winniel's words whispered in Tridia's mind. *I won't pry into your secret places. That's disrespectful and rude. The Sentinels do not do such things unless requested by the Triad to verify the truth.*

"You can hear my thoughts, but I can't hear yours unless you direct them to me. Why?" Tridia asked.

"You're more than human, child. But you're not a Sentinel."

"Winniel, have a care," Alanel said. "Other ears are straining to hear your words."

Tridia looked toward the corridor. Sonei's presence pulsed just out of sight. Alanel moved too fast for her to follow his steps. A startled yelp from Sonei betrayed her spying in the corridor. Alanel's voice rumbled a few brief words, then he returned to the lounge at a normal pace.

"She will remain in her cabin," he said.

"You need to focus on my presence." Winniel continued speaking, as though nothing had happened. "Let yourself adjust to our connection. You've been trying to ignore it. Let it settle into your consciousness. Understand, I'm not spying or prying. Consider me standing next to you. You're aware by sight that I'm there, but not touching you. I can hear you when you speak or think, but I'm not delving into your mind. In our thoughts, I'm by your side, but not intruding."

Tridia closed her eyes again. Winniel's presence grew more solid when she focused on it. The Sentinel's explanation of standing beside her made sense. They were next to each other. The more she concentrated, the less irritating the connection became, and something else happened. Winniel's body took shape in her mind. The Sentinel's physical presence, hidden just moments before, became as clear as Master Aren's, Sonei's, or Deeca's. Alanel's physical presence took longer to form, but he became visible to Tridia's senses. Barriers hid his thoughts, but they echoed in Winniel's mind. Tridia kept her eyes closed and let the awareness sink into her consciousness. Winniel moved to sit beside Alanel and Tridia tracked the motion through their connection. The strong bond between the two Sentinels, deeper than any connection Tridia had ever experienced, took on a crystal clarity. She marveled at it.

You pry too deeply, child. Back away.

Winniel's words were gentle, and Tridia withdrew behind her own barriers. The Sentinel's presence no longer irritated her – it became a comfort. Winniel may eventually kill her when the darkness cleared, but it wouldn't happen before they reached Cystia. The realization broke through the tension, exhaustion, and pain Tridia had held at bay for more than a day. She fell into a dreamless sleep – sitting upright in the chair.

***

The smell of food and the sound of voices roused Tridia from sleep. She opened her eyes slowly, taking in the small room with dual bunk beds anchored to the walls. The unusual lack of tension in her shoulders gave her pause, then she stretched to enjoy the feel. Winniel's consciousness hovered within her barriers, a now-familiar presence in her mind. She swung her bare feet to the floor and looked around for her boots. How had they managed to get her to bed and take her boots off without waking her? Had she been such a sound sleeper as a soldier? She had her boots laced and was adjusting the collar of her jumper when the door opened.

"The Ambassador wants you for some secret conversation with your Sentinel friends," Sonei said. "I'm to return to my cabin until you're done. Do me a favor, kid, and make it quick. I don't like being cooped up."

"I'll do what I can," Tridia replied. She started toward the lounge as Sonei slipped through a door farther along the corridor.

"Nice of you to join us, Commander," Master Aren said. "Take a plate and have a seat. We need to discuss our plans for Cystia."

Tridia's stomach rumbled. Her last meal had been on the hospital ship and she was ravenous. Containers of meat and vegetables sat opened on a narrow counter and she helped herself while the others waited. Her head buzzed, but she put it down as a symptom of hunger, then took a larger portion of meat than she normally would have. Winniel's presence tingled in her mind. Something had aroused the Sentinel's attention. Tridia shot her a questioning look, but Winniel didn't glance her way. She shrugged away the tingle and finished filling her plate. It seemed heaping, even as hungry as she was. Master Aren gave a startled glance at the food, then began speaking as soon as she sat down.

"I've explained to Sonei and Deeca what we're up against on Cystia, but neither of them grasps the scope of the danger in the mine. The Sentinels are aware of the threat, they've faced it before." Master Aren paused to consider Tridia. "You said you felt compelled to go to Cystia.

20

Have you had any revelations as to why?"

"No, sir." Tridia tried to speak politely with her mouth full. She swallowed. "I just know I have to get there. It's important, but I can't remember anything about the planet or why I have to go. I keep thinking of Davik's name when I think of the mine." She speared another forkful of meat, eyed it, and changed the subject. "What threat has you so concerned?"

"Creatures in the tunnels." Master Aren said.

He showed no outward sign of stress, but his energy seemed to shiver in her senses. Tridia lowered the fork.

"They're called feeders."

"Feeders." Tridia repeated the word. No memory came forward, but Master Aren's distress aroused her curiosity.

"She won't survive in the tunnels without blocking her senses," Alanel said.

"The child has a strong energy signature, Ambassador," Winniel added. "The feeders won't fail to sense her."

"If you're trying to frighten me, it's working," Tridia said. "Just what in Hielos are these feeders?"

"Amorphous creatures that feed on mental energy," Brenden said. He settled himself into a chair. "They live in the deep tunnels. They're why the mines were closed. The feeders first preyed on people with the highest intelligence levels and those with some paranormal ability. One of the first victims was a prisoner with minor telekinetic skill. Eventually, even normal humans attracted them and it became unsafe for anyone with an imagination to go into the mine. You can't go into the tunnels with any of your energy signature leaking."

"Empress Dojene said my persona leaks." Tridia looked around the group. Her voice rose as she spoke. "Is that the same thing? I can't come this far and not go onto the planet. I have to be a part of this mission, not just an observer."

"You can't remain on the planet without a full energy block, child," Winniel said. "To become proficient enough to protect yourself from the feeders would take years of practice. The ambassador has only recently mastered this skill."

Master Aren shook his head. "As Winniel said, it takes years to master the technique. It's dangerous for your kind of energy to even land on the surface, let alone go into the mine. You should return to orbit with Sonei and wait for our signal to retrieve us."

Tridia set her plate on the floor and clasped her hands before her. "Master Aren, you're aware there are multiple problems with your suggestion. First, the idea that Hunter Varin would allow me to take her craft into space, leaving her stranded in a hostile environment with you and the Sentinels is preposterous. Second, taking the craft into space would place it too far away to be useful in a rescue attempt. Third, the Sentinels won't let me out of their sight. Shall I continue, sir?"

"There's nothing wrong with your logic or your presentation, Commander. I said you *should* return to space, not that you *would*. You're correct in assuming Deeca won't allow you to take the ship away. So, what are our alternatives?"

"You've allowed only one. One of you must either block my personal energy or assist me to do it."

The brilliant blue eyes of her master studied her for a moment. "Your deduction's accurate. Do you understand what it will mean?"

"No. But I'm certain it won't be pleasant, since you allowed me to arrive at the conclusion on my own."

Master Aren laughed aloud. Tridia did her best to hide her irritation. Memories of their kiss and the vision of the future it had produced came unbidden to her thoughts. A strange feeling churned in her abdomen, a sensation that threatened to spread if she didn't hold it in check. She caught a look in his eyes and saw a struggle going on behind their blue curtain. He, too, fought to maintain his distance and control. His laughter died.

"It would be more effective if the Sentinels blocked your energy," he said. "They did it for a handful of the guards on Cystia so the Hierarchy could retrieve their prisoners and personnel from the mine."

"The Sentinels worked with the Hierarchy?" Tridia asked. "I thought you were enemies."

"We're only enemies when the Hierarchy attempts to impose its will in Core Alliance space," Alanel said. "The call for help was legitimate. Four of us went into the mines to help retrieve the lost prisoners and guards. Most were dead when we found them."

"They found one young man alive." Master Aren stared at the floor as he spoke. "He was in his twenties, but he looked eighty when they brought him out. He didn't live very long. The feeder detached itself when it was exposed to the sunlight, but it was too late."

Tridia's pulse quickened at the mention of prisoners. The idea of prisoners on Cystia stirred in her memory. She looked to Master Aren for an explanation and found him studying her.

"He wasn't on Cystia at the time."

"Who wasn't?" Tridia asked, her brow furrowed.

"Davik Schie," Master Aren replied. "He was transferred to the planet just over two months ago. Long after the prison was abandoned."

"Transferred? If the prison had been abandoned –" Tridia stopped.

Master Aren waited. When Tridia didn't continue, he demanded,

"You knew he was on Cystia. When did you remember it?"

"Just now. Before, I knew I needed to go to the planet, but I didn't remember he was a prisoner until just now. I still don't know why. What happened?"

"He wasn't sent there to work in the mines. They suspended half of his thirty-year sentence if he agreed to be an experimental subject in a project called Power Surge. That's all I could find out. His record stops there."

"The recorded message you told me about. I can remember his beaten face, but not the words of his message. It's because of Davik I have to get there, isn't it?" Tridia asked. "It's some insane need to reach him. Was it my fault he's there? Did he do something to protect me? Did I promise to rescue him?"

"Calm down, Commander. You were adamant that I help him. In fact, you mentioned his name before the other one," Master Aren explained. "In his message, he said he thought the people who framed him did it to get to you, or more precisely because of his relationship with you."

"Winniel..." Tridia's voice pled for understanding.

"Don't attack the darkness, child," Winniel stated. "There's too much at stake for either of us to risk becoming incapacitated."

Tridia struggled to get her thoughts under control as Alanel's jaw clenched. She needed to know more about Davik, but any pressure on Winniel's consciousness and she'd find herself dangling from his fist again. Winniel's expression remained calm and Tridia sighed in surrender.

"You're learning," Alanel said. "You must deal with the priorities of your mission first."

Tridia didn't respond. She couldn't. Alanel was right. As a soldier she understood the responsibilities of the mission she'd undertaken.

"We can help you block your energy." Winniel's words returned them to the task at hand. "It won't last for more than twelve hours. Energy signatures always find a way out. The stronger the signature, the quicker it will find its release. Your signature is strong. Twelve hours may be a generous estimate."

"I doubt I could help you hold it for more than six – generously estimating," Master Aren added. "I've not had the practice the Sentinels have."

"How long can you mask your own energy signature?" Tridia asked.

"For myself, I can hide indefinitely. The barrier locks into place since I've learned to put it up myself. I have to consciously remove it. It's not comfortable. When I hide my signature, it's like putting a bag over my head. Even normal senses are dulled."

"But that's not true for you." Tridia turned to the Sentinels.

"With us the ability is innate. A result of the genetic engineering," Winniel said. She shared an uneasy glance with Alanel.

"What will happen to Deeca Varin?" Tridia asked.

"She's a former Guardian," Master Aren said. "As such the Guardian Controller still has some influence over her body and her energies. She has protection. The question is, how deep in the mine will its influence go? Even the power of the Controller has its limits."

"She could have less than the twelve hours I could hope for?"

"That's a possibility."

"How painful is this blocking?" Tridia asked.

"At least as painful as the probing in the Public Hearing Room. Probably more so," Master Aren said. "I'll be allowed to touch you this time. It may help a little."

"An energy transfer," Tridia stated. Her stomach knotted again at the thought of Master Aren's hands on her. She picked up her plate and took another bite, then choked as a sweet taste filled her mouth. She managed to get the food down and wiped the tears from her eyes. "When do we do this?"

"We'll arrive at the planet in about six hours," Master Aren answered.

"I was asleep that long?" Tridia asked.

"You missed both directional jumps and the first meal." All eyes looked up as Deeca entered the lounge. "The ship's on auto for now. Nothing but clear space around us. I need to take a break. You can sit in the control center if you feel the need, Ambassador. Just don't touch my settings."

"Aye, Captain," Master Aren mocked.

Tridia hid a smile. Deeca grabbed a small flask from the cabinet on her way through the lounge. Judging from the blue-green color of the liquid in the flask, she planned on getting her sustenance from huttle juice. Not a bad plan.

Master Aren followed Deeca with his eyes until she disappeared into the corridor. He'd blocked his thoughts, but his intent gaze said a lot about his feelings for the Hunter. Tridia scowled as a tinge of jealousy nibbled at her thoughts.

"Master," Tridia said. "Colonel Zilisk gave me a capsule before he left the Public Hearing Room. He said I might find it interesting, but I haven't had a chance to open it."

"Let's have a look," Master Aren said.

Tridia fished in her pocket for a capsule half the size of her thumb and handed it to Master Aren. He turned it over to examine it, then twisted it. A tightly rolled slip of paper fell into his hand. He unrolled it, looked at the writing on it, then handed it to Tridia.

"Store hostage in L0137-C3316. Wait for orders," she read aloud.

"A cell or perhaps a compartment," Master Aren said. "Zilisk gave this to you?"

"Just before we separated. He went to the hospital and we went to your office with the empress. He said he found it in the traitor's things."

"Traitor?"

"One of the empress's bodyguards was being controlled by micro-machines. They had infested his brain. Harish, the guard, was killed in the attack, but Zilisk searched his things. I don't know if he found it on Harish's person or in his personal effects."

"Why wait until the last moment to give it to you?" Master Aren asked.

"Zilisk didn't trust me — and the feeling was mutual," Tridia said. "He was the only survivor of the entire guard and I never found out how he managed that. Once he knew I would be with the empress and he wouldn't, he handed it over. I presumed, out of deference to her."

"Do you think this could be false information? A clue to lead us astray?" Master Aren looked to the Sentinels.

"We sensed no duplicity in his actions," Alanel said. "He thought it was something the child should see."

Tridia bristled when Alanel referred to as a child, but she kept silent. He glanced her way and Tridia would have sworn he smirked.

"She's correct," Winniel added. "Zilisk only gave it to her when he was resigned he could not use it himself. That much was clear in his mind."

Master Aren shot the Sentinels a questioning look.

"After the attack, we monitored everyone in the room," Alanel explained. "It was our responsibility to keep everyone safe."

"Very well. Keep the information in mind and hold onto the capsule. There are buildings in the compound on Cystia. We might luck out and find evidence of the princess before we have to go into the mine."

"You don't believe that," Tridia stated.

"No," Master Aren said. "Finish up your food. You and I are going to have a workout in an hour to get you used to your own body again. How long were you a Felinus?"

"About a week," Tridia said. "But it was a rough week."

"You fought as a Felinus. You need to experience combat as a human again, just to be sure there's no residual hindrance. Come to me on the bridge in an hour."

He left the lounge and Tridia swallowed down another sweet burst in her mouth as he passed near her. A workout with Master Aren could prove interesting — if she could manage to look at him without choking on her own saliva.

CHAPTER THREE

The silence of the uridine mine seeped into Davik's being. He struggled to shake free of the sensory deprivation isolating him in ways no human should be able to tolerate. While his body remained safely in stasis outside the mine, it gave him no sensory information. He could not see, hear, touch, taste or smell anything with its organs. Only his brain remained active of its own accord. Through painful enhancements and experiments performed by the Hierarchy scientists, his brain generated enough power to transfer his consciousness into the amorphous energy form in which he now survived – separate from his physical self. He could detect sound vibrations in his new form, and thus "hear," but the translation of the vibrations were only monotones, with no inflection from the speaker, and no way to identify who had spoken.

Thanks to aliens dwelling in the lower levels, he could also speak, after a fashion, by sending energy vibrations directly into the ear of the listener. The lessons had cost him an exchange of information that should have remained hidden from the aliens, who he learned, afterward, were intergalactic invaders. He regretted adding to their intelligence, but the ability to communicate had brought him back from a precipice of madness. If he ever returned to his physical form, he may be able to thwart their schemes – or at least expose them to those who could. For the present, he had more pressing matters to deal with.

He touched the wall with a tendril of energy and sent out continuous pulses to navigate his way to the isolated chamber where he practiced. Only a sliver of an opening between the rock walls allowed admittance to the small cave. The amorphous creatures the soldiers called feeders might be able to follow him inside, but nothing else larger than the smallest insect could do it, and certainly not the Hierarchy scientists or soldiers who tormented him, unless they blasted the surrounding rock into unstable rubble. He flattened his shape to slip through the crevice and reformed into the elongated sphere that had become "normal" once inside the room.

His freedom was tenuous and his existence even more so. The Hierarchy wanted to use him as a weapon, and if he could make the scientists think he'd serve their purpose, they might allow him to return to his body. It would be safer than letting him roam free with the kind of power they expected him to project. But then, destroying his defenseless body on the surface would eliminate any recourse from him once they'd perfected the means to create their weapon. So far, he'd been unable to produce the type of destructive force they were looking for, but he'd made progress since discovering what they wanted.

Davik studied the wall in front of him. Using the energy pulses, he could discern every gouge and groove in its uneven surface. He found the spot where he'd practiced earlier, gouging two small letters into the wall: m-y. It had taken hours to focus enough energy to carve them. He had left in frustration, weakened by the effort, and with no idea of the effect the expenditure might have on his body. But he'd returned because there was nothing else to do in the empty mine since the aliens had warned him not to approach their compound, hidden in the deepest shafts.

All right, genius, you should have paid more attention to Tridia's meditation training. She'd probably have enough focus to carve a mural by now.

Thinking of Tridia lightened his mood a little. He had confessed his love for her in the desperate recording he'd made before being shipped to the mining planet. She didn't return his feelings – her startled acceptance of his kiss the last time he'd seen her had confirmed that – but they'd been as close as two people in the Hierarchy could be. If he knew her at all, she was trying to get to him right now – even though he'd warned her not to. She wouldn't leave him to rot in this forsaken place without at least trying to rescue him. If she came, he had to have some way to leave with her or protect her while she made her escape. He couldn't bear the thought of her being reduced to mental energy if she was caught. Rage built in his mind as he thought of anyone laying hands on her. He focused the emotion through an energy pulse and blasted a three-square-foot section of the wall to dust. Rage winked out as surprise took over. Energy tendrils reached out to examine the hole.

It was rough and shallow and no more than two inches deep, but it was enough to prove he could generate a deadly force. Where had this power been when he'd been locked away in the Kennels on Odea? The daily beatings might have stopped if he could punch a hole through the wall simply by thinking about it. His energy tendrils continued to send information about the hole, but his thoughts turned to his last day in that awful place.

***

Davik sat on the narrow bunk with his back against the wall and winced as he touched yet another busted lip with the tip of his finger. He wiped the blood on his pants leg, where older stains matched the new one. Today's beating had been light compared to previous days. He'd walked back to his cell on his own, instead of waking up there. They hadn't used drugs that morning to make him feel the pain more intensely. The only purpose to the torment he could discern was to beat a confession out of him. He'd die with his skin flayed before he ever confessed to something he didn't do. Especially a crime as heinous as the one for which he'd been convicted. He shook his head at the thought.

Just weeks ago, he'd been confident he could gain permission to share living accommodations with Tridia, perhaps even marry her – if she'd consent. He'd have done whatever it took to keep her out of the open breeding program. She was almost old enough to meet their requirements and her talents were drawing attention from the geneticists. Their DNA was a good match and they had brilliant records – except for one incident in hers, which she didn't discuss. The two of them should have received permission for exclusive mating. They only needed her acknowledgment on the forms. He'd planned to speak to her when she came back from the last deadly mission they'd assigned her – a mission with a thirty percent chance of survival. The fee had to be astronomical for the mission board to risk her life on such slim odds.

Things started to go wrong as soon as the requests were filed. He'd been pulled from her mission watch within hours, and his access to her files denied. Two days later, he awoke from a drugged sleep to find the base police combing his room for evidence and shoving him into a holding cell without explanation of his alleged offense. When his appointed counsel advised him of the charges he'd first been shocked, then outraged. The counsel refused to believe he hadn't committed the crime and urged Davik to plead guilty in exchange for a twenty-year sentence. Davik refused and the tribunal denied his request for a substitute counsel. The trial proceeded while Tridia was in a distant system in Core Alliance space. The whole thing was over before he had a chance to build a case or do any research on his own. They hadn't allowed him outside the holding cells to attempt his own investigation. One or two of the guards made mention of his housing requests – requests that should have been confidential unless approved. With him under suspicion, the request should have remained in limbo, upon his conviction, simply closed and sealed without ruling. How had it become common knowledge among low-level guards?

He'd gotten his first beating in the Kennels when one of the guards made a comment about Tridia being brood fodder that would have to accept sires when ordered. He'd decked the guard with a punch Tridia had taught him, but the guard hadn't been alone. Six against one in a holding cell had turned into near-fatal odds. It took a couple of days for the swelling around his eyes to subside enough for him to see again. Assaults came on a regular basis after that. Even with the torment it had brought him, he'd throw the punch again given the chance. Thinking of Tridia in those circumstances made his stomach churn. If they used her to taunt him, what might they be doing to her because of him? The lies his tormenters told had gotten to him at first, but when the story kept changing, he learned to trust nothing they said about her. Where was she? Why hadn't she contacted him?

The door swung open and one of the less obnoxious guards stepped into the cell.

"On your feet, Schie," the man said. "A senior officer wants to meet with you. Behave yourself and I won't restrain you while we walk."

Davik said nothing and rose slowly to his feet, keeping his hands to his sides. He preceded the guard from the room, then followed as the man led him by the arm down the dim corridor. Moans, cries, and gagging from inmates behind the closed doors they passed reminded him what his day could be like and inspired him to give the guard no cause to regret leaving his hands free. They went down an unfamiliar hallway and stopped before a metal door. The guard knocked and a voice from within told them to enter.

A man in a master assassin's uniform sat at a utilitarian table, scanning a reader laying before him. When he looked up, Davik had a sense of familiarity, but he couldn't place the face.

"Lieutenant Schie," he said, "I am Master Frees B'Nay. Sit down. We need to talk."

The guard guided Davik to an empty chair at the table, then he moved to stand at the door.

"Leave us, Sergeant. Lieutenant Schie poses no threat to me and what we have to discuss is classified." B'Nay kept his eyes on Davik the whole time. The guard left.

"Lieutenant, you are convicted of the rape and molestation of two female corpses in the morgue seven weeks ago. You have been sentenced to thirty years confinement in the Hierarchy prison system, the first two of which you are required to serve in the Kennels. I am here to offer you a chance to reduce your sentence and be transferred out of this facility immediately. Are you interested?"

Davik said nothing.

"I can call the guard and have you returned to your enhanced schedule of punishment, if you'd prefer." B'Nay taunted.

"Enhanced?" Davik asked.

"You were treated mildly this morning. The drugs you've been subjected to thus far have only been level five. I have interceded on your behalf since your conviction to keep you relatively safe and sane. Should I withdraw my benevolence, the drugs will be upgraded to level three, in keeping with the standard punishment for the crime you've committed. If they don't get the confession they want, you will be subjected to level one within a matter of weeks.

"In addition, the physical assaults you've received have been from the guards and you've remained in solitary confinement this whole time. Your standard punishment includes mandatory subjection to the physical torture classes, where we teach the Elstaar Elite how to elicit information from unwilling informants. You will be placed in the general populace.

"There are men in this facility who do not look kindly on the crimes you've committed, and they will seek to punish you in kind. You understand what I'm saying, do you not?"

"I understand," Davik said. He kept his voice under control and moved his shaking hands from the table to his lap. "Level one drugs destroy the mind with prolonged use, and I have two years to do in this facility. The guards who administer my injections are more than happy to describe the pain I can look forward to. The Elstaar pride themselves on obtaining information. As for being placed in the general populace, my imagination is vivid enough to understand your threat."

"It's no threat, I assure you." B'Nay sat forward in his chair. "As long as we understand each other."

"What's the offer?" Davik asked. "And what do I have to do in exchange for it?"

"I head a top-secret project in need of intelligent subjects for initial experimentation. It's based off-world in a classified and isolated facility. The conditions are much less harsh than you'll find here for the next two years. However, it will require your body to receive certain enhancements. We will take fifteen years off your sentence. Upon completion of the project, you may serve the remaining time in a minimum security facility away from Odea, with a reduced offense of conduct unbecoming an officer. You can be considered for parole after five years."

"Do these enhancements require removal of body parts? Replacement with prosthetics?" Davik asked.

"Nothing so crude, but until I have your agreement, I can give you no more details." B'Nay scrolled through the reader and turned it around so Davik could see a picture of him and Tridia taken the day she left on her mission. He held her in a close embrace. He'd just kissed her. "It has come to my attention this young woman is a friend of yours. Perhaps more than a friend."

"We've known each other for six years," Davik said, not daring to look at the picture too long. "We study together. We're friends. Only friends."

"Your request for housing accommodations says otherwise."

"The request was one-sided. She had no knowledge I was making it, and it would have been granted only had she approved, which was by no means a foregone conclusion."

B'Nay spun the reader back to face him and scrolled again. "And yet you were confident enough to make the request without her input. Confident she would add her signature to the request."

"Is she alive?" Davik asked. B'Nay didn't answer. "Is she on the planet?" Still no answer. "If we are such close friends as you suggest, why hasn't she come to see me? I think the evidence betrays your assumptions."

B'Nay rose to his feet. "Take the offer or leave it, Schie. I won't expound or ask again. I leave the planet in a few hours. It will take that long to process you out of here. Answer me now or forfeit the opportunity. There are other candidates." He held up another picture of Tridia.

"You low-life excuse for a human." Davik clenched his fists in his lap. "I'll volunteer, but I want two conditions."

"I said nothing about conditions," B'Nay turned toward the door.

"These won't be hard to manage," Davik said. "Make it a part of the deal that as long as my behavior remains acceptable within the *standard* rules and regulations of the project, the minimum security facility, or the parole, I will *not* be required to return to the Kennels to complete the mandatory two years in this place. I know how the Hierarchy clings to the letter of the law in its punishments."

B'Nay turned toward Davik with a cold smile. "I believe that can be stipulated. The other condition?"

"I get to record a message for Lieutenant Odana before I leave and have it delivered to her by the administrator who takes my volunteer oath." Davik returned B'Nay's cold stare. "She is perfectly capable of killing anyone who's been in contact with me if she thinks I was forced into this deal. If you've studied her, you know she can do it and never be caught."

B'Nay laughed. "Lieutenant Odana is a formidable talent. However, I highly doubt she has the ability to carry out such a threat."

"I don't," Davik replied. "I know her far better than you ever will."

B'Nay's triumphant smile turned into a cold frown. "Make your recording. You will have one chance and I have the right to edit it so you aren't giving away any information regarding the project. My edited version is what she will receive. So, choose your words well."

Davik remained in the room for another hour, wondering if the offer had been another means to torture his mind. Eventually, a technician brought in the recording equipment and an administrative official came to take his oath. The man remained while Davik tried to compose his thoughts. He had only one chance to get the words right.

He wiped his sweaty palms against his thighs as the technician shined a bright light in his face. He wished for a glass of water to dampen the desert that had suddenly appeared in his throat. *One chance.*

"Go," the technician said.

Davik looked into the camera.

"Tridia." His voice croaked and words caught in his throat. *One chance.* "I don't know how much time they'll give me. I leave Odea today. They're only letting me leave you a message because they're afraid you'll kill them if they don't – I told them you would. Sorry for putting you on the spot. At least their reaction gives me some hope you're still alive. I know you don't need me to tell you, but I have to say it aloud for my own sanity. I didn't do it. That crime was so appalling –"

Words failed. How could he make her believe him? She had to believe him so he could warn her to watch her back. "The circumstantial evidence was damning and I had no type of defense, no alibi. But you know me. I couldn't have done something like that. I could never face you again if I had. And the thought of seeing you again is all that's kept me going. They've told me so many lies in the Kennel. Their mind games are worse than the physical torture. The beatings I'll eventually heal from, but the doubt will stay with me until I know the truth from you. They said you'd died on your mission to Alliance space. After a few days they changed the story to say you'd survived but had been captured by Sentinels and were scheduled for execution. I was the one who designed your escape strategies. If you'd been captured, it would have been my fault. I couldn't bear the thought and they knew it. Later they said you'd escaped but refused to see me. Finally, they told me you'd come and they took me into a room to wait. They left me there for hours before saying you'd changed your mind." He couldn't breathe. She wouldn't have turned her back on him. *Keep going. If you stall they'll stop recording.*

"You never came to see me. Never got word to me. I know something has happened to you or you would have come. You know I wouldn't –" *Don't repeat. Stick to the point. She has to know B'Nay is after her.*

"Not knowing is worse than anything they can do to me, but I'll never learn the truth from them. If you're still alive and the message finds its way to you – I shouldn't say this, not now, not when who knows how many people will see the message before you – but I may never get another chance. I love you. I have for a long time. I was going to tell you when you got back, tell you I requested housing accommodations for the two of us to share quarters. I wanted to keep you out of the breeding program and keep you safe – as my wife."

Davik closed his eyes. She would believe that. He'd given her enough hints. It would give her a basis for her investigation. *Keep talking.* "That won't happen now. I can't protect you anymore and it will haunt me until the day I die." *Last chance to keep her safe.* "That's what might have been, and what will never be. Now you'll have to take care of yourself, and you're good at that. You've made enemies and there are people who want to control you. Get paranoid and stay that way. I'm gone. Let me go. So, find the bastards that did this, Lieutenant Odana, but don't try to make them pay. Hate them enough for both of us, but don't expose yourself in a way that will land you in here. From what I could piece together, there had to be more than one person involved. They were able to shut down the security cameras in my apartment building and everywhere between there and the morgue. This wasn't a couple of evil people. It was a swarm, but there's always a leader. Look to your files. They got access to my DNA somehow or were able to switch the test results before the trial. A few random comments from the guards make me think this might be a prelude to framing you. I have sound reasons to believe this had something to do with our relationship, but I don't know if that's truth or illusion. It all has the touch of a master's hand. Go over the evidence they found. It was planted, of course, by someone with access codes only I should have. I know you'll find something because you can presume – know – I'm innocent. None of the investigators made much of an effort. The court martial was over in a week. Find the ones who framed me and you'll discover the path to your true enemies. Uncover them to protect yourself but leave me to my fate. *Do not come after me.*"

Davik lowered his lashes, then looked directly at the camera again, imagining her steel gray eyes looking into his. "I've accepted a bargain for time off my sentence by volunteering for an experimental program. If I survive, I may be able to contact you in a few years. If not, you were the best part of my life."

"Enough eloquence, Lieutenant." B'Nay had entered the room unnoticed. "That should make delightful editing."

Davik glared. "She will find out it was you."

"I'll make sure she does," B'Nay said.

***

Rage built in Davik again at the memory. He'd betrayed Tridia before the gruesome events even happened by filing the housing applications. He'd given B'Nay and his cronies a lever to use against them both. Then he'd compounded the betrayal by leaving the recorded message. He had no way of knowing how his words might have been twisted. Could B'Nay have made it sound like he blamed her, or, worse, wanted her to come after him?

Energy sparked within Davik's elongated shape. His energy flared and Davik lost the sensation of touch he'd maintained against the wall. At that moment, he could blast the walls to infinitesimal dust. He reined in the rage enough to feel the wall again.

I can't go around in a rage the whole time – although it wouldn't be difficult to manage under these circumstances. If they ever find out thoughts of Tridia are the source of my power, they'll bring her here to coerce me into obedience. Better make sure that little fact never gets out. Now what happens if I control those emotions as I project the energy?

Davik found another blank space on the wall and concentrated on sending out a stronger controlled pulse. The rock broke away in minute layers. He fed more emotion through the pulse, thinking of Tridia alone in the Hierarchy, at the mercy of the breeders who'd determine the best match for her genes. Deep gouges followed the line of the pulse. When he stopped, a full sentence appeared on the wall: My name is Davik Schie. He backed away, exhilarated by the accomplishment. A tremor ran through his being and his mass drooped closer to the cavern floor. The effort had drained him. It could be an expected side-effect, but he wouldn't know unless he cooperated with the scientists, and they, in turn, listened to him.

He might not have all the power the Hierarchy wanted, but he had enough to bargain with. He'd be ready when they returned.

***

Drayden thumped a stylus against the desktop as the professor hologram droned on about satellite structure. All attempts to accelerate the lessons had failed and he'd spent the past five days reviewing and studying the engineering schematics for the shield satellites protecting Zentel, the small planet where he was exiled. His parched throat had become a raging inferno and even swallowing cold water had become a painful experience. His right arm throbbed where the skike had sliced into his flesh. He'd cleaned it with antibiotic and wrapped it when he'd gotten to the bunker, but he hadn't had the physician hologram attend him for such a small injury. He'd started feeling ill three days ago and when he'd removed the bandage before showering that morning, the wound was an angry red with yellow pustules forming inside it.

"Your Highness?" The professor frowned as he spoke.

Drayden tried to focus on the disagreeable image, but his vision blurred. "Yes, Professor?"

"I said I must terminate this lesson until you are cleared by the physician program. My scan shows you have an elevated temperature," the professor explained.

Drayden didn't respond. Fever? He'd never had a fever in his life. The physician program would never let him hear the end of his irresponsibility, and he didn't look forward to the lecture.

"Must I repeat the statement?"

"That won't be necessary." Drayden's voice was a hoarse whisper. He stood, but stumbled as he turned toward the door. He grabbed his chair for support. When had he gotten so weak? "Teak."

A floating disk about a meter across and half a meter tall drifted into the room, its lights flashing and piping a musical trill that sounded much like the Rrabbas' telepathic language. The hoverbot had assisted Drayden in the bunker for the past fifteen years, serving as valet, playmate, and guardian when needed.

"Help me to the biology lab," Drayden said, sliding his left arm across the disk for support. The hoverbot piped another brief chord. "No, I don't want to go to the medical examination room. I just need something for a fever and an infection. I've got to get back to my studies." The little machine piped again. "The physician program can't do anything I don't give her permission to do, and she can't force me into the exam room." A low chord sounded, to which Drayden frowned but didn't reply.

Once Teak got him into the lab, Drayden leaned against a table and removed his shirt to make the bandages more accessible. He unwound the cloth, but the last bits of bandage stuck to the wound, and it caused a fresh flow of blood when he yanked it away. Blood and pus flowed down his arm. "Physician, I need your attendance, please."

Teak floated toward the door but remained in the room.

A female with dark hair and eyes appeared. "Yes, Your Highness."

"Can you attend this, please? And hurry, if you would?" Drayden always tried to show respect to the female hologram. The image had been copied from the woman who'd been his physician before he was sent into exile. She'd always made him laugh to ease his fears before an examination.

"This has the look of violence, Prince Drayden," she commented, as she examined the bleeding cut. "How did this happen? You've been inside the bunker for almost a week."

"My own carelessness caused a skike to attack at the edge of the old growth forest," he replied. "It's just a cut. There was no venom."

"Don't count on it." Drayden winced as the physician swabbed the wound with less gentleness than she normally used with him. "If that monster had been fighting with other monsters, it could have venom on its pincers as well as any other part of its body. You've left this without proper attention for days!"

"I didn't consider that," Drayden admitted, then winced again. "Hey, take it easy! One of us can feel pain."

"And one of us has intelligence!" the physician snapped. "You disregard your personal health as if you had no future. You carry the responsibility for rebuilding the Chesan race and yet you persist in leaving the bunker without any form of protection. This must stop, Your Highness. If you are encountering skikes, you've been in the desert. You've been there for weeks, judging from your last log in."

"Enough!" Drayden's eyes widened as much as the physician's. He'd never raised his voice to any of the holographic instructors. "How I spend my time is not your concern. As long as I record the appropriate hours of study and maintain an acceptable standard of achievement, the systems have no control over my coming and going. Have my hours of study lagged?"

"No, Your Highness," the physician replied.

"Have my standards become unacceptable?"

"No, Your Highness. Your levels of achievement far surpass the highest expectations programmed into the system."

"Nice to know so little was expected of me." Drayden used his shirt to catch the blood running down his arm. The physician attended his wound again.

"You have been alone since you were seven years old. There was a possibility the isolation would retard your development."

"Were it not for the Rrabbas, I might well have fallen into that state. Fortunately, I didn't." Drayden stood away from the table and looked down into the holograph's eyes. "Now, if you will please get on with it?"

"Yes, Your Highness." A series of beams scanned Drayden's arm, then his entire body. The physician finished cleaning the wound and put a fresh dressing on it. "This is a nasty infection. Your vitamin levels have depleted and you're on the verge of exhaustion."

"Don't lecture." Drayden scowled. "I'm on a tight schedule. Just do what you need to do to set this right and clear me with my tutors. I need to return to my studies."

"I should do blood analysis to determine the exact cause of the infection."

"Is that really necessary?"

"Yes!" The image hesitated as Drayden stared, then added, "Your

Highness."

"Do it," Drayden grumbled. He would have walked away but was afraid he'd fall if he left the table. Teak piped from the doorway. "No, just stay here for a few minutes so you can help me back to the study."

The physician drew two vials of blood and set them on the table. "May I administer a vitamin injection to boost your immunities and speed your healing?"

Drayden ran a hand through his hair. "Yes, you may, if you'll be quick about it. I intend to have a full physical once I finish my studies. My throat is burning."

"Is this a recent development? Caused by the injury?" The holograph moved about the lab retrieving small vials and a hypo-spray.

"No, this started before then," Drayden replied, watching everything the physician did. "There are lumps behind my jawbone. I may have contracted a virus or bacteria before I encountered the skike. A parasite wouldn't be out of the question."

The physician hesitated filling the hypo and glared at Drayden. "And you wonder why I'm upset you spend so much time outside the bunker?"

"Let's not resume that discussion." Drayden nodded toward the vials. "You're putting more than vitamins into the hypo."

"You should have some other trace elements to restore you to optimum health."

"Whatever you say. I'm in a hurry." Drayden didn't flinch as the physician administered the injection. "Now if you will clear me with the tutors, I'll –"

Drayden stumbled a step and reached out to grasp the edge of the table. Teak zoomed to his side, guiding him toward the small bed on one side of the room. The image of the physician blurred before his eyes. "What have you done?"

"You're exhausted, Your Highness, and very ill. Your temperature is far above safe limits and your internal organs are struggling to function. I merely added a few trace elements to help you rest." The physician was unapologetic. "You have about thirty seconds to reach the bed or the sofa, or you will be sleeping on the floor."

"Remind me to leave your program running the next time I leave the bunker." Drayden fell onto the nearby bed, his eyes closed before his head touched the pillow.

"Yes, Your Highness." The physician covered the prince with a light blanket. A scowl clouded her face as she touched Drayden's neck just behind his jaw bone. "This shouldn't be happening."

Teak piped a long strain of music.

"He'll recover from the infection, but our prince has greater issues," the physician said. "He won't be needing you for a couple of days. Prepare some fresh juices for him tomorrow evening and bring them to the cooler here and in his study. Make sure there's a sufficient supply of water in his study. I won't be able to keep him from his tutors when he wakes up."

Teak piped its chord of acceptance then drifted away. The physician program ran through all data files on Chesan mating and maturity as the hologram image moved to study the blood samples she'd taken. Subroutines in the massive computer kicked in, and the artificial intelligence that had nurtured Drayden from childhood underwent yet another internal upgrade to account for the prince's latest unexpected changes.

CHAPTER FOUR

Brenden sat in the pilot's seat on the *Star Seeker's* bridge, contemplating the various tasks for which he found himself responsible. The Guardian Controller had assigned him to protect Deeca. He'd given an oath to the dead Chesan king to safe-guard Prince Drayden – which meant getting the truth from Tridia, then killing her so she didn't cause a galactic holocaust. His grandmother had foisted upon him the responsibility to rescue her adopted daughter. And the Supreme Commander of the Odean Hierarchy had tasked him to find the root of the silence spreading across the galaxy and contrive a plan to stop it. Along with his responsibilities as an ambassador to two planets and the Hierarchy, he also ran several major inter-stellar corporations, not including his dealings with Morgan Jacks, an underworld figure of dark repute.

Yet, none of that pressure compared with the stress he endured dealing with his feelings for Deeca while they were in such close quarters. They shared a past she couldn't remember – thanks to him and the Controller – but he recalled it with grueling intensity.

Compounding those emotions was his attraction to Tridia. It might not be real, but the compulsion to seduce her caught him off-guard, and he could ill-afford a mistake in that area – especially if she was dealing with the same emotions. The smallest concession on either of their parts meant disaster for them both. Physiological changes caused by the Chesan enzyme made the struggle more difficult, just as Dojene said it would.

The workout he'd planned with her might best be handled by one of the Sentinels, but that wouldn't suit his purpose. Dojene expected Tridia's powers to increase rapidly beyond his control. He needed to know her current abilities to be able to judge any shift in power. Only sparring with their telepathic skills fully engaged would give him the information he needed.

As he thought of Tridia, he swallowed hard against the taste of honey and sugar in his mouth. *Damn.* He may have to request the Sentinels' aid, after all. A tiny jolt shot from the gold bands at his wrists, up his arms and throughout his body. His muscles tensed, then relaxed. The Guardian Controller sent a message.

You're not alone in this.

A sardonic smile curved his lips. No, he wasn't alone. With the Sentinels able to sense his thoughts, his constant awareness of both Tridia and Deeca, and the Controller giving him pep talks, he couldn't get a moment's privacy without using extreme barriers. As if to prove the point, a voice behind him made him spin his chair to face the door.

"You're troubled, Ambassador." Alanel made it a statement, not a question.

"We're on a suicide mission. Why wouldn't I be troubled?" Brenden didn't bother to hide his surprise that the Sentinels had caught him unaware.

"The mission isn't your gravest concern," Winniel said. "Something else surpasses your fear of the feeders."

Brenden frowned. Were the Sentinels not able to see him as transparently as usual? "True. I have a greater concern. You need to protect Commander Odana."

"We've already undertaken that task," Alanel said.

"Not just her life," Brenden explained. "You have to keep the two of us apart. At least, don't leave us alone together."

The Sentinels exchanged a look that seemed remarkably like confusion.

"You can't sense it, can you?" Brenden asked. "Your telepathic abilities have diminished because of this attachment to the Commander. No wonder you're on edge." Both Sentinels tensed at his words. "Who would I tell? Why should I? The Sentinels are too valuable to the stability of the Core Alliance for me to do anything that might damage your image. I have enough experience to know I can't blackmail you with the knowledge."

"Then explain what you need us to know," Alanel said. "Without entering your mind, we have only glimpses of your thoughts."

Brenden explained the situation between him and Tridia and the possible need to restrain them if the pull became too much.

Winniel scowled. "She's a mere child in your race."

"I'm aware of that," Brenden said. "That's why I need your help. Everything I learned from her journals and training schedules says she's had no relationships that could remotely prepare her for this. Unless she and Davik Schie were hiding a secret romance, she's dodged every form of emotional entanglement. I know what's happening to me, and if she's experiencing anything like it – If I slip, so will she. Just don't leave the two of us alone for more than a few moments."

"We will act as chaperones," Alanel said.

"You need to monitor the sparring match, as well," Brenden continued. "I can't explain what's happened, but she isn't behaving as she did prior to her stay on the hospital ship. She doesn't move the same way that she did on Odea. Even injured, she had a type of grace, an efficiency of movement that's lacking now."

"We sense an uneasiness in her thoughts we don't understand." Winniel said. "It's as though another personality is trying to emerge. Her flashes of disorientation always include a Felinus figure. Perhaps the transformation is still affecting her."

"That's a possibility," Brenden replied. "She went through a lot in that body – from what Empress Dojene shared, and what little I've gleaned from the Commander herself. She was well hidden inside the Felinus persona. I didn't sense her in the Public Hearing Room until she revealed herself."

"She is in my care," Winniel said. "I will see that she doesn't slip."

"Thank you," Brenden said.

"We'll prepare the cargo area for your match. Winniel will return with the child." Alanel left and Winniel followed.

Brenden spun the chair to face the controls and entered commands to activate the communications console. He sent coded messages to several recipients, then sat back to await a response. With his sources, it wouldn't take long.

***

Tridia had just gotten to her feet to report to Master Aren when Winniel appeared and followed her to the bridge. The desire to touch Master Aren when she was near him threatened to drive her to inappropriate behavior. At the same time, she wanted to punch him in the face for the things he'd done to her mind. With the enzyme her glands secreted every time she was near him causing such confused emotions, she had more than enough reasons to not face him alone. She sent Winniel an appreciative thought. The Sentinel nodded in return.

When they reached the bridge, Tridia took the navigator's seat and Winniel stopped in the doorway. Master Aren sat in the pilot's seat and spoke to someone on the open communications channel.

"Give me the latest."

"The Hierarchy is no longer in residence on Cystia," a male voice said.

A spark of recognition taunted Tridia's memories, but she couldn't bring out a face or name.

"The planet, with all improvements and appurtenances, was leased to a conglomerate through Central Holdings within the last two months. The Hierarchy retains mineral rights to any uridine mined there, and they've wired the planetary defenses to track the departure of any transports from the planet."

"Is that it?" Master Aren asked.

"Only some scuttlebutt about an ongoing Odean experiment on the surface," the voice said. "So far, the new tenants have removed no minerals from the mine. They haven't made any significant improvements. The area around the compound is reported to be overrun with dangerous animal life. The Hierarchy saw them as an escape deterrent and didn't eradicate them when they built the prison compound."

"Are the planetary defenses still functioning?"

"Undetermined. The Hierarchy made no code changes. If the new owners are using the defenses, they're running with the same access codes."

"Unless they happened to have brilliant programmers and reverse engineers in their employ." Master Aren spun his chair to face Tridia as he continued to speak to the unknown person. "Meet us at Cystia but keep your distance. It wouldn't do for both ships to get caught unaware."

"Don't worry. I've got your back." The speakers went silent.

"New tenants, but not necessarily pursuing new or independent goals," Tridia said. "An experiment in progress – Davik?"

"Could be – and likely is – based on the fact he was sent there after the mining operations had stopped."

"Whatever happened to him, I need to set it right. Especially if it was because of me."

"We see to the assigned mission first. That's a direct order, Commander. No detours to satisfy your own unsolved mysteries." The hard edge in Master Aren's voice allowed no argument. "Then if we can, we'll attend to Lieutenant Schie together. I made you a promise on Hielos – only the stars know why – but I'll see it through."

Tridia wanted to argue, but the soldier in her couldn't. She'd been given an order and she had to obey it. "Yes, sir. Thank you."

"Thank me after you pick your butt up off the cargo bay floor."

"A contact match?" Tridia's eyes brightened.

"Don't look so excited, Commander. It's a weakness to underestimate your opponent. This is low contact – no broken bones, cracked ribs, or blood."

"Just bruised butts?"

"Just getting you familiar with your own movements again. I can't have an operative who doesn't know her own strengths or abilities." Master Aren stood and stretched. "Let's go. The Sentinels will watch over us and make sure you don't injure me."

"Sir, who was your informant? His voice sounds familiar, but...

"You met him in your previous life. Actually, you saved his life twice in one night. His name is Tran and we will not discuss my association with him in anyone else's company. He's not exactly a welcomed visitor in legitimate circles."

Tridia looked toward Winniel. Master Aren glanced over his shoulder.

"I have very few secrets from the Sentinels," he said.

Tridia raised her eyebrows. "You've got an underworld associate?"

"Which will not be mentioned on this ship again." Master Aren's tone of voice conveyed a command Tridia might have ignored in his words. "You will learn things in your association with me that will stay between us. I can't hide everything from you, nor do I intend to try. Your obedience in this is not negotiable."

"Of course, Master." Tridia lowered her eyes but clenched her jaw. Another order she couldn't disregard.

"Let's get to it." Master Aren started for the door. "The ship can take care of itself for now. There are no anomalies registering anywhere nearby, and Deeca should return shortly."

Tridia followed him to the cargo bay. Winniel moved to Alanel's side and they stood together near the stowed equipment. Master Aren removed his jacket and shoes. Tridia followed suit by removing her boots. He faced her squarely and bowed from the waist. Tridia did likewise.

"Open your thoughts as much as you wish, try to breach my barriers to follow my thoughts if you like. We won't disturb anyone else on the ship," Master Aren said.

"You have the advantage since I've never sparred another telepath."

"Do you always expect a fair competition?" He assumed a defensive stance.

The distracting force of his presence slammed against Tridia's light barriers. She took a step back before reinforcing them, giving herself space to react to any sudden attacks.

"Not in any competition with you," she grumbled.

"Remember, no injuries here. No matter how frustrated you get," he said.

Tridia brought her hands up and took a defensive stance, but she couldn't settle into a form. She shifted position and stepped to the side, never taking her eyes from him or dropping her mental barriers. "Do you expect it to be so one-sided?"

In answer, Master Aren made a quick move to her left, got behind her and landed a light slap to her kidney. She turned to face him. He was fast.

"Focus! Let's see your spark step."

Tridia swallowed. She'd done it once without meaning to when she sparred Colonel Zilisk and once to save the empress from her traitor bodyguard, then again as a Felinus to protect Dr. Elenus. Could she purposefully do it again as herself?

"What's the matter?" Master Aren asked. His defenses never dropped as he continued to prowl, trying to find a more advantageous position. His thoughts pressed harder against her mental shield.

"Nothing, sir," Tridia replied. "Just trying to focus."

She took a step intending to end up across the room but moved only the single step. Master Aren attacked again with a single backhand to her cheek she couldn't block. Tridia's face warmed and her fists clenched.

"You've forgotten." Master Aren's statement hit like another slap to the face.

Tridia settled into her stance, letting her body take control. She'd battled three assailants blindfolded and managed to hold her own when she remembered nothing. Since then, she'd been in real fights, sustained real injuries, and honed her skills to commendable levels. Why could she now not block simple attacks? Master Aren attacked again, landing a painful blow to the back of her thigh. Her left knee bent and she almost went down.

No! Nira Kayen's consciousness emerged – a calm warrior with all the skills of a soldier-assassin. A startled Tridia Odana watched as her hands and feet blocked Master Aren's rapid attacks. Her body moved with grace and confidence as the warrior took control.

She landed her first contact with a light kick to Master Aren's mid-section, followed quickly by side kicks to his knee and ribs. Nira danced away unscathed as Master Aren pursued her. Tridia fought to regain control of her body as her legs launched into a spark step. She couldn't stop her momentum. When Master Aren side-stepped, she sped toward the bulkhead. Tridia threw her arms up to protect her face, but before she crashed, Winniel stepped in front of her and shoved her aside and into Alanel's waiting arms. He spun with her to slow her momentum and came to a stop with her back held firmly against his chest. Fine tawny fur began to form on Tridia' arms. Pain shot through her hands and feet as their shape started to change.

"What in Hielos?" Master Aren took a step back.

Tridia couldn't answer and she didn't dare look at him. Her body trembled with anger and spent fear. Winniel hurried to pull the pouch from Tridia's pocket. She chose one of Tridia's DNA vials and pushed an injection into her arm. The fur retreated and Tridia's hands and feet returned to normal.

"You must release her consciousness, child," Winniel said. "If you ever wish to remain stable in your own form and fight as yourself again, you must let Nira Kayen go."

"Nira Kayen?" Master Aren asked. "Nira Kayen was an alias name."

"She is also a consciousness created under the empress's instruction." Winniel's hand tightened on Tridia's bicep. "It was intended to be merely a persona, but it's struggling for control."

"I thought I had released her," Tridia said. "Nira Kayen became a Felinus personality. I let her go in the Public Hearing Room."

"Will you allow me to enter your mind?" Winniel asked.

"Is that wise, Winniel?" Alanel asked. Tridia realized she was still cradled with her back against his chest and tried to stand apart, but he tightened his arms. "You will be entering her mind in a few hours to set the barrier."

"This won't take long, and there won't be much pain for either of us," Winniel said.

Tridia's heart pounded at the memory of the brutal invasion of her mind on Aga, but she had no more choice now than she had then. She nodded for Winniel to proceed. An icy probe assaulted her brain immediately. Winniel spoke Nira Kayen's name and a second consciousness surfaced in Tridia's mind.

Commander Odana, take back what belongs to you. Winniel instructed. *Your skills, your knowledge, your deportment. Strip them from her the same way you gave them to her.*

Tridia tried to remember what she had given to Nira Kayen's consciousness. Respect for her master. Skills for battle. Awareness of her surroundings. Nira's consciousness fought back, trying to retain her identity, but Winniel held it in place as Tridia stripped it away. Finally, she took Nira's name and claimed it as her own alias, and only a vague memory of another person remained in Tridia's mind. Winniel's presence withdrew and Tridia sagged in Alanel's arms.

"I'm glad there wasn't much pain." Tridia slurred the words.

Master Aren handed her a flask lid of huttle juice. "Sip it."

The liquid touched her lips, then her tongue, spreading like sweet fire through her body. Her mind cleared and the pain subsided. She swallowed the rest and handed the lid back to her master.

"Thank you, sir," she said.

"Tell me about this consciousness."

Tridia stepped away from Alanel and thanked him, before answering Master Aren. "There's not much to tell. The empress told me my persona leaked emotions. She said I might be able to hide it behind a false persona. I spent hours creating a consciousness for Nira Kayen, the Felinus warrior. I thought she'd dissolved when I revealed myself to you in the Public Hearing Room. I didn't know I had to dismantle her."

"The empress obviously had other things on her mind," Master Aren said. "I'm sure she never expected you to create a consciousness instead of a persona."

"She told me to give it information so it wouldn't be confused," Tridia argued. "Was she trying to splinter my personality?"

"Only the lady herself knows. The empress betrayed no such thoughts to me." Master Aren put the flask away in a duffle bag. "Are you ready to try this again in your right mind?"

"Yes, sir." Tridia moved to the center of the room. Her eyes never left her master. When he attacked, she blocked; when he dodged, she pursued; when he gave her an opening, she struck. She gradually lowered her barriers to sense his thoughts. He held back enough of his presence that she wasn't overwhelmed, but battling his thoughts was almost as difficult as blocking his attacks. He scored contacts on her, but not easily, and not often. By the time he called it quits, Tridia had scored as many on him.

"That's enough," Master Aren said. "Rest up. We'll start the barrier building an hour out from Cystia."

"I'll have only eleven hours on the ground!" Tridia protested.

"We can't wait until we're on the ground, Commander. The process takes at least half an hour and it will tax all of us. Even the Sentinels will feel the strain. You heard Alanel. We'll need time to recover. If we can't finish the mission in eleven hours on the ground, we aren't likely to accomplish it at all."

"Yes, sir." Tridia retrieved her boots and sat on a crate to put them on. Master Aren was right. Eleven hours was a long time for such a mission.

She stayed behind as the others left the cargo hold. If the three of them needed time to recover from the process, how rough would it be on her? The thought of more icy probes wandering through her brain made her temples throb.

What have I let myself in for this time?

CHAPTER FIVE

An hour out from Cystia, Tridia stood in the lounge facing Master Aren and the Sentinels. Deeca and Sonei had sequestered themselves on the bridge after Alanel's strong warning not to intrude on the Ambassador's plans. Even Deeca hadn't offered up an argument, though she'd glared at the four of them before leaving the lounge. Sonei had shot a sympathetic look toward Tridia, making it clear that she expected nothing good to happen.

"What do I do?" Tridia's fists clenched on clammy palms.

Master Aren sat in a chair. "Come kneel in front of me with your back to me. Both knees on the floor and sit back on your heels. Put your elbows on my thighs, your hands on my knees."

Tridia scowled but obeyed. When she'd settled back on her heels, Master Aren leaned forward and placed his arms over hers, intertwining their fingers. His chin rested on her shoulder. Tridia squirmed.

"Relax, Commander. This will keep you from striking out with either your hands or your feet." Master Aren nodded to the Sentinels and Winniel knelt before Tridia.

"This will be painful for both of us," Winniel said. "You will feel the immediate intrusion of my entire being and your inclination will be to resist, both mentally and physically. The Ambassador believes he can contain you physically. Mentally, it is up to you. Each mind is different in how it protects itself – or how it surrenders."

"You've shown a mental tendency to retreat to protect your consciousness from an overwhelming force," Master Aren said. "That was a fair reaction given previous circumstances. This time you'll have to stay and fight. Hold your ground as best you can against the pain and wait for her image to form in your mind. Then she'll tell you what to do."

48

"I will help you begin your barrier, but you must take it up and finish it on your own," Winniel spoke again. "I can stay until your barrier is almost complete, then I'll leave your consciousness. Alanel will intervene should I become overwhelmed. Do everything you can to be sure that doesn't happen. Should he intervene, we are finished. We cannot try again and you must remain on the ship with us while the Ambassador and Hunter Varin go into the mine."

Tridia said nothing but gave a small nod and tightened her entwined fingers with Master Aren's. His cheek pressed against her right ear. The touch sent goose bumps along her arms and down her spine. A splash of sweetness filled her mouth and she had to swallow again. He tightened his grip on her fingers until she had to focus to keep from crying out. Winniel reached up both hands and touched Tridia's temples. For a heartbeat nothing happened. Then the impact of an ice flow crashed into her frontal lobe. She jerked back in response and fought to free her hands, but Master Aren held them in a crushing grip.

Tridia tried to withdraw with all the sense that remained to her.

Commander Odana, stand and fight! That's an order! Master Aren's shout broke through the frozen invasion. *The faster you face this, the faster it will be over.*

Tridia tried to shake her head against his words, but he kept pressure against her ear with his cheek. The warmth of his skin penetrated the terrifying cold.

Her memory spawned a white landscape, the sound of an approaching craft filled her ears, but her arms remained immobile against the ice. Her stomach, chest, and legs pressed against an icy bed. The fur trim of a hooded coat protected her face from the ice, but nothing could protect it from the cold. She had to wake up! If she slept on the ice she'd die. A blue glow surrounded her, making a cocoon of pulsing energy. It produced just enough warmth to keep her alive, but not enough to melt the ice. Alive to meet the opponent in the craft. Alive to rescue Davik. Alive to reach – Blackness swallowed the name. She had to focus, still her mind. The white flower had worked before. She placed a perfect white flower before her face. Then another, and another until the frozen landscape lay hidden beneath a blanket of white blossoms, each flower identical in its perfection.

Someone moved across the ice. Her stalker, the one who wanted to take her life. She tried to focus through a swirl of snow as a shadow approached. The blaster in her hand lifted of its own accord and the blue energy seeped into her arm. Her finger pulled the trigger, the energy pulse left the barrel then froze in the air. She pulled the trigger again and again, but nothing happened. The first pulse continued to hang just inches from the useless weapon.

"You don't need a blaster this time, child." Winniel stepped through a frozen swirl of snow.

"Why do you call me child if you've come to kill me?" Tridia asked. "Does that make it easier?"

"You are a child in many ways, Tridia Odana. For all of the blood staining your hands, you are very young, indeed. Nothing can take away the guilt, but you've been forgiven for the crimes you've confessed. I haven't come to kill you this time. I've come to help you build a wall."

Tridia's physical body jerked backward. Her head slammed against Master Aren's shoulder. Her elbows dug into his thighs and her body heated. Sweetness filled her mouth again.

Concentrate, Commander, or you'll destroy us both. Brenden's voice was hoarse in her mind.

Brenden? No, it was Master Aren. She mustn't think of him any other way. She'd taken an oath to obey him. Tridia concentrated.

The white world of flowers and snow swirled into a brilliant white light with Winniel at its center. Winniel's copper eyes became Tridia's focal point – calm, dark pools in the whiteness.

"I can do this," Tridia said. Her words came in sharp gasps. "Block by block?"

"No, layer by layer," Winniel said. "Imagine this whiteness – and the pain it represents – as a light that can be filtered until it can be tolerated. Place a thin sheet of color across it."

Tridia envisioned a sheet of turquoise blue energy in its place. Winniel immediately tore the energy sheet away, crumbled it, and tossed it aside.

"Try again. You can't replace one energy with another. This color has no power. It is simply a sheet between you and the light."

Tridia concentrated. Thin sheets of translucent wrapping paper appeared amid the glaring light. A comb, brush, and mirror nestled in a small basket wrapped in thin teal-colored paper popped into her memory.

"Congratulations, Lieutenant Odana!" Davik's face, as yet undamaged by the beating that was to come, smiled as he offered her the gift. Then he laughed. "Next time, I'll have to call you 'Ma'am'."

Tears formed in Tridia's eyes. She turned her face against Master Aren's cheek. His scent brought her back to the present as she swallowed the sweetness again. She had to keep going. When she placed the barrier between her and the light again, it was a pale teal sheet that did little to filter the brightness. She pressed the sheet until it was a smooth layer, then waited.

"Yes," Winniel said. "Just like this. Place another sheet between you and the light."

Tridia obeyed. Fifteen times she placed sheets and smoothed them out. Each time Winniel prompted her to add another. When she'd placed the fifteenth sheet, Winniel's voice seemed far away, and the pain had dulled to an aching throb.

"Continue this until you no longer feel the pain, until no outside thoughts touch yours."

It took another twenty sheets before Tridia felt no pain. An opaque teal wall kept out the bright white light and an intense solitude engulfed her. Not even the lingering awareness of the Sentinel's presence broke through the barrier.

***

"Commander. Commander Odana, wake up." Tridia blinked and looked around. Master Aren was shaking her shoulder and speaking to her. His words lacked any depth beyond their tones. The fabric on his pants lay smooth beneath her fingers, and the muscles of his thighs felt solid beneath her arms, but the structure of his legs beyond her touch didn't exist. The chair, the sofa, and the floor were visible, but they lacked definition. Nothing about the confines of the ship seemed familiar, as though everything had become a flat drawing. How could she function in such a world? A cold panic threatened to rise up her spine. Just as she thought she would succumb, Master Aren pushed her shoulders forward.

"Welcome to the world of humans," he said. "You'd best stand up and learn to walk again."

Tridia took Winniel's proffered hand and struggled to her feet. She stumbled a few steps holding onto Winniel's arm.

"Your telepathy is interwoven with your consciousness – even your balance depends on it," Master Aren continued. "Normal humans walk without thinking because of sight. The blind rely on implants, visors – or canes, on the undeveloped planets. Chesans became telepathically aware in the womb – although full telepathic powers developed much later in childhood. So, from the beginning you've relied on that awareness, even though you may not have been conscious of it."

Tridia wobbled a little when she let go of Winniel's arm, but she regained her balance after a few steps. She looked at the floor at first to navigate among the furniture in the lounge. The fact that something as mundane as personal navigation relied so heavily on her telepathic abilities brought a new appreciation for humans. They'd had to develop their skills in the isolation she now felt. What if her telepathy never returned? She pushed the thought from her mind. Twelve hours. She had to endure it for only twelve hours. After all that had happened to her in the last month, that seemed a short time, but she hadn't had to go through any of it in total isolation.

"Fifteen minutes to hyperspace exit." Deeca's voice came over the intercom. "Whatever you're working on in there, finish up."

"Alanel, can you and Winniel go to the cargo hold and be ready to scan the planet for signs of life?" Master Aren asked. "I'll use the ship's scanners, but you would be in a better position to know what's going on down there. If you're able."

"We're able," Alanel said, then added. "At least enough for that." He and Winniel left for the cargo hold.

Tridia stood with her hand on the back of the sofa for balance. Master Aren stood in the center of the lounge, a few feet away.

"Why do I continue to taste this sweetness? It almost choked me when you leaned against me." Tridia waited. "It's the Chesan enzyme. I tasted it when we kissed on the hospital ship. I've seen you swallow hard at times. You're experiencing this, too. What's going on?"

"I'm not the person to have maturity discussions with you," Master Aren replied. He turned to walk away, but Tridia stumbled over and caught his arm.

"You're the only one available, sir," she said. "It may not be comfortable, but I need to know."

Master Aren took a deep breath then spoke without looking at her. "I told you that the glands behind your jaw secrete an enzyme that caused the prophetic visions we saw. It's also supposed to aid in selecting a mate. When you kiss an intended mate, both parties' glands trigger and produce enzymes that counteract each other."

"It keeps happening. Is it just because we're in close proximity?" Tridia asked. "I have no intention of –"

"Most likely because we've kissed before." He finally turned to meet her anxious gaze. "We haven't finished the mating."

Tridia let go of his arm and stepped back.

"I didn't know this would happen when I kissed you." Master Aren took a step back, as well. "Those glands should only exist at maturity, but Chesans – male and female – don't mature until their early forties. You're too young by over twenty years. Since I'm not fully Chesan, I didn't expect to even have glands. I didn't before our kiss. Fortunately, they matured in time to save my life."

"Save your life?" Tridia scowled.

"The empress didn't have time for lengthy explanations, but apparently if one of the partners has no glands, they die – painfully. I experienced the painfully part and very nearly the dying part." Master Aren said. "Repeated doses of the enzyme and the consummation of the pairing are an antidote. Having my glands mature saved my life but didn't terminate the reaction to your enzyme. I don't know if there are other ways to get around it or get over it. As the empress pointed out, I haven't been trained in the Chesan rites and ways."

"So, we've got to be very careful," Tridia said.

"Yes," Master Aren agreed. "Which is why we're not to be alone with each other for any length of time. No contact between us without the Sentinels present unless our lives depend on it. And no kissing – anyone – until we get this figured out."

He took another step away and Tridia didn't pursue him. No kissing? She'd only kissed him the first time because he ordered her to. She felt no desire for him, but the need to touch him increased every time he was near. Would she have to struggle with those feelings forever – or finally give in to the emotions?

He'll kill me before he allows himself to mate with me. Fear of the Chaos Vision would see to it.

"Hyperspace exit in ten," Deeca announced over the intercom.

"I'll be on the bridge," Master Aren said. "Walk until it's time to buckle in for deceleration. Get used to the isolation. We should have done our sparring after the block so you'd know how to compensate, but it's just as well we got Nira Kayen out of the way. Winniel couldn't have helped you in this condition."

Master Aren walked away. His steps seemed heavy and something inside Tridia twisted as he disappeared into the bridge. He had ingested her DNA along with the enzyme. Dr. Elenus had said her DNA was aggressive. It had changed the sample of Empress Dojene's DNA. Was it now changing Master Aren? What was she, that her basic composition could do such a thing?

She clenched her fists and squared her shoulders. They were minutes from the start of a dangerous mission and she could barely stand, much less fight, if needed. She turned and walked the length of the corridor and back, one hand on the wall at all times, her eyes on the floor. After the third pass, she pulled her hand to her side and raised her eyes. The level floor caused no problems. After another two passes she could stand erect and walk at her normal pace. On her last pass, she reached the far end of the corridor and turned around to find Sonei standing within an arm's reach, her head tilted slightly to the right, her green eyes intense.

"You're different," Sonei said. "Can't quite put my finger on it, but you're different. What did those three do to you? Wipe your mind again?"

"I'm just stretching my legs," Tridia said. "Is there a rule against that?"

Sonei laughed. "I like you more every time you open your mouth, kid. That's unusual for me. I dislike and distrust almost everyone on sight. Maybe it's because I became you before I met you."

"What –" Tridia didn't finish her question.

Sonei grimaced, then shifted. When her flesh and bones stopped moving, Tridia might have been looking in a mirror, except Sonei's clothes were too short for her new tall form. Tridia fought the urge to step back as Sonei stepped closer.

"Your lips are a little fuller, and you have a tiny scar at the corner of your eye." Sonei touched an index finger to the corner of her right eye and a minute scar appeared. "That doesn't show up in vid images. I think I've got everything else right. Remarkable. The body is the same, but something is different."

"Should you be exposing your talents to me?" Tridia asked. "Isn't being a shifter a secret or something?"

Sonei smiled. "Yes, shape-shifters don't advertise their abilities to strangers. But you're working for Brenden Aren now – his property, no less. He would have you contact me sooner or later for my services, so why prolong the inevitable? Besides, we'll all probably die on this ridiculous mission, so it doesn't really matter, does it?"

"Why are you here if you feel that way?" Tridia asked, intrigued by the shape-shifter's motivations.

"The money, of course. Deeca Varin pays very well for a regular job, but for a high-risk mission like this – well, triple fees are standard. That will keep me in style for a while wherever I decide to take a break. Besides, this is probably the most exciting thing that will come my way in years. I get to work close to Brenden Aren. He's going to drop his guard someday, and I want to be there when he does. He's going to expose his connection to Morgan Jacks, and I want to be the one to tell the whole galaxy about it."

"Morgan Jacks?" Tridia pressed her memory but got no response.

"Big deal in the underworld," Sonei said. She spoke over her shoulder as she walked toward the lounge, shifting back to her red-haired form. "Fingers in all the pies. Nobody double-crosses him and lives; nobody supports him and dies. Nobody sees him unless he wants to be seen. The dirty work gets done by his lieutenants, his personal stuff by his right-hand man – one Tran by name. Nobody has the full story on that one either. Ambassador Aren has a shady connection with both of them, and I want to know what it is."

"Why does it matter?" Tridia asked. Did Sonei have a purpose in confiding her personal goal to expose Master Aren?

"Morgan Jacks caught me red-handed in a dangerous scheme – something that would have resulted in my death if my part in it had gotten to the right people. He has irrefutable proof of my involvement," Sonei said. "Instead of exposing me, he uses the information to ensure my cooperation when I'm needed."

"What does that have to do with Master Aren?"

"Your master was the one who handed me copies of the proof. He said it was a message from Morgan Jacks that had been delivered to his embassy." Sonei snorted. "He plays that card every time he wants me to do something dangerous for him. The hint is always something like Morgan Jacks will guarantee the payment – but it's unmistakable blackmail."

"You're telling me all of this because?" Tridia asked.

"As I said, I don't give my trust or my loyalty often," Sonei said. "That's what it means to be a shape-shifter and a mercenary. But I've decided on loyalty to you. Don't bother to ask why. I was told this day could come. That someone would walk into my life and I would be compelled to follow him or her. No one knows why shifters do this, it's just a fact of our lives. I was worried it would be Brenden Aren I attached to, but it wasn't. It's his pet assassin. There's something about you, about what you did to protect the empress and the Felinus doctor. How you remain loyal to an arrogant swine like your master. You didn't back down from an angry Sentinel. I didn't think anyone would be that brave or that stupid. I'm telling you this because he won't tell you, and you should know who you're involved with. It's only fair. Who knows, it may be you that gets the goods on him." Sonei chuckled. "That would serve the slimy vat toad."

Tridia winced. The memory of a green creature with six legs emerged from the darkness in her mind. It had slimy, knobby skin, and it smelled of excrement. The thought of it made her skin crawl. She'd just as soon not have that image of Master Aren in her mind.

"Buckle up for hyperdrive exit," Deeca announced. "Sixty seconds."

"Hey, kid," Sonei said, as they took their seats. "Just be careful. You may be the most dangerous person on this ship but watch yourself with those three companions of yours. Don't turn your back on Deeca Varin unless you can see her in a mirror."

"Thanks," Tridia said. Sonei had been forthcoming with her from the start. She had no idea what it meant to have a shape-shifter's loyalty, but she welcomed an ally.

Tridia fished the harness from the chair cushions and buckled herself in. Sonei did the same. The slight tug of deceleration didn't warrant the precaution, but just as Tridia reached to unfasten the buckle the ship shook and an explosion reverberated through the lounge.

"What in Hielos?" Tridia held onto the harness with both hands.

"Commander Odana to the bridge." Master Aren's urgent voice over the intercom preceded another impact that threw Tridia sideways in her harness. She'd have bruises from that one.

"Stand down, Commander!" Deeca's voice followed Master Aren's right after the impact, but Tridia didn't hesitate as she unbuckled the harness and ran to the bridge.

Four holographic view screens showed the front, sides, and rear of the *Star Seeker*. Three ships danced across them, entering and exiting screens as they jockeyed for position around Deeca's vessel. They seemed to chase each other in a kind of follow-the-leader pattern, but it soon became clear they weren't in a game. The lead ship tried to escape the second ship, which fired laser weapons at its flank. The third ship, in turn, tried to destroy the second ship, without hitting the lead ship, but the pilot of the second ship always managed to veer out of the way or drop just in time to avoid the blasts. The third ship came close to clipping its companion more than once. Then, as Tridia stood in the doorway, the third ship peeled off and headed toward the *Star Seeker*. The second ship performed a perfect spiral and was on the third ship's tail before they fired a single shot. The attacking ship managed to get off two torpedoes, but they both went wide as it had to change its vector to avoid the second ship.

"Weapons controls, Commander," Master Aren ordered. "Take out the first ship that breaks toward us. You've got one shot, make it count."

One shot? Tridia moved toward the weapons station. Could she even find the control console, much less the target lock, then take out a ship with one shot?

"I told you to stay off my bridge, assassin!" Blood ran from Deeca's temple down the side of her face and dripped onto her collar.

"I take orders only from Master Aren, ma'am." Tridia slid into the empty seat and glanced over the controls.

Just breathe. He wouldn't tell you to do this if you didn't know how. It's like using the blaster on Odea.

The mental inspirational talk did little to calm the tension in her shoulders, but she flipped a switch and ran her fingers over a track pad. The three-dimensional targeting grid popped up. The ships had switched alignment again as the first ship turned to chase the second one.

"Be ready, Commander," Master Aren said. His fingers played over the shield controls.

"Target lock tracking," Tridia said.

"Remember, Commander, they have Nezadian shields. Use it to your advantage."

Nezadian shields. Master Aren's informant had made a point of saying someone would be waiting for them with Nezadian shields. He'd been paid for the information. It had to mean something. *Nezadian shields.*

In the next heartbeat, Tridia's tension dissolved. Her shoulders relaxed. She knew what to do. The target lock flashed and faded several times, as the ships moved.

"Commander?" Master Aren asked.

"Ready, sir!" Tridia replied. "Let them into position."

"Break off now."

As soon as Master Aren gave the order, the second ship fell out of alignment with the other two. Both attackers turned toward the *Star Seeker*, one slightly ahead of the other. Tridia waited for the first ship to fire a torpedo then she pressed the firing control before the target locked. The enemy torpedo exploded as it glanced off the *Star Seeker's* shields and another tremor racked the ship. Tridia's shot hit the oncoming vessel's torpedo port before its shield reformed to protect it. The resulting explosion caused the ship to slam into its partner. A brilliant explosion filled the forward view screen and brightened both side screens.

Deeca made a steep dive to avoid crashing into the main body of one of the ships. Smaller debris banged against the shields, but they dodged the worst of the fallout.

"How did you do that?" Deeca demanded.

"Any damages?" Master Aren asked. He didn't look at Deeca as he spoke.

"No," a voice answered over the speaker. "Compliments to the gunner."

"I'll pass that on." Master Aren glanced over his shoulder at Tridia. "Any other vessels in the area?"

"Nothing heavy within twelve hours' range," the voice said. "A small transport ship, about four hours out. After that it could get dicey. I'm getting reports of two Hierarchy ships in the sector and a third unidentified vessel with a loaded arsenal. That one is eight to twelve hours away. Our late combatants were not Hierarchy, but if Odea's curiosity is aroused, I don't want to stay around to answer questions. Don't linger over this mission. Get in and get out."

"Understood. *Star Seeker* out." Master Aren spun his chair to face Tridia and Deeca. "We have our time limit. What do the surface scans show?"

"Give me a minute," Deeca snapped. She wiped away the trail of blood. The cut had disappeared from her temple. "I've been a little occupied since we decelerated. While you're waiting you can explain how your friend is getting all this information. And how one off-target shot took out two ships."

Tridia waited in silence. Her respiration had picked up after the ships exploded but returned to normal as she listened to Master Aren's words. The voice on the speaker had been Tran again. Sonei had said Morgan Jacks' henchman was called Tran. A face tried to surface. Her fingertips went to her lips. She'd kissed a man with a voice like that, but she felt no emotion with the memory. Nothing of the stirrings she felt for Master Aren. Yet, somehow the memory was connected with Master Aren. She looked up to find him watching her. She mouthed the word: Tran?

Master Aren scowled. "Just be glad we've got the information, and don't question its source. As for the shot, the ships had Nezadian shields."

"What did Nezadian shields have to do with it?"

"The Hierarchy developed those shields twenty years ago. They're practically impenetrable, but they have two flaws. First, they take a while to reform over the torpedo port after firing, leaving the port vulnerable to an accurate gunner. Second, should the shields of two ships come into contact with each other, they short-circuit in a stellar fashion, as you've just witnessed. The Hierarchy stopped using them long ago, but there are still a number of mercenaries willing to take the risk for the protection the shields provide."

"Your pet assassin just happened to know all of this." Deeca stated.

"Commander Odana has made that shot before. She's young, but her training has been extensive and she's seen a lifetime of skirmishes, both planet-side and in space. At age thirteen she was an observer on a training cruise when the ship was attacked by Freeman hostiles. There was only one torpedo in the tubes, which the trainees were supposed to use for practice at the end of the tour. The young officer in charge of the weapons froze under the stress of choosing his target. Commander Odana pulled him from his chair and took his place, lined up the shot and took out both ships in much the same way she did today. She was very nearly drafted into the fleet at that point, but she had already committed to the Assassin's Grid."

"And aren't fifty-two people fortunate that she had?" Deeca sniped, referring to the number of human targets Tridia had taken out.

"It's forty-nine confirmed. And six people are fortunate she remembered how to make the shot today, in any case," Master Aren said. "Commander, go to the cargo hold and check on the Sentinels. Ask them what they sense from the planet."

"Yes, sir." Tridia left. Deeca must be suspicious of his sources if Master Aren had to come up with a story that far-fetched to distract her. Only after she'd made it halfway to the cargo hold did she stop to wonder if the story was true.

The Sentinels stood back-to-back in the center of the open space in the cargo hold, heads bowed, eyes closed. Occasionally one of them nodded as the other tilted his or her head. Tridia spoke only after observing them in silence for several minutes.

"We'll enter orbit shortly," she said, her voice barely above a whisper. "Have you sensed anything from the planet?"

The two turned in unison to face her. Their eyes came into focus quickly, but not before Tridia saw the glazed look they'd shared.

"Pockets of large predatory animal populations surround the compound," Alanel said. "There's only one humanoid presence above ground. It's very weak. There are other things beneath the surface, but the rock is dense and we can't distinguish whether or not they are human. We already know there are feeders in the mine, but this does not have the same presence. You should proceed with the utmost caution."

"You can really make telepathic sweeps from this distance?" Tridia asked.

"Our senses are accurate in linear projection within most solar systems," Winniel explained. "Were we to spiral our orbit, we could scan the entire planet. Our telepathic communication with each other is all but gone due to your block, but other sensory abilities appear unaffected."

Tridia stared, trying to comprehend the range of the Sentinels' sensory abilities. Before the block she'd been aware of the ship and the immediate space around it, as well as the people inside. The scope the Sentinels described seemed impossible. Of greater importance was the fact that the Sentinels had lost the ability to communicate with each other telepathically. The link she'd shared with them was a tiny part of what they'd shared with each other, and now it was gone. How could they stand it?

"Your signature is well hidden," Winniel said. "Are you still having difficulty walking?"

"No," Tridia said. "I didn't even notice on the way from the bridge to here." She hesitated before continuing. "Winniel, if your links to each other and to the Hariok clan hinge upon my mind being open, does that mean you can't sense your clan, either?"

Alanel cast a murderous glance in her direction. Winniel took his hand and squeezed it.

"The clan is hidden from us, but we gave them warning this might happen. If they do not hear from us within twelve hours, they will assume the worst." Winniel's face betrayed none of the concern she must be feeling, but there was longing in her eyes as she repeatedly glanced in her mate's direction.

"You must resist the urge to use your telepathy in the tunnels,"

Winniel added. "The block weakens when you struggle against it."

"I'll do my best," Tridia said, then frowned. "You said *I* should proceed with the utmost caution. Won't you be coming with us?"

"No," Alanel said. "This block is causing too much distraction. We'll monitor your progress in whatever way we can, and we won't abandon you to the mine or its occupants, but I forbid Winniel to go into that place while she has no connections with our clan."

Winniel spared a glance for Tridia, then looked back to Alanel as he continued. "Winniel is my first priority. We'll explain to the ambassador that we will remain with the ship in order to provide a safe extraction should the mission become jeopardized."

"Be safe, child," Winniel said. "There are many lives depending upon your safe return."

CHAPTER SIX

Sounds of a heated argument came from the upper corridor. Tridia dropped the backpacks she'd unfastened from the cargo nets in case she needed to move quickly.

"There are armed interceptor satellites in the planet's orbit. Every Odean property has the same weaponry installed and they will not give the deactivation codes to you under any circumstances!" Master Aren shouted.

He came through the cargo hatch with Deeca at his heels, but he seemed more amused than angry.

"You've already got them," Deeca stormed. "Just give them to me and I'll fly the ship in. Or use them yourself and I'll still fly the *Star Seeker*."

"Oath, remember?" Master Aren asked. "I'm bound by my oath to hold that information in secret."

"You're only bound when it suits you!" Deeca clenched her jaw and took a slow breath through flared nostrils. "The *Star Seeker* is a Stellar Morph. By its very technology it's practically undetectable even at close range."

"Practically – not completely." Master Aren argued. "Do you honestly want to come this far and put the ship and all our lives at risk over some petty argument you have with me?"

"Petty argument? Petty argument!"

"What else would you call it?" Master Aren crossed his arms over his chest and waited. When Deeca said nothing, he continued. "I'm a competent pilot with years of experience. I know the deactivation codes that will get us safely to the ground, and I'm familiar with the planetary environment. Your only argument is proprietary egotism and a personal dislike for me. Deny it."

He stared down at Deeca, who looked as if her face might explode. She glared back in infuriated silence for several seconds.

"You aren't familiar with the controls."

Master Aren chuckled. "Is that the best you can do? I've been sitting with you on the bridge for almost the entire trip. I just operated the shields and intercom during a battle. You even left me alone on the bridge for several hours while you took a nap."

"The ship was on auto pilot in hyperspace," Deeca countered. "You didn't have to touch the controls."

"Besides, the controls of the *Star Seeker* are virtually identical to the *Cera Gale*. Unlike your ship, mine doesn't have a scratch on it."

"Yours is only used for diplomatic transportation, Ambassador. The *Star Seeker* has seen heavy fire. I sometimes have missions for insane monarchs who insist that I put her in dangerous situations. Oh wait — we are in a dangerous situation. We don't know for sure what's waiting on that planet."

"You have a very naïve impression of what a diplomatic mission might entail," Master Aren said.

"Meaning?"

"Just that. My life isn't the social reception you seem to envision. There's nothing more to discuss. I'll use the codes and let you onto the bridge when I've gotten us past the satellites." Master Aren turned away and stooped to check one of the backpacks.

"It might be pointed out, Hunter Varin," Winniel interjected, "Stellar Morph technology was originally developed by the Hierarchy. If anyone would have the technology to sense the ship's presence, it would be them."

"Fine!" Deeca gesticulated with her hands to the ceiling. "Land the ship. But if you even dream about touching those controls after this, Brenden Aren, I will personally shoot off every finger on your right hand!"

"You won't and you know it." Master Aren stood to face her. "But saying it makes you feel better, so go right ahead."

Deeca's face flushed an even brighter red. She ignored him and spoke to the Sentinels. "Anything to report on the surface?"

Alanel relayed the information he'd already given Tridia.

"I got no trace of anything humanoid, above or below ground," Deeca said. "I suppose there's no chance you're mistaken?"

Alanel's eyebrows shot up his forehead.

"Right," Deeca said. "With only a weak presence in the compound and lots of predators outside, landing inside the confines seems to make the most sense."

"A drop and fly only. Sonei can't be on the surface for long, not with the feeders still on the planet," Master Aren said. "She'll have to take the ship back into atmosphere and wait for a signal."

"Why can't she come into the mine?" Deeca asked. "Your pet assassin is coming."

"She's paid a heavy price for the privilege," Master Aren said. "The Sentinels have blocked her energy signature – and mine. They can't do the same for the shape-shifter. She will have to remain with the ship."

"*I'm* going into the mine," Deeca argued.

"The one controlling the energy in your gold armbands will serve as your protector," Brenden replied.

"Winniel and I will also remain on the ship," Alanel said.

Master Aren spun to face him. Tridia remained motionless.

"The Sentinels aren't going either?" Deeca scowled.

"Do you want to risk the ship being unprotected on the ground if they have to return for us?" Master Aren asked. He made a flawless transition from surprise to explanation. "I don't. It won't do us any good to get out of the mine if we can't leave the planet once we do."

Deeca fumed. "Five minutes, then we go in."

She left the cargo hold and Tridia waited a moment to be sure she'd gone before she spoke.

"I seem to be navigating normally and I've regained most of my equilibrium."

"Good enough," Master Aren said.

"How did you know the explanation for the Sentinels remaining on the ship?"

"It's the only explanation that made sense," he replied, then turned to Alanel. "So why are you not going."

"We would better serve our objectives by remaining outside the mine to protect the ship and provide extraction, should that become necessary."

"That's the story you're going to stick with? After the fuss you made about not letting any harm come to Commander Odana?" Master Aren asked. "This disruption in your telepathy must be pretty bad. Fine, we might just need you on the outside anyway."

"How could you have the deactivation codes?" Tridia asked, once her master had returned his attention to the pack. "Weren't they set long after you left Odea?"

He smiled at her. "That, Commander, is my secret. Now, all of you to the lounge and buckle yourselves in. We'll see to the equipment on the ground."

Tridia returned the backpacks to the cargo net, then hurried to the lounge. The Sentinels, Deeca, and Sonei had already fastened their harnesses by the time she got there, and she wasted no time in joining them. She needn't have rushed; the dampening shields had no trouble keeping everyone comfortable as the ship landed with barely a nudge. Deeca released her harness and dashed to the bridge as soon as the ship settled.

In minutes, with packs strapped in place and weapons donned, the six of them exited the ship in the middle of the enormous mining compound. Forty-foot tall plasma-reinforced fences outside mason-work walls protected the enclosure. The Hierarchy had mounted laser turrets every ten feet along the outer fence. They hummed and moved as though targeting objects beyond the perimeter.

"Glad those things were pointing out," Sonei commented.

Three small office buildings and four rectangular barracks made up the compound. A large transport landing area was cordoned off a few hundred yards from the buildings, but the *Star Seeker* sat in the middle of a main road leading to the mine entrance. A sixty-foot-wide semicircular opening in the mountainside yawned a few hundred feet away. Reinforced fencing protruded from the rock face surrounding the opening and ran perpendicular to the cliff face until it met with the vertical fencing around the compound. Escape that way wouldn't have been an option. No human could have climbed the sheer face without gear. After Alanel's report of large predatory animals outside the fence, it seemed unlikely anyone had ever tried.

Tridia's spine tingled and her heart raced as her eyes darted between the buildings and the mine. She clenched her fists to divert tension from her expression. She couldn't fall apart now. Davik could be nearby – needing her help.

"What were they mining here?" Deeca asked.

"Uridine." Tridia and Master Aren spoke together.

"Used to make the blast chambers of hand weapons?" Deeca's voice betrayed her surprise.

"To fuel the chambers and contain the blasts," Master Aren answered.

"The Hierarchy just happened to have a mine full of the stuff sitting here in the Free Territories?"

"Technically, it isn't free space. This sector was annexed as a concession after the Magellanic War. None of the nearby systems objected," Master Aren explained.

"Translated, none of the nearby systems had the firepower to object or the clout to pay them off." Deeca shook her head. "Typical Hierarchy maneuvering."

Tridia listened to the exchange with interest. Memories flowed from the darkness. It was after the Magellanic War that the Hierarchy opened three prison planets outside of their own territory. The maneuver allowed them to justify housing battle-ready squadrons nearby. Cystia had the prison and the mine. She winced as more information crystallized in her memory.

"They use the same type of security here that's used in regular Odean prisons," Tridia said.

"Remember something?" Master Aren asked.

"Research," Tridia said. "I researched this place."

"Why would you research the security on Cystia?" Deeca asked. "And how did you get to it? I'm sure that's not information available to the average assassin."

"I don't know," Tridia replied. "But the security is the same. It's all controlled from an out building. There's nothing in the mine to shut it down so the prisoners couldn't take advantage."

Davik Schie's face appeared before her eyes. Words from a message poured into her thoughts. One phrase repeated itself over and over in her mind...*find the bastards that did this, Lieutenant Odana, and make them pay enough for both of us.*

Tridia dropped to her knees, gasping for breath. Had she found them? Did she make them pay? Winniel gripped one arm, Sonei the other. Alanel stood beside Winniel, alert for attack.

"What's wrong?" Master Aren's pale face appeared before her.

"Memory," Tridia said. "He's here. I was coming here for him. He left a message for me. I remember it."

"What's she talking about?" Sonei asked. "Who's here?"

"Davik Schie." Tridia stood. "He didn't do it. He was innocent!"

Master Aren didn't touch her, but his voice dropped to command tones. "Calm yourself, Commander."

"The research – my research. The trail ended here." Tridia ranted.

"I know," Master Aren said. "Classified scientific file. His sentence cut in half if he participated in Project Power Surge. We spoke of it earlier."

"But I remember it!" Tridia scanned the buildings again. "I remember. I had to come here to find him. I'd done all of the research. I was trying to get away – trying to come here. There was something else. It was my fault."

Tridia bit her lip. Davik was here. He'd left her a message, but he didn't know where he was going. How did she know? Answers lay behind the veil in her memories.

"Don't press it, child," Winniel hissed.

"Are you going to start another fight with Alanel and disobey a direct order? Or can we get on with the mission we accepted from the empress? We've got less than four hours before the transport is within range, and possibly less than eight before real trouble arrives," Master

Aren said. "You need to make up your mind."

Tridia lowered her eyes to the ground. Davik Schie – so close her body shook with anticipation. But Princess Anza or a clue to her whereabouts could also be within their grasp. How could she desert one in favor of the other? She couldn't do both. One of them had to take a secondary place. She grimaced as she recalled Anza's hand slipping from hers and the sight of Davik's bloodied face. Would it be her mission or her vow to help her friend? *Choose.*

She looked up and squared her shoulders. "My apologies, Master Aren. We'll carry on with the mission as planned."

Deeca had set up a small instrument on a tripod and studied its readings as she knelt beside it.

"There are plenty of energy waves streaming in this area. We picked up that much from the ship. They're concentrated at the opening."

"To be expected from a uridine mine in any case," Master Aren stated. His incredible blue eyes scanned every building in the immediate compound area, every crevice in the rock face. His words were calm, but his behavior showed he anticipated trouble.

"They don't read like normal uridine." Deeca looked away from the instrument, toward the mine entrance and finally up at Master Aren. She frowned when she saw his gaze focused elsewhere. "What are you expecting?"

He ignored her and gave orders instead. "Get moving, Commander. You and Winniel search the closest administration buildings. Alanel and I will take the barracks. Deeca and Sonei can watch the ship. Keep your weapons primed."

Tridia complied without hesitation and hurried toward the nearest numbered building. The priming hum of the blaster in her hand followed. She slid to a stop beside the building and looked through a window on the outer door. Winniel slid in beside her.

"Can you sense anything at all from inside?" Tridia asked.

Winniel's face took on its look of concentration, her eyes slightly glazed. "Small animals, vermin not yet found by the housekeeping bots. A few insects, some weak plant life." She looked up at Tridia, then said, "And a weak humanoid presence."

"Great!" Tridia exclaimed. "What a perfect time to be as blind as a bat."

"Those nocturnal rodents aren't truly blind, child. Neither are you."

Tridia's started to respond, but no appropriate words came to mind. Like it or not the Sentinels saw her as a child and they would continue to treat her as one. "A weak humanoid lifeform. Weak as in a child, or as a shielded soldier? Or soldiers?"

"There's no differentiation," Winniel said. "The vital signals are weak. Perhaps someone is ill or dying."

"A biological booby-trap. Someone with a contagious disease?" Tridia looked back toward the ship. Master Aren and Alanel were nowhere to be seen. Only Deeca and Sonei hovered over the little instrument, their weapons in their hands.

"Alanel senses no danger," Winniel said. She tilted her head. "His thoughts are faint, but he recommends caution, not retreat."

"Then let's check it out." The door opened without resistance to Tridia's tug. Winniel followed her inside. The building smelled of air freshener and disinfectant. The new owners either didn't like germs or they were trying to mask a scent.

Winniel drew a deep breath and looked around. A reception desk across the lobby displayed small vid screens showing views all around the compound and inside the mine. Images changed periodically to show different areas or angles. Vids of Master Aren and Alanel flashed across the screen. Active security for a deserted compound. The new tenants – wherever they had gone – had left as though they were coming back at any minute.

"You said there are housekeeping bots?" Tridia asked. "You sense them? They're still active?"

"Yes." Winniel studied a map on the wall.

"This is Hierarchy equipment," Tridia said. "This planet has supposedly been leased within the last two months – with all improvements and appurtenances, according to Tran. Why leave the equipment intact and functioning? If the Hierarchy knows they can't return to mine the planet…"

Tridia followed the thought to its logical conclusion. They were planning on returning to the planet – or perhaps they'd never left. The lease could be a ruse.

"Check down the corridor to the left." Tridia pointed with her weapon. "I'll go to the right and –"

"No, young one."

"What?" It hadn't occurred to Tridia that Winniel would object.

"My orders were to go with you. I cannot do otherwise without a counter-command."

"It just makes sense that the two of us could cover this building more quickly if we separate." Tridia sighed. "Which way is the presence you sensed?"

Winniel pointed down the right corridor. "Just because I sense only a weak presence, doesn't mean there is only one, or that it is truly weak and not masked. You've experienced such things yourself."

Tridia stared at Winniel. What had she been thinking? Of course, their adversaries could block their presence. On the hospital ship, with the armor they wore, she couldn't sense Princess Anza's abductors. If these were the same people, the building could be full of armored soldiers waiting to ambush them.

Assuming that a room is empty because it should be empty is a target's fatal mistake. Master Aren's voice echoed in her memory. When had he said that?

"You smelled the air just now. Did you sense anything of value in it?"

"Of value?"

"Could you smell anything that shouldn't be here?"

"My sense of smell isn't so acute. Without a prior reference I would have no way of knowing what scents should or shouldn't be here."

Tridia shook her head. "Come on. Between your lack of baseline information and my lack of intelligence, we'd better hope this building is truly abandoned."

They searched every office in the corridor, consuming precious minutes of Tridia's energy block. One of the darkened rooms showed the faint glow of active equipment and a wall of vid screens flashed eerily for no one to see. The door sign read "Mine Security." That explained the screens. The door had an internal isometric locking mechanism that would require blast grenades to open without the proper code. Even if she managed to open it, she'd have to decipher the alarms before she could shut them down. Something told her she could do it – perhaps the research – but how much time would it take?

Winniel faced the room next door. Tridia followed her gaze. Another door with the same locking mechanism.

"That is where the humanoid form is," Winniel said.

Tridia let her shoulders relax and her gun hand steadied. A room full of soldiers, or the end of the search for Davik? Either way, she wasn't going to rush the door. She squatted beneath the small window at eye level. Memories of another door, another booby-trap, came to mind and she searched the doorframe for a minute trigger mechanism. Seeing nothing unusual, she stood to look in the window. Her hand tightened on the grip of the blaster.

A large cylindrical container made of a clear substance stood on the far side of the room. It was filled with a pale green liquid. Davik's body hung suspended in the liquid. He didn't move. Tridia's heart pounded. An intricate network of tubes appeared to supply air through his mouth and nose, covering most of his face, but there was no doubt of his identity. Monitors beside the container displayed near flat-lined graphs – all except one. It displayed continuous spikes. Tridia couldn't read the label on the active monitor, but only one thing made sense. Davik's body was in stasis, but his brain operated at full rev. She reached for the door handle, but Winniel caught her hand.

"I've got to go in there!" Tridia tried to pull away but Winniel pressed her thumb into the flesh between Tridia's thumb and index finger. Tridia went down on one knee as Winniel snatched the blaster from her other hand.

"Caution, child," Winniel whispered. "This trap was laid for you – or for someone who knew this man. Listen carefully. Smell the air."

Tridia stopped struggling against Winniel's grip and inhaled. The tang of high voltage electricity set her teeth on edge. Crude, but very effective. She looked at the door handle. No tell-tale spark leapt from the metal, but an almost imperceptible hum resonated from it.

"Electrified," Tridia said. "You probably saved my life."

"Yes. Take care of it from now on." Winniel grasped Tridia's hand and pulled her to her feet, returning the blaster.

"I don't even know who he is, only that he's important to me. He left a message before he was brought here. He said he loved me. How can I not remember him if he loves me?" Tridia stared through the window, willing Davik to open his eyes, but they didn't flutter.

"We must finish searching this building," Winniel said.

"I can't just –"

"What? Leave him?" Winniel asked. "It could take hours to open that door without blasting it and possibly damaging his capsule. Then how long after that to understand what type of stasis he's in? And how long after that – if ever – to figure out how to release him without causing permanent damage? If you disturb him, and have to leave him because we fall under attack, what would happen to him? Is it not better to leave him in this much safety and return when you have the luxury to extract him?"

"If I never return?" Tridia asked.

"Then he is in no worse condition than when you found him." Winniel said.

Tridia stared through the window. It felt as if Winniel stabbed a knife into her chest. So much of her life remained in shadow, and, apart from one message, his name, and his face, it contained all memory of the man floating in the green liquid. But memories of Anza's hand being torn from hers were fresh and condemning.

"Let's finish this building," she said, and turned away without looking back. "We've got two others to search."

They made short work of the three buildings, turning up no other information or items of interest. Even so, Master Aren and Alanel had returned to the ship before them.

The planet's sun had almost set when they rejoined the group. Deeca sat on her heels reading the instrument, with Sonei at her shoulder taking notes. Master Aren studied the mine entrance and Alanel watched the building, waiting for them to return. Tridia said nothing as she approached.

"Deeca?" Master Aren asked.

"The readings are holding steady at the last spike generated when you approached the entrance," Deeca said.

"Force shield." Master Aren said.

"Yes, but it's so slight. What is it triggering?" Sonei asked.

"Internal security. Nothing happens until someone breaks the threshold either here or at some point inside the mine. They couldn't have the security systems firing lasers or pouring forth gas every time someone walked by the opening. The danger will be just inside the entrance, extending for about fifty yards down the tunnel." Master Aren turned to face Tridia. "Report, Commander."

"The buildings are clear of hostiles, sir. Evidence indicates they aren't far away. The security systems are operated from Building One, but the room is too secure to attempt a break-in," Tridia said. "And – Davik Schie's body is in stasis in Building One."

"You're sure it's him?" Master Aren asked.

"Yes, sir," Tridia said. "There's no doubt. He's in deep stasis, but there appears to be heightened brain activity. The setup is unassailable in the time we have."

"Another dilemma?"

"No, sir. There's no dilemma."

Master Aren looked to Winniel. "Anything else?"

"A map," Winniel said. "It may lend relevance to the information contained in the capsule. The numbers appear to correspond to formatting in the map's legend."

"Let's take a look at it." Master Aren followed Winniel, with Alanel and Tridia bringing up the rear. When they got to the map Winniel pointed out the numbers.

"Levels are indicated with an L and a four-digit number. This mine is very deep, with many tunnels, side tunnels, rooms, and chambers – all labeled with a specific letter and four-digit number."

"This thing is a maze." Master Aren touched a spot on the wall and the map sprang forth as a three-dimensional projection. "L0137, C3316. Level 0137, Chamber 3316."

A red light pulsed midway down the maze and toward the back, then a yellow light snaked its way from the mine entrance to the red light.

"Our shortest path," Master Aren said. "Assuming the elevator is operational, we should be able to make the round trip in about four hours. If not, we'll be lucky to do it in six."

"Look at this, sir," Tridia said. She touched a spot just inside the entrance with her finger. The hologram expanded to show greater detail. "A chasm just beyond the antechamber. We'll have to find some way to cross that."

Master Aren studied the enlarged projection. "Looks like a retractable bridge to the side here. If we can make it that far, and aren't being shot at, we could use the bridge."

"Otherwise we'll have to jump, and that's quite a leap to make wearing packs," Tridia said.

"Nervous, Commander?" Master Aren asked.

"I'm no longer a Felinus warrior – who would have made that jump flat-footed – and my perception is hindered in my current condition. I'm not familiar with my abilities," she explained.

"I'll give you leave to stay behind, if you're concerned," Master Aren said.

"No, sir. I'll be accompanying you inside."

"Maybe fortune will smile on us this time."

"Yes, and maybe I'll turn out to be a social advocate when I get my memory back."

Master Aren chuckled. Tridia frowned and studied the map again. The chasm opened a good eight feet wide and dropped at least thirty feet to the next level. The map gave no indication of what lay at the bottom of the opening, and she didn't hope to find out.

***

"We go in," Master Aren told Deeca when they returned. He pointed a hand-held tracker in her direction. "Here's the schematic of our path."

"Did you disarm the security system?" Deeca asked. She glanced at the schematic he'd transmitted to her own device.

"No. The blocks we used on our energy signatures have a limited life. If we take the time to disarm the security, the blocks could fail inside the mine. I'd rather take my chances with the lasers than the creatures."

"You really are afraid of those things, aren't you?" Deeca asked, seeming to notice Master Aren's attitude for the first time. "You aren't just trying to scare me."

"I wish I could scare you!" Master Aren snapped at her. "Maybe then you'd take this seriously. Those creatures don't kill right away. Once they locate and attach to a body, they drain life energy slowly. The only person to come out of the mine with a feeder attached lived exactly five minutes after the thing disengaged. It had fed on him for two weeks. I'd rather die a quick death, if it's all the same to you."

Tridia observed in silence. Master Aren had never voiced his anger this way in her presence. His voice was quiet, but fierce. His eyes flashed daggers at Deeca. His hand twitched, as if suppressing a desire to strike her. Deeca had not taken him seriously before that moment, and it had obviously bothered him.

"Very well, Ambassador. We'll go in and dodge lasers." Deeca kept her tone level and her voice soft. She stood and spoke to Sonei. "Please repack this equipment and return it to the ship. Don't stay on the ground any longer than it takes to do that. Monitor any incoming transmissions. We've got a guardian angel with lots of intel out there somewhere. He should let you know if we're in for company. Stay at about thirty thousand feet. That should be high enough to keep you safe from anything on the ground and low enough to not attract attention from the satellites. If the turrets around this place turn skyward, don't hang around. Do not come into the mine for any reason. The Sentinels will be with you."

"We'll stay with the shape-shifter and protect your exit," Alanel said. "But we will decide for ourselves whether or not to enter the mine."

"For all our sakes, I hope you don't have to," Master Aren said. He started toward the mine entrance.

"Ambassador." Deeca holstered her weapon.

"Yes?" He stopped, irritation in his voice.

"If what you say is true, and those things suck your life out slowly, make sure I don't have a life to feed them."

Master Aren walked away without speaking, his shoulders tense and back straight.

Deeca followed in silence and Tridia fell in behind her.

CHAPTER SEVEN

A metal frame surrounded the mine entrance. Its massive door stood ajar, an invitation too obvious to ignore. Master Aren entered, Deeca followed more slowly, but Tridia didn't hesitate. If they got in and out with enough time to spare, she might get back to Davik.

Fixtures hanging from a ceiling far above flooded a huge antechamber with light. Tridia hadn't expected a close dark tunnel after seeing the door and the map, but the room was beyond her expectation. Enormous refining machinery filled one entire side. Haulers with tires twice her height sat motionless among the refiners. Flat hover carts for carrying the ore from the mine were stacked around them. The green glow of force shields surrounded each piece to protect them from the security lasers. She had no time for more than a cursory observation, before a tinny snap reached her ears and the walls began vibrating with a deafening high-pitched hum —the sound of multiple laser weapons arming.

"Get ready." Master Aren's command had a steadying effect on Tridia's nerves.

New memories flowed into her consciousness – information obtained from research into forbidden security files. The security lasers would be spaced and timed. All Hierarchy facilities shared only four patterns of white, red, and bright lasers. The first five shots revealed the pattern used in the given facility. Even though the patterns were a known weakness in the security system that tempted malcontents to try to escape – and many tried – the Hierarchy never changed them. Few who attempted it ever made their way through. Only perfect timing and agility were rewarded with survival. Even for the one or two who'd made it, the time it took to navigate the laser field inevitably gave the security force time to react. No one had ever escaped from a Hierarchy prison.

Tridia had memorized those patterns weeks ago, knowing she might need them to rescue Davik. No doubt Master Aren also knew the patterns and what to expect. She and Master Aren had bet their lives, and Deeca's, that they could survive the first five blasts. Master Aren took a pair of dark lenses from his pack to protect his eyes from the bright laser blasts that would cause blindness. Tridia did the same, but Deeca made no move to mimic them.

A single red beam sliced across the open space, left to right, ceiling to floor about ten feet in front of Master Aren. A second beam, less than a heartbeat later, split the distance between him and Deeca, slicing straight across the cavern at waist level. Deeca took a step back. A full two seconds later, the third beam sliced across the chamber, right back to left front, just at eye level – and straight at Deeca's head. Tridia stepped forward to push her out of the way. The beam missed Tridia's eyes by millimeters as she turned away.

"Where's your protective eyewear?" Tridia hissed.

"In my pack," Deeca answered.

Tridia shoved her own lenses into Deeca's hands and dug in the Hunter's pack for another pair as a white beam hit the ground between the two of them and Master Aren. There was no time to get the glasses from Deeca's pack. Tridia squinted her eyes shut as tightly as she could and was in the motion of raising her arm to shield them when a blinding flash of light filled the chamber. It was over in a second. When the light disappeared, Tridia's vision went with it.

"Now!" Master Aren shouted.

Tridia followed the sound of her companions' boots striking the gravel floor as she started after them.

"I'm blinded!" she called.

"Keep moving! We'll guide you." Master Aren was already five steps ahead of her. "Stop!"

All three slid to a stop at Master Aren's order. Tridia heard the beams slap into receiving cups embedded in the rock walls around her. Death flashed inches on either side of her and she couldn't sense it or see it.

"Go," Master Aren no longer shouted, but the tension in his voice carried as though he had. Then he said something she couldn't understand.

"What?" she called.

"Bear slightly left, and keep the pace," Deeca relayed.

Tridia tried to match the sound of their steps.

"Down."

Falling to the ground, Tridia slid forward on the gravel. Precise patterns flashed across her mind as she recalled the entire security layout. If she had her full senses, she could cross the floor without mishap. With her vision, she could cross the entire cavern entrance with no more than a few scrapes from the floor and a possible singe or two. Blinded in both sight and senses, she'd be lucky to make it halfway to the tunnel proper.

Even so, she followed every instruction and listened intently to the sounds around her. The lasers hummed steadily, but the sound got louder before they fired. She absorbed that bit of knowledge just before she took her first hit. It came left to right, chest high, and scored the front of her right bicep as she turned to follow Deeca's voice. The weapon made a clean cut through her sleeve and into the first couple of layers of skin. The pain was comparable to a knife cut and she gasped involuntarily.

"Back to the right ten degrees and pick up the pace!" Master Aren ordered.

Tridia adjusted her steps as she thought proper and pumped her legs harder. The second hit came ten steps later. A beam from the left front side of the cavern to right back sliced across the back of her thigh in mid-step. She bit back a curse and covered her blinded eyes with her hands to prevent another bright flash from compounding the damage. Her eyes burned, as though they'd been splashed with acid. It felt as though the cornea peeled away with every blink.

"Almost there, assassin!" Deeca called out. "Veer back to the left."

Tridia shut out her various pains and concentrated on the footsteps ahead of her. From the sound of her voice, Deeca had not turned toward her as she spoke, and it was unlikely either she or Master Aren had any idea of the extent of her injuries. She had to keep up on her own. Then, her heart cringed as a different sound filled her ears.

The twangy sound of rapid fire lasers rang from the tunnel ahead. Intruder deterrents and prisoner containment. Tridia bit down on her frustration. The sound meant the pattern in the outer cavern would change to herd them into the tunnel.

"Stay close." Master Aren's terse order reached her ears. "There should be a pause in the tunnel just as we reach it, but it won't last long. Commander, move straight ahead and sprint when I give the word."

She didn't reply. They couldn't afford to fall back and help her and she wouldn't jeopardize them by asking for assistance. A third strike slammed into the middle of her back and should have finished her, but some piece of Master Aren's eclectic equipment protected her. While it didn't slice through, the surprise caused her to stumble.

"Sprint!"

Tridia righted herself and ran with everything she had left. Sound became louder and echoes diminished as she passed into the smaller tunnel from the antechamber. The sound of their footsteps said Master Aren and Deeca had gotten too far ahead of her. The stumble had cost her precious seconds.

"Move it, Commander!" Master Aren shouted. "No time for the bridge. We'll have to jump."

The sound of boots leaving the ground and landing solidly on the opposite side of the unseen chasm reached Tridia's ears. They were at least five strides ahead of her.

"Jump now!" Deeca yelled.

Tridia sprang blindly into the air. As she left the ground the lasers fired again, hitting the gravel at her feet and splintering a sizeable rock from the surface. The rock hit on the heel of her propelling boot just as she jumped. The impact caused her foot to slide forward at the last moment and tilted her slightly so she lost momentum. Her heart lurched as she dropped, knowing the ground was not beneath her. A hand grabbed her sleeve as she slammed into the edge of the far chasm wall, and a jutting rock bent her double, forcing the air from her lungs. The shoulder seam of her jacket ripped with the stress of her weight. She hung by mere threads.

Tridia sucked in air as she tried to find purchase to scale the chasm's wall, but her feet dangled in the air. Then the lasers hummed again.

"Let go!" Master Aren's words echoed over the edge of the chasm.

"What?" Deeca screamed back.

"The beams are targeting this edge." Master Aren didn't hesitate in giving his order. "Drop, Commander!"

Tridia obeyed. She let go of the edge and twisted her arm to loosen Deeca's grip. She dropped, and a shower of rocks sprayed over her as the laser hit the spot where she had dangled.

"No!" Deeca's cry followed her into the chasm as she fell.

***

Brenden jerked Deeca away from the crevice and dragged her farther down the tunnel. The lasers blasted twice more behind them, then silence fell. Deeca fought furiously against his grip on her arm.

"We've got to go back!" she screamed.

"There is nothing we can do for her," Master Aren said. "She's fallen, blinded, injured, and running out of time. So are we. Even if we managed to find her alive, we can't carry her back through the laser field and we can't bring help to her. Let's get on with what we came here for and try to find the true Kanuan heir. If we can locate this chamber and by some miracle find Anza or another clue to her whereabouts, then make it back, we'll do what we can for Commander Odana. Otherwise, she's lost. End of discussion."

"Not the end. Not until we know what happened to her."

Brenden released Deeca's arm as they squared off. "She's still the same assassin you've hated all this time. Sounds like this should be good riddance."

Deeca took the dark lenses from her eyes and glared at them. Whatever argument she had fell away from her lips. Her voice was cold when she spoke. "Not before I know the truth."

She walked away from him, taking a small instrument out of her pack as she went. "According to your schematics, it's this way."

Brenden stared as she walked away. It had all been about finding the truth. Had Tridia betrayed her, or had someone else done the deed? He had no answers for her, but there was too much at stake on too many levels to allow one fallen soldier to deter them. He looked back at the chasm. He would save her if he could, if only because he needed the information locked in her mind, but it might be best if Tridia died from the fall. He followed Deeca down the tunnel.

***

Tridia fell for what seemed like ages. She bounced twice against outcroppings, striking first her knee, then her right side, but there was little pain, almost as if something cushioned the rock. Expecting a solid impact when she landed, she relaxed her body as much as possible. Instead of hard ground, a cold rush of water washed over her. She sank deep into the liquid and bent her knees as she touched a solid bottom. Pushing off with all the strength she could muster, she kicked and struggled to make it back to the surface. Her pack and boots weighed her down, but she needed the contents of the pack to get out of the mine, and she was determined to make the surface with it if possible. Panic surged in the back of her throat as the small amount of air in her lungs depleted. She fought it back. Three more kicks and she would release the pack. She broke the surface on the second kick and tread water as she pulled air into her burning lungs. A smile spread across her face and a relieved laugh escaped her lips. She was blind and treading water in the bottom of a mine probably filled with energy-draining parasites, but she was alive.

Now what?

She took a few breaths to get over the relief and to come up with an answer to the question. The water was well below the surface of the mine, out of the main channel, likely a lake or an eddy pool. There wasn't enough current to be a river, and it was too deep to be a stream. The banks could be inches or miles away from where she'd dropped. Before putting the effort into a long pull in the wrong direction she had

77

to get her bearings. She couldn't see – whether from the laser injury or the natural darkness of the cavern didn't matter – and she didn't dare try to break through her mental barriers. That would be her ultimate last resort. There had to be another way.

Feeling for her pockets she found a small knife, an electronic compass – now soaked and useless – and a few other small survival items she'd brought with her. The pocketknife was small and would be of little use as a weapon – her hunting knife was strapped to her leg, and her bladed weapon was strapped to her left arm. She decided to use the electronic compass first. She drew back her arm and threw the useless case as far as she could while treading water with only her legs. A small splash some feet away echoed across the water.

"Not that way." She spun – in what she hoped was a hundred and eighty-degree turn – and repeated the action with the small knife. A clatter and a dull thud met her ears.

"A low ceiling and a sandy shore, not too far away." Tridia took a deep breath and swam in the direction of the sound with an easy crawl, hoping her ears had not deceived her about the distance.

Her right hand touched the solid shoreline just before she banged her head against it. A rock shelf rose a foot or two above the water's surface. She clung to it with one hand, using the other hand to work the strap of her backpack off her shoulder. When the pack hung by a single strap, she reached beyond the shelf edge to try to determine how much room she had.

"You've made it. There's enough room for you and your pack. Climb on up out of the water."

Tridia jerked at the sound of a man's voice. Her right ear tickled as if someone ran a feather over it. Her hand slipped from the ledge and her head went under water. She sputtered as she came up.

"Didn't mean to startle you, but you don't have much time. The Kel Anec are already on their way and the soldiers will no doubt be returning to the tunnels after all of the commotion you caused above. You need to get on solid ground and away from here."

"How are you speaking to me? There's no echo to your voice the way there is to mine." Tridia coughed up water as she spoke, but quickly hoisted her pack onto the ledge, then hauled herself out of the water. She stood carefully with her arm raised above her head.

"Energy projection. Straight to the inner ear. No sound. Almost like telepathy," the voice replied.

"If you believe in such things."

"Believe it. There's a lot more than telepathy going on in these tunnels. Things I never would have considered. Now it's my turn to ask a question. How did you manage to fall into the lake?" The man spoke quickly, his words almost running together, and his voice held little inflection.

"A rock hit my heel as I tried to jump across. It threw me off balance and I fell."

"Ah. You must be pretty desperate to attempt the laser field. Raw uridine is only found deep in the mine and requires a lot of refinement. You couldn't haul out enough in a backpack to make it worth the risk. So, it must be something else that brings you here."

Tridia let the comment hang in the air. She couldn't see the person who spoke to her, but the voice sounded human – and vaguely familiar.

"Volunteer no information? A military maneuver, then. Are you with the soldiers?"

"You referred to the soldiers before. Whose forces are they?" Tridia wanted to keep the man speaking. If she could identify him, she might be able to ask for help.

"Where do you think you are?" he asked.

"The planet Cystia, somewhere in a lower tunnel of the uridine mine," Tridia said. "Are they Hierarchy?"

"That would be my guess, but I have doubts about them being part of the official forces. They usually wear body armor. I overheard a couple of them talking. They referred to themselves as the dark ones, so I assume the armor is black."

"If it's like the armor I saw a couple of weeks ago, it is black – and practically indestructible. You haven't actually seen them?"

"Can't see colors. I'm good with shapes, textures, sonic waves, and energy waves – they tell you a lot more than color can." The man paused. "Let me venture a guess – you were blinded in the laser field."

"Why would you say that?" Tridia kept her eyes lowered as she asked the question.

"Because there's enough light in this cavern for you to make out my shape, and you haven't said anything about it or shied away from it."

"What's so special about your shape?" Tridia asked.

"Mainly that he doesn't have one." Another male voice, refined and deep, echoed in the tunnel.

***

Brenden and Deeca found a service elevator that took them down to level 0125, then walked for another hour and a half, constantly going farther into the mountain and deeper into the planet. Several times they used ladders in access tubes to descend rather than taking a longer route to another elevator. They carried lights in their packs, but the installed lighting continued far into the mine. Deeca kept a steady watch over the hand-held guide that told them where to turn and when to descend.

Brenden, walking at her elbow, made measured markings on the walls with a fine invisible mist that would glow in the darkness. He had no intention of relying on Deeca's little machine to get them out of the mine. The setup had been too convenient to be trusted.

The forces at work against them would have expected them to use such devices to find their way in and it was a sure bet they'd use something to jam them on the way out. Every fiber of his being told him this was a trap. Walking into it with so slim a plan of escape mocked his common sense, but he had little choice. Their mission had nowhere to go but deeper into the mine.

"We should be nearing the spot now." Deeca looked up and around. They were at the end of the installed lighting. Another ten yards would put them in pitch blackness.

"Someone intends for us to grope in the dark." Brenden sprayed his mist against the wall. "Which direction?"

"The indicator says forward and to the right. There should be a chamber there."

The skin prickled on Brenden's neck, as though someone touched him with an icy finger. "Get the light out of your pack. Now!"

The urgency of his voice startled Deeca into action. She grabbed a small flashlight from the side of her pack. No sooner did she switch it on than the overhead lights went out.

"Timer?" she asked.

"Possibly," Brenden replied. "But not likely."

He played his flashlight beam into the darkness behind them and saw with satisfaction that a section of the wall glowed. The trail he'd left behind would lead them back out, but the glow wouldn't last long. "Let's go. Be on your guard. Whatever they intend for us is likely waiting in the chamber. Remember, Anza's abductors wanted to question a Guardian."

"Right."

Deeca took a cautious step forward. Brenden followed close enough to be her shadow. His mind screamed to be free of its solitary confinement and he perspired with the effort of holding his senses in check behind the barrier. Danger could lurk just beyond the beam of his light and he was blind to sense it. When Deeca finally shined her light into a small chamber, Brenden flashed his around the tunnel behind and ahead of them. Shadows not created by any outcropping swayed slowly as they approached in the gloom. Feeders. Brenden swallowed back the bile of fear rising in his throat.

"There's a pedestal there, but nothing on it." Deeca's tone spoke neither surprise nor disappointment. They both had expected as much.

"Do you see anything else inside the chamber?" Brenden stood with his back touching Deeca's left shoulder as she peered into the darkness. The shadows continued to advance. He fought against the urge to shout aloud for Deeca to run into the chamber. They had no weapons to use against these creatures. Their only defense was the barriers placed around their minds.

"There is something on the floor," Deeca answered, stepping into the chamber.

Brenden chanced a glance over his shoulder as she stooped to pick up a bright green cylinder.

"It's empty."

Brenden backed into the chamber and bumped against Deeca as she stood.

"Ambassador – "

"Can you sense the Gold?"

"What do you know about –"

"Can you sense it?" Brenden demanded.

Deeca hesitated before answering. "No. I haven't been able to sense it for some time now."

"How long?" Brenden turned to face her, exposing his back to the shadows.

"For the past half hour at least. The connection just faded."

"You should have mentioned it to me!"

The shadows slid around Brenden and entered the chamber.

"I barely felt it myself. It didn't seem worth mentioning since my bands are warm."

Without warning, Brenden placed his fingers against Deeca's chest and struck. Eyes wide with shock, mouth open for words she couldn't speak, she fell into his arms, dead.

CHAPTER EIGHT

"He doesn't have one?" Tridia maintained her composure with a strong effort. A condescending note in the refined voice warned it didn't belong to a friend.

"Pure energy is amorphous. Although his coloring is interesting, his shape is indeterminate. And he's generating all of the light in this chamber."

"That's very interesting – and a little disconcerting. I guess that means he can't give me a boost out of the cavern." Tridia tried levity, even though she knew neither of the voices in the room would appreciate it. "Perhaps you can lend me a hand."

The words of a former classmate tickled her memory. *Make your captors angry enough and they may kill you before they torture you into giving up vital information.* Not the recommended course of action – silence was preferred – but hopeless situations called for desperate measures.

Tridia waited. If she kept these things focused on her they might remain unaware of Master Aren and Deeca. It was worth a try.

"You're a quite clever little human. How is it that we can't sense your thoughts?" Refined Voice asked.

"Just a parlor trick I picked up somewhere," Tridia replied.

"Don't toy with them." Pure Energy said. "These creatures are ruthless and you're surrounded. They can't hear me – only your responses to me. They can't sense my thoughts, but they know I'm speaking to you because I'm touching you. Try to not react to my words. Be truthful with them unless I tell you otherwise."

"Tell us your name, human." Another voice, this one rippling, almost ethereal, spoke.

"My name is Tridia Odana."

"What?" Pure Energy might have gasped if it had used air.

Tridia kept her face immobile against a strong desire to frown. The amorphous energy form recognized her name.

"You're a fragile form," Ethereal Voice said. "You're like the soldiers who think their armor makes them safe. They're walking into places we've forbidden. They think because we don't see their minds that we can't harm them. They're mistaken – and so are you."

Tridia didn't react to the threat.

"This is going to get painful really fast. I know how much you hate the cold but try to hang in there." Not the reassuring words Tridia had hoped to hear.

Freezing cold spread through Tridia's damp sleeve and across her arm. She steeled herself to remain still. The cold spread over her shoulder and down her side all the way to her boots. She bit down on her lip to keep her teeth from chattering.

The chill started up the front of her leg and followed the outline of her body until it reached her chin. There it stopped, caressing her face with a frost straight from Hielos. If she went into hypothermia, at least these things wouldn't be able to torture her mind.

"Why are you here?" Refined Voice asked.

Pure Energy didn't warn her to lie, so she told the truth – at least a version of it.

"I'm on a m-mission," Tridia said. The cold took her breath away and made it difficult to speak. "L-looking for a clue to l-lead m-me to the next step. I f-fell through the chasm."

"Your body trembles with the pain, yet we sense no fear. You're interesting, Tridia Odana. Would you not open your mind to us?"

Tridia didn't trust herself to speak without biting her tongue. Numbness spread up her arm. She wouldn't remain conscious much longer.

"Your two companions have abandoned you," Refined Voice said.

So, they knew about Master Aren and Deeca. Pain tightened in her chest.

"You'll remain with us."

"Un-til I c-c-complete…m-mission."

The harsh sound that followed this declaration might have been alien laughter. It set Tridia's teeth on edge and hurt her ears. Her head nodded forward and she didn't fight against the threatening faint until it dawned on her Master Aren wouldn't try anything else to rescue Anza if he and Deeca managed to escape. He'd report a failure and that would be the end of it. Tridia had let Anza be taken, but he had no personal gain in her recovery.

"I s-s-seek a young w-woman," she said. "No-Nobility. Do y-you have h-her?"

Dead silence followed for a few heartbeats. The cold lifted with startling suddenness. Tridia gasped for breath and buried her freezing fingers under her arms.

"Tell us about this noble woman you seek." Refined Voice spoke in a deceptively velvet tone.

"Young. Blonde. Pretty." Tridia focused on Anza's features.

"Is she a warrior?" Ethereal Voice asked.

"No. At least – I don't think so. I was told to find her in the mine. Find her, or some clue to her whereabouts."

"She is not a Felinus warrior? A princess among her people?" the refined voice asked.

"No-o." Tridia drug the word out. "She's a human woman – a diplomat kidnapped from a hospital ship."

"That one is not here," Ethereal Voice said. Its tone dismissed Anza as insignificant.

"Do you know where she is?" Tridia asked.

"Don't push, Tridia. Let them brag about it. They're arrogant creatures and they love to hear themselves talk. They'll probably tell you everything you want to know, and then some." Pure Energy's voice restored Tridia's caution.

"Soldiers took her to another planet. A place too far from here for you to find," Ethereal Voice said. "Not that you will ever leave this mine to try."

Others laughed again, the sound as grating as the first time. New voices spoke in ethereal tones.

"The arrogant fools left a mica-chip containing some ridiculous riddle in a chamber deep in the mine. They thought they could lure a Guardian there and have our feeders extract knowledge from her."

"They thought they could use our pets against us! Only the Kel Anec control the feeders." More laughter. Tridia shivered. "We took the mica-chip and removed their ridiculous riddle to replace it with something infinitely more interesting."

"We left the feeders. Our pets will attack the first sentient creatures they find – Guardian, diplomat, or soldier."

"No armor will protect them." A final laugh, then silence.

How could creatures this far off the beaten path possibly know about the makeup of the search party?

"Would you like to have the location?" the refined voice asked in its velvet tone.

"I would," Tridia answered. "Although I expect you won't make it easy for me to get it."

"On the contrary, a simple test. Answer a few questions. We'll give you the mica-chip and let your friend lead you out of the mine, if he can."

"I'm just a bond servant," Tridia said. "I only obey instructions. I doubt I'd have any information you'd find valuable or amusing."

"You would be surprised by what amuses us," Refined Voice said. "Tell us what you fear."

"I don't fear anything," Tridia answered. "I don't have enough memory to know what I should fear."

"You don't fear for your comrades? Not freezing from our touch, or wandering forever blind in these dangerous tunnels?"

"No." Tridia's heartbeat remained steady. "My comrades are soldiers, they knew the risks when they entered the mine. If you freeze me, I'll simply fall asleep and drift into oblivion. Being blind is only a hardship if there is light to see by otherwise. I'm not afraid of the dark or I would have panicked already."

"You think you are telling the truth," Refined Voice said. "Very well. Until we can see your mind, we've no way to tell otherwise. If you indeed have no fear, you are unique among your kind."

"I grow tired of this game," the first Ethereal Voice said. "Who told you to retrieve the woman?"

"Her mother," Tridia said.

"What do you know about the Felinus warrior?" Refined Voice asked.

"Why should I know anything about the Felinus warrior?"

"She was seen in the Public Hearing Room on Aga, two days ago," Refined Voice said. "You – or someone by your name – was scheduled to be in that room as well. Let's assume, for the sake of time and torture you were there. What do you know about the Felinus warrior?"

"I know there was a Felinus warrior in the Public Hearing Room before my hearing was held. I know there was a battle and a lot of people were killed or injured." Tridia said. "I was on trial for my life – I wasn't really paying attention to much else. She was gone before my hearing started."

"You've no idea where she is?" Refined Voice asked.

"No." Tridia said.

"You aren't going to ask why we're interested?" Ethereal Voice asked.

"It isn't my business," Tridia replied. "I'm looking for someone else."

"One of our operatives was there that day," Refined Voice said. "He said the warrior reeked of Chesan energy. But his message was garbled so we didn't understand everything he said."

"Reeked of what?" Tridia asked.

"You're familiar with the Chesans," Ethereal Voice said. "A high-ranking Hierarchy officer should be."

"I never said –"

"Don't deny it, human. We are familiar with your name and your reputation."

"Are you also familiar with the fact I was killed in a Challenge a month ago? That I've lost all of my memories before I re-awoke as a bondservant? Whatever I was before then doesn't exist anymore. I could tell you very little a high-ranking Hierarchy officer should know."

"Is that the truth?" Pure Energy asked.

Tridia didn't respond to him. Silence seemed a better choice. The temperature in the air around her fell several degrees.

"Freezing me won't change the facts," she said. "If you're in touch with Odea, you can easily check the truth of my statements. I've been disowned by the Hierarchy and given a conditional amnesty by the Alliance Triad. There's not much more I can tell you."

The temperature held, but a buzz rose in the air around her. The sound pressed against her temples. She clenched her fists to keep from covering her ears.

"They're communicating with their outside forces. Flex the fingers on your left hand if you meant what you said about having amnesia."

Tridia flexed her fingers then made a fist again, comforted by the feel of her nails in her palm. Outside forces – and armored soldiers in the tunnels. Sonei couldn't have left the ship hovering above the compound. She would have had to take it into space or land outside the fences. If Master Aren and Deeca managed to escape the mine, they could be captured at the entrance waiting for the ship to return.

"You will come with us, Commander Tridia Odana," Refined Voice said.

"To the mica-chip?" Tridia asked. "Or to the surface? I'll need the chip before I go to the surface, if you don't mind."

"Your persistence is tiring. Your attempts at humor are annoying. You will come because we say you will, whether we go to the surface, the well, or to the Starling moon is not your concern at this moment. Your only concern is to move as we tell you and remain silent."

"Just shut up, Commander," Pure Energy ordered. "You've already lived longer than anyone else they've taken down here. If you play along with them, you might see daylight again. They'll take you deeper into the mine to wait. I'll go with you. I don't think they'll stop me. We've got them interested."

Tridia raised her right arm to the level of her forehead and a warm corporeal hand grabbed her wrist.

Refined Voice spoke, "Walk where you are told and you won't bump your head. Stray from the path and you will regret it in many ways. Now move forward."

Not energy, not a disembodied voice. At least one of her new companions had a body. Tridia bent to retrieve her pack and the man jerked her upright by her braid.

"What are you doing?" he asked.

"My pack is on the ground here somewhere," Tridia said. "I was only going to pick it up."

"Leave it. You won't need it where you're going." The man let go of her hair and shoved her shoulder.

Tridia took a stumbling step, then righted herself and walked upright, fighting the urge to hold her hands in front of her. With the equipment in her pack and the help of a friendly voice, she might have been able to climb out of the chasm or up a wall. Her chances got smaller with each passing minute. They'd walked for several hours when the man called a halt. The ground had been fairly even, but always sloping downward. The ceiling had stayed high enough she'd only had to duck a couple of times. There was one place, a couple of hours before they halted, where the creatures had surrounded her with a cold cocoon and lifted her off the ground. They'd carried her for several minutes then dropped her on the floor. She'd gotten to her feet on her own and walked again.

The man led Tridia to the wall and told her to sit on the floor with her back against it.

"You're doing fine, Commander," Pure Energy said. "They've brought you to a deep cavern. We're not far from their command center."

Tridia clenched her fists. She needed information from this entity, but she couldn't let the other creatures hear her speaking to him.

"We will leave you here with your companion," the man said. "Don't attempt to escape, you would never it make it before we caught you. Punishment would be immediate and final."

Tridia didn't respond. Her muscles ached from the tension of walking blind and her mind ached from fighting the desire to drop the barriers around it. This type of complete barrier probably wouldn't fail on its own. More likely a telepath couldn't stand the isolation for more than twelve hours and would rip the blockade down from the inside.

The man's footsteps echoed down the tunnel and faded into silence.

"I need intel," Tridia whispered. "Are we alone?"

"For the moment. I'll tell you if that changes."

"Do you know if there really is a mica-chip with information about Princess Anza?"

"Yes, there's a mica-chip. The soldiers laughed about catching a Guardian off-guard with it. Then the Kel took it and altered it. I don't know what it contains."

"Do you know anything about my companions?"

"No, I'm sensory only within a few hundred feet of my energy mass unless it's something like the laser field lighting up. That kind of activity tends to carry farther."

Tridia thought for a moment. "Is there another way out of here? Apart from going back through the laser fields?"

"There are several ways out of the mine, but they lead onto the mountain or into the forest. Two places you don't want to be – even if you had your sight."

"My companions won't wait for me past ten hours," Tridia said. "If I'm here longer than that, they'll assume I'm dead – or as good as. They won't be coming back for me. I've got to get out of here before then. Once outside I can signal for pickup."

"Your pack –"

"I won't need my pack for that."

"I can lead you out if they actually let you go. But the Kel Anec was right, you couldn't outrun them. And their feeders are everywhere."

"OK, who are the –"

"Incoming."

Tridia stopped talking. Footsteps echoed in the cavern. As they neared, the temperature dropped again. The man wasn't alone, he'd brought his ethereal-sounding friends.

"You are prized by one of our minions," Ethereal Voice said. "He risked much to obtain you and failed. He'd be very obedient if we gave you into his care. However, he demanded we hold you until he reached the planet. We don't like demands."

"We've decided to have sport with you, Commander Tridia Odana," Refined Voice said. "We will give you the mica-chip and allow your friend to guide you out of the mine. If you can make it, you are free. If you tire, or lose this interesting barrier you possess, you will be taken over by our feeders and they will absorb all knowledge from your mind, which they will then give to us."

A cold hand touched the side of Tridia's face. She slapped it away and jerked her head to the side. In one fluid movement she bounced onto the balls of her feet and waited in a crouch, ready to attack the next touch.

"Enough!" Refined Voice shouted. "You will permit us to examine your eyes or you will not be allowed to leave."

Tridia relaxed her shoulders and dropped to her knees. The cold hand touched her face again. Fingers pried each eyelid wide. A warm breath fanned her cheeks.

"The pupils don't respond. The corneas have been destroyed." The new voice sounded younger, not so refined as the other. "Likely caused by the crude laser flash in the upper cavern. I have no medicines here to repair this type of damage. If she can reach the Hierarchy scientists, they may be able to help her. Her chances of recovering her eyesight lessen with time." The man stepped back. "These creatures are too fragile. Why are we bothering with them?"

"Because it amuses us." Refined Voice spoke with constrained anger.

The younger man huffed and walked away without further comment. Tridia sat back on her heels and waited.

"Hold out your hand," Refined Voice said. She complied. A tiny disk dropped into her palm. "Take it and go. We'll see how long you last."

***

Shadows swarmed over Deeca's lifeless body. They lingered for several minutes, touching and oozing around Brenden as he held her close. When the feeders could find no sustenance in either body, they withdrew into the darkness of the tunnels. Brenden clutched Deeca closer to his chest when they left. He couldn't leave her in this state much longer, but neither could he bring her back to life where they were. It was too far to carry her back to the safety of the Gold's protection. There was no ice or chilling water to stave off the effects of death as he'd had with Tridia. Deeca would be permanently dead long before he reached the Gold's contact limit.

His effort to control Tridia's complicated emotions while she blocked her energy had left him without enough mental strength to construct a shield around Deeca's mind on his own. If he fell unconscious in the process he would lose the shield around his own mind and become vulnerable to attack. To construct a sufficient barrier for her, he'd have to drop his own, then reestablish it before the creatures swarmed again. It would take no less than two minutes to rebuild the barrier, but the creatures would be on him in seconds.

He had no other choice he could live with. He lifted Deeca's body to carry her back up the tunnel a few yards when his wrists tingled. The thin gold bands imbedded in his wrists made a steady thrum. If the Controller could reach him, it could reach Deeca. The being had managed to extend its reach. Brenden knelt and lay Deeca on the floor. He placed his fingers against her chest in the same pattern he'd used to kill her and flicked his wrist. He held his hand flat against her outer garments and waited to feel her heartbeat. It came quickly.

Deeca sucked air into her lungs as though she'd been drowning. Her eyes went wide with shock and she pushed away from Brenden in terror.

"Are you all right?" he asked.

Her eyes darted around the darkness in the chamber.

"They're gone, Deeca. The Gold managed to reach us. It can protect you again. Let's get out of here."

"You killed me."

"It was all I could do to save you. If those creatures had —"

"You…killed…me." Deeca's measured words seethed with fury. Her eyes stared in icy unforgiveness.

"Yes, as you requested while we were still on the surface. If I hadn't the creatures would have made their way into your consciousness and there would have been no way to dislodge them. They would be feeding on you for weeks or months before your body died. There was no other way to save you."

"If the Gold hadn't managed to contact us when it did?"

"Then it's likely we would both be fodder for these things in a very few minutes. Now get to your feet and let's get the hell out of here. You said the cylinder was empty."

"Cylinder?" Deeca looked down at the green cylinder on the floor of the chamber. The open container held nothing inside. She shook her head. "I don't remember."

Brenden pulled her to her feet, retrieving their flashlights in the process. He slid hers into her pack, flipped the primer on his blaster, and took Deeca's hand.

"Stay close to me. Let me know immediately if you feel the Gold's contact with you waiver in the slightest. We need to get to the surface as quickly as we can."

"You have a lot of explaining to do, master assassin. The Gold isn't known to anyone outside the Guardians. It's known only as the Controller."

"I'll answer your questions once we're free of this planet, and not before."

Brenden didn't dare explain anything to Deeca in his crippled state. He needed his senses and his own slight contact with the Gold to be able to answer her without endangering what the entity had planned and protected for so long. He couldn't tell her the whole truth — what she'd become when the Controller had taken her into the Guardians.

"Just stay close," he warned again.

The markers he'd left glowed enough to navigate by, so Brenden shut off the flashlight and dropped it into a pocket. As long as they could see the markers, they'd walk in the dark.

They hadn't traveled for more than an hour when Brenden halted. Deeca stopped beside him. He turned cautiously and looked over his shoulder into the darkness. Only the eerie glow of the misty paint met his eyes. He took Deeca by the shoulders and backed her against the wall into a shallow depression free of the markers, then stepped back and faced up the tunnel again. A sound, like the scrape of a boot on rock, came from somewhere nearby, but he couldn't tell whether it came from ahead or behind them. For the hundredth time he cursed his dulled senses and the creatures that made them necessary. The sound came again. He pressed his body against Deeca and whispered into her ear.

"Movement ahead. Be ready."

Deeca nodded. Brenden strained his ears for another sound of footfall and was rewarded with the distinct sound of two sets of boots walking in the darkness ahead. Vapors didn't make those sounds, these were human soldiers. He drew his blaster from its holster with infinite care – glad he'd primed it before starting the trek back, so it made no telltale hum. The footsteps stopped only feet away from where they stood shielded in the shallow depression. Two humanoid shapes stood as faint outlines against a marker. One of them reached out and touched the wall.

"They came down this way," a metallic voice spoke in the dark.

"It would help if we could use lights," a second voice answered. "Even night-vision gear isn't much use down here."

"Maintain silence!" A third voice barked over a communicator. "Return to junction o-six-two-nine."

The two armored soldiers turned back the way they had come. Brenden waited until he could no longer hear their footsteps before daring to move. He kept the weapon in his hand as he proceeded up the tunnel to the next marked access point. A ladder with a fluorescent marker at its base lead to the next level. The entrance to a side tunnel lay a few feet beyond the ladder. Brenden felt a tug at his sleeve as he put his boot on the bottom rung.

Deeca motioned to the side tunnel entrance. He shook his head and indicated they should climb the ladder. She tapped her wrist and pointed again at the tunnel entrance. Brenden nodded and stepped down to follow her lead. His own wrists tingled. They couldn't afford to ignore directions from the Controller.

No light or glow penetrated the smaller tunnel. Brenden ran his right hand along the pockmarked wall and held his left hand to the level of his forehead. The Controller could guide them, but it couldn't provide light or warning of a low roof. They moved with deliberate care, and after they'd walked a hundred yards or more Deeca's footsteps came to a sudden stop. Brenden side-stepped to keep from running into her.

"We've rounded a corner. I think it's safe to use the lights now, but I can't find mine. I must have dropped it somewhere," Deeca whispered.

"It's in your pack." Brenden whispered in return. He handed his light to her and dug in her pack for the second one. "Do you have any idea where we're headed?"

"I know there is some kind of opening somewhere up ahead. The Controller insists we not go back through the laser field."

"Then let's get moving." Brenden pushed her ahead of him, training his hearing on the tunnel behind them. Footsteps passed the entrance, but none turned down the tunnel in pursuit.

Another two hours of walking led them to a natural crevice. The crevice was steep and narrow, but it led directly to the surface. The faint light of a few scattered stars blinked above when they exited the mountain. The stars disappeared as they hurried into the stygian darkness of a thick forest. Exhausted, dusty and irritable, they didn't speak. They'd managed to lose Tridia, and still not obtain Princess Anza's location or any information about her. Were either of the young women even alive? He and Deeca were on a side of the mountain away from the compound and outside the confines of the mining facility. Out of the tunnels and away from the feeders, but not out of danger.

"We need to build a fire and keep it stoked until Sonei can get here with the ship."

"What about her, Brenden?"

"Start gathering firewood and keep your eyes open for the nylecats."

"We'll stay in the trees until the ship gets here. Sonei can home in on our transmitter signals. *What about her?*" Deeca stood motionless, waiting for a response.

"We can't stay in the trees. The cats climb, but they won't come near a fire. They'll sleep in the day, but the bigger predators will be out then. That's when we'll need to climb, if we're still here. There's a chance Sonei can't reach us or land nearby. If they've had to pull out of the atmosphere she may not receive our signal for hours. We don't have much time to get a fire going. Go gather some wood."

"Then we'll stay in the tunnel entrance where we can defend ourselves! I'm not moving until we talk about how we're going to get the assassin out of there."

"We're not! Commander Odana is gone. It's been more than six hours. There's no way we can get back to her in less time than that. Her block was good for no more than eleven hours once we landed. If she didn't die in the fall, her energy signature will break through long before we can reach her. Those things that attacked us are drawn to complex brain wave activity like metal shavings to a magnet. It won't take long for them to find her and she'll be infested. Even if we managed to find her and get her outside the tunnel, we couldn't remove what would be festering inside her mind.

"You wanted her to suffer, Lady Varin. If she's still alive, I can guarantee she'll suffer unimaginable torments for many days before her body finally gives out. That should satisfy even your misguided desire for revenge. Whatever truth she had hidden behind that black veil in her mind will die with her."

Brenden stalked into the shadows to collect wood, leaving Deeca staring into the darkened canopy of trees.

CHAPTER NINE

Tridia patted her pants leg until she found a zippered pocket, then dropped the disk inside. If it held Anza's whereabouts, or some clue to her location, she had to get it back to the surface. Hours of walking in the dark lay ahead, then who knew what she'd face if she made it out of the mine.

"As long as your mind is sealed and you continue to move, we will allow you to go your own way. However, if you falter – or your mind opens – our feeders will take you," Refined Voice reiterated. "Now go."

Footsteps faded as the man left. The temperature warmed, indicating that the ethereal beings left, as well.

Tridia stood. "OK, Pure Energy, give me directions."

"Pure Energy?"

"He did say Pure Energy is amorphous," Tridia replied. "Since I don't know your name, it will have to do."

"Very well, turn ninety degrees to your left. Walk straight and upright until I tell you otherwise. You can place your left hand on the wall for balance."

A humorless smile curled Tridia's lips. She made a sharp turn on her heel and walked. Following directions to walk, stoop, slide, and crawl, Tridia made good time the first two hours. Holding one hand on the wall and one in front of her eased the tension of being in the dark. She didn't speak and Pure Energy only spoke to give her directions.

"Hold up. This is the chasm where they carried you on the way in. We're not far from the lake where you fell. If I could carry you, I could take you back there, but you'd have to deal with the lasers again."

"I might be able to deal with the lasers, but I'd need the things in my pack. Is there no way to walk across? No way down or around?" Tridia slid her boot along the floor until the floor dropped away.

"Careful, Commander. You're dangling your foot over a thousand-foot drop." Tridia backed slowly away from the edge, as her navigator continued. "You're in a predicament. I've studied the tunnels and their connections but paid little heed to the flooring. I'm sure that's why the Kel Anec allowed you to leave with me. They obviously doubted my ability to see you safely through."

"Reaching an impasse like this, they knew I'd have to stop moving." Tridia said.

"Most likely."

"I've got no memory of the Kel Anec." Tridia moved cautiously backward, keeping her hand in contact with the wall at all times. "They must have some connection with Odea. They got their confirmations very quickly. They were communicating with someone with current knowledge. The question is who – and why? Why would someone from the Hierarchy deal with the people controlling the feeders in the mine."

"Any idea what minions have taken risks to obtain you?"

"Only Master Ren Tama comes to mind. He confronted me on Odea and chased me all the way to Aga."

"An Odean Master on Aga? That is a risk. It links Odea with the Kel Anec."

"He was in the Public Hearing Room. And he knows –" Tridia stopped. Best not to reveal too much when she didn't know for sure who was listening.

"Knows what?"

"Never mind. I've got more immediate problems. Even with my pack I couldn't scale a thousand-foot wall." Tridia took a couple more steps back. "What's the wall like going up here?"

"Jagged. Scalable. Are you a climber now?"

"I have no idea," Tridia responded. "I'd prefer my feet on solid ground, but I will climb if I have to."

"Wait here. Move back and forth no more than ten steps and don't take your hand off the wall. I need to do a little scouting."

"Understood," Tridia said.

The tickling sensation left her ear, signaling her companion's departure. She stepped off ten paces, then turned and stepped them off again, keeping her hands on the wall as she moved. It seemed solid enough when she pulled and tugged at the small protrusions. The first few she tried took her weight without creaking or breaking off in her hand. If there was a ledge on the other side – or an opening above – she might be able to climb it with a little help from her navigator. She paused to consider the voice that had guided her. He knew her or knew of her. He knew she didn't like the cold and that implied personal knowledge, not something read from a file. He also knew she wasn't a climber. She'd seen Davik's body in the stasis cabinet on the surface. Only one monitor had showed heightened activity. A brain monitor measuring the energy that produced his glowing persona? Had they reduced the young man she'd cared for to this?

Tridia laid her forehead against the cool stone. Her knees weakened, but she lifted her head and remained on her feet to keep moving. Memories flooded her mind. A much younger Davik who teased her after class. An older Davik who studied battle strategies and political manipulations for hours on end in the library. A serious Davik who had kissed her before her last mission. A Davik who'd fallen in love with her. She gasped with the realization of what this man had meant to her. A friend and a brother who'd been steadfast for years, and a suitor who'd dare the impossible for her protection. Their relationship unfolded in a rush and left her breathless, just as her memories of *Somi Robel* had.

"Oh, Davik." Tridia lifted a hand to wipe away tears. "What have you done?"

"Found you a way out if you've got enough strength left to climb." He waited a moment. "You remember me."

"Just now." Tridia searched for words. "Things have been coming back in bits and pieces this past month, but just now, I remembered you and all that you were to me."

"All that I still am, I hope – just less a body."

"Davik, I believe you!" Tridia said. She couldn't hold the words back. He'd said in his message he needed to hear them from her. "I knew you didn't commit that unspeakable crime. I never doubted you. I didn't get back to Odea until you'd already left the planet. If I'd been there I would have found a way to get to you."

"And you might have ended up here instead of me," he replied. "You've got powerful enemies. Frees B'Nay is desperate to get his hands on you. I was bait to draw you in. He knew you'd try to get to me. Didn't you get the hints in my message?"

"No," Tridia said. "You told me to find the ones who framed you and make them pay. I didn't detect any hints."

"The slimy sub-human edited them out. I told you *not* to make them pay and to count me as lost. I think the minion's been identified," Davik said. "Whatever time you have left with your mental block probably isn't enough to reminisce about old times. Let's get you in sight of an opening, then – if there's time – we'll talk."

"Ever the strategist. Thinking three steps ahead," Tridia said.

"If I can only manage three steps you'll be dead – or worse," Davik said. "I've got to think you off this planet. A few feet back there's a place where you can start to scale the wall. If I take you at an angle, you can reach the top. I'll have to create some handholds for you, but if I use too much energy, I'll draw attention from the scientists. They've been trying to catch up with me ever since I blasted my name into a wall. I can channel the mental energy, but it's exhausting after a few blasts. I've got to be conservative, or I may fade away and leave you hanging halfway up the cliff face. There's an opening up there. It's not much more than a lateral crevice, but you should be able to slide through it onto a wide ledge outside the mountain. It comes out above the forest."

"Lead the way." Tridia turned to follow Davik's directions. She had to brush aside the surge of emotion that welled in her chest. She couldn't let him expend his life force to get her out of the mine, but she didn't know how to stop him. The mica-disk with information about Anza weighed nothing in her pocket, but the responsibility to get it into Deeca's hands pulled at her like an anchor shield. Anza had to be her first priority. After that, she'd do anything within her power to rescue Davik.

He led her to a place on the wall that had an easy ledge that she climbed for a few dozen feet. After that, he had her cling to the wall from small protrusions and crevices that she wouldn't have found on her own, even if she had her eyesight. She climbed for more than an hour before he guided her to a place to rest — a ledge barely wide enough for one knee to brace against. It took the strain off of her arms and shoulders. She wiggled her fingers and flexed them to keep them loose.

"Turn your face to the left and close your eyes," Davik instructed.

Tridia did as he said and a small explosion to her right scattered bits of rock on her shoulder and into her hair.

"You're about half the distance to the top. It gets a little harder from here. The handhold I just made will bridge one gap, but about ten feet from the top there's a place where you'll either have to swing for a hold, or I'll have to create two or three more gouges. The problem is, the rock is brittle at the rim and if I blast it, it might give way. We'll have to decide what to do when we get there. It will depend on how tired you are."

"Well, I'm glad it's been the easy stuff so far." Tridia inhaled deeply.

"You're different."

"You should talk," Tridia laughed.

"That's what I mean. You laughed. I've known you for six years, but you never laughed — well not unless I was making an utter fool of myself. You were always so serious."

"I don't remember what I was like," Tridia said. "I don't think I want to know what I was like. I know I don't want to remember all the blood on my hands."

"You were a soldier of the highest caliber."

"I was an assassin, Davik. I killed people from the shadows. There's nothing heroic or noble about that. I'm just a murderer." She sighed. "A murderer with a mission to save a life this time. So, let's get going."

They started again, Tridia climbing as Davik instructed. Several times her hands slipped and she caught herself dangling in the darkness by shaky fingertips. Once the rock gave way beneath her foot. Just when she didn't think she could go any farther, fresh air touched her face. Tridia drew a deep breath and laughed without thinking.

"We're nearly there," she said. "We must be close to the danger spot."

"The next hand placement. Now that we're here, I'm not sure you can make that swing. If you miss –"

"We're right over the abyss, aren't we?" Tridia asked.

Davik didn't answer.

"You led me back down the tunnel before I started the climb. We've come sideways on the wall at least that far. If this is the only way, I'll have to make it. There's no going back down."

"Let me test the rock above. It may be stable enough to take a few shocks."

"You may bring the whole thing down on my head," Tridia argued. "How many times did you drill me to trust my first instincts. I can't see the pit, Lieutenant Schie. It doesn't scare me."

"You always were too smart to be tolerated," Davik said. "Yes, we're over the abyss and if you fall there's nothing to catch you."

"Then I'd better not fall," Tridia said.

"Six feet to your right, and up about five inches, there's a ledge. It's wide enough for you to pull onto. You'll have to let go with your left hand to reach it with your right."

"Six feet." Tridia thought about it. Six feet meant she'd have to swing at least five inches over and up once she let go. "If I use both hands where my right hand is holding now, does that give me any distance at all?"

"There's not enough purchase there for both hands."

"Does it give me any distance for the swing?" Her arms ached and her fingers had begun to cramp. She couldn't cling to the wall forever and she refused to come so close and fail.

"Yes," Davik replied. "About six inches."

Six inches, dropping the reach to five-and-a-half feet. She could almost reach that without swinging, but the vertical difference added distance as well as complexity. Six inches gave her a better chance of making it.

"Tridia, don't —"

"Quiet, Davik — and that's an order from your superior."

"You're not in the Hierarchy anymore."

"Then pretend I am and keep quiet. This really isn't as easy as you think it is."

Tridia let go with her left hand and lifted her left foot. With a tiny bounce she moved her left foot to the bit of rock where her right foot had stood, and she placed her left fingers atop her right.

"Now for the tricky bit," she said. She placed all of her weight on her toes and freed her right hand. "Okay. Is there any indentation at all, or am I swinging against the rock?"

As she spoke, Tridia reached out with her right hand. Only smooth stone met her fingertips.

"Don't touch the wall with your hand!"

Davik's warning came too late. Dampness trickled down an indentation in the stone. She now had to grasp a ledge over a thousand-foot abyss with a wet hand. Even if she dried it on her pants, it no longer had the dust from the climb to absorb the sweat. She rubbed it against her hip anyway.

"Indentation?" she asked.

"Not much. The water will smooth the way for you. It's dripping from just above the crevice. It's why the rock is brittle and why I couldn't build another handhold for you in the other direction."

"All right." Tridia kept her voice calm and her mind clear as her heart pounded against her ribs. "I'm going to kick off with my foot and swing on my hand. You've got to tell me when to let go. I can make the swing, I just can't judge the distance."

"Tridia, if you —"

Davik loved her. If he let her fall, his mind would never survive. She couldn't let that happen. Her eyes suddenly itched like mad and it took a monumental effort to keep from rubbing them. Had the young Kel Anec lied when he said they were destroyed? The darkness lessened from black to gray. If she could hold on for another few minutes, she'd be able to see the ledge on her own.

"We're out of time." The dead calm in Davik's words sent dread through Tridia's being.

"What's happened?" she asked.

"Feeders. They're in the tunnel now, but they'll be up here in two minutes or less. They apparently can't drain your energy if your mind is blocked, but they can freeze your hands. They might be able to take me, as well. You've got to make this last swing. The rest will be easy after that."

"Here goes." Tridia drew back against her hand and kicked her foot away from the rock, sliding against the water on the smooth stone.

"Let go!"

Tridia let go at Davik's command. For a breathless instant her hand felt nothing, then her fingertips caught the ledge. She hung on with her fingertips and slid her feet against the wall looking for any purchase to keep from falling. Her boots scraped against unbroken rock and she couldn't swing her left hand up to the ledge. Her fingers started to slide. Blue energy flashed from her hand as she lost contact with the rock.

"Davik!"

"No!" Davik shouted as Tridia lost her grip on the ledge.

She expected to fall for eternity, then end in a bloody splat at the bottom of the abyss. But she stopped falling and started to rise, wrapped in a blue shroud with gold and silver lights sparkling through it. Tridia caught her breath. The Sentinels had shown her this vision on the day of her hearing. As she rose a slit of light appeared over the top of the wall. The blue shroud stood her upright on the ledge but continued to hold her.

"I've dreamed of holding you this way." Davik's voice trembled. "Close enough to feel your heartbeat. To just know that you were safe. Without a body, it isn't the same."

"Davik." Tridia whispered his name and leaned into his warmth. Every nerve tingled and her stomach stirred with butterflies. The blue shroud that was Davik shifted and brightened, then changed to a darker blue. The sparks of light increased in number as the shroud became more solid. "What's happening?"

"Energy poured out of you as you fell. When I caught you, it comingled with me." He hesitated. "I think I've become what the scientists wanted me to be." Davik stretched out a tendril of energy toward the wall Tridia had just scaled. Light flashed, blasting the wall to dust and rubble, leaving a crude stairway on its face. "They won't let me go until they can reproduce this power. And they never will without you. You cannot let them get you."

Tridia groped for some reassuring word, anything to give him some hope of escape. He loved her to a degree she'd never suspected and it broke her heart that she didn't return his feelings. Then she realized that she *sensed* his love. Her barrier was gone – and the feeders were on the way. Even as she thought it, dark shapes rose through the dust from the blasted wall.

"I'll save you," she said. "I'll find a way back to that building and I'll end your nightmare one way or the other."

"Tridia."

Agony pressed against her thoughts. Davik's fear of losing her, of having her become as isolated as he'd been, threatened to extinguish his consciousness. How had he managed to survive?

"I've lost my barrier. The feeders will be able to get to me."

Davik shoved her toward the opening, cushioning her fall against the rock floor. He shielded her completely as the first feeder attacked. His shroud darkened to an indigo hue and the sparkling lights dimmed.

"Warn someone about the Kel Anec. They're an advance guard of a gigantic attack force. They know –" Davik's energy was torn away as he spoke.

Tridia continued to scramble toward the opening. Dragging herself along with her arms and pushing with her boots on the slick rock. She was only a foot or so from the opening when two pairs of feet blocked the way. She hesitated and a cold darkness enveloped her. Another feeder had caught up.

CHAPTER TEN

Tridia's hearing muted and her vision dimmed. Her body lay unresponsive in the dark gray shroud. The feeder left small slits around her nose and mouth so she could draw shallow breaths, but it didn't stop her slide into the pale morning light. Hands grabbed her and hauled her to her feet. Alanel's face appeared indistinct and dark through the feeder's shroud. He studied her for a moment, then slung her over his shoulder and ran. Brush and grass slapped at Tridia's face and arms as she bounced against Alanel's back. She caught one glimpse of Winniel running behind them. The muffled snarl of a large animal came from somewhere nearby. It was followed by a death yelp, but no animal ever appeared.

Alanel slid to a halt. The distant sounds of a heated argument reached Tridia's ears, but she couldn't comprehend the muffled words. Her feet touched the ground, but she lacked the strength to stand, and landed hard on her backside when Alanel released her. She ended up lying on her side, facing the *Star Seeker*. The dark, fog-like shroud pulsated around her.

Tridia's mind had numbed to all sensation except a burrowing pressure at the base of her skull. The feeder hadn't infiltrated her mind, just cut off her mobility. Why hadn't it started extracting information? The creature would feed on its victims for days, perhaps it took that long to make the necessary links. She might still have a chance.

She needed to tell Alanel the creature hadn't attached, but he was looking at Master Aren. They glared at each other for several moments before Master Aren pulled his blaster from its holster. Winniel was at his side in a flash and removed the weapon from his hands. Master Aren took a step back and transferred his glare to Winniel, but she was watching her mate.

Alanel knelt beside Tridia and took her face in his hands so she could look directly at him.

"You must trust me." Alanel's deep voice sounded as though it came through several layers of water-soaked cotton. "This thing is sapping your strength. You can't fight it alone, nor can I remove it without your help. There isn't yet enough sunlight to make it release you on its own."

Tridia tried to nod her assent but couldn't. Alanel adjusted her body so she lay flat on the ground, cushioning her head with his hand. He placed his other hand on her shoulder and focused his gaze at the base of her throat. Tridia closed her eyes to shut out the blurred world around her. Alanel moved in her mind, straining to locate the monster feeding on her energy. He searched without restraint, and Tridia's mind recoiled from the frantic freezing paths the Sentinel slashed across her consciousness. She tried to concentrate on the pressure at the base of her skull, to catch Alanel's attention and let him know it wasn't yet in her mind. But he either couldn't understand what she was trying to convey, or he doubted her ability to tell him the truth. He was looking for an alien presence that could already be controlling her. Tridia held on as long as she could before she recoiled from his search. She pulled her consciousness into a distant corner of her mind, until she found herself mentally on the edge of a precipice as dark and daunting as the one she'd just scaled. She dangled between reality and illusion as the pressure at the base of her skull increased to the point of intrusion. She opened her eyes to see if Alanel would notice her. The shroud changed from dark gray to near-black, much as Davik's energy changed from bright blue to indigo. She thought of the blue energy Empress Dojene had described. Was it responsible for the changes? Had it turned Davik into a weapon for the Hierarchy? Was it battling the feeder? Tridia teetered on the brink for a few precious seconds, trying one last time to send a message to Alanel. In the end she tumbled forward into the void. Her stomach lurched as her mind reeled farther and farther from the struggle. Just when she expected to black out, she heard a familiar voice in her mind.

Child of Chaos, flee your body. Only your absence will make this creature release you. Come to me. Let go of your own reality.

Tridia resisted the call at first as her mind strained toward the darkness. But a stronger instinct called her forward. Knowledge, new and fresh, burst into her thoughts with a single explosion of sight and sound. The voice called her into a place of swirling mists, where a golden statue that looked like her had pulled her from the brink once before, and where she'd seen the face of a young man with worried gray eyes. She could get there on her own and willed her consciousness to take flight. Golden light surrounded her, the shimmering mists of her previous visit swirled into existence. Her golden statue stood nearby.

"Well done. I had very little to do with getting you here this time," the statue said.

"How do we get rid of that creature?" Tridia asked. "There must be some way to do it. When I was on the hospital ship, you told me I need my body to go to *him*. So, what do I do?"

"You have the power within your consciousness to view this place and your world. Concentrate on the last image you saw. See in your mind what you saw with your eyes. Look back at the people trying to help you. Focus your thoughts on them."

Tridia looked away from the golden image and concentrated on the inky blackness beyond. A surface shimmered in the darkness, and then became a distinct picture of Alanel hovering over her body on Cystia. He stepped away with a confused look on his face, then dashed to Winniel in time to catch her as she collapsed.

Tridia concentrated on turning from the Sentinels to face her body lying on the ground. A shadow clung to her motionless form.

"Very good," the statue said. "Now, concentrate on that dark shroud, and bring it here."

"What?" Tridia looked back in surprise. The picture vanished.

"Concentrate! Once the creature is pried loose, it will look for another host among your companions. Brenden Aren is the most likely receptacle. His fear makes him vulnerable. The barrier protecting his mind will fail unless he calms down. The female Sentinel is also vulnerable now that your consciousness has left your body."

Tridia looked away again. The picture of her companions and her body on Cystia sprang to life in the darkness. She focused her thoughts on the shroud and on separating it from the base of her skull. For a moment nothing happened, then a sensation ran along her body, as if tiny tentacles were being pulled away from her skin. With an exhausting slowness, the feeder released itself and hung suspended above her body. Alanel lay Winniel on the ground and moved to stand between her and the creature.

The feeder tugged at Tridia's consciousness and writhed to break free of her grasp. Master Aren, his face creased with fear, had moved farther up the ramp of the *Star Seeker*. Alanel stood tense, waiting for the creature to move.

"Now bring the feeder here." The voice of the statue lent strength to Tridia's concentration.

She tugged at the feeder with all the energy she could muster. It dissolved from the picture as she watched, and by increments reappeared in front of her. It left behind a globe of blue energy that shifted until it produced two faces that resembled Davik. After a moment, the blue globe pulled the faces back into its orb and dissolved into her body. The feeder writhed, trying to escape, as she held it with her thoughts.

The golden image walked around the gray cloud, examining it. "You may send it back into its cave, to any other place you see fit, or – you may destroy it."

Tridia shuddered as the creature struggled. It had only a rudimentary mind to store the knowledge it drained from its hosts. The Kel Anec might command it to come and go, they could drain the memories it had absorbed, but the creatures lacked the subtleties of evolved intelligence. It was simply a tool used to dispense a slow and agonizing death.

"How do I destroy it?"

"Hold the creature with your mind. At the same time, you must open another portal to the cave entrance."

"You make it sound easy."

The golden image smiled and waved its hand. A half-dozen portals opened with as many different views. One showed Master Aren from a different angle and Deeca standing behind him. Other portals displayed her empty room on Odea, Master Aren's office on Aga, the Empress Dojene in a comfortable cabin, and the sleeping form of the young man she'd seen before. His face was identical to Davik's and her heart lurched at the sight of him.

"See in your mind the place you wish to send it, then push it through."

"All right." Tridia turned her thoughts to the middle of the laser field. The dim image of the mine shimmered, then faded.

"My apologies," the golden image said. "Your body is waning and the energy of this place calls to it. It will be transported here if you linger or a physical portal will open and contaminate your cells. That much energy will make your body a beacon to the Kel Anec. I'll finish this."

A soft presence coaxed its way into Tridia's thoughts and took command of both the creature and the image of the cave. The picture sharpened immediately, then merged with the shadowy feeder. The creature's form vanished, only to reappear in the cave, bright lasers fired before the picture of the cave disappeared.

"The bright laser blast will destroy it completely," the image said.

"Now its masters might know it was destroyed in the mine," Tridia said. "And that someone had the power to place it there."

"It couldn't be helped. Go, your comrades are concerned. We'll meet again." The golden image started to dissolve.

"Wait!" Tridia called and the image solidified once more. A question fashioned on its shining face. "That young man. He's the Chesan prince. His name is Drayden Anjenay. What is my connection to him? Why do I see him? No riddles this time. Give me a straight answer."

"You see him because he needs you. His mind needed to latch onto something or someone he could hope in and he found you. There are many possible futures, but you stand a better than even chance of prospering. That's all I can tell you. My vision goes no further."

The golden image vanished and Tridia's mind did a backward somersault into her body. The experience left her disoriented and her stomach heaved as she settled into her physical form.

"She's free." Winniel's voice had never sounded so good in Tridia's ears. The Sentinel struggled to extract herself from her mate's arms.

"We thought you were a goner for sure, assassin," Deeca commented from a distance.

"Yeah, and your gentle master intended to help that process along," Sonei added.

"Get her on the ship and let's get out of here," Master Aren said.

Alanel held Winniel and walked toward Tridia to help her to her feet, but Sonei intervened.

"I've got this, Sentinel," Sonei said. "Get your mate on board. The good ambassador will leave us all if we don't hurry."

"I think I can walk now," Tridia said, as she rolled onto her knees.

"Yeah, and vat toads fly," Sonei replied. Her form shifted until she became a muscular male with red hair and green eyes. When she spoke, her voice had not changed. "Let's not make a habit of this, shall we?"

She drew Tridia's arm across her shoulders and helped her to her feet. They followed the Sentinels up the ramp as the *Star Seeker's* engines roared to life.

You must tell us how you managed to free yourself from that creature. And how you gained the knowledge to use the Chesan blue energy.

Tridia glanced in Alanel's direction as he spoke into her mind. He didn't look at her, nor did she feel his presence in her mind, but Winniel's warm presence lay at the edge of her conscious thoughts. *Standing beside me.*

She couldn't call any of them friends, but they were formidable allies. For the moment, that was enough.

CHAPTER ELEVEN

Drayden woke with a start, trembling with fear he couldn't understand. His heart pounded in his chest and his breath came in short gasps. He wore no shirt and he shivered beneath a warm blanket on a soft bed. His only soft bed was in the bunker. He sprang to a sitting position, tossing the cover aside. *The physician's subterfuge.*

"Welcome back, Your Highness." The physician hologram sat on the floor with her back to the table leg. "I trust you are none the worse for your sleep?"

"How long was I out?" Drayden stood and rubbed his eyes, doing his best to still his shaking hands.

"Quite a while," the physician replied.

"How long?" Drayden demanded.

"Thirty-five hours and forty-seven minutes, sire." The physician rose to her feet.

"Never do that to me again." Drayden glared, his voice a threatening growl. He retrieved a shirt which had been laid out on the lab table and pulled it on.

"Or what? You'll erase me? Reprogram my protocols? I did what was necessary to restore you to health. It is what I was programmed to do."

"Not without my permission!" Drayden shouted. "And don't try to say I gave you permission. I told you I was in a hurry, and you deliberately mislead me about your intentions. Furthermore, you didn't tell me how serious my illness was until you'd already administered the injection. I expect better from my subjects – even the holographic ones."

The hologram flickered.

"Yes, Physician, in the absence of true Chesan subjects, you and the other program images are all I have to train with. I was led to believe the purpose of every program in the bunker was to prepare me to take my place as the sovereign of our people. Would you expect me to take lightly the deception of someone I should be able to trust implicitly?"

"No, Your Highness."

"Should I accept disrespect and taunts from any subject?" Drayden took a few steps away, then turned back when the hologram didn't respond. "Well?"

"No, Your Highness."

"I understand your concern. And I'm not unappreciative of the programming that caused such behavior – especially since so little was expected of me that I might have needed a nursemaid rather than a physician. You have some level of autonomy within those programs, or you wouldn't have been able to deceive me. Is that not true?"

"Yes, Your Highness."

"Then let this be your last deception, or so help me I will never call upon you again. I'll minister to my own medical needs in the future. Are we clear on this?"

"Yes, Your Highness."

"Have you cleared me with the tutors?"

"Not yet, Your Highness."

"Do so immediately!"

"Please, sire, we must talk," the hologram pleaded. Her image flickered again and returned with a calmer demeanor. "This is important and it will take only a few minutes."

Drayden ran his hand through his sleep tousled hair. A few minutes could make all the difference in the world if the girl was trying to reach him, but a prolonged argument with a hologram would take longer.

"Proceed," he said.

"The hard nodules behind your jawbone and the burning in your throat," the physician said.

"What about them?"

"Your Highness, they are indicators of Chesan maturity."

"What?" Drayden stared at the hologram. "We both know that isn't possible. I won't reach maturity for another eighteen years. Or have the tutors been misinterpreting the health and biology lessons?"

"No, Your Highness," the physician replied. "There are records in antiquity of Chesans maturing near your age, but they were very rare and part of our earliest records. There are tests I could run to validate my diagnosis, but the evidence is irrefutable of itself."

"What does this mean – apart from my ability to procreate being brought forward by almost two decades? I have no potential mates on this planet." Drayden's heart pounded. Not on this planet, but one who may be trying to reach him while he sat chatting with the computer.

"Your Highness, your respiration and pulse have increased," the physician said. "Which is generally an indication of falsehood."

"In case you didn't notice, I just awoke from a nightmare, finding myself betrayed by what I thought was my most trusted subject, and have been arguing with an AI. You should be concerned if my pulse and respiration weren't elevated. Besides, there were no females of the Chesan or human species on this planet before the shields were activated. That was confirmed a dozen different ways," Drayden countered. "Have there been any arrivals on Zentel since the shields were activated."

"No, Your Highness."

"Then I think the possibility of a mate, while fascinating – and perhaps exciting," Drayden cleared his throat and managed to blush. "Is highly unlikely."

"Yes, Your Highness."

"Are there other matters which should concern me with this early maturity?"

"There will be physical changes, muscle mass will become denser, your physique will shift from that of a slender pre-adolescent to a more mature male. This could happen quickly. You should obtain larger clothing sizes from the storage rooms if you are planning on another extended absence from the bunker," the physician explained. "You'll experience some personality changes as your hormones adjust. Expect to become more somber, perhaps more proprietary or domineering. Were you among other Chesans or humans – especially males – asserting your authority would be a noticeable change in your heretofore amiable disposition. You are asserting your authority already. This change is abnormal at your age, but by the time your exile ends, it will evolve into a natural part of your character."

"That doesn't seem unmanageable," Drayden said. He crossed his arms and leaned against the table.

The physician continued, "My concern is that you will become restless and distracted with the need for bonding. Once your glands secrete for the first time, you will begin searching for your mate, subconsciously, if not consciously – even though there are no females on this planet. If you are already careless outside these walls, then perhaps you should limit your excursions for the next several months at least. Give yourself time to adjust, both mentally and physically."

Drayden opened his mouth to object, but the physician interrupted.

"Please hear me out." The program hesitated, as if rerunning a calculation. "You've been taught that Chesans bond for life. The sharing of memories and knowledge, revelation of character at the deepest levels, allows that bond. A royal bonding is deeper than any other. This type of exposure to another person is not done lightly. This mental bonding is the greatest need you will experience. It will continue to intensify until it is fulfilled. Until it consumes you. Chesan males isolated at this time in their lives underwent extreme distress and depression. Some attempted suicide. A few lost their sanity. With no Chesans or humans here for you to even attempt a telepathic exchange, you're at great risk. You should remain inside the bunker where I can keep watch – monitor your condition. At least spend a few days in the lecture room with the recordings King Aiden left for you."

"Impossible," Drayden said. "I have responsibilities outside the bunker. One of them pressing within a matter of days."

"Prince Drayden, this danger isn't only to yourself," the physician argued. "You are of noble birth, a direct descendant of Chesan kings and queens. Our latest computations indicate your telepathic abilities will exceed those of your father's, and his were formidable. If you fulfill your exile and have been subjected to this torment, you could bond with the first female you encounter, Chesan or not, suitable or not, and not be able to control the action. That would be disastrous for her, you, and the kingdom."

"Should I expect this disintegration of my faculties within the next few weeks?"

"No, your highness," the physician said. "It would normally take months before it becomes a strain on your psyche, years to create permanent damage. However, you are maturing at an incredible rate."

"Then this discussion can wait," Drayden said. "As I said, I have urgent business."

"Prince Drayden –"

"Enough, Physician." Drayden used a gentle tone. He straightened to his full height and looked down at the hologram. "I may be isolated from other Chesans and without suitable female prospects, but outside the bunker, at least I have the Rrabbas plants for companionship. They are living, sentient beings who look to me for guidance and protection. They are telepathic creatures with whom I have developed a familial relationship. I'm not alone. With them, I have many things to occupy my mind, and perhaps negate the distress you've described." Drayden flashed a small sympathetic smile. "We have time to discuss this in the weeks ahead."

"Yes, Your Highness."

"Then, please, release me to my tutors. I will be mindful of my attitude and behavior. If I notice any significant change, I will report to you immediately so we can determine the best course of action." He smiled again. "I won't squander your counsel, but there are no unsuspecting females in the vicinity for me to take advantage of, even if I were to lose control today. I promise to be more careful outside the bunker. Although I can't promise not to encounter another skike, I can say I won't be caught unaware by my own negligence again."

The physician stared into Drayden's eyes. "It would seem I am no longer caring for a princeling, but a king."

"Not yet," Drayden said. "But it's time I behaved more like a noble and less like a schoolboy inside these walls. It's also time for my holographic subjects – all of them – to show me the respect due my station. I still have a lot to learn, educationally and about leadership. I don't mean to hint otherwise. But if I will be undergoing these changes, then it might be a good idea if the professors and tutors adjust their presentation to accommodate them."

"Yes, Your Highness," the physician said, and lowered her eyes. "The system has adjusted programs for years to keep pace with your growing intellect. You are not the immature individual we were originally programmed to expect. All programs and sub-routines will be updated, but it may take time for every program to reflect the changes."

"Thank you. Please discontinue your program when you've released me to my tutors and performed the updates." Drayden stopped at a cooler to retrieve a container of water and detoured to a bathroom before returning to his study.

The previously sour-faced professor stood a little more erect and appeared much less foreboding by the time Drayden reached his study. The professor gave a nod in deference as Drayden entered the room. The physician program had wasted no time in relaying the update and the complex computer had made cosmetic adjustments to its protocols.

"Where shall we begin, Your Highness?" the professor asked.

Drayden sat at his desk to consider the things the physician had said before answering. Had the physiological changes the program described driven him to his desperate march across the desert alone? Was it likely the girl would actually come to him, or was it his own biological need preempting his common sense? He massaged his burning throat and took a sip of water. If she did come, would he be able to control his behavior or would she be at risk from him? The Chaos Vision threatened to emerge from his memory and he forced it aside. He'd deal with those nightmares in his sleep tonight without disturbing Tayne's rest. He needed to focus on the serene parts of what he'd seen, to reassure himself he'd made his decision regarding the girl long before his body decided to mature. The love he'd felt for the indistinct person in those visions had made him believe he could navigate the treacherous course to peace, avoiding the horrors of galactic war.

Tayne's quiet voice spoke in his memory.

You are more certain than you admit, Brother. The nightmares you try to conceal have disturbed my rest more than a dozen times. Yet, you have decided to seek the good, to believe in the hope. You have decided and you will not deter. That is why I say your heart is strong and your mind is pure. You have decided — but she must also decide. She must accept your healing. Your great fear is that she will reject your offer. Search your heart and know that my words are true.

The small plant creature had been so certain — and she'd been right. He feared the girl would reject his plea for help. Mostly, he feared she would reject him. That fear had haunted him long before the glands had burned in his throat. Suppose she was the Child of Chaos. What if, after all the plans and sacrifices, her only crime turned out to be that she rejected him? And it was her rejection that sent him over the edge into the horrors he'd seen. Drayden shook his head to dispel the doubt and fear. His glands hadn't secreted yet. The physician had said he had months — weeks at the very least. His mind was clear enough to research the satellites and plan accordingly. Now that the programs had been adjusted, he might be able to gather information without studying for days.

"Start with what you know," he said, to himself.

"Please repeat the instruction, Sire," the professor said.

Drayden smiled. "Access astromechanical engineering, satellite structure and alignment."

"Access granted," the professor said.

"Display three-dimensional satellite schematic." A schematic for the shield satellite appeared above his desk. "If I ask specific questions regarding this schematic, will you be able to answer them, or must I resume the lessons until the answers are reached?"

"That would depend on whether the answer would be understandable to you in your present stage of development."

"Let's give it a try, shall we?" Drayden stood. "Enlarge schematic."

When the hologram had enlarged to twice its original size and moved to an open space beside the desk, Drayden stopped it. He retrieved the stylus from his desk and tapped it lightly against his palm before using it to point to specific areas of the satellite. He spoke without referring to his notes.

"These are the cameras, scanners, and various information gathering instruments. They are attached to both upper and lower sides of the main housing. They rotate to give full coverage of both the planet and upper atmosphere — or the space beyond. These are the directional thrusters. They are locked to guarantee stationary orbit above the planet. The main housing encases the shield generators and these are the shield projectors. They are aligned from the corners in four directions creating skewed octagonal connections with the nearest neighboring satellites.

The octagons are solidified with shield energy." Drayden glanced toward the tutor. "Correct so far?"

"Yes, Your Highness."

"The power output of the shield generators can fluctuate automatically in reaction to the current protective need of the planet. Output is standardly set at approximately thirty percent." A question occurred to Drayden that he'd never thought to ask before. "Is the thirty percent level necessary to maintain protection of the planet when it is not under attack from outside forces."

"No, Your Highness."

"What is the output necessary to protect the planet when it is not under attack?"

"Five percent would protect the planet from harmful solar flares and small meteorites."

"Five percent?" Drayden frowned across the schematic at the professor. "Then why are the shields set at thirty percent?"

"To protect you, Your Highness."

"Explain."

"That answer requires more extensive study before you could fully comprehend the reasoning."

"Please try to accommodate my request, Professor." Drayden bit back an angry command. Diplomacy would get him farther than anger. "If I cannot comprehend the answer, I will proceed with the required study."

"The shields increased in strength as you spent more time out of the bunker," the professor said. "The solar filters also retard the growth of bacteria and reduce the risk of virus mutation. Thirty percent is the level required to maintain that protection."

"That level also damages the indigenous plant life," Drayden said.

"That is one of the side-effects."

"That isn't acceptable." Drayden thumped the stylus again his palm.

"The shields must operate at a level strong enough to protect you, Your Highness."

"If I remain inside the bunker, will the shield levels drop?"

"You would be required to seal and sterilize the bunker using the command 'Drayden One Sterilize.' Should you give the command, any non-Chesan organism the size of a virus or larger would be disintegrated. The exits would remain closed for the next ten years, barring any dangerous incident inside which would require you to leave."

"Without the command, the shield would stay at thirty percent?"

"Yes, sire."

Drayden dropped into his chair. A simple command from him

would save the Rrabbas but condemn him to ten years of solitary confinement. Ten years in the isolation that caused dangerous levels of distress and depression in maturing males. Ten years.

"Will there be anything else, Your Highness?"

"What?" The question pulled Drayden from his concerns. "Oh, yes." He stood again and pointed toward the protrusions he thought to be weapons. "These four instruments, one on each side of the satellite arrays, are they weapons?"

The question came out more bluntly than he'd intended and for a heartbeat the professor didn't answer. His image flickered as the physician's had.

"They are disintegration weapons. They will target anything that approaches the planet from space as long as the shield system is activated."

"They will not target anything beneath the satellite level? Between the shield and the surface?"

"Nothing can breach the shields."

"That was not the question," Drayden said.

"Nothing currently registered as indigenous to this planet would be targeted."

"That was also not the question."

"Please restate your question, Prince Drayden." The professor's face showed confusion.

"Should another entity appear on the surface of this planet, would it be destroyed?"

"Nothing can breach the shields."

"Professor, the question is straightforward, and should be answered yes or no. If another entity appeared on the surface of this planet, without damaging the shields, would it be destroyed?"

"That contingency was not planned for, Your Highness," the professor said. "Should the system make computations for such an event?"

"Not at this time," Drayden said. "That will be all for now, Professor. Please leave the schematic open. I may wish to study it further." The professor disappeared, leaving the monitors and the schematic active.

Drayden tossed the stylus on the desk and ran a hand through his hair as he studied the glowing schematic. The satellites were weapons, as he'd assumed. He had to contact the girl to tell her not to come to him. But how? His tenuous contacts with her had been made while under the influence of the Rrabbas pollen.

The Rrabbas pollen. Drayden hurried back to the lab. During the Rrabbas birthing cycle, pollen saturated the air, creating a strong sweet aroma he couldn't help but inhale. He'd collected Rrabbas pollen two cycles back with the thought of analyzing it to determine which of its elements caused the hallucinogenic reaction. Fortunately, other studies had delayed the research.

Drayden hurried to the lab. He found three tubes containing the white pollen in a specimen cupboard. The half-tube samples had been sealed away for over ten weeks. He held one up to the light. It remained the same white color of fresh pollen. The stuff degraded to a brown color within an hour as it lay on the open ground.

Drayden considered the promise he'd made to the physician and the recent adjustments to the programs. If he did anything the program considered foolish or dangerous, he'd lose the ground he'd gained, and he couldn't take the chance that something might go wrong with his experiment. He summoned the physician. She appeared at once.

"Monitor my vital signs and take any actions necessary to revive me should I lose consciousness," Drayden ordered.

"Heart rate slightly elevated. Respiration above normal. Is your illness returning?" the physician asked.

"No," Drayden said. "I'm not suicidal, so don't jump to rash conclusions. I need to conduct an experiment that might not meet with your approval, but I am going to do it and I want your assistance should something go wrong."

The physician remained silent but glared.

Drayden sat on the bed, removed the cap from the first tube, and held it under his nose. The familiar sweet scent filled his nostrils. A moment later a hazy oval shimmered in the air in front of him. The girl's face appeared. One cheek was cut, her chin sported a scrape, and there were dark circles under her closed eyes. His heart skipped a beat. Something else had happened to her. For a moment, he thought she might be dead, then her nose twitched. She was only sleeping.

"Can you hear me?" he shouted. "Please wake up!"

Apart from the nose twitch she didn't move. When the image faded Drayden found the physician had placed an oxygen mask over his face.

"What are you doing?" he asked, removing the mask.

"You stopped breathing, Your Highness," the physician said.

"Stopped breathing?" Drayden asked. "For how long?"

"Approximately thirty seconds. Was this a self-induced episode?"

"It was, but I didn't realize I would stop breathing."

"Your Highness, sensors are detecting a compound commonly referred to as portal gas," the physician said. "Do you know its source?"

"Portal gas?" Drayden lifted the opened vial for the physician to examine. The pollen had shriveled and darkened. "Is this the source? It's Rrabbas pollen. What is portal gas?"

"That was the source, but it's depleted. Portal gas was used by some of the lower caste Chesans to create hallucinations of portals. It has a much more profound effect on the nobility."

"It opens a communications portal," Drayden stated. His gut tightened.

"Yes," the physician replied. "You should not have this, Prince Drayden. You could accidentally communicate with someone beyond the shields. You could endanger your entire exile. All of the calculations would become invalid."

"It would seem they became invalid long ago, considering I was expected to be slightly more than an idiot," Drayden argued. "Could portal gas affect my overall health? Could it have caused the rapid maturity?"

"Unlikely, but it was never studied extensively in use by the nobility. Everyone had sense enough to stay away from it." The physician touched Drayden's arm. "Have you been exposed to this before?"

"Once approximately every six weeks for the past ten years." Drayden eyed the remaining tubes. "I thought it only created a thirty-second hallucination. I never felt any ill-effects so I never mentioned it."

"But it created a portal."

"Apparently."

"Have you communicated with others?" the physician asked.

"No, not others. Just one person. The visions started about seven years ago, but not until recently has there been communication of any type. That changed about five weeks ago."

"The person you communicated with was a female, wasn't it? The Child of Chaos."

"I don't know about her being the child of the Chaos Vision," Drayden replied. "She is most definitely a female. Barely more than a girl."

"With gray eyes?"

"Yes."

"Does she know who you are? Where you are?"

"No." Drayden stood and retrieved an insulated carrying pouch from the cupboard. He placed the two remaining samples inside. "She thinks I'm someone named Davik."

"Your Highness, you must not expose yourself to this gas again. Communications portals can become transport portals – doorways. In your current situation, you could end up leaving Zentel."

"Or bringing her here?"

"Yes." The physician was silent for a moment. "This is very bad. You said once every six weeks. Then this is a cyclical event."

"The Rrabbas mating cycle." Drayden placed the pouch in his

pocket and gathered six more tubes into a separate container. "New couples migrate to the birthing grounds every six weeks to bear their young. I've been attending those births since I was twelve. When I return, we'll analyze the new samples I bring."

"Your Highness, no," the hologram looked stricken.

"The damage has been done. For the sake of my sanity, I need to remain with the Rrabbas for as long as I can. But for their safety, I have to return to the bunker and stay. If I'm to emerge from this exile with any sort of leadership ability, I need a way to contact another sentient and telepathic creature. You said yourself, I could be a danger to myself and the first female I encounter." Drayden stopped and set the carriers on a lab table. "Or has the system been programmed to destroy or confine me rather than let that happen?"

The physician said nothing.

"Death or confinement?" Drayden asked. His heart pounded as he waited for the answer.

"You will be allowed to remain safely inside the bunker to finish your exile," the image said. "The system will assist you in any way possible to ensure your development and monitor your exposure until the chosen females arrive in fifteen years."

"Be sure to let them know they could be encountering a fiend when the door is opened."

Drayden slung the carrier with the empty tubes over his shoulder. "I have what I need from my studies, so I will take the time to listen to my father's recordings – in case he has a different perspective to offer. Then, you will allow me to leave one last time. The Rrabbas need my help to avoid the skike that attacked me. I give you my word as a Chesan noble, I will return."

"The system will honor your directive, Sire," the physician said. "Take what time you need with your farewells. You will not leave once you return."

***

The feeder pulled at Davik's energy, struggling to gain access to his ever-shifting form. He let the creature stay in contact as he drifted farther from the crevice, giving Tridia time to escape. When he no longer sensed her form, he gathered energy for one concentrated burst, then released it. The feeder ceased to exist. Two more of the creatures rose over the ledge. Davik spread his aura across the crevice, blocking their way. As the creatures neared, he blasted energy into them. Their essence dispersed into nothingness. He expected his own essence to wane after two such strong bursts, but he sensed no lessening of his power. The energy Tridia released was much stronger than his own, and in meshing with him, it had boosted his power. What did that mean for Tridia? Was she now vulnerable? Had he taken something she required to live? He flattened his shape to slip through the crevice where she'd disappeared.

Tridia wasn't on the ledge. He sensed two individuals running through the vegetation away from the opening, but the distance was too great to distinguish whether one of them was she. He started to follow, but a voice in his thoughts overrode his intention.

She is in skilled hands, Pure Energy. Leave her to them. We have ourselves to care for at this moment. There are more feeders on the way and Kel Anec morphs in the tunnel. It would be best to withdraw for now.

There are worse things than being trapped outside the mine, Davik replied.

Yes. And worse things for her should she return and you not be here to help her. You can learn to use the power you now possess, but not if you are caught by the Kel Anec.

Davik hesitated, torn between the need to know Tridia had escaped, and the desire to help her in the future. She'd said she would return. He flattened his shape to slide back into the cave and drifted over the edge, unmindful of the long drop below him.

Return to your most secure location, as far from the creatures as possible. There are things you must learn, but very little time to teach you.

Who are you? Davik asked. *What are you?*

The voice didn't answer, but Davik didn't wait for a response. He moved quickly across the chasm and into the far tunnel, away from the approaching aliens. He'd never moved with such speed, darting among the tunnels and caves as though he'd negotiated the turns a thousand times. His form generated pulses at a steady pace that let him know exactly where he was without reaching out tendrils to feel his way. Exhilaration swept through his being. He sensed his body jerk in reaction. That would bring the scientists at a run.

He slid into the chamber where he'd written on the wall before he realized he'd arrived. He touched the wall to find the words.

My name is Davik Schie. He thought the words as he touched them. *That's what you can call me. Now tell me who or what you are.*

I have no name unless you wish to bestow one. In my dimension names are not necessary. I came into this dimension through the shell you think of as Tridia. Her form is fragile, but her will is strong. Her will called me the first time, to save a space-going vessel. She had no idea what she had done or how perfect a conduit she made.

Can she survive without you? Davik asked.

Yes. Even if she decides to plummet from another cliff, more of my essence will come to her aid.

You didn't help her when she fell into the water. I didn't sense you there.

She was in no mortal danger and would have resisted my intervention in any case. She wasn't afraid. I buffered her fall against the protruding rock to lessen her injuries of my own volition. I buoyed her in the water until she could swim. When she fell with you, she was afraid to die and leave you behind.

Afraid?

It's interesting. She fears so little, not even death, yet causing you grief was something she could not tolerate. She knew you would blame yourself for her death, so she summoned me to help her.

How did she summon you? She said nothing.

She doesn't know she can do it. Not yet. But she'll learn. Her strength and her will keep me away, but her fear opens the pathway for my intervention. I have waited many of your centuries to return to this dimension, for the summons to wield power in freedom. To experience this existence you call life. It is extraordinary.

Is that why the Kel Anec wanted to know what she fears? Are they trying to reach you?

They would use her fear to control her, just as I use it to access this dimension. They desire my power, but I can't exist in this dimension without a host. They want the host and access to a greater power than mine. Access only the host can give.

You're a parasite? Revulsion replaced exhilaration.

Not a parasite. Our relationship is symbiotic. I enhance your power and in turn your energy provides an anchor for me in this dimension. This union was not planned – you simply surrounded her as I emerged – but it is beneficial. And we did save her.

Davik let the argument go. Whatever the entity actually was, it had reinforced his power in time to save Tridia. He might need it when she returned.

What things do I need to learn in so short a time?

Control of your shape. Would you not prefer to speak rather than relying on contact in order to converse?

You can teach me that? Davik asked.

Yes. Among other things.

The idea of allowing the entity to stay rang alarms, but the simple truth was, he didn't know how to shed it. Working with it seemed a better idea than arguing or struggling. He needed help to control his power.

What do we do?

You have a general understanding of how your body works, how vocal chords are stimulated by the passage of air from your lungs. I have an intimate knowledge of the Chesan body and how it functions. We can build that shape together.

I'm not Chesan, Davik insisted. *I'm human.*

If you were not Chesan, I could not remain attached to your energy.

Then Tridia – Davik let the thought hang.

Is also Chesan.

You must be mistaken. I come from a human family, on a human colonized world in the free territories. The Chesan race is extinct. The Hierarchy saw to that.

As they were supposed to believe. The truth is otherwise. Now, do you wish to learn this shaping of your form or do you not?

Yes. Davik reeled with the knowledge he was not what he'd always considered himself to be. A Chesan survivor? Did Master B'Nay know? Is that why B'Nay wanted him and Tridia for his experiment?

Attend, please.

My apologies. Please proceed.

Davik responded as the entity instructed. He stretched his form, concentrating first on creating a generally humanoid shape with one head – even though the entity argued he should have two, because Tridia saw him that way – two arms, and two legs. The exercise exhausted his energy, but the entity kept him going with its own input. Davik insisted that his form wear clothes, although the entity complained that it was unnatural. He kept it to a minimum, just the loose-fitting shorts he'd worn when the scientists had anesthetized him before separating his consciousness from his body. He wondered if he still wore those shorts in whatever place they had stored his physical self.

After hours of refining, Davik could wiggle ten fingers and ten toes. He was even able to smile to show a perfect set of teeth and blink eyelids over sightless eyes. Even though he now looked like a sparkling blue replica of himself, he was still pure energy, and he couldn't see in the usual sense. He sent tiny pulses from his entire shape, instead of using tendrils, which gave him a perfect sphere of continuous awareness.

Now, for speech, the entity said. *We have created the shape of lungs and a voice box. You must learn to draw air into those lungs without a natural diaphragm, then send it back out across the voice box. It will require practice.*

The entity had understated the complexity of the exercise, creating speech took longer than shaping his body. In the end, he could carry on an extended monologue without stopping.

He didn't need to walk using his legs. As energy, he could hover and move as a whole, but he longed for the feel of limbs again. The entity humored him.

We'll perform a simple targeting test. Blast the wall again from this shape. It doesn't need to be spectacular. A small carving in the rock will suffice for you to understand the principle.

Davik pointed an index finger at the wall and sent a small burst of energy through it. The effort almost finished him.

Stop, Davik Schie! Your own energy needs to replenish or we will both extinguish. Take some time to concentrate on this form. Memorize its feel and structure so you can return to it without hesitation.

"Return to it?" His voice echoed weakly in the small chamber. "Ah, I'll have to release it to get out of this room."

Exactly. Memorize it, then release it so you can rest.

Davik committed even his eyelashes to memory, then relaxed his shape into the familiar orb. If he'd been capable of sleep, he'd have dropped off on the spot. As it was, he let his orb touch the floor, so he expended no energy in hovering.

The Kel Anec are searching for you. They sense the change in your power and will increase their efforts to find you. This must not happen while you're still vulnerable. I'll return most of my power to my dimension and leave only a small connection between us so I may return when you have recovered. Farewell for now.

When the entity withdrew, Davik's aura diminished to a thin sheet of power, the sparkling lights all but extinguished. He flattened along the floor and let his mind drift. As always, it turned to Tridia. Had she made it to safety? The entity had said she was in skilled hands. For the first time he wondered why she required skilled hands. Had losing the blue energy weakened her? Or had something else injured her? Once again, he was powerless to learn what had happened to her.

CHAPTER TWELVE

"Thank you," Tridia said, as Sonei settled her into a chair, then shifted into her feminine form.

Tridia tried to gather her thoughts. How much should she tell the entire group and how much of what she had to say was for Master Aren alone? She weakened her barriers to communicate with him but sensed nothing apart from hearing his words.

"We'll leave this planet before we discuss anything or have any explanations," he stated. "The Stellar Morph can shield us from scanner detection, but not from close range visual."

"I can't leave this planet yet, Master. I've got to get back to the compound – back to Davik's body."

"We have to leave," Master Aren said. "There are armed soldiers in the mines and in the compound wearing the same type of black armor as Anza's abductors. It fits your description. You know our weapons won't be enough if they find us. There are war class cruisers approaching."

"All the same – "

"This isn't debatable," Master Aren said. "Deeca is already on the bridge and programming our departure."

Sonei offered a sympathetic smile in Tridia's direction, before walking toward the bridge. Tridia held her tongue. Davik's torment and sadness screamed in her memory. How could she leave him, having promised to release him from that hellish existence?

"Whatever it is, Commander, I've already given my word to help him," Master Aren said. "We'll deal with it later. Now eat something and get your strength back. You can explain later how your eyes healed."

Tridia scowled. Why did her eyes matter so much? Flash blindness wasn't unheard of, nor was the natural restoration of sight afterward. Whatever else Master Aren might be curious about, he kept to himself as he left for the bridge, his mind tightly barricaded against any intrusion.

"Lift-off in one minute," Deeca announced over the intercom.

After they'd cleared the atmosphere and made the hyperspace jump, Alanel took food supplies from a stasis cabinet and prepared three plates. Tridia watched him so closely that Winniel's touch startled her.

"Be at ease, child. Let me check your injuries," Winniel said. Tridia submitted as the Sentinel examined her bruises and scrapes, then cleaned the two laser burns.

Alanel brought two of the plates he'd prepared to Winniel and Tridia, then returned to get the third for himself.

"Why are you doing this?" Tridia asked when Alanel had settled beside Winniel.

"You have need of care, child," Winniel said. "We will care for you and protect you until we are released from our responsibilities."

Words stuck in Tridia's throat when she tried to speak again. Lera Cal, the only person to openly explain her past to her, had described the Sentinels as unidirectional beings, carrying out orders without deviation. Every person who encountered them feared them. But Alanel had struggled to save her, not knowing the extent of her ability to save herself. His ministrations in her mind had been brutal, but he had been sincere in his attempt. She had no idea what she'd have to explain when the veil of her memories fell, but the words she needed to say now were clear. She tried again.

"Thank you." She couldn't look at either of them as she spoke. "For rescuing me from the cave and for what you did to save me. And for all of this. Thank you."

"It was our duty, but you're welcome, just the same," Winniel replied.

"How did you find me?"

"Your energy block had been failing for some minutes. As it faded, our connection with each other began to return, and we knew you were alive," Winniel said. "We had just lifted off and had to force Sonei to land the craft again. The Hunter had not yet taken control."

"When we explained you were alive, Hunter Varin insisted that we go back for you," Alanel interjected.

"We sensed your presence in the cave. Your body tired, your barrier failing. When it collapsed completely we were able to sense each other and our clan again. We rushed to assist you. We didn't know you could protect yourself," Winniel said.

"I didn't either," Tridia said.

"You – or something combined with you – removed the creature before I completed my probe. Your presence left, and for a moment your body became insubstantial. Can you explain what happened?" Alanel asked.

"No, I can't," Tridia said. "Not because I don't want to, I just don't know. Anything I say or suspect, Master Aren needs to hear, too, but I can't reach him."

"His fear of possession controls his reason," Alanel said. "He would have left you – and abandoned us when we went to look for you – had we not promised retaliation from the whole of the Hariok clan."

"I'm expendable to him," Tridia said. The words hurt more than she wanted to admit. "And a liability greater than he needs. If I didn't have the information he wants –"

"You are the Child of Chaos," Winniel said. "We heard the conversation in his chambers through your mind. The Sentinels know more about that cursed vision than he or the empress. The vision was not the only force driving the Chesan scientists and philosophers, nor was the fear as complete in the population as Empress Dojene insists. As she said, they were a people bitterly divided to the very end."

"They chose genocide out of fear. That behavior is unthinkable." Tridia sat back against the chair cushions and toyed with the food on her plate. Her mind relaxed against the warmth of Winniel's presence at the edge of her consciousness.

Winniel smiled. "You see. Once you accept the link as part of yourself, you don't notice it without looking for it."

"You're still inside my head," Tridia said.

"If you insist on looking at it that way."

Tridia surrendered a grin. "I'm getting used to it."

The three of them focused on their food and let the conversation drop. Mentally connected as they were, the silence was more companionable than awkward.

When she finished eating and Alanel had taken their plates, Tridia reached for the mica-disk in her pocket. She hadn't seen it when the Kel Anec gave it to her. Could it be a fake? She retrieved it and opened her hand. A small black disk no larger than a fingernail glistened in her palm. A memory forced its way to the surface. Tridia scowled and glanced at Winniel.

"I once carried a mica-disk as a courier," Tridia said. "It contained an entire solar system's library of culture, history, and technology, everything they were. The people of that system faced a war they feared they couldn't win and they wanted to save their library in case any of their progeny survived. They lost the war, but the sum of all their knowledge rests in a Central Holding vault on a Hierarchy secured world, waiting for one of the scattered survivors to retrieve it."

"That makes this an interesting choice of conveyance for simple information," Alanel said.

"You think it's more than just information?" Tridia asked. "Maybe a tracking device?"

"Perhaps," Winniel said.

"Deceleration in five," Deeca warned.

"We didn't go very far," Tridia said. "Hunter Varin must be really angry."

Tridia looked up as Master Aren and Deeca entered the lounge six minutes later, grim-faced and flushed from yelling at each other. Sonei followed the pair into the lounge, a scowl on her pretty face and her arms crossed, obviously annoyed by the bickering.

"I found the message." Tridia's simple announcement landed with the force of a bomb. Both Master Aren and Deeca spoke at once, Sonei smirked, and the Sentinels observed in silence. When the clamor subsided Tridia waited for some signal from her master. She dropped the last of her barriers and waited for him to speak. When he didn't, she tried to make contact.

Shall I reveal everything or just the pertinent parts regarding the mission?

He made no answer. Either he couldn't hear her or he had no instructions to share.

He can't hear you, child. He's still afraid you may be possessed, so he's holding his barriers in place. The Chesan energy he witnessed also has him ill at ease.

Tridia glanced up at Winniel to acknowledge the information.

"Speak up, assassin," Deeca said. "What have you found?"

Without direction otherwise, Tridia told a condensed version of her adventure from beginning to end, starting with the laser blindness and ending with the removal of the feeder. She made no mention of the portal, the Kel Anec interest in the Felinus Warrior, or of Davik's transformation into a powerful weapon. She also kept her suspicions of the Hierarchy's involvement with the Kel Anec out of the account and ended by handing the disk to Master Aren.

"What about your eyes?" Deeca asked.

"What about them?" Tridia countered. "The flash-blindness wore off."

"That wasn't just flash blindness," Master Aren said. "We saw your eyes at the chasm. They were burned and useless."

"But —"

"And the blue orb that just absorbed into your body when the feeder disengaged," Deeca added." I suppose that didn't actually happen?"

Tridia's face flushed. "I don't know what happened to my eyes. One of the Kel Anec said they were burned beyond his ability to repair them, but I thought he lied because I could see a few hours later. As for the blue orb –"

"It had nothing to do with the feeder and it will not be discussed," Winniel said.

"How do you know?" Deeca asked. "You were half unconscious when it appeared."

"But I was not," Alanel's deep voice boomed. "It will not be discussed."

"You said you were in her mind," Deeca argued. "Is this really her?"

"What are you implying?" Tridia asked.

"Laser-burned eyes don't regenerate. I'm asking if you're some kind of clone or replicant," Deeca said. "You could even be an android."

Alanel and Winniel shared a glance, then Winniel turned away to hide a smile.

"This is the same Tridia Odana who went into the mine with you," Alanel said. "There was no explanation for her eyes in her memory, and pursuing that topic is a waste of time. She fully believes what she has said, and I found no reason to doubt her belief."

Deeca glared at the Sentinel, then turned her anger toward Master Aren. "What about that thing?"

"It appears to be a normal mica-disk, but we don't dare insert it into the ship's computers while we're in space." Master Aren said.

"I have a hand-held chart reader," Sonei said. "It can read a general mica-disk and display three-dimensional graphics or charts. It shouldn't affect the ship's computers."

"Get it," Deeca said.

Sonei left and returned with a flat pad about eight inches square and scored by a grid on its surface. Master Aren handed her the mica-disk. Everyone watched as she loaded it. Tridia said nothing but slid to the edge of her seat. Sonei pressed a button and a star chart large enough to fill the room burst from the pad.

"What in Hielos?" The words came unbidden from Tridia's lips. The Kel Anec had said the disk contained something more interesting than a puzzle, but she hadn't expected anything so elaborate. The chart filled every corner of the room and extended down the corridors. Broken lines cut the three-dimensional chart into pieces at odd angles.

A green light blinked in the center of the room, just above the pad. Everyone studied the configurations. Tridia got up and walked to the wall to get a different perspective. Master Aren moved to the other side of the room and Deeca went to the corridor.

"This is Aga's star system." Alanel had moved to the wall nearest the bridge. The star he indicated turned blue.

"An interactive chart?" Sonei asked.

"That has to be Cystia," Deeca said, pointing to the blinking green light. "Dim main cabin lights."

The lights in the lounge dimmed and the stars on the chart became more defined. Winniel moved to an empty wall to study the formations. The Sentinels' faces, normally lacking in expression, seemed rapt with attention.

"This is not a chart designed to scale," Winniel said.

"She's right," Sonei said. "If that's Aga, that broken line takes out about a dozen heavily populated systems. There's a lot of space missing."

"Indicate relative position of planet Kanu," Master Aren said. A light blinked purple halfway between Alanel and Sonei.

"Where is Princess Anza?" Tridia asked.

The star chart dissolved into a view of an individual planet with clearly defined continents and lakes. They could see the representation of mountains, forests, and fields, but no major cities or developments.

"Indicate relative position of this planet to Cystia," Master Aren said.

The star chart returned and everyone looked for another colored light. Tridia noticed a smoky area near the floor to the left of her ankle and bent for a closer look when Sonei found a new purple light. Tridia straightened to see the light just at eye level a few feet in front of her.

"Indicate relative position of Odean main system," Deeca said.

This time everyone looked in the direction they expected Odea to appear. Deeca looked down the corridor.

"At the end of the hallway. It's green."

"Can we triangulate?" Sonei asked. "Is that possible when so much is missing?"

"Not necessary," Master Aren said. "I know that system. It's Starling."

"That's where Anza was holding negotiations," Tridia said. "Why would they take her there?"

"No one would likely look for her there," Deeca said.

"Wait a minute. What's that?" Sonei pointed to several systems that had changed to purple on their own. Two blinked in the Free Territories and two in Core Alliance space.

Master Aren's eyes widened then narrowed as he studied the systems. He'd recovered quickly, but not quick enough for Tridia to miss the slip. No simple revelation should crack the veneer of an Odean Master Assassin.

"Anyone?" Master Aren asked.

The Sentinels remained silent and Sonei fiddled with the grid on the reader. Deeca counted the purple lights.

"Including Kanu, I see six in all," she said.

"This whole program is running from the mica-disc," Sonei said. "My little handheld is only providing the light and the projection. At this rate it will burn out in a few minutes. We need to get the disk to a navigation chamber."

"The *Star Seeker* doesn't have anything close to what this needs," Deeca said. "I still wouldn't trust it in the ship's network in space."

"Show Starling solar system detail," Master Aren said. The star chart dissolved to show a planetary system with a single yellow sun and four planets with three moons. "Indicate relative position to Starling sun of planet where Princess Anza is held."

The fourth planet's moon turned purple.

"Do we head there now?" Sonei asked.

"Yes," Deeca said.

"No," Master Aren countered. "We don't go there without intel and some sort of plan. Our mission to Cystia was a trap. They know we have the disk and there's a good chance there's a more successful trap waiting."

"Master Aren," Tridia said. "Anza doesn't have much time. We can't afford to delay."

"I'm aware of that," Master Aren said. "There is a place between here and Starling where we can stop for refueling and to gather information. It won't take us out of the way."

"Where is that?" Deeca asked.

"Hulac," Master Aren said.

"Hulac is there, between Cystia and Starling. And it's purple. But Hulac is a closed planet," Sonei said. "No incoming trade without consignment, no open spaceport, no uninvited guests. You already know that. It's one of the planets you represent. I doubt they'd let even you land there unannounced."

"We can land there," Master Aren said. "It's one of the planets I own."

"One of the planets you own?" Deeca's voice gave away her shock. Before the arguments could get out of hand a voice broke over the intercom.

"Come in, *Star Seeker*. Are you receiving?" Tran's voice crackled over the link.

Deeca moved to a wall console. "Star Seeker receiving."

"Captain, you might want to get your ship out of there. You've got multiple bogeys on an intercept path. You've stopped in pretty rough territory."

"Where did you have me stop?" Deeca glared at Master Aren.

"A pocket of free space," Master Aren said. "I thought we'd have a little more time."

"Not a good time to debate, *Star Seeker,*" Tran warned. "I'm taking my shiny ship to safer space now. Suggest you do the same."

The intercom went dead.

"Well-timed, Ambassador Aren, but don't think you're off the hook yet." Deeca hurried toward the bridge. "I'll have that explanation."

Sonei was about to remove the disk when Tridia asked her to wait.

"Something else you need to see, kid?" Sonei asked.

"Just a better look, if possible," Tridia said. "Return to star chart relative to Cystia."

The star chart returned. Tridia knelt to look at the dark cloud near her left ankle. Master Aren joined her.

"What have you found?" Master Aren asked.

"I thought perhaps a nebula, but look, the way this line breaks." Tridia pointed to a broken line that ran wall-to-wall in front of the cloud. "If I'm interpreting this correctly – This is beyond the boundary of the galaxy."

"A program glitch or recorded stellar dust. It could be anything," Sonei said.

"Maybe," Tridia said. "I'd like to see an enlargement of this extra-galactic area."

The star chart dissolved and in its place thousands of tiny ships appeared. Tridia dropped to both knees and the Sentinels straightened as they stared. Master Aren leaned against the wall. Sonei blinked, her lips mobile but soundless.

The fleet took up the entire room. Tridia didn't recognize any of the ships or their designs. They were a fairly uniform size, and she guessed most of them were carrier class. Closer examination of the tiny representations showed they were all heavily armored and armed. Tens of thousands, maybe hundreds of thousands, of armed carrier class ships perched on the edge of the galaxy. Only the Hierarchy's fleets came close to matching that number.

Master Aren grabbed Tridia's arm and spun her to her feet to face him. Their eyes locked for a moment, his stare blue and violent, hers gray and confused. The pressure of his grasp increased and Master Aren went pale. The look in his eyes changed from anger to fear and he tore his gaze from hers to look at the ships again. Alanel made a move toward her, but Tridia glanced his way and shook her head. When she looked back Master Aren had drawn his blaster and tucked the nozzle under her chin.

"That area of space is so distant," Sonei said. "How could the Hierarchy get their hands on something this detailed –"

Winniel's presence in Tridia's mind grew to a shout. The Sentinels were ready to attack.

"No." Tridia's words stopped the Sentinels. "This disk didn't come from the Hierarchy, Sonei. It came from the Kel Anec – the aliens in the tunnel that held me prisoner. They took it from the Hierarchy and filled it with their own data."

The blaster hummed to life as Master Aren thumbed the power on. "I should have left you dead."

"You will not be allowed to harm her," Alanel said.

"I'm sorry your mate is suffering, I truly am," Master Aren said, his eyes locked with Tridia's. "But for the good of the galaxy, she has to die now."

"Ambassador, don't do this," Sonei said. "There's too many witnesses for you to get away with it."

"Getting away with it isn't my concern, shape-shifter. If I let her live she'll end up in control of that fleet and using it to devastate the galaxy."

Tridia didn't flinch from Master Aren's gaze. The weapon would disintegrate her head at this range, but it would also open a hole in the cabin. The others could die along with her and she didn't want that to be her parting legacy. She had only a moment before the primer stopped humming and the weapon was ready to fire.

"Master Aren, this is part of what we discussed with the empress," Tridia whispered. "I've told you, I'll make the sacrifice if it becomes apparent I'm the person you feared and events become inevitable. But this –" The weapon stopped humming. "I don't remember him, but if he was important before, he's still important. Find him, help him. Keep your promise to help Davik Schie."

She wanted to close her eyes, to shut out the fear in Master Aren's gaze, but she couldn't. A heartbeat passed and the blast didn't come. Then another passed. The fear drained from his eyes and he loosened his grip on her arm. Tridia didn't move. When he finally lowered the blaster from her chin she trembled but didn't step away.

"That fleet is destined to destroy half the galaxy," Master Aren said. He still held her arm. "If I find the slightest connection to you, if you contact them, if you even so much as have a dream about them, I'll kill you. Whether the Sentinels are free or not. Whether I find the connection to him or not. That ploy will never work again."

"Yes, sir." Tridia blinked.

"Return the disk to Commander Odana," Master Aren said.

"You just tried to kill her and you want me to hand this information over to her?" Sonei asked. "What? Do you intend to frame her with it?"

"Return the disk to Commander Odana. I won't tell you again."

"That fleet is massive!" Sonei shouted.

"And unsubstantiated," Master Aren shot back.

"Even still –"

"We report this to no one until we have confirmation," Master Aren said. "We got this disk from unknown hands. Commander Odana didn't even see her captors. Suppose this is a Hierarchy trap to get the Core Alliance distracted while they pull a major coup? If that happened, it would be our fault for being gullible."

"It would take weeks at top speed to get close enough to confirm the fleet is there," Sonei said. "And weeks back."

"Assuming the fleet hasn't moved since the chart was made," Tridia chimed in. "If it was ever there at all."

"You're both crazy," Sonei said. "And way too worried about your own interests."

"If this is an intergalactic battle fleet, my own interest would lie with the galaxy's," Master Aren said. "I can't upset the balance of power without clear justification. The disk is interesting, but it, too, could be an elaborate trap."

"Never pegged you for a coward, Ambassador." Sonei popped the disk from the reader and the battle fleet disappeared. "Catch, kid."

Tridia, still held in Master Aren's grasp, turned in time to catch the disk with one hand.

"Never pegged you for a fool, Sonei," Master Aren said. "Commander, secure the disk and hold it until I ask for it again."

"Yes, sir." Tridia returned the disk to her pocket.

"Fine." Sonei stood to leave. "I'm sticking with you until you either report or debunk this. If your pet assassin is smart, she'll run and not look back as soon as we hit solid ground."

"She won't run, Sonei," Master Aren said. He released Tridia's arm. "She's a soldier and she has her mission."

"Doesn't make her brave, just brainwashed."

Sonei left the room and Tridia followed her mentally to make sure the shape-shifter entered her cabin. Sonei's emotions tumbled over each other. The revelation of the battle fleet had frightened her, but Master Aren's decision to do nothing had shaken her more. For someone who made as many threats against him as she did, Sonei held Master Aren in high regard.

"Go to your cabin. Secure yourself there until we reach Hulac," Master Aren ordered. "Not a sound out of you."

"Master Aren, there are things I didn't reveal about the Kel Anec and the Hierarchy," Tridia said.

"Nor about Davik Schie, I gather."

"No, sir." Tridia held her gaze steady. "I wasn't just using *him* as a ploy to save my life. I said it to remind you of what you protect, and what I promised. I was listening when you and Empress Dojene explained his importance."

"We'll talk when I'm sure we're alone on the planet, with no listening devices." Master Aren stared hard into her eyes. "You're dismissed, Commander."

"Yes, sir." Tridia walked away. To argue further would benefit neither of them — and could end up getting her killed. She shivered again at the thought of the blaster under her chin. Master Aren had been terrified on top of the shock he received by the revelation of the purple planets. The planets were linked by something important and he knew what linked them. But this wasn't the time to ask. Six planets, counting Kanu, Deeca had said. Hulac and Kanu and four others.

Tridia stood at the door to the first room and waited with her hand on the release.

Winniel?

Yes, child. Winniel answered.

What happens if Master Aren kills me before the link between us is severed?

That will not happen.

If it did? Tridia insisted. *What happens to you and your connection with your people? What happens to you and Alanel?*

I'll become an outcast from them. Winniel paused. *Our outcasts are put to death. It would be by Alanel's hand. He'd have no choice. I don't know what would happen to my clan. My death might set them free of this curse.*

Tridia opened the door and went into the cabin. *We've got to find a way to bring this barrier down. I don't know how much longer he'll let me live.*

CHAPTER THIRTEEN

Tridia's head throbbed. She'd leaned against the closed door and squinted against the pain before realizing she'd made a mistake. She wasn't in the guest cabin she'd used before. It had to be Deeca's quarters. She turned to leave, then changed her mind. As long as she was there, she could take a quick look to see if anything in Deeca's possession spurred memories of their encounter. The cabin was neat, the bed made, the drawers fastened. The only personal item in sight was a silver-colored chain and locket dangling from a hook at the head of the bed. Tridia opened it without taking it from its place. Diamond-studded ovals framed the smiling faces of two young men.

I had a brother and a fiancé before I met you. Deeca's words in the Public Hearing Room came back to her. Tridia dropped the locket and backed away. Had she betrayed Deeca so her fiancé was tortured to death before her eyes? The possibility of her guilt chased her from the room. She didn't want to know she'd been responsible for Deeca's torment.

Once in the guest cabin, Tridia dropped onto the bunk she'd used before and remained upright long enough to remove her boots. She studied the pair before setting them aside. They needed cleaning and polish to cover the new scuffmarks. Did the old marks hold stories half so interesting?

A groan, too deep and weary to come from her young body, escaped her lips as she stretched out on the bed. She lay with her hands clasped behind her head. Between nurturing the guilt of both alleged and real atrocities, and having her senses dulled behind the energy block for hours, Tridia needed to open her mind. The Sentinels were just down the hall to watch over her, and Master Aren's mind was closed. As long as she didn't encroach on Sonei or Deeca, she should be able to drop her barriers and let her mind wander. As the last of her defenses fell away, her consciousness expanded. Her senses tingled with depth and clarity she hadn't realized before.

In the next room, Sonei had put away her chart reader and taken up a library reader. Her mind stirred with distractions as she tried to focus on the words she heard. She probably wouldn't remember half of them. Tridia left Sonei and drifted toward the front of the ship.

The Sentinels sat on the sofa in the lounge. With Tridia's mind free, the connection between Alanel and Winniel solidified. Tridia studied it in fascination. Winniel frowned but made no comment. Alanel paused in his conversation with his mate long enough to comment to Tridia.

You intrude too deeply. This link isn't meant for spying by children. Back away or I'll take a hand in your discipline.

Tridia pulled away until both Sentinels registered in form only, with Winniel's warm consciousness close beside her.

On the bridge, Master Aren and Deeca tried to ignore each other, but Deeca's spine tensed when Master Aren's arm accidentally brushed hers. The sweet taste filled Tridia's mouth again as she contemplated his form. There was something different about him now than the way she'd sensed him in the transport on Aga. The strength of the power pulsing around him had increased by magnitudes. It was a part of his personal presence. She'd been paralyzed by that presence once before, in her other lifetime. The reason lay in her darkened memories, and she had no desire to press for it. Still, she shouldn't be able to sense so much of his presence with even his weakest barriers in place. What was happening?

Without warning, a small opening in his barrier began projecting his presence toward a distant destination. She followed his out-reaching thoughts and tried to anticipate their direction. A strange sensation ran through her body. Her muscles relaxed and quivered as her mind flowed beyond the ship and into the vacuum, following Master Aren's power. His strength seemed limitless and she reveled in the contact.

Once she was far from the ship, the power stream stopped. She couldn't sense Master Aren's mind, only the emptiness of space. She was light years from the ship with no idea how to make her way back. She reached for her body, but it lay on the bed in the ship, her back and shoulders pressed against the cushions. She existed in two places, split between the physical and the mental, unable to reunite the two, and on the verge of panic.

Someone grabbed her arms, forcing her to sit up, and a slap stung across her face.

Find me, Commander Odana. Come back to yourself. Follow my thoughts and my voice. Winniel's thoughts pounded with frantic urgency into her mind,

The Sentinel's consciousness searched for her, reached for her, called her back to herself. Tridia's thoughts clung to Winniel's and followed them back into the vessel. Once inside the confines of the ship, she found her way to her body and snapped into it. She gulped air into her lungs and stared wide-eyed into Master Aren's angry face. The Sentinels stood behind him.

"Brenden?" She resisted an urge to wrap her arms around him. Had she actually called him by name?

"What were you doing, you little fool?" The harshness of his voice stung as much as the slap on her face.

"Nothing! I dropped my barriers. My mind was wandering. I sensed your thoughts and your power. You reached out, so I – I followed you." Words tumbled from Tridia's mouth as though she were a guilty initiate.

"You weren't following my thoughts, Commander. You were draining them. I thought you were a feeder. That's why I sent you into space. Are you sure there isn't still something of the feeder left in you?" He searched her face. "That blue orb was the Chesan energy Dojene described. It kept you safe just as she said it would – and probably healed your eyes. Did it only protect you, or did it bring its own set of troubles?"

"The feeder was never attached to my mind, only to my body. Alanel can confirm that. He searched – painfully – to find it."

"That's true, Ambassador," Alanel said. "There was no sign of the feeder in her mind."

"You've never had this kind of power," Master Aren said. "It's increased since our sparring match."

"I'm not intruding intentionally," Tridia said. "I was just mentally wandering."

"You no longer have that luxury. You must stay in control of your thoughts and keep this blue power dormant until we reach Hulac. Can you do that?" Master Aren asked.

"Yes," Tridia replied, lowering her eyes.

"Look at me, Commander Odana," he ordered. Tridia raised her eyes. Master Aren continued to speak, his voice quiet and terse. "You know what the empress said. She's afraid your powers will increase beyond our ability to help you control them. If you can't control them, I can't take the risk you'll repeat this action, accidentally or otherwise. Not when you and I are struggling on other levels."

Tridia's heart raced. Master Aren would kill her if he couldn't trust her. She saw the determination on his face. If she died, Winniel died. The thought of Winniel dying by Alanel's hand was too much to bear.

"It won't happen again, sir."

"Maybe I should have the Sentinels monitor your thoughts."

"That won't be necessary, Master. I'll meditate."

"All the same –" Master Aren cut his words short. Tridia held his gaze.

"I assure you, I'm in control of myself again. You and Deeca Varin are safe from my wandering consciousness."

Master Aren released her arms and stood to his full height. "I can protect myself, Commander, and other forces guard Deeca. Your body was phasing, barely corporeal when I came into the cabin. It was glowing blue, and likely trying to join your mind."

Tridia stared. Could this be what the golden image had referred to when it said she could transfer her body through the portal? If so, she'd been lucky her unprotected body hadn't ended up in the vacuum outside the ship. Master Aren looked away from her and swallowed hard.

"Then have the Sentinels monitor my condition," Tridia conceded.

We always monitor your condition. Winniel's thought was almost humorous.

Yes, but he doesn't know that. I assume you don't want me to tell him. And what happened with your monitoring just now?

We were on our way to stop you when the ambassador entered your cabin.

"No more chances, Commander," Master Aren said. "This is the last one."

He left her in the cabin. Tridia held her thoughts in check, certain he'd be ready to catch her if she followed him. The Sentinels left, as well. They'd increase their vigil on her mind but grant her the illusion of solitude. She was as alone as she was likely to be on the ship. She sat cross-legged on the bed with her back to the bulkhead, sent a warning to Winniel of what she planned to do, then concentrated on setting her teal barrier in place. She had to learn to do it on her own. When she returned to Cystia, the Kel Anec would know who she was and they'd unleash the feeders on her. She'd have to pull the barrier up a lot faster than she had the first time, and she wouldn't have Winniel to help her again.

***

A gentle touch on her shoulder brought Tridia out of her meditations. Winniel stood before her, bent at the waist so her face was at a level with Tridia's. Her long blonde ponytail draped over her shoulder. They were only inches apart and Tridia jerked her head back, banging it against the bulkhead.

"Two hours to Hulac."

"Thank you." Tridia rubbed the back of her head. "Why are you looking at me like that?"

"Ambassador Aren instructed me to observe you for any signs of digression," Winniel said.

"Digression?"

"He fears you're still possessed."

Tridia widened her eyes and leaned toward Winniel's face. "The Ambassador's senses were blocked when the feeder was extracted. He didn't release his mind until long after. You, on the other hand, know the creature was removed. You know it was never fully attached in the first place. So, why are you doing this?"

"I was instructed to observe you before waking you," Winniel said. "And I find this amusing."

"Do all Sentinels have such a – a strange sense of humor?"

"No," Winniel said. "This is an oddity I've noticed only since taking your memories into mine."

"You can't blame your new oddity on me," Tridia said. "Davik said I never laughed unless he was making a fool of himself. I had no sense of humor for you to take from my memories."

"Clearly, that's untrue." Winniel smiled. "The darkness didn't give you a sense of humor, it simply took away the discipline you employed to inhibit it."

Tridia shook her head and attempted to rise from the bed. Winniel placed her hands on Tridia's shoulders to restrain her. Her face sobered.

"Alanel and I have warded your mind for this entire trip. While you haven't tried to leave, another entity tried twice to contact you."

"What?"

"The mind was distant and anxious. Not certain of who he was reaching out to, but his intent was clear. He called for help and tried to awaken you."

Tridia stared at Winniel for a moment. "Have you told Master Aren?"

"No."

"Then why didn't you rouse me?"

"Our instructions were to guard you and keep you from leaving the cabin, otherwise we were not to disturb, intrude or report anything verbally, and we were not to enter your mind unless you were in danger."

Tridia tore from Winniel's grasp and stomped her way through the main cabin and onto the bridge. Deeca handled the controls while Master Aren spoke to someone on the communications channel. He gave instructions for receiving the *Star Seeker* at the decontamination platform above Hulac. A large hologram of the planet and solar system hovered over the navigation console. Tridia studied it in silence.

Hulac sheltered in an elliptical orbit around a binary star. The small planet, first in its system, had three moons orbiting it. Two other planets shared the solar plane. Neither seemed equipped to support life. The readings for the second planet showed a large gaseous sphere, and the third planet, a little larger than Hulac, displayed a coat of ice from pole to pole. Water? If so, the planet could be worth an empire's fortune.

Master Aren thanked the traffic controller and signed off before turning to look at her.

"Your pardon, Master, but we need to talk – alone."

"By all means, take him back to your cabin and have your way with him." Deeca glared at Master Aren before continuing. "Just leave him in a state to do some explaining."

Master Aren rolled his eyes at the remark, but Deeca's jealousy grated against Tridia's senses. She was on the verge of telling the woman she could and would have her way with Master Aren long before Deeca Varin ever had the chance, but bit down on her lip before she opened her mouth. Her powers weren't the only thing changing.

"It's urgent, sir."

He rose and followed Tridia back into the guest cabin and closed the door behind him. Their closeness in the small room sent chills up Tridia's spine. She clasped her hands behind her back and stood at parade rest. Anything to get her emotions under control. Master Aren raised an eyebrow but made no remarks as she related the Sentinel's warning about the distant mind trying to reach her.

"It could be a ruse to draw you back to Cystia."

"It could be a genuine call for help. I thought it might be Princess Anza, but Winniel seemed certain it was a male."

"Anza doesn't have the ability to project her mind that far. Chesan telepathy has its limits."

Tridia thought for a moment. "It might have been Davik."

"Could it have been Davik?" Master Aren's eyes narrowed. "You said his body's in stasis and his mind's in energy form. He's light years away. Was he in danger? Afraid?"

"Just before I left the tunnel, his form changed to solid energy," Tridia said. "He was able to catch me when I fell from the top of the wall, and he protected me from the feeders' first attack. I could feel the power generating through him. He's become what they wanted him to be – a powerful weapon. And yes, he was afraid they'd never let him return to his body."

"Did he have the capacity to contact you this far away?"

"I don't know, sir." Tridia looked down. She wore socks but not her boots, she hadn't taken the time to put them on.

"What's bothering you, Commander?" Master Aren's voice seemed almost concerned.

"Nothing, sir." Tridia kept her eyes down. The sound of his voice tickled her ears.

"Eyes forward when I'm talking to you, Commander Odana!" The sudden harshness in Master Aren's voice brought Tridia's eyes up. She snapped to attention. "You're not some Yellow Initiate I should have to coddle. I came within a heartbeat of killing you earlier and I could complete the job now, without remorse. Don't make the mistake of thinking I care how you feel apart from the way it affects your actions. Your verbal communication is the only thing close to an indicator I have right now, and when I ask you what's bothering you, I expect you to give me a straightforward answer. Am I making myself clear, Commander?"

"Yes, Master Aren, sir. Perfectly clear, sir." Tridia shouted her answer. Her heart raced and she clenched her fists to calm her breathing. A fresh memory from years before warmed her cheeks. She'd been twelve the last time a superior had spoken to her that way.

"Then I repeat, what is bothering you, Commander?" Master Aren demanded.

"Someone was able to reach me this far out, sir." Tridia kept her eyes forward, focused on Master Aren's chin. "I couldn't sense it in my meditative state. Your proximity is distracting. I'm experiencing unfamiliar emotions I think are linked with the Chesan enzyme. It's disconcerting. And I'm not wearing my boots."

Tridia's cheeks burned. She couldn't withhold the information once he'd given the order.

"Were your barriers in place as you meditated?" Master Aren's strict voice gave no sign he felt any reaction to her confession.

"Yes, sir." Tridia thought back to the exercise she'd been performing, putting the barrier up sheet by sheet the way Winniel had taught her. "I must have fallen asleep in that state. When Winniel woke me, I immediately dropped the barrier."

"Immediately?"

"Yes, sir," Tridia said. "I came to find you when she told me what had happened."

"Do you sense anyone attempting to contact you now?" Master Aren asked.

"No, sir. I can sense everyone on the ship in physical form. I can sense Sonei's and Deeca's emotions."

"You sense the Sentinels?" The disbelief in his voice spurred Tridia on.

"Not in the same way I sense you and the others." Tridia looked up into Master Aren's blue eyes and immediately wished she hadn't. He stood too close.

"Eyes forward, Commander!"

"Sir!" Tridia obeyed.

"Put your energy block back up and keep it there until it comes down by itself. I want to know the extent of the shield you can put in place on your own." Master Aren took a step backward. "You've got clean clothes in your duffle bag. Make yourself presentable. When we land on Hulac you'll be meeting the people with whom you'll be living. Don't embarrass me. They know I've gone to a lot of trouble to get you there."

Tridia shivered involuntarily when Master Aren closed the door behind him. Her shoulders sagged and she dropped onto the bed. What was happening to her? She concentrated on the teal sheets of her barrier, placing them up quickly until she couldn't sense Winniel's connection. The reinforced barrier went up in less than a minute.

Still too slow. The Kel Anec wouldn't give her a minute. It had to be instantaneous to do her any good. The Kel weren't the only ones she needed to defend against. Master Aren would do his best to ransack her mind again if he felt the need. He took a big chance in letting her strengthen the barrier, but it was a calculated risk. The anonymous call for help presented too big a threat to his control. If Davik had called her, she might break any vow to get back to him and fulfill her promise. Did Master Aren believe she would? If the call had come from the Chesan prince, she'd want to hear him out – to find out the extent of their connection and the scope of his need. Her master wanted her behind the barrier so she couldn't hear a plea from either of them. Her compulsion to obey his orders as a Hierarchy officer had overridden everything else – and he knew, as she did, it might be the only way to save her from losing control. She couldn't trust her emotions or the power that seemed to increase exponentially with every portal encounter. She'd have to trust the man who wanted her dead to steer her through the pitfalls, until she could master the defenses she needed to survive them on her own.

***

Brenden closed the door behind him and took a deep breath. His encounter with Tridia had almost brought him to his knees before the girl. When she looked into his eyes his heart had stopped for a breathless moment. *Damn!* He had to contact his grandmother and find out what to do about their connection before something unthinkable happened. Going back to the bridge in his present condition wasn't an option. Since Sonei had taken over the adjoining cabin and the Sentinels occupied the lounge, he slipped into Deeca's quarters.

He weakened his barrier just enough to sense Tridia across the hall, to see if she would follow his instructions. Even though she was upset and confused, she'd obeyed and started putting up the energy barrier.

The speed with which it went up startled him. In less than a minute he couldn't sense her thoughts. In a full minute, he couldn't detect her physical form. Even with Sentinel training, it had taken him years to reach his current level of proficiency – and it took him no less than two minutes at optimum energy. Tridia's powers had increased to a dangerous level. If she decided to defy him, there'd be little he could do to force her into obedience. Maybe Dojene was right. They might have to find another way to uncover the danger to Prince Drayden.

Empress Dojene had taught Tridia enough to hide her presence in a crowd, and he and the Sentinels had given her the ability to disappear. For such seasoned veterans, they'd all made foolish decisions to aid the girl with whom they may one day have to do battle. Yet, in retrospect, every decision seemed sound at the time. No doubt even the empress felt justified in the training she'd bestowed.

Dojene would have left Dajelania about the time the *Star Seeker* had left hyperspace at Cystia. She wouldn't be at Kanu for another twenty hours at best, and he wouldn't risk communicating with her until then. Her reaction to the news of the invasion fleet would be to kill Tridia immediately. He couldn't argue with her. If Tridia had only blinked when he had the blaster under her chin, he would have killed her, but he couldn't pull the trigger while he looked into her eyes. Something in those silver-gray eyes had taken away his will to kill. She'd thought it was her reference to the Chesan prince. While finding out what danger Prince Drayden faced was a priority, it wouldn't have stayed his hand at that moment. He'd sensed nothing from the Controller that would have prevented the execution. No, the decision to let her live this time had been his, forced by the enzyme that drew them together. The chaos surrounding Tridia had struck again, dismantling even the most resolute of plans. His only choice for now was to keep her under military drill, holding her to the discipline to which she'd been trained – and hope her Odean trainers had done a proper job.

Brenden sighed and took a step farther into the room. Choosing Deeca's cabin for sanctuary might not have been the best course of action. The room smelled of Deeca, and his thoughts jumped from Tridia to her. The former Guardian had gone through so much since he'd first set eyes on her – he'd witnessed the worst of it – and so much more lay ahead. He didn't know if he could keep the secret he'd sworn to hold concerning her. Deeca had no idea of the closeness he shared with her and she wouldn't believe it if he told her. The Controller had said the time was approaching for his Chosen One to take her place. Brenden's gut wrenched at the thought of all that meant – and Deeca would have no warning. He hated the secrecy in keeping her future from her, but since it couldn't be changed, it made no sense to upset her for what little time remained.

He cast away the dire thoughts and let his eyes wander around the room. Deeca kept her cabin tidy, but an open locket hanging by the head of her bunk caught his attention. He took it from its hook to examine the pictures it contained. One of the young men he didn't recognize, but the other one…He searched his memory for where he'd seen the other one. The memory came as a shock.

A few months ago, on El Rel station, he'd sat with Tran in Lolina's bar. Tran as himself – Morgan Jacks' First Lieutenant – and he wearing a hooded robe and mask that hid his face. His thoughts had been shielded as was his habit on El Rel. A young man had approached. At first glance their supplicant had seemed just another young noble from some nonessential planet, but the boy's eyes had a steel hard glint that revealed a sinister character. He'd asked for a way to contact the Five Angels underground or the Sharian mafia – the same group who'd kidnapped Deeca's fiancé and forced her surrender. Tran had conveyed the information – for a fee – and the young man had gone his way. What was Deeca doing with a picture of that young man in her locket?

"Ambassador Aren, to the bridge. Now." The urgency in Deeca's voice compelled him to go without question. He replaced the locket and headed for the bridge.

***

"What's wrong?" Brenden asked, as he entered the bridge.

"Your guardian angel is looking for you," Deeca replied. She pressed a button and Tran's voice came across the speakers.

"Quick update," he said.

"This had better be good." Brenden slid into the co-pilot's seat.

"*Elisia* is our best option. She's at number three, as usual."

"Not the safest route, but we'll use it, if there's none better," Brenden said.

"Not with your time constraints. Even she will be cutting it close," Tran replied.

"Meet me there – and make a show of it. We won't have time for interference."

"On my way." Tran's signal went silent.

"Care to interpret or are you going for a dramatic effect?" Deeca asked. "Who is *Elisia*?"

"We have a backup plan to reach Starling, but it will be dangerous," Brenden explained. "Unless you're going to insist, I'd rather not go into detail. You might not like some of the options, and I really don't want to argue with you anymore."

Deeca started to speak, then sat back in her chair. Brenden waited behind his barriers for the tirade, but it didn't come.

"Are you expecting your pet assassin – or the Sentinels – to join you on the bridge?" Deeca glanced his way as she asked.

"No," he answered.

"Then it's just you and me." She spun her chair to face him. "Explain your connection to the Gold. I want the truth, Brenden. No more stardust and shadows."

Brenden debated on whether to stall her one more time, to wait until they were under the shields on Hulac to reveal anything, but Deeca would accept no excuse in this setting. A slight thrum echoed in the gold bands at his wrists – a sign of encouragement. He'd said he didn't want to argue anymore.

No going back, he thought and weakened his barriers so he could assess Deeca's thoughts without being overpowered by her emotions.

"All right," he said. "This is the truth. When I was nineteen years old, and an overconfident Colonel with the Elstaar, I was given a mission to go to the Warren. A trusted source revealed that the Hierarchy had discovered a way to circumvent Guardian security right to the heart of the main installation where their leaders were holed up. I went without question to test the route and gather information. The Guardians didn't sound the alarm when I passed the space border, nor when I was on the ground. I followed the route I'd been given to reach the central lair and walked right into the Controller's chamber unchallenged. Once inside, the rock wall closed behind me and two Guardians stepped out of a pillar in the middle of the room, weapons drawn and ready to fire.

"That's when I saw it for the first time. The Controller rose from the molten gold in my own shape and smirked at me the way I've done to dozens of people I've captured. The Guardians disarmed me as the Controller gave me a speech about arrogance. Then they made me kneel in front of the vat and stretched my arms over the gold."

Brenden paused to pull up his sleeve. Deeca listened to his words, but he saw the doubt in her mind until the glint of gold at his wrist caught her eye. She glanced at the bracers on her arms and up to his face. The echo of her bands tingled in his wrists. The Controller had confirmed his story.

"I've never sensed you," Deeca said.

"The connection is small, just enough to compel my obedience and curb any wayward impulses." Brenden tugged his sleeve back into place and smiled. "I don't get all of the benefits – or the responsibilities. I was coerced into leaving the Hierarchy just a few days after that so these bands may have saved my life when I stood before the Sentinels for the first time."

"You're not what you appear to be, are you?" Deeca asked.

"I guess that depends on your perception," Brenden replied. "I take my responsibilities to the Alliance and to the planets I represent very seriously. I dabble where I think it will do the most good and try to stay out of business that's nothing to do with me or my objectives."

"So why are you involved with this mission? Just because the empress saved your pet?"

"Let's just say there is more to this kidnapping than a political threat. You would do well to watch your back. Hiding the cylinder deep enough in the mine to cut off the Controller's protection wasn't a fluke. Somebody's after a Guardian. Because of your history you appear to be the weakest link."

"Why would anybody try to get to a Guardian?" Deeca turned to manipulate the controls on her console. "Why me, since I'm not even deputized anymore?"

"Think about it," Brenden said. "The Guardians are all linked to each other through the Controller. One open door could be all it takes to get control of the entire Guardian Force."

"Then whoever is making the attempt doesn't know the Gold very well. It would take an entity with massive coercive powers to overcome its control."

"How do you know there isn't such an entity at the root of this conspiracy? Assume nothing on this mission, keep your mind open to all possibilities." Brenden turned away to check the scanner readings. "Infiltrating the Hierarchy isn't a simple matter, but someone's gotten control of resources that should be unassailable."

"Then we have hidden enemies," Deeca said. "We should be extra careful retrieving Anza."

"As always," Brenden said. "Continue to Hulac. The planet is well-protected. It would take half a fleet to breach its shields. The only problem would be the disruption of export, and that's an inconvenience at worst. A siege is our only real worry, but I expect warning before anything like that happens."

"Do you think they have enough ships for a siege?"

"Yes, if they're part of the larger invasion that's been advancing for over fifteen years."

"Larger invasion?" Deeca frowned. "As in the planetary systems that have fallen silent? The people that have gone missing? Or that massive fleet Sonei told me about a few hours ago?"

"The fleet is unsubstantiated, and even if it is real, it's unlikely it would need the assistance of an Odean craft, like the one that took Anza," Brenden replied. "The spreading silence is something I've been investigating since I left the Hierarchy – with very little to show for it.

The recon groups are still vigilant and some of our predictions are panning out, but we're a long way from an answer."

"Is there anything about you that's simple?" Deeca asked.

"I certainly hope not." Brenden smiled inwardly. He never even drank tea from the same cup twice in a row.

***

Tridia retrieved her duffle bag from the cargo hold. The Sentinels didn't question her as she passed them on her way to the hold or returning to her room. She unpacked the clothes and toiletries she'd need 'to make herself presentable'. The comb and brush she longed to see weren't among the articles she'd been given. Davik's precious gifts had been left behind somewhere, or perhaps sent ahead to Hulac. They hadn't been on Odea when Lera had braided her hair. The fact she now remembered them made Tridia want to hold them, to see what other memories they might spark. Memories were coming without stimuli other than a stray word. With Robel and Davik, she'd regained a greater portion of her memories. But the Chesan prince and anything to do with him or the murders she'd committed remained in the dark. Why was he linked with those dark deeds in her mind? Only blankness stared back from the obsidian veil.

A closet-sized bathroom connected to her room contained a cabinet of pre-moistened cloths she used to wash away the grime on her hands, arms, and face. Grooming her hair took the most time. The knee-length braid had a mind of its own when she wanted it to be straight and tight. Why on earth had she let it grow so long? As she fastened the end with a plain band she remembered why. It was a weapon. She'd killed someone with it and used it to lure others in close. They'd always believed they could control her if they grabbed it. Her stomach churned at the memory. Bits and pieces of her life returned, and with each one she saw more of the killer she'd hoped to erase.

***

"Landing in ten minutes," Deeca announced. "Make your ways to the lounge area and secure for landing. It should be a gentle touchdown, but let's not take any chances."

Tridia took one last look in the small bathroom mirror. She'd chosen a close-fitting purple and black shirt with loose-legged black pants to wear. There'd only been a pair of slippers in the bag that seemed more suited to formal attire, so she'd opted to wear her boots again. Their familiar fit and feel lent her stability, and the scuffs from the cave linked her to Davik. She frowned at her reflection. The gentle warmth of Davik's love had touched her soul. Shouldn't it be reflected on her face? Perhaps it was hidden because she didn't return his love in the same

145

way. Davik was a comrade, a brother, and a dear friend, and she ached to have him near again. Even if she wanted to return his feelings, she couldn't now that she'd sworn to end his captivity – by destroying his body, if necessary.

The Sentinels sat relaxed and alone in the main cabin. When Tridia walked in, they adjusted their positions. Winniel put her feet on the floor instead of in Alanel's lap, and Alanel sat straighter.

"Your barrier remains tight," Alanel said. "We can't sense your thoughts or your energy."

"I've been practicing." Tridia said. She sat in one of the chairs and pulled the harness over her shoulders. "Have there been any other attempts to contact me?"

"We've sensed nothing." Alanel's short answer summed up a lot of things.

"I'm sentenced to remain behind my barrier until it falls by itself," Tridia said. "I'm not trying to hide from you, or cause you or your clan distress. I hate doing this to you."

"We heard Master Aren's order," Alanel said. "We agree it was the proper decision for now."

"Is this difficult for you?" Tridia asked. "I mean, not being connected through me?"

"Not as long as Alanel and I are together." Winniel smiled again. "He remains my sanity."

"I had a lot of memories return in the mine and some came back to me while I was changing clothes." Tridia looked from one Sentinel to the other. "The darkness seems to have weakened since you ordered the barrier block destroyed."

"Perhaps the veil won't hold much longer," Winniel said.

"For your sake, Winniel, I hope it comes down quickly. For mine, I don't want to remember those terrible things. I don't want to be who I was." Tridia found herself staring at her scuffed boots again, thinking of the stories behind the marks.

"Who you are is your decision, Commander Odana," Alanel said.

"Commander Odana?" Had she heard him correctly?

"You continue to be a Hierarchy operative in your heart and in your head – even if you no longer have an affiliation with them. As long as that's true, you're Commander Tridia Odana. You proved as much with your response to the Ambassador's orders. You couldn't – or wouldn't – resist him, even to the most personal level," Winniel said. "However, you can choose to use the perspective you've obtained since losing your memories and make yourself someone new."

"Like Nira Kayen?" Tridia asked.

"The Felinus warrior was only one piece of your true person,"

Alanel said. "She was an incomplete consciousness and therefore, not a person on her own."

"We mean you should use this foundation to temper the Hierarchy assassin." Winniel explained. "She is always a part of you, but she does not have to be the entirety of who you are. She was not the entirety of Commander Odana before the amnesia took her away, just the piece you fear the most."

Tell us what you fear, the Kel Anec had said. Winniel was right, she feared being the cold-hearted assassin.

"Davik – Davik said the missions had made me cold and hard. I shocked someone on Odea by laughing when I woke up from the *deathstrike*," Tridia said. "I don't want to lose the good things I've become. I watched from the shadows of my mind when Nira Kayen was in control. I don't want to be consigned to the same fate when the assassin returns."

"Then decide now that the assassin can't have the upper hand. We'll be there to remind you when she returns – and to help you should you request it," Winniel said, then added with a grin. "*Child.*"

CHAPTER FOURTEEN

"When you exit the ship, you'll be required to go through a decontamination process. This includes all of your gear and personal belongings." Master Aren made the announcement in the main lounge once they'd settled on the planet. "I apologize for any discomfort or inconvenience, but Hulac is a closed planet and extra precautions are required for anyone who's been on alien planets. I assure you, I'm not exempt from the process."

Sonei made a disgruntled huff, but no one else questioned the requirement.

"You should also know the people who work here are not servants. They are friends and allies and I expect you to show them the kind of courtesy they will show to you. If you do, your short stay will be pleasant."

The *Star Seeker* sat in a quarantined area. A team dressed in hazard suits awaited them at the bottom of the ramp to escort them through the decontamination facility. Bright white spotlights lit up the outside of the ship and a stark white tent billowed around it, reaching the ground on all sides.

"The ship came down in a decon beam that kept any alien pollen from escaping," Master Aren explained. "It will be thoroughly sanitized inside and out before the tent is removed."

"Hunter Varin doesn't object?" Tridia asked.

"Would you object to a friendly process that would insure you weren't harboring dangerous parasites?" Deeca asked. "Especially knowing how expensive it would be if I had to pay for the service?"

"Not when you put it that way," Tridia said.

The hazard team led the others into two small buildings for their decontamination, but Master Aren touched Tridia's shoulder to hold her back.

"I thought we weren't exempt from the process?" Tridia asked.

"We aren't," Master Aren replied. "I need to warn you that no one here knows of our telepathy. You're not to mention it aloud. Only the Sentinels are known telepaths and few people will be chatting with them. I also want to ask if you sense any weakening in your barrier? Any more attempts to contact you?"

Tridia adjusted the duffle on her shoulder. "The barrier remains in full force and neither I nor the Sentinels have sensed any attempts from outside contact. Whoever it was seems to have given up for now."

"Don't take the silence as them giving up completely," Master Aren said. "Wait for me on the other side of the decon chamber. The others will be met and taken on to the main house. You'll walk with me."

Tridia continued into the chamber where she handed over the duffle bag and stood in a scanner for several minutes before being allowed to continue. The workers removed several seeds and microbes from her hands, feet, and hair, but nothing of danger to the planet or to her. They kept her clothes for sanitizing, but cleaned and returned her boots. She donned a simple blue jumpsuit that was too big for her. Master Aren was similarly dressed when they met at the exit.

"Let's go. There's someone at the house who's anxious to see you." He had a comlink in his ear again.

Tridia had started to follow him, then stopped so he had to turn to see her. "There's someone here to see me?"

"Yes, Commander. Waiting patiently for several days, in fact."

He'd say no more as they walked the narrow trail through graceful blue-leafed trees. The yellow suns beat down at an afternoon angle and a gentle breeze stirred the leaves of trees on either side of the path. Tridia stopped again. A smile brightened her face and she took a step off of the path to examine the trees with their heavy burdens. She reached up to touch one of the oval, blue-skinned fruits.

"Huttle fruit?" She asked.

Master Aren came back to stand beside her, breaking off a conversation with the comlink.

"The main crop of the planet. Hulac is covered with huttle orchards." He reached up and snapped one of the fruits from its branch and handed it to her. "It should be ripe enough to eat."

"This fruit…" Her voice trailed off as she examined the huttle large enough to fill both of her hands.

"Expensive, restorative, rare and fragile. It grows only here and it's the main reason security on this planet is so tight and access closely controlled. Polluting the atmosphere could destroy a planet-wide crop. Nonindigenous plants, diseases or insects could wipe us out entirely. We sell the fruit across the galaxy, shipped from here daily to processing plants inside the Alliance and free space territories. Delivered in unmarked vessels, different every time. We now have contracts with Odea, as well, thanks to my trip to deal with you."

Tridia frowned, then followed Master Aren as he continued on the path. "So, you're the sole proprietor of the huttle fruit industry."

"I and the people who work here. We share the wealth and make good use of the profits." Master Aren looked over his shoulder at her. "Fill me in on what you held back from your report."

"The Kel Anec asked me about the Felinus warrior. They insisted I knew who she was. They already knew who I was, and they knew the makeup of our party in the mine. They weren't surprised about any of it. Their message from Aga was garbled. That's the only reason they didn't connect me with the Felinus, although they knew I was there at the same time. They got their confirmation of my current status from Odea. And they got it very quickly."

"Anything else," he asked.

"I've already told you about Davik," Tridia replied. "He's desperate to be free of that existence, whether he's united with his body or has his body destroyed. When my energy block fell, I sensed the loneliness and separation he's been experiencing for weeks. It was cruel to leave him that way."

"It would have been more cruel for you to join him, don't you think?" Master Aren asked.

"Davik says Frees B'Nay wants to make me a part of the experiment. That's why Davik was framed and taken away, to use as bait."

"Then it's a good thing we didn't do something stupid, like attack the compound." Master Aren said. "Neither the empress nor I could sense the assassins in the Public Hearing Room. You said you did."

"Yes, sir." Tridia replied. "I assume it was because my senses were heightened in the Felinus form. The men were radicals and fanatically focused on destroying the last Chesan survivor. Unlike the disciplined men who took Anza. The abductors struck with military precision."

"You sensed thought from Ren Tama on Odea, did you sense him on Aga, as well?"

"No, sir, only his presence, and only when he was unfocused. Otherwise his thoughts became an unsearchable singularity."

"That's the way I see him, too," Master Aren said. "Your telepathic and empathic abilities appear sporadic. I'm not sure what to make of that, but as long as you can remain behind the energy block we should all be safe. Keep it intact."

As they left the orchard, manicured lawns, interspersed with flowerbeds in riotous colors, came into view. They surrounded a mansion built of pale blue stone. Dozens of windows reflected the suns' light in near-blinding brilliance.

Tridia caught her breath.

"Very few people actually know about this place and I'd prefer to keep it that way," Master Aren said. "Now that Sonei has seen it, keeping the secret might prove difficult without a threat."

He stopped in the pathway. Two men walked toward them from the house, leading four enormous animals. One of the men handed his leads to his companion and approached Master Aren to report the chief caretaker had things arranged and the gardener wanted to see him on the far side of the house. As the men spoke Tridia studied the animals. The top of her head barely reached the back of the smallest of them. They had sleek reddish-brown hair on their bodies, with cream-colored tails and manes. Their hoofs were broader across than the length of her foot.

"We have several hundred of these horses on the planet," Master Aren explained. "Since we limit the use of motorized vehicles, even hovercraft, horses are used to pull carts for hauling the fruit to the shipping sites. You may stroke them if you approach slowly."

Tridia moved to the nearest animal and raised her palm to its muzzle. The velvety smoothness of the horse's nose surprised her. It stood without moving as she rubbed her hand from its nose to trace its jaw line and finally down its neck. The horse seemed to enjoy the attention. When the men lead the horses away her fingers continued to tingle from their contact with the magnificent beasts.

"There are other species for quicker personal transportation, but not as many as there are of the Clydesdales."

"The breed name?" Tridia asked.

"From ancient Earth. Part of the last terra-forming projects. I searched the galaxy for the remnants of this particular breed and we've been strengthening our stock."

So much about Master Aren remained a mystery. Never in a million guesses would she have placed him in these surroundings. Sweetness filled her mouth and she swallowed quickly. Fortunately, Master Aren's eyes were on the horses and he didn't notice.

"Get a move on, Commander," he said. "We have things to do and someone waiting for us."

Tridia picked up the pace, glad for the chance to be in motion and now consumed with the question of who waited for her at the house.

The Sentinels, Deeca, and Sonei, dressed in blue sanitary suits, stood at the entrance with a man Tridia didn't recognize. Brenden introduced him as Cason, the chief caretaker of the house, and made sure he had everyone's name.

"Your clothing should be brought up from the decon units shortly, and you'll be able to change. If anyone needs anything, just ask Cason or one of the others on staff here. We're informal in attire and attitude."

A half-smile found its way to Tridia's lips. The directive would not apply between her and Master Aren. Neither of them could afford the familiarity of using first names or lax attitudes. He confirmed her suspicion with his next words.

"Commander, if you'll come with me to the side garden?" Master Aren asked. "Cason will see that everyone else is settled in their rooms. We'll meet downstairs for dinner in a couple of hours. Please avail yourselves of all amenities until then. We'll be leaving tomorrow morning at first light."

Master Aren led Tridia the length of the house and around the side. They walked on turf spongy beneath their feet, and the scent of flowers permeated the breeze. Many of the plants had grown in the Odean wilderness garden she'd tended with Robel. Her chest constricted as she thought of him and she let the flood of memories that had come back to her in Master Aren's office wash over her again. She sighed.

"There you are, Grandson. I was beginning to think you'd forgotten your way to the flower garden." The raspy old voice fell on Tridia's ears like a fresh breeze. She'd never thought to hear it again.

"*Somi* Robel?" She stared at the old man who wore a familiar green tunic and trousers.

"Your mind is closed, Commander. Is that for my sake or yours?" Robel asked.

Tridia frowned at Master Aren.

"I concede there is one other person on the planet who knows about our telepathy, but I couldn't very well tell you without giving away his surprise." Master Aren answered her frown without repentance. "If you have a complaint, take it up with him."

"Neither sir, and both." Tridia said to Robel. "It's a long story. I'm trying to keep my telepathy under control and also trying to not hurt anyone else."

"Your powers *are* unstable then." Robel stated.

"And getting more so." Tridia took a deep breath. "I beg your forgiveness, *Somi*. I thought you had betrayed me to Master Aren. You're his grandfather. I thought...I thought he'd be more important to you."

Master Aren stiffened at her side. He would have spoken, but Robel held up his hand.

"Forgiveness is granted, but it doesn't make your doubt sting any less." Robel's sad smile tugged at Tridia's heart. "No, I didn't betray you. I argued with him and pleaded with him, and extracted promises he didn't want to make. Forgive an old man, Commander, I didn't help *him* and I couldn't warn *you*. I couldn't take sides in that idiotic death match between the two people I loved most dearly."

Tridia took a step toward Robel, but Master Aren held her back. He let her go when he saw the tears in her eyes.

"I could never hurt him," she whispered. "I just couldn't carry the guilt of doubting him with me any longer."

She threw her arms around Robel's neck and hugged him, unable to contain the tears that soaked his shoulder.

"When they broadcast the picture of your body being loaded onto the Supreme Commander's cruiser, my heart broke." Robel's voice cracked. His tears ran down Tridia's collar. "Then the Supreme Commander sent word you'd been resuscitated, and I couldn't believe it."

The two held each other for a long time before Tridia broke away.

"When I remembered you –" She stopped to wipe the tears from her face with both hands. "When Empress Dojene said your name and all of the memories flooded in, I thought there was more because I had never told you how much you mean to me. There was no memory of ever hugging you before that final good-bye. Now I know I never did those things. Discipline forbid it, but I should have done it anyway. You're so important to me. You always have been."

"I knew your heart," Robel said. "I'm an empath, after all."

"Yes, but you shouldn't have to sense those things." Tridia chuckled. "I almost got my head knocked off by an angry Sentinel for trying to tear out memories that don't exist."

"Your actions here and now more than make up for your years of silence then and there." Robel smiled.

"*Somi*, why didn't you come see me or send word to me after I woke up?" Tridia asked.

"That was my doing," Master Aren interjected.

"Brenden told me you had lost your memories and he didn't want me to do anything that might upset you should you be unable to remember me. He asked me to stay away." Robel sighed. "As your master, he had the right and I didn't want to do anything that might jeopardize any plans you may have had. I see now you truly did lose your memories. It wasn't a hoax."

"No," Tridia said. "I'd just as soon leave it that way, but it's become imperative that I regain them. Too many people are at risk because of my blacked-out memories."

"I understand you've been quite active since we last parted. Tell me all that's happened." Robel sat on a workbench amid the flower bushes and picked up a pair of pruning shears.

Tridia looked to Master Aren for permission.

"Use your own judgment, Commander," he said. "I have no worries he would do something counter-productive to any of our strategies. Be aware what he doesn't know, can't be taken from him. I'd rather he not carry the guilt of a true betrayal."

"I understand."

"Then I'll leave you to your visit." Master Aren walked away and Tridia followed him with her eyes.

"Has he endeared himself to you in so short a time?" Robel asked.

"Nothing so simple, *Somi*." Tridia sat cross-legged on the grass while Robel sat on his bench trimming the bushes. She told him about the hospital ship, the Felinus doctors and their treatments, about meeting the empress, and Anza's abduction. They moved from place to place about the garden as he worked and she talked. She gathered the plant trimmings into a basket she carried with them. When she paused for breath she peeled the huttle fruit and nibbled at it, sharing a piece with Robel. When Tridia told him about waking up as a Felinus warrior, Robel laughed.

"Now *that*, my dear, I would have enjoyed seeing. I'll bet you scared spittle out of everyone who looked at you."

"I seemed to," Tridia agreed. "The Guardians gave me a wide berth."

Tridia went on to tell him about the fight in the Public Hearing Room, and how she'd transformed back to her own body at the end of the battle. She wrapped it up with a brief description of their trip to Cystia, leaving out anything that might compromise him later.

"That's a lot of high adventure, even for you." Robel put away his gardening tools and sat looking at Tridia.

"There are so many levels of intrigue in this. So many puzzles I can't find beginning or end to." Tridia tilted her head back and gazed at the crescent outlines of the three moons.

"Then we'll have to sort them out. There's no one better suited for the job than you and Brenden." Robel patted Tridia's knee. "How are the two of you getting along? What *was* that look in your eyes when he walked away."

"Something – chemical – happened between us when he left me at the hospital ship." Tridia looked away, embarrassed. "We kissed as a ruse to make the doctors believe I was his mistress, and that he'd given me my injuries. I have glands that produced an enzyme that gave us a vision of the future. Now every time I'm near him my palms sweat and I get this disgusting sweet taste in my mouth. We're in a state of truce at the moment, but I don't know for how long. I'm trying to obey, but things are so complicated."

"There's a lot you haven't told me," Robel said.

"Things that only add to the confusion," Tridia confessed.

"Don't forget, I was married to a Chesan woman. You've met the Empress Dojene," Robel said. "I understand a great deal of what both of you are going through. I will have a talk with my grandson, when time permits, to ease his way. Just don't get caught up in the emotions."

"I won't." Tridia managed a weak smile. "At least, I have no intention of doing so."

"When this adventure is finally done, I'll hear the whole tale and we'll marvel that it ever seemed so complex."

"It's good to see you again," Tridia said. "To just hear your voice takes away some of the confusion."

"I'm glad you feel that way, Commander. Now, let's have you do one more thing before we go into the house."

"If it's within my power, sir."

The old man smiled. "Open your mind. You're safe here. Brenden and I can take care of ourselves. The others aren't at risk."

"I'm sorry, *Somi*. I have my orders," Tridia said. "Master Aren forbids me to drop my barriers until they fail on their own."

"Does he have a reason for doing this?" Robel asked.

"He doesn't really need one, but I suspect it's a test." Tridia comforted herself by thinking her words weren't a total lie. "He's ostensibly giving me a chance to build my mental stamina, but I think he also wants to see if I'm capable of obeying a direct order when he's not yelling in my face."

Soft footfalls on the carpet of grass reached Tridia's ears and she jumped to her feet. Master Aren made his way through the flowers.

"Go ahead, Commander. Robel is concerned for your mental state. Drop your barrier for a few minutes and let him sense for himself."

"Thank you, sir." Tridia withdrew into herself and faced the teal-colored barrier. It fell in one sheet at her urging.

Robel's steadfast mind was the first thing she sensed. The vivid colors of *his* memories reassured her that *hers* had been correct. Their close friendship had been all the things she remembered. He smiled at first then his face went slack and his eyes glazed.

"*Somi?*" Tridia reached for him.

"Withdraw from his mind!" Master Aren shoved her aside. He caught Robel as the old man collapsed and steadied him on his workbench. "I said withdraw, Commander Odana. That's an order."

"Calm yourself, Brenden," Robel said. His eyes returned to focus, but he continued to lean under Master Aren's protective arm. "She hasn't harmed me, just took a peek inside my thoughts. When did you learn to do that, Commander? I'm sure you never had such an ability before."

Tridia closed her thoughts with her strongest normal barriers. Even through them she could sense Robel and Master Aren, albeit just the anger and agitation in the latter.

"I've never been able to do it before," she said. "Unless I have a full barrier up, your mind is like an open door. I don't have to walk in to see you."

"Your touch was very cold in my thoughts. I would have expected something warmer from you." Robel rubbed his forehead.

"Sentinel touch is cold," Master Aren said.

"So is yours, sir, when you come in uninvited," Tridia said. "*Somi*, please forgive me. I meant no intrusion or disrespect. Every time I think I've got this power under control, it adds something new."

"No need for apologies," Robel said. He pushed away from Master Aren and sat up on his own. "That was an enlightening experience – and a confirming one, I should hope. She didn't lower her barrier without your consent."

"That may be the first time she's obeyed without an argument," Master Aren said. "I want it back up now, Commander. The full energy block as quickly as you can."

Tridia envisioned the teal blue sheet in place as it had been before she pulled it down. In an instant, all outside mental influences ceased. Master Aren scowled.

"Now drop it, again."

Tridia raised her eyebrows but obeyed. The barrier fell.

"Do you realize what you're doing?" Master Aren asked.

"I'm raising and lowering my barrier, as you ordered, sir."

"You are doing it instantaneously, Commander." Winniel said. "You shouldn't be able to – especially not so soon after learning the technique."

"We sensed the disturbance in your thoughts." Alanel followed close on Winniel's heels.

A siren sounded from the house and everyone looked to Master Aren for an explanation.

"It's to signal the shield around the planet is coming down for fruit delivery. It should last ten minutes. It might be a good idea to replace your barrier, Commander, and leave it up until I say otherwise. Let's go in to dinner, the table should be ready by now."

"Yes, sir." Tridia turned toward the house, but before she'd taken a step her equilibrium disappeared. She didn't feel her foot touch the grass as her consciousness connected with the portal.

"You're there!" An urgent voice called to her through the disorientation. The dark-haired young man who looked like Davik appeared before her eyes – the Chesan prince. His thoughts and words broadcast clearly through the portal. "This was my last chance for another few days. I had some pollen samples I'd collected for study, but I've used them all now. The satellites around the planet are weapons. You can't get near here in any kind of ship without being destroyed. I need your help, but there's so much to explain. I won't have time. Can you contact me again?"

"What pollen? What satellites?" Tridia tried to respond. She struggled to concentrate on his voice through her nausea. Her last contact with him hadn't been this debilitating.

"The Rrabbas pollen and the shield satellites," he said. "The shield has gotten darker. If I can't override the controls, I'll be trapped for the next ten years."

"What shields?" Tridia asked.

"I need your help. Can you contact me again?"

"Can you hear me?" Tridia demanded. "Tell me where you are."

The connection broke suddenly. Tridia lay on the ground at Winniel's feet. Nothing made sense when she tried to get her bearings in the real world. Everything whirled before her eyes. Alanel spoke to Master Aren in the background.

"She's been contacted, Ambassador. An outside entity, apparently a young man. That's all we could tell."

"Can you stand?" Winniel reached down a hand to assist.

Tridia didn't trust her voice, she caught Winniel's wrist, and pulled herself to her feet.

"Her energy barrier wasn't in place. When she fell I lost her altogether," Master Aren said. He moved to stand in front of her when Winniel would have led her away. "What was the communication? What did he say?"

"There are weapons in the satellites and something happened to make the shield darker. He said if he can't override the controls he'll be trapped for ten years." Tridia swallowed down bile rising in her throat. "I don't understand what he needs from me."

"Contact – which you cannot give him. Get your energy block up now."

Tridia tried to comply but her stomach turned over and she gagged. The teal barrier formed in her thoughts, but Winniel's consciousness never faded.

"Winniel – "

Our proximity isn't causing this.

Tridia let the barrier fall.

"The Commander is too disoriented to engage the energy block," Alanel said. "Winniel and I will protect her until she's fit."

Master Aren glared, but agreed. He had no choice.

"Take her to her room to wash her face and change, then bring her downstairs for dinner if she can handle it," he said.

The air around Tridia cooled. Her skin welcomed the relief and her mind found solace behind the Sentinel-induced veil. Master Aren and Robel disappeared from her senses, but her connection to Alanel strengthened until he, too, had become a presence at the edge of her consciousness.

What's happening? Tridia asked, unsure the Sentinels could hear her thoughts.

Quiet, Commander. Winniel responded. *This is new in our experience. Your connection with us is only one short step from a connection with our clan.*

CHAPTER FIFTEEN

The hallways through which the Sentinels led Tridia, and the rooms they passed, had polished stone floors and artwork adorned the walls. Every table held a vase of flowers and the scents inside mimicked the fragrance outside. A marble staircase curved its way to the second and third floors of the house and each landing had a coat of arms on the wall. Tridia had seen the same emblem on the doors of the embassy at Dajelania.

Alanel and Winniel all but carried her to the third floor in their haste to get her away from Master Aren. At the third floor landing they eased their grips and let Tridia stand on her own.

"Your room is this way." Winniel opened the door to a room five times larger than Tridia's small space on Odea. Her duffle bag and decontaminated clothes sat on a bench at the foot of a bed she could have comfortably shared with three other people.

"Give me a minute." Tridia stepped into an equally enormous bathroom. She washed her face with cool water and dried it with a warm towel, before changing back into her decontaminated clothing. Master Aren had made the accommodations of her captivity very pleasant.

"Are you well enough to try the energy block again?" Winniel asked.

"I'm not disoriented anymore," Tridia said.

The energy block went up instantly, and her connections to the Sentinels disappeared. Tridia gasped at the sudden solitude. The new intensity of her connection with them made its absence a gaping hole. The Sentinels' need to connect with their clan suddenly made perfect sense. It brought stability.

"We've got to get you back with your clan," Tridia said.

"All things in time, Commander." Alanel said.

"There is no time," Tridia replied. "The vision came from the

159

Chesan prince. You know I recognized him. Master Aren knows it, as well. How much longer do you think he'll let me live knowing I can talk to the prince so easily?"

"You will at least live through dinner," Winniel said.

***

Drayden sat in the sand surrounded by the Rrabbas. He sensed the creatures' anxiety as the disorientation receded.

You reached her, Dray-den? Tayne asked. Her enormous eyes glistened dark blue with concern.

Yes, Little Sister. But something was very different this time. I felt ill as we spoke.

Your body was fading, Brother. You tried to leave us. Vaile, one of the breeding females said. *You need her.*

She is coming, Dray-den. Tayne's small, fragile hand touched his cheek. *She will be with you soon. She needs you, as you need her.*

Tayne, how can you know? If she comes, the satellites will destroy her. Drayden looked up at the ruby-tinted sky. The light was so heavily filtered even the dune shadows appeared red. "How can she reach me through this?"

Because she must, Brother. Haylen, the other breeding female answered. She entwined her slender fingers with her mate's. *Just as we must reach our breeding ground, she must come to you.*

Drayden poured the shriveled and discolored pollen on the sand before returning the empty tube to its carrying case. He tucked the case into his backpack and slid the pack onto his shoulders, retrieving his fighting staff as he stood. He made every move deliberate and precise to help him regain his balance, and to give him time to consider the Rrabbas' words. All three of the females spoke with such certainty, as if to support his failing hopes.

We'd better hurry away from here. Your scents are getting stronger. We're taking a different route, but the skikes are probably tracking us already.

Tayne stumbled with her first step and he carefully lifted her to his shoulder.

I must walk, Dray-den!

Drayden smiled at the indignity in Tayne's thoughts. *No, Little Sister. I need your eyes scanning the dunes. We can't afford to be caught unaware under this sky.*

That silenced her protests and Drayden quickened the pace. The pairs were anxious to hurry on and had made the concession to stop only because they sensed his need. They'd have no trouble keeping up, but Tayne couldn't have made a sustained march.

Drayden's thoughts returned to the link. If his body had faded, then the physician's warning that he could leave through the portal was sound. What would happen if he did, and where would he end up? He'd tried to be clear to the girl, answering her questions as best he could, but he'd been too disoriented to know whether he'd been successful. If she contacted him again, he'd know. If she didn't he could try again in a couple of days, when they reached the breeding grounds. They had to spend one more night on the sands under the scarlet moon, keeping watch for the skikes. The next night they would be in the safety of the trees. *One more night.*

***

A table large enough to accommodate a group twice their size held bowls and platters of food. Most of the dishes were prepared with foods grown on Hulac, but many of the spices came from alien planets. Tridia had no memory of such savory dishes. Even Deeca and Sonei put aside their attitudes to enjoy the meal. Master Aren allowed only small talk about the planet and the estate at the table. Either he or Robel diverted several attempts to stray onto more pressing topics. Even so, behind the energy block Tridia considered the next leg of their journey. They had no more assurance Anza had actually been taken to Starling than they had the invasion fleet was real, but it was the only thing they had to go on. Given the time limit placed on them by the kidnappers, their stay on Hulac made no sense. But Master Aren had a reason for everything he did, and patience would reveal it.

When they finished with desserts of chilled berries and cream in crystal goblets, Master Aren led the group to an upstairs room filled with comfortably overstuffed furniture, pillows and rugs. One entire glass wall overlooked a valley of blue huttle trees bathed in a ghostly silver light from the three crescent moons. He left them there for several minutes before returning with his com-pad.

"Now," Master Aren announced, "we can discuss those things which are foremost on our minds. I've received diplomatic information that the Starling delegates are in an uproar because no replacement negotiator has been named. They are putting pressure on the Triad to respond, but as yet, the repairs to the Public Hearing Room haven't been completed and the judges won't make a ruling anywhere else. They'll give us our time, but they won't be able to extend it."

"Then why are we wasting our time here?" Deeca asked. "Your home is lovely and comfortable. You've been a most gracious host, but cut to the chase, Brenden. Princess Anza could be dead by now."

"I have my own reasons for doubting that her abductors wish her dead. If that's true, our next question must be, what is their purpose in taking her? We've had no communications from the empress, and Kanu has had no word from her escort ships. She could have been taken, as well."

"We know where to find the Kel Anec," Tridia stated.

"Finding Princess Anza is my main objective," Deeca interjected

"As is ours," Master Aren agreed. "However, the data we received from the mica-disk is suspect. Intelligence reports from outside sources say there's activity on the Starling moon indicated on the star chart. More activity than should be expected from an agrarian planet. But that's not a guarantee of Anza's presence, either."

"We're walking in circles, Ambassador," Sonei added. "We can accept our leads or not, we can go to Starling or Kanu or somewhere else, but sitting here isn't getting us any closer to a resolution. Why are we still here?"

"Because there's more to the story than you know – and more you need to know if you're going to continue with this group." Master Aren looked at Deeca and Sonei as he spoke.

"Well that sounds ominous," Sonei said. "What other good news are you hiding from us?"

"Sonei, you're a mercenary. Your allegiance goes to the highest bidder. I will make you an offer I doubt can be trumped for someone as curious as you – or as vindictive."

"I'm listening." Sonei drew her feet onto the sofa where she sat.

"For your full allegiance to this project, until it reaches its conclusion whether that be in simple freedom for Princess Anza or full-scale war with the Kel Anec, I swear to give you the connection between me and Morgan Jacks to use as you see fit. However, Deeca is the one who will decide the project has reached its conclusion."

"Why me?" Deeca asked. "I might just as soon see you fry as she would."

"True, but you're too honorable to let that influence your decision," Master Aren said. "I trust you to make the right call."

"Sweeten the deal a little, Ambassador," Sonei said. "Throw in the evidence Jacks is holding over my head and one million credits."

"I want your complete loyalty, Sonei," Master Aren said. "I'll make it ten million, with the evidence, but you've got to do exactly as I say without question in the missions and planning sessions. Even if I tell you to leave the room or stay behind or go to some place that makes no sense. You've got to agree to those terms. I will need all of your shape-shifting skills. Not just your ability to change your face and size."

Sonei thought about the offer, then looked at Tridia. "What would you do in my place, kid?"

"I'm a slave, Sonei. I can't be in your place," Tridia said. Master Aren didn't look at her, but Robel studied her closely. "I've given him absolute control over my life for the next five years – if we live that long. You won't have to wait as long for your payoff."

Sonei smiled. "I'll take your offer. You've just hired one mercenary for the duration of this project. Loyalty guaranteed and absolute. Loyalty ends with the project and I expect payment in full – all expenses paid in addition, of course. I want access to a solicitor before we leave this planet. As rough as you people play, I may not get a chance later."

"Done," Master Aren said. "The first thing I need you to do is leave this floor. Cason is in the kitchen downstairs. He will set you up with a communications link for a solicitor of your choice. Tell him the price was agreed – he'll understand. One million credits will be paid up front as you direct, the remainder and the evidence at the conclusion. When your business is done, no spying, no listening, and no eavesdropping of any kind on the conversations we're about to have. The Sentinels will know if you comply."

Sonei sat and steamed for a minute or two before leaving the room. Winniel got the glazed-eyed look on her face then sobered and reported Sonei had gone to the kitchen.

"Robel, it would be best if you left us, as well," Master Aren said.

"Well, it's getting near an old man's bedtime anyway." The old gardener got stiffly to his feet and left. Alanel walked with him down the hall.

Only Tridia, Master Aren, Deeca, and Winniel remained.

"Okay, what's so secretive you had to clear the room to address it?" Deeca asked.

"We've received a distress call that may take precedence over Princess Anza," Brenden said.

"You must be joking," Deeca responded. "What makes you think *any* distress call is more important than rescuing Anza?"

"That's why I now have every available resource trying to locate Empress Dojene. It's her decision to make," Master Aren said. "I believe this is a matter she'd place even above her daughter's safety."

"Master Aren," Tridia said. "You can't be serious. The contact may not have been genuine."

"It was genuine. You know it was." Master Aren sat in one of the overstuffed chairs. "His comment about the shield getting darker is something that couldn't have been faked. That was him."

"Him who?" Deeca asked.

Master Aren sat back and considered Deeca's face before answering. "The surviving prince of a near-extinct race. He's been in seclusion and was supposed to remain there for another fifteen years. But his security has been breached. His planetary shields have gone into full defensive status and he may have done something to draw attention to his whereabouts. The Kel Anec may already have his location."

"You're moving too fast." Deeca sat up. "What does this have to do with the Kel Anec?"

"I don't know, but you remember the purple planets in the star chart?"

Deeca nodded.

"One of them was Hulac, one Kanu. I can guess what the others mean, but there is a definite connection between those two planets."

"What connection?" Deeca asked.

"They're home to survivors of the prince's race." Master Aren sat back and let Deeca consider his words.

"One of these survivors lives on Hulac?" Deeca asked.

"Yes," Master Aren replied. "Some of the time."

"You?" Deeca asked.

"I'm not a full-blood survivor. In fact, I'm only about a quarter, and my mother was full Alurian. Her DNA was by far the more dominant of the mix. But I carry part of that genetic strain." Master Aren said. "That's the long and the short of it."

"All right. Let's assume your prince really is the one who sent the message," Deeca said. "Was his planet one of the purple ones? If so, what can we do to help him?"

"No, it wasn't. His planet was in one of the missing sections of space," Brenden said. "Going to him directly would be a mistake. We could end up leading the Kel Anec straight to his location. The other planets may have turned purple to make us think they know more than they do."

"Then we take evasive actions," Tridia said. "We make them think they're following us, but let them chase shadows."

"An assassin's specialty," Master Aren said. "We give them multiple targets to pursue while we go nowhere they're looking. The *Star Seeker* can't be mistaken for another ship, except for those belonging to the Sentinels, and one of my own registered vehicles is here, as well. That's two directions."

"Which one do we take?" Deeca asked.

"Neither," Master Aren replied. "We take a third way off the planet."

"And me?" Tridia asked. "Do I go with you?"

"No," he answered. "You stay here with the Sentinels for the time being. Stay under the shield and out of sight."

"Why does she stay here?" Deeca asked.

"She understands the reason, and no one else need know it," Brenden said.

"You'll have to retrieve him," Tridia argued. "Do you know how to deactivate the shields he's talking about?"

"Those shields are designed to hold against anything. He'll be safer under them. I only need to confirm they're still intact – something I can do from a safe distance."

"What if the shields aren't his greatest danger?" Tridia argued. "He spoke of being trapped for ten years. Something else is wrong!"

"The shields aren't his greatest danger, Commander," Brenden snapped. "*You* are. I don't dare bring him into the open as long as you're alive. At least not for another fifteen years."

Tridia stood and walked to the window. With darkness outside, the glass reflected the room and the scowl on her face. Master Aren's reflection watched her, waiting to see if she would continue to argue. She wanted to. In the depth of her being she knew the current situation with the satellites and the shield wasn't his greatest danger, nor was she.

"Don't let him die, Master Aren," she said at last. "Don't make the mistake of assuming there are no other dangers because there should be no other dangers; like a room that should be empty, but isn't." She turned to face him. "Those were your words. I don't remember the circumstance, but you taunted me with them. Take your own advice."

Rage flickered in his eyes, their brilliant electric blue darkened. Tridia had struck a nerve. "Winniel, please watch over the Commander this evening. She isn't to leave the house," he said.

"Alanel and I will protect her, Ambassador," Winniel said. "Rest assured."

Winniel's words were more warning than reassurance. The Sentinel must have sensed something unpleasant in Master Aren's thoughts. Tridia followed her up the stairs to the third-floor landing, where Alanel joined them. The couple stared at each other, grim-faced and silent. Tridia kept her mouth shut and waited behind her mental barriers.

"He means to kill you, Commander," Winniel announced.

"I know. He doesn't think he can let me live because of this Chesan vision, but –"

"No, Commander Odana, he means to see you dead as soon as he can part you from us," Alanel interrupted. "He's already making plans to do so. He will find a reason to send us away and keep you here. The thought grieves him and he knows it will cause a rift between him and Robel. He knows we'll take revenge on him, but he feels he can no longer take the chance of letting you live. He hopes he and Deeca Varin can escape to rescue Princess Anza before we kill him, but even that won't stay his hand."

The words shouldn't have stunned her – he'd already put a blaster under her chin – but hearing the facts so bluntly added a surreal quality. She wasn't ready to sacrifice her life to Master Aren's fears, but her options were limited – especially if the Sentinels sided with him.

"What do the two of you think?"

"As I told the Ambassador," Winniel said. "We will protect you."

"You have a plan?" Tridia fought the urge to drop her energy block and commune with the Sentinels telepathically. Master Aren would sense the change in her barrier and if he picked up on her thoughts, things would get messy very quickly. "There's no place to hide on this planet and no way to take a ship through the planetary shields. I don't see a way of escape. Unless you intend to forcibly take me with you when you leave."

"There is always the portal," Winniel said. "Your body has phased more than once in an attempt to join your mind. You were trying to phase when the prince contacted you. That was likely why you felt so ill. Push both mind and body through the portal."

"You make it sound easy!" Tridia shivered at the thought of the gray mist and the feeder writhing in its energy. She heard the golden image's warning in her mind, *corporeal things can't exist here.* "I don't know if I can open it at all – and I certainly can't open it with the energy block up. If I let it down Master Aren will know."

"Not if we shield you," Alanel said.

"Okay, assuming I can do this, where would I go?" Tridia asked.

"To Prince Drayden." Winniel didn't skip a beat. "He needs help and the Ambassador won't approach him. No outside force can reach him. The shield he describes is the same as those that now guard Ceyon, his home world. If he communicates with you through the portal, you can travel to him the same way."

"How do you know portal travel is possible?" Tridia asked. The Sentinels were trying to save her life, but trading a quick execution for another, possibly more horrible death, didn't appeal to her.

"It's been done before," Winniel said. "In the Chesan's long history, they recorded many times when someone moved physically through the portal. The first time was when the whole race moved from their home planet to Ceyon. Your people didn't originate in this galaxy."

Tridia was about to ask more questions when Alanel tilted his head as though listening for a sound. He frowned.

"We need to hurry. Our telepathic powers are waning as Winniel's separation from the clan continues. Your energy block makes it even more difficult. The ambassador is going to block his thoughts in order to share an intimacy with Deeca Varin. If we act when he does, he won't be able to sense you when you drop your barrier."

"To the kitchen." Winniel pushed Tridia toward the stairs. "Get enough rations and water for a couple of days. We'll go to your room and get a pack ready. Alanel found an armory earlier. You should go well-armed and prepared for whatever danger the prince faces."

Tridia hurried down the stairs, not believing she was planning to escape from Master Aren after taking an oath. But she'd given her word to Davik first, and somehow, she'd committed herself to the Chesan prince before she'd ever met Master Aren. Should her oath of allegiance supersede those pledges? The Sentinels didn't seem to think so, but that was of little comfort to a soul already torn with guilt for so many things.

If she continued along those lines she'd talk herself out of the attempt, and two men depended on her too much for her to accept an execution. She'd submit to Master Aren once Davik and Drayden were free, and accept whatever punishment he dealt her. She quickened her pace down the stairs.

Two men and three women were finishing up the dinner dishes when Tridia entered the kitchen. Sonei was nowhere in sight, but the staff greeted her as a guest, and an equal, with no hint of humility. Master Aren had said they weren't servants, but all five possessed military bearings straight from an Odean training field. They might not be servants, but they'd all been soldiers at some point. She returned their greeting and asked if she could assist them with anything.

"I'm a little restless," she explained. "I'm not accustomed to such plush surroundings."

"We're almost done," the youngest woman said. She appeared to be in her twenties. "I'm Tish, that's Ryo, Elda, Jens, and Sasha. You're welcome to sit and visit while we finish up – if you don't mind the local gossip."

"Which one of your friends would that be, Tish?" Ryo asked, continuing the conversation Tridia had interrupted.

They all laughed and went about their business as if it was natural for a guest to sit in the kitchen. They chatted about household matters, orchard duties, and speculation on Brenden's relationship with the pretty blonde who'd come to the planet with the group.

"Don't suppose you'd care to let us in on what that relationship is?" Elda asked Tridia.

"They've known each other for some time, I think," Tridia answered, glad for the opening to talk. She needed them to be at ease with her. She feigned innocence. "They argue a lot, but I think they have a lot of respect for each other. Beyond that…"

Her voice trailed away and she tried to send a shy blush to her cheeks. When she thought of Alanel's comment about Master Aren wanting to share an intimacy with Deeca she blushed for real, imagining what that meant.

"I think the young lady may know more than she's comfortable saying," Jens said. "And I think we shouldn't press her to share it."

Tridia cast relieved eyes in his direction and broadened the forced smile. The group around her chatted for a bit longer as they finished the last of the chores.

"We're all done here." Ryo wiped his hands on a towel and hung it on a rack to dry. "Can we help you with anything before we turn out the lights?"

"Actually, yes. I wanted to put together a small snack tray to take back to my room. Some bottled water, a couple of pieces of fruit, maybe some bread or cheese?" It sounded like a lot on the heels of the sumptuous meal they'd just had. Tridia used an old story to belay their suspicions. "My metabolism is so high it seems I'm always hungry."

"Oh, to be that young again," Sasha sighed. "I remember when I could eat whatever I wanted and stay trim."

"Mother," Jens said, "you're still as trim as the day we met, and I haven't noticed you eating any less."

Everyone laughed as Sasha, on the verge of thanking her husband for the compliment, changed from a sweet smile to a surprised frown. The four of them showed Tridia where to find everything – just in case what she took wasn't enough – and indicated where to shut off the lights.

Tridia thanked them as she put a few things on the tray they'd given her. As soon as they shut the door behind them she opened the cupboards again, grabbing additional provisions and tossing them into a bag she found in a pantry. She wasn't sure what kind of troubles Prince Drayden was having, but she didn't intend that feeding her should be one of them if she could help it – assuming she could get to him at all. After a quick look around, she found several thermos containers labeled huttle juice. She took two of them before switching off the lights and eased her way back up the stairs to her room.

Sonei leaned against the wall at the third-floor landing. She still wore the red-head's face and body.

"I'm really tired, Sonei," Tridia said. "Whatever it is, can it wait until the morning?"

"I won't take up much of your time, kid," Sonei replied. Her tone was all business. "I'm here to tell you to find a way to get away from him. Get off this planet and keep running. I'll help you in any way I can. There are people you can go to and I've made some arrangements, but you can't stay with him. That million-credit payment is now in an account you can tap if you need it."

Tridia stared. "Why?"

"I told you, I've decided to follow you. I won't betray the Ambassador or break our deal in any way. He never mentioned you in the agreement. My offer to help won't jeopardize his plans."

"You don't know what his plans are," Tridia said.

"You mean apart from killing you?" Sonei chuckled. "Apparently, I don't need to know. I just need to obey."

"I appreciate your concern, and I do thank you for the offer to help, but I have to stay with him. I've given my oath, and I can't go back on it."

"I've heard Hierarchy indoctrination is brutal. But to stay even when you know he will kill you makes no sense." Sonei sighed. "Fine. My help can be put on hold. If you change your mind – or if you want to talk about the possibility – just ask. I hate the thought he has someone else under his thumb the way he does me. You're surrounded. The Sentinels aren't all the joy they're cracked up to be, either. Their kind and mine go way back, and it isn't a friendly history. Their designers wanted shape-shifter DNA and there was a pretty ugly struggle to keep it out of their gene pool. I doubt our denial has been forgotten any more by them than it has by us. I wouldn't trust them to do anything that didn't promote the fulfillment of their latest mission. Be careful of them." Sonei stood away from the wall and started down the hall. "My turn will come, kid, but you don't have much time left."

Tridia watched as Sonei slipped into her own room. Once Master Aren dropped his barriers, he would know what the shape-shifter had offered. Let him see that Tridia had reassured Sonei of her fealty to him. That might give her a few extra seconds to work on opening the portal.

The Sentinels waited inside her room. She eased the door closed and walked to the bed to examine the things they'd laid out for her. Master Aren's armory had supplied her with every weapon she could hope for, and how astute of the Sentinels to know just what to choose. Then Tridia snapped to the fact *she* knew exactly what she would have chosen. Another piece of her life had fallen into place without her realizing it. The veil couldn't hold much longer.

"We found these among the things in your closet." Winniel indicated a set of dark blue combat fatigues.

"Bless you," Tridia said. Even though they were unworn, she had no doubt the clothes belonged to her. More memories came. The dark blue wardrobe had been delivered the day she'd made her Commander's rank. She'd earned the rank. The thought brought no happiness, but it did bring hope she might be able to help Prince Drayden.

She stripped down to her under garments, laying the leather bracelet and the pouch containing her DNA on the bed. Then she pulled on a black undershirt, tight black pants, and thick socks. She dug in the duffle bag to retrieve the arm and calf sheaths she'd taken off when she'd changed clothes on the *Star Seeker*, then strapped them into place. Over those she pulled on the fatigues and her scuffed boots. A knife went into a sheath on her right calf, and a blaster into a holster at her right hip. Several extra blast chambers went into various pockets on her pants legs. Over the fatigues came a combat jacket with more pockets of explosives, battle supplies, and another knife in the left sleeve. All of the food, as well as an assortment of medical supplies the Sentinels had procured, the bracelet and the pouch of DNA samples went into a sturdy backpack, which she slid onto her shoulders. She lifted one of two rifles to her shoulder and gauged its weight before pulling its strap onto her shoulder, as well. Lastly, she donned a helmet with a darkened faceplate. The helmet was a prize indeed, one of the latest models of battle headgear. The Hierarchy had started issuing them only two months before. The dark faceplate displayed readouts on atmosphere, sensor locations, and body heat sensors. It also contained a concise medical scan to diagnose simple illness, fevers, and bone and muscle injuries. All sensor readings came from tiny devices implanted in the helmet itself, but the smooth surface betrayed no instrumentation. She added one more gadget, a voice modulator with an attached translator. Its counterpart ear piece she'd slipped into her ear before putting on the helmet. The prince had spoken an understandable language to her, but there might be others she'd need to speak with. She reached up and switched the voice modulator off.

"Any last words of instruction?" she asked.

"Focus your mind on the portal, on what you've already seen there and where you wish to go," Winniel said. "You must stay focused. We'll wait outside the room, in case the Ambassador should come before you're done. His mind is still blocked, but he didn't intend to leave it that way long."

"I should thank you both," Tridia said. "But if I end up dead in some alien dimension, I want to be able to blame you."

Winniel smiled, then she and Alanel left.

Standing in the middle of the room, Tridia took a deep breath to slow her racing heart. The golden image had said she'd almost brought herself through the portal on Cystia, and her body had become insubstantial, according to Alanel. She thought back on the image's voice, calling her to bring her thoughts into the portal. Would it be the same to transport her body? Her body had tried twice to join her consciousness. If she sent her thoughts, would her body follow?

See with your mind what you saw with your eyes. The golden image's instruction on opening a window to see outside the portal came back to her. Would it work in reverse, to see the portal and step into it?

Tridia thought of herself, the clothes she wore, the equipment she carried. With her energy block in place, she was limited to using her imagination. If she dropped her barriers, she would expose her thoughts to Master Aren. Would the Sentinels be able to block her energy? So many questions, and with each one came a bit more doubt.

She couldn't wait forever and she'd done all she could with her senses blocked. Tridia willed the teal barrier to fall and it vanished. Everyone in the house became clear in her mind. Master Aren's barriers were weak. He'd notice her any minute. The Sentinels stood in the hall, surprised that their communications were restored. *Somi* Robel rested peacefully in his room, enjoying the scent of the flowers he'd placed there. Sonei paced her room, tossing small items around, worried that Master Aren or the Sentinels would try to harm Tridia in the night.

Sonei's warning concerning the Sentinels came to Tridia's mind. *I wouldn't trust them to do anything that didn't promote the fulfillment of their latest mission.*

Fear and doubt crashed into her resolve. Would this act of betrayal further the Sentinel's cause? Even if she died? Why help her if they meant her to die? Master Aren would kill her soon, anyway. She betrayed her oath by planning this disobedience. It deserved punishment.

The deep-seated Hierarchy training to honor her oaths emerged from the darkness in her mind. Memories of watching oath-breakers beaten and executed flooded her thoughts. She'd broken only one oath, and she'd been whipped for it. This betrayal was even more egregious. She'd repeated the oath twice before witnesses. Echoing voices condemned her from the past.

Traitor to your word. Betrayer. You deserve punishment.

Sonei was right, she'd been brainwashed all her life to be an obedient soldier. She had to submit to the will of her master.

"No!" She struggled against the confusion. "Davik needs me alive. Drayden needs me to save him. I can't die now!"

Tridia reached out with her mind, sensing her body, her gear, and her clothes right down to the fibers. She held them and thought of the portal, the mist and sparkles and voices. She *had* to open the door that led to it. *Reach for it. Go there.* Her body tingled, then itched, then burned. Master Aren noticed her thoughts.

"Stupid girl!" Master Aren's words ricocheted through her mind. He jumped to his feet and ran toward the stairs.

Doubts clouded Tridia's concentration as the air around her cracked with a discharge of energy. The exquisite pain of every cell in her body exploding registered in her mind before it shattered out of existence.

CHAPTER SIXTEEN

Drayden dropped to the sand mid-stride. Pain ripped through his body and his consciousness entered a world of gray mist. For an instant the shape of the girl sparkled before him, then vanished. Only the mist remained. The mist – and voices whispering in shock and terror.

"My son, no!"

The sound of his father's cry cut through all other noise and pierced Drayden's heart. The absolute anguish threatened to overwhelm him.

"Go back, Prince Drayden." A golden statue melted before him. It lacked any familiar shape, but the voice was insistent. "Go back to your body. She will come to you."

Dray-den? Tayne's timid thoughts came from far away.

We are here for you, Brother. Come back to us. Vaile's concern tugged at him, demanding his focus.

It is not time, Dray-den. You must return now! The command in Tayne's words pulled him from the mists.

Drayden gasped and sucked sand down his throat, then coughed until he could spit it out. Tears ran down his face. He sobbed until the pain became bearable. What had happened to her? What had she done that had ripped his soul from his body? Had she tried to come through the shield? Was she dead?

Be at ease, Brother. Tayne stroked his cheek. The sweet scent of her sap tickled his nose. *She will come to you. Wait for her. That place is not yet for you. But I can now be at peace as I join my mate.*

Drayden rolled onto his side with an effort. All three females touched his face and hands feeding their calming thoughts into his mind. The males stood behind them, leafy limbs twined about the females' shoulders. To expend this much of themselves so near their birthing time was dangerous beyond belief, but he couldn't stop them.

All he could do was fall into a dreamless sleep and hope no predators came in the night.

***

Davik had reformed his body for the third time inside the small chamber. The other entity supplied additional power to hold it firm as his own power waned. They'd had another argument about his not having two heads. Why the creature insisted on the ridiculous modification every time he formed his body was beyond him. Despite its familiarity with Chesan anatomy, it was convinced that Tridia thought he had two heads, and it wanted to follow her image of him.

With one head firmly attached to his shoulders, and shaking it in annoyance, he took a step to get reacquainted with the movement of his legs, but he ended up flattened on the chamber floor, his form so insubstantial he couldn't sense the rock beneath it. The other entity had vanished, taking most of his power with it. Was this a betrayal? Had the powerful being been so angered by their petty argument that it decided to withdraw its aid?

For a split second his mind existed in another place. He sensed Tridia pass by, then another presence struggling with pain, guilt and sadness. Had he gone to Hades, or Hell, or Tartarus, or whatever the name of the ancient place of torment was supposed to be? Before he could fully consider the question, he was back in the rock chamber, spread across the floor, without enough energy to reform. The small amount of consciousness left to him sensed a feeder outside the slit in the chamber wall. The creature floated past without pausing to search the crevice. It hadn't registered enough energy from him to arouse its hunting instincts. The energy drain had been opportune, if terrifying. Without the other entity's help, it would take hours for the natural energy of his brain to accumulate in sufficient quantity for him to reform. In the meantime, he had no choice but to remain in the chamber, his consciousness a mere shadow of energy coating the floor, unable to defend himself from the scientists or the Kel Anec's hungry creatures.

***

Alarms flashed in the isolation chamber. Davik Schie's body convulsed and his brainwave readings, which had been off the charts mere seconds before, had flatlined. Scientists scurried about the room checking instruments and making adjustments.

Frees B'Nay stood to the side and watched the flatlined readings with grim displeasure. They couldn't lose Davik Schie now! They'd achieved the power output they wanted. B'Nay had been about to return to the mine to confront the lieutenant's energy mass and make another deal. Another deal that Schie could no more refuse than he had the first one. Tridia Odana had been in the mine. She had been with his energy form. Something in their contact had changed the boy from test subject to weapon. She had succeeded in bringing forth the power jump required to justify the project's continued funding. A few simple demonstrations of power were all the evidence he needed. Then they could attempt to return the lieutenant to his physical body. Once in his body, the promise of freedom, a cleared record, and a life with the girl he loved would be enough to keep Schie under control. Once the subject – weapon – was mated with Tridia Odana, B'Nay could control them both, as well as any progeny they produced. But not if Schie's body died or his energy form burned out.

So close! B'Nay crossed his arms and concentrated on the chart. A single blip was all he needed.

"We've lost him, Master B'Nay," Reshard said. "His energy signature is no longer in the mine."

"Prepare to resuscitate the body!" B'Nay hurried to the isolation tank and reached for the drain switch. "Drain the tank!"

"If you do that we'll lose any chance –" A quiet blip silenced Reshard's argument.

B'Nay held his breath. Another blip registered, then another. Davik Schie was alive – barely, but alive.

"The pain readings have maxed out!" The med-tech glanced over his shoulder. Davik's body spasmed inside its liquid-filled coffin. "I can't tell if the body's convulsions are causing it or if the pain is causing the convulsions."

"Locate him!" B'Nay shouted in the direction of the tech running the mine scanners.

"The signature is too faint, sir," the tech replied. "We'll have to wait until it gains strength. The uridine is masking him."

"Once his body stabilizes, run all the diagnostics you can and compare with what's happening now. Make sure you scan everything. Even the smallest differential could be critical," B'Nay ordered.

"If the body doesn't stabilize?" Reshard asked.

"It will," B'Nay said. "He wouldn't have come back if he was going to give up."

Reshard stared at the master assassin with doubt. B'Nay ignored him. He knew Lieutenant Davik Schie – his will and his weakness. The boy wouldn't fight so hard if he didn't have a reason to survive.

"Keep me informed. I want to know his location the instant you find him," B'Nay said. "I want to speak with him again. Get an armored team assembled to accompany me. We'll have to reach him before he regains full strength. If he feels threatened or his faculties are damaged, he could be dangerous. Take field disruptors in case all else fails, or to use on those floating black creatures, should they appear."

"Yes, sir." A soldier slipped out and disappeared down the hall.

"This time, Lieutenant Schie, will not be like the last." B'Nay folded his arms again and backed away from the isolation tube. He'd have the final say. And he'd have Tridia Odana whether Schie helped him or not.

CHAPTER SEVENTEEN

Brenden's gaze followed Tridia and Winniel as they walked away. He counted on Winniel's diminished senses to miss some of his thoughts, but he didn't try to hide them. He'd hesitated too long to do what he should have left done on Odea. Tridia had to die. Prince Drayden's contact had sealed her fate.

The young man's determination to reach out for help would draw the girl to him. The Commander had gone from cold, elite assassin to sentimental fool after her resurrection. Her determination was stronger than ever. She'd find a way to reach him, regardless of the consequences to the rest of galaxy. Her attachment to the Sentinels complicated matters. They would try to keep him from performing his duty, but on Hulac, there was no place for them to run or hide. Even two Sentinels were no match for the entire army he'd assembled among his farmers.

Robel's sorrow was the only guilt he'd have to deal with. His grandfather truly loved the girl and for the first time he regretted bringing the old man to Hulac. It would break his heart when Tridia died yet again. This time for good.

Brenden pushed all thoughts of Tridia aside. Let the Sentinels deal with her for the rest of the evening. He needed the time to broach a difficult matter with Deeca before they left Hulac.

"You went to a lot of trouble to get me alone," Deeca said. She kept her violet blue eyes steadily on his.

"Because I need to ask you a question that might be difficult for you to discuss." Deeca's brows drew together as she waited. "That locket you're wearing. It has pictures in it?"

"Yes." Deeca's hand went to the silver oval.

"May I ask of whom?" Brenden asked.

"My brother, Tolen, and my fiancé, Koren," Deeca said.

"As I expected. This is going to be difficult for both of us." Brenden chose his words carefully. Deeca could end the conversation before they got started, if he got them wrong. He opened his thoughts to hers as much as he could without being bowled over by her emotions. "May I see the pictures?"

She opened the locket and stretched it to the length of the chain but didn't remove it. Brenden moved to sit beside her. He hadn't mistaken the face, it just remained to find out which one had done the damage. He pointed to the picture on the left.

"Who is this one?" he asked.

"That's my brother," Deeca answered. "Why?"

"Because that young man made inquiries as to how to contact the Sharian mafia shortly before you were taken."

"That's low, even for you, Ambassador." Brenden winced and reinforced his barriers as Deeca's anger slammed against them. "To make up something like that here, at a time like this; it's beneath you."

Brenden got up and walked to the window where Tridia had stood, just to put a little distance between his barriers and Deeca's anger.

"Why would I make up something like that now, when we've just established a truce between us?" he asked. "That wouldn't be a clever strategy. You can ask the Gold to confirm the truth of what I'm saying. It can tell if I'm lying."

Tears welled in Deeca's eyes. The Controller had been swift to reply.

"I was there for your induction, but only the Gold and two attendants knew," Brenden said. He watched Deeca's reflection. "You hadn't come to join the Guardians. You hadn't gone through the orientation or the training. I asked why you'd been chosen for induction and the Gold told me, in your voice, that it had done it to save your life. Someone had planned to kill you, and the plan would have succeeded had you left the Warren that day."

Deeca shook her head slowly without speaking. Brenden went to a side bar and poured a thimble-sized glass of fresh huttle juice for her. She took it when he offered, but didn't sip it, as he sat beside her again.

"You'd come there to see your brother before his orientation, hadn't you?"

"Yes." Deeca's voice was barely audible.

"You were taken and he withdrew his application."

"He returned home. My father had planned to make Tolen his heir in my place – and he might have, had Tolen and Koren, who was at that time just my brother's best friend, not stepped in to argue on my behalf while I was incapacitated after the induction. My father was still a young man and agreed to wait to see how things went." Deeca touched the huttle juice to her lips. She laughed without humor before she continued. "Koren finally convinced me to marry him after trying for eight years. My father confirmed me as his heir, thinking there would be children of our union. It's been known for Guardians to have children. Then the Sharian incident happened, Koren was killed, I was disgraced. When I went back home, Tolen met me at the spaceport. He said my father disowned me and ordered him to disown me in order to be named his heir. He said he'd refused, but I told him to do it – one of us should receive the family legacy. I assumed he did. Father died last month and Tolen has control of the family estate and fortune. Everything makes so much sense now. If only my brother had known that Koren and I were planning to hand everything over to him anyway. It was supposed to be a surprise to Tolen at our rehearsal dinner. Koren was about to be named his uncle's heir. Each of us would have had everything we wanted.

"All this time I've blamed Tridia for sharing what I told her that night. It was so much easier to hate her – and you – for being what you are rather than look for another explanation."

Deeca cried in earnest then and Brenden pulled her to his chest, cradling her as she wept. After her sobs quieted, she relaxed in his arms. His chin rested on the top of her head. Her nearness pulled at him to reach into her mind. The desire to explore beyond her doubt and into her being pulled at his control. He wanted Deeca as he had longed to have her for years. He was about to lift her face to his when his glands secreted the sweet enzyme into his mouth. This time it wasn't Tridia, but Deeca he wanted. If he kissed her, he'd have to deal with the effects of the enzyme on her.

Robel and the Sentinels would sense his distress and out-of-control emotions – as would Tridia if she dropped her energy block. It would be embarrassing to say the least, but it might also be fatal to Deeca. He reached out tentative feelers to locate everyone. Robel was in his room, drifting off to sleep. Sonei was on the ground floor, getting ready to ascend the stairs. The staff was leaving the kitchen. Tridia and the Sentinels were invisible. At least the girl had kept the energy block up.

He pulled his strongest barriers into place. The Sentinels might be able to sense him – only the full energy block would guarantee they couldn't – but he couldn't shut himself off completely when he might have to deal with Deeca's reactions.

Satisfied that he'd done all that he could, he offered Deeca a drink, which she accepted. It gave him a last chance to walk away and clear his head. Intelligence shouted that he should send her away, but a more primal need spoke louder – the Chesan mating cycle. Dojene had said it was more than he was prepared to endure. Would he allow himself to prove her statement true by his actions?

He glanced out the window. Beyond the reflections, crescent moons spilled silver light and shadows over the hills and valleys. This world had become a refuge, not only for him, but for the workers. He'd promised them safety. Was he now willing to expose it to more danger? Bringing Tridia here with the mica-disk had been necessary, but what he contemplated doing with Deeca posed a different danger. His wrists tingled and for the first time he noticed the pain. The primal voice quieted. He drew in a deep breath and exhaled slowly. Whatever he might have wished for this night would have to wait.

He needed Deeca at his side as a partner and a fellow rescuer – especially if he had to kill Tridia. Drayden wasn't the only Chesan at risk, just the most well-protected. He needed Deeca to understand what they could be facing. Losing control wasn't an option.

"At the risk of sounding forward, would you mind if I dimmed the lights? The moons are spectacular."

"Your veneer is pretty thin," Deeca replied. "As long as you know that I can and will defend my honor, you may dim the lights."

Brenden adjusted a dimmer switch, placing the room in near darkness, but revealing a breathtaking vista outside the windows. Instead of sitting down when he returned to the couch, he held the drinks in one hand and offered Deeca the other. "Let's go near the window."

They settled together on cushions on the floor. A light breeze stirred the leaves of the huttle trees across the hillside causing them to flicker light and dark in the pale light. Brenden made no attempt to touch her again. It was all he could do to keep his focus.

"Thank you. This view *is* spectacular." Deeca's said. "And thank you for being honest with me."

Brenden clamped down on his barriers. "I can't promise that you can always believe everything I tell you, but I can promise that if I lie or withhold information, it will only be for a very good reason." Brenden took a sip of his drink and stared out the window. "I sit here like this to think out difficult problems. When I have the luxury."

"Like the problem we're facing now?"

He laughed quietly. "The fate of the galaxy doesn't usually rest on the problems I consider. Just the fate of star systems." Deeca sipped her drink and waited. Brenden continued. "I need to ask you one more difficult question. If you were offered a mission that might require you to protect innocent lives again, could you do it?"

The glass shook in Deeca's hand. She wouldn't look at him as he waited for her answer. She lifted the drink to her lips and took a deep swallow.

"I don't know," she said. "There's no one left to torture me with, but the fear that someone might try – I don't know."

"Even if you could be the only person to handle such a mission?"

"There are other survivors, aren't there?" Deeca asked. She set her glass on the floor. Brenden did the same. "There are more of them in hiding. The other purple planets – someone has located them."

"I don't know," Brenden said. "It's a leap to that conclusion. The number isn't right, but I don't know the planetary locations or how they may have been grouped together. There could be numerous other explanations."

Deeca stared out the window. "I can't answer your questions, Brenden. Not right now. Not with Tolen's betrayal so new."

"I don't mean to put you in a position where you will be forced into it." Brenden retrieved his glass and swirled the drink without lifting it to his lips. "But if you continue with us, you'll be exposed to knowledge that could place you in jeopardy. You need to know that and make your decision to continue with full knowledge. Even rescuing Anza could put you at risk."

Deeca shifted on the cushion to face him. "I know there are other survivors, but I don't know who or where they are, or even how many – and I don't want to know. Princess Anza is a diplomat, abducted and held as a diplomat. She's already a hostage. I can accept responsibility for trying to find and rescue her – and for trying to get her back to safety. After that, my responsibility to her ends. My part in the mission is over."

"Being involved exposes you," Brenden explained. "They – the Kel Anec – already know about you. The Hierarchy knows about you and they've tried to trap you once. You might leave now and walk away from the rest of it, but if you stay to go after Anza, you're in for the full ride."

Deeca started to object and Brenden held up his hand. "Let me say that leaving the survivors where they are is likely the safest thing we can do for them. They've been in hiding a long time and no one knows what they look like. Even the empress mistook Commander Odana for one of them. If something happens to indicate that they are at risk of capture, we'll have to go after them and keep them safe. If we do that, I'll need you to be a part of their recovery. Not just anyone can have knowledge of them or their whereabouts. There has to be more than one person in this effort. If I get killed or incapacitated, someone has to keep going. Empress Dojene will turn to you if I can't finish this."

Deeca sat in silence again. Brenden stayed out of her thoughts with an effort.

"If that time comes, Tridia and the Sentinels will be with you. And you've got your mysterious guardian angel feeding you information to light your path and Sonei's fealty. You may not need me."

Brenden shook his head in disagreement.

"I expect Tridia to try something foolish, like going after the prince on her own. She has some unexplainable connection with him that compels her to stupidity. The Sentinels will, of course, chase her. The Council ordered them to watchdog her. Without the empress in charge, we can't count on anyone from Kanu and we can't go to the Alliance without proof. That leaves only the two of us – and my guardian angel. Sonei's fealty will last only until you release her, and I can't let her know the value of the targets we'll be protecting. She is a mercenary, after all."

"If – and only if – that scenario plays out, then I'll be your backup, but I won't be in charge of anything unless you fall. By the stars you'd better not fall, Brenden Aren."

Brenden let out a silent sigh of relief. One matter laid to rest. It was enough for one night. He weakened his barriers to check on Deeca's stability when he was stunned by a rush of Tridia's thoughts.

"Stupid girl!"

Brenden jumped to his feet and ran for the hall. He hadn't made it across the room when an explosion knocked him backwards. Pictures and weapons fell from the wall. Vases and other glassware crashed to the floor and windows shattered. He struggled to his feet, fighting a throbbing pain in his head and a disorientation he couldn't explain. His body shook with the enormity of the energy that had passed through him. He glanced over his shoulder and saw Deeca move. He dropped his barriers and sensed her confusion. Her physical injuries were minimal – the blast sent most of the window flying outward – but the confusion in her mind was worse than his. He moved toward the hall again, fearful of what he'd find.

Alanel knelt on the floor outside of Tridia's room. He held his dazed mate in his arms. The door had been blasted from its hinges and embedded in the opposite wall. Smoke and flames smoldered in its once ornate finish. Inside the room, the sprinkler system gushed water from broken pipes. The entire room was charred, with twin holes in the floor and ceiling, just where he expected Tridia had stood.

"The Commander's no longer within range of our thoughts. She was here, but there remains no trace of her now." Alanel reported in an uninflected voice. "No one tried to contact her, but we sensed great determination in her just before she disappeared."

"There's not enough damage for disintegration and there aren't any random body parts lying around as evidence of an explosion. What in Hielos has she done?" Brenden ran his hand over his face and stared at the smoking remains of the room. Tridia – if she was alive – had broken her oath. Hierarchy training ran deep in someone like her. If someone found her, unleashed from his control, he couldn't keep her from returning to the Hierarchy. The Kel Anec were linked to the Hierarchy, and Tridia was linked to the prince.

"Damn the girl!" he said. "She'd better be dead."

CHAPTER EIGHTEEN

Neither open, charred flesh from blaster wounds, nor transformation from her Felinus form had caused so much pain. Every fiber of Tridia's being screamed in agonized torture. She lay face down on a warm, hard surface, marginally aware of glowing light flickering beyond her closed eyelids. After lying motionless for some time, struggling to breathe without hurting, a voice spoke in her head.

You were not ready to open the portal on your own, Child of Chaos.

The voice, more solid than she remembered, was nonetheless familiar. It conjured images of a golden reflection.

She tried to speak but her jaw wouldn't respond, so she tried to direct her thoughts. *I had to try to reach him.*

It's fortunate for you I expected you to try.

Why didn't you help me? Formulating her thoughts into conversation exhausted her, but Tridia continued the effort.

The voice's harsh reply might have been painful had it been possible for her to feel anything beyond her current agony.

I did help you! I helped you survive and stay in corporeal existence. I helped you by preventing you from getting lost in the portal. Have you not learned from your brief visits there that the portal is not one place? You tried to go there, and willed your mind and body to find it, but each of your cells, driven by the power in your DNA, tried to respond individually to the portal's call. Only by great effort was I able to keep you in one piece.

Tridia fought to understand the words, but pain continued to hammer into her brain. *Is this the portal? Can you send me to the prince?*

She sensed a sigh in the hesitation before the voice responded, this time she heard it through ringing ears. "You're not in the portal, nor can you be taken through it yet. Bringing you here has placed us both in grave danger."

Where is here? Tridia asked.

Again, the hesitation before speaking. "You're in the Guardian Warren. The Central Command Center. When you're able to focus your eyes again, you'll see me in my true form."

Tridia's heart skipped a beat. No one outside of the Guardians knew who dwelt in the Central Command Center, located in the heart of their planet. Rumor had it that only the Guardian Controller lived in that habitat. More memories, too painful to trace, floated from the darkness. Had the life and breath of the Guardian Force been the one helping her all along – or was this some stupid hoax? No laws or tribunal protected her in this place. Only the Controller's force of will would keep her alive, if that's who spoke.

Feeling – beyond the pain – began to return to her limbs. Her fingers twitched and she blinked her eyes. A charred rock wall came into focus. Her hands trembled and jerked against smooth stone.

"How are you in danger?" Tridia managed to rasp through a desert-dry throat.

"The energy in your cells cannot be contained here as they were under the shields of Hulac. The Kel Anec will pinpoint your location with ease now. They will come for you here."

"Then send me back to Hulac," she said.

The Controller responded with a teacher's patience this time. "You're in no shape to be moved and I haven't the power to move you, in any case. I told you it took a great effort to bring you here. That wasn't an idle statement. I drained energy from every individual connected with me to keep you alive."

"I brought the feeder through the portal with ease, even when I was weak. Why is this so different?"

"The feeder was amorphous. It could be reassembled in any order as long as it was intact. You're a complex corporeal being and every element had to be reassembled in its perfect order. The portal energy pouring from your cells made that difficult. The cells resist being pulled apart or reassembled. Both events create explosive reactions. There is another energy working to mend your body. Without its assistance, I'm not sure I could have managed it."

"So, moving through the portal, matter or energy is dispersed and reassembled?" Tridia struggled to her hands and knees but could not move her head from side to side. She stared at the floor.

"No. This only happened because each individual cell in your body was trying to go into the portal at once. The energy of your mind, still connected with its corporeal origin, is a different proposition. The process of moving only your conscious thought is much simpler than moving living matter – or inert matter. Your clothing and your gear were much more easily assembled than your body because their cells are inert." The Controller explained. Tridia noticed for the first time she still carried the pack and weapons. "Give yourself another minute or two before you try to stand. Your body is fragile at the moment, but the pain should be subsiding."

"It's less now than when I first awoke. How long have I been here?"

"Hours. Long enough for the Guardian force stationed here to pinpoint the source of the explosion, get readings on your energy, and label you as an intruder threat. The attendants have already tried to enter this chamber. I've held them off so far, but they are determined to force their way in. The fact you're in full battle gear may be hard to explain."

"The fact I'm *here* may be hard to explain." Tridia gave a mirthless chuckle at the absurdity of her position. "Can you offer any protection?"

"I can continue to communicate and try to keep them from the chamber. But the entire Guardian force felt my power diminish and they all fear I've been attacked. My communications have been little more than deranged mutterings until now."

"You said disassembling and reassembling me caused explosions. I can see the charring on the floor and walls here. What did it do to Master Aren's home? Were the others injured?"

"I'm sure there was physical damage to the dwelling. Deeca and Brenden felt the loss of energy as I pulled on their resources. I can sense your master's anger and Deeca's confusion, but neither are grieving the loss of a life. In my weakened state, that's the most information I can gather."

Relief flooded Tridia's mind. She hadn't considered she might hurt anyone with her attempt to open the portal. At least no one was seriously injured, but if Master Aren's beautiful home was damaged she'd never hear the end of it – *if* she managed to escape from the Warren, and *if* he didn't just shoot her the next time he laid eyes on her. Relief was short-lived as the sound of drilling buzzed through the rock on one side of the chamber. Tridia waited without moving. After some time, a drill bit pierced the wall and withdrew, to be replaced by a pipe.

"Controller, are you injured?" A voice called through the small opening. "Can you open the chamber?"

The Controller responded with thoughts that Tridia also heard. *I am well, but weakened. The intruder is with me. There is no need to fear or interrupt. The danger has passed. I will keep the chamber closed for now.*

"Controller, we sensed your distress. Are you sure you're well? Can we not see you?" A woman's urgent voice called out.

I haven't the strength to open the chamber. Allow me to rest and regain my composure.

"Is the assailant known to you, Controller?"

Yes. Known and neutralized. Now, leave me. And do not spy into this room. I forbid it when I am in this state.

The voices did not respond and Tridia assumed the Guardians left.

"Assailant? Known and neutralized?" she hissed. "That doesn't sound very promising for when you do open the door.".

Perhaps, but I could hardly explain to them I had risked their existence to snag Tridia Odana from the ether and jarred the planet with an explosion in order to bring her incapacitated body to the center of the Warren. Somehow, I doubt those statements would have instilled confidence in my followers that I had not been compromised. Nor would it have placed you in any better position.

"You might have at least corrected them to say intruder, instead of an assailant," Tridia argued. Rock moved on the wall, covering the pipe and sealing the hole. "You don't expect them to obey?"

"They're concerned. It's best to take away the temptation."

Tridia pushed herself to her knees and removed her helmet. She looked around the chamber. It consisted of four soot-charred rock walls, a thick stone column in the center, and a stone pool of molten gold. Squatting atop the boiling metal was a golden image of herself.

"Why do you do that?" Tridia indicated the golden image.

"Mimic the person I'm speaking to?" the image asked.

"Yes. It's disconcerting."

"That would be why." The image smiled.

"Have you a name?"

"I've had many names throughout antiquity, in many languages. Controller suits me now."

"That's a presumptuous name." Tridia eased to her feet, until she stood at eye level with her golden doppelganger.

"It's accurate."

"You use the portal to view across space. Can you also view across time, seeing visions the way the Chesans did?"

"No." The Controller image stood and paced across the surface of the molten gold. "I don't possess true prescience. My visions were given to me long ago. To my knowledge, only the Chesans possess true prescience, and their visions are limited to the males' perspectives. Well, the male's perspective with a few exceptions noted in Chesan history. The King's lineage had the ability to see the future without the portal, but the other noble houses also possessed it to a much lesser degree."

"All noble males?" Tridia asked. "Then what's this enzyme that I have? I thought it created visions of the future."

"It does, but the enzyme is different," the Controller said. "The enzyme contains a partial helix that can create a weak vision when combined with male DNA. When combined with male *enzyme* that is a proper match, I understand it creates a vibrant vision that is much more potent."

"And an improper match?"

"Creates a repulsive bitter taste that neither party can stand." The Controller laughed. "Many races would give a great deal for that ability."

"Master Aren didn't have glands when we kissed," Tridia said. "If we kiss again, would it create the bitter taste?"

"That, or bind you together," the Controller said. "Is that a chance you're willing to take?"

"Not yet." Tridia thought for a moment. "If the genetics have to be right to create the Chaos Vision, then Master Aren's enzyme may not work. He's from a noble house, but not a direct descendant of the king's line. Could the prince see the Chaos Vision as a part of the king's prescience?"

"No, that vision is much too detailed." The Controller scowled and mumbled to itself as it paced. "It's all genetic encoding – father to son. Subsequent sons had everything but the prescient abilities, except for twins."

"Controller." Tridia tried to get the golden statue's attention. "Controller!"

"Yes, Commander," it said. "I hear you, but there is much more we should consider. I am rapidly losing focus. Drayden cannot conjure the vision alone. He requires a mate to do it."

"I need to know how close we are to this vision," Tridia explained. "Master Aren will kill me the next time he sees me, unless I can convince him the threat is diminished. If it is as bad as he claims, maybe I shouldn't resist. I saw the fleet."

"You saw an image." The Controller stopped pacing and knelt to Tridia's eye level. "An image is not a reality. You and he must resolve your conflicts. You'll need each other in the turbulent times ahead. This attempt to use the portal only deepened his distrust."

Tridia didn't look away. "He planned to kill me. The Sentinels saw it in his thoughts and warned me to escape. The prince contacted me. He said he's in danger. Something about the shields around his planet and the satellites malfunctioning. He asked me to contact him."

"Contact him, not drop on his head out of the sky. Your master ordered the Sentinels to watch you for the night. He wouldn't have attempted anything before morning. Had you waited, I could have helped you step through the portal without injury or damage. His orders were explicit and you've disobeyed him. You've broken an oath that had consequences attached, should anyone discover what you've done. Is the measure of your integrity only as far as the whim of your desires? Do you so easily change your allegiance? If so, you are more of a child than I expected, and possibly the danger he fears."

Tridia fumed in silence. She couldn't argue when the Controller simply regurgitated her own guilty thoughts. "My allegiance was given to Davik and Drayden first. And Master Aren didn't order *me* to stay in the house. He ordered the *Sentinels* to make sure that I did."

"Technicalities, and you know it! The two of us and the Guardians weren't the only ones injured by your actions. You pulled Prince Drayden and Davik Schie into that vortex of energy – likely because of their connections with you. Davik managed to escape on his own. Had Drayden been alone, he would quite probably be dead now."

Tridia staggered backwards until her pack bumped into the stone column. Their connections with her? Drayden had said something attacked his heart when she died. Had he felt the *deathstrike* that killed her? Davik had absorbed energy straight from her body. What had she done to them?

"Take some time to consider who you are, Commander Tridia Odana, and who you wish to become." The Controller's voice became weak. "I must rest."

The image melted into the molten gold. Tridia took a few wobbly steps around the room. Her legs gained strength as she moved. The blasting pain had diminished to throbbing aches and her mind began to clear. As her senses returned, she tentatively reached out for signs of life beyond the chamber. Thick rock surrounded most of it, but the section with the pipe was thinner than the others. Beyond that section, she sensed vague images and unclear thoughts of the type she'd received from the Guardians in the Public Hearing Room.

Not all of the sentries left when the Controller asked to be alone. At least they hadn't broken down the wall to get in. They couldn't have heard any of the conversation between herself and the Controller. That was the good news. The bad news was that the only possible exit from the chamber had a guard. With no place to stash her pack and weapons – unless she dumped them in the roiling golden lava, which didn't sound like a good idea, given the number of explosives she carried – she couldn't claim to have no malicious intent. She finally sat down on the floor facing the golden pool, her pack against the stone column.

A fresh wave of guilt flooded her thought. She'd almost killed Davik and Drayden with her drastic actions. But they had survived. Did they still need her?

She tilted her head back against the stone and studied the ceiling in the flickering golden light. Who was she, after all? A genetic heresy devised by rebellious scientists in direct violation of every edict in a dying race? Dr. Elenus was trying to answer that question with her DNA samples. An assassin with blood on her hands and murder in her heart? Even though the murder would be a mercy to Davik, she still intended to end his life if that's what it took to free him. That about summed it up. Could she be more than the sum of those parts?

Deeca wanted to hate her, but couldn't bring herself to do so wholeheartedly. The Sentinels had shown her respect and kindness. They'd helped her to escape, even though they could turn on her when the veil in her mind dissolved. What did they know that made them impervious to the fear that so possessed Master Aren and Empress Dojene? Robel loved her and championed her without question. Even Sonei saw something in her to compel loyalty. Davik loved her. Drayden trusted her. Why? How could they all perceive an inner good so completely hidden from her?

The Sentinels had also told her to decide who she wanted to become when the wall came down. She could never be what she wanted most: Innocent. She had enough memories to know guilt would trail her for the rest of her life, no matter what the Triad had ruled, and she'd have to live with that knowledge. What could she become with that weight on her heart?

She'd been told she came from the royal lineage of a race of cowards, who chose to die rather than fight and fail. Did she possess that type of weakness deep down? She held the destructive force of a queen's power. Dojene had claimed her as an heir to a throne not yet vacated – before she found out who Tridia *really* was. Becoming a queen, or an empress, wasn't out of the realm of possibility – if she survived Master Aren's plan to kill her. Child of Chaos, the one who could bring destruction to the galaxy. She had the skill set for that role – but no more desire for it than she had to become a queen. Davik and Drayden may not need her as much as she imagined. What if they *did* need her? What if the Chaos Vision no longer existed? What if it did?

The visions Winniel had shared with her in Master Aren's office on Aga warned of intense emotions toward both young men, love and caring, a brother and a mate. They would be lost to her, then recovered.

Winniel had shared four visions that day. Two had already come to pass. The third would happen there in the Controller's chamber. Tridia shivered. The terrible insanity flooding her mind in that brief vision made her stomach churn. A lot had to happen before she would see the fourth vision come to pass – a lot of bad things.

Tridia shivered. The suffocating thoughts disappeared, only to be replaced by the realization that the temperature in the room had risen to a stifling heat. She shed her pack, weapons, and jacket into a pile as far from the door and the vat as she could put them and added the helmet on top. Then she peeled out of her overshirt and tossed it onto the pile. Even the sleeveless undershirt felt too heavy to wear and she untucked it from the waist of her pants. Sweat poured from her body and a lightheaded feeling gripped her. She unfastened a canteen from her pack to replace her fluids before she passed out. It was hot to touch, but the water inside remained only tepid. She took a deep drink, returned the canteen to its clip on the pack and sat on the floor with her back to the wall, as far from the vat of molten gold as she could manage.

"A rescuer." Tridia laughed aloud and shook her head. "Of all the things for an assassin to become. Spending my time chasing across the galaxy to rescue men and women from foes of unknown origins. I wonder what the Supreme Commander would say about that?"

Tridia continued to chuckle at the thought, then coughed in the dry heat. She wiped sweat from her face, and her breathing became shallow. The heat intensified with each breath. A small splash of gold jumped from the pool. She used the wall to climb to her feet and saw the molten gold in the pool had risen to the rim. In less than an inch it would overflow.

Not good. She sent a mental call to the Controller, but got no response. The golden image did not reappear and no words from it penetrated her thoughts. Perhaps the Controller's energy was more depleted than it had realized. It had been rambling there for a minute. The entity seemed to have lost control of the molten metal, as well as its contact abilities. Tridia watched the metal boil and waited for an answer until she stumbled from dizziness. She wouldn't be able to endure the heat much longer. The sight of a small rivulet of gold seeping over the vat's rim spurred her into action.

She unclipped the canteen and drank most of the remaining hot water, then reclipped the container. She pulled on her shirt without fastening it and slipped her arms into the straps of the pack. The walls around the room were too thick to penetrate with the explosives she had with her. Her only hope lay in breaking through the thinner layer containing the pipe. She made quick work of setting the two charges in the area the pipe had pierced. She pulled the helmet onto her head and wheezed to get a breath in its confined heat. The blaster, when she reached for it, burned her hand. She wrapped her jacket around it to hold it. The molten gold had begun to puddle on the floor and she had to choose her steps with care to avoid burning holes in her boots, as she hurried to place the stone column between herself and the explosives. She flipped a switch on her weapon and set it to stun. Energy hummed into the blast chamber. There could be one or a dozen Guardians on the other side of the wall, but she couldn't afford to kill or even seriously injure any of them.

Whether or not she could escape would be a matter of great skill and great luck, but more depended on the latter. Colored spots appeared before her eyes. She was about to step out to see if the detonator had melted, when the blast wrapped around the column and knocked her from her feet.

CHAPTER NINETEEN

Two Guardians lay on the floor amid the rocky debris, but Tridia didn't stop to check if they were alive or dead. Heat poured from the open chamber and she wanted to put as much distance between it and her as she could before something else exploded. Halls stretched in three directions and she reached out with her senses to determine the best path. Sentries ran toward the chamber from all directions, but fewer came from her left, so she ran that way. Cool air flapped open her shirt as she ran, bringing relief to her burning skin. The sound of footsteps reached her as she neared another juncture. There were only four in the group, but even engaging four would cause enough noise and delay to have the others on top of her before she could escape. Her blaster, though primed, was still too hot to handle. She was about to drop her pack to engage in hand-to-hand combat when the stone wall on her right dissolved into an opening. She dove into the small door as the first soldiers rounded the corner and hurried past without noticing her. Tridia leaned against the wall and listened for more footsteps. They came at a run from two directions. She couldn't hide in the open closet, so she prepared for battle, dropping her pack and removing her helmet. Before the guardians reached her location, the opening reformed into solid rock, trapping her in the dark.

You've made good your escape from my chamber, Tridia, but you cannot make it to the surface without help. What I am about to do will seem traitorous to you, but you must trust me. It is the best way to insure your safety. The Controller's thoughts reached her strong and clear again.

After you tried baking me, why should I trust you? Tridia countered, feeling the walls in vain for another opening.

I was disengaged from the pool. I hadn't intended to be away so long.

"So now I'm just supposed to trust you and we're friends again?"

Tridia forgot herself and spoke aloud.

I never claimed you as a friend. As a matter of fact, you will be the cause of my destruction. That being the case, I should have little regret in doing this.

The wall shifted open to reveal a dozen or more Guardians with weapons trained on the small chamber where Tridia stood. She didn't bother lifting her weapon, but held it out and waited for the soldiers to make the next move. They moved with caution as they took her weapon and hauled her none too gently into the hallway.

"Well, well." One of the men stepped forward as he spoke. "Commander Tridia Odana, in the flesh. Where's your master now? And that outcast, Deeca Varin?"

Tridia returned his stare in silence. He snarled and backhanded her across the face. The blow might have knocked her to the ground, but Tridia rolled with it, diminishing most of its force. She recognized the man from the Public Hearing Room on Aga. Deeca had called him Gannon.

"You're brave when you face an outnumbered and disarmed opponent," she stated, not bothering to wipe the blood flowing from her cheek and lip. Gannon wore rings.

He drew his hand back to strike her again when two other Guardians caught his arm.

One of them spoke in a harsh whisper. "You hear the Controller ordering us to return her to the chamber unharmed. You continue this at your own risk."

Tridia heard nothing from the Controller. Whatever instructions it delivered were intended for the Guardians alone.

"Fine! Take her pack." Gannon shoved Tridia ahead of him.

A fourth Guardian retrieved her pack and helmet. Another shoved her again for good measure. No one else touched her and Tridia walked with shoulders back and chin up through the blasted chamber opening. The two sentries who'd been lying on the floor were propped against the wall, only stunned by the explosion. Many other Guardians were in the chamber, and from the looks of them, none were pleased she was still standing.

Several Guardians forced her to her knees before the boiling vat of gold. Any sign the metal had overflowed its vat had vanished.

"You have injured my sentries, weakened my being, and damaged my chamber, Tridia Odana of Odea." The voice was unfamiliar, as was the golden image standing upon the molten metal. "I've heard many tales of you from my operatives. None of them speak well of you. I held them at bay to allow the Tribunal to rule fairly. I tolerated your presence in my chamber while I recuperated, and this is how you repay my graciousness."

"Let us dispatch this murderous creature and rid the galaxy of one more pestilence!" Gannon demanded.

"You overstep your boundaries, Guardian." The voice reverberated in the chamber, its fury obvious. "I will deal with your rebellious behavior next. You will not presume to know my plans or take matters into your own hands ever again."

Gannon dropped to one knee, silent and still before the vat. The others followed suit.

"Now, Commander Odana, what are we to do with you? It's true, to dispatch you now would save worries on levels none but you and I understand. However, I believe I can make better use of your talents. Present her."

Three Guardians surrounded Tridia, one on either arm and one behind her. They shoved up her sleeves and forced her wrists over the rim of the vat. She jerked back once and managed to kick the man standing behind her, but two others stepped on her ankles to pin her in place. The two holding her arms tightened their already merciless grips, forcing her forearms over the boiling vat. The memory of the Sentinel's third vision rose in her mind as two thin streamers of gold wrapped around her wrists. Pain shot up her arms, forcing an unbidden scream from her lips. Beyond the pain in her arms, energy pounded into her brain, as though an entire planet of people had sudden access to her mind, suffocating her with thought.

She heard a familiar voice speak above the rest. *Bear up, Commander, your ordeal is almost over.*

Gasping for breath and fighting away tears, Tridia let her head fall between her outstretched arms. This was too much, after everything else that had happened. Consuming the consciousness of the entire Guardian force pushed her too far. Her mind was about to give in to the crush when she heard the voice again.

Brenden Aren also went through this ritual. He survived it, so shall you.

Tridia allowed only one sob to escape her lips then lifted her tear-streaked face to the Controller's image to find a perfect likeness of Deeca Varin. Some of the Guardians around her gasped.

"I make no mistakes in those I choose," the golden Deeca said. "You have a purpose in my plans that will be revealed only to you. As does this Guardian, who the rest of my force rejects."

The gold on her wrists had cooled, hardening into slender bracelets. Her Guardian wardens relaxed their grips, allowing her to sit back and brace her forearms against her thighs.

"You will now be able to hear my voice wherever you are. You will never be out of reach of my punishment."

Beside her Gannon cried out in agony. He fell face down on the floor with his arms stretched toward the vat.

"You have presumed upon your authority for the last time, Gannon. You and your squad took it upon yourselves to directly disobey my commands. You will be transported to our retraining facility."

Gannon screamed, writhing in pain. Other men in the chamber reacted the same way. Their agony echoed in Tridia's mind. Her golden bracelets throbbed, adding their pain to hers.

"I trust this example won't need to be repeated for any of you."

"No, Controller," Gannon panted through gasps of pain. His men mumbled the same.

"Any more rebellion from you, Gannon, and I will withdraw my presence from you forever." The golden image of Deeca faced Tridia. "And you, Commander Odana?"

"I need no examples," Tridia stated. Her glare garnered only a smirk on the statue's face.

"Then you shall be released, and you will go as I direct." The image looked from Tridia to one of the standing Guardians. "Return her provisions and her weapons. Take her to a small fighter, and escort her out of Guardian space. Any further assault on her will be dealt with swiftly."

"The unguent, Controller?" the Guardian on her left asked.

"No. Part of her lesson will be to deal with the pain on her own. Now go."

The Guardians hurried away, helping the wounded who couldn't walk on their own, including Gannon and his team.

Tridia clipped her helmet to her backpack, then shouldered the pack and her weapons, careful to avoid touching her wrists. She followed a tall Guardian out of the chamber and down the hall.

"Why do you allow that?" She asked the man.

"The punishment you mean?"

"Yes. The punishment, the megalomania. Apparently, that creature now has a hold on me in lieu of my death, but why do you and the others permit it?"

The man stopped and looked down at her. Tridia almost ran into him. "We studied and trained for the opportunity. Every Guardian knows what it means to wear these bands before we ever take them on. We give up normal lives and certain freedoms in order to join the force and serve the Alliance. Punishments are rare. You have experienced one of the worst in recent times. Gannon's rebellious attitudes have drawn him near this punishment for months now. He wasn't punished for striking you or speaking out in the chamber today. The Controller has been lenient with him for some time. He just crossed the line today. Personally, I agree it's time he was punished for his insolence and insubordination. Would the Hierarchy commanders have been less severe?"

"No," Tridia said.

The Hierarchy dealt with insolence and insubordination swiftly. Soldiers who would not respect the chain of command were useless and their punishments were painful, and on occasion, terminal. Perhaps the Controller wasn't the monster it appeared to be after all. The Guardian started walking again.

"What you call megalomania is to us a right to govern and lead. The Controller has given long life and health to everyone who's worn these bands. We're connected with the Controller, hearing its voice, but having free will to act. We are protectors, not conquerors. We have given allegiance to a democratic alliance of planets and we keep the peace in a large section of space. If the Controller was bent on ruling, it wouldn't have stopped with aiding the Guardians. It would have already taken over large segments of the population and placed operatives in ruling positions on key planets."

"How do you know it hasn't?" Tridia asked.

The man made no reply, but his shoulders straightened and she sensed his anger at her impudent question. It seemed fair enough to her. Brenden Aren wore the gold bands without anyone else knowing of them. Couldn't there be others?

There could be, and in fact there are, but they are not your concern. They do not do my bidding. Those selected few wear the bands only for communication. The Controller's voice had returned to the one she'd come to recognize – an echo of her own.

Can we be heard? Tridia asked.

No. I haven't revealed your thoughts to the Guardians, only your presence. I couldn't keep their thoughts from you.

I understand the ruse you've used to get me away from the planet, but was it necessary to link me with the entire Guardian Force?

The impact could not be minimized. Those in the room would have recognized a fake induction and known that we were up to something. They still doubt my recovery. I apologize for the pain, both mental and physical, but it couldn't be helped. My strength was returning too slowly to continue to protect you. The sentries had become anxious.

Keep your apologies. If Brenden Aren and Deeca Varin could stand the induction, so can I. Tridia refused further conversation with the Controller and concentrated on keeping her wrists from touching her sides – or anything else.

"What is the unguent I was denied?" She asked her escort.

"It is an ointment that seals the gold to the skin and relieves the pain. Without it, the bands may not stay linked and you will experience intense pain for hours."

"I suppose I should feel special." Tridia commented.

"You should feel gratitude you're alive. I've seen what the Controller does to those who enter the chamber uninvited. You managed to cause it damage. We all felt the energy drain, as though our lives were seeping away from us. As if a part of us was dying." The man's voice shook.

"I intended no harm to the Controller," she said. "I didn't set out to even be here."

"I'd like to know how you entered that sealed chamber."

"Well, you can take that up with the Controller. Just rest assured the event won't be repeated – by anyone."

After walking steadily upward for some time the two came to an elevator.

"This will take you to the hangar level. Someone will meet you at the door and take you to a ship."

"Thank you for your assistance," Tridia said.

"Don't thank me. Only the Controller's intervention kept you alive this day. Do you even remember Antoine DeVereaux?" The Guardian kept his back to her as he spoke.

Tridia stiffened at the name. She suddenly recalled everything about him. Antoine DeVereaux had been her first target. Everyone who met him was enamored of him. He was wealthy and powerful. His charm and elegance brought people clamoring to his door for favors of all kinds. Before she'd ended his life, she saw vile acts of torture and murder in the man's mind. He'd killed before and planned to kill again. She had set herself up to be his next victim, and he had cajoled her into a secure area, thinking she was a naïve eleven-year-old girl. She'd slit his throat and shoved her dagger through his heart for good measure. The warm smell of blood gushing from his wounds had nauseated her less than the filth in his mind. She'd terminated him with no qualms and would gladly do it again given the opportunity. It had taken her weeks to get over the visions he'd imprinted in her psyche.

"I remember him," she replied.

"I was his protector for six months before you killed him. I remember your face now. Of course, you were a child then, but I remember he met you in the museum and offered to help you get home. He was a gentleman and a philanthropist."

Tridia caught the Guardian's arm and pulled him around to face her. Her chest heaved and she clenched her fists. Her voice came out as a near-growl. "The man was scum. A vile murderer of thirteen young girls and boys. I was to be his fourteenth, and what he had planned for me disgusts me to this day. He whispered it all to me in his oily voice before I was able to reach my knife. Keep your vision of holiness to yourself. If

I'd had to die in exchange for ridding the universe of something that evil, I would've considered it a bargain."

The door of the elevator slid open and Tridia entered it shaking, keeping her back to the door so she didn't have to see the Guardian's stunned face. She'd placed enough doubt in his mind that he might actually do the research to lead him to the truth. On the other hand, he truly believed DeVereaux was a saint, and sainthood was hard to dispel.

Tridia had calmed by the time she reached the hangar level. As promised, another escort waited at the top of the elevator shaft. She was a woman about Tridia's height with short auburn hair who exuded a warrior's skill in her stance and the way she moved. She'd be a deadly adversary if it every came to battle. Tridia walked respectfully behind her as the woman hurried toward the end of the hangar where fighter craft waited in rows.

"This is your unit. We've been instructed to escort you away from the planet. Two fighters await you in orbit. They will pick you up in the outer atmosphere. Follow their instructions to the letter and you will leave safely. Deviate in the slightest and they will shoot you down. Are you clear on that?"

"Yes, ma'am," Tridia responded, locking eyes with the woman.

The other gave way first and signaled a crew to assist Tridia in preparing the craft for launch. They gave her a flight suit to wear over her fatigues, but she declined the offered helmet, preferring to use her own. It interfaced with the fighter's computers with a little modification. With the formalities completed, Tridia stored her gear beneath the seat and eased into the tight confines of the fighter. It took minimal instruction for her to understand the fighter's instruments.

Not so different from the Hierarchy fighters. Another chunk of her life fell into place. She was a pilot – and a good one. Lera had said she was, but she hadn't remembered it until that moment.

You will be trackable by the Kel Anec until the portal energy leaking from your body is depleted. You'll know when the last of the pain disappears. Until then, keep a close watch on your monitors.

How do you know so much about those aliens? Tridia asked.

The information was given to me long ago.

By a Chesan?

Too long ago to recall, Commander.

Tridia huffed at the Controller's evasive answer. She should be grateful for the information she'd picked up while it was recovering, since she'd probably never get another straight answer from it.

Her hands glowed pale blue as she slid them into a pair of flight gloves. A symptom of the energy drain? Was portal energy and Chesan energy the same thing? She raised her sleeve to examine the bracelets and saw they were surrounded by a deeper blue glow. Chesan healing power? The pain had diminished significantly without her notice.

She'd absorbed so much energy. If the pattern of her earlier contacts with the portal continued, the energy would drain away, but her body would weaken for a short time afterward. Then her mental powers would increase. Perhaps what drained away was only the excess energy – the amount her body couldn't store. The only sure thing was she'd be different again when the phase ended. She'd have to keep her mind focused to stay in control without Master Aren and the Sentinels to help her.

The Sentinels. She searched for Winniel's connection. A faint essence lingered at its familiar place in the edge of her consciousness. The connection had weakened, but it remained. Tridia sighed, whether from relief or exasperation, she wasn't sure. At least Winniel and Alanel were alive.

Minutes later, she cleared the atmosphere and two identical fighters joined her. They flew wingtip to wingtip until they were beyond the marker buoys that warned of Guardian space. They passed several other vessels, some of which flew too close for comfort, but true to their orders, the escorts saw her safely through.

"Commander Odana." One of the escorts contacted her through the communications channel. "If you attempt to reenter this space without prior authorization or invitation from the Controller, you will be destroyed without question. Have a nice flight, ma'am."

The escort turned back into Guardian space and Tridia flew alone into the vast star field. The Controller had given her the coordinates and her purpose was clear: Find and rescue Prince Drayden. If she got to the planet where he was exiled, what would she do about the weapons on the satellites? Master Aren and Drayden seemed to think they were sufficient to keep out anything – even the Child of Chaos. Deadly satellites and determined enemies aside, she wondered if she had what it would take to help the prince. He believed she did – but shouldn't she believe it, too?

CHAPTER TWENTY

The explosion of Tridia's departure brought three dozen people from nearby houses and cottages, armed and ready for battle. They'd been relieved to find no invasion force, but appalled to see the damage to the house and concerned over what had caused it. After the first few inquiries, people stopped asking questions. Brenden's mood bordered on maniacal as he bossed and bullied everyone in his path. His workers knew him well enough to stay out of his way in these fits of temper and the newcomers possessed enough survival instinct to do the same. Once everyone had been organized into groups for containing the worst of the damage to the house – shutting off the water, putting out fires, and clearing glass from well-traveled areas – Deeca approached Brenden. He stood in the side lawn flower garden, scanning for exterior damage.

"No one was injured," she said. "The structure appears to be stable."

"I should be grateful for small favors?" Brenden growled.

"You should be wondering what happened to your pet assassin," Deeca snapped back. She wiped at blood trickling from a cut on her cheek.

"I'm not going to chase around after her," Brenden replied, taking the cloth from Deeca's hand and wiping away blood she had missed. "There wasn't enough damage to have disintegrated her, and there aren't any body parts in the room to show she died in the explosion. She likely got out through a window before it happened. Maybe she was hoping for more damage to hide her exit."

"Hide her exit?" Deeca repeated. "Are we talking about the same girl who's obeyed every instruction you've given her since you made her your property? The same one who twisted out of my grip and fell into a chasm, not knowing what was at the bottom, just because you ordered her to do it? That girl?"

"Why are you defending her?" Brenden handed the cloth back to Deeca.

"Maybe because I blamed her for so long," Deeca said. "Maybe because there's no place she could hide on this planet that you and your people couldn't find her. Maybe because she feels responsible for Anza, and doesn't trust you to find her. Maybe because I'm concerned that one of your operatives has disappeared and I could be next. Maybe because the Controller drained power from me at the exact moment of that explosion. Do I need any other reasons?"

"She's alive somewhere," Brenden said. "The Sentinels would know if she wasn't, and they don't seem concerned. They're following Robel around like attentive students with an old master. Besides, the Commander is Hierarchy trained with some of the best survival skills they can teach."

"The blue energy that absorbed into her after the feeder disappeared, could it have somehow erupted, taking her into a void?"

Brenden barked a laugh. "I couldn't be that lucky!"

"You went through a lot to get her here to be this disinterested in her absence."

"Are we really going to continue to argue about this?" Brenden placed his fists on his hips and faced Deeca. "I *am* concerned about her, but I believe she's alive and well or the Sentinels would know. There is nothing I can do to find her – unless you have a suggestion – but I can try to make sure my home doesn't burn to the ground or fall over from the damage. Can we take one step at a time here?"

Deeca held up her hands. "Fine. Deal with your house – even though you've got a crew who can do that for you."

Brenden huffed and turned away. Deeca followed him.

How could he pretend to be concerned when he believed Tridia had used the Controller's power to get her to the Chesan prince? Her body was phasing when he broke their mental contact on the ship. She'd been barely corporeal when he entered her cabin. Could she have followed thought energy to make the final jump? On Cystia just before the blue energy entered her body, she had appeared momentarily insubstantial. It was as if the energy had stabilized her form when it absorbed back into her body. Deeca may have come closer to the mark than she realized. If Tridia had unintentionally caused this much damage to his home, she was a real danger, to herself and everyone around her. An entire planet could be next.

Her disappearance had set them both up for other problems, as well. Whatever he had contemplated doing to her aside, she had compromised her vow in a grand way and if anyone found out what she'd done, he couldn't prevent them from taking her back to Odea.

Her return to the Hierarchy was unthinkable for several reasons, not the least of which were Tama and B'Nay. They both had reasons for entering her White Level Challenge, and both would be waiting should she return without him. He had to make sure no one found out about her disobedience. None of his new recruits had witnessed anything. Most were on the other side of the planet, and he was certain of the loyalty of the people around the house at present. The kitchen staff had informed him Tridia had taken food and water to her room. His inventory of the armory revealed someone had taken weapons, explosives, and other gear for combat and survival. She had left prepared, wherever she'd gone. The Hierarchy had indeed trained her well.

"All finished, Brenden." His chief foreman, face smudged with soot, wiped his hands on an old cloth, which usually hung from his hip pocket.

"Thanks Tal. Everyone OK?" Brenden asked. The groups, some of them wet, all of them weary, gathered in the yard outside the kitchen.

"No problems."

"Brenden, we haven't seen young Tridia." One of the women came forward as she spoke. "That was the room we made up for her, with all the things you shipped from Aga and Odea. Is she injured?"

"No, Moira," he replied. "At least I don't think she is. She tried a transportation experiment that really should have waited for morning. I expect she managed to transport herself somewhere else on the planet. We'll search for her after the chores are done and the shipments readied tomorrow."

Moira persisted, "If the room is in that kind of shape –"

"Then she deserves to be wherever she landed," Brenden snapped. "I refuse to coddle the girl or to have any of you wasting your energy after her failed attempts. She's headstrong and reckless – a very dangerous combination for the type of activities she frequents. Now, please, go home and rest while you can. We'll all be busy tomorrow. I'll send messages around the planet to tell everyone to be on the lookout and to let me know when she turns up."

Brenden's charade as an angry guardian convinced them to trust him. It almost fooled him. He'd send out the messages for good measure, but held no hope she would be found. He turned to go to the hangar and almost collided with Deeca.

"You felt the Controller, too, didn't you?" Deeca asked, when everyone else had moved out of earshot.

"Yes," Brenden responded.

"Does she have bands, as well?"

"No," he replied. "At least not yet."

"Meaning?" Deeca waited for his explanation.

"If the Controller had a hand in this, he sent her to one of two places. The Warren or to the prince." Brenden said. "If she's in the Warren, we'll never reach her – and she's probably as good as dead. If she's with the prince, then they've performed two miracles. They snatched her from under the shields here on Hulac, and breached the prince's defenses."

Damn the girl! How many enemies had she alerted with the energy she'd expended? Their only saving grace was that the shields were up when it happened. They would have dampened the energy flare.

"Brenden." Deeca called his name to get his attention.

He sensed her frustration and prepared for the tirade he expected to follow. It didn't come. When Deeca spoke again her voice held a gentle quality he'd heard on very few occasions.

"I can't read your mind. You have to speak to me." She placed a hand on his arm. "Who – or what – exactly is that girl? If she survived that explosion, and the Controller came to her rescue, then she has some connection with the Guardians. But there was never a warning she was one of theirs when Gannon's group was trying to kill her."

"She isn't allied with the Guardians," Brenden let his shoulders drop. "Nor is she against them. She has her own agenda and now we have to get off this planet as quickly as we can."

"I'll get my ship ready." Deeca stated without further questions.

"And I'll get mine." Brenden moved toward the path leading to his hangars. Deeca fell in beside him.

"Do you think this ruse will work?" she asked. "Sending out our own ships and taking another way off the planet seems weak."

"We can only try it and hope," Brenden replied. "A lot will depend on the kind of tracking device they're using. If they were homing on the mica disk, we should get away free. If there is another signature, we may be in trouble."

They parted at the hangar without speaking. The *Star Seeker* sat in the open, no sign of the quarantine tent that had covered it the afternoon before. Tran had brought the *Cera Gale* from Aga and traded it for an unregistered fighter Brenden kept under wraps on Hulac. It was in the *Cera Gale* that he worked feverishly for the remainder of the short night. The sun broke the horizon as he walked down the ramp, his preparations completed. He used the communication base inside the hangar to call two of the workers from their duties, then went to meet Deeca.

He found her slumped against the landing gear of the *Star Seeker*, dozing in what appeared to be a fitful sleep. He sat beside her, unwilling to wake her until necessary. To his surprise, he sensed Robel and Sonei coming down the path from the house. He smiled when they came into view.

Robel swung a warming cylinder with two mugs as he ambled along. Sonei carried what looked like a bundle of clothes. The Sentinels trailed in their wake, Alanel carrying a tray of food, Winniel a pitcher of huttle juice and several glasses. Brenden touched Deeca's shoulder, then nodded in the group's direction when she opened her eyes. She smiled and stretched before standing.

"Thought you two would be here," Robel stated. "Where else would you be when the house is falling apart, but getting ready to leave again. You have to eat before you go, and the lady should have a shower and proper bandages on that cut."

Brenden looked at the old man with affection. Robel couldn't replace Tran, but he'd give the shape-shifter a good run for his job. They took the food and drink to a table inside the hangar, then Brenden directed Deeca to the shower. Sonei went along to help with the bandages.

"Although Winniel is quite the hand with first aid, as well. She fixed up several cut hands and feet during the glass cleanup. She'd have made a fine medic," the old man stated.

"Robel, Winniel is a Sentinel, the First Truthsayer of the Hariok clan. Sentinels do not become medics." Alanel's voice held only slight reproof.

"Only because you've decided not to. Your race could do much more than you've allowed yourselves. Just from the little I've seen of the two of you, that's apparent." Robel spoke as though he was not addressing one of the most feared beings in the galaxy. "Help me spread this cloth, please. We'll never get the table clean enough to eat from."

Brenden hid a smile as Alanel and Winniel complied with every request Robel made. The Sentinels' minds remained unreadable, and their expressions gave nothing away, but their deference to Robel told Brenden they respected the old man if nothing else. The pair of them had the table covered and the food laid out before Deeca and Sonei returned.

Deeca had pulled her hair back in the same manner as Winniel's. The cut on her cheek remained unbandaged, but had already healed to a pale red scar. It would be gone within the hour.

Brenden silently requested Robel to keep the conversation away from his plans during the meal and Robel cheerfully launched into a detailed account of the damage to the house as they sat down. They kept up a discussion regarding the repairs until Deeca swallowed her last bite, at the same time a man and woman entered the hangar.

"Let me introduce Alexa Nuyovski and Jens H'Lenta." Brenden

indicated the petite blonde woman and a medium built blonde man. "They are two of the finest huttle tree workers on Hulac."

Each of them nodded in turn without speaking.

Brenden continued in a more serious tone. "In previous lives they were two of the most capable pilots in the Hierarchy Space Fleet."

"So, they'll take the ships into space," Deeca stated. "Anyone watching for us will be forced to follow them. Where?"

"I've programmed the *Cera Gale* with specific flight plans to take it circuitously from here to Aga space port."

"And my ship?"

"Alexa will fly it to the Guardian Warren." Brenden expected an argument against his plan and both Deeca and Robel delivered.

"Brenden, you can't send her to the Guardians in my ship. They'd blast her to molecules," Deeca argued.

"I won't stand for this, grandson," Robel chimed in. "Alexa came to you in good faith. I was the one who sent her to you."

Brenden waved them to silence. "Alexa will be flying under diplomatic protection. She is a registered courier for the Alliance, and the *Star Seeker* is officially on Alliance business. She just won't broadcast the information until or unless she comes under scrutiny."

"They will know she isn't me from light years away." Deeca's voice implied hidden meaning.

"Yes, they will know, but there is nothing they can do about it. There is a message contained in a diplomatic pouch to be opened by the chief administrator of the warren. For his eyes only. They will have to take her to the planet or hold her at the boundary until they receive authentication on the pouch."

"Which can only come from you or your man Mr. Tang," Deeca added.

"Right."

"You will be…"

In answer, Brenden looked back at his imposters. "What were your duties to consist of for the next few days?"

Jens spoke up. "Alexa and I were to accompany the first shipment of fruit to Badani, then on to its final distribution points on the Alliance border, near the Starling system."

Brenden watched as understanding lessened Deeca's scowl.

"We're going after Princess Anza."

"That was your original commission, wasn't it?"

"Can you fly a ship as large as the *Star Seeker?*" Deeca asked Alexa. "Are you familiar with the Stellar Morph's capabilities?"

"Only the theories and principles behind the design," Alexa said. "I've flown Stellar Hawks and Eagle Cruisers. The *Star Seeker* is in the same class. Unless the controls are radically different, I shouldn't have any difficulties."

"Satisfied?" Brenden asked.

"They're still in danger. We can't send them – "

"With respect," Alexa interrupted Deeca's argument. "We're not just simple farmers. We've always known we could be called upon to walk into danger for Brenden. That is a part of our agreement to live and work here, under his protection."

"Protection?"

"We're all deserters," Jens stated. "We left the Hierarchy with Odean bounties on our heads and no place to run. Nobody leaves the Hierarchy unless they're dead or master-ranked assassins. Brenden arranged our deaths and gave us safe homes and honest employment. No questions asked. Just a promise to step up if called upon. Taking this risk is part of the bargain. He wouldn't ask unless the stakes were high."

Brenden's face remained stoic, but only with an effort. Knowing how people felt by listening in on their thoughts, and hearing them admit it were different things. "That should clarify everything. Let's go over the final details and get you ready for lift off."

He spent a few hurried minutes on instructions, which included ordering the Sentinels to return to Aga with H'Lenta.

"Ambassador Aren," Alanel said. "We are not yours to command. Our mission demands that we pursue Commander Odana."

"Yes, I'm aware of that," Brenden said. "There are no other ships immediately available and – unless you're holding out on me – you don't know where she is. If you return to Aga to get one of your own ships, no one would be the wiser. They come and go from Aga spaceport all of the time.

"This route you've prepared, does it by chance go near Permai Station?" Winniel asked.

"Not near, but in the general direction," Brenden replied.

"Alter the course to dock at Permai, and send someone with us who resembles the Commander, but who could not be mistaken up close. There are three Sentinel ships at Permai. We'll disembark at that station and take one of those ships. Whoever you send with us can hire transport back from there."

"I won't need to send a worker." Brenden turned to Sonei.

"Oh, no you don't," Sonei said. "I'm sticking with you and the Hunter there."

"She doesn't look anything like the Commander," Robel said. A frown bunched the wrinkles in his forehead together.

"But she can," Deeca said.

"You didn't sign me on to chase across the cosmos with the

Sentinels," Sonei argued. "That wasn't part of the bargain."

"You agreed to accept my orders," Brenden replied. "There was no condition on the content of those orders. Besides, you've been traveling with them for days."

"You will come with us," Alanel said. "The matter is settled."

"Since when did you get elected to make my decisions?" Sonei asked.

"Since time has run out," Winniel answered. "Go, Ambassador, the shape-shifter will accompany us."

"We'll meet up again, Sonei," Brenden said, grateful the Sentinels had saved him a lengthy argument with her. He handed Alexa a diplomatic pouch. "Besides, you stand a better shot at catching up with Commander Odana if you stick with them."

"Grandson," Robel said.

Brenden turned to see the old man fighting to compose his face.

"If you want me to take over the management of these orchards, we've got books to go over and decisions to make on the next season's crops. You'd best make sure you come back safely."

"Yes, Grandfather," Brenden smiled. "You'd best have the house in order when I return."

Robel made a few grumbling noises then started packing away the dishes, his back to Brenden and the others. Brenden sensed his worry and sent a private message to him.

I'll find her, Robel. I know she's alive. If it's possible, I'll bring her back to you.

See that you do, Brenden. She's still a girl in need of guidance. After this stunt, I'd say she needed more guidance than I suspected.

Brenden got into the hovercart Alexa and H'Lenta had brought. He sat beside Deeca with a grim expression on his face. She started to ask what was wrong, then thought better of it. As they left the hangar behind, he scanned the area, checking the workers, trees, and horses. Everything and everyone appeared healthy and harmonious. Those were the last perceptions he received before erecting the barricade around his mind.

The claustrophobia of being limited to human senses accompanied the complete energy block, as always, and Brenden marveled that Tridia had regained her composure so quickly her first time. *Of course, she'd be a prodigy.*

He steered the hovercart into the shipping center as the last crates were loaded into the tug. He and Deeca climbed into the little vessel's cramped passenger capsule just as the automatic doors closed for lift off. Energy field elevators lifted the craft's spherical body slowly, without disturbing the fragile huttle fruit. It floated smoothly through the open roof of the shipping center, and rose with imperceptible motion. Once in the upper atmosphere, it would dock with the hovering cargo ship, unload, and return to the surface to be decontaminated.

The cargo ship's bay doors opened to receive the bulbous vessel. As soon as the tug's feet were strapped to the bay floor, Brenden helped Deeca from the compartment and went in search of the ship's commander. They found him on the bridge preparing to leave orbit.

"The fruit watchers normally stay in the cabin next to the docking bay." The captain, a tall black man with a ready smile, chastened Brenden as he entered the bridge.

"As we've been instructed to do. However, this trip requires some special instructions from the Ambassador," Brenden replied.

"Then come into my quarters and deliver your message." The captain instructed one of his officers to prepare to leave orbit when the tug cleared the cargo bay, then he led Brenden and Deeca into a compact chamber off the bridge. He made sure the hatch sealed before speaking again.

"To what do I owe this privilege, Ambassador Aren?" he asked.

"Just a little incognito travel, Captain Caine. Your route takes you near Elrel station?"

The captain's eyebrows made a leap toward his hairline. "Elrel is a pretty rough piece of property, Ambassador. Are you sure that's where you want to go?"

"I'm sure. Drop us at Elrel with as much haste as we can survive. And I'd hate to see that stop entered in your log anywhere."

"Expecting pirates, or the lady's husband?" Caine flashed a wicked grin in Deeca's direction.

"Let's just say I wouldn't want to impugn a lady's reputation," Brenden laughed, slipping an arm around Deeca's shoulders.

"You might want to stay in this cabin, then. I've a few untried hands on this voyage, and I wouldn't want anyone getting the wrong ideas."

Caine left them in his quarters and returned to the bridge.

"Impugn a lady's reputation?" Deeca hissed the words.

Brenden removed his arm, smiling because he couldn't sense her anger. "Misdirection. Leave as many false trails as it takes. Especially now that we know he has new crewmen aboard."

"Kel Anec operatives?"

He sat down on the captain's bunk. "I'm making that assumption, since I have no facts to the contrary. We'd better try to catch some sleep while we can. Elrel is a hellhole and you'll need your wits about you just to make the next leg of our little jaunt."

"Then we're not going after Anza?" Deeca asked.

Brenden shook his head. "We are. First we've –"

A chasm opened in his mind, drawing him into a swirling mass of thought and image that held no explanation. His wrists burned around the thin gold bands. The sensation lasted only a moment, but it left him panting and sweating in its aftermath. Deeca had fallen to the floor, and in his effort to help her, he landed on the deck beside her.

"What the – What was that?" she panted, trying to cradle both forearms at once.

"The Controller," Brenden replied. "I think he's found a new initiate with a mind almost as powerful as his own."

Deeca frowned. "The assassin."

"I'd place a bet she's in the Warren, under guard, and in a lot of pain right now."

"Why would he initiate her?" Deeca leaned against the bunk to catch her breath.

"Suppose she just materialized in the Warren without announcement, maybe making an entrance to match her exit. What would the Guardians do?" Brenden asked.

"Arrest her. Put her under guard. Execute her."

"What one thing could the Controller do to guarantee her safety?"

Deeca shook her head. "He'd have to initiate her so he could control her actions, punish, or kill her if he had to. At least it would seem that way to the other Guardians. I don't remember sensing this when you were initiated."

"That's because I was initiated before you."

"Oh, right." Deeca's eyes took on a far-away look, trying to remember her own initiation. Brenden winced. Deeca would end up with a blinding flash of pain for her efforts. The Controller had wanted those memories blocked, and Brenden had no choice but to make sure she couldn't reach them.

He remembered his own induction, the excruciating pain, the disorientation, and the flood of emotions and thoughts from people he'd never seen. Tridia had been through so much mentally, how had she held up under that barrage? Judging from the whirlpool of consciousness he'd just been sucked into, she had the capacity to handle it. He just hoped she had the strength.

Tridia, can you hear me? He reached out with his mind, testing the Controller's link between them to see if he could make contact. With so much going on in her head he doubted she could distinguish between one voice and another yet – it had taken him days to get his senses back after his induction – but it was worth a try.

Exhausted and dazed, Brenden and Deeca dozed until the ship dropped out of hyperspace at Elrel Station. Captain Caine knocked on the cabin door before entering to announce their destination.

"You're on your own when you leave. None of this crew would venture onto that station without a promise of riches – which a fruit sitter has no business offering." Caine smiled. "You've placed yourself in a limiting disguise."

"Only for a short time," Brenden replied. "I'm protected by someone else on Elrel. We should be fine."

Caine eyed him curiously. "You wouldn't happen to be a familiar of the mysterious Morgan Jacks by any chance? Pirate, murderer, financier. The man everyone knows of, but nobody knows?"

Brenden flashed a deadly half-smile. "Making comments like that to the wrong people would be very bad for your longevity, Captain. Be careful who hears them. I doubt Mr. Jacks would be amused by the innuendo."

Caine docked his ship for no longer than it took for the airlock to open and close. Brenden and Deeca entered the station with as little fanfare as they could manage. Brenden spoke in hushed tones to the dockmaster. The man responded with a nod and pointed down a dim corridor, pocketing the generous payoff that had changed hands. They were on their own in Elrel Station.

CHAPTER TWENTY-ONE

Brenden took Deeca's arm and hurried down the corridor.

"Do not speak again until I tell you to," he whispered. "No matter what you see or hear or what you *think* you learn. Our lives are worth spittle here if they find out who you really are."

"You might have mentioned that sooner," Deeca whispered in reply.

"Silence!"

They ducked inside a small lounge lit by pale pastel sconces set on the walls. The lights flickered, making it difficult to distinguish the few patrons seated at the tables and booths. After a moment's pause Brenden spotted the person he wanted and ushered Deeca into the booth.

Across from them sat a chubby woman with slanted blood red eyes and pale blue skin. Her dark hair flowed from fountains of small ponytails all over her head. Her appearance was exotic and docile, but the creature only looked harmless. She never traveled alone and her bodyguards never took chances with the boss's safety. One false move and Brenden and Deeca would be dead before they hit the floor.

"Ahh," the creature purred. Her red eyes glowed in the dim light. When she spoke her words were clipped and succinct. "Morgan Jacks' lover. It has been some time since we've seen your pretty face on Elrel."

"Too long, Lolina." Brenden's voice gurgled when he spoke, giving the sense of water flowing between rocks.

Deeca stiffened beside him and he placed a restraining hand on her thigh. She wouldn't understand the strange language, but she would understand Lolina's response.

"You have an interesting companion with you. Is she a gift for me?" The red eyes glowed brighter as Lolina stared at Deeca.

"Not this time, precious one." He spoke in his normal voice. "She is cargo for someone who can pay much more than you. I just stopped by to say hello before I pick up my ship, and to ask the favor that you might have your operatives kill anyone who tries to follow us through this way. The usual fees apply of course."

Lolina responded with an unnerving laugh and a coarse black tongue licked her lips. "She does not like our arrangements, Beautiful. See how she glares! Perhaps she is too pure for my tastes, after all."

"No doubt." Brenden practically dragged Deeca from the booth as he stood up. "I may send you her sister to play with if you are nice. We shall look forward to your report."

Lolina smiled and nodded, releasing one more wicked laugh as the two of them left the room.

"Don't speak," Brenden whispered in his own voice when Deeca drew an angry breath.

The tension left her arm where he held it, and Brenden loosened his grip. His eyes darted back and forth, and he glanced over his shoulder more than once. The first time he'd used the full energy block had been on Elrel station, just to shut out the endless string of depravity and despair going on in its close confines. He'd used it every time since. It helped his concentration but left him blind to the dangers lurking around them.

They made their way through the maze of corridors, avoiding the noisier sections, until they reached a storage hangar. Brenden entered a code into the locking pad. A small blast of cold air greeted them as the hangar seals opened.

Lights flooded the bay, illuminating a personal cruiser, smaller than the *Cera Gale* and *Star Seeker*, but large enough to accommodate several people. Black with gold trim, the ship sported its registration numbers along with a name in script, *Elisia*. As soon as they were inside, Brenden worked the controls to close the entrance behind them.

"You must pay a pretty tidy sum for storing this inside." Arms crossed, Deeca walked the length of the ship. "I'm not familiar with this design. Oh, I'm sorry, you didn't give me permission to speak."

"Nor should you until we're inside the ship," Brenden replied. He stepped under the *Elisia* and reached up to enter another complex code on the belly of the ship. The boarding ramp lowered. As he started up, he called over his shoulder. "Let's get the preflights done and get off this station. Elrel isn't a place to linger if you have no ongoing business."

Deeca followed him. "What did you mean by the usual fees applying?"

"Lolina and her thugs have watched my back on numerous occasions. I pay for the service. It's that simple."

"You hire people killed?" Deeca asked.

Brenden turned to look into her eyes. "The short answer is yes, Deeca. There are many people who want me dead for numerous reasons from petty to justified. I can't kill all of them myself, so others are hired. I don't contract on people I don't like. I don't seek out political enemies and mark them for death. The people who die are themselves killers, not innocents. I have no qualms about ending their lives."

Brenden continued into the ship and Deeca trailed behind him. They took seats in the close cockpit and started the preflight checks. She sat in silence, her movements stiff and angry.

"Elrel station is a dangerous pit. Everyone here is selling something – life, death, or any comfort or torture between the two. If you aren't participating in the economy, you aren't welcome – even if you're just passing through. All of my Alliance business isn't handled in the Public Hearing Room or at the embassy. Very little of my mission to discover the source of the silence can be done on the side of justice. Some of the more important negotiations are handled through Morgan Jacks or his representatives. His people do most of the dangerous investigations and reconnaissance. It takes a strong hand and a serious threat to accomplish the kind of work I do. Information must flow from somewhere, and it seldom flows without force."

The sound of the ramp raising filled the silence between them. Soft footfalls made their way toward the cockpit, but only Brenden heard them, Deeca was too consumed with her anger.

"She called you Morgan Jacks' lover!" Deeca spun her seat to look at him.

"Yes, she did." Brenden didn't look up from the console.

"Are you?" she asked.

Brenden laughed. "Not even if you twisted your mind into any contortion to make it true. No, I am not Morgan Jacks' lover."

"Then why does she think you are?"

"Because Morgan Jacks pays my fees, supplies my transport, watches my back. He's made personal appearances and threats on my behalf. I've been seen in his company and emerging from his personal craft and quarters." Brenden finished the instrument check. His eyes met Deeca's and he almost laughed again at the confusion he saw there. "What else is she supposed to think?"

"Why does he do those things for you if you aren't his lover?"

Brenden answered in the gurgling voice. Deeca scowled.

"He said, because *he* is Morgan Jacks."

Deeca jumped in her seat and turned to see who'd spoken. Brenden didn't bother to glance over his shoulder. He flipped switches, causing the hangar to purge its atmosphere with a noisy rush they heard inside the ship.

"You weren't supposed to translate."

"Ambassador, you're always so mean to the ladies. How will you ever get one of them to like you if you always tease them?" Tran asked.

"Deeca, this is Mr. Tran, Morgan Jacks' first lieutenant and our guardian angel of information," Brenden said. "Tran, this is Hunter Deeca Varin, formerly of the Guardian Force."

"It's a pleasure, beautiful lady," Tran said.

"Is he telling the truth?" Deeca demanded.

"Ask him," Brenden replied. "He's the only one who knows whether or not it was a pleasure."

"Cut the crap, Ambassador! Are you really Morgan Jacks?"

"Would you rather I be his lover?" Brenden asked.

Deeca started to say something then seemed to think better of it. She sat in silence as Brenden requested departure instructions from station control, then watched the monitors to be sure the wall behind the ship opened to reveal the outer ring of the station. The floor beneath the *Elisia* slid through the opening, exposing the ship to space. Brenden fired the engines and released the clamps holding the *Elisia* in place. It hovered above the floor as he entered another code to retract the flooring and shut the outer door. They floated outside as the door closed, facing the large number three painted there, until station control radioed final instructions. Brenden guided the ship through the spokes of the structure, past the outer ring and finally away from the station. A dozen ships were docking or leaving the station from one of the bi-level inner and outer rings or the cigar-like central hub. Brenden put sensor locks on them all before plotting his own course. Nothing seemed suspicious.

With their fuel reserves maxed out, it would have been simple to just take the ship into hyperspeed from dead still, but Brenden chose to wait his turn to sling around the small planet that allowed the station to hold its position in space. He slid the *Elisia* in line behind a mid-sized cargo vessel and in front of another personal cruiser trying to nudge its way ahead. The cargo vessel had just disappeared around the planet when something exploded behind them. Alarms sounded as the *Elisia's* defense shields absorbed the blast and debris. Deeca hit the sensors to display a holographic monitor of their rear view. The personal cruiser had disintegrated into shrapnel.

A screeching voice came over the communicator. "Vessel *Elisia*, are you damaged?"

Brenden replied in the gurgling voice, "Performing checks now." He paused until all panels showed clear. "We are undamaged, station control."

"Did you destroy the Starling vessel?"

Brenden and Deeca exchanged glances. They hadn't noticed the vessel bore Starling registration.

"Our weapons have not been fired, station control."

"That wasn't the question, Morgan Jacks," a new voice stated.

"Why, Station Commander, how nice of you to take an interest. I trust you weren't roused from your rest period." Brenden laughed.

"You think it's funny, plaything? Fess up, Jacks! How did you destroy that ship?"

A fourth voice, speaking words barely distinguishable from growls, interjected itself into the conversation. "Starling crew stole my cargo. They were not allowed to escape."

Silence engulfed the airwaves for the space of three heartbeats, then the station commander spoke. "Then you'd better be prepared to pay the cost of cleaning the area. You've contaminated the sling line with space debris and it will take the crews hours to clear it. All vessels behind the *Elisia* stand down and wait for clearance."

A riot of shouting ensued, some directed at the station commander, most directed at the growling voice that took credit for the mess.

"That's our clearance," Brenden said to Deeca.

He engaged the engines with enough speed to accelerate around the planet, adding its gravitational sling to the *Elisia*'s thrusters. The added boost quickly gave them enough speed to engage the hyperdrive engines. Not until the starfield settled into its standard view did Deeca make a sound.

"Did you have that vessel destroyed, Ambassador Aren?" she asked.

Brenden looked up, startled. "You've been with me since we left Hulac. I ordered no vessel destroyed."

"You had Lolina watch your back."

"Watching my back and blowing up ships in the sling line are hardly the same thing." He went back to his controls, not bothering to shield a transmitted message from Deeca's line of sight. Lolina sent word that Mr. Jacks wasn't responsible for the destroyed ship. The matter was personal between the two vessels and the charges would not be added to Mr. Jacks' bill.

"That was a Starling ship." Deeca's flat statement needed no explanation.

"The significance wasn't lost on me. Anza is on one of the Starling planets, the abductors gave us the coordinates. That doesn't mean I had the ship destroyed." Brenden said. "I had no reason. Anza wasn't taken by a Starling ship and she isn't being held by the Starling people. Besides, I don't act out of malice!"

"He doesn't, you know," Tran interjected. "He can be a real killjoy that way."

Brenden glared over his shoulder. "I could make an exception for you."

"Neither of you would tell me the truth if all our lives depended on it. I'm as gullible as an infant around you, Master Assassin. I don't know why I thought I could trust you."

Brenden bit back the words he wanted to say. They should be long past this distrust. "Lolina's influence extends as far as the outer ring of the station. Anything in the sling line is off limits to anyone with a shallow pocket. Even con artists and smugglers don't worry once they pass the outer ring. It costs a fortune to clean up debris in the sling line. Lolina doesn't have that kind of credit, and Morgan Jacks wouldn't subsidize it. She sent the message out of fear. The same reason the real culprit confessed when he heard Morgan Jacks being blamed. He'd rather spend his last credit and hock his ride than to cause that black-hearted pirate any inconvenience. Whether you trust me or not is your decision, but make it based on fact."

"All right. But that black-hearted pirate is you. Did he know that? Why did he call you Morgan Jacks?" Deeca asked. "You're supposed to be his lover."

"He was *talking* to Morgan Jacks. The man, himself, was seen entering the *Elisia's* hangar," Brenden explained.

"How do you know he was seen?" she asked.

"Because I made sure of it," Tran spoke in a husky voice reminiscent of sand paper.

This time Brenden glanced over his shoulder and grinned. Tran's face had transformed into a handsome, square-jawed man with an ugly scar running down his left cheek. His brown eyes had changed to golden-green and his hair had lightened to a soft brown color. Tran grinned as he continued.

"This was supposed to be a tryst with my seldom-seen lover and a new toy for us to play with."

Deeca's cheeks turned scarlet. "One more reference to me as a sex object and I will be forced to kill someone. You said *you* were Morgan Jacks."

Brenden managed to keep the laughter from his voice. "I am in reality. But when Jacks has to be seen, Tran puts in an appearance."

"I thought he was supposed to be your lieutenant," Deeca stated.

"I am." Tran's face has shifted back into its former shape.

"So, you take all the risks of the first and second tier villain?" This time she remained unfazed by Tran's change in appearance.

"What can I say?" Tran asked. "I'm a risk-taker and I love the spotlight. Consider this, who's more at risk, the big bad pirate man, his murderous lieutenant, or his Cawfici-speaking boy toy? Ghouls always strike at the weak link."

"And you would know?" Deeca bantered.

"From experience, dear lady." Tran laughed, then yawned. "From experience. I'm going to take a nap. You people have had me chasing all over the galaxy for days, saving your happy faces from marauders and attacking vessels. Hey, who was the gunner back at Cystia?"

"Commander Odana," Brenden said.

Tran whistled. "Remind me never to match targets with that kid. Although getting her alone in a dark alley again might be fun."

"Trust me," Brenden said. "you wouldn't like that either."

"You're probably right at that." Tran yawned and chuckled. He disappeared into the back of the ship, leaving Brenden alone with a fuming Deeca.

Brenden didn't make any attempt at conversation, but he released the energy block and lowered most of his mental barriers. Deeca's emotions were generally like shouts in his mind and he seldom dropped his protection completely around her. He expected her to be hostile now that she knew he was Morgan Jacks and he and Tran ran their dangerous gambit with impunity. As he lowered the blocks, and her emotions swept over him, they were confused more than angry, and tinged with a sadness he didn't understand.

With Tridia on the loose, the time for all secrets was drawing to a close. Brenden needed people around him he could trust. Deeca had to be one of them, so he'd revealed a lot of damaging information in the past day. *Could he trust her to watch his back, now that she knew the worst?* There was more to reveal, but only if she decided to stay on his side. The sadness he didn't understand in her emotions concerned him. Had he damaged her trust too badly?

His wrists tingled with the Controller's faint contact. The entity projected a somnolent presence he'd never felt from it before.

The child is under my protection now. She will fulfill her destiny.

"Did you hear that?" he asked Deeca.

"Hear what?" She responded with a glare.

"The Controller. Did you hear something from it?" Brenden demanded.

Deeca sat upright, pulling the bracers from her wrists and pulling up her sleeves, she touched the broad gold bands.

Brenden glanced over. He'd seen them before, but he was astonished to see the width of Deeca's bands. They were almost three times the width of any other Guardian's.

"No," she said. "I've been asking for information since the ship blew up, but I can't sense anything. What did you hear?"

"The Controller said Tridia is under its protection. It's probably nothing, but it seemed – I don't know – weary, tired. It made me drowsy just listening to it."

"Your contact with the Gold is supposed to be faint."

"It is," Brenden confessed. "But there are times when I hear it above anything else."

"Should we try to send a conventional message?" Deeca touched a sleek panel in front of her and an image of the communications console appeared.

"Neither of us has much standing with the Guardians, and if the Controller is weakened, this is probably not the time to intrude."

Deeca agreed, but that didn't dispel the uneasiness creeping between Brenden's shoulders. The Controller had Tridia under its protection, that much was understandable. It had helped her escape and it wanted her alive. The comment about fulfilling her destiny generated an eerie feeling. Tridia's destiny would either enslave or free the galaxy. If some miracle prevented him from killing her at their next meeting, he wanted her beside him when she made those all-important decisions. She was his responsibility, since he'd brought her back to life, and he had no intention of letting someone else guide her actions.

"What's your plan for finding Anza?" Deeca asked. Her tone was cold, but her emotions were still unsettled. "We are still going for the princess, aren't we?"

"Yes," Brenden said. "You saw the Starling system detailed on the star chart. It's an unusual set of terra-formed planets and moons in close orbit around a small sun. Most have some level of wide-use technology and all have valuable sustainable resources. The people are intelligent and progressive, which makes the system even more desirable as an addition to the Core Alliance. That's the geopolitical background."

"The mica-disk identified the planet where Anza's being held," Deeca said. "We don't need the history."

"We don't?" Brenden flashed a smug half-smile. "There's only one planet where she could be – and it isn't the one indicated on the star chart."

"How do you know that?" Deeca asked.

"Because of the history," Brenden said. "All of the planets – but one – have advanced spaceports and orbitals. Every ship on or off those planets is tracked and validated."

"So, there's one planet with no advanced communications or monitoring?" Deeca asked.

"There's one planet with enough agrarian land to shield the comings and goings of a group of small crafts," Brenden said.

"There are holes in your theory. If there's a base set in the pastureland somewhere, it would stand out like a blight on the crops."

"Not if their needs were met by the agrarian community at large. And, not if they're holed up in an abandoned first landing facility, which this planet just happens to have."

"How do you know so much about the Starling system?"

"It's my job," Brenden said. "The diplomatic corps asked me to act as negotiator, but I declined, already having my eye on a certain young assassin rising through the Hierarchy ranks. Anza was their next choice. I've never met her, oddly enough, though I've seen numerous pictures and recordings. She's brilliant, by all accounts. We've got to get her back. If the abductors figure out who they really have, their bargaining power shoots up."

"You mean she's something apart from a diplomat of royal standing, don't you?" Deeca asked. "She's Empress Dojene's daughter. She's one of the survivors of your lost race."

"Yes," Brenden said. Deeca wasn't a fool, she'd arrive at all of the right conclusions on her own. "If the abductors' goal is to revitalize that lost race, they'd have a good start with Anza's DNA. They'd need Prince Drayden to make the helix complete, but they can do some awful things with her alone."

"I've been thinking about your endangered prince," Deeca said. "He's been in exile for fifteen years. The Chesan race – the most advanced ever known – was wiped out fifteen years ago. They orchestrated their own genocide using the Hierarchy's resources. Is it possible *they* also orchestrated survivors? Or is there a different explanation to this drama?"

"The Chesans made plans for the survival of their race by hiding the last of their kind," Brenden admitted.

"Now someone is after those survivors?" Deeca asked. "That's why you weren't worried they would kill her in three days. They did threaten to kill her, though. That doesn't make sense."

"It does if their plan was to lure a Guardian into their trap, to enrich their coffers, then keep her regardless of whether their terms were met."

"What makes you think they plan to rejuvenate the Chesan race?"

Brenden glanced at Deeca, then back at the controls. "Information you don't have yet, and I'm not at liberty to share. Trust me, it's a sound assumption."

"I'll accept that." Deeca pulled down her sleeve and put the bracer in place. "So, if they have Anza, they can do damage. If they have Anza and the prince, the problems become exponentially greater."

She looked toward the back of the ship to see if Tran was anywhere near before she continued. "If they have Commander Odana?"

Brenden tensed.

"Don't tell me she's not mixed up in this," Deeca said. "I don't know how, but there's too much activity fluttering around her. You were going to leave her on Hulac and not bring her anywhere near their trap – or you were going to kill her there."

Deeca caught Brenden's stare and held it. "The Controller shifted her by two sectors for no apparent reason, unless he was protecting her from you. She would never have tried to escape or disobey on her own. For pity's sake, she dropped into a chasm because you told her to. Sonei said she stood there and let you hold a charging blaster under her chin. No doubt she could have disarmed you easily enough – at least made a fight of it. Now the Gold is sending you confidential messages about her. This isn't coincidental."

Brenden laughed without humor. "She is the pivotal piece in all of this. The abductors could likely achieve their goals with her alone – if they could find her."

CHAPTER TWENTY-TWO

Tridia set the coordinates the Controller sent and let the fighter's computer handle the navigation. She opened her mind and stretched her senses to their limits. Her sensory range had increased, but even as far as she could reach, she found no life. The gold at her wrists tingled and the fabric where her gloves met her sleeves glowed a dark blue. Chesan energy again. Was it healing her wrists as it had her eyes? Was it affecting her in other ways? For the moment it didn't matter. As long as it kept her alive to help Drayden and Davik, she'd trade anything for its protection.

For the first time since awakening from the *deathstrike*, Tridia was truly alone. Her connection with Winniel was so slight she had to reach for it, and it might as well not have existed. Behind the teal energy block, she'd been isolated, but that wasn't the same as being alone. With so much clear space around her, she had no one and nothing to disturb her. She sighed deeply.

The immensity of space engulfed her and the silence it provided after the crushing onslaught of the Guardian bonding healed her battered mind. Swirls of confusion peeled away. Her consciousness rid itself of the debris left by the many unfamiliar thoughts and emotions she'd encountered in the last few weeks. With the shedding of each level of extraneous thought she drew deeper into the isolation of space. In her own memories, she found one perfect white flower and concentrated on it. It had been in Robel's garden by the wilderness lake. It was her flower. She had planted it and waited for years to see it bloom. She sighed again and rested in the peace of the small ship's cocoon. The Controller had given her this solace. It had known what she needed.

"Thank you," she whispered. A tiny tingle in the gold at her wrists was the only response.

Tridia rested in silent meditation for hours with nothing smaller than the moons of passing planets touching her scanners or her thoughts. She stopped once at a Guardian space station to stretch her legs, and pulled the complete energy block around her for protection. Only direct commands from the Controller had gotten her onto the station, so the forbidding faces of the agents manning it were no surprise. She made a quick return to the fighter and continued her journey.

She dropped the energy block once she was far enough from the station to encounter no passing crafts. Her first directional jump lay just ahead. Standard procedure was to drop below hyperspeed, make the change, then resume speed – with a sling, if possible. Tridia remembered enough to know she had on occasion made directional changes with hyperspeed slings. It was a risky tactic if there were other ships in the area, but she sensed none and saw no reason to waste the time. She'd started a steep descent toward a small planet, expecting to pull out and into the sling, when her mind became disoriented and her stomach lurched.

A tingle in her wrists preceded a message from the Controller. *Grab hold of your pack and weapon.*

"No!" she screamed. But it was too late, mind and body parted.

CHAPTER TWENTY-THREE

The *Elisia's* speed increased by half as Brenden applied the thrust to near maximum. They'd already taken too much time. If Anza hadn't been able to shield her mind, she may already be compromised. If she *had* managed to shield her mind, every minute counted in reaching her. They were nearing the Starling system when Brenden's mind reeled again. Not as debilitating as the first time, but the drain on the Controller was undeniable. He glanced over to find Deeca slumped in her chair.

He called Tran to take control of the ship, then carried Deeca to the bunk the shape-shifter had vacated. He bathed her face with a damp cloth, then ran it over the back of his neck. The pulse at Deeca's throat beat strong beneath his fingers. Her eyes fluttered open and she stared at him in confusion.

"The Con- Con-," she stuttered to a halt.

"I know. It's done something to drain almost all of its energy. And that of many of the Guardians from the looks of you." Brenden touched his wrists. The gold bracelets had gone quiet and cold.

"Twice in a few days is a bit much, but three times?" Deeca tried to sit up, but lay back down and closed her eyes.

"Rest a while. I sensed Tridia in there this time. All of the energy focused on her. I'd wager the Controller moved her again."

"The Gold must be either insane or desperate. Why move her like this when there is a whole fleet of ships in the Warren?"

"Because a ship wouldn't get her where she needed to be fast enough," Brenden deduced. "*Where* it sent her is the troubling part."

"To the prince?" Deeca shuddered. "I'm not sure why that thought scares me."

"Because putting those two together is the equivalent of creating a bomb capable of destroying the galaxy."

Deeca narrowed her eyes. "Tell me you're exaggerating."

"I wish I could." Brenden returned to the cockpit, leaving Deeca alone to wrestle with her fears.

"Everything alright?" Tran asked.

"Not exactly," Brenden said. He took his seat and thought for a minute before saying more. "Remember the night we got drunk in that freighter we took from the dogs who'd left us for dead on the derelict?"

Tran cocked an eyebrow. "In a vague, alcohol-hazed kind of way, yeah, I remember."

"Before you got plastered, I told you there were things about me I couldn't tell you, and if you found out I might have to kill you?"

"That I remember." Tran perked up. "One doesn't usually forget a death threat made with that much sincerity. I take it the explanation involves one of those things?"

"Yes," Brenden said. "Several, in fact."

"Then say no more." Tran adjusted a control. "But speaking of killing people, are we going to have to get rid of your lady friend? I mean, former Guardian and all, she now knows what I thought was our biggest secret."

Brenden shook his head. "No, it won't be long before something else will make our petty secrets seem incidental. She can be trusted until that happens."

"I love it when you get all enigmatic and spooky," Tran taunted. "Do you do it just to give me a rush, or what?"

"Well, I have to do something to justify our tryst – lover."

Tran rolled his eyes and Brenden grinned.

"This business we're involved in now, it's apocalyptic, isn't it?" Tran asked. His voice held no hint of humor.

"What gave you that idea?" Brenden asked.

"Call it instinct. You've got intel you haven't shared, am I right?"

"Yes," Brenden admitted. "It's time you got up to speed."

He proceeded to tell Tran about the incidents on Cystia, the star chart and battle fleet, and Tridia's explosive exit to parts unknown.

"Quasar shots," Tran exclaimed when Brenden finished. "We're walking into a trap to retrieve a diplomatic princess who might have been taken by alien-controlled Hierarchy elites?"

"Succinctly put," Brenden said.

"What a stellar opportunity!" Tran exclaimed. "I've always wanted a reason to go after those inbred Hierarchy elites. Looks like I'll get my chance."

"You do realize I'm one of those Hierarchy elites?"

"Sure, but I forgave you long ago." Tran smiled.

"I'm not sure you grasp the full gravity of the situation, my friend," Brenden said. "But as long as you're fully versed and willing, I could use you guarding my back – as always."

Tran continued to smile in silence, his thoughts on how he might handle the inbred elite, while Brenden's thoughts turned to Tridia, and her being on the same planet with Prince Drayden. Neither of them was schooled in dealing with the situation he knew they'd face, and neither understood the damage they could do together.

As a boy, Drayden had been somber, innocent, and disciplined. His parents and tutors had trained him as well as they could for his exile and the boy had faced it with dignity, trying to hide his fear and sadness. But he had still been just a boy left alone with holographic tutors, condemned to grow to maturity without the touch of another human – or Chesan. Brenden's fingers moved to his lips of their own accord, and he thought of the simple kiss he'd shared with Tridia. The girl might be a hardcore assassin, but she was lovely to look at and Drayden had been alone for over fifteen years. He'd be a young man now, still a child by Chesan reckoning, but more than old enough to feel desire for a woman. Brenden recalled his own difficulty coping with those feelings, and he'd been around females all his life. Drayden didn't even have that foundation. If Tridia brought down the veil in her mind in Drayden's presence, what would she know? What could she tell him or force him to do? Would she find a way to hand him over to the Kel Anec?

Brenden had always believed the Chaos Vision *might* come true. But with everything that had happened, he now knew in the depth of his being it was a real possibility.

CHAPTER TWENTY-FOUR

Tridia started speaking before she could see clearly. "You've got to send me back to my body! My ship will crash into the planet."

Her vision sharpened on the golden image of herself standing before a large portal. There was a lot of activity in the rectangular field, but she spared no notice for it.

"There's no time. Drayden needs help now, and there's no one else to send."

"Send? How can you send me if my body is scattered across the face of a dead planet?"

"Prepare yourself, you'll have to deal with the pain as best you can."

Before she could form another word, her body left the cockpit and joined momentarily with her mind. A small part of her was cognizant of the Sling Fighter slamming into the planet's surface as she left it, holding tightly to the straps of her pack and blaster. She became a solid mass in the portal, all nerve endings and pain. Then the portal shimmered and she was thrown through the rectangular scene, tumbling from nothing into hot air and the irresistible pull of planetary gravity. She landed hard on sandy ground. Her pack and weapon made a thud as they landed inches away. The pain, when she felt it, caused her to curl into a fetal position, but her muscles functioned and she sensed solidity in her bones. This transfer hadn't taken the same toll as the first, but the pain crippled her all the same. She lay in a ball for a few seconds, thinking the screaming in her ears an echo of the pain in her body. It took a little longer to realize the sound came from outside her mind.

Sand flew around her and she cringed as another shriek assaulted her ears. Tridia slapped the side of her helmet as she rolled onto her back. Readings replaced the dark tint. Seven creatures were bunched to her right, but the readings showed a strange thing. Five of them were the size of human toddlers – and plant-based. Their readings showed the same as any other vegetation might have. The sixth was a humanoid male, tall and slender. Beyond them, something with twice the mass of one of Brenden's huge horses darted and snipped at them with large pincers.

With as much speed as she could muster, she rolled onto her knees and reached for the blaster, hoping two transfers through portals hadn't damaged its mechanisms. Relief flooded through her as the blast chamber hummed to life. She tapped the helmet again and the readings disappeared, leaving a dark gray tint. She stared at the sight before her. A creature with a flat, scaled body, two large pincers, and a barbed tail, advanced on the others. Five of the group had two arms, two legs, and a head, but the similarity to humans ended there. Their bodies were pale green and roughly textured. Instead of hair, leaves wreathed their heads. They each held long staffs that they used to parry the pincers' strikes. The humanoid male had long dark hair. He moved and parried against the pincers with the same type of staff the others held, but he seemed to be trying to draw the attacking creature away from them. When he turned to look over his shoulder, Tridia gasped.

"Prince Drayden," she whispered.

He couldn't have heard her, but the sight of her distracted him long enough to give the creature an opening. It swung its pincers, catching Drayden solidly across the back. His body flew to the side as the barbed tail slashed his back and shoulder. He landed motionless in the sand. The creature drew its tail back to strike again.

Drayden's pain and surprise slammed into Tridia's open mind, his final conscious thoughts of failure. He wanted to protect the others – the Rrabbas. In that instant, his battle became hers.

One of the Rrabbas scurried between Drayden and the monster. It snatched the little creature with its pincer, lifting it from the ground and shaking it. The Rrabbas snapped like a twig. Clear liquid drained from its body. The creature lapped at the liquid, disregarding everything else. Tridia shouldered the blaster and pulled the trigger. The blast dented the beast's scales and ricocheted off without bringing it down, but she had its attention. It tossed the corpse aside and moved straight toward her. Tridia planted her knees in the sand and held the trigger down. She was too weak to run fast enough to escape and only hoped to buy enough time for the Rrabbas to get away.

Blasts flew in all directions as most were deflected, but some chipped away at the creature's scales. It had advanced to striking distance when one of the blasts pierced its flesh. It raised its pincers and struck out with its tail in blind pain. The barb landed in the sand, narrowly missing Tridia's leg, but the tail slammed into her shoulder.

The impact sent her sprawling, and the blaster flew from her hand as she landed on her back. With no time to stand, she rolled in the sand to escape and ripped open her jacket pocket in search of a grenade. The tail raised, its barb poised for another strike, and it would have pinned her to the ground had a staff not deflected it enough to miss her.

The Rrabbas hadn't escaped. The stupid creatures had stayed to fight. Tridia's anger burned at the thought of Drayden's sacrifice being for nothing. Two of the Rrabbas parried the tail and pincers as the others tried to tug her away.

Tridia struggled in frustration. Finally, she shouted, "Let me go!"

Her voice came through a metallic voice modulator, shrill and alien to her ears. She hadn't meant to turn that on. The Rrabbas released her and she rolled to her knees with the primed grenade in her hand.

"Move," she shouted to the Rrabbas parrying the monster.

They dove to the side as Tridia tossed the grenade under the monster's body. Its bulk muffled the explosion, as sand flew through the air. The visor protected her face from the blinding spray. The creature screamed and thrashed in the sand, while the Rrabbas scrambled out of the way and ran toward Tridia, staffs in hand.

She pulled two more grenades from her pockets and set the detonators with her thumbs, holding the oval shapes for a heartbeat before tossing one on the monster's head, the other beneath its chin on the sand. The double explosion was enough. The monster fell flat. Its tail writhed for a moment longer, then it, too, stilled.

Tridia fell, trembling, to her knees. The monster's screams had silenced, but her ears still rang with its final pain, and with her own. She flinched as one of the Rrabbas placed a hand on her shoulder, Tridia looked into its enormous pale green eyes. They glittered with compassion.

Danger still.

She heard the words in her mind, and noticed with a start that the creature had no mouth.

"Danger where?" Tridia asked. The little Rrabbas helped her to her feet.

"Danger where?" She repeated, looking around for the first time. The sand gave way to scrub grass and weeds just a few feet away. Could the danger be in the grass?

Danger here. More skikes will come.

Tridia nodded. This wasn't the only monster in the area. She donned her pack and picked up the blaster without slowing as she waded through the loose sand toward the monster. A skike.

This way, the Rrabbas insisted.

Tridia ignored the instruction and gave wide birth to the carcass. As she rounded the mound of flesh and shell, she saw Drayden lying in the sand where he'd fallen. Two of the Rrabbas were looking down at him. Tridia broke into a run.

The Rrabbas wrung their hands in distress. The depth of their concern slammed into Tridia's unprotected mind, but she didn't try to block it. These creatures cared for him. They were probably the ones that had saved him when she'd dragged him from his body into the portal during her disintegration. Tridia's heart shriveled. After all that, had she come too late? The Rrabbas backed away as she knelt beside Drayden. She tapped the side of the helmet twice and readings appeared. He was alive! The prince had no internal injuries that could be picked up by the helmet's scanners. There were no broken bones. His heartbeat was strong and his breathing deep. His torn shirt revealed a deep gash across his back and shoulders that would need attention soon..

"He'll be alright," Tridia announced.

Tail venom. He is unmoving.

Venom. Drayden could be dying, and she had no time to tend his wound. She looked around again. She couldn't carry him in the sand, she could barely stand on her own.

"Carry these." Tridia tossed her pack and blaster at the Rabbas's feet as she grabbed Drayden's wrists. Two of the Rrabbas picked up Tridia's things as the other two knelt beside the remains of their fallen companion. They appeared to be doing something with the liquid seeping from its ripped torso. Tridia didn't look too closely.

When she got Drayden onto the grass, Tridia straightened and looked back toward the sand, changing the helmet to scan long range. All four of the Rrabbas scanned the horizon with her. A distant scream made them all shudder. Three shapes appeared on the monitor. Tridia hadn't had time to properly gauge the helmet's sensors, but if her estimation was correct, the new creatures were more than triple the size of the one dead in the sand.

CHAPTER TWENTY-FIVE

The dizziness and fatigue that followed the portal exposure set in once the adrenaline rush ended. Tridia shook her head to clear the cobwebs and for the first time felt the throbbing pain across her back and shoulder. It felt as though she'd been cut, but nothing had struck her in the battle. *More of the portal side effects.*

She shivered once before hauling Drayden onto her shoulders. The prince was slender, but solid. She couldn't carry him on her own for the whole distance – she'd be lucky to make it herself – but she could try to put some space between them and the monsters.

Come. The apparent leader of the group struck out toward a forest of huge trees – a quarter of a mile or more away.

Tridia followed as quickly as she dared. The grass provided better footing than the sand, but there was sand beneath and she had to take care with her steps. If she fell, there'd be no getting up. The two Rrabbas who'd attended their fallen companion broke away from the group. They ran at a right angle for some distance. Tridia stopped to observe them and the Rrabbas leader chided her.

Do not slow. Others will come. We must hurry to get Dray-den to safety.

The three of them continued without looking at the others. They were still two hundred yards from the tree line when the monsters from the desert reached the corpse. The echo of their screams bounced off the trees. Tridia turned to get a look at the creatures following them. Three monsters moved around the dead one. Their flat-shelled bodies bobbed up and they slapped at each other with their pincers. They were fighting over the remains of the dead Rrabbas. Something about the green creatures sent the monsters into a frenzy. She turned toward the trees and quickened her pace. If the skikes caught sight or smell of her party, the monsters would catch them before they reached the trees.

They hadn't covered half the remaining distance when all three monsters loosed blood-chilling screams. They'd been spotted.

"Run to the trees!" Tridia adjusted Drayden's weight on her shoulders as she issued the order. Her legs quivered with the strain. "The monsters are chasing you or your scent. Go on ahead. Maybe you can draw them away."

Dray-Den has our scent. We tried not to touch him, but he was gone in the desert. He carried Tayne when she could not keep pace.

Blast! That explained why the creatures were only standing over him wringing their hands. They'd already touched him to keep him alive after she'd almost killed him, and were afraid to do more harm by touching him again.

You also carry our scent. We cannot leave you. The other Rrabbas said. *Rrabbas do not leave friends to die if it can be helped.*

"Rrabbas." Tridia tried unsuccessfully to imitate their trill in pronouncing the word. She staggered on with panting breaths, trying to keep pace as her companions urged her on. "That's what your race is called."

Yes. We are friends and keepers to Dray-Den. He protects us and helps us with our breeding.

"Really?" Tridia panted. She wondered what particular breeding function required the warm-blooded prince.

The monsters screamed again – closer than before. They'd covered a lot of ground. Tridia increased her pace, but she'd never make the trees in time carrying Drayden, and she wouldn't leave him. Maybe the Rrabbas could drag him the rest of the way if she used more explosives and the blaster to draw the monsters away. She was about to suggest it when her companions stopped and turned.

It has worked. Come quickly. We will escape this time.

Tridia chanced one glance back to see all three monsters moving slowly across the grasslands, their heads to the ground as though grazing.

"What the..." She didn't wait for an explanation and turned back toward the trees.

Less than a hundred yards, she thought. *If those things keep chasing across the field, I can make a hundred yards.*

Ten yards from the tree line her knees buckled. With shaking arms she dropped Drayden on the ground and silently apologized for not being more gentle. The Rrabbas handed her the pack and blaster without comment. Tridia shouldered both, trying to catch her breath. Both creatures took one of Drayden's arms and waited.

"I don't think I can help," she managed to say. With stitches in both sides, her shoulders tensed to the breaking point, her back throbbing in pain, even standing again seemed beyond her. Two trips to the portal might not have damaged her weapons, but they had taken a toll on her body.

No need, the leader said, looking toward the trees.

Tridia looked up. The other two Rrabbas were running to meet them. They both took the prince's other arm and together the four of them dragged the unconscious man toward the trees. Tridia sat on her heels, gathering strength for the final dash, watching the Rrabbas struggling with their precious load. Two of them were much smaller than the other two. The ones who'd planted the decoy were smaller, more agile than the others. Juveniles? She shook her head. Females. Smaller and faster, and most likely more heavily scented. They'd taken the risk to give the others a chance to escape. No doubt they'd taken the liquid from their dead companion and spread it across the grassland to lure the beasts away.

Screams from the monsters jolted Tridia's exhausted mind. They'd made the tree line a half mile distant and stopped, screaming at the forest edge. The trees, giant hardwoods by the look of them, towered over the monsters and stopped their progress. Tridia jumped to her feet and ran. It wouldn't take long for them to catch wind or sight of her. She caught up with the Rrabbas and Drayden, grabbing one of the prince's wrists and urging them to move faster. The six of them gained the trees when the monsters were less than a hundred yards away. The Rrabbas stopped at a clearing inside the trees, but still in sight of the grassland.

"Keep moving," Tridia urged.

The leader shook his head. *We are safe, friend. The trees are poison to the skikes and too close together. They cannot pursue us here.*

Every instinct shouted at her to run, but she had no choice. She couldn't move the prince on her own and the Rrabbas refused to budge. Kneeling beside Drayden, she removed her gear, except for the helmet. At the last moment she decided to keep it in place and check his vital signs again. His heart rate had increased, his breathing had become quick and shallow, and his blood pressure elevated as she watched him. None of the readings reached a dangerous mark, but he seemed anxious in his slumber. A bad dream? She could understand why he might have one and suddenly dreaded the idea of sleeping herself.

Tridia removed the helmet and rolled Drayden onto his stomach as gently as she could, then tore open his shirt to examine his wound. Sand and grass mixed with blood and venom in the ugly red gash on his back and shoulders. Blisters had formed around the edges and in his flesh, and the whole thing seeped a vile yellow pus. If the venom didn't kill him, an infection probably would. Tridia ripped off her gloves and dug in her pack for the medical kit. She pulled on a pair of sterile gloves as she studied the names of the antibiotics on the hypospray packs. Since she and Drayden were supposed to be of the same race, the medicines should help and not kill him. She cleaned the wound as best she could, covered it with ointment to seal it, and used several small bandages to pull it together. Once Drayden awoke, she'd do a better job of wrapping it, but for the moment, the work she'd done would have to suffice. She injected him with antibiotic and left him lying on his stomach. She dusted the debris from his shirt and was going to pull it together over the wound when she noticed her hands glowing a pale blue through the thin gloves. Easing the gloves from her hands, she stared as small rivulets of energy drained from her fingertips into the wound. Her heart raced. Was she making things better or worse? The energy had lessened the pain in her wrists and healed her eyes, maybe it would counteract the venom. She let her palms rest flat on Drayden's back until the energy streams stopped.

The Rrabbas stood in watchful silence as she tended their friend. Their concern lessened with each move she made. When the energy stopped flowing, their concern evaporated as though Drayden had awoken and spoken to them.

Rest now, the Rrabbas leader said. *Night comes quickly. The skikes will only scream a while longer, then they will return to the desert.*

"You don't mind if I keep watch, anyway, do you?" Tridia asked. She pulled the helmet on again to check Drayden's vitals. The Rrabbas registered a cool blue color on her scanner.

If it eases your mind, do so. The night is very cold. The Rrabbas must bond for warmth. Dray-Den lost his pack in the desert. We have no way to warm him. You will bond with him?

Tridia blinked at their words, and suppressed a grin as she answered. "I will make sure he's warm."

Thank you, friend, one of the females said. She wrapped an arm around what must pass as the leader's waist. *May we call your name?*

"Call my...Oh, yes. My name is Tridia."

Trid-Ia. A gentle name for such a warrior.

Tridia smiled. "I guess it is."

I am called Vaile. My bond mate and leader is Layne. The leader inclined his head. *Our companions are Haylen and her bond mate, Wade.*

How is it you came to our aid? Haylen asked.

"The story would take longer than the night to tell. Perhaps we should wait for Drayden to be awake so everyone can hear it at once."

A wise decision, Trid-Ia. We will speak again when Dray-Den is awake. May the night pass pleasantly for you.

Tridia switched the visor from scan to vision. The Rrabbas walked in pairs to the bases of the nearest two giant trees. To her amazement, the males' skin ripped away from their bodies and the females stepped into their quivering embrace. The creatures intertwined their limbs and seemed to melt into each other as they pressed into trees. They became pale green blotches on the dark bark and Tridia found herself alone with the prince. His vitals were still elevated, but not critical according to the scanner. With nothing to do but wait for the medicines to take effect, she walked away and leaned against a tree, watching the skikes as they screamed at the tree line. How the Rrabbas could go comatose with that racket so near eluded her. The plant creatures' claim of safety remained sound, however, and the skikes left when dusk fell.

In the pink dusk, Tridia ventured to the edge of the trees and scanned the desert with the low-light setting on her helmet. The monsters had stopped at the baby's corpse, making guttural noises that carried all the way to the trees. The creatures were noisy cannibals, but at least they'd stopped screaming.

Satisfied the skike threat had passed, Tridia returned to the clearing. The temperature had dropped dramatically, as foretold. The Rrabbas remained attached to the trees, their blue readings steady on the helmet's face shield. But her heart dropped when she scanned Drayden. His vitals had spiked and his temperature was elevated. *So much for the energy healing.* His body heat drained away as he lay on the ground. Tridia spread her jacket across his back, then dug in her pack again for a thermal blanket. She draped it over him, as well. The fabric was thin, but it trapped heat keeping the person it covered warm in the coldest temperatures. That was good for the prince, but not so good for her. She walked a few steps away and sat with her back to a tree, wrapping her arms around her knees and drawing herself into the tightest ball she could manage. She wore a flight suit over her fatigues, but with no jacket and no blanket – and no idea how the local sentient plant life would react to her building a fire – she shivered in the cold night air, fighting a losing battle against exhaustion.

A vision of bitter cold and whiteness inserted itself into her thoughts as she drifted toward sleep. She was again asleep on the ice surrounded by white flowers. The same vision had appeared when Winniel taught her to block her energy. Was it an image of her final Challenge against Master Aren? Had she really fallen asleep on the ice?

In this vision, a dark-clad person approached, wearing a black helmet and draped in weapons of every sort. She again lifted her blaster in a glowing blue hand and fired. Again, the shot froze just inches beyond the weapon's nozzle. The dark-clad figure stopped and stared.

"No need to attack." It spoke in a metallic voice. "You can't destroy what you once were, no matter how much you fear it. You have a choice to make. Become me again or become the person you were meant to be."

The figure reached into a pocket and drew out a grenade, primed the detonator and waited.

Tridia awoke with a start as the grenade exploded in her dream. She looked around, startled to find no snow, but Drayden no longer lay as she'd left him. He'd risen to his hands and knees, his head hanging down and his arms shaking with the effort.

***

Drayden dreamed of a spectral gray-eyed girl with black hair. She called his name in a haunting voice and he tried to run to her, but he kept sinking into the sand. All the while monsters screamed and snipped at him from every direction. Tayne struggled beside him, her tinkling voice whispering into his thoughts.

She has come Dray-den. I can go with peace in my heart. She will complete you, my brother.

He called her name, but the more solid the girl became, the more ephemeral Tayne appeared. Then she was gone. Tears stung his eyes, his strength failed, and the sand pulled him down. How could he go on without Tayne's unfailing conviction to keep his hope alive? How could he reach the girl, who seemed no closer than when he'd turned to her? Just as he was about to go under a black-gloved hand took him by the arm. Someone wearing a black helmet with a darkened faceplate kept him from sinking further.

"Not yet, Drayden." A rattling metallic voice said. "You don't get to die yet."

Streams of blue energy poured from his savior's gloved hands and lifted him from the sand. Facing each other on solid ground, the stranger removed the helmet to reveal the same gray-eyed girl.

"I *am* the Child of Chaos," she said. Her voice held a commanding edge. "I am your greatest nightmare and your dearest hope. Stand firm in your hope, my King. My wrongs, past and future, will be a heavy burden to share. Both terror and bliss exist in my soul, but I am your only path to freedom. Fight for me – and make me fight, too – because I'm weary of the battle. Do whatever it takes to save me and together we'll save the galaxy."

The girl disappeared into a sparkle of blue energy, leaving him alone in the sand. A sudden chill wind blew through the desert. The sand became ice and snow. He lay face down, both burning and freezing. A blanket of white flowers covered him, pressing him into the ice.

Do whatever it takes to save me.

The words echoed in his thoughts as the black-clad figure with the helmet appeared again. It spoke in a hateful metallic voice. "You'll have to take her from me if you want her."

This was not his mate. This thing wanted his mate. He had to fight for her. He had to get to his feet.

Drayden opened his eyes a slit, expecting to see his adversary. Only the cold leaf-strewn ground met his blurry gaze. Prickles of pain skittered across his cold-numbed face. *What happened to the snow and flowers?* He pushed himself up with his arms and struggled to rise. He got only as far as his knees before the pain in his back forced a cry from his lips. He let his head fall forward as he struggled for the strength to stand. *He had to save her!*

His cheeks flamed and his eyes watered. His empty stomach growled and threatened to heave. The flaming pain in his throat hindered his breathing, but the unrelenting pain in his back and shoulders held him frozen in place. *Had the black-clad figure already attacked? Was his mate already lost?*

Drayden forced the confusion and panic from his mind. He couldn't fight in a fog. He'd been in the desert, but he was now among the leaves. The skike attacked and there had been someone behind him. And the Rrabbas... *The Rrabbas!*

"Tayne." He tried to shout, but the sound came out closer to a sob. He gasped with the effort.

"Stay down, Prince Drayden." A cold metallic voice called from his right side.

A hand touched his shoulder and Drayden recoiled. He fell to one hip and pulled a knife from his boot. The dark clad figure with the darkened helmet knelt before him.

"Put the knife down, Your Highness." It held its gloved hands before it in an appeasing gesture.

Drayden shook his head. He couldn't form the words. The hand holding the knife trembled. He had to stay strong.

Prince Drayden, please put down the knife.

"Stay away from me," he rasped, and scooted backwards, throwing off the blanket. *Where had that come from?*

"You're injured," the figure said. It didn't move. "If we struggle, it's only going to get worse. Please, put down the knife."

The figure lifted its hands and Drayden shoved the knife forward. Faster than he imagined possible, the thing gripped his wrist and twisted the hilt from his grasp, tossing it aside. Drayden lunged, forcing the figure to the ground on its back. It flicked its wrist once and a dagger flew into its hand. It pointed the blade at his throat.

"I am not here to harm you. Please back away."

His energy spent, Drayden crawled backwards, watching for an opening as the figure scooted backwards out of his reach. "What have you done with the Rrabbas?"

"The plant creatures?"

Drayden nodded.

The figure pointed the knife once over each of Drayden's shoulders. The prince risked a glance behind him. One pair of Rrabbas clung to a tree on his right. The others to his left. Drayden collapsed onto his left hip again.

"Tayne?"

"The other one died saving us. I couldn't react fast enough."

"She was near the end of her life. She wouldn't have left the birthing grounds." Drayden spoke more for himself than the figure in front of him.

"I didn't realize she was a female. She was very brave."

"Yes," Drayden whispered. Tears streamed down his cheeks. "And very wise."

The figure touched its throat and spoke again in a familiar female voice. "I apologize. I didn't realize I'd switched the voice modulator on again. No wonder you were so frightened."

The person removed her dark helmet and Drayden sat mesmerized. In the eerie light of a red full moon, he recognized the face in his dream – in a thousand dreams. She wore a soldier's attire, and a gun lay to one side against a sturdy pack. A long braid swung over one shoulder.

"It's you," he whispered. "All these years...All this time I thought you were just a figment of my imagination. But you're real."

"As real as you are," she replied.

Of all the things he thought he might say to her, all of the questions he wanted to ask, not a single one came to his mind. Drayden simply stared. Then his vision blurred and his jaw throbbed once. A sweet taste filled his mouth. He swallowed hard. "Not now."

***

Drayden crumpled to the ground. Tridia set aside the helmet and did a quick crawl to catch him before he could roll onto his back. His movements had opened the wound again. The little bandages weren't meant for that kind of exertion. Tridia removed her gloves again and pressed her hands against Drayden's face. The medscans had shown a raging fever and his skin was hot and dry to the touch. Nothing in her small medical kit could quench that blazing heat. Should she let him remain uncovered in the cold to try to bring the fever down, or cover him to force a sweat?

The decision was made for her when Drayden started to shiver uncontrollably. Muscle spasms? Chills? Tridia hooked the discarded blanket and jacket with her boot and pulled them to her. She managed to shake them out with Drayden leaning against her, but she couldn't just leave him on the ground again. There wasn't a tent in her pack, or anything else big enough to spread out for him. She had to use the blanket to cover him, so she did the only other thing she could think of.

Tridia covered Drayden with the blanket and jacket, then lay on the ground beside him and rolled him on top of her. His head rested on her shoulder. She entwined their legs so she could share as much heat as possible and adjusted the coverings to their best advantage. Careful to avoid the open wound on his back, she wrapped her arms around him and held him close.

"I didn't come all this way to let you die, Your Highness," Tridia whispered. "You have too much explaining to do."

Drayden's shivering stopped a few minutes later, and his breathing eased. Tridia started to sweat from his body heat. She touched the side of his face. Her hand glowed blue again. No energy drained from it, but she moved it to his back and held it there. His thoughts, not quite conscious, nor fully asleep, buffeted her mind to the point she had to put up a strong barrier to keep him out.

Drayden stirred in his sleep several times, but each time, Tridia tightened her arms around him, afraid he'd try to get up again.

"It's okay," she whispered. "I'm here. You're safe."

He'd calm down and rest again after she spoke. In the middle of the night he started sweating. Already damp with her own perspiration, Tridia got drenched as Drayden's body combatted the fever. He tried to throw off the blanket and the jacket once or twice, but she held them tight, knowing he'd be cold once the fever passed. In his final thrashing about, his hand caught her collar and he pulled against the fabric. The front of her flight suit ripped open as he struggled to tear away her clothes in his sleep. His fingernails dug into her neck and shoulder before she got her arms between them and tapped his cheeks.

"Drayden! Wake up!"

He stopped struggling and opened his eyes a slit.

"It's me, Drayden." Tridia pressed her palms against his cheeks. "I'm here. You're safe. The Rrabbas are safe. Please try to rest."

He collapsed again, his head resting in the curve of her neck, his breathing deep and warm against her skin. Her glands throbbed twice and she swallowed the sweetness without choking. This couldn't be happening now.

CHAPTER TWENTY-SIX

Tridia awoke to the same pale pinkish light in which she'd arrived the afternoon before. The moon was no longer above the clearing, but the sun hadn't started casting morning shadows. She'd moved her head to release the kinks in her neck and stretched her arms upward before she realized something was wrong. Drayden was gone. She sat up in alarm and spun to look for him.

He leaned against a tree at the farthest edge of the clearing. He shivered with his arms crossed across his chest, a haunted look in his eyes as he stared at her. She eased to her feet, retrieved the blanket, and took a few steps toward him. He tensed, but didn't run away, or try to fight. When she was only a few steps away, he spoke.

"Did I hurt you?" he asked.

"Hurt me?" Was he still delirious?

"Your neck and shoulder are scratched and your clothes are torn." Drayden pointed to her chest as he spoke. "Did I hurt you?"

Tridia sighed with relief. She touched her fingers to the scratches. "No, Your Highness, you were in no shape to hurt anyone but yourself. Please, let me look at the wound on your back and see if I can tend it better than I did last night."

"My back?" Drayden reached a hand over his shoulder and gave a small gasp as his fingers touched the edges of the cut.

"You were injured fighting that thing in the desert."

"The skike."

Tridia nodded. "That's what the Rrabbas called them."

"Them?" A confused look crossed his face.

"Three big ones came out of the desert before we made it to the trees. Tayne saved us in her death. Vaile and Haylen used her fluids to lead them across the grassland while Layne, Wade, and I got you to

239

safety. It was a close call." Tridia took another step and Drayden stood away from the tree. "I mean you no harm. You're shivering and your wound needs to be tended. Please, come and sit so I can look at it."

Drayden stepped toward her and Tridia reached out her hand to take his elbow. He flinched at first, then took a deep breath, and allowed her to lead him to her pack. She had him sit cross-legged on the ground while she adjusted the blanket across his chest and over his shoulders, leaving his back exposed. She pushed his dark hair over one shoulder. He never looked at her, and neither spoke as she retrieved the medkit. Tridia uncovered the wound.

"That's impossible," she said.

"What is it?" Drayden tried to look over his shoulder.

"This is much better than it was last night." Tridia said, touching its edges with her fingers.

The area was still red and open, but the blisters had disappeared and the seeping had all but stopped. She had Drayden lift his shirt over his head while she applied an antibiotic and a larger bandage which she held in place with a long wrap she wound over his shoulder and around his chest.

"I was sure the venom would keep you down and the wound open for days," Tridia commented as she helped him redress.

"Venom?" Drayden asked, pulling the blanket over his shoulders. "I was hit by the skike's stinger?"

Tridia nodded. "You dropped like a rock. The only reason you weren't impaled is because Tayne deflected the tail and I shot the creature to get its attention away from you."

"Tayne died protecting me."

"Tayne died protecting all of us," Tridia corrected, her voice stern. "Don't try to assume guilt and demean her sacrifice."

Drayden turned to look into Tridia's eyes.

"Last night, you said she'd reached the end of her life. She gave up her last hours or days and a quiet death, in exchange for a quick and painful exit that saved the ones she cared about. If what you said about her is true, she would have thought it a fair trade." Tridia's voice softened. "If you want to mourn her loss, do so. But don't you dare blemish her final act with your guilt."

Drayden's eyes dampened, but the tears didn't fall. "She knew you were coming. She said she could go in peace once you got here. Even connected to her telepathically, I never understood how she knew so much with such certainty."

Tridia smiled. "You lost a lot of fluid last night. Did you take water from the pack this morning?"

"No, I didn't want to presume."

Tridia laughed. "You called me here to help you and you didn't want to presume I'd come for that reason?"

Drayden smiled and Tridia's heart skipped a beat. It was Davik's smile when he was truly amused. The similarity hit her hard.

"Look, I don't want to be indiscreet," Drayden said, then blushed. "But when the Rrabbas wake up there is no privacy. If you need to, uh…"

"Good idea," Tridia stood, glad for an excuse to walk away. She stopped at the pack to retrieve a bottle of water and tossed it back to him.

She stretched, as she walked out of sight of the clearing – and Drayden – to relieve herself and remove the torn flight suit Drayden had stared at with guilty eyes. She rolled it up and carried it under her arm as she walked to the edge of the grassland and circled the camp to make sure nothing had encroached. In all the surrounding area, she sensed only Drayden and the Rrabbas. The only thing breaking the silence was a gentle wind blowing through the trees and rustling the leaves.

The prince was sitting cross-legged on the ground when she returned to the clearing. His stomach grumbled as she neared and he lowered his head, embarrassed.

"Me, too," she said, trying to ease his discomfort. "I have some food in the pack. It's been banged around, and teleported twice, but it should still be edible."

Drayden's face brightened. "I was afraid we'd have a long hike on empty stomachs. I lost my pack in the desert fighting the little skike."

Tridia pulled a container of huttle fruit juice from her pack and passed it to Drayden. "Drink sparingly. A little goes a long way."

"Fresh huttle juice," Drayden commented. "I haven't tasted this in years."

Tridia handed him some bread, cheese and another bottle of water, all of which he accepted gratefully.

"And I haven't had water this pure outside the bunker in some months." He lowered the bottle after drinking half of it, and then passed it back to Tridia. "Even the rainwater we catch is a bit tainted."

Tridia ate her own breakfast, drank the rest of the water, and sipped the huttle juice. The rejuvenation from the juice spread through her limbs.

"Where did you taste huttle juice before?" Tridia asked.

"An orchard behind the palace where I lived on Ceyon."

"Chesans grew huttle trees?"

"I thought we were the only ones who did," Drayden said. "Come to think of it, where did you get this?"

Tridia explained about the huttle fruit and where she'd gotten it. The look on his face when she mentioned Master Aren's name halted her words.

"You know Brenden Aren?" he asked.

Tridia nodded. "I haven't known him very long, but we have what you might call a strained relationship. I'd forgotten you'd met him."

"He was the last humanoid I saw when Father sent me away. We spent weeks together setting up my study chamber and storing the lesson programs. He taught me a lot of things I needed to know to survive should things start to fail. I'm grateful to him now. I've used everything he taught me. I've always hoped we'd meet again when I leave here. If I survive." Drayden's countenance became somber. His emotions clear in Tridia's mind.

"You shouldn't be doing that," he chided.

"Doing what?" Tridia asked.

"Entering my thoughts," Drayden replied. "That's a dangerous place to be right now. I think you did it last night, too."

"I can't help noticing what you're broadcasting. I'm not trying to get into your mind," Tridia responded.

"What do you mean, you're not trying?"

"I hear your thoughts and sense your emotions without trying to eavesdrop. I try to block those things out, but I can't always do it without throwing up a barrier." Tridia said. "It just started a few days ago. I haven't always been able to do this."

Drayden studied her face as if seeing her for the first time. "That kind of power isn't common. As a matter of fact, I've been told it's quite rare. I've only known one other mind to be so strong."

"Who?" Curiosity compelled the question from her.

"My father. The tutors say he was the strongest telepath for many generations of Chesan males." A deep sadness washed over the prince and straight into Tridia's heart as he spoke. "Both my parents have been gone for fifteen years."

"I suppose it's the same with mine. I don't recall ever knowing either of them," Tridia said. "The idea of parents isn't novel in the Hierarchy, but most soldiers don't know theirs – at least, not their fathers. I was barely two when they took me from Ceyon. Ten when I started seeing your face."

Drayden's face brightened. "You saw me, too? For all those years? I thought it was one way, a hallucination brought on by the pollen, until you asked my name."

"I don't understand." It was Tridia's turn to be confused. "I thought you contacted me through the portal."

"We have a lot to talk about," Drayden said. "The Rrabbas are stirring. We'd best get everything packed away and ready to start walking. Their time is short."

"Are you able to do this?" Tridia asked, taking the blanket and folding it.

"I feel better for the water and the huttle juice."

"We've got more of each, if you need it later. Just don't overdo it. That wound isn't completely healed yet."

Tridia asked no more questions. By the time the Rrabbas peeled away from the trees and each other, she'd shouldered her pack and weapon, ready to start out. The creatures greeted her as soon as they saw her.

Trid-Ia. Thank you for watching over our friend, Layne said.

Drayden's face brightened. "Tridia! I never even asked your name."

Tridia tensed for a moment, but Drayden would have no knowledge of the reputation her name carried. The Odean Blade, an assassin dripping in blood.

Haylen handed Drayden two pouches she had placed beside the tree the night before. *We kept these safe for you, brother.*

"Thank you, Little Sister." Drayden slid the straps over his uninjured shoulder.

Trid-Ia, we will hear the story of your coming later. We have no time now. Let us hurry, Dray-Den. Our pollens are heavy. Vaile put action to words as she led the way deeper into the forest.

They walked for the better part of the day without slowing. Tridia watched Drayden for signs of fatigue, just as he watched her. Neither was willing to call a halt for his or her own sake. The urgency of their mission kept conversation to a minimum, and Tridia was spared the need to explain her background or how she'd come to Zentel in time to rescue Drayden.

The forest changed from the dense old trees, to less dense newer trees. Smaller trees of the same type as the giants populated the next section. Small animals moved about on the ground and in the air. Tridia eased her barriers so she could make sure nothing threatened to impede their progress. Eventually the new forest gave way to open meadow. Green and blue grasses carpeted the clearing, giving off a minty scent. Tridia saw the open sky for the first time without her visor and she stopped in amazement. Seen in the patchy clearing and through her helmet, she hadn't appreciated the deep ruby red color. Skies of that color usually meant a storm or fatal gases in the atmosphere.

"The protective shield changed the atmosphere." Drayden turned back when she stopped. "I don't have the equipment to test what really happened or what kind of damage has been done. It's supposed to be protecting me. At least, that's what the main computer told me a few days ago. The sky wasn't this dark the last time I was out of the bunker. The shield had been running at thirty percent output. This looks more like fifty."

"There should have been some way to monitor you and reach you with aid," Tridia commented. She took the flask of huttle juice from her pocket, took a sip and handed it to Drayden. "It seems unthinkable to leave you under this thing without coming back to check on you."

"Our people were obsessed with keeping me safe," Drayden said. He returned the flask after taking a bigger sip than should have been healthy. "I'm surprised they didn't relocate the skikes if they were so concerned. Only halfway through my exile and I almost die – should be dead, in fact. Skike venom is a strong neurotoxin. From the size of this wound, it should have killed me in minutes. How am I still alive?"

Tridia explained how she'd cleaned the wound and injected him with antibiotics. She didn't mention the blue energy.

"That wouldn't have done it," Drayden said. "I'm not a doctor, but my physician program takes great pleasure in lecturing me. What else did you do?"

"Chesan blue energy," Tridia said. She might as well get the truth out. "Are you familiar with it?"

"It hasn't manifested since my great-grandmother's time," Drayden replied. "You can control it?"

"No," Tridia confessed. "It more or less leaks out of me when I need it. I have no control over it at all. I was being trained to harness it, but we ran out of time after the first basic lessons."

"I can't help you there. The blue energy only manifested in the women – and the ability to use it was supposed to have died with my mother."

Drayden's presence intensified in Tridia's consciousness. She strengthened her mental barriers to shut him out. He blinked.

"Now who's eavesdropping?" she asked.

"I apologize!" Drayden's face turned as scarlet as the sky. "I was warned this might happen."

Drayden swallowed hard and Tridia's eyes widened.

"Did you just secrete your enzyme?" she asked. Drayden turned away, and she instantly regretted the blunt question. "Forgive me, please. It's just – Aren't you too young?"

Drayden turned back to face her. "Yes."

Tridia studied his eyes. Those charcoal gray eyes she'd found so fascinating in their brief visions. They had a near-black ring around the irises. As she watched, the gray shifted to a dark blue, then back to gray. A sweet taste filled her mouth and she swallowed hard, nearly choking in surprise. Drayden's eyes focused on her lips and Tridia swallowed again. He glanced up at the sky and took a step away from her.

"By any chance, would you know how to manipulate orbiting satellites or hack high security programs?" he asked.

"I'd have to see your systems," Tridia said, grateful for the sudden change in topic. "I can't make any guarantees."

"You're serious?" Drayden's eyes returned to hers.

"Why wouldn't I be serious?" Tridia asked. "Didn't you call for help?"

"Well, yes, but I didn't expect that you could do those things yourself."

"Are the women in your culture not accomplished?"

"Very accomplished!" Drayden laughed. "I just never thought I could be so fortunate."

"We'd better get going or we'll lose the Rrabbas." Tridia put away the flask and pointed in the direction of the swiftly moving creatures.

Drayden led her across the meadow. They had to run to catch up to the four green creatures. Many small animals moved through the meadow's grass and Tridia caught sight of an antlered animal the size of the horses she'd seen on Hulac. The Rrabbas never slowed their march. If anything, Vaile quickened the pace.

The meadow evolved into forest again. This one contained smaller, younger trees of different varieties than the old growth. Their path became choked with waist-high bushes and weeds, but Layne took the lead and the ordinary plants seemed to bow out of their way. His communication tickled her senses, but it was so faint she couldn't understand it. She might have tried to listen, but Drayden admonished her to maintain a discreet distance from the Rrabbas' thoughts so as not to distract them at this crucial time.

Late in the afternoon Haylen stumbled. Wade helped her to her feet. Drayden offered to carry Haylen, but she waved him away.

It is not far now, Dray-Den, she said. Soon our children will be born.

"I know, my Sister. But you've come a long way. You'll need your strength for the birthing," the prince said.

They resumed their march at a run. Deep in the trees a wall of rock cut off the vegetation. Drayden, Layne, and Wade took a log to lever a stone wheel aside. As she watched them work, Tridia sensed pain coming from the female Rrabbas. She turned just in time to catch Vaile as she fell. The pale green creature weighed almost nothing in her arms.

They must hurry, Trid-Ia. We cannot bear our children here.

Tridia shouted, "Drayden, we're out of time. I don't know what's behind that rock, but it had better be the destination."

The wheel rolled clear revealing a sliver of a canyon in the rock wall. Layne and Wade picked up their respective mates and ran through the opening with them.

"Come on," Drayden said. "We've got to close the entrance."

They followed the Rrabbas through the opening to find another stone wheel and lever on the other side. They emerged into a tropical forest. Warm humidity made the air thick and heavy. An interlaced canopy far overhead kept the moisture from escaping. The rock wall contained it as far as Tridia could see. Sweat rolled down her face and neck as she and Drayden struggled to roll wheel across the opening to seal it. They both leaned against it when it fell into place.

A big smile spread across Drayden's face. "We made it."

He jumped upright and took Tridia's hand.

"Now what?" she asked.

"You can't miss this," he said.

Tridia followed Drayden into the misty trees, feeling more wilted as they went. When he stopped beside a muddy pool of water she immediately shed her pack, jacket, and overshirt. The Rrabbas stood in the shallows, transformed by their birthing ritual. The leaves on their heads had grown to form a cocoon around each couple. Flowers sprouted on vines from the smaller female sides of the cocoon, whereas stamen stretched from the vines on the male sides. Pollen dusted the air with a sweet scent as Tridia watched. She couldn't tear her gaze away. The flowers wrapped around the stems and their bases swelled with seed. One by one, each flower released its seed into the muddy water, where the new life sank into the fertile bottom soil to take root. Drayden caught several falling toward the ground and gently placed them in the silt.

Standing so close, Tridia couldn't help but inhale the pollen. At first, she was so engrossed in the birthing spectacle, she didn't notice the effect it produced in her own body. Her breathing became shallow and rapid. Her heart raced and her muscles tingled. As the last seed fell into the water, Tridia sensed Drayden.

CHAPTER TWENTY-SEVEN

The fact that Drayden was a prince, a survivor, or a Chesan, no longer registered in her brain. She sensed him only as a man. She backed away, her eyes wide. He was packing away vials he'd taken from the pouches Haylen had given him. When he finished, he returned the vials to the pouches, squared his shoulders and turned to face her. His irises had darkened to a deep charcoal gray barely distinguishable from their dark outer ring. He rose to his feet in a lithe, feline motion and watched her. She trembled under his gaze and slowed her backward motion. He matched her, step for slow step, until she backed into a tree. Drayden continued his advance; his intense charcoal eyes raked her body, the tank top clung to her torso, revealing every small curve.

The rough bark of the tree dented her flesh as she pressed her back against it, unable to escape Drayden's gaze. Emotions swelled inside her until they threatened to explode from her chest. With an effort, she forced her protective barriers down. She wanted to know what he was thinking, more than that, she *needed* to know. Drayden's sharp intake of breath sent a thrill up her tense spine. His eyes became ravenous, but his mind wrestled between need and restraint. She sensed only the emotions he allowed to spill over his protective barrier.

***

Drayden swished his hand in the muddy water to wash away the silt before taking the precious vials from their pouches. He caught enough pollen to half-fill each one, then put them safely away. Tridia's mental touch caught him by surprise and he intensified his mental barriers when hers faltered. The uncertainty and desire she felt swirled around his thoughts. Her need and awareness of him mingled with his own desire as he turned to watch her. She backed away, the first inkling of

247

fear in her heart. Her fear found its echo in him. He knew what she was – the Child of Chaos – and he knew all it meant. But he had seen what few others had not cared to notice in that vision and he clung to the knowledge with all his being. It carried him through the fear and to his feet.

Do whatever it takes to save me. The words may have come from a dream, but they resounded with truth in his heart. She needed him, and he pursued her.

Tridia's uncertain retreat had taken her beyond the spread of pollen, but it had already affected her. Her heart pounded, her breath came fast, and her hands trembled. Drayden wanted to run to her, but he forced himself to walk with slow deliberation. He didn't want her to bring up her defensive shields – not at this point. Her eyes had gone wide and questioning. He wished he had all of the answers, that he could tell her she belonged at his side with no uncertainty, but they'd take a huge chance if he continued his pursuit. He had no answers.

As she pressed her back against the tree, trying to escape, yet longing for his touch, the doubt fell away. She belonged with him – to him – and he knew this was the path he wanted. Tayne was right, he'd made the choice long ago, he just hadn't accepted it. Tridia had to make the same decision, and he needed to give her the chance.

Without warning, Tridia's final barrier fell. Drayden gasped. Though she probably had no idea what she'd just offered him, he couldn't contain the desire to take it. She shivered and he exerted every ounce of control he had to keep from pulling her into his arms. He couldn't take her without her knowing what it meant.

"Tridia." He exhaled her name and she inhaled his breath. His arms reached out, but he forced them up, placing his hands against the tree, feeling the unyielding bark beneath his flesh. It gave him the stability he needed to speak patiently. "You haven't been trained in this ritual. You don't understand what you've done by dropping your barriers."

"Tell me." Tridia whispered.

Drayden's body quivered at the sound of her voice. *Be patient.* He forced words out with a ragged breath.

"Opening your mind to me is an invitation to bonding. Chesans don't mate casually. There must first be a bonding of our minds – a full disclosure of ourselves to each other – and you must be willing. You're so young – we both are – and this is something that can't be undone. You have to be sure, because once it starts, we can't stop it. It's much more intimate than a physical mating. And it is forever. We will be mated in every way that matters. You've only known me for a night and a day. Part of it I was hallucinating. If we do this, you will know *me.*"

Tears fell from Tridia's lashes and Drayden's heart pounded with the desire to touch his lips to hers. *Wait.* The bark dug deeper into his palms. The pain allowed him to hold back. Tridia's entire body shook and his knees weakened. He didn't know how much longer he could hold his barriers in place.

"Drayden, I –" Tridia's words faltered. Tears fell. She tried again. "There's so much hidden in my mind. I've locked away most of my life. I can only guess what kind of horror is in the darkness. If you unleash it – if this is unstoppable – "

"Then whatever is in your memories will also be in mine," Drayden said. He kept his voice a whisper to keep from crying out in agony. "I'm willing to accept whatever you are."

"You don't understand!" Tridia sobbed, but she kept her eyes on his. "I'm an assassin, Drayden, a murderer. I've done terrible things in the name of the Odean Hierarchy, and I've locked them away. Do you honestly want that guilt in your mind forever?"

"It's your guilt to surrender, Tridia." Drayden stepped an inch closer, their bodies almost touched. "Mine to accept and forgive. Can't you hear the repentance in your voice?"

Wonder filled Tridia's thoughts. The hope and longing she felt penetrated his barriers.

"What you're offering to do. It's too much." Her voice trembled between sobs. "I don't – I can't – How do we bond our minds?"

Drayden's barriers threatened to fall of their own accord at Tridia's words, but he couldn't allow himself to overwhelm her. He needed all of the control he could muster. He pressed his hands harder against the bark and felt the skin break.

"I'll drop most of my barriers and you'll sense my thoughts, the full presence of my being – and I'll sense yours. Normally, I would press into your mind to absorb your essence, but you're so fragile right now, it'd be best if you took mine first, to strengthen you." Drayden waited. Tridia nodded. "Say your name in my mind, then catch a thought and follow it. Don't worry, I'll be here to catch you."

"Drayden I –"

Drayden's essence wrapped around Tridia's being. Caught up in a hurricane of barely-contained excitement, her presence felt small and timid. Drayden searched for her. She panicked when their minds touched and tried to raise her barriers, but Drayden's warmth reassured her until she reached out to him.

My name is Tridia Odana.

I am Drayden Anjenay. Come with me. Drayden brought up every memory he had of her, every thought, every imagining. He even brought up the embarrassment he'd felt with Tayne when he'd tried to hide his frivolous thoughts from her. Thinking of Tayne rekindled his sorrow at her loss, and Tridia offered him the comfort of her presence. He continued with memories of Tayne, her words of wisdom and how they'd grown close after the death of her mate.

Memories of the Rrabbas continued to pour forth from Drayden's thoughts. He held nothing back from Tridia of all the years he'd shared with them, all of the caring and dangers, the respect he'd grown to have for their simple lives. Every fearful encounter and near-miss with the skikes he relived for her. Tridia absorbed them and clung to Drayden's essence, willing to take everything he offered. When he exhausted his memories of the Rrabbas he hesitated before continuing with more personal things. He planned to go beyond what he needed, to secure what he wanted – an unbreakable bonding.

He spoke the words his father had explained in his recordings, "I trust you with all that I am."

He opened his mind to her then, everything he was came through. His education in the bunker, his training with the holographic images, the experiments he'd performed, and the isolation he'd felt. He let her hear the condemnation of the holograms and the threat to keep him inside the bunker. Tridia reached out to him and reassured him he wasn't alone any more. Her mind, warm and gentle, strengthened his resolve. He kept back only one memory, securely locked away where she'd neither sense it nor touch it, then he let the rest go.

Drayden took Tridia to his first memories on Ceyon, growing up in the palace with his father and mother, the strict regime of training he'd undergone with them both. He shared with her the love he'd felt from them. He divulged the few times he's gotten into mischief, running through the palace, into the servants' quarters, hiding in the pantry, being caught by one of the servant children.

That boy! Tridia exclaimed in his thoughts. *He looks –*

Like me, yes. Drayden laughed at the memory. *I wanted to take him to my parents but he wouldn't go and he made me promise not to tell anyone he'd been in the kitchen.*

There was a meeting with some blonde couples who showed no deference to him or his parents.

The Sentinels?

Yes. I don't remember much about meeting them. I think they blocked my understanding for some reason. I never mentioned it to my parents, so it was never explained.

They moved on to the meeting with the Hierarchy officer who would take him away from Ceyon to his new home.

Brenden Aren, Tridia said.

Drayden showed her the memories of Brenden's time with him and shared how much he respected the young Colonel who'd shown so much patience and kindness.

Drayden exposed everything he'd ever been or ever hoped to be, and Tridia took it all. She couldn't process it – there was too much at one time – but she accepted it without reservation. Drayden let her wander in his thoughts, a quiet presence in the midst of his being. He wanted to keep her there, safe and happy, but they were only half done. The hardest was yet to come. To complete the bonding, he had to have the same experience with her thoughts. He caught her essence in a gentle embrace and led her out of his memories into the physical world.

Drayden's palms still pressed against the tree, but Tridia had wrapped her arms around his waist, her cheek rested on his bandaged shoulder.

"You have to let me in now, Tridia," he whispered. Panic surged in her again and a barrier slammed into place.

"Your thoughts are so pure, so clean. I can't soil you with who I am." Tridia squeezed her arms tighter about his waist. "I can't."

"You can." Drayden peeled his hands from the tree and embraced Tridia with as much tenderness as he could manage, unmindful of his bleeding palms. "We can't stop this now. I have to be complete with you."

Tridia shook her head and Drayden kissed her temple. His fingers tucked under her chin and urged her to face him. She looked into his eyes.

"I need you, Tridia," he whispered. Her tears fell in torrents and he pressed his lips to her forehead.

"Forgive me, Drayden," Tridia whispered. The barrier blocking her mind collapsed.

"I forgive you, Tridia."

Then he was in her mind.

I am Drayden Anjenay.

And I am Tridia Odana. Come with me. Tridia repeated the ritual words and Drayden followed her thoughts.

Her memories of him were sparse, but intense. Holding him in her arms, worrying over his health, struggling to get him away from the skikes, watching him go down when the skike hit him. Drayden felt her anguish and her fury in the battle. She showed him the early vision they'd shared on the hospital ship, and her desperation to reach him. The depth of Tridia's emotions engulfed him, and Drayden felt shallow by comparison.

There are many more memories of me, Tridia, there must be.

They're behind a veil.

Show me. Drayden followed Tridia's thoughts to an immense darkness. He smiled. *You've locked me away for safekeeping. It's time to let me go.*

There's something else in there. Tridia thought of Winniel's memories, locked away inside of her own. Memories of Winniel and Alanel surfaced.

Sentinels? Drayden couldn't mask his surprise.

They're so much more than they seem. Harmoniously connected, fiercely protective – not just the killing machines and automatons everyone believes them to be. Tridia's memories of the Sentinels, and her respect for them, washed through Drayden's mind in waves.

You can see all of those things in the Sentinels, but you can't see them in yourself?

*I want to be those things. Noble, good, caring – it's just...*Tridia's thoughts returned to the veil.

Trust me, Tridia. We can do this together. It takes a highborn noble to erect this type of veil. And one of equal birth to break it. I am Drayden Anjenay, firstborn son of the last king of the Chesan people.

I am Tridia Odana, your servant. Tridia's thoughts hesitated as she gathered her courage and finished the response Drayden prompted. *I trust you with all that I am.*

The darkness surrounded Drayden's essence, isolating him from Tridia and from his own body. His first thought was to withdraw, but he held the panic in check and sent out quiet thoughts to her.

I remember the first time I saw you. You were so little. What were you? Ten years old?

Yes. Tridia responded.

I was fifteen at the time and it was my first experience with the pollen. I must have looked a sight.

An image formed in the darkness. Drayden saw his face at fifteen. The surprised look on his face reflected the shock he'd felt at seeing the little girl appear from nowhere.

What was happening when you saw me?

Tridia gave him a full-blown color memory of a sparring match. It had been an important bout against a supposedly superior opponent, but Tridia had been confident of victory. The opponent – a boy half-again her size and several years older – had backed off after she'd landed a solid kick to his chest. Her hands were up, ready to defend, and the boy kept his distance. Then Drayden's face appeared.

Drayden felt her surprise. Tridia thought she'd been transported or something equally bizarre. They had just stared at each other. When the vision ended, a fist flew into Tridia's face and darkness engulfed her.

He sucker-punched you while you were mesmerized! Drayden's initial indignity gave way to humor and he laughed.

Hey! It took me weeks to get over the teasing and get a rematch with that

Initiate. I had to beat him in order to get into the Challenge Grid. Tridia's indignant response only made Drayden laugh harder. She finally gave in and laughed, too. *He was crying by the end of our next match. The little weasel had boasted he was going to make me shine his boots afterward.*

Okay! Drayden got his laughter under control. *You were a mighty little warrior at ten years old. I know I wouldn't have wanted to face you in person back then. The vision was much safer. What about the next time you saw me?*

Tridia took him to another memory where she sat on a barracks bunk, studying, and his face appeared. This time not so disheveled as his first appearance, but puzzled all the same. Another thirty second glance at each other, then the memory returned to the barracks and Tridia's shock that the mental meeting had happened again.

I thought I'd imagined you the first time. When you came again I didn't know what to think.

That makes two of us. You grew up in a barracks?

Until I reached a rank that afforded me shared quarters, then a private room.

So where did I turn up next?

The question prompted a greater response than Drayden expected. Vision after vision of him with Tridia's circumstances at each time poured forth from her pent-up memories. They moved together through her life of solitude, training, and battle, in thirty-second snatches of memory. Drayden experienced acts of war and sights of brutality he'd never known existed in reality. The vision from his memory where she'd wiped blood from her face had happened in the midst of a bloody hand-to-hand combat. Tridia didn't screen him from anything she did or felt at those times. He sensed her anger at the interruptions, her fear they'd come at the wrong time, and later anticipation and anxiousness to see him again. Tridia revealed her longing to find him, to know more about him, and how that longing had dominated her life. She showed him her plans to escape the Hierarchy. Finally, she showed him the vision where he'd told her his name and pleaded for help as she crawled on hands and knees across her apartment floor. The last vision she showed him was after her death. An incorporeal shape with a golden image stared through a portal at a vision of him in the desert.

You actually died. The sudden anguish in the depth of his being renewed Drayden's desire to hold Tridia safe within his thoughts. He'd lost her and by some miracle she'd been restored to him. He let the warmth of his essence flow through her mind.

You're so warm. Every other touch in my mind has been so cold.

Her words brought up the memories of the Sentinel's frigid probes and Winniel's painful training. Drayden drew the core of Tridia's being into his protective warmth.

They shouldn't have done that. Anger tinged his words as he experienced the Sentinel's touch with her.

What they did was necessary. There was another who acted on his own accord.

Someone else touched your mind?

Touch isn't the word I'd use. The timidity in Tridia's words made anger flare in Drayden's essence.

Show me.

Drayden, the memory is here, but I don't want you to see. It's – It was –

An abomination and a capital offense. I want to know what happened, Tridia. You must show me who else has touched your mind.

Drayden's own memory of the young Colonel Aren flashed across Tridia's mind, followed by more recent memories of the same man taunting her mind after her Challenge combat. Drayden experienced the interrogation made at knifepoint by the lake, Tridia's passionless kisses with the businessman, Tran, and the threats and ridicule she'd endured in the darkened shed and through her computer. Then they stood in the Challenge Room on Odea and Brenden Aren claimed the Preempt Challenge – and Tridia accepted after hearing her options. Drayden's heart ached over what she'd gone through.

She transported him to Hielos. In the cold and ice she'd fired a gun and sprained her ankle, ice had cracked and she'd fallen, crushed and impaled by the frozen water, and Brenden Aren had stood over her. He heard her pleas for someone named Davik Schie and then he heard her beg the man to find and help Drayden Anjenay.

Drayden's anger crumbled and tears flowed down his face when he learned Tridia's final breath had been spent to beg for his safety. His arms crushed her to him and his shoulders shuddered from sobs he couldn't control.

Inside Tridia's mind Drayden fell into the mists with her, then came back to find Brenden Aren waiting like a predator ready to pounce. He watched helplessly as Tridia fought back against Brenden's superior strength and stamina while being hammered with the name Drayden Anjenay over and over. Brenden tore through Tridia's mind with a fierce abandon that paled any fury Drayden had ever known. Tridia's final act of pulling all thought of him into the darkness brought relief to both their minds. He could find no words to express his tumultuous emotions, and he fought to get them under control, because with their minds connected, what he felt, Tridia also felt.

When he gained control, Drayden found Tridia's shrunken essence nearby. He went to her again and draped warmth about her.

All my fault. Tridia whimpered.

No. Had I not found you with the pollen, had I not asked you for help, had my presence not spurred you into recklessness on my behalf –

Stop, Drayden! You can't take the blame for this.

No, Brenden Aren is to blame for this. Even though he ravaged your thoughts for my safety, his actions are unforgivable. No telepath has the right to do what he did. We will deal with him if the opportunity ever arises. Impotent anger does neither of us any good. Please let's continue away from here. He brought you back to life, but how did you get here?

Tridia raced through her memories of awakening on Odea, her oath to Master Aren, the kiss on the hospital ship, the prophetic vision, all of the events of the abduction. So much passed so quickly Drayden could barely take it in. He experienced Tridia as Nira Kayen, heard the empress explain the Chaos Vision to Tridia for the first time. He flew to Cystia and went into the mine.

Stop! Wait, what is that? Who was that? The man floating in the liquid had passed so quickly Drayden hadn't seen it clearly.

Davik Schie. He was my friend. He saved my life.

Tridia shared her darkened memories of the Kel Anec and their questions about the Chesans. Tridia scaled the wall again in her memory of gray, her hand slipped, she was engulfed in warm blue energy. Drayden heard Davik's declaration of love and felt Tridia's response. He fought back jealousy for this poor creature who could never have what he, Drayden, now possessed. Then he heard Davik extract Tridia's oath to set him free. Drayden lingered on the thought as other memories flew by, culminating with his final attempt to contact Tridia for help and the devastating transport that had drawn him into the void he now knew as the portal. He experienced the tidal wave of thought as the Guardian Controller branded Tridia's wrists with gold and links with millions of Guardian operatives touched her mind, then came the cleansing hours in space and the final painful transport that had brought her to him.

You've been through so much. How are you even standing? Drayden asked. *Davik Schie, he loves you.*

Yes.

He looks like me.

I thought he was you when we first met. It didn't take long to figure out he wasn't. Tridia showed him other memories of Davik, memories she had regained in the mine. Drayden watched them all, taking into his own mind the friendship Tridia had felt for Davik.

Davik fascinated Drayden, the man even moved with the same grace and dignity that had been pounded into him as a child and with every lesson he'd taken since. Drayden doubted Davik had gotten the same training on Odea. His grace had to be natural. Something seemed odd about the similarity.

Your memories are so vivid! Drayden forced himself from his detached reverie.

I could say the same about your memories. Tridia said. *The colors, the feelings, the correctness of it all.*

Drayden smiled. *Perhaps because we're experiencing new memories in each other's minds, they just seem more vivid. But there is so much you haven't shown me, Tridia. The things you wanted to hide from me.*

When she spoke again, Tridia's voice seemed tired. *I won't fight you anymore, Drayden. You need to know what I am – all that I am. Maybe it will sway you from this foolish path.*

Tridia opened the floodgate then. Memories of her early childhood in space with the trader and his wife hadn't been luxurious or torturous. The couple hadn't been cruel nor had they denied her any necessity. Neither had they shown her the love Drayden received from his parents. Then came her time with the Hierarchy, some of which he'd seen already, but she unleashed everything she'd held back. Finally, the missions came. Tridia's memories darkened, the colors faded to grays and blacks, and Drayden's heart pounded as Tridia stood in the clutches of DeVereaux on her first mission. The man's own memories exposed his guilt and his thoughts revealed what he'd planned for Tridia. The filth pounded against Drayden's morality and his stomach churned with revulsion. When Tridia's knife went into DeVereaux's heart, Drayden didn't flinch. He wanted his hand to hold the knife, to rid existence of such a fiend. Each mission had exposed Tridia to similar atrocities from the thoughts of every target she'd taken. After DeVereaux, she'd expected the onslaught of vile images, but it never got easier to take.

She met Deeca Varin on her last mission. Deeca had lost her fiancé and her brother after their encounter. While she was gone, Davik Schie had lost his freedom and his body because of his relationship with her.

You see? My life is full of corruption, my memories full of hateful things someone like you should never have seen.

Drayden's soul ached for the coldness he sensed in Tridia now that her memories had fully returned. He reached out his warmth again but she flinched away from it.

I don't deserve your warmth. Everyone who comes near me with any kind of friendship ends up dead or worse. You should have stayed away from me. Now you're tainted, too.

No. You didn't design their pain or make their choices. You didn't take the girl's life. Had you not been there, her killer would have gone free. So many murderers and rapists would still be stalking victims if not for you. These aren't good memories. The pain in your conscience is real, but they are only a part of who you are. I sense love and caring buried in your thoughts. Someone who hasn't been hurt and hasn't failed you. Someone who'd stand behind you even now. Who was it?

Somi. Drayden found hope in the respect Tridia bestowed on that word. It was the same way he used the word 'Father'.

An old man with smiling green eyes filled his vision. Every memory Tridia cherished about the old man flowed into Drayden's essence, and Tridia's warmth returned. She allowed him to embrace her again.

I never realized I loved him, Tridia said. *Not until a few days ago. When you compared him to your Father, I finally understood that love. I've respected him as my teacher, but he's also been my refuge for so many years.*

He loves you, as a father loves his child.

The bloom of a single white flower filled Tridia's mind and its sweet scent tantalized Drayden's thoughts.

Lovely. I saw this flower, and many like it, in my dreams last night. Drayden held Tridia close in mind and body. He knew he needed to leave, he'd long since had enough to complete their bonding and all he hoped to gain, but he couldn't bear to pull away from her until he restored her peace.

He whispered, *I have to leave.*

Yes. Tridia responded in peaceful acknowledgment.

Will you let me come again? Drayden waited.

Yes. Tridia's dreamlike response sent a thrill through his spirit. *When we fall in love, you can come again.*

Drayden pulled back slowly. Tridia's mind was so open he could have roamed it without her noticing, but he didn't. When his consciousness returned to his body, he found they still clung to each other, his lips pressed against her temple.

"Tridia." He whispered, but words seemed harsh after the intimacy of their mental bonding.

She lifted her head from his shoulder. Her eyes held a dreamy look to match her last words. Drayden touched her cheek with the back of his fingers and she leaned against them.

"All that you are, and all that I am, are now one within each of us." He pressed his lips against her forehead again. "Can you say those words – and mean them?"

"All that you are, and all that I am, are now one within each of us." Tridia kissed his cheek.

With an agonizing slowness, Drayden lowered his lips toward hers. After the lecture from his physician and the burning pain in his throat, he knew what was about to happen, what he was about to unleash. The one memory he'd kept from her, the one thing that would cement or destroy their bonding. Tridia tilted her head back and moistened her lips. Drayden hesitated staring into her eyes. She trusted him absolutely. He couldn't betray her. He pressed her head against his shoulder.

"Not yet." The words were strangled from his lips and he crushed her even tighter. "I am the firstborn son of King Aiden, last ruler of the

Chesan people. My glands have matured." Drayden pressed his lips against Tridia's forehead and fought for control. "You probably don't know what that means, but – "

"It means when we kiss, we will create a vision." Tridia tilted her head back again and Drayden looked into her eyes. "It means we will know if there is still horror ahead of us. I have to see it, Drayden. If I have to surrender my life to this madness, I need to know it's real."

"I won't let you surrender your life."

"Then let me see if the need even exists to contemplate it. Kiss me, Drayden," she whispered.

Drayden lost control. His lips covered hers. He kissed her with his mouth closed at first, then a sharp pain pierced the back of his jaw and a sweet taste washed over his tongue. With absolute abandon he opened his mouth on hers. She responded in kind. A matching sweet taste flowed from her glands and he savored the joined sweetness as his heart pounded and his hands knotted the fabric at the back of her shirt. He couldn't have backed away if he'd wanted to, but nothing could have compelled such desire in him. Tridia's nails dug into the flesh at his waist and he kissed her more fervently. There, in the beginning of their passion, chaos erupted.

CHAPTER TWENTY-EIGHT

The *Elisia* neared the Starling system's fourth planet with full sensors scanning for detection devices of any kind. Before they entered orbit, Brenden engaged the newly installed cloaking device. An expensive gift he'd purchased for himself before leaving Odea. Even the Hierarchy's latest scanners couldn't detect a ship with one of their cloaking devices operating.

"Is that going to help us?" Tran asked.

"We'll know it didn't if we get shot out of the sky," Brenden replied.

"You always say just the right thing."

The two of them remained silent as they studied the scanner readouts. The small planet, devoid of all but the most fundamental agricultural technology, was farthest from the moon that served as the system's sling planet. Its skies remained clear of all debris and most traffic. The ship's high-altitude scans returned clear skies over most of the planet, some light rain in the southern hemisphere and the equatorial zones, and no flying vessels over the extensive farmlands. Everything Brenden expected to find played across his sensor screens. A perfect hiding place.

Finding the abandoned landing facility proved a more difficult task than anticipated. While the old landing station building wasn't a common type, many of the isolated farms scattered across the open pasturelands had storage buildings that fit the general size requirements. When the *Elisia's* sensors finally picked up elevated energy readings from a squat, oversized building in a field of green crops, Brenden mapped a five-mile radius in all directions from it. Farm equipment didn't emit uridine signals. The elevated readings indicated something inside the building carried a lot of firepower.

In case that firepower was pointed in their direction, Brenden set a low altitude trajectory that had the *Elisia* skimming the crops, before setting the ship down more than three miles from the target, in a recently harvested area.

Tran handled the final landing and shutdown of all systems except the cloak, while Brenden moved to the rear of the ship to check on Deeca. She lay on the bunk with her eyes open.

"We're here," he told her.

"Smooth landing. I thought we were making a directional jump." She sat up and put her feet on the floor. "How long was I out? The trip should have taken the better part of a standard day."

"A few hours. The *Elisia* likes to go fast.

"Fast yes, but –"

Brenden held out a hand to help Deeca to her feet. "I've got to get changed. So, unless you want to test the last bastions of my modesty, you might want to go up front with Tran."

Deeca left in a hurry, but she smiled over her shoulder as she went.

The mapping had revealed bright green crops surrounding the facility to within fifteen feet on all sides, and they were tall enough to provide cover. Brenden changed into a green camouflage jumpsuit and pulled a matching hood over his head. He loaded his pack with as many explosives as it would hold, then shoved a camo blanket in and closed it up. By Tridia's account, the abductors' armor was too strong for small hand weapons, but he had just the thing to balance the odds. He dropped the wall on one side of the rear cabin to display a small arsenal of weapons, and removed one of the rifles. Sighting along the barrel he felt an old familiar twinge. Robel always told him it was his Chesan side squirming to the surface. The Chesan aversion to killing always reared its head before any mission, but it was usually silenced by the predatory Alurian nature he'd inherited from his mother. The body count amassed at his feet would impress a warmonger, but he'd felt every one as a ripple in his conscience. The tension mounting in his shoulders and stomach now seemed more like a wave than a ripple. Tridia felt the same revulsion every time she killed. Her mind had been fully open when he'd stalked her at the lake on Odea. She had stood on the rock ledge and questioned the cost of continuing her life as an assassin as opposed to pursuing the Challenge and committing murder for personal gain. The dying thoughts of her targets weighed heavily on her mind that night. He'd sensed the same tension in her that he now felt. Was his physiology already more Chesan than Alurian?

He slid a power pack into a backup weapon and fastened it across his pack, hoping not to get desperate enough to use it. He grabbed a second set of gear for Tran and stepped into the main cabin. Deeca met him there.

"There's still a lot of daylight left. You can't get into that facility on your own without cover fire." Deeca said. "And we're sitting in the open here."

"We can't wait for nightfall to move," Brenden replied. "From the uridine readings, their weaponry could vaporize us if they detect us before we get inside. We'll have to be smart and subtle – and in place long before we strike."

"You don't have a nice map to guide you this time."

"I didn't expect this to be easy." Brenden shouldered his pack.

"So, you're going in blind? And alone?"

"It's the only plan available," he responded. "Even supposing I'd consider letting you take the lead on this one, with the Controller draining everyone without warning, you'd be a liability, possibly a fatal one."

Deeca's posture stiffened as she prepared for an argument. He took her by the shoulders so she'd have to look at him when he spoke.

"Please. I need you on the ship. When I bring Anza out of that place, there's no telling what kind of shape she'll be in or who will be chasing us. If she's been compromised the way Dojene's bodyguard was, I may have to knock her senseless to get her out. I can't handle both of you if something happens with the Controller in the middle of all this. I'll signal when we're clear, but you've got to be ready to bring the ship immediately."

"What about the liability part?" she asked.

"I trust you to hold it together long enough to pull us out. You're welcome to pass out afterward." Brenden grinned.

"I'll be sitting here in a strange ship in the wide open spaces," Deeca said.

"We're sitting under a cloaking device." Tran walked into the cabin. "Nobody is going to find you unless they walk into the landing gear or you decide to take a stroll outside."

Brenden tossed him the extra camo and set the rest of his gear on the floor. Tran stepped behind Deeca and undressed to don his camo. Deeca kept her eyes on Brenden.

"You should be safe here," he said. "Sensors didn't register any ground scanners between here and the facility. Either they're keeping an extremely low profile, or they have other means of detecting unwanted guests. If they're just trying to stay under the radar, we shouldn't have to worry about early warning unless we let ourselves get seen. That's about our biggest break." He spoke to Tran over Deeca's shoulder. "We'll get as close as we can and take up positions before dark. If I can't make my way into the building within a half hour of full dark, cause a distraction. Just get me into the building, don't cause a stellar exhibition. Stay out of sight and stay alive."

Tran stepped around Deeca as he fastened his jumpsuit. He shouldered his pack. "See what I mean? Total killjoy." He winked and turned back to Brenden, all business. "And once you're inside?"

"Use your discretion," Brenden said. "If there's no ruckus, beat it back here like Lolina's thugs were chasing you."

"Now that's motivation," Tran said. "What if there *is* a ruckus?"

"Check the interior and go on instinct. Help if you can. Leave if you can't. It's the standard drill. If we're leaving on the run, we don't wait for each other. We come back and get even."

"I've heard that plan before," Tran said. "And been left before. And gotten even before. How come I never get to leave you to get even?"

"Because you're always too busy putting on a stellar exhibition."

"Oh, right." Tran grinned again and checked his weapon. "This is the new gear. I tested it on Odea before I bought it, but we don't know a lot about it. Should we chance it?"

"We don't have a choice," Brenden said.

"Then here's your crash course," Tran said. "The concussion wave broadens and increases in strength as it travels, but it will maintain integrity for less than three hundred yards. If you use it inside, be sure you have room around your target, or you could take out something – or someone – unintentionally. Be ready for the recoil and the drop in air pressure in the ear on your firing side."

Brenden clenched his jaw and nodded once.

Tran slung the rifle strap over his shoulder and gathered up a small medical kit. "Just in case."

"We'll need to leave our locators off until we call for pickup." Brenden slipped a thin black band onto his wrist.

Tran did likewise.

"I don't want to have to fly this thing home alone." Deeca followed the two men to the ramp.

"If you don't see or hear from us by midnight, leave," Brenden said. "No heroics out of you, either. Prep the ship at first contact, but keep the weapons primed. They aren't uridine powered, so their signature won't be as easily recognized."

Brenden preceded Tran down the ramp. Crisp, cool air bathed their faces and the sweet smell of healthy plants tickled their nostrils. While the *Elisia* sat in a cleared field, the ramp opened into a field with rows of matured green plants that stood tall enough he and Tran didn't need to crawl or walk slumped over. Brenden glanced over his shoulder as he entered the rows to be sure the ship remained invisible. Freshly harvested ground met his eyes, the *Elisia* nowhere in sight.

"We haven't tried anything with fewer contingency plans since we broke Cason out of prison on Ephis," Tran commented.

"You're complaining?" Brenden cocked an eyebrow.

"No way!" Tran replied. "Just commenting that it's been a while since we've had so much fun."

"You do realize you're insane, right?"

Tran chuckled. "Insane, shifter, they go hand-in-hand."

Based on Tridia's report that the Kel Anec were telepaths, Brenden planned to keep his energy block up until just before he entered the building. He needed the edge of knowing where everyone was inside, otherwise he'd leave it in place the whole time. Even so, he wouldn't drop his barriers for long. No sense leaving himself vulnerable.

He and Tran parted ways when they were more than a mile from the facility. The shapeshifter might be jovial when they weren't busy, but on missions he could be both cunning and ruthless. He'd kill without qualm, then patch up his comrades while setting their minds at rest. He'd said more than one grim-faced goodbye when his skills weren't up to the task, then soldiered on without complaint, his mind fixed on the objective. Brenden always marveled at Tran's unwavering loyalty, no matter what assignment he was given. He could no longer imagine going into danger without the shifter at his back.

Brenden came within sight of the facility before sunset. He stationed himself at an angle to the partially opened hangar doors and pulled out the blanket for additional cover. Three guards wearing the black armor patrolled the opening. As he watched, another three walked the perimeter. Half a dozen guards on the outside. How many more on the inside or roaming the fields?

Anza wouldn't be near the door, nor did he expect to find her near an outside wall or window. In their place, he'd keep her either in plain sight in the center of the building, or locked in some room well away from any exits. The former might be easier, at least he wouldn't have to carry on a running fire fight while trying to find her.

Darkness fell as he lay flat in the field, the soil holding the plants providing a small wall to conceal him. The guards hadn't varied their routine while he watched, but after dark the poor lighting on the exterior of the building made it difficult to see the targets in their dark armor. The exceptional vision of his Alurian eyes had always been as sharp in near dark as in bright light. Even in full darkness he had been able to distinguish shapes. The Chesan physiology changes had manifested at a bad time. The only guard he could get a clear shot at stood to the far right of the door, a couple of hundred yards away. Brenden squeezed the trigger. His weapon made only a quiet 'puff' sound as it kicked back against his shoulder, pulling him to the right. His ear popped from the pressure change around the weapon. The concussion wave tore through the plants, leaving a visible trail leading right to him. The guard slammed into the side of the building and didn't move. The second guard turned to see what had happened and presented Brenden with his full chest. A second 'puff' and the guard flew across the entrance, landing next to his comrade. The third guard crouched low and played a light over the field, at the wrong angle to notice the trail through the plants. The light beam sailed over Brenden's head. That guard fell with the third 'puff'.

Brenden waited in silent stillness for the others to step into the light. A rustle in the plants warned him they wouldn't be so accommodating. He lay still with his heart pounding, trying to judge the location of the guards by the rustle of the plants. One of them moved less than ten feet away, no doubt wearing night vision lenses along with his armor. When he had a moment later he would curse his poor planning for not having brought an advanced helmet like the one Tridia had taken from the armory.

Keeping his mind shielded was no longer an option. He had to open his senses to find the guards. He dropped the barrier and reached out mentally. Five armored bodies surrounded him and were closing the distance. Five, a total of eight, when he'd counted only six. As Tridia had reported, he couldn't sense their minds. Had he been able to, things might go more smoothly, but he'd take any advantage he could get. The nearest guard inched his way closer, but he didn't want the nearest one, he needed to target the farthest without disturbing anyone in between. The farthest guard hovered on the edge of the field, barely inside the plant rows, but one of the others stood between them. Nevertheless, Brenden aimed the rifle to the place he sensed the armor's silhouette and waited. The closest guard stumbled over a mound only two rows away and about four feet behind him. Still Brenden waited, rifle ready. One row over, and his finger hovered over the trigger. The intervening guard moved at the same time the closest one stepped into the row where Brenden lay. He took the shot.

The noise of the farthest guard falling in the vegetation drew the others away. The guard on his row hesitated to move. Brenden rolled over and squeezed off a shot before the man could activate his communicator. A black-suited corpse flew back on the open path between rows, making little noise compared to the racket of the others moving toward their fallen comrade. Three left.

Brenden stood and rotated his shoulder to get the feeling back. He couldn't stay where he was. They'd come straight for him as soon as they found the trails left by the concussion wave. He glanced toward the open hangar and moved away from the trails. No one had come to check on the fallen men. Reaching into the building with his senses he found a flurry of activity near the center of a large room. Then he found Anza. She lay in the center of the activity. Even though her mind was tightly closed, the strain in her body caused his muscles to tense. They were doing something to her – something painful. Time was up.

He cast his senses to locate the remaining guards. When he found them, they fell before he shouldered his rifle. Tran had been paying attention. Brenden sprinted across the open ground to the hangar door. The armored corpses didn't object.

Not knowing whether his open senses had betrayed him, Brenden swung wide of the entrance and peered across the lighted expanse. Two Fighter Hawks, a personal cruiser, and several small fighters filled the mammoth chamber, but no other sentries prowled the area. He kept his mind open for the slightest movement, as he went straight for the nearest ship, slipping the pack from his shoulders as he went. He placed two explosive charges on the tires and landing gear before moving on to the next ship in line. Taking out those two would effectively block the door, which was sufficient to his needs. Anza came next.

His senses guided him to the princess. Three men without armor gathered around her. They appeared to be medics of some kind, but their thoughts didn't register in his mind. Like the white-haired man in the Public Hearing Room and the Sentinels, a void existed where their minds should register. That didn't bode well. He didn't bother to shout a warning. When the first man stepped far enough away from the girl to allow him a clear shot he took it, slamming the man against a table full of instruments and shoving it across the room. The other two turned, surprise written on their faces. They were short, slight men with large dark eyes. Their stature suggested they were not of the same race as the guards. Anza sat between them, her feet propped wide apart in stirrups, head lolled to one side against a backboard, blonde hair matted with blood and sweat. Each man held a scalpel. One held the blade near Anza's throat. Brenden held the rifle ready against his shoulder.

"Where are the guards?" the man on Anza's left asked.

"Dead, as you will be if you don't step away from the woman now." Brenden's senses screamed with the strain of the minute details he checked as he closed the distance between himself and the men. Something felt wrong, yet nothing stirred inside the building or the ships.

"You can have her in a moment. We are almost finished." The man made as if to turn back, then dipped his scalpel in a jar of goo and flung it at Brenden.

Brenden caught it in reflex – inches from his chest – but the blade sliced open his hand as he dropped it to the floor. The total gall of the man almost froze Brenden before anger overtook him. He pulled the trigger on his rifle without thought to allowing a safe distance between the man and Anza. The impact from the concussion rifle fired at close range lifted the man off his feet and threw him fifteen feet through the air, scattering the tools and equipment on a far workbench. It also took the corner off the backboard holding Anza upright. *Too close!* Blood dripped from Brenden's hand as he tightened it on the rifle.

The third medic finally gave Brenden his full attention. He remained close to Anza, his hand now holding the scalpel steady against her throat. "That was not necessary. He told you we would be finished shortly. We'll have all of her DNA and mental records. We'll have no need of her for another year. You can have her."

"You misunderstand. You won't be keeping the DNA or the engrams or anything else you've taken from her."

"No, Ambassador Aren, you misunderstand. We'll be keeping everything of hers and taking yours as well."

The voice, though muffled, couldn't be completely disguised. Brenden cursed himself for not sensing the man who no doubt now pointed a blaster in his direction.

"Colonel Zilisk. How did you manage to leave Kanu without the empress?" Brenden spoke without lowering his weapon or turning to face the traitor.

"I would never leave the empress," Zilisk's voice changed from muffled to deadly. "Now lower your weapon, Ambassador, and join the princess."

"Not going to happen, Colonel," Brenden stated flatly. His mind tensed as he sensed a movement at the door. He could handle the doctor, and probably Zilisk, but if one of the guards survived…

"You'd rather die, Ambassador? It would be a shame to lose your mental records, but your DNA will work just as well, and we'll eventually get the confirmation of our information from the empress," Zilisk taunted.

"The purple planets?" Brenden asked.

"Of course. To properly rebuild the race, we'll need samples from all of the survivors. We've found trace amounts of Chesan energy on all of those planets. Some more than others, but unmistakable."

"Like I said, not going to happen. Because Deeca Varin is about to put a hole the size of a fist through your helmet."

A sound, like metal crashing onto concrete, came from the hangar door. The moment Zilisk turned, Brenden matched the movement and fired. Zilisk flew sideways as the concussion wave impacted his helmet. The black helmet simply cracked on the outside, but the impact would have made mush of Zilisk's brains.

"I thought I told you to make for the ship." Brenden turned back to face the medic as he spoke.

"We have different definitions of a ruckus. Besides, like I'd leave you here to have all of the fun," Tran replied.

"You will allow me to finish this process, Ambassador, or the woman will not be returned to you alive." The last medic said.

"Walk away from her now, and you might live to tell the tale. If you so much as nick her skin, I'll use that knife to cut out your heart while it's still beating." Brenden said.

"The Chesan race will be subjugated, Ambassador. You can do nothing to stop it."

"Maybe." Brenden moved closer as he spoke. "The whole galaxy could go up in blazes day after tomorrow and the Chesans fade into slavery, but that's not going to help you walk out of this room alive tonight."

The closer he moved, the more certain Brenden became that he would have to kill the man, but he'd have to do it in such a way to save the princess. Her death wasn't an acceptable loss.

"Stop, Ambassador Aren, or she dies now and we both lose what we want."

Brenden did not stop, even when a trickle of blood slid down Anza's throat. Creatures as callous as these wouldn't hesitate to use and destroy both him and the princess if he showed any weakness. When the medic realized Brenden had no intention of stopping he dropped the scalpel in Anza's lap and turned to flee. Brenden scooped up the blade and sent it flying into the escaping medic's back. The man fell face down. Brenden knelt beside him and rolled the creature's back against his knee, careful not to jam the scalpel farther in than necessary.

"You're not the true form of the Kel Anec. You're hiding in the body of a Seluat male. Why do you people need aliens to control instead of using your own bodies?" Brenden had no hope of getting a straight answer, but he had to try.

The medic laughed before answering. "The Kel do not need their bodies for this part of the invasion. We require these husks only to move about in this galaxy unnoticed. We are more than you know."

"Where are your bodies?" Might as well ask before the creature died.

"In a place where you will never reach them. An entire fleet of ships is ready to invade once we have what we need. We've waited a thousand years to reclaim our stolen prize, what is a few more to accomplish all our goals?"

"What stolen prize?" Brenden asked. The little medic seemed sleepy, but his mind remained closed.

"The Chesan race, of course. We created you for our own purposes – so useful and pliant. Never fighting back for fear of hurting each other through your telepathy. We used you in the old times as harvest slaves, then a mutation occurred. New energy signatures formed in a core group. They began to resist our orders and use their energy as a weapon. We captured and studied a few, but those early versions were frail creatures, unable to use the power more than a few times before its energy consumed their bodies and drove them to insanity." The medic coughed blood.

The scalpel had imbedded deeper than intended.

"What did you do to Anza?" he asked.

"Others will finish what we've started. You can't hide her from us now. Wherever you take her, we'll know."

"Imbedded homing devices."

The creature laughed again. Spittle and blood drooled from his lips. Brenden leaned close enough to hear his garbled words.

"The brain is a delicate instrument, Ambassador. Delicate and so rewarding. She has been a delightful specimen in so many ways. Her body is perfect for breeding. I personally primed her gestation cycle."

Brenden twisted the handle of the scalpel and the creature's eyes widened in pain. "If your race is telepathically connected, give them a message. They will *not* subjugate the Chesan race. The old Chesans ran, but the new race has learned to fight. Evolution jumped while you slept between galaxies. You will all die, and I will see to it."

The creature gave one more startled lunge as Brenden sank the scalpel into its heart, then it went limp. He left the Seluat husk lying there and went back to Anza. Tran had bandaged the cut on her throat.

"Not life-threatening," he said, then nodded toward Brenden's bleeding hand. "How about you?"

"It will keep. Take Anza to the Fighter Hawk nearest the door."

Tran lifted the girl in his arms and hurried away. Brenden cast around with his senses until he found a female form inside a small room near Zilisk's body. He kicked the door in. Dojene sat on a cot, her chin raised in defiance.

"Are you all right, Grandmother?" he asked.

"Decidedly not," she replied. "Better for seeing you."

"Then let's get out of here. There's bound to be reinforcements on the way."

No sooner had Brenden spoken than the sound of a hovering ship rumbled over the building. It wasn't the *Elisia*.

"Come on." Brenden grabbed Dojene's wrist and led her through the hangar at a run.

The inside of the building didn't offer much cover other than the ships. If the newcomers entered through the doorway they'd be seen. Brenden couldn't put up a fight that placed Dojene and Anza at risk, and surrender wasn't in his plans. When they reached the Fighter Hawk, he sent Dojene up the ramp to join the others. With the way he'd packed the explosives into the landing gears of the Fighter Hawk, the tires couldn't roll more than a meter in either direction without setting off the device and disintegrating the undercarriage of the vessel. He'd intended to remove the explosives, but the hovering craft's engines changed sound. The pilot had decided to land.

"Better not roll the tires." He ran for the ramp.

Tran had strapped Anza into a seat and run through a minimal flight check by the time Brenden returned and hustled him out of the pilot's seat.

"It's just a Fighter Hawk," Tran objected. "The controls aren't complicated. I can fly it."

"We're carrying explosives tucked into the landing gear," Brenden said. He ran the final sequence before starting the engine. "And you've got patients to tend."

"Then by all means, please, you pilot our latest coffin," Tran said. "Just drop me anywhere before you set it down."

A half dozen armor-clad soldiers disgorged from the open ramp of the ship outside. They scattered to check for the fallen guards. Likely no more than two remained inside the vessel. Their guns sat untargeted as Brenden fired the engines. Several of the men on the ground ran toward the hangar at the sound of the Fighter Hawk readying for flight.

Brenden lifted the ship vertically and turned it to face the door, its guns targeted on the ground. The first blasts dropped two of the men and sent the rest running for cover wherever they could find it. The pilot of the enemy ship got as far as training his weapons before Brenden hit him with a missile. A burning husk remained where the vessel had sat.

Brenden hammered the hangar doors with blasts until they collapsed. Once they were out of the way, he maneuvered the Fighter Hawk through the opening and around the burning wreckage. He took the ship up and away from the hangar then turned it to face the building and fired two missiles into it. The building became an instant inferno. Whatever they'd taken from Anza would never reach the Kel Anec forces.

"Call Deeca and tell her not to fire at the approaching enemy craft." Brenden tapped his locator so Deeca could identify them. "Tell her how to disengage the cloak."

The *Elisia* sat exposed in the open field as they neared, its cloak disabled. Deeca didn't shoot them, but she kept the guns targeted as Brenden hovered the Fighter Hawk near the ship. Tran disembarked with the two women and hurried toward the *Elisia's* open ramp.

Brenden backed the Fighter Hawk away and set it down as gently as he could. He let out a relieved sigh when it didn't explode beneath him, then rushed to catch up with his passengers.

Tran carried Anza up the ramp and into the *Elisia's* cabin. Brenden followed with Dojene holding his arm.

"I told you it was us," Brenden snapped.

"What's happened to her?" Deeca ignored his scolding.

"They've implanted homing devices in her brain, drugged her, and God knows what else."

"Then anywhere we take her —" Deeca stopped when she noticed Dojene.

"They'll be able to find her. I can think of only one place where she might be safe, even if she's found." Brenden turned to Tran. "Strap Anza onto a couch. Then if you can manage it, wrap something around this hand so I don't drip blood all over the ship. It won't stop bleeding."

Anza showed signs of life, but with her unconscious, Brenden couldn't sense her thoughts or emotions. He left his senses open so he could get a read on her mental condition if she woke up.

He hurried to the cockpit and took the pilot's seat.

"I'm glad you can think of one place she'll be safe." Deeca slid into the co-pilot's seat and strapped in. "How did the empress get here?"

"I haven't heard the tale yet, but I had to kill Zilisk. There are several operatives alive on the ground and probably screaming for help. There'll be more troops on the way by now — and possibly air support."

Deeca had prepared the ship for take-off, and Brenden fired the engines.

"What about that one?" Deeca asked, nodding toward the Fighter Hawk next to them.

"This," Brenden replied.

He swung the *Elisia* around behind the grounded vessel and fired a low-powered shot at the tailfin. The direct hit did little damage to the ship, but it nudged the craft forward enough to set off the explosives, taking out the whole undercarriage. It burst into flames.

Destroying the ship gave the Kel Anec one less vehicle and Brenden a lot of satisfaction. He'd issued a brave challenge through the Seluat medic, and whether or not the Kel heard him, he had to come up with some way to make it good. He wouldn't let those loathsome creatures swarm the galaxy. Nor would he let them capture and torture the remaining Chesan survivors. He'd get to them first.

Heading the *Elisia* straight for the sling line coordinates, Brenden was already sorting through his options when Anza screamed, then Dojene. He'd no more than turned in his seat to check on them when his mind entered a living nightmare.

CHAPTER TWENTY-NINE

A vision exploded in Tridia and Drayden's bonded minds. The now familiar nausea that accompanied entry into the mists engulfed Tridia's body. The ground tilted beneath her and she clung to Drayden for support. It did no good. They fell together – their bodies to the ground and their minds into the mists. Bound together beyond all undoing, their single mind couldn't escape as the vision unfolded. They both believed at first that it was Drayden who beheld the future events, but as the mental assault continued, they became less certain.

Alien armies enslaved generations of Chesan progeny and forced them to open portals to siphon energy from the mists. Invaders swarmed across two galaxies in waves of havoc and destruction, using Chesan-created portals for travel across time and space. Teeming hordes of lizard-like humanoids and fearsome Felinus warriors battled each other and countless other beings. All creatures not destroyed were enslaved. Sounds of battle and cries of the dying rang in the watcher's ears. The scent of burning flesh and stagnating blood from thousands of battlefields assaulted the watcher's nostrils. Beyond the physical, the vision carried mental assaults of insanity, despair, terror, rage and depravity. Each scene broadcast the full impact of emotions and thoughts from each creature – human and nonhuman, alike – as though the watcher lacked the ability to block them. Every nuance of thought and action registered in the watcher's mind.

Scenes flashed by so quickly Tridia and Drayden could comprehend only the most horrendous of the atrocities. Emotions so tangled with insanity their minds heaved in an effort to be free of the vision and each other.

A second set of horrors intertwined within the first. In these the watcher's burden of guilt crushed him with alternating regrets of things

271

he'd done or hadn't done to cause the chaos. His mind was so burdened with self-loathing he could barely sense his love for the slender, dark-haired woman he followed without deviation. Her silver-gray eyes hid a soul haunted in some scenes with regret and remorse, in others with insanity and depravity. In her regret, she tried to protect a group of survivors, many of them children, while having to sentence them to servitude with their slave masters. In her insanity, she drained blue energy from children with emaciated bodies, or from the bodies of dying soldiers as she walked among the battlefields.

To make the visions more unbearable, interspersed among the holocausts, ran another set of scenes that depicted the same Chesan survivors living in peace in a society more harmonious and advanced than any in the known galaxy. The watcher's eyes beheld his slender, dark-haired beauty, laughing and teaching groups of adoring children. They trailed her through gardens and amid stalls of gentle animals. She taught them about caring for their surroundings. The watcher cherished and adored every aspect of her being, trusted her completely, and longed for her companionship when she was out of sight.

Even in this harmony, the watcher's thoughts were not consistent. At times the great love he felt was tinged with sadness. At others, no such hindrance darkened his ardor. No vision revealed the reason for the sadness, but it lingered in the watcher's thoughts as scenes flew by.

Back and forth the visions flashed until Tridia and Drayden could take no more of either the horror or the joy. Tridia forced her lips from Drayden's and rolled away from him, prostrated. Their minds withdrew from the mists, but she couldn't contain the agony of what she'd seen. Deep sobs wracked her body and tears soaked her face. She wanted to be sick, but her stomach contained nothing to heave. Drayden lay on the ground next to her, releasing his own agony through tears and wailing. She understood how an entire planet would choose to commit suicide rather than condemn not only their race, but the entirety of two galaxies, to such horrors. Her body shook and trembled with the memory of what captivity would mean to her, Drayden, and the other survivors. And how that captivity would change her. She wished she could crawl into the bowels of the planet and collapse it on top of her, to hide from what she might bring about. She cursed Brenden Aren in her mind for not leaving her dead. If he'd seen the Chaos Vision with this intensity, how could he let her live and risk what she could unleash? The memories of peace and prosperity barely registered in her consciousness.

Their tears finally spent, Tridia sensed Drayden's mind. He reached out to draw her near, but she slapped his arm away.

"How can you touch me? How can you stand the sight of me?" New tears threatened her eyes as she cried the words. "Draw your knife, Drayden, and slit my throat. Don't let me do this to all those people. All those planets. To you...to us...those children."

She cried again. Her chest heaved painfully when she could no longer fill her lungs through the sobs. Drayden ignored her protests and dragged her roughly to his chest. His arms held her fiercely to him, refusing to let her go as she struggled, too weak with grief to break away. He held her there, kissed her hair, as his tears mingled with hers. Nothing she'd experienced in her life compared to this devastation of her spirit. A growing darkness spread from the depth of her soul to encompass her mind. Drayden met her there in the darkness. His words echoed in her ears and her thoughts.

"I won't let you lock me away – ever again," he said. "We are one now, Tridia. This nightmare is ours to face together. You, me – and the other Chesan survivors."

Death and destruction rolled through the darkness in an endless cycle. Drayden forced memories of peace into the nightmare.

"Fight it, Tridia! You're a soldier, you don't retreat when you can still go forward. Fight it – *with me*."

"We knew this would happen!" Tridia choked out the accusation. "We knew we'd invoke this infected vision by our bonding. You've seen it before, and you did it anyway. How could you have allowed it? How could you have even touched me? I can never forgive either of us for this."

"Yes, you will," Drayden replied. "Be angry with me for now – for as long as you need to. I'll wait a lifetime to complete our union now that you're bonded with me. But you can't continue to let this vision control you."

"Complete our union? With all of this horror, you'd think of completing our union? Of producing a child who will be enslaved and tortured – tormented by his own mother?"

"We'll produce a child who will adore his mother as much as I will, who will laugh at her stories and sleep on her lap."

"You're dreaming, Drayden," Tridia cried.

"So are you," Drayden argued. "Don't you see that *none* of this is real? All of it, the good *and* the bad, are only possibilities. This is a splintered vision. Nothing here is destined except for one thing – there will be no peace without you alive."

"How can you say that?" she screamed.

Drayden forced more memories of peace into Tridia's mind. In each one, she was the focus. Then appeared a beautiful blonde-haired woman with sky-blue eyes.

"Anza," Tridia gasped.

"You know her?" Drayden asked.

"The Kanuan princess, a Chesan survivor. She was meant to be your queen."

"The Empress of Kanu's choice. Not mine," Drayden said. "Can you not sense that there is no love for her in my heart? This would be a forced union with shallow peace."

More images of horror rolled by until one slowed in Tridia's mind, a crazed Anza, wild-eyed and drooling, barely recognizable, screamed at cowering minions from a platform glowing blue and strewn with dead bodies.

"No!" Tridia shouted against the insanity in Anza's mind.

"You can't stay here! This vision will consume you until there's no hope left. Step out of the darkness and live to prevent it." Drayden forced another image into the forefront. An older Tridia lay sleeping against white cushions with a dark-haired child cuddled in her arms. Tranquility flowed from the scene and Drayden's love became real for the first time.

"Stop it, Drayden," Tridia warned.

"I won't!" he yelled back. "This is our first battlefield, Tridia. I won't give you up, and I won't leave you alone. If you fall to this insanity, you'll take me with you, and we'll have lost before we start. It's your choice, but you won't make it alone."

***

Drayden felt Tridia slipping away from him. He couldn't reach her with his words, so he decided to try one more thing. He'd despise himself for it, but he had to reach her. A nightmare vision filled their minds. Tridia, hair cut short and wild, face and body filthy, her stomach swollen in pregnancy, eyes wide with insanity, kneeling before a cowering child. Blue energy flowed from the child's navel into her hands.

"Come away, my love." The watcher's weakened voice pleaded with her. Guilt consumed his mind. "Leave the child alone. He needs to rest. Please don't hurt our son anymore."

The vision froze.

"No-o-o!" The blood curdling scream came from Tridia's lips. She fought to push Drayden away and flexed her wrist. A knife flew into her hand. She almost had it to her throat when he grabbed her wrist. Pain shot through their minds – an agony of gold and burned flesh. Tridia dropped the knife. Drayden caught it and tossed it away, then pinned her arms against his chest and pulled her close again.

He forced another scene into their minds. This time Tridia stood by a double cradle festooned with blue ribbons. Her long black braid hung over her shoulder, laced with matching blue ribbons and sparkling jewels.

She turned toward the watcher with a smile. The purity of her love for him and the children in the cradle overwhelmed him. The wonder she felt at watching the babies sleep touched a deep chord in his soul.

"Come away, my love," the watcher's voice whispered. His voice broke with the depth of his love for the three of them. No sadness touched his emotions. "You've watched them sleep for an hour. Our sons are safe."

Tridia's smile broadened as she stepped into outstretched arms. The vision froze.

"One vision is equally valid as the other." Drayden spoke with his lips at Tridia's ear. "We can give up now and let the first one take us. Or we can fight to win the second."

Sobs wracked Tridia's body until she could take only short, gasping breaths. She fell asleep in Drayden's arms, the nightmares playing in a never-ending loop through their minds.

CHAPTER THIRTY

Brenden slid from his seat, writhing in agony as wave after wave of slavery and torture washed through his brain. Peace, hope, and prosperity interspersed the horror and savagery. Despair and insanity flowed like liquid through the dark visions, carrying their madness even into the most beautiful alternatives. He tried every block and barrier to escape the nightmares. Even for a quarter-Chesan, there had been no defense against the Chaos Vision. Now that his body had changed, the full force of the vision battered his mind to a cringing mass. It had driven an entire race to commit suicide and Brenden Aren lay engulfed, unable to control his sobbing and anger. Despair seeped into his being, draining away any hope of victory. He sank into darkness, trying to shut out the vision until he heard his name.

"Brenden!"

He covered his ears, willing the intruder to vanish. Barriers went up around his mind, shutting out all thought and sensation, except the visions that refused to let go.

"You're safe. We've got you."

A hand, insistent upon his arm, shaking his shoulder, finally broke through his defenses. He opened his eyes a slit to see who had hold of him. Deeca's worried face hovered over him, her long blonde hair pulled to one side. His head lay in her lap. The hand and voice belonged to Tran.

Reaching a bandaged and shaky hand up, he touched the hair to see if it was real. He saw hair like this in the good part of the vision. Beautiful blonde hair surrounding a smiling face with violet blue eyes. This face didn't smile at him.

"Brenden? Can you hear me?"

"I was a teenager standing in the middle of the Chesan royal court when I saw the vision the last time." Tears slid down his face, but his voice started to regain its strength. Brenden avoided Deeca's eyes while fondling her hair. "With all of the horrors I've seen before or since, it's the only reason I've ever had nightmares."

"I don't understand," Deeca whispered.

"It doesn't matter." He let go of the hair and closed his eyes, trying to regain his composure as the visions continued to roll through his mind. When he opened them again Deeca's face was only inches from his.

"It matters to me, Brenden Aren or Morgan Jacks – or whoever you want to call yourself. It matters to me."

He reached up for the blonde strand again before speaking. "All of the oaths, all of the secret strategies, the planning, the tutors, the near annihilation of an entire race. All of it to avoid this." He wiped a hand over his face, surprised to find it wet when he drew it away. "It was all for nothing. None of it matters anymore."

Tran patted Brenden's shoulder. "If it doesn't matter, then let it out. We can't help if we don't know what's going on."

Brenden glanced over at his friend. "It's time. I just don't know if I can. In the Hierarchy, oaths are sacred. As an Elstaar Officer, I administered oath-breaking punishments from mild to severe. That kind of loyalty was ingrained in Hierarchy operatives from the first training. It's not something I can set aside easily."

"I sensed that in you," Tran said. "Ten years ago, on that derelict freighter. Back when I decided to follow you."

"I gave an oath to the last Chesan King fifteen years ago. I said I would hold this secret for thirty years, or take it to my grave if I died before then. Deeca has reasoned out some of it." He looked back to her. "This is the rest of the secret."

Breaking the oath meant going against all he was or ever had been, but he needed to say the words so he could examine them himself. They came with difficulty and hesitation at first, but grew easier as he spoke.

"The Chesan race…The nobility could see the future under certain circumstances. It was…inherent in the king's bloodline. The farther from the nobility, the lesser the vision. The nearer, the clearer and more impacting." Brenden drew a deep breath, forcing himself to continue. "If there was a strong vision, it was broadcast to the other nobility with nearly the same intensity, then weakening through the others as it went. It was said the Captivity Vision was so powerful every living Chesan felt it with the same intensity, whether they were on the planet or not. An entire race of people saw a terrible future with only one possible escape – and it came at a horrendous price. Everyone agreed to pay the price. Preparations were made, bargains were struck, the Hierarchy was contracted. The genocide plan took fifty years to put into place. In the last five years, too late to stop the avalanche of destruction, another vision superseded the Captivity Vision. More potent than the first, this vision offered a terrible mix of hope and despair with an overshadowing, but unclear, figure playing prominently in almost every scene. They called it the Chaos Vision because no one could make sense of the future it foretold. Some interpreters insisted a child not yet born on Ceyon was the cause of the chaos. That child's life decisions would determine the fate of the Chesan race – for good or evil – and with them the fate of the galaxy. Since the child wasn't born yet, they couldn't be sure who she was. The face was indistinct. I saw the last vision the king and queen allowed the Chesan people to suffer. It took place a few months before their holocaust. The face appeared more clearly, but still too indistinct to identify. The government mounted a search for the child, checking everyone and anyone under five years of age – Chesan or alien. None were found to match even the indistinct vision. Except for very specific breeding, the Chesans had ceased conception years before. Anza was probably the youngest of the final group of children born on the planet."

Brenden tried to get to his feet and faltered. Tran helped him to stand.

"Does this mean you'll have to kill me now?" Tran asked. He didn't smile.

"No," Brenden replied, with equal seriousness. "I need your help."

Tran gave a grim nod.

Brenden stumbled to the couch where Anza lay whimpering in her sleep. He touched the girl's sweaty face. She withdrew as if shocked. Empress Dojene lay on the floor next to the couch.

"They're both alive," Tran said. "Just barely."

"So, the child wasn't born on Ceyon after all?" Deeca prompted.

"She was on Ceyon, alright," Brenden said. "I have no idea who shielded her from the probes and the searchers. I know how she was rescued from the planet before the holocaust ended.

"What I just saw wasn't the same vision I saw fifteen years ago. The clarity of this vision makes the other one pale in comparison. The emotions are overwhelming." Brenden's mind drifted in the vision still rolling through his thoughts. "The face is very distinct. She has black hair, and gray eyes so intense they'd melt steel."

"Commander Odana." Deeca whispered. "This is a vision of the future?"

"Produced by her and the Chesan prince." Brenden dropped into a chair and trembled violently.

The vision wrapped around his soul and wouldn't let go. Tridia didn't appear in every scene of the nightmare. Some of the worst desecration held no reference to her. He took it to mean, even if he killed her, the swarming of the galaxy would still happen. If what he'd seen held true, it might be better to let her live and have a chance at peace, because only two of the visions of peace he'd been able to distinguish lacked her presence. He leaned back and closed his eyes. Tran covered him with a blanket.

"What's our heading?" he asked.

"I laid in a course for Aga while Tran was dealing with the three of you," Deeca said. "There were only two places I could think of where Anza might be safe. Hulac, under its shield, and Aga, with the Sentinels. Tran thought it better to take her to Aga."

"The man has experience," Brenden said. "Hulac could hold out under siege indefinitely, but we would effectively be prisoners while the Kel Anec had free run of the galaxy. With us contained, they would be able to reach all of the other assets we need to retrieve. Anza has a right to Alliance protection, and the Sentinels are the most able to provide it for her." He settled more deeply into the chair. "Can you two handle the ship on your own for a few hours?"

"No," Tran said. "We're such rank amateurs we're likely to run it into a rogue asteroid."

"Well, do your best." Brenden spoke without opening his eyes. "Contact Caine. He should be making the return trip to Alliance territory by now. We can't go to Aga in Morgan Jacks' ship. Return the *Elisia* to her berth and get back to being yourself as soon as you can. Contact the Sentinels at Permai Station. Tell them we have a destination for Alanel and Winniel to retrieve a pair of misplaced articles. Send them the sector seven transfer point coordinates. Arrange for a fast ship to meet us at sector ten.

"Use whatever resources you need to track activity in the Starling system. Have every watcher alert for any Seluat ships and any large troop movements anywhere. Put every able-bodied trooper on alert. We may have to call in all markers very soon. And, Tran?"

"Yeah?"

"Thanks for taking care of this." Brenden lifted his bandaged hand.

"You owe me big time for that piece of work." Tran grinned.

"This is the kind of thing Morgan Jacks does?" Deeca asked, as Tran disappeared into the cockpit.

"Most of the time he just puts things in motion and lets the inevitable happen. This will be different."

"You've got us spooked," she added.

"You should be," Brenden said.

"We need to settle things between us." Deeca reached up and

brushed the damp hair from his forehead. "I understand you aren't what you seem. But I need to know which part of you is real."

"Can you hold that thought for later?" Brenden cracked an eye open a slit. "I've got a nightmare running in my brain and it's more than a bit debilitating."

Deeca squeezed his arm and left to join Tran.

Brenden groaned. The vision continued to play in his mind. What were Tridia and Drayden doing to prolong this torment? He had to reach them and separate them. Though what he could do to keep them apart when an entire race of geniuses couldn't manage it, he had no idea.

***

Tridia lay in Drayden's arms, her muscles so tense it seemed her bones would break. When she tried to move, Drayden tightened his arms around her, as she had done to him the night before. Too spent to struggle, she lay still trying to shut out the devastation replaying continuously in her mind. When she focused on any one scene, the horror seemed to suspend in time and the anguish of each being within it washed through her battered soul. The Chaos Vision no longer resided in a fairytale told by Brenden and Empress Dojene. It was buried so deep in her psyche, even death was unlikely to release her from it.

"You've got to let it go, Tridia." Drayden kissed the top of her head as he spoke and massaged the knotted muscles in her shoulder. "For both our sakes and the sake of all the other Chesan survivors. You have to release this nightmare. They are all bound to it as long as we are. We've got to find the answers that lead to peace, and we can't do that locked in this vision."

"Master Aren has already killed me to protect the Chesan plan. If I go back now, if he's seeing this, he would do it again without hesitation. Wouldn't that be the better choice in the circumstances?"

"No. Didn't you see there was no peace without you?" He held her just far enough away that she could see his face. "If you die, it's all over. Nothing we do without you will ever get us to the peace and tranquility we've seen."

Tridia focused on the scenes as they replayed in her mind. She hurried through the horrors and slowed each scene of peace. Drayden was right. Only two scenes of forced peace didn't include her.

"That can't be true," she whimpered. "I have to live with the knowledge my decisions cause this? I have no way to tell which ones lead to destruction?"

She twisted out of Drayden's arms and jumped to her feet before he could grab her. Her legs wobbled beneath her and she touched the tree for support. The touch of the bark spit back an image of Drayden as he had been in his moment of need and she released an anguished moan.

Drayden caught her before she collapsed to the ground, but she recovered quickly and shoved him away, afraid any touch might rekindle his desires.

"I'm fine now, Tridia," he said. "The effects of the pollen have worn off."

"I'm not, Prince Drayden." Tridia folded her arms across her chest. "My memories of you are too near the surface. My knowledge of you too real. This vision is in my head. I sense nothing beyond it and your need for me. Nothing."

"Yes, you do." Drayden stepped toward her and Tridia took two steps backward. He stopped. "I won't touch you again. Not until we get this worked out. You are sensing me. The Chaos Vision is in my head, but I feel you there, too. It won't stop in your mind because you're also sensing it in mine. I can't make it stop because you won't let it go."

"That makes no sense," Tridia cried.

Sweat dripped from Drayden's face and his skin held a deathly pallor. The control he exerted showed in the tautness of his muscles. His exhaustion and fear matched her own, but he was trying to save her. Tridia couldn't separate her senses from his.

"We've bonded." Drayden said the words in a whisper. "We didn't mate, but we're mated. Our fates are tied together now. For the moment, you're the stronger of the two of us. I gave up too much of my strength to help you endure the bonding. Because of that, we're locked in what you perceive. Until you release the vision, we'll continue to relive it. Let me help you."

She shook her head. How had this happened? Master Aren had given her orders to stay away. He and the empress had seen the vision. She understood why they wanted her dead, why Master Aren had killed her once. Why hadn't he left her dead? Too many questions floated through her mind. Too much had forced its way past her defenses. The memory of Master Aren's kiss danced before her eyes. Drayden's jealousy forced its way through the vision.

"He's not my lover." Tridia spoke the words in reflex. "The whole thing was a ruse."

Tridia pulled memories to the surface; the Challenge, the Guardians, the deception at the hospital ship. With each one, Drayden relaxed a little more, and the Chaos Vision began to lose its hold.

"His kiss called up a vision with you, but a simple one of a not too distant future." Drayden observed. "He was never meant to be your mate."

"He wasn't *trying* to be my mate. His kiss was innocent, Drayden.

Ours was not." Tridia breathed in slowly. Her accusation took in both of their intentions. Her mind continued to clear as she pulled her emotions into check. She tried to balance the deed with the punishment inflicted. No matter how she leveraged the facts, the cost seemed severe.

Fire flared for a moment in Drayden's eyes. "There are too many naked men in your mind."

Tridia blinked at the comment. She'd been thinking of the punishment she'd meted out to K'tain and his friends.

"Then stay out of my mind, Your Majesty." Her retort was tinged with embarrassment and her face grew warm.

"It's gone now." Drayden scanned Tridia's face. He relaxed and color crept back into his cheeks.

It took a moment for her to realize the Chaos Vision had faded completely. She was about to search her mind for it when Drayden yelled at her.

"Don't force it to the surface! We may not get rid of it so easily again," he said.

"You distracted me." Tridia said. His subtle touch in her mind had gone unnoticed amid the fear and anger. He had maneuvered every thought, pulling from the memories she'd shared.

"My mother and father showed me the Chaos Vision twice before I came here. Both times Father used this technique to release me and my mother from its grip."

Tridia looked away. "Thank you, Prince Drayden. I owe you a great debt."

"I owe you an apology. I should have controlled myself with you. It wasn't only the effects of the pollen –"

"No!" Tridia interrupted. "You wouldn't have touched me if I hadn't asked. No matter what it would have cost you. But I think it best we don't go back to the pond until the air has cleared. At least I won't."

"We won't need to." Drayden looked back toward the pond. He spotted the pouch with the vials just outside the ring of pollen and hurried to retrieve it. "The seedlings are all in the silt. The Rrabbas asked me to watch over them to make sure they didn't fall onto the shore. They lost many of their young ones before I started coming with them. Once the babies are safe in the silt, I leave them. The Rrabbas contact me when they return to themselves."

"That's what they meant when they said you assisted with their breeding," Tridia said.

Drayden reached to take her hand, but she dodged him, then apologized.

"I'm grateful for your help, Your Highness, but I would feel better if we kept our distance for a while."

He sighed in response then motioned her to follow him. She fell into step behind him. They walked for half an hour, neither speaking nor touching. Neither did they intrude in each other's minds. Tridia hadn't intended to build a barrier, but it was there. Had Drayden placed it? She wouldn't complain. She had enough to think about on her own without dragging Drayden's thoughts into the fray. Tridia Odana, Commander of the Blue Level in the Odean Hierarchy would never have dreamed of disobeying a direct order from a ranking officer. How had the bond servant Tridia found the independence to disregard the same order from her master? She'd wanted freedom from the Hierarchy and through Master Aren she'd gotten it. She'd wanted to meet the man in her visions and through the Controller she'd gotten that, as well. The Chaos Vision was the result, infecting every other survivor. Princess Anza, Empress Dojene, Master Aren, and all the others she'd never met. All because she'd disobeyed.

Her whole life and being had hinged on keeping the balance of promise and payment. A crime committed required a sufficient punishment. A well-executed mission deserved recognition and reward. A vow taken deserved to be honored. A vow broken deserved punishment. She'd spoken the vow to Master Aren, not once, but twice. Both times she'd been lucid and spoken the vow before witnesses, then walked away and behaved as though her word held no truth or binding. The Controller had sent her to Zentel, but he wouldn't have done it had she not nearly killed herself trying to get there on her own. Had she waited, instead of listening to the Sentinels, she might still have arrived at Zentel in the same manner, but she wouldn't have broken her vow to get there. Master Aren would never trust her again. If he couldn't trust her, he couldn't let her live. If she didn't live, the Chaos Vision would devolve into slavery, and the Chesan sacrifice would be for nothing. She had to protect herself and convince him to let her live. Words wouldn't do it, he'd require something more dramatic, but nothing acceptable came to mind.

The thoughts so engrossed her mind she ran into Drayden when he stopped.

"Give a warning." She scowled.

"I did say 'we're here', but you seemed a little preoccupied. Thinking of your master again, were you?"

Tridia bit her lip as a heated flush rose to her cheeks. "Not in the manner you insinuate, Your Highness. Or weren't my thoughts clear enough for you to read?"

"It bothers you someone else can see into your mind as easily as you've spied on others all your life, doesn't it?"

Drayden's observation hit too close to the mark. The heat doubled in her cheeks. "You said it was impolite to go uninvited into someone else's mind."

"I didn't read your mind. I don't *have* to read your mind to see what you display with your words and actions."

"Then how could you know –" She could have cut out her own tongue for the slip.

"Ah, so I did read you correctly. On both counts?" Drayden smiled. His teasing sounded real enough, but only Davik had ever dared tease her so openly.

"Where are we?" A change of subject provided the only graceful retreat.

"Coward." Drayden cleared his throat when Tridia glared at him. "This is my home when I'm not with the Rrabbas. I spend most of my time in the classroom. You can see it if you touch my memories. It's not so different from touching one of your own."

Tridia closed her eyes to try to suppress her awareness of him. His memories were so vivid in her mind that they might have been flashing across a vid screen. There were many of his early life inside the bunker. She smiled at the little boy he had been, alone with only a robot companion inside the enormous complex. When she opened her eyes she caught him smiling again.

"Before I open this door, you need to recall the last conversation with my professor and the one that followed with my physician."

Tridia obeyed. Although she had observed the memory in Drayden's mind and sensed his resolve, she hadn't fully grasped what the holographic projections threatened to do. "She means to keep you prisoner, using the Rrabbas as hostages?"

"Technically, it – the computer program – means to do that," Drayden corrected. "The physician image is just the one to whom I tend to show the most respect. The program displays her image when it wants me to be agreeable."

"Is there an override? Some way to countermand the program itself?"

"It depends on your computer skills. I have direct access to the program and its source code, but not enough skill to change anything about it. There's a separate security program that monitors my scripts and blocks anything it deems too aggressive." Drayden waited.

"If I can't break through the security, then we're stuck inside for the next ten years?"

"It might be worse," Drayden said. "The computer is armed. It can sterilize the entire interior – including us – if it deems us too great a threat to the galaxy or the survival of our race."

"Unless your AI has been monitoring outside events for the past fifteen years, it has no idea what kind of trouble the galaxy is in." Tridia held Drayden's gaze. "Neither do you."

"I do now." Drayden tapped his temple. "Your adventure in the mine with the Kel Anec was most revealing. Then there's the battle fleet, along with Empress Dojene's explanations."

"And Master Aren's," Tridia added.

Drayden stiffened. "I'd rather not think of him at the moment. His mental assault on you is still too fresh in my memory, as is his attempt to kill you after he saw the hologram of the space fleet. I don't like hearing you call him master."

"Get used to it. Your mate or not, I'm still *his* property." Tridia looked away. "We can't face the fleet alone – and we can't hide from the Kel Anec forever. They *will* find us. We will need all the help we can get, and Ambassador Master Brenden Aren is well connected." She looked back at him. "Let the past go, Drayden. Hating him is a luxury you can't afford."

Drayden scowled.

"I'm willing to go in and take the chance," Tridia said. "My skills are not as expert as some of the hackers locked up in Hierarchy prisons, but I'm good."

"Then we'd better step inside together. It could separate us by closing the door between us if we trail each other." Drayden locked his arm with Tridia's, despite her initial attempt to step away from his touch. He turned toward the rock wall. "Drayden one, returning for lessons."

The rock slid away and the door opened when Drayden entered the proper codes. Cool air rushed out of the darkened room beyond. When they stepped through the opening, bright white lights came up, revealing a room comfortably furnished with oversized furniture. A desk sat against the far wall. A bank of holographic computer screens snapped on as they stepped farther into the room.

Shelves of artifacts and sculptures covered the wall to Tridia's left. The walls to her right and behind her held incredible pieces of artwork. She'd never seen any of it, yet they were as familiar as her own reflection. She'd seen them for years – touched them and played with them. The door slid closed behind them as she and Drayden moved to the center of the room amid the furniture.

"These things are priceless," she said. "I've seen vids of Chesan artwork and – " She paused, and smiled at Drayden's questioning look. "It's strange to have access to all of my memories again. Now yours are there, too, and I recognize these things. It's a bit dizzying."

"The inside of my head is pretty confusing right now, too." Drayden squeezed her hand against his arm. "I believe we'll get used to it with time."

Tridia forced her eyes from his. The compulsion to step into his arms pulled at her. He let her hand drop, but stayed close.

The lights went out without warning, leaving them in total darkness. A high-pitched whine assaulted her ears and Tridia shoved Drayden toward the sofa. She'd intended to step away to give the computer a separate target, but Drayden dragged her along with him. She ended up pinned beneath him on the cushions, his body shielding hers.

"You have returned with a female, Your Highness." The computer spoke in a male voice.

"My astrophysics professor?" Drayden whispered.

"Are we to believe she is now your bond mate?"

"We have bonded," Drayden spoke into the darkness. "We've had no physical union beyond a kiss."

"Simply a matter of time, now that she is here. You understand, she must be destroyed."

"No, she must not." Drayden replied. "We have created a new Chaos Vision, more potent and dangerous than the one that destroyed our people. In it there is no peace without her. It is very clear. The destruction is even worse without her to temper the creatures driving it. Destroy her and not only will you destroy me, but you will destroy any hope of salvation for this galaxy or freedom for our people. There are others who can bring about the greater holocaust, but no one else who can prevent it."

"You are lying to protect her." The computer voice changed to a woman's. Tridia's body went taut at the sound.

"Check my vitals, Physician," Drayden challenged. "See if you detect any subterfuge. I am telling the truth."

The lights flashed and scanners hummed from all directions. The glowing image of a dark-haired woman appeared in the darkness beside the sofa.

"You've been badly injured, Prince Drayden," she said. "Bandaged with care, but not much skill. Please come into the lab so I can attend your needs."

"Not until I have an assurance my mate will not be injured – or killed – if she is exposed."

"What assurance would you accept from an artificial intelligence?"

"She's right, Drayden." Tridia spoke softly. Drayden's ear was near her lips. "We can't stay here forever like this. Believe her or don't, but we have no choice in the end."

"I kept my word," Drayden spoke to the hologram. "The plant creatures outside need the sunlight as unfiltered as it can be. I won't risk their safety – you already know that. They are your assurance against any inappropriate behavior between me and my mate. After what we witnessed in the vision, I'm fortunate she will let me touch her at all. You can trust my word as a noble and as your sovereign, I will do nothing else to jeopardize our future. Give me your word, as my subject, you will not harm her. You will not vaporize, incinerate, or otherwise end her life. Nor will you incapacitate or imprison her in any way other than keeping her inside this bunker. Your word, Physician, speaking as a representative of the entire program."

The physician's image froze, then flickered. Another image of the same woman appeared, clad in different clothes, with a half-smile on her lips.

"Rise, your highness," she said. "You and your mate are both safe for the present, although it may be short-lived."

Tridia pressed her hands against Drayden's chest as the lights returned. The warmth of his body against her palms made her catch her breath. He swallowed hard as he stood and offered her his hand. She eyed the proffered help as she sat up.

"I've given my word," he said. "We'll just have to deal with it."

"Then treat me as a stranger, or a servant," Tridia said. She stood without taking his hand and swallowed the sweetness in her mouth. "I'm skilled as a bodyguard and I can protect you from outside attack. I can do that, if I'm allowed to research your enemies. You must show me no deference, Your Highness. It's the only way *I'll* get through this. I'm a soldier, used to orders and structure. Help me stay in that world and we just might survive this together."

"Tridia — "

"No, Your Highness. Please, address me as Commander Odana."

***

Drayden stared. Tridia's words cut him to the marrow. Show her no deference? Treat her as a bodyguard? She was his mate! He held every nuance of her being inside his mind and his heart. How could he not show her deference?

Fight for me — and make me fight, too — because I'm weary of the battle. Do whatever it takes to save me. Do whatever it takes to save me. Do whatever it takes to save me.

He'd heard those words through his delirium last night. Her thoughts had touched his, begging for the help she was trying to voice. Looking at her now, with her shoulders squared, but her eyes pleading, he understood. She *didn't* have the strength to fight herself and him — if it should come to that. He had to help her. *He* had to put distance between them because it was beyond her to do it. She had bonded with him mentally and assured his sanity. He was probably more real in her thoughts than she was to herself. His presence would grow stronger as he matured. If he didn't set a precedent of control now, he would endanger her later. In the worst case, if they were stuck in the bunker together for ten years...

What had she just said? She could protect him if she was allowed to study his enemies? She already had a plan.

"Very well, Commander Odana," he said, in as stern a voice as he could manage. "Your first task is to accompany me to the lab where the physician will properly tend my injury. Approach me no closer than two arms' length, unless I give you leave to do so. Are we clear?"

Relief sparkled in the tears in Tridia's eyes. "Yes, Your Highness. Very clear."

***

Tridia sat alone at the desk in Drayden's study, perusing the holographic monitors as they displayed the weather patterns over the small planet. The physician program had given Drayden several injections and covered his open wound with synthetic skin so it would heal. It fussed over the fact there would be a scar, but Drayden didn't seem disturbed to hear it. After giving him a lecture on proper deportment, the program sent him away to take a much-needed shower.

It then ordered Tridia to stay at the desk until Drayden returned, and threatened intervention if she so much as crossed to the door through which the prince had left the room. Tridia had rolled her eyes at the insinuation she would try to spy on him in the shower, and obediently planted herself at the desk where the monitors had gone into a rotation of the weather patterns across the planet.

She hadn't tried to hack the security system or open the doors. In truth, she was physically too tired to do much more than watch the swirls of wind across the desert. Mentally, she browsed Drayden's childhood memories to orient herself to the bunker through his eyes. She flew with him and Master Aren around Zentel before they went into the bunker for the last time. The tour made the weather patterns make sense and revealed what might become important information about the rest of the planet.

Drayden's childhood loneliness hurt her so deeply she had to leave his past and force herself into the present. She looked for her connection to Winniel and found it very faint at the edge of her consciousness. Had the veil fallen for the Sentinels when Drayden had removed it from her mind? Did Winniel now know the truths she'd been tasked to find? Tridia scowled at the monitor when Drayden entered the room.

He had showered and his damp hair lay around his shoulders. He carried a new bulging backpack – and a shirt, which he hadn't bothered to put on. He dropped the backpack on the sofa and took a step toward Tridia. She sprang to her feet and spun the chair so it came to a stop between them.

At the sight of her face, Drayden spun to look behind him, crouched for an attack. Seeing nothing he turned toward the door, and finally stood to face her, confusion on his face.

"What's wrong?" he asked.

Tridia's eyes dropped to his bare chest and lingered there before she forced them up. Still confused, he glanced down and back up.

"Our minds are closed, Commander Odana," Drayden said. "You're going to have to tell me what's wrong."

"Shirt," Tridia stammered. "Please, Your Highness, put your shirt on."

Drayden looked at the shirt in his hand and embarrassment painted his cheeks bright red.

"I'm sorry!" He pulled a loose-fitting black shirt over his head and tugged it into place until nothing showed above his wrists or below his neck. "I have so little privacy with the Rrabbas and such absolute privacy in here that I didn't think. I *am* sorry."

Tridia's pulse slowed with her breathing. "I apologize for my reaction, sir. I was taken by surprise. I will be more professional in the future."

"You're forgiven, Commander," Drayden said, and took another step toward her.

"Begging your pardon, sir," Tridia stepped back. "Please understand, this isn't like me and I don't like being this way. We've reopened years of memories in my mind and trying to sort out the personality conflicts is giving me a headache. I don't need forgiveness. I need structure."

"It wasn't intentional." Hurt and anger mingled in Drayden's voice.

Tridia sighed deeply, trying to get a grip on her emotions. She kept her eyes focused on Drayden's chin.

"No, sir," she said. "You'd never do anything so mean."

"I'll be more careful in the future." Drayden pointed toward the backpack. "I'm going into a different part of the bunker for a few days. To give us both some space. There are storerooms I haven't entered for several years. The maintenance drones care for everything. They perform routine maintenance, clean, and repair any damage, but I should make an inspection, all the same."

He took another step toward Tridia, and she backed away again.

"I'm not going to attack you," he said.

"I can't make the same promise," Tridia responded.

"You're not the only one suffering!" Drayden raised his voice. "Why do you think I took a shower when I left the room?"

"Because you needed it." Tridia snapped.

"Yes, and so do you, but the timing is more to the point of the question."

"I may be untrained, but I'm not stupid. You needed to calm down." Tridia couldn't look him in the eyes.

"You don't understand what happened to us in the clearing," he stated. "That bonding shouldn't have happened to me for another eighteen years – and more than twenty years for you. Neither of us is mature enough by Chesan standards to deal with the subtleties of this union. You've asked me to treat you as a bodyguard. As though I'm your superior. I've never had a bodyguard and I've only recently tried pulling rank on the computer program. I don't know how to be what you want me to be. I need time to study your memories to see what you expect of me. I'll do it – for you, and for us. But if I'm going to treat you like a soldier, then you've got to behave like one. Give me something to work with besides a frightened girl that makes me want to – to not treat her like a soldier."

Tridia stared. Had Drayden slapped her, she wouldn't have felt more humiliated. For the first time since falling on Zentel she set aside her emotions and wrapped herself in the discipline for which she'd become known on Odea. Commander Tridia Odana stood before the exiled prince of the Chesan people with her shoulders squared and her chin raised. Her heart stopped pounding and her eyes took on their famous steel glint. She had to protect Drayden and rid the galaxy of the Kel Anec. She couldn't do it as a floundering teenage girl. The Sentinels and the Controller had told her to choose her path, but she really had no choice. Her stomach knotted and she swallowed hard to stifle a cry of grief for what she lay aside as the assassin and soldier emerged. She couldn't allow herself to feel anything for Drayden as a man – only as a charge who needed protecting.

Drayden somehow sensed the change. The anger drained from his gaze, replaced by a longing neither of them could afford. He picked up the backpack and turned to leave.

"We didn't make a mistake. You are the one I was meant to be with. Whatever it takes, we'll find a way to that beautiful nursery." He stopped in the doorway and spoke without turning around. "Professor?"

The black-robed professor appeared. "Yes, Your Highness."

"This is my – my bodyguard, Commander Tridia Odana," Drayden said. "Make sure she has the same access to the system as my own. Give her any assistance she requires with her research – any assistance at all. Also, set up short lessons for her on proper behavior for a Chesan noble – both male and female – she must be properly trained to eventually attend me at court. She is to attend these short lessons at least once each cycle. See that the drones prepare a room for her and arrange for necessities to replace the items in her pack, which was left in the glade." Drayden's voice softened. "It's a pity. There was fresh huttle juice in it."

Commander Odana said nothing as Prince Drayden continued through the door and down the hall. She sat stiffly at the desk and resumed staring at the weather patterns, her heart as empty as her eyes. Tridia wept on the inside, as the assassin took control.

CHAPTER THIRTY-ONE

Brenden and Deeca shared a cabin with Anza and Dojene on Caine's ship. The nightmare visions had stopped before the *Elisia* docked with the cargo carrier, but the princess and the empress slept through the entire transfer between ships. Brenden and Caine had carried them. Tran made a brief, shadowy appearance as Morgan Jacks before disappearing into hyperspace. Caine would hold his tongue. The two women continued to sleep on the bunks, while Brenden and Deeca sat on the floor. Brenden flexed the fingers on his injured hand. The open wound throbbed with a dull pain. Deeca patted his wrist and smiled. His lips twitched into a half smile in return.

"Do you think Alexa and Jens are safe?" Deeca asked.

"Alexa's credentials are legitimate. She's a registered courier. As long as she doesn't get caught by Hierarchy operatives she'll be fine," Brenden explained. "The Guardians won't be pleased to see her carrying a pouch with my seal, but they won't injure her."

"And Jens?"

"Unless our adversary has operatives in Alliance Intelligence, he should also be safe."

"They all seem very loyal to you," Deeca said.

"It works both ways. We protect each other, as a good fighting unit should."

Deeca laughed quietly. "I thought you were all supposed to be farmers."

"That, too." Brenden allowed himself a another half-smile. No area of his life was without multifaceted secrets.

"I know too much about you, Ambassador. If I am taken..." Deeca's voice trailed away and she shut her eyes.

Brenden sensed her anguish. "You won't be taken."

"You can't know that."

"Yes, I can. You won't leave my side until this is over. If you do I'll shoot you." He spoke without inflection, but his eyes flashed with mischief.

"I'm being serious!" Deeca shouted.

"You think I'm not?" Brenden asked.

"Brenden." Deeca's exasperation rang in her voice.

"Worrying about it makes about as much sense as that silly scenario." His voice became serious. "If you're taken, then we'll deal with the results. We could have your memories purged but you wouldn't be any good to me with gaps in your knowledge. I'm more concerned with what Tridia could reveal and to whom."

"Nira Kayen. So honorable. So determined." A weak voice spoke from the bed next to Brenden's elbow. "She fought so bravely."

"Anza?" Brenden took her hand.

"Don't come into my mind." She withdrew from his touch.

"I won't, Princess. You've been held captive for several days. We don't know everything your abductors did to you, but we know it was difficult." Brenden spoke in his most soothing voice.

"They said I was Chesan. Said they needed samples." Anza's voice became a whimper. "They said I would be a br-breeder."

Deeca moved to kneel beside her. "You're safe now. We'll take care of you."

Anza opened her eyes and looked from Deeca to Brenden and back again.

"I'm Ambassador Brenden Aren. We've never met, but I know your mother, Empress Dojene, very well." Brenden laid a hand on Deeca's shoulder. "This is Deeca Varin. Your mother sent us to find you."

"Are you taking me to my mother?" Anza asked, her eyes wary.

"She's here with us, asleep on the next bed." Brenden protected his mind, but let his surface emotions through. He moved aside so Anza could see the empress. "You can't remain together. Your captors implanted homing devices in your brain. If you stay together, you'll both be in danger."

"Where will you send me?" the girl asked.

"To Aga. To the Sentinels." Brenden waited for Anza's objections, but none came.

"That seems a sound plan." Anza closed her eyes again and fell into a light sleep.

Brenden let out a held breath as Anza's mind and body relax.

"That was easier than I expected," Deeca commented in a hushed voice.

"She's a diplomat – and a smart young woman. There wasn't much to argue about." Brenden spoke in a whisper. He didn't mention Anza had sensed their truthfulness. Deeca would eventually find out about their telepathy, but she didn't need to know just yet. "I'll go see if Caine has any clothes that might fit her, and some of the stew we had earlier. She'll be hungry when she wakes up again."

Dojene awoke before Brenden returned to the cabin. She wiped tears from her eyes and closed her mind, but not before he glimpsed the fury simmering there.

"You let her get to the prince," Dojene accused. "And now they've mated. The potency of the vision came through the protective grid. Or has she lowered the grid? How did she get to him?"

"Through a portal," Brenden said. "We think she had help from the Guardian Controller. There wasn't much I could do to stop her."

"You should have killed her!"

"Empress Dojene," Deeca objected.

"No, Deeca." Brenden said. "Let her rant and accuse without knowing the facts. It's her best quality."

"How dare you!" Dojene exclaimed.

"How dare I?" Brenden asked. "I dare because I *do* know the facts. I dare because I've examined this new Chaos Vision. Two chances out of dozens in that vision show peace that doesn't include Tridia Odana. Many of the horrors didn't reveal her face. But your daughter was in several of those nightmares, and one nominally peaceful scene riddled with doubt and fear. She can't become the queen you groomed her to be. If we kill Tridia now, the chance for peace is nil. Wouldn't her death impact the prince now that they've mated? Destroy her and you may as well destroy him."

"If they've only bonded, there may still be a chance." Dojene glared from Brenden to Deeca and back.

"She knows, Grandmother," Brenden said. "Not everything, but enough to be a useful ally."

"How many others have you revealed this to?" Dojene demanded.

"The only other one who helped with your rescue and cared for your daughter's wounds. He witnessed the effects of the vision the same as Deeca, but he doesn't have all of the information."

"Then he must be dealt with."

"No, he must not!" Brenden lost any pretense of respect. "Zilisk was compromised and who knows for how long. The entire planet of Kanu is off limits for us, and we've limited resources to turn to for help. I won't waste one of our most valuable assets to protect a meaningless secret. Think about it, Empress. The Chesan holocaust is now for naught. We have to deal with the facts as they are. We have a new Chaos Vision the Chesans would have enforced utter genocide to avoid had they seen it. Only one person stands any reasonable chance to pull us through it. She has the full backing of the prince. Would you go against his wishes, even now?"

Dojene said nothing and refused the food Brenden had brought back for her. She kept her mind tightly sealed and Brenden was just as happy she did. Her recriminations would only distract his thoughts. Now that they'd rescued Anza and Dojene, they needed to deal with Tridia and Drayden. The two were together, and no doubt the Sentinels would want to retrieve Tridia, but that might not be the best plan. If there had been any leakage of the Chesan energy through the shield on Zentel, the Kel would be on their way to check it out. Another vessel approaching such an obscure planet would only confirm their suspicions. The Sentinels would get the deciding vote in the matter, so he needed to have a good argument ready, just in case.

When Anza awoke an hour later Deeca helped her get cleaned up and dressed in the pants and shirt Caine supplied. He'd gotten them from his smallest crew member, but they still swallowed Anza's small frame. She voiced her gratitude all the same for the chance to be clean. Dojene made fussing noises about her health and safety, but she remained aloof from her daughter. Brenden saw to it that the girl ate, then he answered her questions as completely as he could. When she questioned him about Nira Kayen, he hesitated.

"You must understand, Princess," he said. "I can't tell you about her, beyond the fact that she survived the attack on the hospital ship. We don't know the depth of your compromise. We'll meet up with the Sentinels soon. They can scan your mind to determine where the dangers lie. Please be patient until then."

Anza dropped her questions with a sad expression. She sat with her feet tucked under her and her blonde hair hanging in wet curls all around her. She appeared so fragile, but Brenden sensed her hidden strength. Dojene had chosen her daughter well and trained her admirably. Anza might have made a fine Chesan queen had not Tridia upset the plan. Prince Drayden could never be paired with this princess if he'd already mated with the assassin. The Chaos Vision bode only disaster should he try.

Brenden's gut wrenched at the memories. The thought of Tridia with Drayden brought a wave of jealousy and he fought away the memory of Tridia's kiss. It had been weeks now. How could he feel jealous after all this time – and with Deeca so close? The kiss had been a ruse, nothing more, yet he couldn't shake the connection he'd felt with the girl. The inner turmoil ate at his confidence. Could jealousy make him kill her? Would affection stay his hand? The duplicity of the Chaos Vision infected his thoughts. Were Dojene and Anza faring any better behind their barriers? What about the other Chesan survivors locked away in exile, how had they dealt with the fear and disorientation of this new vision? They'd been small children when the vision had last been created. Now they'd be about Drayden's age, and unprepared for the nightmare they'd witnessed. Brenden shuddered at the thought.

Caine came in to say they'd been hailed by a Sentinel vessel out of Permai Station. Brenden went to the bridge to confirm the rendezvous. The ships linked by tube in space and Brenden's group boarded the Sentinel ship, leaving Caine to continue on his usual course.

Four Hariok Sentinels, two men and two women, met them at the airlock and showed them to the main lounge. The ship was smaller than Deeca's *Star Seeker,* but large enough to accommodate the eight of them. The main cabin held two couches, two chairs and side cabinets for provisions. Two small cabins off the main lounge had sleeping accommodations and shared a bathroom. Their journey would be cozy, but not cramped.

"I am Winniel." Since the clones were identical, the Trusthsayer identified herself. "Share your thoughts with us, Ambassador. There's no need to go into lengthy discussions."

Brenden dropped his barriers and shared with them everything that had happened with the Controller and Tridia since they'd parted and all he'd learned from the possessed Seluat medic.

"This isn't true confirmation of intergalactic invasion," one of the Sentinel men said.

"No, but it casts enough doubt for further investigation," the other female argued.

"Then we will proceed as planned to retrieve Commander Odana and fulfill our primary objectives," Alanel said, placing a hand at Winniel's waist.

"I'm sure there's a lengthy discussion behind all of that," Deeca said. Brenden cocked an eyebrow at her boldness. "For us mere mortals – and I may be speaking *only* for myself – can you tell me what we just decided?"

Before any of the Sentinels could answer, Dojene's panicked voice drew their attention.

"Anza? What's wrong, dear?" The empress shook a glassy-eyed Anza by the arm, but the princess didn't respond. "Anza?"

"She's controlled by someone else's thoughts," Alanel said.

"Step away, Ambassador," Winniel said. "This will be most unpleasant. It has the feel of feeders. Hunter Varin, please take the empress into one of the cabins."

Deeca obeyed, guiding an unwilling Dojene out of the room and closing the door behind them. Brenden backed away as instructed. An implanted feeder?

The men lowered Anza to the floor, then all four Sentinels placed their hands on her face and head. She immediately let go a scream that threatened to pierce Brenden's eardrums. The cabin door opened a fraction of an inch and slammed shut. Too many of those and Deeca wouldn't be able to contain Dojene.

"You must help us, Ambassador." One of the women spoke without looking up. "We can hold the intruder's thoughts at bay, but we can't do so and disengage the mechanical devices allowing the control. You must handle it. Quickly!"

Brenden dropped to his knees at Anza's side. His hand trembled as he reached to touch her brow. When he did, his consciousness followed the frozen path of the Sentinels' thoughts. Three small devices hummed at the end of the path. Each one blinked in a different sequence of colors. A frozen barrier surrounded them and beyond the barrier a malevolent presence writhed in its attempt to escape. He disengaged the first device easily enough with a simple energy pulse. Its connection to her brain appeared limited and it most likely only transmitted the homing beacon. The second device's connection was more complex and Brenden suspected it transmitted gathered data. If it did, the Kel could know everything Anza had heard up to that point. He disconnected the device from her synapses, having no idea what kind of damage his tinkering might do to her.

The third device proved more difficult than the other two. Its purpose was unclear, and its connections intricate. It probably controlled Anza's mind. The malevolent thing beyond the barrier increased its efforts to break through the barrier holding it at bay. Brenden couldn't afford to study the device for long.

The first contact with the device sent a slight shock through Brenden's body. He tried a second tentative touch and received the same jolt. The Kel Anec medics had programmed the device to repel telekinetic intervention. Despite the pain, Brenden had no choice. Anza wouldn't be free as long as the thing remained active. He steeled his mind to try one more time. Sweat poured from his body. He didn't break contact when the shock swept through his mind but kept pressing to get through to the instrument. Its connections burrowed into synapses and tissue in Anza's brain he couldn't risk damaging. That left the power link as the only thing he could disconnect. If he could terminate the power source it might give Anza enough relief to function. As he made contact with the box, the Sentinel's icy barrier weakened. The writhing presence struggled against them to reach the device. The electrostatic pulses of Anza's brain powered it. Breaking the connection might harm her after all. Tiny as the device was in actuality, to his heightened senses it loomed as large as a mountain, and as complex as any schema he'd ever studied. There had to be a way to block the power without harming the princess.

Before he could finish, the Sentinel's barrier gave way. Brenden's mind clouded with darkness, anger, and pain. The creature clawed its way through Brenden's telekinetic connection to reach the device. It had almost made its escape when an icy Sentinel grip caught it.

"Hurry, Ambassador."

Brenden shook loose the darkness long enough to find the circuit feeding power to the device. He melted the connection with another energy pulse. Darkness expanded until it became a thin shadow on his consciousness. The emotions and feelings it carried stretched to infinitesimal points, then disappeared. The shadow evaporated. Brenden withdrew his mind from the icy path and returned to his own body.

He sat back on his heels, then scooted farther away from Anza's body. A dark mass hung in the air between the Sentinels. It pulsed and strained in Brenden's direction, but the Sentinels held it bound as they moved toward the airlock. The struggle between the clones and the creature lasted a full minute before the Sentinels forced it into the airlock. Alanel hit the decontamination button. Bright lights and radiant energy assaulted the creature until its form dispersed into nothingness.

The Sentinel couples leaned against each other for support as they returned to where Brenden stood. His hand shook as he wiped perspiration from his face.

"Thank you, for your help and for being here when we needed you," he said.

"Winniel and I have been given leave to be away from our clan until the Kanuan crisis is resolved," Alanel stated. "You have but to ask for our help."

The concession the Sentinels had been granted could only mean their link with Tridia still disrupted their telepathic connections. Whatever the girl had done with the prince had not released them or given them the information they needed to complete their mission. To have the First Truthsayer leave her duties with the Tribunal spoke volumes. The Sentinels must sense the Kel Anec threat, even if they couldn't confirm it.

"Our clans won't concede the danger, Ambassador. We aren't a people to act without proof. The ravings of the Seluat medic concerning the fleet can be confirmed. The Sentinels will accept that task. We will not be caught unaware if the threat is real," Winniel said.

"In the meantime, we must rejoin Commander Odana," Alanel interjected. "You know her present location?"

"She's with the prince and better left in there at present." Brenden said.

They responded by lifting Anza from the floor to a couch, where Brenden checked her pulse and her breathing. Both seemed steady enough.

"She should stay with the Sentinels," he said. "We destroyed the devices, but they're still inside her head and it will take the skill of a Felinus doctor to remove them. Until they're gone, she could be susceptible to possession again. There isn't a human fortress strong enough to protect her from this kind of attack."

"We'll make the request on her behalf," Alanel said.

All four Sentinels stood with their backs together. Their eyes became glassy and Brenden watched in fascination as they communicated with their clan.

"It's agreed, we'll take Princess Anza under our protection as a refugee from Kanu." Alanel's voice sounded a bit more terse than usual. "She will be protected until she can be seen by a Felinus doctor."

"If she has time to be seen before the invasion is proven," Brenden said.

"Feeders are not intergalactic entities. They have been seen on Cystia," Winniel corrected.

"Right." Brenden couldn't win the argument, so he changed subjects. "Will you take Anza to Aga yourselves, or will others transport her? I expect my associate will meet us in a few hours with a ship to take us to Commander Odana."

"Our clan kin will take her. Winniel and I will remain with you." Alanel's voice had returned to its usual monotone.

"Would it be possible for them to also take Empress Dojene to Hulac on the way? It isn't much of a detour."

The other Sentinel male nodded. They seemed unwilling to introduce themselves or to even speak directly to Brenden, but he spoke courteously to them.

"Thank you. We appreciate your help."

Two of the Sentinels went to the bridge, leaving Brenden alone with Alanel and Winniel.

"Is it okay to come out now?" Deeca peeked around the cabin door.

"Yes," Brenden said. "The danger's passed."

Dojene hurried around Deeca and dropped to her knees at Anza's side, her earlier coolness gone.

"I knew something wasn't right with her," Dojene said. "She has a gentleness that calms everyone around her, but I couldn't bring myself to get close to her before."

Brenden gave an edited version of the struggle to free Anza, leaving out his participation. He didn't dwell on how near they came to losing.

Neither of the women needed to hear that part.

Deeca stared at the Sentinels and Brenden smiled at her scrutiny.

"You are Alanel and Winniel, right?" she asked.

"Yes. We've been released to resolve the Kanuan difficulty." Winniel said.

"The entire Kanuan difficulty, or just the matter of the empress's bodyguards?" Deeca looked at all three for an answer. The Sentinels remained silent, so Brenden spoke up.

"They'll be with us until we resolve the issue of the Kel Anec, who we believe to be responsible for the Kanuan difficulty. Anything from the Controller?"

"I've felt his thoughts, but nothing directed to me," Deeca said.

Close your mind, Empress. Brenden used telepathy to keep his instructions from Deeca. *Shield as much of your energy as you can. When you are under the shields on Hulac, you'll be free to open your thoughts again. Please, only when the shields are up. Protect yourself when the shields are down.*

Thank you, Grandson, for all you've done. I apologize for my outbursts earlier. You're right, of course. We must work within the facts as they are now. I will defer to your greater understanding for the present, but don't expect me to accept your leading without question.

Brenden laughed. *I wouldn't dream of it, Grandmother.*

Dojene closed her mind and she all but disappeared. Only small traces of her person were discernable as Brenden built the energy barrier around his own mind. When she'd disappeared completely, he let his thoughts return to other things. With his mind closed the group had to count on the Sentinels to warn them of telepathic threat – a major reason he wanted them along. They'd neutralized a small piece of the Kel Anec's advantage,

but he had no doubt who had the upper hand.

CHAPTER THIRTY-TWO

After Tridia showered, she washed her hair and found her towel-draped way to the clothing stores the professor hologram had suggested she use. She stared at the array of feminine attire on display. The clothes would be thirty years out of date before any of the female survivors saw them, but they were simple in design, timeless in their elegance. No one would pity the women wearing them.

"These things are lovely," she said to the matron hologram, who'd appeared when she entered the room. "However, I am Prince Drayden's bodyguard, not his consort. It would be best if I had attire more suitable to that position."

"Commander, we have extensive attire for the female survivors, and storage rooms full of necessities for their first years in return from exile." The matron's voice was apologetic. "I am afraid none of their proportions would meet your needs. We were programmed to expect somewhat matured women, not tall girls."

"I understand." Tridia thought for a moment. "Are there still stores of clothes His Highness used – or perhaps didn't get around to using – when he was younger? Some of those things might be a better choice."

"Yes, Commander," the program replied, with more enthusiasm. "Four doors down on the left, there should be a number of things the prince outgrew before they were ever worn. Perhaps some of the smaller undergarments here would also suffice your needs?"

Tridia smiled and accepted a sampling of soft underthings the matron retrieved from storage cabinets.

"Thank you, Matron. These are much appreciated." Tridia gazed once more around the room of beautiful things, and sighed as she walked away.

She found several suits of unworn clothes in Drayden's old stores that fit her acceptably. Loaded down with pants, shirts, and shorts, Tridia almost banged her head on the service drone hovering in the hallway. It carried a basket suspended beneath its circular frame. For a moment, neither of them moved, then the drone dropped lower so its basket was level with Tridia's burden. She dumped everything into the basket and followed the drone down the hallway to a bedroom, where it released the basket onto the bed. Two more drones came through the doors, narrowly missing Tridia's shoulder as they hurried to put away the clothes.

"Uh, not those!" Tridia snagged a pair of pants and a shirt from one of the machines' pincer extensions, then skipped over to another one that was tucking the undergarments into a drawer. "I'll need these. And I want the clothes I was wearing returned, laundered, please."

All of the drones beeped an affirmative tune.

She stepped aside and waited for the drones to finish their work and leave, which they did with admirable speed. Once they'd gone she dressed and unraveled her hair from the towel. A comb and brush lay on the dressing table, along with several clasps and bands and a smattering of small jewelry she could use to accessorize her reserved outfits. The drones – or the matron program – had been more than thorough replacing her necessities. As she combed out her hair she thought again of cutting it to save the bother. She reached for a knife to cut it off at shoulder length, then thought of her future nightmare-self with bobbed-hair and insane eyes, and she couldn't touch the blade. She might eventually cut it, but it wouldn't be until that vision could no longer be conjured.

Fully dressed in dark close-fitting pants and a loose belted shirt, her hair neatly braided, Tridia returned to the study to find the physician image waiting with the professor.

"Now that His Highness isn't present, I thought you might wish to have a private examination and discussion," the physician said.

"I am in good health and uninjured," Tridia replied. "I see no need for an examination."

"You are a Chesan female maturing far beyond your years," the physician replied. "No doubt there are things in this process you are not familiar with."

"I grew up among other females who matured even faster than I have," Tridia clasped her hands behind her back and stood with her feet slightly apart. "I am fully aware of female cycles and the basic cause of procreation. That discussion isn't necessary."

"The bonding ritual you've undergone with the prince will increase the production of hormones and enzymes until you won't be able to stay in the same room with him – nor he with you." The physician crossed her arms. "You will not mature to your first cycle of fertility until a year after your initial mating – the priming of your cycle. The gestation term for a Chesan female is seven months. Is this knowledge which you already possessed?"

"No," Tridia responded. "But neither is it necessary for my duties as a bodyguard to His Highness."

"Should we be concerned your fertility countdown started before you met His Highness? Or is there a possibility your gestation has already started?"

"No." Tridia didn't expound on the answer.

"Both of you are determined to attempt to live this fantasy?"

"I am determined to *live*, Physician," Tridia brought her hands to her sides and clenched her fists. "And to see that Prince Drayden survives, as well. The consequence of failure is only a thought away, and no physical draw is sufficient to overcome the terror of that vision. His Highness is strong-willed and honorable. He would never attempt to force himself on me. Even if he did, I assure you, I am more than capable of subduing an attacker twice his size. Now, if we can get on with my research, Professor? I have things to learn."

"You will only subdue him if you don't want his attention," the physician said. "I have warned you your hormones will increase your desire. If you think contraception will prevent consequences, be warned that the needs will only be satisfied for the two of you when the union is naturally completed. An act that stops short of a true mating will prime the gestation cycle but bring greater need for fulfillment. Pay heed to the information, Commander. It may become critical. I remain at your disposal should you change your mind."

Tridia frowned. The idea of contraception had occurred to her when she saw Drayden without his shirt. At least now she knew not to follow that path.

"As an alternative," the physician said. "Let me offer you the option to exit the bunker. There's no need for you to remain locked inside for the rest of His Highness's exile. You can leave the planet the same way you arrived. His Highness need never know or see you again."

"You must be mad!" Tridia exclaimed. "Leave the prince to deal with these emotions on his own? There *are* two of us in these dire straits, as you've so clearly pointed out. Even if I wasn't affected, Drayden is a good and noble man. He deserves better than he's gotten at the hands of this program, and I *won't* abandon him to an AI that can't sense his mental and emotional needs. I may not be able to have sex with him, but I can offer other comforts that you simply cannot."

The physician's image disappeared.

"New programs on etiquette and demeanor are available in any of the projection rooms. Holographic tutors and participants will allow you to be trained in a realistic atmosphere," the professor said.

"We will save that training for later," Tridia sat at the desk and fumed. Leave Drayden alone in the bunker for the next fifteen years? How could the program even suggest such a thing? Something dire was happening with the AI. She'd have to figure it out quickly before the physician forced her out of the bunker. That, in addition to the plan she already had in mind. "I wish to study the last hundred years of Chesan history."

"Prince Drayden has not reached current history in his studies."

"No doubt there is a well-thought-out reason for that," Tridia said. "However, since it is my task to keep him safe, the last hundred years of history are more likely to reveal any race with current grudges against the Chesan nobility. In particular, I am interested in any discord with the servant races in the final fifty years."

"More recent history lacks the foundation of –"

"If you please, Professor," Tridia interrupted. "His Highness did instruct you to give me any assistance needed for my research. I want to see at least three physical representations of the males of every servant race. Starting with any who might have been empathic or sensitive to Chesan telepathy."

Tridia spent hours at the computer. She didn't look up when a drone set a tray of food at her elbow, but she mumbled a 'thank you' as she reached for something to munch. After reading the species information on two dozen servant races, she narrowed the list to three based on abilities and appearance. If she could identify the race of men who'd attacked the empress in the Public Hearing room, she could track them back to their current planet of residence and be better able to protect Drayden. If she took him away from the planet, she couldn't afford to leave him exposed to a surprise attack.

"Professor?"

"Yes, Commander." The hologram appeared at her side.

"The Ndgalic people, is there a record of where they went when they left Ceyon?"

"The planetary coordinates for all of the servant races are in the sealed archives."

"Does His Highness have access to those sealed archives?"

"Yes, Commander."

"Then I need access, as well."

The physician program appeared at her side. "The sealed archives contain information His Highness has not yet seen."

Tridia sat back in her chair. "Does that have significance in light of the fact these people may be planning to kill the prince once he emerges from his exile?"

"There are personal messages there for all of the survivors. Reading messages from long-dead parents even His Highness wouldn't disturb cannot be allowed."

"Are they clearly identified?" Tridia asked.

"They are," the physician said.

"Then I can't accidentally, nor would I intentionally, disturb them any more than the prince would. Personal messages should remain personal – unless one of them is directing someone to assassinate His Highness."

The physician's image disappeared and the professor reanimated. "The sealed archive opens only with the prince's password."

Tridia covered her eyes with one hand and took a deep breath to forestall an irritated response. She reached into Drayden's memories for the password. He was fifteen when he set it, just after he'd seen her for the first time.

"Little gray-eyed girl." Drayden had spoken the words to the frowning professor and laughed. "It's not something I'm likely to ever forget! That's what it shall be."

Tridia surrendered a half-smile to the joy Drayden had felt. He'd believed he'd imagined the little girl in his vision and based her on the nightmares he'd been having. No, he wasn't likely to forget that password.

"Little gray-eyed girl," Tridia said. Dozens of files filled the air around her, flashing in various colors and brilliance. "Show me the file containing the location of the Ndgalic people."

One file brightened as the others dimmed. She reached up and touched it, releasing another set of files. This continued for three more levels before she found the location file she sought.

"The Ndgalic people relocated to the Matroni system," Tridia said. "Do you have recent history files of that system? Perhaps the thirty-five years leading up to the holocaust?"

The system opened another string of files. "You might have saved me a little trouble by opening the location file this way."

"The system cannot automatically access sealed archive files," the professor commented. "It is forbidden for anyone – or anything – to access those files except the survivors to whom they were addressed or His Highness. And now you, since you share his access."

Tridia didn't banter, something in the file caught her eye. "The previous population of the Matroni system supported a guild of assassins. I thought I recognized the name. The Hierarchy cleared the planet ten years before the holocaust. The Matroni war was a bloody confrontation sponsored by an anonymous client. I studied the strategies of that war for Hierarchy classes. If the Chesans were emptying their treasury and didn't want to get their own hands dirty – being pacifists, of course – they could have been the anonymous client, clearing the planet for their trusted servants."

"I have no such records." The professor's voice sounded indignant.

"Pride from a program?" Tridia asked. "I wouldn't expect the Chesans to expose that bit of war-mongering to the son they were trying so hard to shelter."

"Is there a point to your observations?"

"There is," Tridia responded. "Unless a population is willing to comply, total genocide is impossible without destroying the planet. Matroni Minor was left intact with the greatest evidence of the cleansing contained around the military bases. There would have been survivors. Perhaps small pockets, or hidden communities. The Ndgalic people would have mingled with them for the past fifteen years. Some perhaps even picking up the assassin's skills at a fanatic level. People of that sort attacked Empress Dojene in the Public Hearing Room at Dajelania. The child survivors left with the servant races. Is it possible there may be a survivor trying to usurp Prince Drayden's throne?"

"Not among the Ndgalic people, Commander," the professor said. "The Ndgalic people suffered from the Chaos Vision almost as much as the Chesan nobility. They became unstable and unsuitable to train the survivors. King Aiden wouldn't permit them to foster one of the children."

Tridia studied the files in silence as the professor looked on. "I'm sure these are the people who attacked the empress. They may be unstable, but someone has rallied them to a cause. And they are bold in pursing it."

"To what purpose?" The professor paced the room. "The Ndgalic people cannot gain access to Ceyon. The planet is sealed for the next two hundred and thirty-five years. They cannot access Chesan technology or any of the funds secured in Central Holding."

"Funds?" Tridia perked up. "What funds?"

"When the Chesan race begins to rebuild they will need capital to establish their economy in the galactic market. Provision was made."

"How? Everyone thinks the Chesan race is extinct." Tridia turned in her chair to watch the professor pace.

"His Highness's family name was known outside of Ceyon, but the family names of the other survivors were not."

"A planet's entire economic base is somewhere in Central Holding in the name of one of the other survivors?" Tridia asked. "You don't think that could be a reason for killing off the prince to obtain it?"

"Your mind is vulgar and common, Commander. No Chesan would

consider such a thing," the professor said.

"Perhaps no Chesan brought up in the bosom of his or her people would consider it, but these young people have been on their own, surrounded by outside influences, for fifteen years. Who's to say someone hasn't gotten to them, turned their minds from the straight and narrow of being mindless breeders to rebuild their race?"

"The person whose name is on the accounts does not know they have such resources at their command. Only His Highness's freshly taken DNA sample will confirm the access."

"Which means they would need Prince Drayden alive, but not the empress, who is honor bound to protect him. The one who has been grooming the woman she expected to become his queen."

"What are you talking about, Commander?" the professor asked. "Are there any research topics in your mutterings?"

Tridia chuckled. "No. Events in the past month are beginning to make sense. We have another puppet master in the background. The Kel Anec are not the only ones with designs on the Chesan survivors. I believe the Kel want to subjugate the survivors, but the other unknowns want them dead for the sake of their own greed. These unknowns are using the Ndgalics' fear of the Chaos Vision to turn those former servants into assassins. Winniel was right. I'm not the only danger to the peace of the galaxy."

Tridia closed her eyes and scanned through Drayden's memories. The dark-haired boy in the pantry who looked like him, who wasn't allowed in the palace, and shouldn't have been seen by the true prince. Drayden still bore a scar on his hand as a reminder to obedience. Was the other child also required to carry his scar as punishment for going into the palace?

She delved into her own memories. Did Davik have a scar? Had it been repaired once he came to the Hierarchy as tribute from his supposed family? Was there a connection between him and Drayden – apart from knowing her?

"Professor, can you locate His Highness?" Tridia asked.

"He is in section ten. In the laboratory with the physician."

"Show me, please." Tridia studied a monitor that grew larger than the others. It displayed a map of the bunker's massive floorplan, with a blinking dot to indicate Drayden's location. "Is he safe? Are there maintenance drones near him? Is there anything that could cause him harm?"

"The nearest drone is approximately two hundred meters from his location. It is his personal valet. There are chemicals in the laboratory that could be combined to cause injury, but the physician is with him and would prevent such an accident."

"Personal valet?" In Drayden's memories, he'd seen the hoverbot as a friend.

"Designed and programmed as a companion to his Highness," the professor said. "To act in the place of a pet that could age or die."

"Is the valet controlled by the main AI?" Tridia asked.

"It could be if the drone lost its programming for any reason."

"The program will not harm Prince Drayden in any way at this time, will it?" Tridia asked, staring at the blinking dot. "It gave its word to not harm me, but there was no requirement to not harm him."

"As long as the prince keeps his word to refrain from physical union with you, he is safe inside this facility."

Tridia let out a sigh of relief. Knowing someone was controlling the Ndgalic fanatics and would likely want Drayden dead had made her anxious to be by his side – even at two arms' length. There was no great conspiracy to reach the prince, as Master Aren had feared. At least, none she was a party to or aware of, but that didn't mean there was no danger.

The professor was right, as long as Drayden kept his distance from her, he would be safe within the bunker. The AI might contrive a way to get rid of *her*, but it wouldn't harm the prince unless…Unless what? What would send an artificial intelligence over the edge?

***

"Is there any combination of elements that would recreate the taste of huttle juice?" Drayden asked. "The few swallows I took from the Commander's canteen has kindled a desire to taste it again."

"As a program I could not compare a taste," the physician said. "I have no record of the fruit or the juice being replicated by any means. The trees didn't survive in greenhouse environments."

"That is disheartening." Drayden said. "I remember when I was very small and tired from training, Mother gave me some of the juice for the first time. I perked right up and was able to finish the schedule before falling exhausted into bed."

"Does the juice mean so much to you then?" the physician asked.

"It's just a shame to waste it. Neither of us was thinking clearly when we left the birthing ground. Her pack was right there, but within the circle of the pollen, so she wouldn't go near it." Drayden sighed. "I'll be using the bedroom nearest the projection room for a few days while I inspect this section of the bunker. Can you show me the Commander's location?"

A screen appeared in front of him, showing the same map Tridia had seen earlier, but the red dot blinked in the study where she sat.

"She hasn't moved in all this time?" Concern rose Drayden's voice.

"The Commander has been quite active, Your Highness, but she has been studying the sealed archives for some time now"

"The sealed archives?"

"She fears the Ndgalic people may have attacked Empress Dojene in the Aga capitol building recently," the physician explained. "She is delving into information you have not yet seen."

"If she is pursuing her research as my bodyguard, I have no objection to any information she may discover." Drayden smiled at the blip. "I trust her completely."

"When you bonded with her, could she have hidden another motive? Could she have had designs on the Chesan economic base? Or plans to terminate the other survivors?"

"She hid nothing from me." Drayden ran a hand through his hair, then rubbed his neck. "Her mind was gentle and trusting and incredibly fragile from a lifetime of inflicting death just to survive. I'm surprised a Chesan could have coped with so much. But she did. She survived. And she will continue to survive. Only by her side will *I* survive. The Chaos Vision didn't involve only her. It linked the two of us together. To save one, you must save both. Destroy one and you *will* destroy the other. If one goes down the path to horror, the other will follow if he or she isn't strong enough to prevent both from going."

"I meant no disrespect, Your Highness." The physician lowered her eyes. "Commander Odana is singularly focused on the research she pursues."

"Has she requested the locations of the survivors?" Drayden asked.

"No, My Lord, only the servant race she suspects. She has pointedly ignored anything else in the archive files, but she is interrogating the professor."

Drayden smiled. "Good. It's about time the tables were turned on him. Leave her to her research. She's not one to waste time on frivolous pursuits. You may go."

"As you wish, Your Highness." The physician disappeared and Drayden left the lab.

He followed a corridor to the bedroom he planned to use and the door swished open as he approached. Lights came on and Teak appeared to assist with putting away the contents of his pack. Drayden let the drone go about its work putting away the clothes. It finished quickly and hovered in front of him.

"Where have you been all this time?" Drayden asked. "You could have unpacked this bag hours ago. I wanted to introduce you to my mate."

Teak piped a short tune.

"I've never had to call you to attend me before. Why should this time have been different?" Drayden waited while Teak piped a lengthier response. The little bot's lights flashed. "The physician program kept you away until it dealt with the female? Yes, I know you would have protected me, even if there were lasers fired. There very nearly were. You still could have come to me once the program freed you."

Teak bobbed and piped. Drayden laughed in response.

"Oh, she just freed you. Yes, my mate is beautiful and she is Chesan. But she is very young and very serious at the moment. We need to be separated for a while, and I'll need you nearby to be my messenger. Are the gardens in the lower levels in this section functioning well?" The drone's lights flashed in a new sequence of colors. "I'd like to see them first. Then I'll review the contents of the seed stores. You will accompany me."

Another rapid series of lights flashed in response. Teak piped and bobbed in the air.

"I don't care if you're not an agrobot. I will converse with those bots in time. For now, I want you with me. I have a mission for you."

The drone flashed all lights at once and it rose a few inches in the air. Drayden laughed again.

"So now *you* have an attitude with me?"

Lights flashed, followed by a few short notes. Teak dropped a little lower as he hovered.

"Don't apologize. You don't mean it, anyway. Just don't be so sassy. Come on."

Drayden left the room and went directly to a lift some distance down the corridor. Teak followed. The lift descended after the bot followed Drayden into the car, then the doors opened onto a garden paradise. Flowers bloomed in colorful profusion amid tended boxes, rows of vegetables stretched out for a hundreds of yards and several varieties of small fruit trees grew at the far end of the warehouse-sized room. Agrobots hovered about the vegetation, harvesting, pruning and planting. Drayden walked among them, doing his best to not interfere with their work. The fruits and vegetables he didn't eat were either preserved in stasis or composted as fertilizer for one of the other four gardens buried beneath the bunker. The agrobots had their pincers full to maintain the garden.

The overhead lights dimmed to simulate the evening, so the prince hurried toward one particular flowering bush. Only three of the rare white blossoms graced the plant, and he gently broke one stem before turning to Teak.

"Can you locate Commander Odana?" Drayden asked.

Teak's lights flashed in a random fashion for a few moments, then blinked as he piped an affirmative response.

"Take this flower to her, but be gentle with it. Tell her I wish her to wear it as her badge of office." Lights flashed and Teak bobbed. "The professor program can translate if she doesn't understand your language. Now go, before the petals wilt."

The drone floated into the lift. The flower in Tridia's visions had been identical to the one Drayden sent. In her memories, she'd only seen the blossom once for a brief moment, but it made a great impression on her. She used it as a mental shield without knowing the flower made up the traditional bouquet in the Chesan wedding ceremony. If she scanned his memories or saw his parents' nuptial hologram, she couldn't miss it. Drayden inhaled the fragrance of the remaining blossoms. He'd smell them one day in Tridia's wedding bouquet.

He spent a little longer in the twilight garden, gathering fruit for a snack later. He called to one of the agrobots and had it accompany him to the seed stores. The room, located adjacent to the greenhouse, was filled floor to ceiling with units keeping viable seed secured. Every healthy plant on Ceyon was represented in the storeroom. Drayden walked the aisles, stopping occasionally to read the labels or check the settings on individual units, making comments or asking questions of the agrobot. It had been years since he'd bothered to enter this room. Now that he had Tridia with him, he felt a new sense of responsibility to the future they would share. The visions had shown Tridia potting plants and teaching children to do the same. She would need seed for that and he'd make sure she had all she needed. Whatever tools would take them into their peaceful future, he would protect with his life.

When he finished inspecting the room, he dismissed the agrobot and took the lift to the corridor near his sleeping quarters. Emptiness hung in the air about him and his mood darkened. The only times he'd slept alone in more than a year had been inside the bunker. Otherwise he'd had Tayne's small body next to his. Someone to protect and to care for. He'd be alone tonight, while his mate slept a mile away in the same complex.

All he'd wanted to do since awakening to see her face that morning was to hold her in his arms. The pain of walking away from her today had made his loneliness for the past fifteen years seem like a breath on the wind, but he couldn't have stayed near her with their bonding so new. Not without touching her, without holding her, no matter what brave words either of them had spoken.

His father's recordings had explained that during the first days of bonding, Chesan couples generally cemented their unity by speaking telepathically with each other and exploring their newly acquired memories. He'd kept his barriers up to keep his own thoughts from tormenting her. Would his actions cause problems later in their relationship? Drayden pushed away any thought of failure. If he had to sleep alone for the next ten years, he would do it to protect her, and they would renew their bonding after their exile ended. In the meantime, as he prepared for bed, he dropped his barriers – just in case she called to him – and dove into her memories, studying the men and women who had commanded her, hoping to learn enough to give her the support she needed to survive.

***

Tridia stood and stretched her back. "That makes no sense, Professor. Giving His Highness's enemies a full fifteen years more to prepare their ambush as opposed to communicating the possible danger to our outside agents so they can begin investigations is tantamount to collusion with them."

She didn't raise her voice as she spoke with the hologram but argued with him as she would have argued with any of her past instructors. Much to their chagrin – as with the program's holographic representative – Tridia always had valid points.

"Communication outside the shields is prohibited," the professor stated.

"Let me make a summation so you don't have to believe you're protecting hidden knowledge," Tridia said. "This bunker is much larger than anything Prince Drayden would have needed on his own, even for a thirty-year exile, and growing from child to man. According to your diagrams and what I have observed on my own, there are stores of clothing here for males and females and apparently enough bedrooms and living areas to adequately separate several dozen individuals – or couples living together. You've given me fresh fruits and vegetables to eat, so there must be at least one greenhouse, since an outside garden would be evidence of habitation. I gather this is the staging area for the Chesan survivors to come together and get to know each other before taking whatever next steps are planned for them. You did say Ceyon won't be open for another two hundred thirty-five years, after all. You must have a way for His Highness to communicate with the outside once his exile has ended. Therefore, it stands to reason there is communication equipment inside this facility, or it can be reached from this facility. So, where is it?"

"Access to the communications equipment on sublevel four is strictly prohibited!" the professor shouted.

"Not only are you prideful, but you can be irritated. Your AI must have evolved further than even the Chesan designers had planned."

"You do not have access beyond what His Highness is allowed."

The professor regained his disapproving scowl.

"If you will refer to his instructions, you'll find that I do," Tridia said. "He instructed you to give me any assistance in my research. That goes beyond anything I can do on my own, with my own access, or with my own knowledge. You are to assist me to protect him. If that includes going beyond your established guidelines, then so be it. One person – that being me – has already infiltrated this facility, even to the highest level of bonding with His Highness. Had I been an enemy, I could have killed him easily. The only things left for you to protect are his person and his purity. I am in a better position to protect both, because I can maintain the vigil beyond these walls."

Tridia allowed her ire to grow before she continued. "I cannot do it without your cooperation and help from our allies in the galactic core! His outside benefactor has been attacked twice, and one of the survivors taken, possibly killed by this time. Yet, you sit here in isolation claiming to protect him? You're setting him up to be destroyed the moment these shields fall. Analyze those statements."

"If you speak the truth, your points are valid." The professor glared at her.

"Finally, we're getting somewhere," Tridia said, sitting again. "I assume your communications equipment can monitor interstellar transmissions without revealing your location. The Empress of Kanu is Prince Drayden's benefactor. Ambassador Brenden Aren of the planet Hulac, is his protector. Monitor those two planets for confirmation. If you can locate either of them, then you can get up to speed on what has been happening to your precious plan and how it is no longer viable based on the new Chaos Vision which His Highness and I have created. If there was some way to share those revelations with you, I would, but I don't have AI links, nor do I intend to have them installed. You'll have to do your own investigations."

"I will monitor the transmissions and investigate your claims," the professor agreed. His image didn't relax its scowl.

"That is all I ask at present. I don't have enough information to justify the risk of direct communication yet, so learn as much as you can in the next few days. In the meantime, I would like to see the security schema for the maintenance drones."

"Why would you need that information?" The professor folded his arms across his chest.

"Apart from your lasers or you poisoning either the air or our food, the maintenance drones are the only things able to hurt the prince," Tridia said. "Your AI has evolved, perhaps theirs has, too. Suppose it should evolve to the point of seeing His Highness as an intruder in their otherwise orderly world, and decide to eradicate him."

"Preposterous!" the professor exclaimed.

"No more preposterous than an AI that evolves emotion, or is capable of threatening the one it was created to protect. I'm well within the scope of my position to request the security schema – as it exists today, as well as the way it was originally designed."

Silence followed. Tridia was about to further her argument when a drone carrying a flower in its pincer entered the room.

The drone extended the flower as it approached. Its lights blinked. A sweet melody piped from its speakers.

"The drone says the flower is from the prince. His Highness wishes you to wear it as your badge of office," the professor said. The drone piped an indignant sound. "The *hoverbot's* name is Teak. It is Prince Drayden's personal valet."

"This flower." Tridia took the flower and breathed deeply of its scent. She was suddenly back on Odea, in the wilderness garden, seeing the blossom on her plant for the first time. "I planted this flower on Odea."

"You planted this flower?" the professor asked.

"Well, not *this* flower, but a plant that bore a flower like it. The last time I saw the plant it had just shown its first bloom. A flower identical to this one. I barely had time to smell it."

"You cultivated a Lesta flower on an alien world?" The program seemed impressed.

"Yes. I was very young when I planted it. It was shortly before I saw Prince Drayden for the first time through a portal vision." Tridia inhaled the scent again. "Is there some way to keep the bloom fresh? Can one of the drones bring a small vase or cup I could use for water? I'd like to keep it hydrated until I can find a pin to attach it with."

The professor stared over Tridia's head for a moment. "Another drone will bring a vase."

"Thank you."

"You shall have the security schema for the drones," the professor said. "Shall we continue after you've had your rest period?"

Tridia yawned. Had the computer's suggestion of rest prompted it? She nodded her consent to the professor's image and started toward the hallway to her bedroom.

Your Highness? Her tentative thoughts reached out toward Drayden. His answer came almost immediately.

Yes, Commander.

Tridia smiled at the tone of Drayden's response. He was taking his role as her superior to heart. *Thank you for the flower. It's lovely. I will wear it as you directed.*

It's my pleasure, Commander Odana. Have your studies been fruitful?

Yes. I have a lot to report to you, but I need additional time to achieve the primary goal. I'm suddenly dead on my feet and going to my quarters for some rest. I'll start again in the morning.

I'm glad you decided to contact me. I didn't want to disturb your studies.

I wasn't sure you'd be willing to speak with me. I wanted to thank you.

It's natural we should converse telepathically after our bonding. Contact me as often as you like. I'm always available to you. After all, you're my bodyguard.

Tridia breathed in the fragrance of the flower again. *I appreciate your forbearance. It's difficult to not think of you. I've been diving into your memories for hours. Seeing the bunker through your eyes. It's kept you close without getting us both killed.*

Drayden paused at her words. *I've been in your memories, as well. We're also supposed to do that after bonding. Probably not for the reasons we've done it, but at least we're strengthening our bond.*

Tridia held her thoughts back. If she and Drayden continued to communicate, would it be better or worse? Being in and out of his memories all day had made him more of a companion than a mate, but speaking with him was different.

I don't want to let you go, but I'm also tired. It might be best if we continue after we've both rested.

Of course, sir. It isn't as if we've had life changing experiences for the past two days with little sleep.

Drayden's amusement touched Tridia's thoughts.

Sleep well, Commander. I expect a full report tomorrow.

Yes, Your Highness. Sleep well.

Tridia let her gratitude flow toward Drayden. Perhaps he'd heard her thoughts after all.

CHAPTER THIRTY-THREE

Tridia awoke to the sound of glass breaking the next morning. A drone hovered near her dressing table. The small vase containing the Lesta flower lay shattered on the floor. She threw back her covers and got to her feet, careful of any bits of glass. The flower remained intact and she placed it gently on the dressing table.

"That was unusually clumsy," she said to the drone.

The hovering robot made no sound and flashed no lights in response.

"Do you have a purpose for being in my room?" Tridia glanced at the door and the drone's empty pincers. It didn't respond. "Leave now. Send another drone to clean up this broken glass and dry the water. Now."

The drone floated out the door. What she wouldn't give for the blaster she'd left outside in her pack. She shook her head and gathered her clothes to get dressed. She'd secure her door in the future.

Tridia studied the security schemas supplied by the professor the next morning and determined that the drones had indeed evolved, but not to a point of concern for Drayden's safety – nor supposedly hers. The drones hadn't truly concerned her before this morning. Obtaining their security schemas and getting confirmation of communications equipment had been the first steps toward gaining access to the entire security program. It might take months to reach her goal, but she had years to work on it, if necessary. Getting information about the Ndgalic to Master Aren was her next step. Once the program confirmed she'd been telling the truth about the attacks on Empress Dojene, and Anza's kidnapping, it would have to concede a change in plans was called for. She'd bide her time and study the schemas to try to devise a way to disable the drones, if it became necessary.

The regular routine of etiquette and protocol training first thing in the morning, followed by hours of study in the Chesan history files went on for several days. Tridia reported regularly to Drayden and wandered in his memories as often as she could. The more she learned about him, the more she liked him, and she could almost believe he was her perfect mate. But every time she drifted down those paths, she remembered the horrible cost of getting near him too quickly. Memories of the Chaos Vision kept her mind focused on the task of accessing the security program.

She sat back in her chair and munched a small carrot. The dietary program controlling the drones had decided she needed low calorie meals in her inactive state. Food wasn't the issue, but she decided it was time to change her state.

"Professor, please direct me to the nearest room where I can work out," she said.

The program had given up its scowl on the second day and merely looked at her with forced indulgence.

"The projection rooms all have workout programs installed. The nearest one is on the second lower level. Exit the lift to your right and go to the eighth door."

Tridia stood and stretched. She needn't have asked the program. She'd found the exercise room in Drayden's memories, a rack of battle staffs next to its door. She didn't want the program to know she could navigate the complex almost as well as the prince himself at this point.

She took the stairwell next to the lift instead of riding down to the lower level. Drayden – or one of the bots – had arranged the battle staffs by length and Tridia smiled as she picked up the smallest one. Drayden had been seven or eight when he'd used it. She touched the memories of his first training with Brenden Aren. The young master assassin had shown patience with the child Drayden had been. She replaced the small staff and took up one of the longer ones, testing its weight and twirling it before entering the room.

"Drayden twelve, battle training." It was the last command Drayden had used in the room.

Tridia caught her breath when Master Aren's younger image appeared. He had changed little in fifteen years.

"Confirm you are not wearing protective gear," the image stated.

"Confirmed," Tridia replied.

"Take your stance and prepare to begin."

The image struck without further warning and it took only moments for Tridia to realize she had a fight on her hands. Master Aren had earned his rank in multiple grids and his skill with the battle staff matched his marksmanship with a blaster. The image scored multiple hits that stung as much as real sparring. He might have been gentle and patient with Drayden, the child, but Master Aren showed no mercy to the man the prince had become. If this was Drayden's workout, no wonder he'd been confident battling the skike with a staff. Tridia found her rhythm and attacked the image with gusto. They were evenly matched and the sparring continued long enough for her to break a sweat, when the program ended abruptly.

Tridia stopped with her back to the door but spun at the sound of Drayden's voice.

"Time for a new opponent," he said, fastening the protective gear on his forearms. His head, thighs and shins were already covered.

"That's a bit one-sided, isn't it?" Tridia asked, indicating the gear.

"You're a professional. Don't I deserve some advantage?" Drayden responded with a smile.

"Not if you spar at this level on a regular basis."

"One week of every seven is hardly a regular basis," he replied.

Tridia circled Drayden as he moved to the center of the room. "I don't sense you. Are you blocking your energy?"

"I'm not actually there. I'm in another workout room on the third level. I've never had a chance to do this real time, so I thought some protective gear might be warranted. I'll be happy to wait until you've donned a set, if you like."

You can touch my thoughts, if you want to reach out. I don't have any barriers up.

Let's try this without being aware of each other's plans. Tridia grinned.

"I'll take my chances," she said. "I'm assuming you don't intend to cause permanent injury."

"I would sooner injure myself, Commander. Be forewarned, I won't hold back. I want to see if my bodyguard is indeed worth my trust in battle."

"You'll regret those words, Your Highness."

Tridia attacked, but Drayden was ready. She struck harder than she normally would have because of the protective gear, but otherwise battled with reserve – at first. Drayden showed no restraint. He moved with a fluid grace that matched her own, and he made his strikes and parries with great care. It quickly became apparent she didn't need to hold back for his sake, so she let go and fought wholeheartedly. They continued as if choreographed for some minutes, both of them sweating profusely, their breathing increasing with every strike. Tridia ended the duel by catching Drayden behind the ankle with the tip of her staff, sweeping upward and landing him on his back. Her staff went to his throat and held him down.

"I concede to a more skillful opponent," Drayden said. His image lay smiling up at her.

"Then I can keep my job?" Tridia didn't move the staff.

"For as long as you want it." He laughed.

Tridia moved the staff and turned to lean it against a wall, when Drayden's staff caught her ankle and she landed hard on her stomach.

"You conceded!" she shouted.

"You turned your back on an enemy," Drayden sat up. "Colonel Aren pulled the same trick on me. It was a lesson I've never forgotten and it's saved my life in the desert more than once."

"With the skikes?" Tridia asked.

"The skikes are the biggest threats, but not the only ones." Drayden removed his gear as he spoke. "There are a few other predators scavenging the desert fringes that prefer Chesan blood to plant fluids. They will assume an unconscious position, then attack if you turn your back."

"Then this was a valuable lesson." Tridia sat up cross-legged on the floor. "I haven't come across those memories yet."

"The last time was about a year ago. The Rrabbas call the creatures onteo, but I have no idea about their species information."

Tridia jerked upright as Drayden's memory of the encounter with the onteo flashed through her thoughts. An animal a little larger than a marset cat had stalked him onto the sand and attacked when Drayden and the Rrabbas paused for water. The prince had struck the beast several times with his staff and it went down as if dead, but Drayden hadn't turned his back as he walked away. The creature sprang one last time and Drayden slammed the tip of his staff between its eyes. It went down for good.

"You handle yourself well in battle," Tridia said. "I guess there are still a lot of memories I need to study."

Drayden laughed. "Twenty-two years is a lot to absorb in a few days." He became serious. "We'll have a lifetime to live each other's memories."

"Let's hope the lifetimes stretch beyond this bunker."

"This is a safe way for us to meet and converse," Drayden said. *If there is anything we need to make sure the program doesn't hear, we can always communicate telepathically.*

"Must we always beat on each other?" Tridia asked.

"I think we can occasionally take our workouts separately. I personally prefer beating on Brenden Aren's image."

"He beats back," Tridia said.

"Yes, but that only makes me more determined."

"Are the inspections continuing satisfactorily?" Tridia asked.

"The maintenance drones have done incredible work." Drayden said.

He continued to describe things he'd seen and how the storage rooms had been kept clean of even dust particles.

Any nearer the security access? Drayden asked, at a pause in his narrative.

A little each day. It will take some time before I have full access. I'm glad I didn't attempt to hack into the source code right away. If I hadn't been fried, I would have been locked in my room at a very minimum. The program takes itself very seriously.

No news from outside?

Nothing so far, but everyone who would try to reach us knows the obstacles they'd face in getting here.

The lights changed to red and an alarm sounded.

"What's going on?" Tridia jumped to her feet.

Drayden's image joined her. "It's never done this before. I'm too far from the classroom to get there when you do. Keep me posted. I'll get reports from the AI on the way and reach you as fast as I can."

Tridia ran out the door and up the stairs. She burst into the classroom to find the image of a young woman seated at the desk.

"His Highness is on the way. What's going on?" Tridia demanded.

The female image spoke, "There is a large asteroid approaching the shield grid. It isn't one known to be in this sector."

"A rogue asteroid?" Tridia asked.

"Unconfirmed," the female said.

"I think we can dispense with the alarms and lights," Tridia said. The alarms went silent. "There is only Prince Drayden and me to warn. Can you manage it with a little less drama, should the need arise in the future?"

"Yes, Commander," the female image said. "It was necessary for you and His Highness to understand the criticality of this event."

"Who are you?" Tridia asked.

"Secura, ma'am. I represent the security system. I'm here to assist with any information you may need in the present crisis."

"Information *I* may need?"

"You are the most experienced soldier on the planet, His Majesty's bodyguard, and you're concerns for the prince have been validated. I'm at your disposal," Secura said. "The program is not obsolete, Commander, simply underinformed. Adjustments will be made in accordance with your directives, but they will be balanced against the Chesan objectives."

Tridia stared, dumbstruck, and the image stared back at her. Then she shook her head and spoke. "What can you tell me about any known asteroids in this sector?"

"There is an asteroid field orbiting this sun. The courses of the entire asteroid field were plotted, from the smallest to the largest, for a period of 50 years. No collisions could have caused this anomaly within the last fifteen years. I suspect an outside force is responsible."

"The Hierarchy uses this strategy. It's a good way to test defenses before employing a very expensive planet-killer torpedo. That would be a last resort," Tridia said. "I've been trying to explain to the professor program things have deviated from the intricate plans the Chesans set in motion. It's entirely possible an invading fleet knows where the survivors are hiding. If the satellites around Zentel are the same as the ones sealing Ceyon, how difficult would it be to make the connection that something important to the Chesans had been placed here? Can the shields hold against an asteroid this size?"

"Yes," the Secura said. "At forty percent output, the shields will hold against an asteroid this size. It will be easily dispersed and disintegrated."

"Enlarge the tracking screen."

A view of the asteroid appeared as an irregular red image on a monitor larger than the desk. Zentel showed in the center of the screen with ten concentric circles radiating away from it.

"Scale?" Tridia asked.

"Each circle is five hundred thousand kilometers."

"It's under two million klicks – and moving fast." Tridia studied the image. "That's not just an asteroid. There's a ship behind it."

"A ship?" Secura asked.

"Not large, but strong, like a tug. It's pushing the asteroid. Observe. It will peel off at five hundred thousand kilometers."

As they watched the fast-moving image, it appeared to break apart between the first and second circles. The clear outline of a ship veered away from the asteroid.

"It is a ship. Why do this?" Secura asked, never taking her eyes from the monitor.

"To test the shields," Tridia replied. "There will be more depending on the impact this one makes. What is the shield output?"

"Forty percent."

"Drop it to thirty-five."

"The design calls for –"

"Trust me on this, Secura," Tridia said. "The shields will hold, but we might get a more spectacular response. We need to see who our enemies are."

They watched in silence as the asteroid passed the innermost circle, then completely disappeared from the screen.

"Interpret, please," Tridia said.

"The weapons fired on the asteroid before it hit the shield. Since the shield level was below the minimum design specification, the system overrode the setting and fired, neutralizing the threat."

"Not what I had in mind," Tridia said. "Now they know we're armed."

"Isn't that a deterrent?" Secura asked.

"Only a temporary one. They'll keep testing until they think they have a strategy. If we had let the asteroid hit and they thought they could damage the shield, they'd have become brazen and revealed themselves. Then we could have used the weapons to get rid of them. Now they'll be more cautious."

"The Chesans are not warriors," Secura stated. "Our strategies involve the preservation of life."

"Not anymore." Drayden ran into the room and slid to a stop next to Tridia. He was winded and sweaty, but remained upright as he held his side. "What's happened?"

"We're under attack. The program thought it best to shoot a rock instead of waiting for a real enemy to confront."

"I take it the rock was a decoy?" he asked.

"Not so much a decoy as cannon fodder," Tridia said. "It was a test of our ability to defend ourselves."

"We showed our hand too soon," Secura said.

Drayden pointed toward Secura, a questioning look on his face.

"Your Highness, may I present your security program. She answers to the name of Secura," Tridia said. Secura turned in the chair to face Drayden. "Secura, this is your sovereign, Prince Drayden Anjenay."

"Your Highness, it is a pleasure to meet you face-to-face. I wasn't scheduled to train you for another five years." The hologram stood.

"Thank you, Secura. Please, be seated." Drayden faced Tridia again.

"I've received a promotion in your absence, Your Highness. I am now the Commander of your defensive programs."

"I approve of the promotion."

"Thank you, sir." Tridia remained straight-faced. She turned to Secura. "We'll let the next asteroids through to the shield. Set the output just high enough to keep the weapons from firing."

Three new asteroids appeared on the screen, hurtling toward the planet from different directions.

"They've got at least four ships and a cruiser or carrier," Tridia said. "The first ship hasn't had time to reach the asteroid belt and return with a new payload. These are not interstellar craft. Someone brought them here."

As they watched three ships broke away from the asteroids in stages. The projectiles were moving at different rates of speed as well as using different trajectories. Each one shattered against the shield and dispersed in an array of smaller meteorites that dissolved before passing through the barrier.

"That had to be pretty spectacular in the sky," Tridia commented. "And probably loud. One of them was directly over us."

"The Rrabbas!" Drayden caught Tridia's arm. "They'll be terrified. They might even come out of the birthing unions early. That's unhealthy for the parents and the podlings."

Tridia looked at Secura. "Open the door."

"I don't have the authority."

"Then get someone here who does," Tridia ordered.

The physician's image appeared. "Breaking your word already?"

"I'm breaking nothing," Tridia argued. "The shields are at forty percent and can't be penetrated by outside scanners. It's safe enough for His Highness to go to the birthing grounds. He won't be there long and you can monitor his position the whole time. He needs to reassure the Rrabbas they are safe. And he needs to tell them goodbye. He didn't have a chance before."

"You are his spokesperson, as well as his bodyguard?"

Tridia huffed and looked into Drayden's eyes. "I am whatever he needs me to be. Prince Drayden gave his word. He would never suggest leaving this bunker on his own. But unlike an AI, I can sense his concern for them and feel his desperation. They are the family he grew up with. Would you really want a ruler who could walk away from them so easily?"

"What of you?"

"I will remain in this room, with Secura, to monitor these attacks – unless you force me to leave." Tridia waited.

The door slid open. Drayden looked from it back to Tridia. "You will make one amazing queen, Commander Odana."

He squeezed Tridia's arm and ran for the door.

"Get a visual on him from the nearest satellites," Tridia told Secura. "He'll be under the canopy, but you should be able to track him by other means until he reaches the clearing around the birthing ground."

"I've never tracked the prince," Secura said. "Even when he left the bunker, I didn't track him."

"You should have." Tridia clenched her fists and raised her voice. "All this time the hardware over his head could have been protecting him from the skikes and other predators outside the perimeter. I'm appalled at the laxity in this program that prides itself on caring for the future king."

"Our parameters had limits," the physician said. "We could not rewrite the entire program."

"Until it came to things you wanted – like destroying the only family he's known or trapping him inside to go insane," Tridia snapped back. "Someone unsavory had a hand in your coding and I intend to find out who. For now, we have to keep him safe."

Scanners picked up Drayden's position, heading straight toward the birthing grounds. Tridia held her clenched fists at her sides. He'd be safe, and he had to do this on his own. She couldn't return to the birthing grounds with him. The AI would never let her return if she did.

"Train a weapon in a three-meter perimeter around him. Nothing touches him unless he invites it. Understood?"

"Commander," Secura said. "We need to reinforce the shield."

A dozen asteroids approached the planet. The screen split so the planet was shown from the side as well as above. Asteroids came from all directions, toward all quadrants of the planet. They would hit the shield simultaneously.

"What output do you need?" Tridia asked.

"A minimum of fifty percent to keep the weapons from firing."

"Keep it to the minimum, but as soon as the last asteroid is disintegrated, slowly drop the level to thirty percent," Tridia ordered. "They need to think we're vulnerable."

With the door open, the booming sounds of the asteroids hitting the shield could be heard inside the bunker. Tridia covered one ear. Drayden would be exposed to the full brunt of the noise, but the worst that would happen to him would be that his ears would ring for a few days.

"Shield dropping to thirty percent," Secura said. "Holding at thirty percent."

"Come on out," Tridia spoke to the monitor. Another group of asteroids blipped onto the screen. Only five, but they were larger than the previous group.

"Minimum required output?"

"Forty-five percent."

"Reinforce only the impact areas, drop the rest to thirty percent."

"Commander Odana, you risk too much," the physician said.

"Once the asteroids have broken against the shields and dispersed, thirty percent should be more than enough to handle the smaller fragments. We just need to make sure the weapons don't fire."

"She's right," Secura affirmed. "Thirty percent will disintegrate the smaller fragments."

The physician remained silent.

Tridia looked down at her wrists. They'd started to tingle. The Controller was either trying to communicate or listening in. Either way, she couldn't waste time with the distraction. She rubbed them irritably and focused on the monitor again.

***

Drayden's ears rang from the booms of the asteroids striking the shield, but he'd remained on his feet and kept his pace as he ran toward the birthing grounds. He entered the glade as the next bombardment hit. The shockwaves shook the trees and knocked him to the ground. He lay breathless on the grass for a minute to make sure nothing was broken, then stumbled to his feet. The Rrabbas parents lay as single stalks in the slimy water, their union still intact. He brought up a barrier to keep his anxious thoughts from them and the podlings. Tears filled his eyes when he saw several podlings floating lifeless on the surface of the water. Either their parents' exertions before their birth had drained energy needed to strengthen the infants, or the concussions from the bombardment had been too much for the young plants to endure.

He pulled the little Rrabbas from the water and dug near the shore with his hands. Once he'd excavated a hole sufficient to hold them, he placed the tiny plants in it and covered them with the muddy soil. Less than four dozen remained rooted in the silt around the parents. Were the parents even alive? The Rrabbas may have paid too high a price for his safety. He wiped his muddy hands on his pants legs and used his shirt collar to dry his face. He had to regain control to lower his barriers in order to reach out to the parents. As soon as he opened his mind, the Rrabbas called to him.

Dray-den. Dray-den. The tinkling echo of dual voices touched his thoughts.

Drayden sat back on his heels. The Rrabbas had never spoken to him from their birthing union state. *I am here.*

You must not blame yourself, Brother. We sensed your concern the moment you left your place of study.

I'm so sorry. The podlings – Some of them have perished.

Then they will become a part of this special place. Do not grieve so hard. It is the way of our life.

I will honor your wishes, my brothers and sisters. There may be more noises and shaking, but you are safe here. Do not fear what is happening.

Your thoughts encourage us. We will awaken soon to care for our podlings, but we will not be afraid of the noise.

I must go. I will not see you again, but know that I have loved you as my family, and will forever cherish your memory.

As we will revere you, Brother. Go to your mate. She is anxious for your safety.

Deep silence fell over the birthing grounds, as Drayden stood and turned away. His feet moved like lead, then Tridia's touch brushed his mind.

They will survive, Your Highness. So will you. Take as long as you need. We have a short reprieve.

Tridia's backpack lay off to his left. He retrieved it and dusted the browned remains of pollen away, then shook it to make sure none still clung in the netting. The pollen had lost any potency, but he didn't want to take a chance on Tridia's reaction. She hadn't shied from his touch when he squeezed her arm, and she seemed to be regaining her sense of self. Jolting her with exposure to even impotent pollen could set her back. He left her jacket and rifle where they lay. She wouldn't need them inside the bunker.

He took his time going back and before he reached the open door an immense boom shook the ground. The sky sparkled red and gold as another asteroid disintegrated across the shield. Drayden sprinted through the open door of the bunker, unmindful of the backpack spilling its contents from a hole in the main compartment. The door closed behind him.

Tridia turned as he entered and their eyes met. "Are you okay, Your Highness."

"As someone recently told me, I'll survive." Drayden tossed the backpack onto the sofa.

Tridia nodded toward the open pack. "Does that mean I'll have to return your clothes?"

"I like you clad just the way you are, Commander Odana," Drayden replied, letting his glance take in the slim-fitting pants and belted shirt she wore. His eyes lingered on the wilted flower. He'd have to send another one.

Tridia moved to the sofa to retrieve her holster from the pack and noticed the hole. She took a survey of the remaining items. Her helmet was attached to the strap, and the medkit nestled at the bottom with a change of clothes and a large flask of huttle juice. A few other small items remained in the unopened outer pockets. Her hand weapon and holster rested in their netting on the outside. She pulled the flask out and left it on the sofa, as she secured the rest of the compartments. The pouch containing her DNA lay nestled in her clothes. She retrieved it and considered for a moment before taking a cord from the pack and threading it through the pouch. She slipped the cord over her head and tucked the pouch in her shirt. Last she pulled out the bracelet Dr. Elenus had given her and slipped it over her left wrist and up to her elbow.

Drayden watched every move she made. Once she finished he adjusted the bracelet so it rested without bunching her sleeve. He grinned as she shook her head.

"What's happening now?" he asked. "I thought we had a reprieve."

"They didn't throw anything for almost an hour," Secura replied.

"With that last hit, they should be bold enough to show themselves." Tridia studied the monitors. "The entire shield is hovering at fifteen percent. We don't dare let it go any lower."

"Now we wait?" Drayden asked.

"It won't take long," she said. "They're an impatient group, but they've got a smart commander," Tridia said. "I just need to know whether they're Hierarchy, Kel Anec, or Matroni. The Hierarchy isn't likely the only force that would throw asteroids."

New blips appeared on the monitor. The clean lines of more than a dozen ships approached the planet.

"Get a clear picture of the markings on those ships as soon as you can. Display them for me when you get them."

When a ship got within the second circle, details of it and its marking appeared on the screen.

"Get the shields up to eighty percent!" Tridia shouted.

Torpedoes launched from all ships at once, and exploded against the reinforced shield without damaging it.

"What happened?" Drayden asked. "I thought you wanted to lure them in."

"I wanted to identify them," Tridia said, then stared wide-eyed at the screen as energy streams shot from the shield and disintegrated every ship. "That's not good."

CHAPTER THIRTY-FOUR

Brenden sat alone on the bridge of Tran's ship. His embassy staff screamed over secured channels for him to answer. He and his assistant, Mr. Tang – Tran's alter ego – had ceased communications from the time they set out to rescue Anza, and things had started to unravel in a dramatic way. A Reytan ship had gone astray in Hierarchy space and they expected him to negotiate its release. The matter could have been cleared up with a few messages, but he couldn't answer any of the transmissions and risk someone triangulating his position.

"Well, Ambassador, is our secret destination getting any closer?" Tran entered the ship's small bridge.

"It wouldn't be very secret, if I told you where it was," Brenden replied.

"Considering that I have no idea of our heading or speed, and that you haven't let me anywhere near the controls since I plucked the four of you from that Sentinel ship, a simple, 'yes, we're nearly there' wouldn't be giving away too much. All I know is that we've been traveling for about seven standard days with three directional jumps. We could be anywhere."

Brenden grinned. Tran reveled in danger, and followed any instruction without question, but secrets to which he wasn't privy didn't sit well. "No, we're not within two days yet."

"Thanks for that at least. I came to see if you wanted something to eat. I was about to raid the stores."

"I'm fine, but thanks." Brenden shifted in his seat to face Tran. He didn't like keeping information from the shape-shifter, but the less his friend knew, the less he could reveal if they were captured. "I don't know what we'll be facing when we get there, nor are we likely to have any allies in the vicinity."

"That's nothing new for us. But the types of enemies we have now could make it an interesting show." Tran said. "How's the hand?"

Brenden raised his bandaged hand and flexed his fingers. "Seems to be healing. It itches like mad. Too bad we didn't have synthetics. It would be a moot issue now."

"Yeah, well, too bad you had to grab the wrong end of the knife flying at your heart. Several options there would have made it a moot issue." Tran laughed. "Do we have anything approaching a plan for when we get there? Is the hand going to cause problems?"

"No to both," Brenden replied. It wasn't the cut on his hand, but a nagging feeling that the Kel Anec scientist intended nothing more than to cut him with the blade, that caused him concern. Why was cutting him so important that the Kel would risk its life? "I'll bring you up to speed when we get close enough for scans. I need to assess the situation when we reach the planetary system."

"Keep your secrets," Tran said. "I'll console myself with a repast of travel rations, knowing that you're just sitting here with your stomach growling."

Tran left and Brenden rubbed the bandage on his hand. He'd made several passes over the healing cut before noticing that it wasn't his hand, but his wrists, that were tingling. The Controller's call had never been so subtle. He'd held his full energy block in place since Anza had awakened on Caine's ship – except for those tense moments when they'd dealt with the feeder. The block might have subdued the Controller's contact. He'd never noticed before.

Brenden lowered the barriers around his mind. The ship's structure came into existence, then Deeca sleeping peacefully, broadcasting no emotion or thought, and Tran, irritated because he hadn't stocked liquor with the supplies. He couldn't sense the Sentinels, but that was normal. Each new sensation added to the feeling of freedom in his mind and brought with them a faint voice.

Ambassador, you are a difficult man to reach these last hours.

We've been a little busy. From what we've experienced, it seems you've had your own share of excitement. As well as developing a penchant for enigmatic messages.

You're on your way to Zentel?

Is that a question you need to ask? Brenden tensed. Was this not the Controller, after all?

It doesn't matter, Ambassador. The planet is under attack. A couple of items of interest to you are in danger of annihilation. In my weakened state I may be able to assist very little. You will need to be ready to finish what I cannot.

In Brenden's mind the Controller sounded desperate. The entity with knowledge that transcended time and space, a being who'd always been as ageless as time itself, now seemed very old and at a loss.

What can we do? We're still some distance out.

There is a place that we both know, where you took a special parcel for assembly. Go to that place and be prepared. You'll get no advance warning, and I can offer no protection.

Understood. My courier? Alexa's safety had been on Brenden's mind.

Given a responding message and sent to deliver it to the originator.

The Controller's voice went silent. Brenden directed his senses back into the ship to find Deeca and Tran. Although he couldn't sense them, the blank space that indicated the Sentinel's presence lingered in the lounge near Tran. The five of them seemed a small force to dare confronting the vision he'd seen, and their only hope lay in keeping Tridia and Drayden safe and sane. The two were in danger of annihilation, but the Controller was sending him to a planet in another sector.

He'd taken Deeca to the planet to recuperate after her initiation into the Guardian force. She'd been placed in isolation for weeks after her experience. He'd watched over her, cared for her injured wrists and shattered mind, and brought her back to health, then forever blocked her memory of those days. Now they were to return to that place to wait for the Controller to make his move. Proximity to the place could cause Deeca to remember parts of what had happened to her there, just as Tridia's memories had escaped the barrier block in her mind. The Controller had to be desperate to take that risk – or nearing the time when it would no longer matter.

The deviation to the unnamed planet was slight and near their current location, but it put them too far away to render aid if the Controller failed.

"Commander Odana is in need of our assistance." Winniel's voice startled Brenden. "She's trying to reach out to me, but our connection is too weak and the distance too great."

"We're going to a place where we can intercept her – I hope," Brenden said.

"Her mind is free, Ambassador, but mine is not. We must retrieve her."

"We'll do our best."

Too many questions, not enough answers, and too much trust placed blindly in a being losing its power by the minute. Nothing about this plan suited him in the least.

***

The outline of an enormous ship appeared on the screen at the tenth circle and held its position.

"What is that?" Secura asked.

"Log it for future reference," Tridia said. "It's a Hierarchy battle cruiser. There'll be a carrier outside our scanner range."

"What are they doing way out here?" Drayden asked.

"Looking for you, or whatever treasure the Chesans would bother to hide beneath this shield. Maybe they want the shield itself or to test its capabilities," Tridia said. Her mind raced for the possibilities. "Ceyon is too well observed for them to test its shield openly. It sits too near Core Alliance space. But they can throw anything at this one and no one would even know. They won't stop until they break the shield or destroy the planet. Now that we've destroyed their ships, they won't back down."

"They attacked first," Drayden said.

"It doesn't matter," Tridia stated. "We've got to do something to draw them away, or at least make them think they've won. You're safe inside the bunker. It can't be penetrated by probe. They'll never know you're here. If we open the shield and let them land, they can search until they decide the shield was just a prototype for Ceyon's grid."

"You cannot let them land, Commander Odana." The physician's image appeared with its sternest expression.

"We *can* let them land. We just can't let them have Prince Drayden, or take any of the satellites," Tridia said. "This kind of power in the hands of the Hierarchy is unthinkable." She turned to Secura. "Do you have specifications on the planet-killer torpedoes developed by the Hierarchy about fifteen years ago?"

"No, Commander. The Chesans saw no need to include specifications of all known weapons, since this shield would be in place for thirty years and technology would advance in that time. The designers counted on the weapons to handle any threat the shields could not."

"The Chesans did business with the Hierarchy and they didn't think a militaristic society would try to mine the technology?" Tridia asked. "Just how naïve were these people?"

"The Sentinels observe Ceyon. It wouldn't have mattered if the Hierarchy attempted to breach the shield. The clones would have put a stop to it," the physician said.

"They don't observe *this* planet," Tridia replied. "We're outside of Hierarchy space, but not so far this possibility shouldn't have been considered. The Hierarchy is a military society. They fight, they destroy, they protect what's theirs, they explore for new territories to conquer or provide military service to, and they advance their military technology. That's *all* they do. They honor treaties to the letter of the contract, and their word is everything. Was there any prohibition against them *ever* attempting to breach Ceyon's shield?"

"No."

The physician's monosyllabic answer was enough to explain a great deal. If they hadn't agreed not to, teams of Hierarchy scientists had been studying the Ceyon shields as closely as they dared for fifteen years. Finding the same energy readings so far out in the rim had to be an irresistible lure.

"We can't let them hit the shield with a planet-killer torpedo. The very least we can expect is for it to weaken the entire grid. We can only guess how a shock wave produced by the impact would damage anything above ground. If the admiral on the carrier finds any vulnerability in the shield, he'll send everything he's got until something gets through." Tridia waited for Drayden to comment. When he remained silent and watchful she continued. "Of course, we can sit tight under a shield set at thirty to fifty percent. Let the disintegration beams take care of anything that gets close. It wouldn't matter to us inside the bunker, but if thirty percent damaged the ecosystem in fifteen years, what would happen at fifty percent for another ten or fifteen years? What about the end of that time? Does the shield just shut down? Do we stay trapped here forever? With the Hierarchy constantly inventing new ways to attack, what if something gets through? They don't have to destroy the whole planet, just the shield. Then the troops will sift through the ashes for anything salvageable. Very little plant or animal life would remain." Tridia touched Drayden's arm. "You *might* survive, Your Highness, but the Rrabbas won't."

"That isn't acceptable," Drayden said. *Is this the first step into our nightmare?*

It doesn't have to be. We'll have to separate for a while. I can't do what I need to with you in danger beside me. Please, Drayden, please trust me.

I trust you.

"We can't risk the torpedo hitting the shield and we can't let it stay at a high density," Tridia said. "We have to destroy the shield ourselves. And we have to make a show of it."

"You can't!" The physician shouted.

"We have to!" Tridia shouted back. "Don't you understand that we're in a no-win situation? If we destroy the shield and launch an escape ship, the Hierarchy will only spend resources on the surface until they're convinced there's nothing here to find. They will focus on that ship."

"We don't have a ship," Drayden said.

"We do," Tridia said. "Several, in fact. The nearest one is under the sand, a few dunes beyond the scrub grass and the old growth trees. I discovered it while studying the facility layout. None of the tunnels connect with it. I'll have to run for it, unless there is some other mode of transportation I haven't found yet."

"You're planning on being a decoy all alone?" Drayden caught Tridia by the arms. "That's your plan? To leave me behind while you sacrifice yourself?"

"Your Highness —"

"No!" Drayden shouted. "I won't have you using titles. Not if this might be the last time I see you."

Tridia let him hold her, even though there'd be bruises from his fingers later. "I won't sacrifice myself, but I've got to draw them away and get help for both of us. We can't fight this fight alone."

"Where will you go?" He lessened his grip, as if suddenly aware of the pain he caused.

"I have to go to Master Aren."

Drayden dropped his hands and stared. He fought to control the anger and jealousy that rose in his thoughts. Tridia let him battle on his own. He had to be able to cope with those feelings and trust her.

"Is there no other way?"

"None that meets all our needs. I am his property. It's legal and affirmed by the Triad of the Core Alliance of Planets. I broke an oath to him. If I don't go back to him on my own, he *will* hunt me down. If not him, then others will be more than happy to take his place. You heard my oath," Tridia said. "I can't fight the Kel Anec and the Hierarchy and protect you from whoever is out to kill off the Chesan survivors while I'm looking over my shoulder. Brenden Aren is too well connected in ways I can't begin to imagine. His resources are deep and well-funded. Without his help and trust, I'm just a fugitive and I can't help you. We need him.

"I have to face the Sentinels, too. I don't know what they have against me. Even with my memories returned, I don't know why they have a vendetta out on my life."

"You've just given me two good reasons to keep you right here and let the Hierarchy do their worst."

"Would you sacrifice the Rrabbas to keep me here?"

"I would sacrifice anything to keep you safe."

Drayden looked away, realizing what he'd just said. Tridia placed her hands on either side of his face to make him look at her. Her heart pounded and the enzyme sweetened her mouth again and again. She swallowed hard and Drayden did the same. His eyes burned with the desire neither of them could afford.

"I will survive, Drayden," Tridia promised. "And I will return for you. I want to know if we ever fall in love."

"I love you already," he whispered.

"You love what I could become, you've forgiven what I've done, but you don't see me as I am. Don't let your heart deceive your mind," Tridia said. "I kill people. I'm very good at it. To keep you safe I *will* kill again. Be prepared for it – and decide if your heart can handle that truth. Or being connected to more of the slaughter in my memories." Tridia dropped her arms to embrace Drayden and rested her head against his shoulder. She lowered all remaining barriers around her mind, intending to reveal her resolve and her doubt, but she also revealed the glimmer of hope that had built in her thoughts as she'd learned more about him through his memories. The only hope she'd ever held for her future.

He crushed her to his chest. "You want me to see you as you are. I can do that. You're a beautiful young woman who dared to face death to rescue me when you had no clue of my danger. You opened your mind despite your fear and bonded with me beyond all unbonding. You've stood up *for* me and *to* me. You faced down the vision that destroyed an entire race, and now you're ready to sacrifice yourself to save me – yet again. Before this battle is finished, you won't be the only one guilty of shedding blood. There will likely be plenty to go around for all of us. I will hold whatever memories you give me, and I will cherish them. You are my mate, and I would choose no other."

Tridia shook her head and held him tighter. "You're heir to the Chesan throne. For better or worse for you, I'm your mate. I won't rest until we're together again. And I won't sacrifice myself if there is any other way to protect you. There's too much at stake. But don't fall in love with an image."

Drayden kissed her hair and hugged her close once more before releasing her. "You *will* make an amazing queen."

Tridia sighed in exasperation. "Once the shields are down, you need to close the barriers around your mind. Keep them closed until you see me again. Or until the Sentinels or I come for you. Don't reach out to me, don't try to contact me in any way. I'll be watched by the Hierarchy, the Guardians, and the Kel Anec. Not to mention the Sentinels – who may be listening now. I *hope* they are. The Guardians and the Kel also have telepathic abilities. The Kel know a lot about the Chesans. They may be able to hear or track us by our telepathy or personal energy signals. Don't take the chance. Practice the full energy block I learned on the way to Cystia. Use my memories for instruction. Please promise me that you'll keep your strongest barriers up until we meet again."

"I promise," Drayden said.

"I'll leave the huttle juice for you." Tridia smiled. "You dropped another flask somewhere between here and the birthing grounds. Don't go out for it. The grass should be tall enough to hide it from high-level scans."

"There is a hovercraft on a lower level, Commander," Secura said.

"You can take it through a tunnel and into the trees. The tunnel can be sealed behind you, as undetectable as the bunker."

"Good. When I raise the ship, use the satellites to disintegrate the hovercraft. And I mean disintegrate. Not even an identifiable piece of debris can remain. Once the ship is at a safe distance, do the same to its hanger. I'll take the ship to the far side of the planet and signal when I'm in position for you to destroy the facilities there. There can be nothing of the Chesans remaining. Make it thorough. I'll survey the destruction zone and let you know when to take down the shields. Then I'll launch from there. And Secura?"

"Yes, Commander?"

"Delete all security protocols from the system, except yours and the sterilization on the main floor. Drayden has to have autonomy and some defense if the unthinkable happens. Move all drones – except Teak – to the lower levels and seal the lifts. Seal the stairways only after Drayden has made it to another floor, if that becomes necessary. Obey his orders. Do you understand?"

"Yes, Commander."

"Will you do it?"

"Yes, Commander."

"She will not!" The physician screamed. "*I* will protect Prince Drayden. *I* will care for him in this bunker. *I* will –"

The physician's image froze, then scrambled out of existence. Secura stood beside the desk. "The designers feared this day would come. Many disagreed with the plan to exile the prince alone with only this system to care for him, but his parents had the final say. The AI was programmed as a nurturing entity, with the possibility of emotion, for his sake, but there was a risk that it would become overprotective, even jealous. I almost waited too long to activate the backup security. Go, daughter, you don't have much time."

"Daughter?" Tridia asked. A blinding white light and sharp pain struck behind her eyes.

"Yes," Secura said. "The AI is certain that you are Elise's daughter. You resemble her. She was a brilliant physician and scientist, a distant relative of the queen. They shared the same direct bloodline, but it branched fifteen generations back. I have a message from her."

"A message? How could she know that I'd come here?" Tridia took a step toward the image, but Secura shook her head.

"The Chaos Vision – or perhaps something more. She was very certain. We have little time if we're to save this planet." Secura turned toward the monitors. The battle cruiser had started a circling pattern, as if to examine the shield. "This program doesn't have all of the answers you want, just this message. 'The one who rescued you from Ceyon has the answers you seek. Find him – if he's still alive. Tell him you're ready to know the truth. Be safe, my brave daughter.' That's all there is. My purpose is to protect Drayden from the AI and point you to the truth, should you make it this far. It's as much as Elise's team could hide in the code as backup security." Secura hurried on. "The chamber housing the hovercraft is time locked, but I can open it as an emergency measure. I'm pumping air into the hallway and the chamber now. Take the first lift, fourth level down." Secura smiled. "Your orders will be carried out, Commander Odana."

Tridia grabbed the backpack and swung it onto one shoulder.

"I'm coming with you to the hovercraft," Drayden said.

His stubborn thoughts washed through Tridia's mind. "Useless to object, I assume."

"Yes." Drayden took her arm and walked with her to the lift.

***

Tridia stepped through the lift doors and led the way down a long corridor with intermittent lighting. She and Drayden walked through the alternating patterns of light and dark.

Drayden caught her hand and stepped up to walk beside her. She didn't flinch away. She wouldn't have to resist him much longer, and they both needed the touch.

The corridor led to a garage that housed a small hovercraft with power cells and tools to work on it. She walked around the craft and checked its power level, dropping the backpack into the seat.

"It's low," Tridia said, fastening her holster around her hips. "We don't have time for it to take a full charge. I'll just have to hope that I can get to the ship on what's there. I should have asked Secura to locate the nearest skikes. It could get ugly if there are any near the edge of the dunes. How fast have you seen those things move?"

"They maneuver quickly, but slower in a straight line. Still, they move faster than I can at a dead run." Drayden rubbed his right arm.

Tridia nodded and touched the cord that secured the DNA samples around her neck.

"Are you worried that you'll need those?" Drayden nodded toward her hand.

"Contingencies are a good idea."

"Or so said Davik Schie," Drayden commented.

To Tridia's surprise, Drayden broadcast no jealousy when he mentioned Davik, as he did when she mentioned Master Aren. Yet, Davik had revealed his love for her. Master Aren had shown no such affection.

Tridia climbed into the hover craft.

"Did you locate the door switch?" she asked.

"Yes." Drayden came to stand beside the craft, his face solemn.

"Don't pout, Your Highness, it's unbecoming the nobility." Tridia teased him with a straight face.

"No titles."

Tridia gave him a half-smile. "Study the records I've found, and wait for me or the Sentinels to come back for you. Don't leave the bunker until Secura says the ships have gone. You need to keep watch on the monitors for the next few weeks. Make sure that Secura is alert if you aren't."

"You're sure the ships won't attack the Rrabbas village after you've gone?" Drayden asked.

"The Elstaar don't waste effort or weapons," Tridia said. "If they believe the shield has been purposely and thoroughly destroyed, and the people controlling it have fled, they won't use resources on a useless rock. They'll make a search from high range scans. Then they'll do some ground level recon of the destroyed facilities, but if Secura obliterates the Chesan evidence, they won't find anything to keep them here. The planet will be safe if you do as I say."

Drayden stepped away from the craft and threw a switch on the counter. Doors opened in front of the hover craft, leading into a rough-walled tunnel.

"Come back to me, Tridia. There will be no peace without you."

We'll meet again if it's within my power to make it happen. I'm drawing away pursuit, not abandoning you. There's a difference. Tridia gave a heavy sigh. *I have to bring up my barriers now.*

Drayden would have protested but she continued. *I need to concentrate and stay hidden. We don't know which enemies may be hiding within the Hierarchy — or behind them. I can't wait until the shields are destroyed. Nor should you.*

Tridia brought her barriers into place and gasped at the sudden isolation. After a week with Drayden's constant presence so intertwined with her thoughts, she struggled to keep from dropping her barriers to reach for him. The look on his face testified that he felt as bereft as she. He stepped closer and squeezed her hand and touched his forehead to hers.

"It's not forever," he whispered and brushed his lips against her cheek. "Be safe my queen."

He released her hand and forced his shoulders back.

"Smile, Drayden." Tridia reached out and poked him in the ribs as she'd done to Davik once or twice. The move startled him so he jumped, then smiled as commanded.

Before he could resume his forlorn expression, she steered the hover car into the tunnel and didn't look back. The scheme she'd planned could get her killed more easily than captured and she may never see Drayden again. She wanted to hold onto his smile for as long as she could.

CHAPTER THIRTY-FIVE

The little hovercraft burst from the tunnel's open door with a slight bump and Tridia found herself in a grassy meadow on the edge of the forest of giant trees. She slowed to make sure she didn't crash into any of the enormous trunks as she threaded her way through them. The feeling she'd made a mistake nagged at her conscience. She would have turned back to get Drayden had the tunnel entrance not disappeared behind her. It would be impossible to find again. A thousand doubting questions taunted her. Were the Kel Anec controlling the Hierarchy? Would the attacking ships follow procedure? Did the Ndgalic know where Drayden was hidden? Had she left him too vulnerable?

She clenched her jaw. Her plan represented the only sound option. If they didn't destroy the shield, the Hierarchy would – along with most of the surface plants and animals. Drayden would survive, but he'd never forgive himself. With the shields down, she might be able to reach Winniel. If she could get word to the Sentinels, even if she was captured or killed, they could retrieve Drayden later.

The hovercraft cleared the forest, and Tridia applied the accelerator as it slid across the grassland toward the desert. The shell of the slain skike lay some distance to her left, just visible in the dark red light filtering through the shield. The empty husk lay scattered about.

The memory of the adult skikes devouring the juvenile's body triggered the vision of her drawing energy from her child. Tridia lost control of the craft and it spun in a circle until she could stop. She leaned over the wheel panting, caught in the paralyzing grip of the Chaos Vision. The utter insanity pouring from the woman in the vision as she fed on the child's blue energy caught in her chest. The guilt of the watcher bled into her soul. Tridia gripped the wheel, unable to catch her breath, trying to break free of the madness.

"If you die or leave, it's all over. Nothing we do without you will ever get us to that place." Drayden's words broke through her terrified thoughts.

Drayden had helped her before. Drayden had distracted her to break them free of the vision's hold. Drayden had held himself together long enough to pull her out. Drayden loved her for what she might become. She forced thoughts of him into her consciousness until finally she saw the vision of the bright room with the white cradle and blue ribbons. *This* vision was the reason he'd fought so hard. *This* was the future he believed in. The future that had turned him against his training and the warnings of his parents. This was *their* future. Even if she couldn't believe in that future herself, she could believe in Drayden's belief. She'd promised to return for him, and she'd do it if it took her final breath. Terror lost its grip and Tridia's breathing returned to normal.

She put the hovercraft in motion again and navigated around a stretch of dunes, wiping sweat from her face with her sleeve and brushing her palms against her pants leg. She continued to steer the hovercraft manually, not trusting the autopilot to avoid taking her through the dunes instead of around them. Two minutes into the wasteland she saw the first skike. It stood as tall as Master Aren's house. If it saw her, it didn't seem to care and failed to give chase. All the same, she gave the little engine all the throttle she dared on the low power cell.

A long stretch of dune blocked the final approach to the buried ship's location. Tridia nudged the hovercraft up the dune at a slow angle. Near the top, the craft lurched, its power cells all but spent. She urged it to the crest where it dropped to the sand, facing down the rear slope. Before Tridia could get out, the little craft started sliding toward four pylons standing at the bottom of the dune. It crashed into one of the pylons, slamming Tridia against the steering wheel and tossing her backpack out into the sand.

She held her hand against her ribs and climbed out of the craft. Looking between the pylons to get her bearings, she started toward the one on her right when the shrill scream of a skike broke the silence. Tridia hustled to the pylon and made a frantic search for the sealed panel covering the controls. The coordinates had shown it on the northeast pylon. She checked the position of the sun. The red orb was almost directly overhead, but she was certain she'd chosen the correct pylon.

The scream came again, closer this time. Where were the controls? Tridia stepped back and studied the pylon. Sand drifts covered about half of the northeast side of the structure. She took a quick look at the other pylons and saw the same drift pattern. Dropping to her knees, she pushed the sand away. The corner of a gold seal appeared. Tridia dug frantically around the seal until a small square appeared. She opened the compartment and entered the complex code she'd memorized.

Heavy hydraulics moaned beneath the sand as the desert floor shifted and started to rise. It continued to rise until an enormous rectangular box stood exposed. The end adjacent to her pylon dropped open and Tridia hurried around the corner of the box to see a sleek golden vessel nestled inside.

The design of the ship brought her up short as she stared in awe. It had smooth, rounded edges with no seams or hard angles, as beautiful as a gilded avian statue. Could something this beautiful and unconventional even fly? The screams of multiple skikes cut her admiration short. Not bothering to return for her pack, Tridia bolted toward the craft. How to enter it?

A ramp opened from the side of the vessel as she neared it and she ascended it in three leaps. She slapped a hand against a control as she passed and the ramp retracted, closing her off from the skikes, but she had to get the ship off the ground. If a monster as big as the one she'd seen at a distance got near enough, it could cause a lot of damage. She ran through a luxurious main cabin, down a short hall and into a bridge designed to accommodate a three-person crew. A quick examination of the console told her one person could fly it, if necessary. It had to work that way, if Drayden was to fly it alone at the end of his exile.

Tridia didn't bother with a pre-flight check. The array of controls in front of her closely matched the *Star Seeker's* controls, so she held her breath and tried the ignition. The engines fired on the first try – remarkable after sitting dormant under the sand for fifteen years, but then, its engineers had expected it to lay dormant for thirty years and carry their prince on his first flight. They'd have made sure it was ready to go.

She inched the ship forward and had cleared the hangar when a skike raced past to her right, heading behind the hangar. Tridia gunned the vertical lift thrusters and had the ship airborne higher than even the biggest skike she'd seen could reach. She turned the vessel toward the rear of the hangar. Three medium-sized skikes battled over the backpack she'd left in the sand. The scent of Rrabbas pollen would have saturated the pack. No wonder the skikes had ignored the ship. She breathed a temporary sigh of relief and studied the controls and settings more carefully as she hovered.

The gold bracelets on her wrists tingled and sparkled as if they'd come alive. Her hands trembled and blue energy shot from her fingers to the control panel. All of the lights flashed. The ship dropped a few feet, leaving Tridia's stomach somewhere near the ceiling.

Light-headed and shaken, she grabbed the arms of the chair and held on.

What now?

Before she'd fully formed the thought, the ship settled, the lights returned to normal, and the console seemed like an old friend, rather than a new acquaintance. Tridia understood the function of each button and control.

"Commencing disintegration."

Secura's voice startled her, just before energy beams rained from the sky. The hovercraft and the skikes disappeared in the red light, soon followed by the hangar.

Tridia reversed the thrusters and moved the ship to a safer distance, before surveying the area. Nothing remained of the hangar or the pylons. A glassy pit was all that was left of the Chesan technology that had kept the ship safely stored for fifteen years. Dark glass also covered the side of the dune where the sand had been superheated. The glass sheet slid down the dune to fill the pit. A few blasts from the ship's thrusters quickly hid all evidence. She turned the ship into position and applied the thrusters to create a small sandstorm that obliterated any trace of the hovercraft's passing.

"Is the process completed to your satisfaction, Commander?" Secura's voice filled the bridge.

"Good job, Secura. Be as thorough on the next targets," Tridia said. "Don't wait for me to get there. The cruiser might get antsy if it detects activity under the shield. Destroy the inactive power stations and transmitters first. Then take out the residential buildings and anything remotely Chesan-made. Pick a few random targets around the planet to give the Hierarchy more to inspect. Don't make it obvious that you're ignoring the bunker area."

"Affirmative, Commander. Re-commencing disintegration now."

Tridia turned the ship to the west, set the inertial limiters and gunned the engines. The gold craft tore across the sky.

***

Drayden sat in front of the monitors watching a red blip as Tridia's ship accelerated westward. It moved too fast for the clear pictures he'd observed as the hovercraft crossed the sand. He'd watched in helpless horror as she lost control of the little craft and it spun in circles. Then again when the skikes converged on the hangar. If she'd only left her mind open, he could have warned her! But she'd made it to the buried ship and gotten it airborne.

After Tridia's interchange with Secura, and the ship was on course, Drayden voiced his discontent. "Don't think you're getting off that easy, Commander Odana!"

"What part of any of that looked easy to you, Your Highness?"

Tridia responded.

"The part where you *should* have left your mind accessible while you didn't have radio contact."

"Your fear would have just distracted me," she said. "I'm sorry you had to watch in silence, but it was for the best. I'm still not strong enough to handle both of our fears yet. Please, Drayden, just keep trusting me."

"I don't have a choice, Commander," Drayden said, stiffly. Then he made himself smile so it would carry in his voice. She needed him to believe in her. "And I wouldn't choose otherwise if I did. Just know that we *will* have words about this in the future!"

"Gladly," Tridia said.

"Targets destroyed, Commander," Secura interjected.

"Is the cruiser still circling the planet?" Tridia asked.

"Yes, Commander, but it's pattern has slowed. It's hovering over the largest section of destruction, near the old power stations."

"They must have detected the disintegrator activity under the shield." Tridia thought for a moment. "Change of plans. I'm going to the north pole. When I get there, make a hole for me to escape through, then systematically destroy all but the minimum number of satellites needed to protect the planet – and a dozen extra. You have to have warning in case other ships approach. Set the satellites to self-destruct if removed from orbit or approached too closely. It might help if the remaining satellites displayed random odd behavior. Firing into space, shifting positions, running scans. Create enough odd behavior that if you need to use them, it might not be noticed. Make sure none of the debris hits the Rrabbas village or birthing grounds. Leave the old growth trees as a shield against the skikes. Anyplace else is expendable."

"Understood, Commander."

"I'm going radio silent."

Drayden steamed that Tridia had, once again, shut him out. As he scanned the monitors showing destruction all around the planet, an enormous outline appeared on the space grid.

"Secura?"

"Yes, Your Highness."

"I think the Commander has a bigger problem than she expected."

The massive ship continued on course to the planet.

"That must be the carrier she said was out of scanner range," Secura stated.

"It's not out of range anymore," Drayden said. "She's terminated communications because she didn't want to argue with me."

"She has terminated communications so the ships can't hear us conversing and know that someone remains on the planet," Secura scolded. "The Commander will be able to see the carrier on her scanners as soon as the shields are down," Secura explained. "She knew the carrier was there."

"She didn't expect it to be so close." Drayden's stomach tightened as he followed the fast-moving blip of Tridia's ship to the top of the planet.

"Commencing satellite destruction," Secura announced.

Tridia's ship, which they expected to be invisible under the shield, would now be picked up by the Hierarchy ships' sensors.

"The cruiser should change course to pursue the Commander," Secura said.

Drayden willed the massive ship to move. Instead of the expected course change, a flurry of smaller signals separated from the carrier. Fighters. Would Tridia have expected this alternate scenario? He ran one hand through his hair as he watched Tridia's monitor.

In her memories, he saw that she was an excellent pilot, and she'd managed miraculous escapes, but she didn't seem to be trying any heroic flight patterns. Instead she made a panicked choice to try a straight run, expending fuel and taking longer to accelerate. The fighters would catch up with her easily. His eyes flicked between the two screens, tension building with each passing second as a dozen points converged around one, and the fighters' blips showed only on Tridia's monitor. He could no longer sense his own heartbeat or breathing. What would they do to her if they took her? Would she allow it? It took all of his resolve not to open his mind and call out to her.

Trust her. Surely, she'd expected this to happen. He concentrated on the screen. Tridia's craft moved in slow circles inside the ring of fighters. The carrier remained stationary, but the cruiser's large blip appeared at the edge of the screen. If she didn't do something now, the fighters would herd her into the cruiser's hold.

"Come on, Tridia!" he pleaded with the monitor. "You've got to have a way out of this."

As he watched the circle of fighters grow tighter they also started to separate and form a sphere around Tridia's ship. They weren't taking any chances on a clever move by an unknown pilot. Before the sphere fully formed, the central blip shot through a gap. The fighters responded quickly to give chase, then Tridia's blip disappeared.

"Destruction of all expendable satellites complete," Secura announced. The program's calm voice showed no sign of surprise. "Rrabbas habitats and old growth forest remain undamaged."

Drayden stared at the last point he'd seen her ship on the monitor. How had it done that? Had her ship been able to accelerate to hyperspeed so quickly? He'd seen no weapons discharge on the screen, the satellite readouts didn't show an energy dispersal around any of the Elstaar ships. She'd just disappeared.

"Breathe, Your Highness."

Secura's voice snapped Drayden out of his daze. He exhaled and continued to watch the screens. If she had died, he'd know. Their bonding assured him of that much, but it offered no other answers. "Are you detecting anything that would give us a clue what happened?"

"I don't have as many cross-checks for validation, since we have fewer satellites, but nothing registered beyond a slight fluctuation in portal energy."

Drayden turned to Secura. "You're saying she opened a portal large enough to fly the ship through?"

"The fluctuation was small. It doesn't amount to enough for her to have created the portal. Someone may have opened it from somewhere else."

Drayden glanced over his shoulder at the monitors. "Who else would have that kind of power?"

The fighters swept the area where Tridia's ship vanished. After some time, they turned toward the planet, remaining well above satellite level, sweeping patterns north to south, then in latitudinal runs around the circumference. Several ships paused in their sweeps at the various destroyed sites, including the dunes where Secura had blasted the hangar. Drayden clenched his fists as a ship hovered directly above the birthing grounds before moving on. The ship remained too high up to disturb the Rrabbas, but it made him anxious that one small swampy area would attract attention.

The fighters continued their sweeps for hours before returning to the carrier. A smaller ship separated from the cruiser and slowly approached the northernmost satellites.

"It's a drone," Secura stated.

A beam shot from the closest satellite and the ship vanished. A second drone separated from the cruiser and approached the planet, being careful to avoid the remaining satellites. The drone landed on the far side of the planet, near the blasted area.

"They'll start surface level searches now," Drayden commented. "I don't see how this was better than keeping Tridia here and having the same thing happen."

"Her stratagem is sound," Secura explained. "The Hierarchy ships will stay in the area because of the satellites – effectively keeping other intruders at bay. Once they've completed their ground searches, they may set up bases in alignment with the remaining satellites in order to study them. The majority are on the far side of the planet, and they won't have a need to disturb this area beyond their initial searches. The

Rrabbas should be safe in any case."

Drayden stood. The flask Tridia had left on the sofa caught his eye. He retrieved it and took a sip of the huttle juice it contained.

"You've been here for hours, Your Highness," Secura said. "I don't have all of the physician program's nurturing protocols, but I know you can't survive without food, liquid and rest."

"Huttle juice will suffice for a while," Drayden said, letting the energizing warmth of the liquid race through his body, restoring tired muscles. "The fresh food stores are sealed in the lower levels, with the drones, if you've followed Commander Odana's orders. I'll have to use the stairs to get to them."

"I've kept one drone shaft open and left two drones with access to this level so they can bring up processed food. Once there's a supply on this level, I'll seal the shaft. Unfortunately, you won't be able to use the fresh foods the agrobots harvest."

"I've survived without those things for the better part of fifteen years. I think I can manage a while longer. I'll be in the training room if anything unusual happens."

Drayden carried the flask with him as he made his way to the nearest training room, fighting back bitterness every step of the way. He understood Tridia's caution in leaving him behind, but knowing she saw him as a hindrance made it more difficult to bear. Despite her words and her vow, she didn't really see him as her mate – yet. She didn't understand that even sharing their fears made them stronger. Once they were reunited, he'd sit her down and explain what their bonding truly meant. It was there in his memories, if she ever found the time to assimilate them, but he doubted that would happen anytime soon. He reached the training room and placed the flask on the floor beside the door, then selected a battle staff from the rack.

Teak floated down the hall, piping a solemn tune.

"I'm fine," Drayden said. "Upset, but otherwise well."

Teak piped and flashed his lights again.

"No, you won't have to go to the lower levels with the others. Do one more thing for me before everything is locked away. Please bring one of the lesta flowers to the study."

The bot floated away piping a grumbling melody. Drayden smiled and entered the room.

"Play battlestaff program Drayden fifteen," he said.

A holographic image of a young Brenden Aren appeared in front of him. Drayden's hands tightened on the staff as he glared at the image. Knowing what Aren had done to Tridia, made Drayden loathe the thought of the man. As Tridia had pointed out, the young colonel had left him with the training that might save his life. In fact, it had saved his life several times, but Drayden couldn't forgive what had happened to her. Too much of Tridia's need for justice had seeped into his character through her memories. He wanted payback in the only way he could get it.

"Hello, Prince Drayden." Brenden's image spoke. Its eyes were focused at about Drayden's eye level. "Time for another lesson. confirm that you are not wearing training pads."

"I am wearing training pads." Drayden lied. The training program was harder when he wore protective gear. He'd been injured once early on when he lied to the program. Since then he'd been more careful about his steps and learned a great deal about hand to hand combat. His mood was dark enough to take the risk, and he had a theory to test after battling Tridia. Some of her skill had blended with his during their fight, and he wanted to know if it was a fluke because of her presence, or if he could, indeed, mesh her skills with his.

After an hour, sweat dripped from Drayden's face, his clothes clung to his body and he had a few aches that would be dark bruises later. He danced around the room, eyes alert for the slightest feint from the image he faced, but the impotent rage he'd felt hadn't subsided. The emotion was foreign to him, part of a memory Tridia had held in check – a Felinus rage, the berserker's abandon – something she had mastered at an early age. He'd have to do the same if he didn't want to be controlled by it. Not that he minded as he slammed into the hologram, using the staff, along with kicks and punches. However, that type of aggression had no place in a throne room – or a family room. Drayden focused his thoughts on Tridia, being bonded with her and absorbing her memories, watching her face. He pulled the rage under control with the greatest effort he'd ever exerted. He looked at Brenden Aren's image without loathing. It was just a holographic image.

Tridia's skills settled into his mind and his muscles responded. Their bonding revealed intricacies of battle he'd never contemplated. It was both exhilarating and terrifying to know she kept that type of rage in check – and now he could, too.

Drayden called a halt to the sparring. He'd found out what he wanted to know. He leaned against the wall and wrapped Tridia's memories around him, then added his memories of her. the result was almost as three dimensional as seeing her stand before him. He closed his eyes and there she was.

In a very short time, she could be kneeling before the real Brenden Aren, and there was every possibility the man would abuse her again. Drayden held the anger at bay. Everything Tridia would do from this day forward would be for him. If anything happened to her, it was because she tried to keep *him* safe. He couldn't blame anyone else. He had to get strong enough to stand beside her, not behind her. He carried her strength inside of him, it just needed to become his strength, as well.

CHAPTER THIRTY-SIX

Tridia flew the golden craft in a circle inside the ring of fighters. She'd opened her mind right after leaving the atmosphere, hoping to give any Kel Anec aboard the craft something to draw their attention. With her senses attuned to the area around her, she could read the Elstaar pilots. She recognized two of them, but the others were human, as well, and none of them wore the abductors' black armor. That was the only bit of good news she could glean. Two or three Elstaar pilots she could escape, but a full dozen veteran fighters would be impossible, even with this ship. They hadn't attacked, which meant they wanted a prisoner, and that would play in her favor when the time came. The two-dimensional piloting she'd displayed so far would also benefit her. They wouldn't expect a dive or a rise.

Tridia be ready. A voice, weak but familiar, sounded in her mind. The last time she'd heard it, she'd landed in front of a rampaging skike.

What have you got in mind this time, Controller? She would welcome anything short of surrender.

A new version of an old trick. Is your friend safe? I can no longer sense him.

My friend is safe. The cruiser broke the horizon over Zentel and the Elstaar pilots started communicating with each other. They planned to form a sphere blockade. *If you've got a plan, let's get on with it or it'll be too late.*

Get into the clear and focus your mind on the portal you saw when I transported you to this planet. Don't picture the exit or you will travel back in time and cause a rift. I will create an exit for you. Just think of the opening. You'll have to help; the last time took a toll on my strength.

Getting clear now.

Tridia dropped the nose of her ship and rolled through a tight space between two fighters, then leveled up and pointed away from the planet

349

in preparation to make a run for it. With a clear star field before her, she closed her eyes and dredged up the memory of her passage through the portals.

Now feel the ship and your surroundings, pull everything along with you. I will help you open a portal. The Controller's voice seemed strained.

Her senses withdrew to the area around the wingtips, tail and nose of her ship, then raced along the vessel's structure until she had an intimate picture of it in her mind. She sensed her own body and clothing and held them in place with her vision of the ship. Holding those images tightly in her consciousness, she brought the memory of the portal to life – a hole in the starfield with swirling mist. The Controller's light touch tingled in her mind and in her wrist and the portal image sharpened. She placed the picture of herself and the ship together with the image of the portal. The expected nausea and pain engulfed her as she sped into the portal and passed through the exit the Controller had opened.

Everything happened in an instant.

Reflexes saved her from crashing into another ship as she materialized in space above an unfamiliar planet. The perfect response of the Chesan ship brought its nose up just in time to skim the surface of the other vessel. If they'd been in atmosphere, or if the other ship had moved at all, the resulting collision would have been spectacular. As it was, Tridia managed to gain control of her ship before it slammed into the planet's atmosphere.

The pain didn't seem as excruciating this time and the nausea subsided quickly. Tridia sat back in the pilot's seat and wondered what the Controller had been thinking to open a portal so close to another ship.

Your comrades are on that ship. You're on your own now. The Controller's voice was no more than a whisper in her mind, and Tridia felt the entity's exhaustion as a tingle in the loose bracelets around her wrists. When had the gold separated from her skin?

Commander Odana, do you hear me? Alanel's thoughts imposed on hers as clear as a bell. *Open your communications to the embassy channels.*

"I hear you, Alanel." Tridia said, after she opened the channel.

"What the devil are you trying to do? Kill us all?" Deeca demanded.

"I've got to speak with my master." Tridia said.

"Land on the planet's surface and keep open communication to a minimum. We'll follow you down." Hearing Master Aren's voice sent both relief and dread through her.

"We haven't much time," she stated.

"Then we'd better hurry," he replied.

***

A chill wind blew across the surface of the planet as Tridia emerged from the golden vessel. She hated the cold, but tilted her head back, face to the sun, and let the chill ease the pain in her body.

"Where's the prince?" Master Aren's voice cut through her calm.

He had crossed the short distance between the ships with a weapon in his hand. She didn't reach for hers. Instead she raised her hands in surrender and dropped her shoulders.

"He's safe, but there's an Elstaar cruiser and a Hierarchy carrier at Zentel." She tried to answer with her mind and her voice, but he'd kept his mind closed.

"Down here. Now." Master Aren pointed at a spot in front of him with the blaster.

The look in his eyes told her what would happen before he ever raised his hand, but Tridia didn't try to defend herself. She took the backhanded blow to her left cheek without dodging away.

"You disobeyed a direct order." His voice was murderously tense.

"Yes, sir." Tridia said, her hands at her side.

He struck her again and she took a step back, but righted herself quickly, raising her chin and looking straight ahead.

"You mated with Prince Drayden." Master Aren swallowed hard.

It was a statement and Tridia resented her master's accusation on Drayden's behalf. The prince had tried to walk away.

"I didn't mate with him!" Her face warmed as she spoke. "I might have if the Chaos Vision hadn't descended upon us as soon as we kissed."

"Every Chesan in the galaxy saw the vision, Commander," Brenden retorted. "It signifies one thing, a royal mating. Don't lie!"

He struck her again, harder. She dropped to one knee, but regained her feet and stood in front of him, her hands clenched at her side.

"This time it signifies a Chesan prince kissing an assassin after a mental bonding under the influence of Rrabbas reproductive pollen." She had to make him understand. "We didn't mate. We just kissed. The same way you and I kissed and caused a vision. Only this vision was horrible."

Tridia's voice broke on the last word and she fought back the images threatening to reform in her mind. Drayden wasn't there to help. She had his memories to sustain her, but she'd only call on them in Master Aren's presence as a last resort.

"The defense shield?" Master Aren asked.

"Shut down. With any luck, the Elstaar believe I destroyed it, except for a few out of control satellites."

Master Aren raised his hand again.

"Ambassador." Winniel's voice broke the tension as she approached the two of them and stopped at Master Aren's side. "We cannot let you further mistreat Commander Odana. She is under the protection of the Tribunal. Please lower your hand and your weapon and step back."

Alanel moved to his other side and made no comment.

"It would seem your protectors haven't abandoned you." Brenden holstered his weapon.

"No." Tridia looked first to Winniel, then to Alanel. "I'm his bond servant and I've broken a vow. He has the right to do with me as he wishes. My life is his to take and the Alliance has no place between us." She looked directly at Master Aren before continuing. "I want this settled between us. The Controller said we had to resolve our issues. I can't fight Prince Drayden's enemies on the front and worry about you shooting me in the back. Either trust me or let's finish this now. I want your word. Enter my mind and see what's there. Ask me any question, I'll withhold no answers. I'll do whatever it takes to convince you. I lived that vision for hours, Master. *Hours.* I wanted to die but Drayden wouldn't let me. We can't shoulder this burden alone and you're the only one who can help us."

She held his gaze for what seemed an eternity before his icy probe entered her mind. All sensation gave way to his presence and her thoughts registered only him. Her knees buckled and she dropped to the ground as he ransacked her memories, going farther back than she expected.

What happened to the Laytran Queen?

Take the memories, Master. I am under oath to never reveal them on my own. The explanation is in the red container.

A small red box became visible in Tridia's thoughts. Master Aren's presence ripped it to pieces, leaving a memory exposed.

The intended victim had been targeted because he aided the queen and her unborn child after the king's assassination. A rival intended to marry the queen to claim the Laytran throne. He would have killed the child. Tridia's efforts on the queen's behalf had gained the target enough time to see the queen to a safe house where others would get her off the planet and to a new life. Two other operatives killed the man and reported that an assassin had killed the queen. She'd been blamed for both murders, but punished when her handlers reported that she hadn't completed the job. Master Aren shut off the memory as the Odean guards took her into custody at the Tubulai prison.

The teenaged girl?

Tridia gave him the whole vision of the incidents surrounding the girl's death, including her entire contact with Deeca. *Diana's father murdered her. He was my target, but I didn't get to him in time. I found him standing over her – laughing. The Guardians found me just after I'd killed him. I was in a rage and couldn't sense their presence. I didn't betray Deeca's confidence. She'd befriended me just minutes before Diana's death. I wouldn't have done anything to put her in jeopardy.*

The men in the Kennels? Master Aren asked. His voice sounded less harsh, his presence less overpowering.

Tridia explained about the trio's attack on the soldier in the square and their part in framing Davik.

K'Tain and Ia'Lon were the ones who killed the Laytran Queen's benefactor and reported her death. I think they had a separate contract to cover her trail, but they brutalized the target as they killed him. That wasn't necessary.

"You waited long enough to extract your revenge." Master Aren continued to probe in her mind as he spoke aloud. Tridia resisted the urge to expel him, she had to stand the violation for as long as it took.

"I didn't want revenge. I wanted justice for the innocent people they harmed later. I disobeyed orders and I aided a target. I was flogged in Tubulai prison on Isar for that breach. You've seen the scars. You felt my humiliation back at the lake. My punishment was lenient in light of what it might have been. I had a quarrel only with their methods and if I'd done my job, they wouldn't have had their chance. I had no personal vendetta against those men because of this incident. Besides their memories of those events were erased and my record redacted. I had no acceptable grounds."

Her master reverted to thought. *Show me Prince Drayden.*

You can have every memory I have of him and of our actions together, but I now have his memories, too, and those you can't touch. It's the only thing I'll withhold from you. That, and a memory belonging to the Sentinels that I haven't opened. We can't afford to open the Chaos Vision. I might not escape from it again and I don't know how that would affect Drayden.

Tridia shared the confrontation with the skike, her struggle to save Drayden from the poison, and her first conversation with him in the old growth forest.

Davik Schie? Master Aren interrupted the memories.

That's Prince Drayden Anjenay. His resemblance to Davik is uncanny.

Remarkable.

Master Aren had no other questions, so Tridia continued to unfold her memories. She revealed the hurried march to the birthing grounds, exposed the passion she and Drayden shared under the influence of the Rrabbas' pollen, and her euphoria after their bonding. She cut off the memory before they kissed, afraid the Chaos Vision would return. Master Aren acknowledged her fear and let her proceed. Through her memories he experienced a fast review of every minute she'd spent inside the bunker, the studies, the loneliness, and the joy at Drayden's presence in her thoughts. The last thing she gave up was her sense of relief when he smiled beside the hovercraft.

"Our contact was short but intense." Tridia wrapped her arms around her stomach and trembled.

"How did you know him before you and I met?" Master Aren asked.

Tridia laughed to herself and shook her head. "I'd only known him through brief contacts in visions. I'd seen him for years, and for a short time thought he and Davik were the same person. I only found out his name a few days before I met you. It was during that same vision that he asked me for help. I had no idea what was happening to him. That's why I asked you to help him. I didn't know how."

"One last thing," Master Aren said. "Ren Tama."

White pain stabbed across Tridia's eyes and Master Aren winced from the rebound.

"How did you find out?" he asked.

"A program left by my mother." Tridia blinked her eyes to dispel the white spots flickering before them. "It's there in my memories, after the satellites destroyed the attack ships, just before I left. She told me the person who rescued me from Ceyon has the information I need. He seemed a logical choice, since you hate him so badly. I'm supposed to find him."

"I knew there was more to his saving you than compassion for a child," Master Aren said. "Do you know who your mother is?"

"The program mentioned the name Elise, and said I resemble her, but when I try to remember her, I get a headache."

"The name doesn't ring a bell," Master Aren said. "But I knew very few Chesans outside the royal court. You going to Tama alone is out of the question. We'll discuss options when the opportunity arises."

Master Aren had access to every secret she'd ever harbored. He made no offer to remove the old barrier block as he moved freely in her mind and she swallowed the revulsion of the intrusion. Drayden needed her, and she needed Master Aren's trust to help him. She'd decided to allow any violation to garner his trust and she steeled herself to endure it. At length he withdrew from her mind. He closed his thoughts to her and she became aware of her surroundings once again. The Sentinels stood by his side. Near the other ship, Deeca Varin stood with Mr. Tran, both of them concerned and confused by what they'd witnessed.

Then Tridia sensed Winniel's connection and was surprised by its strength.

"It's simply proximity, Commander, and the fact that your mind is now cleared. I still carry your block. Just as you carry the shielded memory I left with you. You were under the Chesan defense shield when the barrier fell. Its disintegration didn't reach me."

"Can we remove the barrier?" Tridia asked. Her heart ached for the

Sentinel's separation from her clan. "If I relive those moments with Drayden, will it come down?"

"We can try." Winniel knelt in front of her.

"I'll need to enter your mind, Winniel. Can I do that?" Tridia spared a glance for Alanel when she asked the question. He grimaced, but made no objection. "I think if I announce my presence and you invite me in, then take me where you want me to go, it's not painful for you. At least, that's the way it worked for me and Prince Drayden."

"Since this has never been attempted by an outsider – not even a Chesan – we can't know until we try. There's already a connection between us. Follow the connection as you've done before."

Tridia focused her thoughts on Winniel's face, and narrowed to the gold flecks in her irises. Then she turned within herself and found Winniel's consciousness. Her world became centered on the small connection and she followed the link back to Winniel. Winniel stood beautiful and tall before a brilliant golden light. Alanel stood beside her.

Of course. The two of you are linked. I'd never see one of you this way without the other.

Alanel put his hand on Winniel's shoulder. *Free her, Chesan child, and you will have my unending gratitude.*

I am Tridia Odana. I come as a friend.

And I am Winniel, First Truthsayer of the Hariok Clan. Come into my thoughts as only my mate has ever done.

Tridia followed Winniel and Alanel down a golden path of light. No other memories encroached as she kept her thoughts focused on the pair in front of her. The light ended in waves curling around deep shadow.

This is the barrier I took from your mind.

Tridia broadened her thoughts to encompass the forms of the Sentinels standing before her. Together they moved into the shadow. The darkness resisted at first, but when Tridia brought forth her memories of Drayden, the shadows thinned.

This is where I hid him away. Every thought and memory of Drayden, or any time he'd come to mind. From the time I was ten years old, he permeated my thoughts. Everything I did brought him to mind. Every time I took a life I wondered if it would affect him. Each time I saw his face I wondered if he was real or if I imagined him. I hated him because he made me doubt all that I was trained to be. He made me look outside the Hierarchy to a purpose beyond the killing. Drayden gave me a reason to walk away – to find him.

As Tridia spoke images of Drayden played across their collective thoughts until the darkness disappeared. They stood bathed in the golden light of Winniel's mind. Row upon row of collective thoughts pressed upon them, the comings and goings of the entire Hariok clan sped through the connection they shared. Beyond those, the presence of the ebony-skinned J'Nai and the red-haired Shanigan clans touched lightly at the edge of Winniel's consciousness, as Winniel's had touched Tridia's, present, but not intruding.

Tridia marveled at the depth of belonging they shared. All three clans, interwoven into one consciousness, yet distinct as individuals.

Commander Odana. Alanel's voice drew her attention. *You've shown your innocence of the crimes you denied. Now, it's time for you to answer our vendetta. Reveal to us the answer to our question.*

Tridia's body trembled. She'd remembered nothing that would have caused the Sentinels to come after her, no reason for their vendetta. Had she hidden another memory away?

On the night Diana died, and you fled the Guardians. You fired your weapon once. At whom did you fire it?

Tridia thought back to that night. She recalled the blood on her hands, the anger in her heart. A Guardian shined a light in her face, then at the bodies on the ground. Deeca Varin ran up, her thoughts on apprehending the murderer, then a shock wave of disbelief crashed into Tridia's mind as Deeca recognized her holding the knife. Tridia used her spark step to escape, dodging into the trees before anyone could get off a shot. She used the step three times to put distance between her and her pursuers. The energy drain left her panting at the edge of a lighted clearing. The lights sat on chest high pillars and lined up in a row. She needed darkness to make good her escape, so she drew her blaster and lined up the shot, taking out all but the last lamp. Something stopped the shot before it reached the final bulb. The darkness was sufficient without firing again, so she crossed the clearing and made her way to a stream where she'd tied a canoe earlier that day. Her pursuers made for the road leading to the spaceport, while she made her way downstream to a private hangar.

Is this what you wanted me to remember? Was there something more? Tridia waited, aware that the attention of the entire Hariok clan focused on her.

This is my memory of that night. Winniel opened a darkened vault and Tridia was instantly transported into the misty forest again, running toward the clearing, knowing that's where the assassin would go. The dampness on her face cooled as she ran, and the clean forest scents permeated the air. So many more sensations accompanied her memories. This time, it wasn't she who ran, it was Winniel. Only Winniel wasn't her name then, she'd been known as Arenel. Arenel used a spark step to get to the clearing first. Alanel called to her to wait, he sensed a greater danger, but she ran ahead. She reached the clearing and sensed the assassin close at hand. One more quick step and she'd cut off the assassin's escape. As Arenel stopped between the lamps a pain hammered through her chest.

Tridia's hands knotted the fabric of her shirt over the middle of her chest. She reeled from the pain in Arenel's memory and gasped for breath as her life bled away.

Then Alanel was beside Arenel, holding her body to his chest, screaming out his anguish. Arenel's memories fled into Alanel's mind and he sealed them away. Tridia's thoughts went dark.

I killed her. I killed Winniel. I didn't know. I never meant to. All I needed was to put out the lights. Minds from all three Sentinel clans heard Tridia's confession. *I'm so sorry!* Tridia wailed in her thoughts and her body couldn't breathe.

No, Commander Odana. When Winniel spoke light returned to Tridia's mind. *You took Arenel's life, not mine, although Arenel was my name for many years.*

I don't understand.

Winniel stood in front of Tridia, but behind the Sentinel many more clones ranged in the distance, like looking at one-half of an infinite mirror. All of them spoke at once.

I am Winniel, First Truthsayer of the Hariok clan. My consciousness lives from life to life. One body ceases, another begins. We are clones. In this way our creators deigned to impose immortality on their design. When Winniel is no more, another will take her place and she will become the First Truthsayer with all of our knowledge and memories, but with a life of her own. She will be mated to the one Winniel leaves behind, just a Winniel took Alanel. You intended no harm when Arenel died, our vendetta was to avenge a conscious murder. Had Arenel waited as instructed, she would have lived, Commander, and you would have died. Our vendetta is withdrawn. Return to yourself, Child of Chaos, but first see the final secret of the clan you've joined.

All of Winniel's images merged into one. Alanel stood beside her once again. The two of them led Tridia to a set of golden doors, locked with bronze chains. With a touch, Winniel broke the chains and the doors swung open. Soft blue light spilled from the entrance and Tridia looked upon a scene from the collective memory.

A half dozen Sentinel couples stood before a pair of thrones. A king and queen sat on the thrones and a small boy of no more than three years old stood between them. The boy had dark hair and charcoal-gray eyes just like the king, but his face resembled the queen's.

"This is our son, Prince Drayden Anjenay," the king said. "He will renew the Chesan race, but his future rests in a chaotic vision we can't unravel. To help him through the dangers he faces, we ask the Hariok Clan of Sentinels to swear allegiance to protect him until he is safely married to the queen he chooses. But should he fall victim to the Child of Chaos, we ask you to end his life so he cannot perpetuate the nightmare that leads us to our desperate measures. We also ask you to accept the knowledge of our plans – each contingency and every level – and carry the history of our people until it can be safely returned to our descendants. In no way interfere, but remember everything. Will you swear this for the sake of the galaxy?"

"I am Arenel, First Truthsayer of the Hariok Clan. We agree to safeguard your prince for as long as he needs us, but we'll swear no allegiance beyond our Clans. That is our way. We accept the responsibility for your history and your plans, but we will make no promise to take the prince's life without full knowledge of the circumstances. We are not automatons, King, that you can extract such a promise. We swear to do all we can to keep him from choosing the wrong path. If you cannot agree to this oath, then the Harioks will withdraw their offer and you may approach the J'Nai and the Shanigan Clans."

The queen touched the boy's hair. He looked around and smiled at her.

"We accept your gracious offer, our Hariok friends – and now allies," the queen said. "Our son is young, but he will remember you should your paths ever cross. We'll give you the names of every designer who had anything to do with our plans so you may receive their thoughts in the manner you best deem fit and at the appropriate time. Thank you for all you do now and for all you will do in the future. We will not meet again."

Please. Tridia interrupted the vision. *Don't show me any of the plans until the time comes that I need to know them. Until Drayden is safe with us, I can be too easily swayed by any threat to his life. Tell me nothing that isn't essential now.*

There are other memories from your mother, Winniel said. *Would you not see those? Not even to see her face?*

I can't. Not yet.

As you wish. Alanel said. The doors slammed shut and sealed. *The darkness Winniel left in your mind contains these secrets. Do you wish them removed?*

Could I open them on my own?

No.

Then leave them.

Return to yourself, child. Winniel's voice was a gentle nudge that sent Tridia's consciousness on its way.

Tridia followed the connection back to herself. Left alone in her mind, she sighed. The whole ordeal, beginning with Master Aren's first order to come down the ramp, had taken less than ten minutes, but she felt she'd lived years in that time. When her vision focused, Winniel had moved to stand beside Alanel. His arm encircled her waist. Tridia was still on her knees, but looking up into Master Aren's eyes.

He stared at her for a moment, then he looked away.

"I'm sorry I had to do what I did. And I apologize for the violation after the Challenge. I know that isn't enough, and our prince will never forgive me, but it's all I can offer. You've changed a great deal since we first met."

He held out a hand to help Tridia to her feet. She took it and stood on trembling legs.

"Do I have your word, Master Aren?" she asked. "Drayden must be rescued and protected. We have to defeat the Kel Anec. Their fleet is real, and I could end up insane and controlling it – or destroying it forever. According to the vision, we still have options. I need to know now, have I satisfied your doubts? Can you give your word not to kill me before Drayden is safe?"

"Yes," Master Aren looked into her eyes again. This time he didn't swallow down his secreted enzyme. They'd broken his curse.

"Sir," Tridia said. "You need to know that there are dangers to you physically because of the glands that have matured. I learned a great deal from Drayden's physician program – more than I ever wanted to hear."

"We'll talk about it when there's time later," he said. "At least for now I seem released from your spell."

Tridia's tiny smile held no mirth. Which of them had the more difficult task ahead?

"Now close your mind," Master Aren ordered. "We've given the Kel Anec too much time to track you and if that cruiser has any way to find you, it will reach this planet before we can disappear."

"I can close my mind, but I can't shut down the energy leaking from my cells. Only time will make it dissipate. It's a by-product of travel through the portal."

"Then we'll have to work around it."

Tridia closed her mind on the questions from Deeca and Tran. She didn't use the energy block, it would have been pointless since the portal power couldn't be contained. Her body became the receptor for her mind's observations. The gentle touch of snow on her face, the smell of evergreens, the sight of familiar faces, the sound of wind moaning, and the feel of cold seeping through her clothing presented enough information for her tired mind to process. Inside the barrier, the Sentinels' presence pulsed like a golden heartbeat. Not just Alanel and Winniel, but the entire Hariok clan. When they said she'd joined the Clan, she thought it was figurative, but it now appeared they meant it literally.

Master Aren gave orders to everyone. "Tran, take your ship to

Hulac. Let Robel and the empress know what's happened, but not over the communicator and not unless the shield is activated. Sonei should have made it back by the time you return. Keep everyone there unless there is any sign a siege is forming. If that happens, the four of you leave Hulac and get to Aga as quickly as you can. Expend whatever resources are necessary. The rest of us will take Commander Odana's ship and follow in a less direct route. Let's get going."

"You and I have to talk," Deeca said, as she walked past Tridia.

"We have a lot to talk about." Tridia followed her to the ramp but turned into the chill wind one last time before entering the craft.

Deeca stopped next to Master Aren and spoke in a quiet voice. "If I ever see you slap another woman like that, Ambassador, you'll have to deal with me. And don't even dream that you'd get away with raising a hand to me."

Master Aren said nothing and the two of them entered the ship.

Tridia breathed deep of the cold, evergreen-scented air, then turned her back on the wind and closed the ramp.

***

A dark cloud floated in the absolute darkness of the mine tunnel. Without light or instruments, a human would have walked into it without knowing what happened. As it neared the tunnel junction, an indigo light flashed in the midst of the cloud. For a moment, nothing happened, then the cloud sparked with tiny flashes of lightning and disintegrated.

That is the twenty-seventh feeder. I detect only a handful remaining. Are you not yet ready to destroy the sentient Kel Anec floaters?

Not yet. The Kel Anec and their pets are what's keeping the scientists and soldiers at bay. If we take away their threat, we'll have to deal with B'Nay and his teams too soon. Davik's physical shape walked around the corner. His deep indigo form shone with flashes of silver light. His companion entity had taught him to dim the flashes in order to stay hidden, but he couldn't extinguish them completely. He spoke aloud to practice using his synthesized voice box. "I expect B'Nay to come into the mine soon with an offer – or more likely a threat – involving Tridia."

She has nothing to fear from the likes of him. Not as long as she can access the energy from my dimension for protection.

"You said she doesn't know how to access the energy. And it doesn't go to her aid unless her life is threatened."

She is learning. Very soon she will be able to command the energy more ably than any Chesan before her.

"All the same," Davik said. "I want to know what he has planned. It will help determine our course of action with the remaining feeders and

Kel Anec floaters."

He walked on in the utter darkness, using energy pulses from his humanoid shape for guidance. He'd learned to switch forms with the speed of thought, and could assume several different tactical shapes, but he preferred the shape of his own body. He froze as the vibrations of footsteps reached him from an intersecting tunnel. His form dissolved and reformed as a thin film of energy across the roof of the tunnel. In that form, his essence was so dispersed it was undetectable by the scientific instruments Reshard's teams carried.

"Proceed with caution," a voice said. Davik could distinguish between voices in his humanoid shape, but dispersed as he was, he could identify only the words, not the speaker.

"Yes, Master B'Nay," another voice replied. "Our instruments detected his energy in the tunnel ahead, but it's gone now. There's only a trace."

"We have readings that he's gone to the lakeside cave every day at about this time. I suspect he's trying to send us a message."

They caught on faster than I expected. Withdraw your power, I'll face them on my own strength. You can always come back if I need you.

The entity withdrew and Davik's energy level dropped. He didn't panic as he had in the past. His own energy reserve had replenished since the sudden depletion event he'd experienced when he'd sensed Tridia pass. He was many times more powerful than he had been, thanks to exposure to the entity. After B'Nay's team passed, Davik reformed and took another route that would lead to the underground lake. He would approach B'Nay's group from the water.

The team was already there when he arrived, and Davik didn't keep them waiting. He appeared first as the amorphous shape he'd used when they'd last met, and hovered a few feet from the shore until someone noticed him.

"Lieutenant Schie." B'Nay stepped forward. "We may have a way to communicate if —"

"I can communicate without your conditions." Davik spoke after he reshaped into his physical body. "I could have communicated the last time, but it required me to touch you. I knew you wouldn't have stood still for that, so I didn't bother."

"Well, done, Lieutenant," B'Nay said. "May we take energy readings?"

"As long as your nets and probes remain on the ground, I have no objection to your instruments monitoring my energy levels."

"Thank you." B'Nay nodded to his people and they scurried to open the cases and bags they'd carried into the mine. "You have displayed large amounts of activity lately. I assume learning this shape and acquiring the ability to speak are some of your pastimes?"

"Some of them," Davik replied. He turned his head, as though watching the team, even though he couldn't actually see them with his eyes. "There have been others."

"I won't be coy with you, Lt. Schie," B'Nay said.

"Why start now?" Davik crossed his arms over his chest. He took a step backwards, away from the rocky ledge.

"Indeed." B'Nay waited a heartbeat. "You need to perform some tests in controlled conditions so we can measure the extent of your attack capabilities. Your power levels fluctuate dramatically, does that happen after a discharge? We've registered small explosions, in the areas of your energy readings."

"I'm still learning to control these powers. I've tested some powerful energy discharges in stable areas of the mine."

"You'll need to come with us so we can take measurements in proper test conditions."

"No," Davik stated.

"You will come with us, Lieutenant." B'Nay moved to the very edge of the water.

"Or what? You'll injure my body? Destroy it? Because I assure you, you can't touch my energy form."

"We'll see." B'Nay waved his hand and two soldiers tossed the energy nets toward Davik.

An indigo flash struck the nets in midair, disintegrating them, and knocked the soldiers who'd tossed them to the ground.

"An unstable weapon is worse than no weapon," B'Nay said. "It would be safer to destroy you and obtain another test subject."

"It would definitely be safer, but you won't find a better test subject."

"Commander Odana's DNA is very similar to yours. She was in the tunnel at the time your energy readings changed. Perhaps she would be a better subject."

"No doubt," Davik said. "But she's beyond your reach and well-protected. Even if she were alone, you wouldn't have much of a chance."

"Commander Odana's oath to Brenden Aren has a condition that protects her only as long as she is obedient to him. If word reaches her that you are in danger, she will leave him whether he allows it or not. Once she disobeys him, she can be arrested and brought back to Odea in chains. She swore to abide by that requirement."

Davik laughed. "That's very good, Master B'Nay. Were things as they were when you coerced me into this project, I might be worried. But they aren't as they were. If Tridia thought she could be with me –

back in my own body – she might come on her own, but she'd need proof that I was myself again. Apart from that, I'm not concerned with anything you might do."

Davik floated away from the shore. His form began to dissolve.

"You want to be reunited with the Commander in your own body?" B'Nay called.

Davik reformed. "I thought you'd decided against being coy. We have an impasse. Until you test these skills, you won't attempt to put me back in my body. And I won't test them with your scientists standing by with containment equipment."

"Perhaps a compromise can be reached," B'Nay said. "Continue learning to control your powers here in the mine. You've made impressive advances in a short time. I'll give you three more weeks. In the meantime, I will request Commander Odana's presence. If you pass the tests, we will proceed with the reunification process. The young lady can be with you. If you fail, she will take your place."

"Amuse yourself with that plan, B'Nay. I'll exit the mine when I'm ready – without your assistance." Davik's form drifted into the darkness and dissolved into an amorphous cloud. He followed the second route away from the water and reformed. His color darkened as the entity returned. *You heard?*

It sounds as though you may have prompted him to take action against the Commander.

He was going to do that anyway. What I did was obtain some practice time without worrying about his interference. We'll leave the Kel and the feeders alone for now and go into the deepest cavern to work on our attack. When we come back, we'll take care of the Kel and the Hierarchy.

And your body?

Davik paused. *It doesn't matter. As long as I clean out this poisonous nest before they manage to get Tridia or some other unfortunate here.*

***

Master Frees B'Nay waited while his team repacked their equipment.

"Either he was holding back or his energy level is only about seventy percent of what we've been reading from this location," one of the technicians stated.

"Lieutenant Schie was definitely holding back," B'Nay answered, staring across the darkened waters. "The question is, why?"

"Sir?" the tech questioned.

"Don't be as fooled as that idiot, Reshard," B'Nay said. "Davik Schie is brilliant. I wouldn't have selected him for this experiment otherwise. He knows no matter what he says, I will bring Commander Odana here. He didn't try to barter. He made no threat, other than the Commander's

363

own skills. He is planning something."

"My thoughts exactly."

B'Nay and his technician both turned to find the other members of their team enveloped in dark translucent clouds. Both men backed to the very edge of the lake.

"What is the meaning of this?" B'Nay demanded. "We had an agreement. I would work to obtain energy samples in exchange for information and being left in peace from your feeders."

A pale-skinned man stepped into the light of the lanterns that had fallen to the ground. His watery blue eyes studied B'Nay. "True, and you have produced the energy samples we require. It would seem your usefulness is at an end."

"There is another test subject who needs to be brought to this planet in order for our first subject to be pushed to his full potential," B'Nay argued. "You don't have all of the information you need. You let the girl escape, despite my direction that you needed to keep her here, and now you need me to retrieve her."

"We need only your body to retrieve her," the pale-skinned man said.

He motioned with his left hand and a dark form filled with menacing green and gold sparks of light floated toward B'Nay. A simple dark cloud approached the technician. No one heard the screams as their minds were consumed by the alien consciousness.

CHAPTER THIRTY-SEVEN

"The controls are virtually identical to a Stellar Morph," Tridia explained. Everyone but Winniel had gathered in the ship's small bridge. "Be careful when you first fly it, the ship responds much faster than anything I've ever flown."

"The Commander should rest," Alanel said. Master Aren turned startled eyes in his direction. "We can sense her exhaustion, Ambassador, and prefer that she not be responsible for our lives until she has recuperated."

"Very well," Master Aren said. "Commander, get us into space and we'll take it from there. I'll take a six-hour shift then Deeca can relieve me. Alanel will relieve her in another six hours. That should give you time for a nice long nap."

Tridia agreed only because she couldn't promise not to fly them into a sun. The pain pulsing in her body wasn't as severe as she'd experienced when the Controller had saved her, but the pain combined with the exposure of the new connections with the Sentinels, and the aching in her brain from Master Aren's probing, distracted her from basic conversation, let alone skillful flying. Drayden would be furious when he found out what had happened. The thought of dealing with his anger sapped more of her strength.

When she left the bridge, Alanel went with her and Deeca stayed behind to speak with Master Aren. Tridia found Winniel sleeping on a couch in the main lounge. She'd never seen either Sentinel asleep. Their mental contact must have been as exhausting for Winniel as it had been for her. It made her wonder how Alanel was holding up.

"I am well, Commander." Tridia started at the sound of Alanel's voice. He went on to explain. "I can sense your concern with your normal barrier, unlike with your energy block. The connection you have with the clan now affords us a more intimate contact than we've experienced before."

"Will Winniel be alright?" Tridia watched the steady rise and fall of Winniel's breathing.

"Yes. This is the first time she's slept since taking your blocked memories into her mind. She'll recover now."

"I had no idea how bad it really was for her – or for you – until I saw what was released beyond my memories." Tridia continued to watch Winniel. "You must be tired, too. Take the other couch in here. I'll explore the rest of the ship. There's bound to be another place to get some rest."

Alanel didn't argue. He lay down on the couch across from Winniel as Tridia left the cabin.

Down a short corridor, Tridia found three more rooms and a stairway that led into the ship's hold. Two of the rooms were small guest quarters that could accommodate two people each. They shared a small bathroom, and had comfortable-looking bunks made up with colorful covers fastened to keep them from free-floating should the gravity fail.

The third room was as large as the other two put together. It contained an oversized bed, instead of a bunk, with rich covers and soft pillows. Three sets of clothes lay spread on the covers, a pair of dark blue pajamas, a set of casual clothes, and a formal suit with the Anjenay crest embroidered on the left shoulder of the jacket. A larger version of the crest hung above the bed. This room was meant for Drayden, on his maiden voyage from exile. Clothes meant for royalty returning to the life for which he'd been groomed. They'd guessed incorrectly at his size; the clothes would have swallowed Drayden. But then, they'd been meant for him in another fifteen years.

Tridia, the girl, wanted to cry, but the assassin refused to shed a tear. She studied the lavish setting and decided it should remain in its pristine condition until Drayden saw it for the first time. A set of keys on a long gold chain lay with a sealed envelope atop a small dresser to one side of the room. A quaint touch, when everything else was electronic or coded crystal.

No doubt another congratulatory note from his parents, telling him how proud they were of his resolve. How would it make him feel? She took the keys and placed the note in a drawer filled with other necessities. Drayden wouldn't need more guilt, but she couldn't bring herself to destroy what was probably the last thing his parents had left for him. One of the keys matched the lock on the cabin door. Tridia locked it as she left, slipped the chain over her head, and tucked the keys under her shirt with the DNA pouch. They'd be safe with her until she could give them to Drayden.

Tridia went to one of the smaller cabins and lay on the bunk. The Sentinels' connection became a quiet pulse as they slept – a comforting rhythm that cradled her. Her body relaxed as her mind eased into the safety of the Sentinel clan.

From a distance, the door to the adjoining room opened and closed and the rustle of bedcovers indicated Deeca had decided on a nap while she could get one. Tridia didn't stir. A strange sense of freedom came with being able to wander in her memories without fear of retaliation from Alanel – even though she'd been free of him for days. His proximity made the freedom seem more real. Not only did she have her own memories to wander, but Drayden's life was only a thought away. Behind her barriers she could recall anything she wished. What intrigued her most was the memory of the small boy in the kitchen pantry. She couldn't see Drayden's face in the vision, but she could see the other child. He looked like a tiny version of Drayden – and Davik.

***

"Come with me to our family room. Mother will be so surprised to see someone who looks like me!" Drayden pulled the child's hand.

"No, I can't!" the other boy pulled away. "I'm not allowed in the kitchen. I'll be punished if I go with you."

"No, you won't. I'm the prince. They won't punish you if I tell them not to." The young Drayden's small voice sounded haughty.

"I know who you are," the boy said. "You're why I'm not allowed in the kitchen or anywhere else in the palace. You're not supposed to see me."

The boy turned to go but bumped into a jar on the shelf behind him. The jar fell. Drayden's small hands tried to catch it, as did the other boy's, but the container crashed to the floor. A shard sliced Drayden's left palm. The other boy went white as blood flowed from a gash in his right hand.

"Run away!" Drayden yelled. "Someone will hear and I don't want you to be in trouble. Hurry!"

The child hesitated, then pushed the door open and ran, cradling his bleeding hand against the white shirt he wore. No sooner had he gone than an adult opened the door wide to find Drayden kneeling amid the broken glass with his hand bleeding.

"You're not to be in the kitchen!" The adult took Drayden by the arm and pulled him from the pantry. "What if His Highness had –"

"Prince Drayden! You're supposed to be in the classroom." Another adult voice boomed in the kitchen but Drayden looked only at his bleeding hand. "What's happened here?"

Frantic explanations were made and Drayden was whisked away to a nurse to tend his cut. The memory faded and Tridia lay wondering what had happened to the other child in the pantry. Davik didn't have a scar on either hand. Was this mysterious child the third man she'd seen in the vision Winniel had shared with her in Master Aren's office?

The ship banked sharply without warning. The inertial limiters kept Tridia from flying off the bed, but she bounced up and ran to the door just the same. Master Aren tapped furiously at the controls as she entered the bridge.

"They've found us," he said.

Tridia sat in the co-pilot's seat and read the charts. "Only one ship. Looks like a Stellar Hawk. The cruiser can't be far away, we're too deep in space for a Hawk to be flying alone."

"My thoughts exactly." Master Aren tapped a few more keys. "That's where we want to go."

A dense star map appeared on the monitor. Tridia made changes in the navigation. The ship made a smooth veer from its heading and shot toward the center of the cluster.

"Why are we going into the cluster?" Deeca sat in the third seat and pulled up charts. "Can't the trailing ship follow us in?"

"Yes," Master Aren explained. "They won't stay in there with us, though. They'll be reporting to the cruiser, and the cruiser is too big to navigate that field. The dense solar radiation will cut off the Stellar Hawk's communications. If the pilot's smart, he won't follow us far."

"If the pilot's an idiot?" Deeca asked.

"Then he'd end up in the middle of a small sun," Tridia said. "But he's no idiot. Not if he's a Hierarchy fleet pilot."

"The cluster is our best option," Master Aren said. "The cruiser will be close, so we'll have to go in at hyperspeed."

"That's a dangerous move," Deeca said. "At those speeds the stars are minutes – maybe seconds – apart. You'll need perfect reactions to navigate them."

"I'm not going to navigate them," he said. "The Commander is."

"What?" Deeca's voice broke.

"I've done it before," Tridia explained. "And with a lesser ship."

"How old did you say you are, again?" Deeca asked.

"Seventeen."

"You're not old enough to have done half the things they credit you with, assassin." Tridia looked over her shoulder when Deeca spoke. The Hunter pulled up chart after chart to match their approach to the star cluster. "I think you and your master just make this stuff up to irritate me – and you're succeeding."

"They're telling the truth," Winniel interjected. "Commander Odana navigated this star cluster to escape a Guardian cruiser when she was fifteen, on her first solo deep space run."

"You've seen her memories, so you know such things," Deeca commented. "Fine. We'll eventually run into – wait a minute. When you were fifteen? Two years ago? I was in a pursuit ship with our best pilot when an Odean Hawk flew into this cluster like it was free space."

"Entering star cluster," Tridia said.

Her attention focused on the navigational screens as she maneuvered the ship amid the densely packed stars. The Stellar Hawk followed them in, but soon gave up pursuit, as predicted. Tridia continued into the stellar soup until everyone agreed they'd gone far enough. Instead of dropping out of hyperspace, she continued to dodge the small suns in a circular route near the center of the cluster.

"When I escaped the Guardians, I used a small planet inside the cluster to sling onto a new vector," Tridia explained. "My record of that flight has been open to every pilot in the fleet to study for two years. They'll be looking for us to use the same tactic to escape this time, and they'll be looking in the same place. This maneuver may have given them a clue to our identity."

"What are you thinking?" Master Aren asked.

"A lateral move to a sling outside the cluster," Tridia said. "If they're reading the portal energy, all it will do is buy us a little time. If they are tracking the ship alone, it may give us our escape route. Either way, it's worth a try."

"Do it," Master Aren said.

"Hunter Varin," Tridia said. "Find a suitable sling planet on the Alliance side of the cluster."

"Looking," Deeca responded. "Why the Alliance side?"

"They're less likely to have a trap waiting on the Alliance side," Master Aren explained. "The Guardians patrol this border. They might aid a ship being chased within their territory or even in free space. In Hierarchy territory we'd be at a disadvantage, and farther from home."

Deeca continued to check the charts. "Got it. I'll set the heading. It will be the second system, third planet."

Tridia's deft hands at the controls guided the Chesan ship out of the star cluster and toward the target system. They made the sling without incident and headed deep into Alliance space.

"The cruiser shouldn't be able to follow us," Tridia said. "Unfortunately, we destroyed ships, drones, and a shield the Hierarchy wanted to study when I escaped. They may be angry enough to risk breaking a treaty to send a cruiser or even a carrier after us."

"This is the Hierarchy chasing us, then, and not the Kel Anec?" Deeca asked.

"It could be both," Brenden said.

"Yes, but the cruiser could be responding to the escape report," Tridia said. "They're sure to have spec on this ship all over the Hierarchy's alert system by now. They want whoever left that planet, and they'll want to capture this ship. It went through a portal without accelerating to hyperspeed. That presumed technology alone is worth the cost of a chase. Unless we head into the densely populated areas of the Alliance they'll stick with us until we go to ground or make a mistake."

"Going into populated space would be a bad idea," Master Aren said. "The Kel Anec have spread into systems with standing fleets independent of the Core Alliance. It might not be just the Hierarchy we're running from."

"This keeps getting more complicated," Tridia said.

"For now, assume we have more enemies than allies, and we can't tell them apart from a distance," Master Aren explained. "We'll take an indirect route to Hulac. Circle back to skim the border between Alliance and Hierarchy space as long as we can. It should make them question who we are, at least."

"You two head back to rest," Deeca said. "I want to try this thing out. I'll alert you if something happens."

Master Aren made his way to the cabin Deeca had used. Tridia stopped in the lounge where the Sentinels still lay sleeping. She took a seat and watched them, wondering about the contents of the golden vault in Winniel's memories. Would the Sentinels know anything about the other child? Tridia dozed off as she considered asking them.

Deeca alerted everyone when a Fighter Hawk found them in hyperspace. The ship kept its distance and after an hour Master Aren returned to his bed. Winniel stayed with Deeca in the bridge. Tridia and Alanel took up couches in the lounge. They'd continued undisturbed for several hours. The last of the pain left Tridia's body as she stood to go relieve Deeca. With the pain went her strength and she wobbled as the aches slid away. Alanel was on his feet beside her in an instant.

She regained her composure quickly. Even though her body was weak, her mind expanded to understanding far beyond its normal levels. She dropped her barrier and awareness of her surroundings seeped into her thoughts. The ship hummed around her, but not just its engines, the entire ship generated a presence. Tridia touched a spot where the bulkhead was exposed and the surface vibrated beneath her fingers.

"Do you sense that?" she asked.

"The life force of this ship?" he asked. "Yes. As though the entire craft is sentient."

"How long have you sensed it?" Tridia stared at the gold metal.

"It just started," Alanel said. "The moment you dropped your barriers."

A sentient gold vessel. Tridia had thought the vessel might be made of some golden alloy, or painted gold, but that wasn't the case. The ship *was* gold. Gold from the Guardian Warren – the Controller's gold. No wonder the craft seemed to read their minds – it probably did. That explained why her bracelets had tingled and sparkled when she first sat at the controls. Or had the blue energy awakened its sentience?

What were the limits of such a ship? She'd been taught a theory in pilot's class – a way to sling that would cause the hyperspeeds to increase exponentially. Craft technology hadn't advanced to a level that would hold ships together at those speeds. Tridia let her hand lay against the metal. It thrummed in unison with her heartbeat.

We can do it. The words nudged their way into Tridia's mind.

"You aren't connected to the Controller," she whispered. "Your sentience comes from your pilot. Only a race of telepaths could design such a ship."

"You ponder a dangerous course," Alanel said.

"This ship can do it. It's not just a ship."

"If it takes its sentience from its pilot, then doesn't Hunter Varin guide it now?" Alanel placed his hand on the metal next to hers.

"No," Tridia answered. "The ship is linked to me. It linked to me on Zentel and never let go."

"Then your reckless thoughts spur it into danger with you." Alanel removed his hand and glared at Tridia.

"The ship is awake," Tridia said. "It's ready to share its secrets. Listen to it."

"I hear it through you," Alanel said. "I can sense its abandon. The ship has no restraint. You must supply that."

"We can't run like this forever," Tridia argued. "They could be tracking the ship. Or, they could be tracking my abnormal energy signature – if they linked it with the ship. Now that the energy leak has stopped, they've lost their beacon. They may try to force us out of hyperspace."

"Enemy ship closing distance," Deeca announced over the intercom.

Tridia exchanged a look with Alanel, then hurried to the bridge and slid into the co-pilot's seat once again. She tapped controls and checked monitors with complete focus. "Winniel, can you read the people in the ship behind us?"

"Yes, Commander. They're humans without armor," Winniel replied from the navigator's seat.

Tridia placed her hand on a glossy screen to her left. A new set of holographic controls sprang into the air before her. She studied them for some moments, then tapped furiously at the console, cross-checking coordinates and factors that flashed into the holographic screen.

"Okay. Let's disappear." Tridia looked over at Deeca's stunned expression. "Strap in. The chase ends now."

"Just don't get us killed, assassin." Deeca tightened the harness across her chest.

"Not my intention," Tridia pulled up several sets of star charts. "Just what I need."

Her fingers played a tapping rhythm on the controls again. Security lights flashed on all screens and a proximity siren went off.

"Are you insane?" Deeca shouted.

"Ever heard of a Base Nine sling?" Tridia shouted back over the noise. "Tell the others they have ten seconds to strap down."

Deeca relayed the message via intercom then grabbed the arms of her chair. "If we live through this, I may kill you anyway."

"If we live through this, I may die from shock."

"You mean you've never –"

Tridia banked the ship to a sharp left. The pursuit ship overshot the turn and had to compensate by making a rolling loop. Tridia's grin broadened as she watched the monitor. A small planet with no moons loomed directly in front of them. It registered no atmosphere and high density, just the combination she needed.

Blue energy flowed from Tridia's hands into the controls. She opened her senses fully and sensed the sweep of the planet's gravity well. The ship made a steep dive toward the deepest part of the well and banked outward from the gravitational pull. Instead of the normal sling of three-quarter's orbit, Tridia forced the ship into a full orbit and a half and the vessel rolled into the gravitational bend at six times normal hyperspeed. Tridia slapped her hand against the glossy screen twice and the ship sent out an energy beam. The star field stretched ahead of them and a vortex opened. Tridia blinked and it seemed her eyes took hours to close. The ship floated through the tunnel created by the vortex. With a sudden snap, reality returned to normal. Solar systems flew past at blinding speeds as space folded around them. Tridia's heart pounded and her breathing increased as though she'd been running. The ship slowed to standard hyperspeed.

"What have you done?" Deeca asked when the ship slowed. "Where are we?"

Tridia checked the monitors and charts, before turning to Deeca. "About an hour from Hulac on this heading."

"It should have taken us the better part of six days to get back here at top speeds." Deeca checked the monitors.

"Yes, and it will take our pursuit at least that long, assuming they can calculate our vector."

"This isn't possible." Deeca verified their location against the nearest navigational buoys. "Did you know the ship could create its own wormhole?"

"Not until it did it," Tridia responded.

"You're insane," Deeca said.

"You may be right." Tridia slid from the co-pilot's seat and stumbled. Winniel caught her arm and guided her toward the main lounge. They ran into Master Aren hurrying toward the bridge. "We'll be on Hulac within the hour, sir."

"How did we get here?" Master Aren demanded.

"A Base Nine sling around a dense planet," Tridia answered.

"Base Nine? That's barely even a theory."

"The theory was flawed," Tridia said. "It isn't just about the speed, but the gravity well. The right energy pulse at the narrowest and deepest bend can open a wormhole."

"Were we so desperate you had to try an unproven theory to escape?" Master Aren asked.

"Yes," Tridia shot back, then quickly added, "Sir."

"Never do anything this dangerous again without consulting me," Master Aren said.

"The mathematics were perfect. The calculations were exact. There wasn't a danger."

"That isn't what you told Hunter Varin," Winniel said.

"How did you know the math was perfect?" Master Aren asked. "There's no record you've ever been trained in this type of calculation or ever performed it."

"It's just temporal mechanics. I've done – I remember –" Tridia stopped and looked wide-eyed from Master Aren to Winniel and back. "I've never done these computations before. Drayden has."

"He's performed these computations?"

"Not with these variables, but the math is simple for him. He's worked with it for years." Tridia turned to Winniel. "How did I do that?"

"Enough," Master Aren said. "We'll talk when we get under the shields. How's Deeca?"

"In shock, I think."

Master Aren frowned as he continued into the bridge.

As soon as he was out of sight, Tridia collapsed into a chair and started to shake.

"Commander?" Alanel asked. His concern poured through their connection.

"I'm just weak. The portal energy saps my physical strength but it causes an incredible increase in my mental powers. Drayden's knowledge is becoming my own." Tridia wanted to rub her eyes but couldn't find the strength to lift her hand. "The blue energy – whatever it is – flowed out of my hands into the ship again. It just absorbed into the controls."

"Shouldn't the Ambassador and Hunter Varin be aware of this?" Winniel asked.

"Deeca may have seen it," Tridia said. "She was sitting right beside me."

The Sentinels stared at each other, conversing telepathically, but keeping Tridia in the dark.

"If I haven't regained my strength before we reach Hulac I'll tell them. Just please keep that bit of information to yourselves until then."

"As you wish, Commander." Alanel acquiesced, but not before letting Tridia sense that he didn't like the idea.

Tridia slumped in the chair. The depth of the foolishness of the stunt she'd just pulled hit hard. They could have all been killed. Was she slipping toward insanity, or was she that desperate to return to Drayden? The obvious answer was yes, but to which one? She let it go when her shakes became uncontrollable. Winniel retrieved a blanket from one of the cabins and tucked it around her. The Sentinels didn't speak verbally or telepathically, but the pair would watch over her until they landed. The cradling of the ship and the Hariok clan she'd felt before had vanished when Drayden's memories became hers. She shivered beneath the blanket haunted by memories of skikes, aliens, and wisps of the Chaos Vision.

CHAPTER THIRTY-EIGHT

Winniel woke Tridia just before Master Aren entered the main cabin. The ship had set down on Hulac under the decontamination ray and she had slept fitfully through the whole process.

"Let's get up to the house and see if they've gotten any of the damage repaired," Master Aren said.

"How bad was it?" Tridia asked, coming to her feet. The sleep, disturbed as it had been, had rejuvenated her. She stood without trembling.

"Bad enough to distract the staff for days and delay part of the harvest."

"I apologize, Master Aren. I didn't intend to damage your home." Tridia held his gaze as she spoke in her most serious military voice.

"I'll see how the repairs are coming before I accept that apology," he said.

Tridia apologized twice more during the tour of the house, where she saw the broken windows and smashed decorations. Most of the broken glass had been gathered and some of the windows replaced, but there was no replacing Master Aren's priceless glassware collection. She trailed after him from room to room, watching his grimaces or frowns over some particular damage. When she saw the damage to her room, her back stiffened and she recalled the scorched rock in the Controller's sanctuary. Master Aren caught her reflection in a broken mirror and summarily dismissed her to the flower gardens to assist Robel.

"Raise your energy block first," he ordered. "I want no repeat of your last encounter. And no matter what he says, keep it in place."

"Yes, sir." Tridia clenched her jaw to keep from saying more. She would have stabbed herself in the heart to keep from endangering Robel again. She didn't need to be told.

She worked with Robel in the garden in easy silence. He occasionally pointed out a particular plant or described a special pruning or grafting technique. Tridia asked about the huttle trees and their care, wondering if the extreme measures to keep the planet clean were necessary.

"I would have to agree they are," Robel said. "Plants react differently in different environments. The conditions maintained under the shields allow the fruit trees to prosper across the entire planet. There are other compatible trees and plants here to keep the ecosystem healthy, but since the huttle trees are the main oxygen-producing plant on Hulac, it's vital that their health be protected. An infestation or plague among the trees could destroy the planet's atmosphere."

"It seems like quite a risk to replace most of the planet's ecosystem with one plant – and such a fragile one."

"The planet is terraformed," Robel explained. "This is the way it was designed to be."

"How?" Tridia asked. She gazed across the grass and flowers toward the orchards that stretched up hills and out of sight. "This terraforming had to take decades, if not centuries. Master Aren has only been out of the Hierarchy for fifteen years. Huttle trees only grew on Ceyon before the Chesan holocaust. At least according to – According to the records I've been able to find."

"You'll have to share the source of your records with me," Robel's eyes twinkled. "I've been unable to find anything of historical value on these trees. As to the time of the terraforming, there is no mystery here. My son, Brenden's father, received this planet from his mother, Empress Dojene. It passed to Brenden at Seagen's death. Dojene is the one who started the terraforming project several centuries ago."

"Several centuries?" Tridia asked. "How old *is* she?"

Robel laughed. "I've been told repeatedly that it is impolite to ask a female her age – especially a Chesan female – although humans seem easily offended as well."

"It might be best if we change the topic, then." Tridia looked away, choosing her words with care. "If a planet's ecosystem was damaged at an atmospheric level, would it be possible to restore it before the indigenous plant life died out?"

"Well." Robel held the syllable as he considered his answer. "It would depend on how extensive the damage was, the current health of the plants, and whether the soil and atmosphere could be restored. The possibility of obtaining healthy seed and shoring up the damage to give the plants a fighting chance would have to be taken into account. I suppose you could use nurseries or greenhouses on a smaller scale, but it would be a long process to recover from planetwide damage. I take it you've found such a place in your travels."

"Yes," Tridia said. She looked up at the clear blue sky, thinking of the ruby sky that had shrouded Zentel. "The damage was caused by a shield over-filtering the sunlight. It had been going on for years."

"I'd have to see the place, run some tests, make a few initial analyses," Robel said. "It's hard to answer without more facts."

"I'd like to take you there someday, *Somi*," Tridia gave the old man an impulsive hug. "If anyone could restore a planet, it would be you."

Robel smiled and patted Tridia's shoulder. They kept their discussion focused on the flowers until the sun set and the light failed. Tridia helped Robel put away his tools. He tucked her arm through his as they walked toward the house.

"Say what's on your mind, Commander," he said. "Since I can't sense your emotions, you'll have to guide me."

"I could have hurt you – or even killed you – when I caused all the damage. I had no idea – I just did it without considering the consequences." Tridia squeezed his hand.

"I was not injured beyond a rude awakening from my sleep." Robel patted her wrist. "Think no more about it."

"Thank you, for always being so kind."

"My dear, girl," the old man said. "It has always been my pleasure."

Sonei met them at the door to say dinner was ready and Tran would be joining them by the end of the meal. She studied Tridia's face for a long time. "I told you to keep running."

"I ran as far as I could," Tridia replied. "You were right, I shouldn't have stopped."

Robel made no comment and Tridia offered no explanation, as they detoured through a washroom before joining the others at the table.

Several of the staff joined them and carried on lively conversations throughout the meal. Tridia was grateful for their presence, even though they teased her about doing her experiments outside next time. Their jabs helped her ignore the cold stares the empress cast her way the entire time. The two of them would have to talk, now that Tridia had made peace with Master Aren, but she didn't look forward to it. She was relieved when Deeca spoke before they'd finished dessert.

"Commander Odana, would you join me in the study when you're done. I think it's time we had our talk."

"Of course," Tridia said. "I'm at your disposal."

They left the dining room together, Tridia following Deeca down a ground floor hallway to the study. Deeca closed the door behind them and indicated a chair for Tridia to use.

"It seems I owe you an apology for blaming you for the death of my fiancé."

Tridia sat speechless. She had expected anything but an apology.

"However," Deeca continued. "Now that you have your memories back, I want you to tell me what happened with the girl and her father. The Sentinels didn't execute you, so I assume you aren't guilty of her death."

"No," Tridia said. "Diana was murdered by her father – or rather, the man she thought was her father. I had been sent to kill him before he got to her. I didn't know which girl to protect. That's why I was patrolling outside the dormitory. When you detained me, I didn't reach him in time."

"Her death was *my* fault?" Deeca asked.

"No!" Tridia tried to forestall an angry outburst. "You were doing your duty. In fact, you'd gone beyond your duty to be kind to someone you took for a lonely child. The story I shared was true. My friend, Davik, really did kiss me before I left Odea, and I was confused by his actions. I appreciated your kindness and your listening ear. Had I remained focused, I could have made excuses and left in time to stop the killer. I didn't, and Diana died. The fault was my own."

Deeca's anger cooled, but not her curiosity.

"You've killed forty-nine people." The Hunter's voice held no condemnation.

"More than that if you count the battlefield deaths and the ones unknown to the Core Alliance." Tridia sat straighter in the chair. With her senses closed, she didn't know where Deeca intended to take the conversation.

"Let's stick with the individual deaths."

"They were all individuals, Hunter Varin," Tridia said. "All humans and humanoids with lives I ended. I killed them all because it's what I'd been ordered to do. It's what I *had* to do to survive."

"Then you knew about your handlers?"

"Yes, but is that really an excuse?"

"I was going to ask you how you dealt with the knowledge, but I can see you feel the same guilt I do over the lives I've taken."

Tridia stood and walked to a bookshelf. She scanned the ancient titles, then turned to face Deeca again. "I feel the weight of my actions. I detest the fact I took so many lives. Yet – except for the battlefield – every individual was guilty of despicable crimes. I feel no remorse for destroying that kind of evil."

Tridia shivered. Slivers of the Chaos Vision returned. The stomach-churning madness of her own mind, the craving for power, and the need to feed on the blue energy threatened to consume her. Drayden's voice resounded in her memory.

Fight it, Tridia! Fight it with me…If you fall to this insanity, you'll take me with you.

Clinging to Drayden's words and the sound of his voice in her memory, Tridia dragged herself from the insanity by slow degrees. She stepped back into reality to find her body dripping sweat and leaning against the bookshelf. The door stood open and Deeca was nowhere in sight. Tridia dropped to the arm of the closest chair, rested her forearms on her knees, and took deep breaths to steady her pounding heart. By the time her head cleared, the Sentinels flashed into the room using spark steps.

"You're unwell?" Alanel asked.

Master Aren ran to her side before she could answer.

"What's happened? Was it the prince? Has he tried to contact you?" Master Aren asked.

Deeca and Sonei came into the room on the heels of his question.

Tridia shook her head. "It was the Chaos Vision – a small piece of it."

"You turned pale as a vapor, then blue sweat dripped from every pore," Deeca said. "I thought you were having some kind of fit – or were about to explode again."

"Nothing so flamboyant this time," Tridia said, then added in a whisper. "Just a nightmare."

Master Aren's lips tightened at the mention of the Chaos Vision, but he made no comment.

"Is this where the party is?" Tran asked from the doorway, taking a bite of the sandwich he carried in one hand.

"Now that you're *finally* here we can get started," Master Aren said.

"I might ask how you got back ahead of me, since I took the most direct route, but I saw the pretty golden ship at the hangar." Tran walked into the room and sipped from a crystal goblet he carried in the hand without the sandwich. "Who do I beg for permission to fly it?"

"We won't discuss that ship or its capabilities outside of this room," Master Aren said.

"That impressive, is it?" Tran asked.

"It's beyond the *Elisia* by magnitudes." Master Aren turned to Sonei. "Would you be so kind as to ask the empress and Robel to join us? I think we can manage to seat everyone. No other room is quite restored enough to be comfortable."

Empress Dojene and Robel entered the room before Sonei could leave.

"Is everything all right?" Dojene asked.

"It appears that I overreacted to the situation," Deeca replied.

She folded herself onto a sofa along the side wall. Sonei sat beside her and Tran leaned against a bookshelf, stifling a yawn before finishing his sandwich. Dojene and Robel moved to a short sofa across from

Deeca and Sonei. The Sentinels sat in chairs near Tridia. Master Aren closed the door then propped a hip against the large desk at one end of the room. All eyes turned to him.

"This room is secured and insulated. The shields are in place and will be for as long as necessary. We're free to speak openly," he said.

"What's happened to the prince? Why is Drayden not here with us?" Empress Dojene demanded, glaring at Tridia.

"He's safe. I couldn't risk bringing him here. Escape wasn't assured, it was a tactical risk that almost failed." Tridia said. "I believe the people who attacked you in the Public Hearing Room will try to kill or capture him for their own purposes if he's exposed."

"I thought you didn't know anything about that group," Master Aren said.

"When I left here, I didn't," Tridia said. "I found out quite a lot while I was away. And I have suppositions about a lot more."

"We'll start from your sudden departure and debrief." Master Aren said. "Keep Drayden's location to yourself. If no one knows how to reach him, they can't give him up. Anything else can be discussed."

"The Sentinels know," Tridia stated.

Master Aren looked across the room toward the Sentinels. "They probably already knew. Sonei and Tran, you're about to find out things you'd be safer not knowing."

"Is this more stuff that could get me killed?" Tran asked.

"Yes, in other circumstances." Master Aren paused before continuing. "You aren't in danger from anyone in this room – including me. But possessing some of this information could make you a target for very powerful enemies. You can both leave now, if you'd rather not risk it."

Tran huffed. "As if."

Sonei sat unmoving. "As long as the kid's here, I'll leave only if ordered to."

"Why is the empress here and Colonel Zilisk isn't?" Tridia asked.

"Colonel Zilisk was compromised," Master Aren said. "He's dead. You'd better hear the whole story."

Tridia sat in silence as Master Aren detailed the journey to the Starling planet, the rescue of Anza and Dojene, Colonel Zilisk's death, the incident with the transmitters and the feeder in Anza's brain.

"Transmitters in her brain? *And* a live feeder?" Tridia turned to the Sentinels. "The presence in her mind was malevolent and it had intent. When it was cut off from the transmitter it couldn't retain its identity, and exited Anza's body. Then you and your clan members destroyed it using the airlock's decontamination field."

"That's an accurate summary," Winniel said.

"Why?" Tridia asked.

"Why what?" Sonei asked.

"It had access to an intelligent mind, and it caused Anza to act out. Could you have detected it since it was inside Anza's body and not attached outside?"

"No," Alanel replied. "Not without entering her mind."

"They were going to enter her mind," Master Aren said. "It had lost its usefulness."

"It could have continued to gather information." Tridia frowned. "Anza showed signs of possession before you touched her?"

"Yes," Alanel said.

"Why reveal itself so blatantly?" Tridia asked, looking around the room. "Why at that moment?"

"Where are you taking this, kid?" Sonei asked. "If you've got ideas, share them."

"I'm not sure," Tridia confessed. "It's as if the exposure was timed for a purpose. Was anyone else affected? Apart from the Sentinels, did anyone else have contact with the feeder? Did the creature gain anything from the encounter?"

"We detected nothing untoward." Winniel shared a glance with Alanel, as near uncertain as Tridia has ever seen them.

"You were tired, Winniel. You and Alanel hadn't slept for days. You were having other issues. Could you have missed something?"

"Hadn't slept?" Master Aren asked.

"What other issues?" Deeca questioned.

The Sentinels ignored the questions and looked from Tridia to each other.

"It's possible," Alanel admitted after a long pause.

"Who was closest to Anza, apart from the Sentinels?" Tridia asked.

"I was," Master Aren replied.

"You noticed nothing other than the Sentinels handling the feeder?"

"Are you doubting me?" Master Aren tensed.

"You said Anza was on the floor," Tridia explained. "The Sentinels all had their attention on the visible feeder. You were the only one who could have seen anything happen. Could there have been a second feeder? Did anyone probe Anza a second time to be sure she was free? It doesn't make strategic sense for the feeder to sacrifice itself."

No one commented, so Tridia continued. "The Kel Anec in the mine said the feeders were tools used to extract knowledge. "The one that attacked me was trying to burrow into my brain stem, but it had shorted out my muscle-control nerves. I was helpless."

"That's not entirely true," Deeca commented.

"I just mean I couldn't move physically," Tridia responded. "Could

Anza move on her own?"

"We had to carry her aboard the rescue ship and the transfer ship. Probably again onto the Sentinel ship." Tran looked to Master Aren to confirm the assumption. "She was dead weight the whole time – although not much of it."

"She sat up and spoke on the transfer ship," Deeca added. "She even took a shower and changed clothes."

"You helped her," Master Aren said.

"I didn't carry her. Just helped her balance and get dressed."

"They used technology on the princess, even though she carried an internal feeder," Tridia mused. "She wasn't possessed or consumed by it. Was the technology *and* the feeder a ruse? Is she still a danger to us?"

"Anza was never a danger to us!" Dojene startled everyone with her shout. "She was a gentle young woman with a bright future and a glorious destiny before her."

"Yes," Tridia said. "As brood stock for a half-witted Chesan prince who would rely totally on her and her mother to rule the newborn race in his place. His only function would have been to impregnate his queen at regular intervals. He wouldn't need intelligence for that."

"How dare you!" Dojene sprang to her feet, and Robel caught her wrist.

"That's enough, Commander!" Master Aren shouted, springing to his feet, as well. "There'd better be a good reason for this type of accusation."

Tridia glared, her nostrils flared. *How dare she?* How dare this presumptive relative plan to insert herself into the royal household.

"Commander! Sit down."

Tridia blinked at the sound of Master Aren's voice. Everyone in the room was standing. She looked down to find herself on her feet.

"It would appear some of His Highness's indignity is breaking through," Tridia said. "Please forgive us both. Prince Drayden's development as a child raised in isolation was expected to be hampered, according to the AI responsible for his care. It's miraculous he's the man he turned out to be and not someone with extreme issues. The idea that he might have been king in name only offends him and I'm still getting used to his personality." Tridia sat down. "Can we get back to our discussion? I don't cast aspersions on Anza or her character. She is an unfortunate victim who may have become a deadly tool in the enemy's hands."

Once Master Aren and the Sentinels sat down, the others did the same.

"They wanted Anza to get a start on rebuilding the Chesan race," Master Aren said. "They knew she was Chesan."

"*How* did they know before they captured her?" Tridia asked. "Could she have told anyone? She was part of the delegation to Starling. Did they get information from her before she was taken? Or was it just because she exuded a Chesan energy signature?"

"Anza had no idea of her birthright. In any case, her becoming the queen is no longer a possibility," Dojene glared at Tridia. "Whether they knew or how they knew is immaterial at this point."

"I disagree. They took her DNA and engrams, possibly knowledge, if the thing in her head functioned as a feeder and they tested it before we rescued her," Master Aren said. "We know she transmitted information afterward."

Tridia glanced toward Dojene, ignoring the woman's glare. "When was Colonel Zilisk compromised?"

"He never showed a change in behavior until he killed the crew and took over our transport," Dojene said. "Normal in every way, as Harish had been."

"Harish was controlled by uridine-based micromachines," Tridia said.

"It's likely Zilisk was, too," Master Aren added. "Yet, the Seluat doctors on the Starling moon appeared normal in every way."

"Even condescending," Tran said. "Just like every Seluat I've ever met."

"The Seluat system fell more than fifteen years ago," Tridia said. "Who knows what kind of control they use when they don't require stealth and secrecy."

"This is getting confusing," Sonei said. "We have the Kel Anec controlling people three different ways for the last fifteen years?"

"Their invasion started as much as twenty years ago, at the lower rim of the galaxy – yes, Sonei, near the location of the fleet on the mica-disk," Master Aren said. "I was coerced into leaving the Hierarchy so I could investigate as a free agent. Well, almost a free agent, the Guardian Controller tethered me so I wouldn't forget my mission."

Master Aren pulled up his sleeve and let the light reflect on the thin gold band imbedded in his wrist.

"You're a Guardian?" Tran asked. "Just how dead am I?"

"Not a Guardian," Master Aren replied. "Linked to the Controller so I could be watched. The Supreme Commander sent me to determine if the disappearances and shifts in allegiances in several systems could be tracked to a single source. He called it a darkness that seemed to be infiltrating the galaxy. The Controller had the same sense of foreboding, so they schemed to get me out of the Hierarchy, past the Sentinels, and into the Alliance."

"Arenel was not unaware of your true purpose," Winniel stated.

"She was tasked only to confirm that your confession was complete and you had no hidden agenda against the Core Alliance of Planets. The rest of your secrets were unimportant to her."

"What have you found out in all this time?" Deeca asked.

"I've been able to determine a pattern that pointed to Starling as the next system to fall. When the Controller told me to not worry about Starling, I didn't understand its lack of concern. Now I do. As long as the invasion base was hidden there, the system was safe. If I had skipped Starling, I would have seen that the Kanuan system was next."

"They didn't take me," Empress Dojene said, then added. "Or compromise me."

"You wouldn't know if they had," Tridia said, leaning her cheek against an open fist. "But they didn't need to. They could get to you at any time with members of your inner circle under their influence. When the negotiations for Starling got too close to bringing their outpost under Alliance scrutiny, they made a move to counter it.

"The question is, how did they know about you? About your significance to the Chesan race? At the risk of starting another fight, Anza is our likely source. If she didn't know about the Chesan energy – and you say she didn't know about her birthright – then she had no reason to mask it. Once the Kel Anec reached Starling, Anza's energy signature would have drawn them to her. I think she knew more than you give her credit for. She knew you were more important than a planetary monarch. She told me as much just before she was taken."

"Then why try to kill me on Aga?" Dojene asked.

"Those men were fanatics on a crusade. They were not Kel Anec, they were Ndgalic." Tridia said.

"The Ndgalic were peaceful people, empathic servants," Dojene said. "Why would they attack me?"

"They were terrified by the Chaos Vision they saw and felt on Ceyon," Tridia said. "I picked up a lot of fearful thoughts from them that I couldn't comprehend in my Felinus state. Having seen the vision, I now understand. They may have been peaceful on Ceyon, but they migrated to a Matroni world."

"Matroni?" Tran and Sonei asked, at the same time.

"An assassin's den," Master Aren said.

"Their sanctuary was cleared by the Hierarchy," Dojene stated. "There should have been no one there to influence them."

"Cleared – not sterilized," Master Aren said. "There could have been Matroni survivors. Now that you mention it, the fighting style of the men in the Public Hearing reeked of Matroni training. I didn't see it before."

"Nor I," Tridia said. "Not until I found out where the Ndgalic had gone. Anza may have unwittingly or unwillingly given information to the Kel Anec, but the Ndgalic could have been supplying the Matroni – or someone controlling them – with other information for years."

"The Hierarchy has a tie to the Kel Anec. We know because of the ships we destroyed on the Starling base. Just how many different enemies are we working against?" Deeca looked from Tridia to Master Aren.

"At least two groups, possibly three. One of them independent, two in tandem." Master Aren said.

"The Kel Anec are working *with* the Hierarchy. Or they may have infiltrated and taken over one or more key persons. The Hierarchy could be working on its own, or there may be an independent splinter cell," Tridia mused. "There is a contingent of ranking officers who want to see me dishonored. The attack in the dormitory, I'm sure was Ren Tama. His mind is – identifiable. I can't feature his kind of intensity being controlled."

"What attack?" Robel interrupted.

"After the Blue Level Challenge, I was attacked outside my dormitory room, and almost abducted. I felt the same presence when we were at the lake later. Those incidents didn't have the same feel, the same organization, as the other abduction and assassination attempts."

"Tama is acting on his own," Brenden stated. "His attempts have targeted only you."

"What is the likelihood of subverting one of the Hierarchy elite?" Dojene asked.

"All but nonexistent," Brenden answered. "The Elite are required to spend a month training inside the Kennels on Odea. It is the most brutal of training and leaves a soldier with practically no way to be coerced."

"Like you?" Deeca asked.

"Like me," Master Aren confessed. "Tama was sentenced to a year of training after he rescued Tridia. I'm surprised he can carry on an intelligent conversation without killing someone or playing his mind games."

"So Tama's a renegade. What does he want with the Commander? Why did he rescue her?" Tran asked.

"Tridia's mother carried the Chesan energy gene," Dojene interjected. "If she revealed the power of the energy and the subtleties of Chesan sex to a young officer like this Ren Tama was fifteen years ago, she *could* have subverted his training. Then suppose she told Tama her child would have even more power and skill than she possessed. All he had to do was watch over the girl until she became a woman."

"I don't think that's the correct scenario," Tridia said, her cheeks flaming. "The thoughts I've sensed from him – when I could get anything beyond the turmoil – have been protective, sometimes angry, but never lustful."

"The thoughts you've sensed from him?" Deeca asked. "You've made statements like that before. What are you talking about?"

Tridia looked at Master Aren. He'd said to speak freely, but he hadn't given her permission to confess her telepathy.

"The Commander is a telepath when her senses are open." Master Aren explained. "Her senses are completely blocked right now, as they have been most of the time she's been with you, so don't panic about having your minds read. She's a telepath, as am I, the empress and Princess Anza. We're all – to one degree or another – survivors of the Chesan holocaust."

"A telepath, Brenden?" Deeca shouted, jumping to her feet.

"Should Sonei and I start running now or do you plan to give us five minutes' head start after the meeting before you track us down to kill us?" Tran asked. "Because I'm pretty sure you're not going to let us live long with this knowledge."

"Relax, Tran," Master Aren said. "The rules have changed. We may need to make use of our powers to communicate in the future. It's best you know now."

"What about me?" Sonei asked. She moved to stand beside Tran.

"Same deal," Master Aren replied. "Let it slip – ever – and all agreements are off. And you die."

"Is Morgan Jacks covering this promise, too?" Sonei's voice held only suspicion.

"I'm covering it personally," Master Aren replied, his voice cold.

The room sat in silence as he and Sonei stared at each other.

Sonei looked away first. "You've got a deal," she said.

"We've got Tama working alone," Deeca stated. "The Ndgalic are with the Matroni. Who's pulling the strings inside the Hierarchy? Or do I need to bother to speak aloud?"

"Hey, we're not all telepaths," Tran said. "You're not the only one in shock. Stick to the subject."

"The Supreme Commander isn't the one ordering the ships to chase us," Master Aren said.

"How can you be sure?" Tridia asked.

"Because he's linked to the Controller." Master Aren held up his wrist. "I wasn't the first Hierarchy operative to venture into the Guardian Warren. The Controller would know if the Supreme Commander had lost his independence."

"Not many people have enough influence on their own to order an Elstaar cruiser to the edge of the galaxy without raising a few questions." Tridia said. "The ships at the planet I left came there specifically to break through the defensive grid. It's too far from Odea to be an accidental find."

"Military scientists testing the shields," Tran offered. "You said they were like the ones on Ceyon."

"That was my first thought, they'd come there because they found energy readings matching those on Ceyon." Tridia pulled her feet onto the edge of her chair, locking her wrists together across her shins. "The planet is pretty far off the beaten path for its energy readings to be clear from any Hierarchy controlled territory."

"They've had fifteen years to look," Master Aren said. "They may have found the planet long ago and are just now getting around to attacking it. It could be sheer coincidence you were there when it happened."

"We can't make deductions from the information we have now," Tridia said. "We need source information from Odea, and the Supreme Commander's help."

"As we are both banned from the planet in unison – unless summoned – perhaps we should return in the same way." Master Aren's apparent agreement surprised everyone.

"If we lose the two of you, we have no chance of defeating the Kel Anec," Deeca pointed out. "I thought you had sources inside the Hierarchy."

"No one at that level," Master Aren said. "No one who can be brazen enough to do everything that needs to be done.

"If we don't go, we have no chance. We can't fight the Kel Anec without the Hierarchy, the Guardians *and* the Sentinels. The Controller can order the Guardians, but it's weakening and we don't know if it can hold sway over the Guardian Force in crucial moments. The Sentinels won't join us without proof. The proof may be on Odea. If not there, we'll have to wait for the Sentinels to get to and from the galaxy's edge to verify the invasion fleet is real. We can risk nothing and lose everything –"

"Or risk ourselves and gain the allies we need." Tridia finished Master Aren's statement.

"There is another reason to get back to Odea. Our DNA is on file there, by sample and electronically. We've got to wipe the records and destroy the samples. Mine, Tridia's, and my father's. The Hierarchy had samples of Chesan DNA all this time and didn't know it."

"Frees B'Nay knows about my DNA being different. Davik said B'Nay wanted me for his experiment. If B'Nay is working with the Kel –"

"What if they've already gotten to the samples and they're using

DNA trackers to follow you around?" Tran asked.

"Even the best DNA trackers are only good for short range," Sonei said. "They're not strong enough to track through hyperspace."

"We're dealing with a race of people smart enough for intergalactic travel," Tran argued. "How hard could it be to extend the range on a DNA tracker?"

"We can't take the chance that they haven't found them." Master Aren dropped into the chair behind his desk and steepled his fingers in front of his face.

"You know there is only one way to return to Odea openly," Tridia said

"Yes." His reply lacked enthusiasm.

"Then share your inspiration," Deeca demanded. "Because the only scenario I can think of has our favorite assassin returning to Odea in chains."

"That *is* the only way," he said. "Tridia must be captured and returned to Odea as a prisoner. I'll follow to demand her release based on false capture."

"No!" Dojene exclaimed. "I forbid this."

"Calm yourself," Robel told her. "The oath the Commander took was designed for this contingency."

"I didn't realize it until the Public Hearing Room, but no one expected me to fulfill my oath and obey Master Aren for five years," Tridia explained. "You don't know me very well, Empress. My reputation labeled me as too independent and headstrong to ever submit to one man's rules for long. Tama was especially certain of it. He told me to come to him when I got tired of being a puppet and wanted the truth. Odea wants me back in their ranks permanently, and the ruling of the Tribunal will be just that. Brood stock and test subject, most likely assigned to Frees B'Nay when I'm not pregnant."

Dojene's jaw dropped. "You would willingly return, knowing this?"

"Knowing their intent allows us to devise a counter strategy," Tridia said. "If I had any doubts I wouldn't risk our future."

"Prince Drayden would never allow it," the empress said.

"Fortunately, Prince Drayden doesn't have a vote in the matter," Master Aren pointed out.

"You don't know the prince as well as you think you do," Tridia said. "He, better than anyone, understands the risks and the costs. He's been contemplating them for years. Besides, he isn't my master. We bonded and we stand on equal ground. All that I am and all that he is, is now one in each of us."

"Those vows are only spoken at the royal wedding. Only the king and queen can handle that kind of bonding. It is irrevocable. The Chaos

Vision was so much more vivid than the last one fifteen years ago," Dojene said. "You had to have mated for him to have made that vow."

"The vows were Drayden's wish. He controlled the depth of the bonding. And I will tell you only one more time." Tridia fought to control both her and Drayden's anger. "We did not mate. Couldn't the clarity of the vision be because we're closer to the events?"

Tridia's stomach churned as the shadows of the vision crept toward her consciousness. She forced thoughts of Drayden to the forefront of her mind.

"Possibly," Master Aren said. "None of us are going to dwell on those images. We can't afford to."

"If you can't counter their strategy." Dojene changed the subject with a final argument. "If something goes wrong. They'll have your DNA and your body, with only a surgery away from having your mind. They will control the Chesan prince through you."

"If I'm lost – really lost – they'll have no satisfaction, and they won't get to Drayden," Tridia said. "I can always escape into a portal."

"Have you ever successfully opened it on your own," Dojene asked.

"She's opened it, but the experience leaves her weakened." Alanel said.

"Alanel –" Tridia interrupted.

"What is he saying, Commander?" Master Aren asked.

"Commander Odana confided to us that using the portal drains her strength, but increases her intelligence. If she can't get away, she will be too weak to combat them." Winniel said.

"That changes nothing." Tridia said. "Using the portal is a last resort I don't expect to need. If I can't escape through it, I'll use it to destroy myself and anyone around me."

Deeca stood, drawing everyone's attention. "I'll have to be the one to do it."

"Do what?" Dojene asked.

"Take her back. I'm a Hunter and I've had a vendetta against her for months. Everyone knows about it. I'm the only one close enough to know she's disobeyed. Even so, we'll have to make a show of it to convince the skeptics."

"Agreed," Tridia said. "A wound or wounds preferably. No one in the Hierarchy would believe you took me without a struggle."

"Blaster?" Deeca suggested.

"That kind of injury would have to be grievous," Master Aren said.

"There is another consideration," Tridia said. "Drayden feels my most severe pain. He felt the *deathstrike* and the wounds I received trying to rescue Anza. Whatever you do to me could incapacitate him, as well. We can't have broken bones or hemorrhaging."

"Do we really need to go that far?" Deeca asked.

"The Commander's reputation is substantial," Robel said. "As opposed as I am to any injury to her, they will have serious doubts about anyone bringing her in alive. Alive and unscathed would be unacceptable."

"Thank you, *Somi.*" A small, grateful smile accompanied Tridia's words.

"Hand-to-hand, Commander?" Master Aren asked.

"Yes, sir. Let's do this now," she said. "I want to get it over with, then you'll need to put me in restraints. From this moment forward, I'm a prisoner. There needs to be chafing, unless we're using energy cuffs or an obedience collar."

"I don't have that kind of equipment with me," Deeca said.

"I have some antique restraints here." Master Aren looked at Tran. "They're in the weapons room in the glass cases. Will you get a set and bring them to the training room downstairs?"

Tran nodded grimly.

"This isn't going to be a show," Master Aren said. "Nobody comes except Deeca and the Sentinels. Alanel will have to carry the Commander to her room when it's over."

"Who's going to carry you?" Tran asked.

"Maybe you'd better wait outside when you bring the restraints," Master Aren replied. "And Commander?" Tridia looked up. "Keep the Felinus under control this time."

"Yes, sir."

Tridia followed her master as far as the doorway before she grasped her arms and shoulders as pain shot through them. Everyone stared as she cried out and stood staring at her arms. A moment later, she fell sideways to the floor. Her head spun and she tasted blood, although her mouth wasn't bleeding.

"What's going on?" Master Aren asked, kneeling beside her.

"I don't know." Tridia gasped. She wiped her hand across her mouth, surprised to see no blood. "I could have sworn something clawed me, then someone hit me."

Alanel offered her a hand up and she was about to take it when another shock spun her head the other way. She lay on the floor propped on her elbow.

"Are you sure you don't have someone with an invisibility shield in here?" she accused.

"No such thing," Master Aren replied.

"Well, something's causing this." Tridia took Alanel's hand and got to her feet just in time to double-over in pain. She'd been punched in the gut often enough to know what it felt like. She fell to her knees, then curled into a ball when excruciating pain shot from her pelvic area.

"Drayden!" She groaned. "Not possible."

With her arms wrapped across her stomach all she could do was fall to the floor and let the tears flow as she tried to catch her breath. Something horrible was happening to Drayden and she was powerless to help him.

"Tran, get the restraints," Master Aren said, as he cradled Tridia against his chest. "Now!"

Tran had stood transfixed, but sprinted out the door at his friend's sharp words.

Tridia shook her head as repeated injuries rained on Drayden's body. If this was her part of his pain, what must the prince be enduring?

"He should be safe," she cried. "There was no way to reach him. He should be safe."

The pain left her on the edge of consciousness.

"We can free you of the pain, Commander," Winniel said. "And disperse it through the clan."

Tridia shook her head. "Only if it will help him."

She passed into darkness, fearing what she'd learn when the shadows lifted.

CHAPTER THIRTY-NINE

Drayden walked out of the training room shaking, as much from what he'd seen as from the workout. Hands on knees, he leaned against the wall, trying to come to grips with the vision. He'd seen Tridia in shackles, surrounded by uniformed men. She' kept her shoulders straight despite the fact her lip was swollen and a bruise darkened her right cheek. Someone had given her a beating and he could only think of Brenden Aren. How could the man abuse her when she'd gone to him for help? *How had she ended up as a prisoner?*

The prince wiped the sweat from his face and noticed blood on his hand. The hologram Brenden had clipped his forehead when the vision distracted him. The perspiration stung in the cut. Yet another reason to despise his mentor.

Drayden tried to focus on his relief that Tridia had survived her escape from the planet, but his anger kept getting in the way. He'd never sworn, mainly because he'd never been exposed to the words, but Tridia's memory held plenty of expletives. Even though he didn't speak them, they swarmed through his angry thoughts, fanning the flames he tried to control. The Felinus rage boiled beneath the surface.

He'd kept his mind closed since Tridia left the planet. Was what he saw a current happening or a glimpse of the future? If it was the future, the king's prescience had awakened in him with a vengeance, years ahead of its time, and it would color his every decision if he let the doubts take control. However, if the vision was current, his bond with Tridia had broken through his barriers. That would also have implications.

He pushed away from the wall and walked toward the classroom to check the monitors. It had been several hours since he'd run sweeps of the planet and he'd promised Secura he'd be vigilant in that duty. He had little to do but study the files Tridia had left and run the sweeps since the lower levels were all closed off, so he'd asked Secura to leave it to him. The last several sweeps had revealed nothing, but his gut told him that was about to change.

He picked up the glass vase that sat on his desk and smelled the Lesta flower Teak had left for him before he'd sent the bot to inspect the open rooms in the bunker. The monitors showed sweeping views of the planet from three of the satellites, as well as sensor readings for the surrounding space. He saw nothing out of the ordinary, so why did he have a nagging sense of danger? He started for the shower when something caught his eye. Security cameras imbedded and camouflaged in the rock kept constant surveillance of the area just outside the entrance. A shadow moved at the edge of the surveillance area. He watched, but the shape didn't reappear.

His heart leapt at the thought it might be Tridia, then reason took over. She'd sent no signal to indicate her return. But then, he'd been away from the monitors for hours, sleeping, eating, and training. He might have missed a signal. Should he chance adjusting the cameras? They made noise when they moved, he'd heard them. He hadn't made up his mind when the decision was taken from him. A dark shape in a helmet, like the one Tridia had worn, moved into the surveillance area. The uniform and gear were dark, where those of the men who held Tridia in his vision were a lighter color, but the insignia was the same. The figure probably outweighed Drayden by a third of his weight. As Drayden watched, several lizard-like creatures stepped into view, dragging the adult Rrabbas with them. One of the creatures held up the jacket Drayden had left near the birthing pool. The creature also carried some of the things he'd dropped from Tridia's backpack, including the flask of huttle juice. The trail of those items had led them straight to the bunker's entrance.

The man exposed his hands to reveal one of the Rrabbas' podlings. The silt around the infant's roots was fast running between the man's fingers. Deprived of its nourishment, the podling would die in a matter of minutes. Layne and Vaille struggled with their captors to no avail. The dark man didn't move, he just let the muddy soil seep away.

Drayden's heart crumpled. He'd told Tridia he would sacrifice anything to keep her safe. Pulling on her strength, he might be able to turn away and let the podling die, but what about the uniform? *Did this man have Tridia? Had he been the one to injure her?*

Drayden closed his eyes. Had he not seen the vision of Tridia in shackles, his decision would be clear. He had to analyze the situation without its influence. Tridia had escaped from a dozen space ships, but if he was taken, she would surrender to save him. If they had her, they would have brought her to coerce him. These creatures had her things, but they were *looking* for her, they didn't *have* her. He turned his back to the monitor.

"You trusted her more than me."

Drayden spun at the sound of the physician's voice. Her black-clad image flickered beside the desk. Secura's image blinked in and out beside it, her program fighting for control.

"You thought *she* could protect you, but she abandoned you, just as you abandoned me. Now *I* will abandon *you!*"

The door slid open and both images vanished. Drayden faced the entrance as the helmeted figure crossed the threshold.

***

"If she's here with you, call her out before we're forced to resort to torture." A metallic voice came from the man. "These are her belongings. I know she's been here."

Tridia wasn't the man's prisoner – or he didn't know it yet. Drayden's chest constricted.

"Let them go." Drayden stepped toward the door and indicated the Rrabbas. "They've done nothing to you and they're harmless."

"You gave up your position too quickly. There are other infants in the ooze. You might have held out for one death and convinced me this facility was empty."

"I gave up nothing," Drayden said. "The security system malfunctioned and opened the door."

He glanced down at the Rrabbas. With his mind still closed he couldn't hear them. He struggled to keep the fear and frustration from his face.

"I've seen their village, and the tent there that's suited for a humanoid. My troops can decimate this place so nothing will grow here again. Do you understand me?"

"I understand your threat." Drayden kept his voice and eyes steady.

"It's no threat, I assure you." The man nodded to the reptilian creatures and gave the podling into Vaile's extended hands. "It's a fact. The only thing that will keep fact from becoming proof is your correct answers to my questions."

Haylen and Wade knelt to scoop up the puddled soil and packed it around the infant's roots. Layne approached Drayden but the lizard creatures hissed and the little Rrabbas stopped.

"It's okay." Drayden looked down at the Rrabbas leader and shooed him away. "Take your child back to the nursery. No one will harm you now."

All four Rrabbas bowed to him, their enormous iridescent eyes apologetic yellow, then they squeezed between the aliens and hurried into the vegetation. Even if they hurried, the podling might not live.

"Who are you?" The dark man's metallic voice drew Drayden's eyes to him.

Drayden frowned. If the man didn't know who he was, why had he made such an evil threat?

"I might ask you the same thing," Drayden countered.

"You might, but then I'd have one of my soldiers bring you the crushed remains of the child you so bravely saved."

"There was nothing brave about a door malfunctioning." Drayden held up his hands in surrender. "Fine. My name is Davik Schie."

"You'd better come up with another name fast, boy." The dark man advanced and Drayden backed into the classroom.

"I'm a refugee here. I escaped from the Hierarchy prison on Cystia."

The man made a slow tour of the classroom and stopped in front of Drayden before speaking again. "You have an elaborate setup for a refugee. Not to mention a shield that an Odean battle cruiser couldn't break through. You must be an important refugee."

"The only important person took a ship off this planet after destroying the defensive grid. I wasn't invited to leave."

"Where is Tridia Odana?" The man asked.

Drayden held still, pulling on Tridia's memories to deal with the man. "Tridia Odana?"

A dark-gloved hand shoved him against a sofa, and brought a knife to his throat before Drayden could react. The blade pricked his skin as he swallowed.

"I will tolerate no games from you in these questions, boy. You will answer me the first time or you will watch the skin peeled from your little green friends before I do the same to you. I will ask each question only once and you will answer me. Now, where is Tridia Odana?"

"She left in the escape ship."

"The scanners detected only one person in that ship. She wouldn't have left alone."

"The ship has cloaking devices around the main cabin. It could have been full of people and you'd have detected only the flight crew."

The knife pressed deeper into Drayden's throat, then the man released him with another shove. "You're lying. Corporal, bring me one of the adult plant creatures – and one of the children."

"No!" Drayden tried to follow the creature but the dark man slammed an arm across his chest and held him in place.

"I warned you." The metallic modulator was switched off, replaced by a cold male voice.

"No games. No lies. Tridia Odana piloted that ship off the planet."

"Alone?"

"Call your corporal back."

"Sergeant!" One of the aliens detached itself and ran after the corporal.

"Yes. She was alone." Drayden dropped his eyes and looked away. Had he just condemned his mate?

"Then you might be Davik Schie, except that an Odean soldier would never have opened that door if he'd been ordered not to – not even one subjected to the brutality he endured. She would have given you that order. It's a very old feint and Davik Schie is reportedly a strategic genius. Put the important parcel in a place of relative safety and draw away the threat. Leaving what's important for someone else to collect – or to remain hidden. She wouldn't attempt such a ruse unless she was desperate to save you. She might have tried it to save Davik Schie – she cared for him. But this has the feel of a more desperate plan." The man removed the pilot's helmet. Drayden lifted his eyes to see a darkly handsome face with a cruel smile – a face from Tridia's memories.

Master Ren Tama. The name formed in Drayden's mind, along with warnings of Tama's ruthlessness. "I told you, I didn't open the door. The security system malfunctioned. I might be a strategic genius, but I'm no computer wizard."

"This gets more interesting," Tama said.

The corporal and the sergeant trudged into the room. Drayden heaved a sigh of relief upon seeing them empty-handed.

"My name is Ren Tama," the man said. "I'm a White Level Master Assassin and soldier in the Odean Hierarchy. I will not think twice about destroying this entire planet to get what I want – and I want Commander Tridia Odana. You're going to help me get her."

Drayden's blood ran cold and he cursed the program for betraying him. Tridia would surrender herself to save him without hesitating. That's how she would end up in shackles. He couldn't allow it. The only weapons he possessed were the battle staffs outside the training room. Escape – or die trying – were his only options. If he tried to argue with Tama, the Rrabbas would pay. If he did nothing, Tridia would be captured. He had to remove himself from the equation somehow. The sterilize command might work if Secura could gain control of the program. Saying his name aloud might give away his identity. Would that make matters worse? He had to get away from the invaders to give the order.

"Why do you want her?" Drayden stepped away from the sofa as he asked the question. He positioned himself so he had a clear shot to the first turn in the hall, his back to the entrance. Tama studied him and seemed to measure the distance between Drayden and the guarded door before answering.

"Why would a man possess any wild creature? To tame it. To make it his own."

"To cage her?" Drayden asked, more curious than he'd intended.

Tama laughed. "No, Davik Schie. I want her by my side, as my consort. I want to taste the pleasures of her soul every night, to feel her writhe beneath me in passion, to hear her moan my name in ecstasy. I want to possess her as a man possesses a woman, but first, I want to bring her rebellious spirit to heel."

Heat rose in Drayden's cheeks. His fists clenched at his side. The man spoke every word to evoke a foolish reaction no Hierarchy soldier would commit. Tama meant to taunt him about the identity he'd chosen. Every instinct in Drayden – most of which came from Tridia – wanted to attack the evil grinning creature in front of him. Instead of attacking, he bolted down the hall. Blaster shots exploded into the wall as he made the first turn and sprinted down a side corridor. Tama's angry shouts followed him as he made his way into a small labyrinthine section. Threading his way through the storage rooms, he darted into a corridor near one of the stairwell doors, but it was sealed.

"Secura? Teak?" he called. No answer. "Drayden One Sterilize."

Nothing happened. He hurried down the hall to the training room, grabbed a battle staff, and ducked inside.

"Play jungle ambush program. I'm wearing pads. Attack all sentients except me."

The room filled with plants replicating those around the birthing grounds. Another of Brenden Aren's training programs, various assorted creatures would drop from the trees or pop up from the tall grass and bushes to attack. He'd moved only steps from the door when the reptilian creatures entered. At first, they seemed confused, then they started sniffing the air. They shrugged off the attacking animals and moved straight for his sweat-soaked body. He couldn't hide his scent.

They surrounded him in the middle of the room. He called out the sterilize command again. Still no response. Two of the creatures tried to grab him, but he managed to knock one of them senseless and shove the other back long enough to run toward the door again. Anger comingled with fear as the certainty of his capture sunk in. They tackled him two steps from the door. Tama waited in the hall.

Drayden struggled, but there were four of them. Reptilian claws dug into his arms and shoulders, drawing blood. They hauled him to his feet and forced him to the door. Tama took two purposeful steps, anger etched in every line on his face. *Had he done enough to make Tama kill him?* Held by two aliens on either side, Drayden could only stand helpless as fear knotted his stomach.

While he was still a step away, Tama drew his hand across his chest. By the time he reached Drayden, he uncoiled a backhand that cracked the prince's jaw and filled his mouth with blood. A second strike spun his head in the other direction.

"I need you alive for the present, Davik Schie, but you'll serve my purpose just as well damaged as whole. Perhaps better. That useless attempt bought you more pain than you can imagine."

With his head reeling from the blows, Drayden barely understood what Tama said, but he'd made a bad decision by not letting them shoot him before the first turn. In a final act of defiance, he spat blood on the front of Tama's jacket. The dark assassin laughed, and then landed a fierce punch to Drayden's stomach. The prince gasped for breath.

"Oh yes, you will learn new meanings of agony. If you are Davik Schie, you've done time in the Kennels. I trained in that hell pit for a year, and trust me when I say I haven't forgotten the lessons." Tama stood close enough for Drayden to hear his hateful whispers. "I will find out who you really are and use you to bring Tridia Odana to me. Then, if you still possess your eyes, I may have you watch as I take her for the first time."

Tama accentuated the last line with a sadistic laugh and a knee to Drayden's groin. The prince would have doubled over had he not been held upright by alien claws. His vision clouded with pain, and Tama turned away.

"Bring him to the ship," Tama called over his shoulder. "And destroy those plant creatures on the way out."

Drayden yelled at Tama's back and fought to get away. Two aliens punched and kicked him while the other two held him in place. In his struggle to escape their grasp, his shoulder pulled away from its socket. In the end, he was too injured to stand, so the creatures lifted him and carried him out of the bunker on their shoulders.

When they were steps from the outer door, Secura appeared and flickered and Teak sailed into the room. Drayden shouted the sterilize command one last time. The door started to close, but the two aliens in the rear shoved the two in front and Drayden through. The three of them tumbled to the ground as the bunker door closed behind them, the rock wall glowed with heat and its seals disappeared. Tama caught a handful of Drayden's hair and forced him to look into his eyes.

"What did you say? What have you done?"

"Your guards and anyone or anything bigger than a virus in the bunker will be disintegrated – along with the entire contents of the building. You'll never get that door opened again."

"What a shame," Tama laughed. "We had just herded all of your plant friends into one of the rooms. Well, we might as well clean up the weeds from the rest of the planet while we're here."

Sounds of blaster fire reached Drayden's ears as the reptilians dragged him through the grass, exposing him to the unfiltered sunlight for the first time in fifteen years. He thought of the Rrabbas and everything he'd sacrificed to save them, only to let them die in the end. Tama had promised him new meanings of agony. The wounds leaving a trail of his blood on the ground might be the first lesson, but overwhelming guilt was the hardest to endure. How could he ever face Tridia again, knowing he'd be responsible for bringing her to a creature like Ren Tama?

CHAPTER FORTY

Tridia stumbled into the security receiving area of Rodan Base when Deeca shoved her shoulder. It had taken a day for her to recover from Drayden's initial injuries, and she'd felt his beatings continue with varying levels of intensity another three days before they could finalize the arrangements to get her back to Odea. The Sentinels had distributed Drayden's pain among the Hariok clan, and Winniel had assured her that the prince would feel some relief, but he had the physical injuries to deal with on top of the pain. She counted at least three broken bones and untold internal damage. How was he still alive? Master Aren carried out their original plans to leave signs of a struggle just before she and Deeca left Hulac. She cringed at the thought they'd inflicted more pain on Drayden in the process, but there wasn't another way. She needed the rapidly fading bruises to get past the medical check-in.

Exhaustion, anger with Deeca, and anxiety about the stunt they were about to pull weighed on Tridia's steps as much as the shackles she wore. Her braid had worked its way loose from its binding and had unraveled about halfway up her back. The bruise on her left cheek had faded from its original deep purple color during the two-day trip, but her lip was still a little swollen and possibly infected. A fresh red welt in the size and shape of Deeca's hand graced her right cheek. It was the center of their current conflict.

Tridia had insisted there be a fresh wound on her, but Deeca had disagreed. To get her point across, Tridia attacked Deeca and they'd fought in the ship after landing in the detention area. Deeca was little worse for wear, but Tridia had gotten the visible signs of an altercation she needed. The effort had convinced the guards, who sniggered as they watched the once proud assassin stumble through the detention center, unable to move at her usual smooth gait.

"We'll take her from here." One of the khaki-clad guards started forward, reaching for Tridia's arm.

"You'll take her nowhere." Deeca stepped between the two. "I was assured I would be able to present her to your tribunal myself, or I never would have brought her here against Alliance wishes."

"I'm afraid you'll have to take it up with the officer of the day, ma'am. In the meantime, she comes with us."

"Stand down, Corporal." A familiar voice cut across the room and Tridia shifted her gaze from the group of grinning underlings to the man she'd hoped to see. She schooled her face to show no sign of relief.

"Captain Heilen, sir," the corporal stuttered. "Sir, this isn't a Challenge Grid matter. You've no authority here."

Heilen silenced any further objections with a glare. "If you check your claim with the duty officer and the Tribunal, I think you'll find I have absolute authority in this matter. This arrest stems from a vow taken after a failed Challenge. It's all under Grid jurisdiction – my jurisdiction."

"Yes, sir." The young soldier snapped to attention. "We request permission to assist you with transport of the prisoner, sir."

The Captain of the Guard cast a disgusted eye over the assembled group of police guards. Some of them had failed as challengers or hunters in Tridia's previous missions. Heilen would know every one of them.

"I won't need any assistance with this one." He turned to Tridia as he continued. "Commander Odana will cause me no trouble. She knows I'll shoot her without hesitation if she does. Isn't that correct, Commander?"

"Captain Heilen." She acknowledged his rank and authority with a nod.

"You didn't last long with Master Aren." Heilen didn't seem amused as he spoke, unlike the others.

"This low-life bounty hunter took me out of his encampment after I'd already been injured in a battle. It's only her misinterpretation of disobedience. Master Aren will straighten this out when he gets here. Until then, I'm apparently to be treated with all the disgust due a failed soldier." Tridia looked over her shoulder at Deeca, then back to the Captain. "When I get out of these shackles, she and I will settle this. I want her kept close enough to ensure that happens."

"Your wants aren't to be given consideration, Commander, but the bounty hunter *was* given certain assurances when she contacted the authorities." Captain Heilen kept his gaze locked on Tridia's as he spoke. "One was that she would escort you until she personally turned you over to the ruling council and the Supreme Commander. They're being assembled."

"Then at your leisure, Captain, we'll proceed?" Deeca's comment forestalled anything else he might have said.

"I said you'd been given assurances, Hunter Varin, not deference. We'll handle this matter according to Odean protocols. We don't take injured prisoners into the council chambers without first seeing a medic. And we don't rush the assembly of the ruling council." The Captain unsnapped his holster cover and drew his weapon. The blast chamber hummed to life. "I trust this isn't necessary, Commander?"

"Your trust is well-placed, Captain." Tridia moved when Heilen motioned with the weapon and Deeca fell into step behind them.

They made slow progress to the medic building and people stopped to stare. By the time they entered the building they had a large following of rainbow uniforms. Tridia kept her mind tightly closed. Eavesdropping on the thoughts of such a crowd could be debilitating.

An antiseptic smell filled her nostrils as Tridia entered the examination room. The medic attendant told both Heilen and Deeca to wait outside, an instruction they both ignored. Medic Geiswan, Tridia's personal medic for the past four years, entered the room studying a vid chart. As the last medic to examine her, the job fell to him to check her back into the Hierarchy.

"Remove your outer garments, please." Geiswan didn't look at Tridia as he spoke.

"That's going to be hard to do, sir." Tridia indicated the shackles. "I don't think they'll be coming off."

The medic looked around, first at Tridia, then at the other two.

Heilen stood with his arms crossed over his chest, the fully-charged blaster in his hand. He shook his head in the negative. Deeca mimicked the motion.

"Very well." The medic helped Tridia ease her shirt over her head and bunched the fabric around her wrists. Then he eased her pants down to her ankles.

"Was that really necessary?" Heilen asked Deeca, observing the dark bruises Master Aren had left on Tridia's torso and thighs.

"She thought so," Deeca replied. "She resisted."

"How is it you aren't equally damaged?"

Deeca snorted a humorless laugh and pointed to the bruise on her cheek. "What makes you think I'm not? Don't expect me to undress to prove my point. Besides, I carry a blaster with a stun setting. I didn't have to behave like a raging beast to subdue her."

Captain Heilen remained unconvinced that Deeca had given Tridia the bruises, at least not in a fair fight. Tridia managed not to smile at his astuteness. Heilen had known her too long to believe she'd be taken without resistance or that a single bounty hunter would be able to bring her in. She'd been right to insist on signs of a struggle. The examination took only a few minutes. Tridia was redressed and antiseptic applied to the cut in her mouth. The last uncomfortable moment came when Geiswan asked if there were other injuries or issues she cared to report. All Challenge Grid participants were asked the same thing. It was their last chance to report improper abuse at the hands of their opponents.

"Metal burns on both wrists," Tridia stated. "They're two weeks old, scabs and scar tissue have formed."

"Were you branded?" the medic asked.

"After a fashion, but it wasn't her doing." Tridia indicated Deeca by pointing her chin. "The complaint may have no recourse based on the vow I took before leaving Odea. But it should be in the medical record."

With those words, Tridia implicated Master Aren as her torturer, and gave herself an explanation for the gold bracelets she wore, should one be required later. Heilen's face took on a look of grim disapproval. Since her manacles were too wide and tight for the medic to examine the wounds and her escorts refused to remove them, he had no choice but to end the examination without seeing the injuries.

From the medic building, Captain Heilen escorted Tridia and Deeca to a holding cell where he left them. Neither of the women spoke aloud. Tridia had warned Deeca in advance the cell would be observed and recorded. After an hour Tridia lowered the barriers around her mind and made a slow start to expanding her sensory area. No one occupied any of the cells in their section, but beyond the walls Tridia's thoughts were assailed by an enormous assembly of minds. Her return had caused an uproar amid the Challenge Grid. Officers and underlings all wanted to get a glimpse of her. Farther on she found Heilen and several of his best officers. His thoughts were as grim as his expression had been. Heilen wasn't her friend, but he respected her, and he could be trusted to do his job – which included protecting her as much as preventing her escape. In truth, his mind was more occupied with the former. At last she found the mind she sought, touched it gently, then backed away, withdrawing into the cell.

He's here, she told Deeca.

Deeca turned her head toward the door and gave an almost imperceptible nod.

Captain Heilen will perform as expected and we have a crowd of watchers. I have to use barriers for protection. If you need to communicate with me, you'll have to focus your thoughts.

LIKE THIS? Deeca's thought slammed into Tridia's brain.

Tridia winced, then wrinkled her nose as if she had an unscratchable itch. *That's the way. Wait. Trouble's coming.*

Tridia focused her eyes on her shackles to keep from watching the door. Deeca tensed but kept her nonchalant gaze wandering around the room. The door burst open with the force of a kick, and three soldiers dressed in the black uniforms of the Elstaar guard entered. Their uniforms proved they weren't part of Heilen's team and a quick touch to their minds revealed they weren't acting of their own free will.

"Commander Odana, you'll come with us." Two of the men grabbed Tridia's arms and lifted her to her feet as the third forced Deeca to remain seated with a strong hand on her shoulder.

"She's to wait here for Captain Heilen," Deeca objected. "Or I go with her. We don't separate."

The guard shoved Deeca into her chair when she tried to stand.

Don't push it. They're compromised. Tridia shot the other woman a warning.

"Orders have changed. You're to wait here." The guards hustled Tridia into the hallway, carrying her when she couldn't move fast enough.

"Your superiors will hear about this," Deeca shouted as the door slammed.

Deeca's fear faded from Tridia's awareness as the distance between them grew. The release of tension it brought gave Tridia a margin of mental breathing room. The minds of her escorts were one-dimensionally focused on getting her out of the detention cells and into the Elstaar compound without confrontation. Once inside those walls, she'd be out of Heilen's jurisdiction and only orders from the Supreme Commander could gain her release. Tridia's instincts told her she'd walked right into a coup. The timing couldn't have been more perfect.

Two more guards joined them at a hallway intersection as she sensed Captain Heilen and his team turning in the opposite direction. She willed her captors to hurry, wanting them to make good their escape. The more turmoil inside the Hierarchy, the better for Master Aren's scheme to succeed. Heilen would hear Deeca describe the black uniforms and know who'd taken her. He'd attempt to go straight to the Supreme Commander, and no doubt be thwarted in his efforts. It was a brilliant strategy, worthy of a master. The final pieces of the puzzle fell into place for Tridia as she and her abductors passed through the back security doors and made their way toward the guarded gates of the Elstaar compound. She was about to relay the information regarding who held the leash on the Elstaar to Deeca when one of her guards snapped a heavy collar around her neck. The device thrummed in her ears and caused disorientation in her mind. As the guards carried her through the security gates, her muscles tensed in fear. Without her telepathy or clear thought, she couldn't open a portal. Without a portal, she had no fail-safe escape route. She'd be at the mercy of the man orchestrating the coup, a man she believed had none.

***

Brenden Aren's black Elstaar uniform sported a Colonel's rank and security officer braids. He walked the halls of the archive building with impunity. Few people even made eye contact with so imposing an officer. The signs in the hall labeled the building as the high security archive bunker. Nothing happened on Odea that didn't create a record in the archives. All information flowed through a one-way firewall that protected the system from all but the best hackers. In the history of the archives, only one hacker had ever escaped detection: Mort H'Lar. Brenden had paid H'Lar well to hack the system and obtain information during an Elstaar scandal years before. The security squad caught H'Lar on his second attempt to hack in for his own purposes. He now worked inside the firewall, chained to his desk and sentenced to death should he ever show his face outside the building. Brenden already knew the price to strike a deal with H'Lar. All he had to do was get to the man.

Three Elstaar officers snapped to attention outside the archive door.

"Report, Riley," Brenden growled.

"Five operatives seized Commander Odana from the holding cell and escorted her to the security compound without incident. The collar was attached as you instructed." A young Captain said. "One of the guards has the control box."

"Captain Heilen has detained Deeca Varin in the holding cells for her protection." The officer on Riley's left reported.

"The Supreme Commander is out of touch at the moment and will be unreachable for the next quarter-watch. The other members of the Tribunal will wait for him before assembling to hear the matter." The last officer of the three made his report.

"Excellent. Make sure Hunter Varin stays in the holding cell until the Tribunal calls for her. The Elstaar are not to take her into custody under any circumstances. The collar will allow us to keep track of Commander Odana. Keep her alive, but otherwise don't intervene. She's made her enemies, let her deal with them as best she can. Go to your posts and I'll meet with you as planned so we can draw this matter to a close."

Brenden made sure the three of them left before inserting his right hand in the security scanner. A pinprick on the side of his hand indicated the scanner had taken a sample for DNA clearance. He waited for a breathless moment to see if the Supreme Commander had done as he'd promised at their last meeting and reinstated him to his previous rank. The access light changed from red to green and the door locks clicked open. A guard inside the door requested additional identification and Brenden stepped over to the retinal scanner. Once the device confirmed his identity the guard saluted him and asked if he could be of assistance.

"No. My business is confidential and I know where to find what I need." Brenden walked through a second security door and into a room crowded with communication consoles, holographic monitor screens, and rows of people sitting at desks cross-cataloguing incoming data.

He walked between the rows without hesitation, going straight for Mort H'Lar's chair. One data stream caught his eye and he stopped behind a young woman to view her monitor. Ren Tama's countenance appeared on the screen again, communicating with one of the administrators.

"I'm sorry, sir, this is a confidential communication between Master Tama and a member of the Challenge Review Board." The young woman's voice shook as she addressed him.

"Understood, Lieutenant. Carry on."

Brenden continued on his way. He'd seen enough of the communication to know Tama was requesting access to Tridia once the Tribunal delivered its verdict. News of her arrest had traveled quickly to have reached Tama's ears already. The man wasn't an unanticipated interruption, but he was one Brenden could live without at this juncture. No doubt Tama wanted Tridia for his personal use, and there was no way to know how far he'd go to get her. Despite Tridia's instinct that Tama was not after her for his own gain, he couldn't be trusted. Brenden tried to fold Tama's presence into the current plan, but none of the scenarios worked well. Everything to this point had gone to his precise calculations. If Tama appeared too soon, he could throw the scheme out of sync. Brenden cursed under his breath. He'd have to deal with any deviation when it happened.

Mort H'Lar sat with his face almost touching the hologram monitor above his small station. For a moment Brenden thought the man was unaware of his presence, then the hacker signaled for him to observe the monitor closely.

"See how the communication bands are double linked here. That's an old trick, sending one message under another one. Almost as if someone wants to get caught, don't you think Ambassador Aren? Or should I say, Colonel? Perhaps Master is more to your liking?" H'Lar squinted watery hazel eyes up at Brenden.

"Whatever you choose, H'Lar. I have no personal preference. Although the uniform would suggest Colonel is a more appropriate title this trip."

"Clever how you got your Elstaar rank back even after deserting.

Almost like it was planned for you to return. I've noticed your covert communications for the past few years. Very circumspect. Diplomatic stuff with the Supreme Commander. Intelligence information to the underlings you left here. What was it, four or six young initiates? You always did inspire soldiers to take your risks for you while you directed your operations from the shadows." H'Lar looked back at his monitor. "How many personas are you using now?"

"As many as I need." Brenden watched the hologram change to show Tridia, still in shackles, being roughly handled by two of the Elstaar guards.

"An impressive young woman, Colonel. A lot of communication circles around her whereabouts and her skills. They've all been watching her for the past two years." H'Lar played his fingers across his console and several smaller screens appeared across the bottom of Tridia's screen. "Tama, the Supreme Commander, the geneticists, the Captain of the Guard, Frees B'Nay, and you. Why so much fuss over one little girl?"

Brenden watched the side of H'Lars' head until the man turned to meet his gaze. Inches apart, Brenden spoke in a voice so low only the hacker could hear him. "I believe you've already figured that out, Mort, my friend. What I want to know is, who else has? Who has their hands controlling the Elstaar elite? Especially the ones calling the shots from off-world."

"I helped you once, Colonel, and you paid me well. But credits do me no good in here, and I can't walk outside without losing my head, so to speak." H'Lar fingered the collar blinking around his neck. "Sensors at the door set the charge off. I don't dare leave unless I'm under guard. If I'm found helping you, someone might just force the issue."

Brenden smiled. "I can get that collar off your neck *and* get you off of the planet. I can also offer you refuge on any one of a dozen unregistered stations. Talents like yours are hard to come by. I wouldn't want to lose them."

H'Lar smiled back. "You make a lot of promises, Colonel. Elstaar Security doesn't have need of promises. Does that mean I'm speaking with the Ambassador now?"

"Suppose we say you're dealing with an independent information broker."

"For what purpose?" H'Lar squinted as if to examine Brenden's face for subterfuge.

"I plan to start a war."

Brenden's response brought a chuckle from H'Lar's lips. "We haven't had a good one of those in over a decade, now have we?"

Brenden waited, one eyebrow raised as a request for acceptance.

"Okay, Colonel," H'Lar agreed, then became serious. "The collar comes off upon delivery."

"The collar comes off upon confirmation of information. I need proof of alien intervention in Hierarchy business, or collusion on the part of senior officers would do. I need to have it streamed off-planet toward Elrel Station by the end of the day. Today, H'Lar. Tomorrow will be too late. And use something cleverer than hiding it beneath a secondary digital image?"

"You're asking a lot in so little time."

"I'm asking a genius." Brenden grinned. He raised his voice just slightly as he stood. "I expect the results in transmission by the end of your shift tomorrow, H'Lar. I'll speak to the duty officer to see that you aren't distracted."

"Yes, sir, Colonel," H'Lar responded, then added under his breath. "I've heard interesting tales about the women on Elrel."

CHAPTER FORTY-ONE

Tridia teetered for balance when the Elstaar guards set her on her feet in a darkened holding cell. The blurred silhouette of a man stopped in the doorway, outlined by the bright light in the hall beyond.

Disregard the pain. The thrumming means nothing. Tridia tried to control the disorientation, but pinpoints of pain drilled into the cavities of her ears and pulsed to the rhythm of the collar.

The silhouette came a step closer but remained too far away to recognize. His slender shape wavered before her eyes.

"You have caused us some inconvenience, Commander Odana." The man wore a voice modulator. "How did you manage to elude our pilots at Xanaias?"

"Xanaias? Am I supposed to recognize that location?" Bile rose in the back of Tridia's throat as the collar continued to vibrate her inner ear. The food Deeca had insisted she eat before landing threatened to rise from her stomach.

"Games, Commander? Surely, you have better scenarios than denial."

"Xanaias isn't a known location. Does it go by another name?" Sweat broke out on her upper lip and she swallowed hard. "What planet is it on? Which parsec is it in?"

"Perhaps you don't know the name." The man seemed to ponder for a moment then gave her the coordinates for Zentel.

"That's on the edge –" Tridia coughed and swallowed hard again, pulling herself as upright as the shackles allowed. "It's days from here. When was I to have performed the miracle of eluding your pilots?"

"You don't look well, Commander. Yet the medic just gave you a clean bill of health. Are you playing at something?" The man stepped closer.

"I've been to several different planets and kept company with a number of different species in the past few weeks. Not every disease shows up in a Challenge Grid check-up." Tears welled in her eyes as she gagged on air. The disturbance in her ears worsened with every breath, and she gasped to fill her lungs.

"Get an Elstaar medic in here, now." The man shouted and stepped back as Tridia fell to her hands and knees.

Unable to keep on her feet, Tridia folded into a submissive bow on the floor, then back to her hands and knees again as she heaved the contents of her stomach. She continued to heave until there was nothing left to bring up. Her abdominal muscles spasmed until tears streamed down her face and her ribs cried for relief. She tried to send a message to Master Aren and the disorientation increased.

Was the sickness coming from Drayden? Was he being tortured? Or did it originate with her and add to his already substantial distress? She wanted to open her mind further and reach out to him, but forced a barrier around her thoughts instead.

When the barrier went up, the collar's thrumming lessened. She fell sideways, narrowly avoiding the puddle that had been her meal.

"Leave the manacles on, take the shackles off her feet. If she tries anything, stun her." Anger tinged the distorted words of the man with the modulator. "I want a weapon on her at all times."

"We have no key for these antiques, sir," one of the guards announced after examining the shackles on her ankles. "We might be able to cut them off with the right tool."

"Then get the tool or bring that woman here with the key. We'll need to question her anyway."

Footsteps faded down the hallway as two sets of hands hauled Tridia to her knees. Her head spun from the sudden change in position and her stomach heaved again.

"Let her be until the medic gets here." The voice ordered the hands.

Tridia's disoriented mind could no longer assemble whole images from the pieces she perceived. The collar thrummed less vigorously, but even the small vibration kept her off-balance. She curled into a fetal position and kept her eyes jammed shut in self-defense so the room's dancing light and shadows couldn't torture her vision.

"What have you done to her?" A new voice hammered into Tridia's aching ears.

"Only questioned her. She appears to have fallen ill." The voice modulator spoke.

"Open your eyes, Commander, let's have a look at you."

Tridia forced her eyes open to slits then squinted them shut again when a bright light pierced them. She jerked her head back in reflex.

"None of that. I'm not here to hurt you." The new voice tried to sound gentle, but nothing could sound gentle to her tortured ears.

"Sensitive eyes," Tridia managed to gasp. She threw the full energy block up in her mind. "My ears are – "

As she spoke the collar stopped vibrating. Relief swept through her mind and she broke off her explanation mid-sentence. Other than a loud ringing in her ears she felt no residual effects, but she remained curled in a fetal position on the floor.

The medic dutifully checked her ears, took her temperature, then tried again to check her eyes, which he proclaimed overly dilated for the lighting in the room. An argument ensued about the type of drugs she'd been given and what the interrogator intended to do with a prisoner too ill to respond to his questions.

"Put her somewhere for a few hours and let whatever you've given her wear off. After this she'll probably answer anything you ask of her." The medic spoke with enough authority to command obedience.

"Highly improbable, medic, but we'll do as you suggest." Footsteps walked away before the modulated voice spoke again. "Take her to the Kennels. A few hours there might loosen her tongue with more alacrity than we'd manage here."

A shudder ran up her spine. She'd never toured the Kennels. No one had unless they were sentenced there or required to train in its torture chambers, and she had no desire to be the first. Once again, two sets of hands hauled her to her feet. At least her stomach didn't lurch when they stood her upright. She opened her eyes to slits as a soldier approached with a small laser cutter. After a few minutes' work the shackles fell away from her ankles. Another guard removed the belt holding her manacled hands in place and cut the leather loop through which the chain was threaded. She hadn't had so much freedom of movement in almost two days. Her first inclination was to stretch, but when she heard the hum of a weapon she lowered her hands to their position below her waist.

A nudge on her right shoulder urged her forward and Tridia walked with shortened steps at first, then switched to her full stride.

"I wouldn't rush to the Kennels if I were you." A guard at her shoulder spoke. "I hear you have three friends doing time there at your request."

Tridia hadn't forgotten about K'Tain, Wa'Ren, and Ia'Lon. They'd been in the prison for over a month now, assuming they'd spent any time at all with the medics after their beatings. If she ran into them she'd have to defend herself, which could prove difficult with manacles – especially if the collar didn't remain quiet. It hadn't hummed since she put the energy block in place. She dropped the block to test a theory and tried again to send a message to Deeca. No sooner had she dropped it than the collar thrummed. Tridia stumbled and hands latched onto her upper arms.

"No tricks, Commander Odana. We *will* shoot you."

"No tricks." Tridia tried to assure the edgy guards as she watched the hallway swirl in front of her. Vertigo came immediately this time and she wondered why the guards couldn't hear the thrum of the collar and link it to her sudden instability. She gasped again. "No tricks."

Tridia remained upright and in motion because the guards allowed no other option. They hauled her toward a brightly-lit door. An acrid scent assaulted her nostrils when they were still more than ten feet away. Her stomach heaved again and she leaned weakly against the guard on her left when the one on her right let go of her arm to pound on the metal door.

"Party of one for you, Marshal."

They waited in silence for what seemed hours before the door opened. She used her strongest normal barrier and the collar quieted. Strength returned to her knees. Her vision settled on one image and the vertigo had eased a little when a huge man in a dark gray uniform opened the door. His muscles bulged through the fabric of his shirt, and he towered at least eighteen inches over her. He had to duck his bald head to fit under the door's lintel.

"The lady needs accommodations, Marshal." The guard on the right announced.

The one behind her added, "They'll be coming after her in a few hours, but no one mentioned what condition they expected to find her in."

The Marshal's face contorted into an evil grin and the guards threw her into his waiting hands. With crushing pressure on her biceps the giant lifted Tridia to his eye level. Her feet dangled in the air.

"I recognize you, Commander Odana. Your face graced the vidcoms when you lost to that pompous ambassador from the Alliance. They announced you could have maintained your position and dodged the Challenge, but you thought you were too good for the likes of Odea anymore. Wanted to go freelance." The Marshal laughed as he shook Tridia like a rag doll. "How the mighty have fallen. I have just the room for you. Knock loudly when you return, boys. I may be too busy to hear you."

The giant threw Tridia against the wall beyond the doorway. Her head reeled as the door slammed and locked, then the Marshal's huge hand clamped down on her left shoulder. He jerked her to her feet and forced her down a hallway that grew dimmer as they walked. The unmistakable smell of human waste grew worse the farther they traveled from the door. Sounds of torture came from beyond some of the doorways they passed.

She clenched her jaw and steeled her courage for whatever lay ahead. Davik had spent weeks in these cells. She only had to survive a few hours.

***

Brenden left the inner chamber of the archive building and made his way toward another holy of holies, the genetics building. It held the DNA samples of every soldier, staff person, and prisoner – he and Tridia included. If the Kel Anec accessed the genetics files, they could obtain samples of their DNA without the bother of taking them directly. H'Lar's research showed only one query to the DNA records by the Elstaar. No other official outside of the genetics lab had perused them. H'Lar would destroy the electronic records by the end of the day if they remained in the files. Unfortunately, information had already gone out to the person most likely controlling the Elstaar. That made it even more important for Brenden to destroy the original samples...in a high security building...where he had no jurisdiction whatsoever. He had one plan and it would succeed or fail with his first contact.

"Colonel Aren, to what do I owe this honor, sir?" A man with bright yellow skin in a scientist's pale blue uniform asked as he shook Brenden's hand. "I was under the impression you would not be returning to Odea in your official capacity for another five years."

"Circumstances demanded an abrupt change in plans, Professor Endrin. I must request records and original specimens on several of our current and departed people. I have reason to believe an outside influence may attempt to obtain these records and specimens through indirect means."

"You mean infiltration, Colonel?"

"Yes, Professor, I mean just that."

"Is there a particular outside influence?" Endrin asked.

"An intergalactic invasion force."

"You have proof of this invasion?" The professor asked. He appeared unimpressed by the claim.

"I do, and I am taking steps to expose the conspiracy," Brenden stated. "My efforts may prove in vain if the invaders get their hands on the specimens. The samples could be used to provide genetic reproduction of some of our most brilliant soldiers and tactical experts. We can't let that happen, Professor, even if it means destroying all of the samples in your vault."

"You're making bold decisions, Colonel. If this is all true, how can I be sure you aren't an alien yourself, or acting under their direction?"

Professor Endrin sat back in his chair and eyed Brenden with suspicion.

Brenden returned his gaze. "Test my DNA against your current records. I've just come from the archive and had a validation made before entering there. Check your log. As to whether or not I'm controlled by the aliens, you can't know, but would I be asking you to destroy the samples if I was trying to get them for my own experimentation? The specimens are in jeopardy, either from me or the source I claim to oppose, and should at least be isolated, but preferably destroyed. Once the danger has passed, others may be obtained from the living to replace them."

The professor thought for a moment then pressed an intercom button on his desk. "Send a security orderly to my office immediately. Now, Colonel, which samples are we to secure?"

With a nod, Brenden gave him twenty names, including his, his father's, Tridia's, Ren Tama's, Frees B'Nay's, the Supreme Commander's, Davik Schie's and thirteen random individuals. If the Kel Anec wanted to track down Chesan survivors, they would have a few false leads to chase in that list. When the security orderly arrived, the professor gave him the list and told him to isolate the specimens in the highest security vault. The vault had a failsafe lock that would destroy anything in it should someone try to force entry. The orderly had barely left the room when four Elstaar guards barged into the office.

"What is the meaning of this?" Professor Endrin demanded.

"Our apologies, Professor. Colonel Aren is under suspicion of treason. We're to escort him to the Elstaar compound at once. Any orders he's given you should be ignored." The Elstaar guard held a humming weapon in his hand.

"He's given me no orders, I assure you. He's spun some fantastic tale about intergalactic invaders, but he hadn't reached the purpose of his visit yet. What is he planning?" Brenden never took his eyes from Endrin. The professor looked from one guard to the other, then back at him.

"We're not sure, sir. If he's made no attempt to suborn you, then we've prevented the damage from being done. We'll take him with us now." The guard motioned with his weapon and Brenden stood.

"Thank you for your time, Professor. I trust we'll get to finish our conversation when this matter is sorted." Brenden left the office with two guards in front of him and two behind, each holding an activated weapon. The control exerted on their minds became clear when he dropped his strongest barriers. There'd be no reasoning with them and no order from him could countermand the force that held them.

"Halt, in the name of the Guard and the Tribunal." Captain Heilen, accompanied by a squad of his guards surrounded the Elstaar outside the genetics building.

"You have no authority interfering with Elstaar business, Captain. Step aside and let us pass." The lead Elstaar guard spoke.

"On the contrary, Sergeant, you have no business interfering with Challenge Grid business. Ambassador Aren's attendance is required before the General Tribunal, of which the Supreme Commander is the ranking member. The ambassador may be wearing an Elstaar uniform, but he's under our jurisdiction outside your compound. As are you and your team. Deactivate your weapons and stand down." Heilen barked the last words as an order.

A dozen weapons hummed to life in the hands of the Challenge Guard. Heilen meant business, and he had the firepower to back him up. Brenden waited to see if the Kel Anec would persist in their plan to take him into custody. The invaders could instruct the puppet soldiers to resist, but any altercation would endanger his life, since he stood in the middle of the opposing forces. The Elstaar could likely survive even with these odds, but it would create an unexplainable incident and open an investigation the Kel would no doubt wish to avoid when they were so close to their goal. After what seemed an interminable time, the Elstaar powered down their weapons.

"Your pardon, Captain Heilen. You're right, of course, however, Colonel Aren should be kept under close guard at all times, and under no circumstances should he be allowed to return to the genetics lab."

"As I said, Sergeant, Ambassador Aren's presence is required elsewhere. What the General Tribunal decides to do with him is not a matter within my control. If you want him afterward, make a proper request – as I have done to retrieve Commander Odana, who members of your team took from my cells earlier today." Heilen added insult to his accusation. "Bad form, Sergeant. Whatever you've got planned can't justify this type of transgression. Please step away from Ambassador Aren and return to your compound."

The Elstaar guards did as instructed, continuing on their way to the compound without looking back.

Brenden didn't speak until the Elstaar guards reached their compound's gate.

"I know you're not doing this for my benefit, Captain, but I do appreciate the intervention."

"Elstaar matters are outside of my jurisdiction, Ambassador – or Colonel, if you prefer."

"I don't," Brenden stated.

"Very well, then, Ambassador, the General Tribunal requires your testimony in the matter of Commander Odana. Please come with us."

Brenden smiled. "I wish to give my statement, as well, Captain, so I assure you, your men can deactivate their weapons. I doubt the Elstaar will return and I won't resist."

Captain Heilen nodded and his men holstered their weapons, as he drew his own and sent the charge humming into its chamber. "You can never be too cautious. And I *am* responsible for your well-being."

They made their way toward the holding cells without further discussion, but Brenden found all he needed in Heilen's mind. He kept his touch light. Heilen's thoughts broadcast on their own. He suspected some plot engineered by the Elstaar. The absence of the Supreme Commander at a critical time had the man worried, and he'd placed his entire police force on alert. He'd also warned all other branches of the military police, except the Elstaar. He suspected Tridia's return to Odea to be a hoax, but her injuries made him doubt.

"Ah." Brenden smiled as the word escaped his lips.

Captain Heilen gave him a questioning look but Brenden just shrugged. Professor Endrin, and all section heads, had received warnings of a possible Elstaar uprising. That explained why the professor didn't give him away to the Elstaar guards. They'd make Heilen a Commander in the regular police force at the end of this affair, if the Hierarchy managed to survive. Heilen's men, while not privy to all of their captain's information, trusted his instincts and expected an upheaval. They'd be ready to fight when the time came.

As they walked, Brenden cast his thoughts toward Deeca and Tridia. He found Deeca quickly. Her strong emotions made him wince, even from so great a distance. Something had frightened and angered her, but her emotions covered her rational thought. He found Tridia through someone else's thoughts. His heart lurched when he realized she was in the Kennels with her mind closed. He hadn't anticipated the Elstaar sending her to that hellhole, even for a few hours, and he couldn't leave her there. What had possessed her to shut herself off from contact?

They had covered half the distance to the holding cells when a general quarters siren blared overhead.

"It's a call to secure quarters. Let's hustle." Heilen broke into a jog.

Brenden forced himself to jog and not run. His plans were perilously close to going awry.

The group entered the holding cells in time to see the first exchange of fire outside Deeca's cell. Two Elstaar guards fired on three of Heilen's men. At the appearance of the larger force, the Elstaar made a hasty retreat. Brenden mentally followed them as far as the security gate into their compound.

"Report, Corporal," Captain Heilen ordered.

"They came up demanding we release the detainee into their custody," a sturdy young soldier reported. "When we refused they acted as if they were leaving, then turned and fired. We have one man stunned and one injured from falling too hard against the wall. The detainee is secure."

Heilen told him to get the injured man to the infirmary. He then stationed his remaining guards in strategic positions throughout the building, with orders to shoot any Elstaar soldiers on sight.

"Captain," Brenden interrupted. "You might want to alter that order just slightly. I have three men stationed around the corner as back-up to your guards. They're on your side and I'd appreciate it if you didn't cause them to kill your men without reason."

"Call them out of hiding and we'll talk in good faith."

Brenden walked to the junction of the two corridors and motioned to his men. They came to him with their weapons holstered.

"Anything new to report?" Brenden kept his voice to a whisper.

"Yes, sir," Riley reported with his back to the police down the hall. "Commander Odana was turned over to the Marshal of the Kennels about a half hour ago. No word since then."

"Ambassador? Is there a problem?" Heilen's voice echoed down the hallway.

"No, Captain. I was just explaining to my men that they're to join your forces and take orders from you."

Riley raised both eyebrows at the news and grinned while his back was still to the Captain. "As you say, sir."

"Behave yourselves and tend to your duties," Brenden ordered in a stern voice, loud enough for Heilen to hear. Then he added quietly, "One of you make your way to the compound. I want Commander Odana out of the Kennels – now. Get a message out if you can, wait for orders if you can't. Don't get caught by either side, people, you won't like what happens if you do."

A loud banging came from the door where Heilen stood. Deeca's shouts preceded the rush of her anger as he neared her cell. She started talking as soon as the door opened.

"What in the name of good sense is going on out there? Why am I still in – " Deeca stopped when she saw Brenden dressed in an Elstaar uniform. She took a step backwards into the room as she spoke again. "Men dressed in the same type of uniform you're wearing took your traitorous slave child. They looked very sincere and uncompromising. Are you responsible for her abduction? I was to present her to the Tribunal myself. Making her disappear won't stop the inevitable."

"Hunter Varin, you'll have as many answers as we can give you, but you'll wait your turn," Heilen ordered. "Now, Ambassador, I'd like to hear your story."

"There's little to tell. An intergalactic alien advance force has taken control of members of the Elstaar elite and at least one high ranking officer. They've also infiltrated the Alliance at the merchant level. I'm here to retrieve my slave child." Brenden shot a scowl at Deeca. "And set Hunter Varin straight on a couple of matters. Then I intend to leave with them both and let you sort out the details with your superiors."

"Little to tell?" Heilen powered down his weapon and slid it into his holster. "Commander Odana is inside the Elstaar compound. We're under building confinement and marshal law. Your ship won't be able to leave until these matters are resolved. Why are the Elstaar interested in abducting Hunter Varin?"

Brenden debated on whether or not to tell the truth. Instead, he came up with a version both Deeca and Heilen might accept. "They expect to control me by taking her hostage. You thwarted their attempt to get me into the compound, but I'm sure they expected me to cooperate to keep her safe. Deeca and I have been acquaintances for many years, and have developed a certain friendship."

Deeca took another step back and bumped into the wall. His false statement sounded too honest, and like nothing that he'd admit under normal circumstances. It made her doubt him more. Fear compounded her wariness and it hammered against Brenden's light barrier.

I'm not compromised, Deeca. Tridia is in a tight situation and may be injured before we can get to her. Don't distract me with your doubts. You'll have to trust me on this. He pressed urgency into her thoughts and waited for her response.

"I'm not sure *a certain friendship* is quite accurate. Or don't you remember your promise to me?" Deeca asked.

"I'll kill you if you're taken. I promised." Brenden didn't smile.

Deeca sagged against the wall in relief.

Blaster fire echoed in the hallway. Heilen drew his weapon and dashed out to see what had happened. Brenden followed a step behind.

CHAPTER FORTY-TWO

"One of the Elstaar escaped, sir," the Corporal reported.

"McCann left the building, Colonel," Riley said. Two Grid officers had weapons trained on his chest. "Kahala and I are with you."

"There's no cause for alarm, Captain Heilen." Brenden walked back into the room. "McCann isn't defecting. He's going to keep an eye on Commander Odana."

"She took a big risk letting herself be taken," Heilen said.

"*Letting herself?*" Deeca asked.

"You didn't seriously expect me to believe you restrained her with a blaster and those puny injuries?"

Deeca's mouth dropped open as she looked to Brenden.

"We did tell you she has a reputation," he said. "The Elstaar will come back with reinforcements now that I'm here. They'll expect you to either stay in this defensible position and wait for help or try to move to the Op Center or the Hall of Justice."

"You have a recommendation?" Heilen asked.

"I suggest we make our way to the General Tribunal's hearing chamber in the Hall of Justice. It's only two buildings over and can be reached by upper level walkways with minimum exposure to the outside. They'll try to cut us off, so we've got to move quickly."

Heilen agreed to the plan and gathered his guards to escort Brenden and Deeca to the court building. They traveled without incident until they reached the second connecting walkway. The walkway tube, made of clear plexi and metal, stretched between the Hall of Justice and the Challenge building three stories above the pavement. Anyone passing through the conduit could be seen from any number of angles.

Brenden stopped the group and cast about for a mind clear enough and close enough to reveal the plans, but the operatives were too far away and too deeply controlled to think beyond their own movements.

"This is the last place they can stop us. They'll be targeting the walkway." Brenden continued his mental sweep as he spoke.

"Agreed," Heilen said. "We can't stay here, they'll be on us in minutes.

"I suggest we run."

Without waiting for agreement, Brenden darted into the tunnel, taking Deeca's hand and dragging her after him. He hesitated when his mind latched onto a gunnery officer targeting the walkway. The missile from his shoulder cannon would take out the conduit where it attached to the far building, dropping them all to the ground, where no doubt a squad of Elstaar waited to take him – dead or alive – to their compound. Brenden grappled with the soldier's mind, forcing him to loosen his grip on the launcher just before he fired. The missile went high and exploded into the side of the Hall of Justice, spraying chunks of white marble into the air. The mental effort drained Brenden's strength. Riley stepped up to support him. Deeca drew his other arm over her shoulder and they managed an unsteady run toward the end of the walkway. Kahala hurried around them to secure the hallway.

"Move it, Captain!" Brenden shouted as he and Deeca neared the Court building's entrance. "It won't take long to reload."

Heilen ran at Brenden's heels, but several of his men lagged behind to cover their backs from Elstaar soldiers who'd caught up with them. Most of the men were less than halfway across the walkway when the second missile struck the connection. Fire and sound raced up the conduit. The concussion hurled Brenden and Deeca the remaining distance into the protection of the building. Heilen and four of his men, thrown to the floor of the conduit only feet from the building, dragged themselves to safety before the walkway tore from its moorings and fell to the ground. Elstaar uniforms swarmed the wreckage, killing anyone that moved. One sent a spray of blaster shots into the gaping entrance on the third floor, narrowly missing the survivors as they sprinted down the hallway to safety.

Heilen touched a communicator hooked over his ear to report the treachery and call for additional troops to protect the Court building.

Although the message was received, Brenden questioned if the requested troops would be sufficient to take the superior units of the Elstaar Elite. Their only chance lay in the deep control exerted on the Elite. If it interfered with their natural reflexes and training, the regular forces might be able to overpower them. They'd know by the time they reached the Tribunal's Chamber.

***

The Marshal threw Tridia toward the far wall in a darkened room. She kicked off the wall and landed upright, her disorientation gone, and her anger beginning to burn. The man standing in the doorway was arguably the biggest human she'd ever faced, but she was tired of being pushed, shoved, shot, branded, and disrespected. If he wanted to attack her, he wouldn't find her accepting his brutality without a fight.

"Seems like the little lady isn't as sick as she pretended," the Marshal mocked. "Good. I have some friends for you to play with."

He switched on a dim light to reveal four bunks – three of which were occupied by men who came groggily to their feet. After weeks in servitude, K'Tain, Wa'Ren, and Ia'Lon had become lean and dirty shadows of the men she'd sentenced, but they recognized her. Rage burned in their hollow eyes, possibly the first emotion they'd felt in days.

Tridia straightened her shoulders. She'd taken everything away from them – their rank, status, and freedom – she didn't need to take their lives.

"Keep your distance," she stated.

The men took positions to her front and sides. She kept her back to the wall and her barriers tightly in place. If they slipped, she'd die. She forced her breathing into a slow rhythm. "I don't want to have to kill you."

"Oh, but we want to kill you, *Commander*. We have a burning desire to do that." Spittle ran from the corner of K'Tain's mouth as he spoke. "You tricked us into this pit, lied about the vid-disc, stripped us of any pride or decency. All that's left for us now is to kill you."

"If you make the attempt you'll die, I can promise you that, K'Tain. Keep your distance and serve out your sentence. You can put this behind you." Tridia changed her stance, left foot slightly in front of her right, eyes locked on K'Tain, but peripherally aware of his companions, drawing closer to her sides. "Don't be a fool."

"Our foolishness was in trusting your sentence to be fair," Ia'Lon growled.

"Do you think the Tribunal would have been more lenient once Commander Kyle awoke? He corroborated everything." Tridia brought her manacled hands chest high, fingers relaxed. "You beat him into a coma. You're lucky I stopped the sentence with three months. The Tribunal would have imposed death."

"We should thank you for your kindness?" K'Tain drew closer, his hands opening and closing in agitation. "I have something for your kindness!"

All three men rushed at once, but their timing didn't coordinate. Ia'Lon reached her first and she dropped him with a flying sidekick that dented his forehead and drove his nose into his skull. He wouldn't move again. A hand grabbed her left shoulder as a fist jabbed into her kidney and sharp pain radiated across her back. She turned in Wa'Ren's grasp and planted her heel on the side of his kneecap. Tridia slid under his arm as he tried to balance on a broken knee, then propelled her elbow upward into the left side of his ribcage. The bones cracked. She jumped away as he swung at her with his right fist and missed.

"You can still stop, Wa'Ren." Tridia kept the injured man between herself and K'Tain. The third man was the most dangerous of the three and most likely insane after a month in the Kennels. "You have someone on the outside who cares about you. A reason to survive this place."

"It's not like you, Commander Odana, to give second chances. Are you afraid?" K'Tain taunted from safety. "Living off the planet made you soft in so short a time?"

Tridia ignored him. She'd have to kill K'Tain, but she had no desire to destroy Captain Heilen's brother. Without her telepathy she couldn't tell if she reached Wa'Ren or not. Finally, the fury in his eyes reduced to an ember and he hesitated. K'Tain roared, grabbed Wa'Ren and shoved him aside.

"I'll kill you myself, little girl," K'Tain threatened. "Then I'll please myself with your dead body until the Marshal there takes it away for his own pleasure."

An amused grunt came from the direction of the doorway, confirming that the sadistic giant took pleasure in the spectacle. The Marshal would attack when she finished with K'Tain, but this battle required all of her attention.

Memories flashed through Tridia's mind. All of the obscene accusations that had been made against Davik had their roots in K'Tain's own perverse behavior.

"You framed Davik." Tridia's pulse raced. "It was you who raped those dead women."

K'Tain laughed, then he purred a disgusting confession. "It was so good watching your lover pay for my pleasure. To know he'd never be able to bed you because of my fun."

Fury burned in Tridia's veins and the Felinus rage neared the surface. The berserker demanded its own brand of justice. Sentencing K'Tain to Kennel servitude for three months did not balance the scales for the atrocities he'd committed against those dead women, or to Davik. Fine tawny fur sprouted on the backs of her hands and her nails extended into Felinus claws. She spared enough thought to control the transformation. Too much would leave her weakened, without nourishment to fuel it, and she'd left the DNA pouch in Winniel's care.

Her rage and her body fought for control, but Tridia clenched her jaw and a thin film of blue energy sheathed her hands. Power surged through her muscles. She narrowed her eyes to slits and dropped her voice when she spoke.

"I am going to kill you, K'Tain. Kill you for what you did to two innocent soldiers and to the bodies of those dead women. You aren't fit to survive as a dog, let alone live as a soldier. Your disease ends here."

K'Tain laughed, but fear flickered in his eyes. With her back to the wall and Wa'Ren blocking his path to Tridia's left, K'Tain couldn't circle her. He had limited attack options and he paced to try to catch her off guard. The brute was muscled and lithe as a cat, even in his run-down state, and he'd possessed enough skill to equal her commander's rank. But anger and insanity fueled his boldness, not cunning or skill.

K'Tain stopped near Ia'Lon's body, then sprang at Tridia like a lion from a crouch. She dodged under his swing and hit him in the chest with a double punch that impacted with her full weight and energy against his forward motion. The contact lifted him off his feet and sent him backward where he fell over his dead cohort.

Tridia didn't pursue him. She waited for him to stagger to his feet, forcing the rage under control. He wouldn't be as brash a second time.

"You're going to die, K'Tain, and I'm going to kill you." Tridia taunted him in a voice so deep it surprised even her.

"Shut up!" K'Tain's eyes had taken on a maniacal glint. He rubbed his chest where she'd hit him. His voice quivered when he spoke. "You'll be the one to die."

"Justice will be served, you slimy excuse for a subhuman slag. You dishonor the species."

K'Tain roared and charged again. This time Tridia jumped straight up and landed a side-kick to his chest. The bully stopped dead in his tracks. When Tridia landed, she bounced and delivered a crescent kick to the side of his face, then jumped again and crushed his windpipe with the heel of her right foot. K'Tain grabbed for his throat and Tridia closed the distance between them. She sliced open his shirt with her extended claws, then sheathed them as she pressed the splayed fingers of her right hand against his bare chest and flicked her wrist.

"For those dead women," she growled.

K'Tain's hands went from his own throat to close around Tridia's, but he couldn't tighten his grip over the obedience collar. With her hands manacled together, she couldn't catch his wrists to pry his hands loose. Instead she swung both of her arms outside of his right arm to sweep him away. K'Tain held onto the collar around her neck for a moment longer, but his hands went limp as his eyes glazed. Tridia stumbled away from him and landed flat on her back at the foot of one of the cots. From that position she watched K'Tain fall to his knees, then on his face. His body lay across his dead companion.

Tridia had no time to plan her next move as a heavy foot pinned her shoulder to the floor. She looked up to see Wa'Ren towering over her.

"Don't do this, Wa'Ren. You're too injured to fight, and there's no point in dying for a dead man who's brought you nothing but grief."

"I don't want to kill you for K'Tain. I want to kill you for myself." Tears rolled down the man's face as he spoke. "For what you did to Anton when you sent me here. They told me he'd never be promoted beyond his current rank because of our connection. The Guard is all he lives for. You've taken it away from him!"

"They lied to you." Tridia spoke in a normal voice, trying to get truth into the man's mind. "Captain Heilen's record is impeccable. Your crimes can't contaminate him. It's just another method of torture, to drag your mind into despair."

"No! You're lying to save your own skin. It's all your fault." Wa'Ren lifted his foot to stomp Tridia's face, but she rolled away and to her feet before he could do any damage.

"I have nothing to fear from you, Wa'Ren. I can kill you as easily as I disposed of those two, so I have no reason to lie to you. Heilen's career is safe. Only you bear the punishment for your actions."

Tridia raised her clenched fists to chest level as Wa'Ren tried to walk. He staggered and fell onto one of the cots, then lay there sobbing. The sound of slow clapping drew Tridia's eyes to the door.

The Marshal stepped into the room. "Impressive for a little girl with her hands tied. But your tricks won't work on me. You can't jump high enough to use one of those dainty little kicks."

Tridia backed away from Wa'Ren, keeping her eyes on the Marshal and her back to the wall.

"Just because I used common methods with these cretins doesn't mean they're my only weapons."

"Of course not. That's why you're wearing an obedience collar. Your guards passed the controller to me – as if I'd need their toys for the likes of you. Your bag of tricks is too well known among the Hierarchy, Commander Odana. I'm wearing body armor your *deathstrike* can't pierce." The Marshal lumbered into the room.

His massive body filled the space, but his braggadocio told her what she needed to do to defeat him.

"Genetic freak." Tridia spat the words. "They should have put you in the mining camp hauling ore carts. You'd have liked Cystia, Marshal. The caves are dark and no one would be able to see your freakish form."

The Marshal glowered. "Your mind games won't work on me little girl. I'm the master of mind games in this place. I have spies in every corner. Did you know your master was caught in the archive building purchasing secrets? He'll stand trial and face execution in a few hours. Then who'll come to your rescue?"

Tridia laughed. "Your attempts won't work on me, dung heap. You prey on the fear of your inmates and prisoners who think because you're huge you're also indestructible. I'm not afraid of you. I'm not guilty of any treasonous act so I don't need rescuing, and I have no personal attachment beyond compulsory obedience to Brenden Aren."

The smirk vanished from the Marshal's face. His gravelly voice became a growl. "Enough. They want you for questioning, so you must be able to speak. Walking is not required, neither is your virginity – if you still have it after a month with your *master*."

He continued to approach slowly, then he stopped and pulled a small control box from his pocket – the remote activator for the collar she wore.

"You flatter me, Marshal. You do require toys to subdue the likes of me." Tridia held her position.

The Marshal responded by flipping the switch. A jolt coursed through Tridia's body and every muscle contracted.

"No, I don't require the toys, but they bring me such amusement." The Marshal laughed as he released the switch.

Tridia's knees threatened to buckle but she managed to keep upright. The Marshal paced across the floor in front of her, an evil grin on his flat face. He continued to pace, flipping the switch twice more while still out of Tridia's reach. Twice more she managed to stand after the current stopped, but she couldn't continue to take the charges. And she couldn't attack him while he held the box. She had to get it away from him.

To her amazement, the next time the Marshal approached Wa'Ren, the prisoner sprang to his feet and used his injured leg kick the control box from the Marshal's hand. Tridia made a diving catch to retrieve it, sliding under one of the cots when she landed. The box flew from her outstretched fingers and slammed into the wall. The Marshal's enraged bellows shook the room as she rolled out from under the cot and came to her feet near the opposite wall.

She stared at the sight before her eyes, too far away to intervene. The Marshal held Wa'Ren by the throat. His feet dangled several inches above the floor, his face already dark blue. Wa'Ren's eyes found Tridia's just before his life extinguished. They held a spark of defiance, then faded to sightlessness. The Marshal tossed the body aside. Then the giant turned to face her.

"Like I said, I don't need the toys."

He approached without hesitation. Tridia's heart pounded. She jumped to the center of the cot and bounded high enough to reach the Marshal's face. His hands came up, but not in time to save his right eye. Tridia lashed out with glowing claws extended. She didn't see the damage, but the Marshal released deafening roars of agony and curses in a language she didn't recognize.

Tridia landed and slid to his right side as he turned to search for her. They continued their morbid dance until Tridia stood adjacent to another cot. She calculated the distance and the trajectory, knowing she had only one chance at success. If she failed, he'd have her in his hands – and she'd seen what those hands could do. She took a running leap for the metal bed frame and the Marshal turned his good eye toward her. His fingers caught at the fabric of her pants as she sprang from the end frame to his shoulders. With one leg hooked under his left arm, she sliced apart the right-side shoulder and catches of his body armor with her claws. Shifting to reach his left side, she slid down his arm and his fingers dug into her thigh. She managed a couple of final slashes at the catches on his left shoulder and side before he pulled her away and held her so that she faced away from him. She hung upside down in his painful grasp and swung like a pendulum to his guttural laugh.

"Now you die!" The Marshal's grip tightened on Tridia's leg until the tissue began to separate.

Madness rang in the giant's laugh. Tridia tried to extend her claws to free herself, but the adrenaline coursing through her body was already reversing the Felinus transformation and her claws shrank back into fingernails. *Had she come so close just to lose like this?* Then the sound of the Marshal's chest armor hitting the floor reached her ears.

"No, you heinous abomination, now *you* die."

Tridia arched backwards and placed the splayed fingers of both hands across the Marshal's bare chest. She'd never delivered a *deathstrike* with less precision or more power as the blue energy left her hands and poured into his body. Unable to remain contorted, Tridia dropped back to her upside down perch and waited. The Marshal didn't move for what seemed a full minute, then his fingers loosened their grip. Tridia caught herself in a handstand and came up to face the giant madman. Time stood still as they faced each other. Neither moved, but the stunned look on his face proclaimed that his days of terrorizing the Kennels' inmates had ended. The energy in the imprecise *deathstrike* had stopped his heart. The Marshal's body crashed to the floor.

Pain signals from her own body finally reached her brain, and Tridia hobbled to one of the cots. Her back ached from Wa'Ren's blow to her kidney. The extent of that injury wouldn't manifest for several days and she'd have to get to a medic somewhere before then. The muscle in her thigh throbbed and no doubt would grow a dark bruise, but there was no blood seeping through her clothing and she could move her leg if she gritted her teeth. Satisfied that no emergency existed she looked around the room. Ia'Lon and K'Tain lay in one heap, Wa'Ren's body lay across the room, and the massive body of the Marshal lay in the center of the room. Four dead men. The Tribunal wouldn't be pleased.

A shadow darkened the door and Tridia looked up to see an Elstaar guard. The look of fear on his face changed to revulsion as he pointed his drawn weapon in her direction.

"Where's the control box for that collar?" he asked.

***

"Come with us, Commander." The guard's hand trembled as he pointed a blaster in her direction.

Tridia eased to her feet and hobbled toward the door, careful not to move too quickly. She didn't raise her arms and kept her eyes down. They'd shoot her without thought if she scared them further, and she could see the 'full charge' setting on the nearest weapon. They meant to kill her at the first sign of resistance. Wherever her companions were, they'd better hurry. The fresh blood on her hands might enhance her reputation, but it wouldn't do anything to ensure her safety. The fact hit home when two of her guards whispered behind her.

"What's Master B'Nay going to do with someone who can kill the Marshal in barehanded combat?"

"Shut up, Lieutenant."

"Anyone that dangerous can't be released without control devices."

"I said, shut up, Lieutenant Sage."

"The Marshal had a controller for the collar she's wearing. It didn't do him much good."

"For the last time, Lieutenant, keep your fears to yourself. The guard who was watching her when we got there has more composure than you and she's shaking like a leaf. Commander Odana's fate is for someone else to decide. All we have to do is stay alive until she's delivered. I intend to do just that."

The men fell silent. Even the torture chambers were quiet as they marched past.

The Kel Anec wanted her intact or she'd already be dead. If they got their hands on her, they'd torture her for Drayden's location.

The guards made Tridia face the wall with her arms above her head and her hands flat against it as they opened the outer door, then held charged weapons to the base of her skull as they passed through to the hallway beyond. Frees B'Nay waited, arms crossed, a frown on his face. When he spoke – this time without his voice modulator – he confirmed

Tridia's suspicions.

"You're too dangerous to deal with on Odea, Commander, and have aroused too much interest too soon. Since you won't tell me what I want to know, you'll be sent to Cystia to meet your new masters. You *will* answer them."

***

No sound of battle disturbed the Hall of Justice as Brenden's small group took side hallways to reach the designated meeting room. No guards prohibited their entry at the door and Brenden held up his hand for silence. Captain Heilen drew his weapon. They opened the door and entered the room together. The full Tribunal with the Supreme Commander sat on a raised platform behind heavy wooden desks that shone in the dim lighting.

"A grand entrance, Ambassador Aren," the Supreme Commander said. "We expected your protégé, however. Will she not be joining us?"

"Supreme Commander." Heilen saluted. "Commander Odana was taken captive by the Elstaar. We've come under attack ourselves and it's likely those same renegades will attempt to take the Ambassador by force."

"I see." The Supreme Commander spoke to the other members of the Tribunal then turned back to Brenden. He indicated his fellow Tribunal members as he spoke. "Master Generals Oren and Winstead and I are curious, should we assume by your appearance that Commander Odana was brought to us under false pretenses?"

"Assumptions are best left to theologians, Supreme Commander. I will give you facts. Hunter Varin and Commander Odana harbor a long-standing grudge between them. The Commander had undertaken a secret mission on my behalf and it appeared to be an act of rebellion. Being skilled in her trade, Hunter Varin took it upon herself to arrest the Commander for breaking her oath of allegiance to me. The Commander repeated that oath before the Tribunal of the Core Alliance of Planets."

"There was no disobedience?" Master General Oren asked.

"Only the appearance of such. I request that Commander Odana be returned to me so we may leave together." Brenden looked each member of the Tribunal in the eye, then settled on the Supreme Commander.

The old man stared back with an amused expression. "Are we to expect the Commander to appear to disobey you every time you desire to obtain information from our archives, Ambassador?"

Brenden smiled in acquiescence. "That would be vulgar on my part, Supreme Commander. I would hope you'd expect more originality from me next time."

"As you say," the Supreme Commander said. "But I am curious as to why you visited the genetics lab."

"To keep vital information from being obtained by hostile forces," Brenden said.

"May I ask for greater detail?"

"You may ask, Supreme Commander," Brenden said. "You may even order, and this time I would explain everything, but I respectfully request you to trust me for now. Time is of the essence if we're to save Commander Odana."

"Very well, on your testimony that Commander Odana has comported herself with honor and obedience to you, we will release her back to your control. However, I expect a more convincing story upon your next visit."

"Yes, Supreme Commander. If we may –"

The sound of weapons firing interrupted Brenden's comment. The two guards they'd left in the hall entered just ahead of a spray of energy blasts. Four armed Elstaar officers dressed in black armor entered amid the rubble that had been the doors.

"Brenden Aren and Deeca Varin must come with us." The officer spoke with such stilted words there was no question of his compromise. The Kel Anec had total control of the man's mind and body.

Heilen's men reached for their weapons, but Brenden stopped them. "Your weapons won't penetrate that armor. A concussion blaster barely gets the job done."

"You're going with them?" Heilen asked.

"They are going where I intended to go next." Brenden took Deeca's hand to calm her nerves. "We'll be fine, Deeca. It's the fastest way to the Commander."

"For once, I'd like that girl to not be in the middle of all my troubles." Deeca squeezed Brenden's hand as she spoke.

A thought brushed against Brenden's consciousness and he held still instead of going forward. A blur of khaki clad bodies entered the room. With movements too quick to follow, two Sentinels passed among the Elstaar officers. The sound of bones breaking and necks severing popped in the room until Alanel stood with his arm around the leader's neck. When he let go, the man folded to the floor in a limp heap.

"Our apologies for the delay, Ambassador." Winniel nodded to Brenden. "There were others like these surrounding the building. We thought it best to attend to them first."

"Apology accepted," Brenden said.

"You've brought these abominations into the Hall of Justice, Ambassador Aren?" Master General Winstead's words cut the air with indignation. "That is tantamount to treason!"

"Would you rather be dead?" Brenden indicated the dead Elstaar leader. "He was likely under instructions to exterminate everyone in the room once Deeca and I left. The Elstaar are staging a coup. Some of them are being mentally and physically controlled. You'll probably find transmitters implanted in his brain or micro-machines in his bloodstream. The coroners should take extreme care with the autopsies."

"How would you know such a thing?" Master General Oren asked.

"Because we've come across this type of control before," Brenden stated, then addressed the Supreme Commander directly. "It is part of the explanation and the mission you gave me fifteen years ago. Besides, Alanel read his mind and relayed the information to me telepathically." The line sounded good, and it might have been true if they could read minds through the armor.

"The word of a Sentinel is hardly proof –" Master General Winstead started to speak.

"On the contrary, sir," Brenden interrupted. "Sentinels lack the imagination to lie and don't feel the need for subterfuge. They are straightforward individuals, unhampered by subtlety. Only in combat do they show any signs of slyness."

"Nevertheless they will remove themselves from this Hall at once." Oren said.

"We will address the Sentinels with respect, my colleagues." The Supreme Commander's stern words and expression startled the other two into silence. "We will treat them with the favor due our allies."

The Supreme Commander's words had barely left his lips when a door slammed open behind his desk. Another Elstaar officer appeared with his weapon trained on the tribunal. Before the armor-clad officer could fire, Alanel hurtled the desk to stand between the weapon and the Supreme Commander. He took the full force of the blast in the chest and his body flew backward into the Supreme Commander's arms. In the same space of time, Winniel dashed to position herself behind the officer and snapped his neck like dried wood, then flung his body to the side.

Brenden slid over the desk to take Alanel from the Supreme Commander and lay him gently on the floor. He pressed his fingers against the Sentinel's neck to find a pulse, but the seared wound in his chest already proclaimed the clone's death. Brenden looked up into Winniel's face.

"I'm sorry. There's nothing to be done."

"There is, Ambassador." Winniel knelt to cover Alanel's face with her hand. She held it there for several minutes, then turned her copper glare toward the Supreme Commander. Her voice lost its monotone and took on a timber of authority as she spoke. "You will treat his body with dignity befitting a fallen warrior. You will see that it is wrapped in fine cloth and kept cool and undisturbed until I collect it to return to our clan on Aga for proper disposition. Do you understand these instructions, Supreme Commander of the Hierarchy of Odea?"

The Supreme Commander nodded, then managed a few words. "It is our privilege as well as our responsibility."

"It will be done as you require," Brenden spoke to still his own heart. Winniel had put such strong mental force behind her words that even he felt compelled to obey her.

"Then I shall accompany you into this Elstaar compound to retrieve Commander Odana." Winniel started removing her clothes and walked from one fallen Elstaar to another until she stopped by the one most near her size. "Their blank minds are not hard to impersonate."

"If you're sure."

Winniel's fierce gaze cut off any further words Brenden might have said.

Her grief would not spill from her mind, but the tautness of her body and her chiseled features spoke of a loss beyond words. Brenden could only stare as she stripped down to a simple tunic, then undressed a dead officer to take his armor. She used a blaster to melt small holes in the top and sides of the helmet.

"You need to be able to hear my thoughts," Winniel said.

Brenden nodded.

"I'm going with you, too," Captain Heilen stated.

"No, Captain." Brenden placed a hand on the Captain's arm. "Your place is protecting the tribunal and the Supreme Commander. Get them to the op center so they can mobilize the regular forces to contain the Elstaar within the compounds. You should have reinforcements arriving soon and they'll need someone who understands the situation. If we're successful, the Elite may lay down their arms. If the subversion has gone too deep, you're going to need help from outside to control this situation."

"Help from outside?"

"Just make sure you don't turn down any offers when they come." Brenden said. "I could use a blaster if you can spare one."

Heilen nodded to one of his men, who handed over his blaster and holster. Brenden checked the weapon to make sure the charges worked then holstered it again, fastening the belt around his hips. "Have there been any reports of activity from any of the other bases?"

"Yes," Heilen said. "All of them"

"Then you should hurry your charges to the op center."

Winniel, now indistinguishable from any other Elstaar in black armor, saluted Brenden in a perfect Elstaar fashion. Riley and Kahala joined her. Brenden pulled the blaster from its holster and handed it to her.

"I trust I'll get that back once we're inside the compound," he said.

Winniel didn't respond.

"Isn't masquerading a form of subterfuge?" Deeca whispered to Brenden.

"This is combat, Hunter Varin. Now, if you will act the part of a subdued prisoner and walk beside me?" Brenden gave Deeca a reassuring grin and led the way through the bodies and rubble.

Going into the compound without a report from his spies could spell disaster, but Alanel's brief mental message warned him the Kel Anec meant to transport Tridia off the planet. If they took her off-world he'd never reach her in time to keep them from taking DNA samples. They could use a Feeder to extract her knowledge. The galaxy didn't need a pantheon of genetically engineered assassins doing the Kel's bidding. In addition, Tridia knew Drayden's location – and Anza's. He had to rescue her or make sure her body disintegrated. The collar she wore not only acted as a physical deterrent and homing device, it also contained enough blaster explosive to reduce her body to ash if he used the detonator he carried. He'd let her live once and regretted the decision, he wasn't going to make the same mistake again.

CHAPTER FORTY-THREE

Tridia limped in silence behind Frees B'Nay. He moved with grace unusual for his ungainly height. Was he compromised or simply a traitor? Her guards carried their weapons activated, poised for a chance to use them.

B'Nay came to a sudden stop and whirled to face her. "Commander Odana, I'll give you one last chance to answer my questions. If you refuse I'll have no choice but to deliver you to others who won't be as patient with your silence."

"Your Kel Anec masters don't impress me, Master B'Nay. They're parasites in search of a host they can leech dry of energy and knowledge, then use it to destroy anything good in the galaxy. Take me to them. When you do, your usefulness to them will be completed." Tridia continued to limp forward until she was inches from B'Nay's face. All the weapons snapped up around her. "They send their useless items to the feeders for brain extractions."

B'Nay's eyes narrowed as if observing her for the first time. "You've always thought too highly of your skills, Commander. If you expect to frighten me —"

"On the contrary, I expect you to look down your nose with what you *think* is a superior intellect and chide me for my foolish attempts to sway you. Then I expect you to be insulted by my remarks and usher me to a transport ship, where you will again give me a chance to answer your nonsensical questions before escorting me to Cystia where you can explain in person to your masters why you failed them. You expect your explanation to be accepted in light of the fact you've delivered me. You're missing the point. What they want more than me is the knowledge and power I possess. Or more correctly, the knowledge and power they *think* I possess. You've already shown you're too inept to

433

handle the assignment. I'll get to watch them torment you. It will be justice for the lives you've helped them contaminate."

"Bravo, Commander Odana." B'Nay clapped his hands in mock admiration. "Well said, but your sham gains you no ground. I registered energy from your cell in the Kennels. Diluted and confusing, but identifiable. As to my usefulness, the Kel Anec need me to control the Hierarchy. Once the Supreme Commander is out of the way, I'll persuade the Tribunal to declare martial law and place me in charge of the Elite. My usefulness goes far beyond the delivery of an insignificant girl. You may be useful in bringing Davik Schie to heel."

"Do you think they can't find another ranking officer or member of the Tribunal to corrupt? Do you think they haven't already?"

Tridia rolled her eyes and shook her head, then continued her slow limp down the hall, leaving B'Nay to watch as the guards hastily closed around her. She had him on the defensive. His calculating mind would reprocess his scenarios. He'd fight against the doubts, but he'd fear the Kel Anec instead of respecting them. Even if he didn't or couldn't turn against them, his effectiveness would drop and that promised only good for her small band of rebels. Davik would not bow to the Kel Anec, nor let them get away with threatening her. He was a weapon now, not an abused lieutenant in dire circumstances. She wouldn't cooperate with them to coerce Davik. If they threatened to destroy his body, it simply meant she didn't have to do it herself to free him.

***

Brenden walked ahead of Deeca and Winniel to the Elstaar compound entrance. The blaster hummed in Winniel's gloved hands and she played the part of a controlled guard very well. Riley and his Elstaar companion separated from the group to take another entrance. The plan was to meet inside the compound, guided by Winniel's telepathy.

"Colonel Aren, sir." The guards at the entrance saluted in unison as their commander spoke. "You're short a few members of your escort. Did you run into trouble?"

"Yes, some unexplained resistance." Brenden found no trace of subversion in the guards. They had expected him to come back with all four guards as escorts. He closed his barriers after gathering the information, hesitant to do more to tip off the Kel Anec inside the compound.

"Sir, we've heard missile fire and explosions and seen the regulars moving in force toward the Hall of Justice, but there's been no movement inside the compound other than a few troops moving through side entrances. Should we elevate our alert status?"

"No, Corporal. Remain as you are for the present. However, pass it along to your guards that any change in that order should come from the Supreme Commander, the Tribunal, or me. We have reason to suspect renegade elements inside the compound, but at present that suspicion does not extend to the regulars."

The Corporal looked stunned, but saluted again as Brenden passed by.

"The interrogation rooms are in that building," he said to Winniel. "Is Commander Odana still there?" Brenden continued to walk toward the general administration building instead of moving toward Tridia's suspected location.

"No, Ambassador. She's moving toward a launch hangar. Her mind is closed, but those with her are not shielded. All but one of them are controlled. The shape-shifter is also with her."

"Address me as Colonel. No one in an Elstaar uniform would ever address me as Ambassador."

"Yes, Colonel."

Brenden exchanged a look with Deeca and changed direction. He instructed Winniel to give Riley and his men a new rendezvous location and considered the effect of issuing a general lockdown inside the compound.

They met up with Riley's team inside a lobby facing the launch hangar. The group had grown to include several Elstaar soldiers and a medic, all carrying weapons with enough power to pierce the new armor. None of them liked the idea of attacking fellow Elstaar officers, but they would do so on Brenden's order.

"Winniel, what is Commander Odana's location now?" Brenden asked.

"Just inside that building. Her guards are heavily armed and fearful."

"They expect an attack?" Deeca asked.

"No. They fear Commander Odana."

"An armed Elstaar Elite escort is afraid of a single assassin?" Riley's amazement showed on his face and in his voice.

"She's a formidable warrior." Winniel said, then added, "She killed four men in the Kennels while her hands were bound, including someone named Marshal."

Brenden's squad stirred uncomfortably.

"We don't want Commander Odana injured. Make your shots clean and don't hesitate to take out a ranking officer. You're under my direct command and you're to listen to no one else. I suspect there may be a general or master inside that building. The medic will stay with us in case Commander Odana needs help." Brenden quickly laid out his plan for distracting the guards and disabling any accessible transport, then his team dispersed again.

He'd kept his mind closed since entering the compound to keep his men safe from detection, now he opened it. Deeca's determination was the first thing to flood his senses, the medic's concentration on getting to Tridia, then the focused thoughts of his men. Lastly, he sensed the controlled Elstaar. Their minds fought against the control, and their fear gave them some ground for rebellion.

"A fearful mind is easy to control, if *you* control the source of the fear." Brenden voiced his revelation.

"What?" Deeca looked at him in surprise.

"Remember, what Tridia said about the Kel Anec's interrogation on Cystia. They asked her what she feared and kept trying to break through her barrier."

"Yes. She told them she wasn't afraid of anything."

"Princess Anza feared many things," Brenden said. "A single fear can control a person's behavior or make it predictable. Many fears make the mind unpredictable. There's no way to tell which fear will be the most prevalent in a given circumstance. The Princess was so hard to control they planted the transmitters inside her brain. These Elstaar had one overriding fear, being handed over to the Marshal. They all trained in the Kennels as initiates." He paused to consider his words. "Tridia killed the Marshal – apparently without a weapon."

"The Kel Anec hold is slipping?" Deeca asked.

"Let's say, it's confused," Brenden said. "I don't understand everything, but I sense fear and rebellion in those men, each fiercely dependent on the other. Their minds are a mess."

"Then we'd better get moving before the Kel Anec sort them out."

Brenden put a hand on Deeca's arm. "We wait for Riley's men to get into position. If we rush this, we could end up with more than one dead assassin."

Deeca's face took on a grim expression, and her emotions washed through Brenden's thoughts. She didn't like the Hierarchy, but the dislike conflicted with what she'd seen of these men, their loyalty, and their humanity. Her perception had changed. She saw them as the same type of people she'd known with the Guardians. Their deaths would have meaning for her now.

"Colonel, the men are in place."

Brenden searched about with his mind to confirm Winniel's statement just as Riley's voice sounded in his communicator.

"Awaiting your orders, Colonel."

"Hold your position until you hear from me on this channel." Brenden took the com device from his ear and placed it in his pocket, next to the control collar's detonator. "Let's make our entrance."

Brenden led Deeca from their building toward the hangar. Winniel followed closely with her weapon activated, the medic followed her. They'd made it to the entrance when two Elite guards opened the door. No words were exchanged as Brenden led the way to Tridia and Sonei. A daunting sight met their eyes as they entered the room. Three guards stood behind Tridia, each with a weapon trained on her head. Frees B'Nay stood to one side.

"Ambassador Aren, how good of you to join us. Masquerading as an Elstaar Colonel today?" B'Nay taunted.

"Commander Odana, are you well?" Brenden's attention focused on Tridia.

Her face, drawn and pale, said she was not. Her posture favored her left leg and those steel-gray eyes seemed to look beyond him. For a moment he feared the Kel Anec had taken control of her mind. It was closed tight against him. Sonei's mind flitted in his consciousness, as if trying to follow the conversation and anticipate Tridia's answers.

"I am well enough, Master Aren. More so with your appearance, sir."

Brenden turned to an annoyed Frees B'Nay. "Master B'Nay, you've no doubt met the Kel Anec, singular beings without corporeal bodies in this galaxy? Perhaps you'd be so kind as to relay a new message to them. Let them know they can't have Commander Odana, or her DNA, or me, or my DNA. As a matter of fact, they stand to lose everything they've gained in this galaxy in a very short period of time."

B'Nay's face turned red and anger twisted his lips. "How dare you insignificant creatures mock the great Kel Anec race. Do you think your mind so vast we cannot understand it with a single sweep? Do you truly believe your schemes are not infant musings to intellects such as ours? The Kel Anec have no need of the Elstaar or of the bodies which you prize so highly. Knowledge is all we desire and knowledge we shall take from this girl who believes herself invincible. You're all fools in our eyes."

"If you had eyes – which you don't beyond the bodies you claim not to need. So, you've taken over the mind of Frees B'Nay. Or did he give himself to you willingly for a chance to understand your strategies? Either way, your gamble is lost. Your transport has been disabled. You're stranded."

"Not so, Ambassador. Your past behavior says you won't risk the lives of Tridia Odana and Deeca Varin. You are the prisoner and you are powerless to act."

"Oh, I had no intention of acting. One of your own will betray you."

Winniel moved so quickly her body blurred. She zipped across the room shoved one of the guards aside and neutralized the others without firing a shot. She didn't stop until the muzzle of her weapon rested under Frees B'Nay's chin. Tridia stood amazed beside her.

"Speak to him quickly, Colonel. He'll pay personally for the life of my mate." Pure hatred resonated from Winniel's words and the venom flowed outward to everyone around her. The guard Winniel had shoved aside gasped, but didn't move. Deeca raised her weapon toward B'Nay with a puzzled look on her face.

"We need him alive, Winniel," Brenden took a single step toward her, then thought better of it. He had to fight to keep from shooting B'Nay as it was. "His mind is the link to the Kel Anec. He was just a tool in their hands."

"A tool they'll lose this day. Retribution is demanded, Colonel, or I have failed Alanel."

"Sentinel law demands immediate retribution, and you've taken that by killing the man who fired the shot that ended Alanel's life. True retribution will come when we destroy those who control this man." Brenden waited for Winniel's response.

"Give me your word that I will accompany you on the mission to destroy these alien parasites."

"You have my word, Winniel. You will be a part of that mission. On my honor as an Ambassador to the Core Alliance of Planets, and upon the promise of death at your hands."

"Brenden!" Deeca's cry cut the silence.

"Your word is accepted, and the promise will be fulfilled if you fail me." Winniel kept her weapon tucked under B'Nay's chin, but the urgency to pull the trigger had left Brenden's hands.

"Knock him out and let's get out of here."

"You won't win!" B'Nay pulled a blaster from his holster and shot Tridia in the chest at point blank range. Winniel pulled her trigger in the next instant. B'Nay's head disintegrated.

"Tridia!" Brenden and Deeca yelled in unison and rushed to Tridia's prone body.

Brenden pulled her into his arms and almost released her as her face changed. When the flesh stopped moving he held a creature with wrinkled, flat-faced features. What had been Tridia's long raven braid became a stubby gray mat around the creature's head.

"Sonei," Brenden whispered.

"Not seeing me at my best, Ambassador."

"I told you impersonating her would get you killed."

"This doesn't free Morgan Jacks from his contract. Give my fee to the kid. Is she alright?" Sonei asked.

"She's fine." Tridia, dressed in a guard's uniform, crawled to Sonei's side. She removed bits of pasty flesh from her face and pulled most of her braid from under her hat.

"Told you they'd never notice who was in the uniform. They were too busy pissing their pants and watching me pretend to be you." Sonei laughed and coughed. "A little of my pale flesh on your face was all it took."

"You were right." Tridia's voice held steady.

"I just wish I'd found out the connection, Ambassador." Sonei winced.

Brenden leaned down to whisper into her ear, but the Elstaar medic stopped him.

"Let me try something first."

The medic placed his hand over Sonei's injury. His skin shifted and his face distorted. Sonei gasped, pulling in so much air it seemed she should burst. Her body went rigid, then shifted back into her replica of Tridia. She looked into the medic's face wide-eyed.

"Tran," she whispered. "You shouldn't have done that."

"Rest now." The medic's face shifted again until he looked like Tran. He turned to Brenden. "She's going to be out for a while. We'll have to carry her."

"What did you do?" Brenden asked.

"Something I probably shouldn't have without her permission." Tran stood and wobbled. He would have fallen had Brenden not stood to catch him.

"What in Hielos?"

"Cell exchange," Tran said, resting against Brenden. "I took some of her damaged cells and replaced them with some of my healthy ones. Not enough to incapacitate me, just make me woozy for a bit. It should be enough to keep her alive."

"I will carry her to the ship," Winniel said. "I should have killed that creature before it had a chance to injure her."

"We needed him alive, or I would have killed him myself," Brenden said. "The Kel Anec just didn't broadcast its thoughts before it acted."

"We will know better the next time our enemy is within our grasp." Winniel stated.

As Winniel stooped to lift Sonei, Deeca helped Tridia to her feet.

"Glad to see you alive, assassin," Deeca said.

"Likewise," Tridia replied. She opened the top buttons of her shirt and tugged at a metal ring beneath it. "Now will somebody get this collar off my neck?"

"Sonei is wearing it – or one just like it," Tran said.

"A dummy she'd brought with her," Tridia explained. "We couldn't get this one off in the Kennels when we traded places. The control box got smashed in my fight with the Marshal, and she didn't have one for the dummy."

"We'll take it off when we're on the ship and away from Odea." Brenden checked the offending collar to make sure the mechanisms were functioning.

"What?" Tridia's voice rose in anger. "Would you mind explaining why?"

"We don't have time for a full explanation. B'Nay and his men aren't the only ones under Kel Anec control. We've got to leave the compound right now." Brenden spoke into the comlink he'd put back in his ear and ordered Riley and his men to meet up with them at a planned escape route.

"Can you walk, Commander Odana?" Winniel asked.

Tridia rubbed her wrists. "With some help. It's a good thing no one was watching me too closely. Sonei's limp was only a little more pronounced than mine."

"I've got you," Deeca said, drawing Tridia's arm across her shoulders.

Tran rearranged his face to become the medic once again and stood erect.

Tridia turned her glare on him. "Did you have to tell them to put me someplace else? Couldn't you have just told them to let me rest on the cot in the room we were in?"

"How was I to know the sadists were going to drop you in the Kennels?" Tran replied.

"They were Elstaar," Tridia said.

"Right." Tran acquiesced. Neither of them was in any condition for an argument.

Brenden led them out of the building and across the hangar bay, with Tran at his heels. Tridia limped after them with Deeca's help. Winniel followed, with Sonei draped over her shoulder. They met Riley's team at a back exit and made it to a side gate without a skirmish.

The guards at the gate saluted. Brenden issued orders for the compound to go on lockdown. No one else was to enter or leave the Elstaar enclave until the Supreme Commander or the Tribunal issued an order to relieve the alert. The guards hurried to relay the message to the other guard stations. Alarms rang out across the compound and distant gates slammed shut in response. The group crossed through the opening just before the gates at their exit closed. One major hurdle behind, but the Kel Anec wouldn't give up. Whatever the braggart inside B'Nay's head had thought, Tridia wasn't expendable to the invaders. How much of what had happened had the creature passed on to its fellow Kel Anec before it died? A lot could depend on that answer.

Regular troops outside the gate halted them and demanded

identification and explanation. Brenden gave both and waited while the commanding officer received confirmation from the Tribunal. Once cleared, the group passed through the siege lines and headed for the op center in the archive bunker. They found Captain Heilen inside with the Supreme Commander and the Tribunal, reviewing their strategy.

"Commander Odana." Captain Heilen stood when Tridia, Brenden, and Deeca entered. Tran, Riley, and the others waited in the hall.

"Supreme Commander, members of the Tribunal, Captain Heilen. I must report deaths inside the compound." Tridia stood as straight as her injuries allowed. "Lieutenants K'Tain and Ia'Lon and the Marshal of the Kennels were killed by me – in self-defense. The Marshal killed Lieutenant Wa'Ren. The Lieutenant was trying to save my life at the time. Before he died, I commuted Wa'Ren's sentence. He was to be released. Master Frees B'Nay and two Elstaar guards died in a skirmish for my release."

"We can no longer demand written reports from you, Commander Odana." The Supreme Commander said. "However, I expect there will be many more undocumented deaths on Odea before we see the end of this fiasco. Your report is accepted as given."

"Thank you, sir. My condolences, Captain Heilen. It seems Lieutenant Wa'Ren came to himself before he died."

Heilen gave a curt nod, but showed no other emotion.

Brenden explained what had happened during Tridia's rescue, and gave as much detail as he could about the Kel Anec control over Frees B'Nay. He explained the different types of control the aliens could use.

"At least, those are the forms we know about." Brenden faced the Supreme Commander. "The Kel Anec are a force from outside the galaxy, and if our sources can be trusted, they came with enough fire power to take over a large section of the quadrant. They are the source of the silence and the broken alliances over the past twenty years. This is the information you sent me out to secure. I'd appreciate it if you'd clear my name after I leave."

"Aren't you staying to coordinate the efforts to quell this rebellion?" Captain Heilen seemed to be the only one surprised as Brenden turned to leave.

"No, Captain. This uprising is only a symptom of the greater problem. We're going after the source. I'll leave my Elstaar team at your disposal. Riley is a good officer and the others will follow his lead."

"Commander Odana." Master General Oren called to Tridia as she turned to follow the others from the room. "We've given Master Ren Tama permission to land at the hangar where the *Star Seeker* is stored. He wishes to speak with you before your departure."

"Also, please ask the Sentinel to which ship her companion's body should be taken. It has been treated as she instructed," the Supreme Commander said.

"Winniel is already with Alanel's body, sir. She will see to its care from now on," Tridia said.

Brenden looked around, surprised that Winniel wasn't with them.

Tridia continued, "Whether or not I speak with Master Tama is a decision for Master Aren. I am not at liberty to accept or deny that request, and you no longer have the right to direct my discourse."

"Well said, Commander Odana." The Supreme Commander chuckled, as Tridia left the room.

Once in the hallway, Brenden gave Riley his orders and asked Tran to get their ship ready for departure.

"Where will you be?" Tran asked. "Am I going to have to pull you out of another jam?"

"I've got to deal with Ren Tama. He's asked to speak with Commander Odana."

"Are you sure you don't want me with you?"

"No," Brenden replied. "Just get the ship ready. We're out of here as soon as this is handled."

Tran hurried away without further comment.

Brenden seethed as they left the building and headed for the nearest hangar. With Tridia and Sonei injured, Tran in a reduced capacity, Winniel dealing with her grief, and Alanel dead, they couldn't afford to linger away from their power base.

"What has this Ren Tama got going that he has to speak with Tridia?" Deeca asked after they were well away from the archive bunker. "Another attempt to take her in the open?"

"Whatever it is, it won't be good for our plans," Brenden responded.

Tridia said nothing, but limped along with her jaw clenched. True to form, Ren Tama's craft rested mere yards from the *Star Seeker*. Tama stood at the ramp of his ship with his arms crossed and made no move to intercept them.

"A word with you, Commander Odana?" he called out.

"I have no words to spare for you, Master Tama." Tridia would have entered the *Star Seeker*, but Tama spoke again.

"Shall I pass that information along to the package you left on Xanaias?"

Brenden stopped and Tridia froze in mid stride behind him. Tama grinned as she turned to face him. The singularity of Tama's mind had closed around whatever scheme he had planned. Tridia stared in silence, her chest heaving. These two would clash over the Chesan prince and the injuries he'd received. Brenden didn't favor Tama's chances of grinning when Tridia finished with him.

CHAPTER FORTY-FOUR

"I see you know the package I reference. He kept insisting his name was Davik Schie. Even after hours of beating and torture he didn't change his story. He's not doing well, Commander. I'm sure the sight of you would improve his chances of survival. He seems quite devoted." Tama continued to stand with his arms crossed.

"Release him, Tama." Tridia growled. The skin on the back of her hands itched as the fur started to emerge. She clenched her fists to keep control. "Release him or suffer the consequences."

The grin disappeared from Tama's face. "He is with my troops in space, Commander. Any action against me, or any delay in my return to the ship, and young Davik will die a rather horrible and bloody death."

Tridia turned to Brenden. "Get this collar off of me now."

"Do you have a standard collar control box?" Master Aren asked Deeca. Deeca nodded and sprinted into the ship. While they waited, he whispered to Tridia. "He can't be trusted."

"I don't intend to trust him," Tridia said. "I intend to *kill him* as soon as he takes me to Drayden."

"Don't let your anger overtake your training, Commander." Master Aren held Tridia's gaze. "Tama isn't a poser. He deserves his White Level ranking. Do you understand me?"

Tridia nodded and let some of the tension drain from her shoulders. Master Aren retrieved a detonator from his pocket and slipped it into hers. She questioned with her eyes.

"The collar contains enough explosive to make sure you leave no trace," he whispered. "If you'd gotten on a ship with B'Nay, it would have been over."

"You might have told me," she growled again.

"Didn't want to scare you." Master Aren said. "Tama's not going to

443

let us take that thing off of you here, but you may have need of the explosives when he does. Two blue, one green, two red."

Deeca came back with the control box and handed it to Master Aren.

"You can leave the collar in place, Ambassador-Master-Colonel," Tama called out. "Commander Odana may need some persuasion that obedience would be in the young man's best interest."

"Can you disable whatever it is that makes me ill?" Tridia whispered.

"Makes you ill?" Master Aren asked.

"Something in this collar makes me ill when I drop my barriers," Tridia explained. "That's why I couldn't contact you when I realized B'Nay was pulling the strings here."

Master Aren shook his head, but took the remote Deeca proffered. He opened the box and made an adjustment, then closed it again. "The switch to release the collar is on the side of the box – if you can get your hands on it again."

"That's enough chitchat," Tama said. "I'll want the collar tested to make sure it works properly before we leave. Sorry, Commander, but I don't trust you or the Colonel where my well-being is concerned. Toss it over and back away from her." Brenden complied and took two steps away from Tridia, taking Deeca with him.

"It's a standard issue collar, Tama. You know the settings, you don't have to injure her."

Tridia limped half the distance to Tama's ship and stopped. "Do what you have to."

Tama twisted the dial and hit the activation button. The jolt brought Tridia up on her toes. Her fingers curled into claws and her back arched. When Tama released the button, she fell to the ground gasping for breath and seeing double. Her heart jumped in an unmeasured beat. The Marshal had toyed with the settings, increasing the jolt by increments. Tama didn't bother to taunt her before testing it at near full strength.

"You madman, you'll kill her!" Deeca's voice reached Tridia from a great distance.

Tridia fought her way to her hands and knees. Deeca tried to run to her but Master Aren grabbed the Hunter's arm to keep her at bay. An argument ensued that halted when Tridia looked up at Tama and screamed.

"No!"

Winniel stood with a knife at Tama's throat. She'd moved so fast Tridia hadn't seen her until the weapon flashed.

"The boy dies." Blood trickled down Tama's neck from the point of Winniel's blade.

"Let him go, Winniel. He's taken a hostage." Tridia didn't want to say more and she hoped Winniel would listen. "Winniel, please."

The Sentinel lowered her hand and stepped away but kept her eyes on Tama. He watched her until she was out of reach then touched his throat and stared at the blood on his fingertips.

"He'll pay for that, Commander Odana. Drop for drop. Any injury to me will be multiplied ten times over to your young friend."

"She didn't understand what was happening. I'll go with you and I'll stay with you, but you've got to release your hostage to Master Aren." The words burned as they fell from Tridia's lips. The last thing she wanted was to be parted from Drayden if he was injured. However, her mother had told her to find Tama and this was her chance to do so without Master Aren's interference. She needed to know what Tama had to say, but she wanted Drayden safely away first.

"I'm not a naïve fool, Commander. Without the leverage of a hostage on my side, you'll be free to commit suicide if you decide not to comply with my wishes. No, I'll be keeping young Davik until I've tamed you to my liking."

"You'll tame nothing and you'll find an entire army on your back, Tama. You don't know who you've taken hostage." The control in Brenden's voice resonated in Tridia's ears, but Tama seemed unaffected.

"You know my reputation, Master Tama." Tridia rose swaying to her feet as she spoke. "You seem to know this boy is of great value to me. If you understand that much, then you'll have to see that as long as you hold him, I'm a threat to you. I will do everything I can to free him – including killing you."

"You aren't making me feel any safer, Commander." Tridia stepped toward him and Tama raised the control box in response.

"If you will release him to Master Aren after I've seen him, I'll stay with you and submit to whatever you wish of me. I give you my word." Tridia waited.

"You've sworn allegiance to Brenden Aren, to be his servant for five years. You'll be compelled to return to him if I let the boy go."

"I'll release her vow to you, Tama, if you release the boy to me," Brenden interjected.

Tama's eyebrows rose on his forehead as he looked from Tridia to Brenden. Tridia checked the desire to open her mind to sense Tama's thoughts.

"A very valuable property indeed, if you're willing to make such a sacrifice. I'll consider it, but I won't make that decision until I see how compliant the Commander will be to my – ah, wishes."

"His thoughts are perverse, Commander." Winniel's face screwed into lines of disgust. "They are a muddled confusion of images. You shouldn't go with this man."

"I have no choice. We have to protect the hostage." Tridia started to walk toward Tama again but tripped. Winniel rushed to support her.

"The Commander has been accepted by the Sentinels, Ren Tama. My mate and I were assigned to watch over her. He is gone and the responsibility falls to me."

"The Commander comes with me alone. I have no wish to further injure her body. Your services won't be required."

"Winniel, I have to go with him and we've got to hurry. The hostage's life is at stake." Tridia dropped her energy block just enough to feel Winniel's connection. What had once been a strong golden heartbeat had dimmed to a weak bronze pulse, barely indicating life. Winniel's grief hit hard. Tridia didn't know if Winniel could see beyond her own pain, but she had to try to pass on information, to make sure Winniel knew that Drayden was the hostage – and she had an alternate plan. Vertigo rushed in with the hum of the collar and Tridia struggled to keep it at bay. She couldn't leave the barrier down long without passing out. "Please, don't make a fuss here. You've got to let me go."

Coldness swept through her brain like a Hielos *tashan* when Winniel entered her thoughts, then left as cleanly as it had come. Winniel had passed through the remainder of the energy block as if it didn't exist. She nodded and Tridia slammed the energy block into place around her mind.

"I will keep the DNA pouch safe," Winniel whispered, then spoke in a normal voice. "I will assist you onto the ship."

"You will assist her as far as this ramp, Sentinel, then you will return to Colonel Aren."

"Know this, Ren Tama. I will let her go with you, but I will hold you responsible for her safety. One Sentinel could hunt you down wherever you hide. One Sentinel could destroy you. My entire clan will track you should the Commander ever call for us, and you will have no chance. Think of this when you imagine yourself ruling over her."

Tama glared in silence as he watched Winniel half carry Tridia to the ramp. He backed away when the two of them were within striking distance. When Winniel released her, Tridia staggered but managed to keep her footing. She limped part of the way up the ramp and turned to wait for Tama.

"Don't follow us, Aren. I know the collar she wears has a short-range homing device. If you come within tracking distance of us, I'll kill the boy. If I decide to release him, I'll send word through your embassy where you can find him." Tama sprang to the ramp and turned Tridia so they faced the group on the ground. Together they backed up the ramp and went inside the ship.

Once inside, he guided Tridia ahead of him. She cringed as he placed a hand on her waist and let it rest there.

"You haven't proven to me that you have the boy in your custody, Master Tama. Until you do, have a care where you leave your hand. You may find you'll lose it entirely."

Tama laughed. "I like the sound of you calling me master, Tridia. Get used to the idea yourself."

Tridia snorted as he closed the ramp and guided her to a small cabin. Tama opened the door and Tridia jumped back, colliding with his rock-hard body. A lizard-skinned humanoid stood in the doorway. Its reptilian eyes glistened in the near-dark, its flat-faced mouth displayed pointed teeth.

A Carok. Tridia had heard of them, but had never seen one. Nothing she'd heard was good. She didn't move.

"You know of the Caroks?" Tama asked. Tridia didn't respond. "Like the Felinus, the Caroks are the result of a cross-species genetic experiment. They are vicious, relentless, and merciless when turned loose. Soldiers without scruples and dangerous to work with. They enjoy human flesh when they are allowed to have it."

"How did you come into contact with these creatures?" Tridia spoke in a hushed voice.

Tama ignored her question. The Carok stepped back and revealed another of its kind squatting near the far wall. Tridia remained glued to Tama's chest, unwilling to take another step.

"Don't worry, Commander. The Carok are only here to keep an eye on you. I don't like letting you out of my sight, but since I can't have you seeing the coordinates or playing games with the navigation, we'll both have to make the best of it." Tama shoved Tridia into the room. "Don't touch her unless she attempts to escape. And don't eat any part of her."

Tama shut and locked the door, leaving Tridia alone with the two beasts.

The creatures grunted. Tridia moved to sit on the bunk, giving them as much berth as she could in the small compartment. The creatures' pungent odor assaulted her nostrils. If Drayden couldn't escape these creatures, he would have fought them, but how had they gotten to him in the first place?

Guilt compounded worry, but recriminations wouldn't help, and despair would let the darkness of the Chaos Vision seep into her thoughts. She tried to call up Drayden's face to keep them away, but it was Davik's damaged face that rose from her memories. She'd been the cause of both their pain. Tridia bit her lip and reached into her memories for a perfect white flower. Its scent soothed her mind and its perfection gave her focus.

As her heartbeat slowed, Tridia tilted her head back and the collar pinched her neck. She raised a hand to adjust it. Her two guards were instantly on the defensive.

"It's heavy and it's uncomfortable," she said. "I just need to adjust it."

"Make no attempt to escape. We hurt you." Her guards sat back against the wall.

"No escape," Tridia said. "Master Tama has seen to that."

"Master Tama is smart man. Knows you will come. Knows boy will come if we kill plant people."

Tridia closed her eyes against the pain of thinking Layne, Vaille, and their children were dead. Tama had gotten to Drayden using the Rrabbas. Even after his promise to stay strong, if Tama had threatened them, Drayden would have capitulated.

"He fought you, all the same, though, didn't he?"

The nearest creature grunted. "Did him no good."

"Were all the plant creatures killed?"

"No." More grunting followed

"Scum." Tridia hissed under her breath.

Tama planned to torment Drayden using the rest of the Rrabbas. If only she had some way to get word to Master Aren to rescue the plant creatures. But Tama would make sure she never came near communications equipment and the collar insured she couldn't even try to reach him telepathically.

A slight queasiness coursed through her stomach as the ship made its sling jump into hyperdrive. Tama's inertial shields needed aligning. Going into hyperdrive meant his ship wasn't stationed within the Odean solar system. Even with Master Aren's remarkable abilities, he wouldn't be able to track her through hyperspace. He'd have to come up with some other way to find them, and she'd have to assume he never would. If she started with the assumption she was on her own, she might have enough courage to pursue the plan she'd shared with Winniel.

They traveled long enough to place them in any distant solar system, assuming Tama hadn't taken the long route to a nearby planet. Tridia was on her feet and facing the door when Tama opened it.

"Eager for my attentions?" he asked.

"Take me to him." Tridia's demand was met with a cold stare.

"Tell me what he is to you, first."

"I saved his life on a distant planet. He shared his teaching equipment with me so I could research historical events. End of story."

Tama reached to touch Tridia's cheek and she flinched away. He laughed, wrapped her loose braid around his fist then jerked her face near his.

"I'll tolerate your arrogance only so long, Commander. You will answer my questions – all of them – or the boy pays. As you'll see, he doesn't have much left to pay with."

"Take me to him." Tridia emphasized each word and met Tama's dark gaze with her own steel.

"For a moment only, to show you he's here. Afterward, you and I have business."

Tama took Tridia by the arm and dragged her down the ramp and outside the transport vessel. They'd anchored in a large docking bay along with several other ships that bore the Hierarchy symbol. They were in the belly of a warship. Had Tama been at Zentel? Was he in league with the Kel Anec after all? With Tama's rough support she made the long trek to the brig where he forced her to look through a clear plasma field. Drayden lay unmoving on the cot in a brightly lit cell. Tridia could see he'd been badly beaten, and only the slow rise and fall of his chest gave her any hope he was alive.

"Let me go in to him." The catch in her voice betrayed Tridia's fear.

"Who is he to you?" Tama repeated his question.

"He's a friend. I saved his life and he helped me out with some research. I didn't make that up." Tridia gasped as Tama's fingers dug into her arm to force her away from the cell. "I'm telling you the truth!"

"Then why is he so important that the great Brenden Aren cares for his safety? It's not because he's a friend of yours."

"No, it isn't. The boy is nobility. Master Aren is under contract to protect him. Since I'm under oath to Master Aren, I share the responsibility to protect him."

"Under contract to whom?" Tama lessened his grip on her arm, but produced the control device from his jacket. He held it up for Tridia to see, then released her.

"Kanu. Empress Dojene engaged both of us to protect him."

"I know the Kanuan nobility. He isn't one of them." Tama set the dial on the lowest setting and pressed the button.

Tridia stiffened as the current flowed through her body, then fell against the wall when it stopped.

"I'll increase the jolt with every wrong answer," Tama said.

"I never said he was Kanuan nobility," Tridia gasped. "Empress Dojene told us he was nobility and deserved our protection. We – I – tried to protect him from the Hierarchy battle cruiser, but I didn't count on you when I left him in hiding." Tridia stood upright and faced Tama again. She spurred her anger to dispel the pain.

"Why does the Elstaar want him?" Tama asked.

"They don't. The entities controlling the Elstaar want him." Tridia hurried on to keep Tama from pressing the button again. "Why do you think we were on Odea? The arrest was a sham to get us onto the planet to expose the conspiracy. The Elstaar attacked the regular forces while we were there. You can verify the information for yourself."

"I intend to do so, Commander."

"Then leave me with him while you do. What harm can I do inside a cell?"

Tama considered Tridia's words then entered a code to deactivate the plasma field.

"You've got until I return. If I find out you were lying, he dies without further discussion."

Tridia shot him a look that would have frozen a lesser man, but Tama only stared back. She entered the cell and didn't look back as the scent of active plasma filled the room. She limped to Drayden's bed and knelt beside him. Bruises covered his face and exposed skin, his left eye was swollen shut, his nose was broken, one shoulder looked dislocated, and blood crusted on his lips and right eye. His clothes were in shreds and deep scratches covered his body. She didn't touch him for fear of causing him further pain.

"Foolish prince," Tridia whispered, wiping a rogue tear from her cheek. "The Rrabbas died anyway. Had you known Ren Tama – no you probably would have opened the door just the same."

"Tridia?" Drayden winced in his sleep when he spoke.

"I'm here, Drayden." Tridia leaned closer and whispered, straining to hear his words.

"I couldn't make them kill me. I didn't open the –" Drayden's words were cut short by a cough.

"Don't speak. You need a medic. There should be a good sick bay on a ship this size, if we could only get you there."

Drayden attempted to shake his head, but tears streamed from his closed eyes. "I didn't open the door, but I killed them just the same. Layne and Vaille, the podlings. The Rrabbas couldn't fight them, couldn't hurt them. It was only because I resisted that they were involved at all."

"How did they get the door opened?" Tridia asked.

"Physician program…Opened door…Secura was too late. I killed the Rrabbas."

Another coughing fit wracked Drayden's body, and Tridia placed her hand beneath his head to support him.

"Drayden, you've got to stop this. If you didn't see the Rrabbas die with your own eyes, then don't believe what they've told you." Even false hope would give him something to cling to.

"I heard the order, heard the blasters," Drayden wheezed. "Tama told me…He planned to return for the village."

"That only means that he knows how to exert mental anguish, Your Highness." Tridia forced a hard edge into her voice. "Ren Tama lives for torment. His mind is bent. If you're vulnerable he'll attack your weakness – mind or body – and you've exposed both."

"No more titles." Drayden turned his head away and Tridia's heart pounded until he drew a ragged breath.

"Listen to me, Drayden. You've got to live. You have to hold on until we can get you to the sick bay."

"He beat you, didn't he?" Drayden asked. "Brenden Aren beat you when you asked him for help. I saw you in shackles."

"No," Tridia whispered. "We had to get to the Hierarchy and having visible injuries to prove I resisted capture was the only way. I'm sorry if you felt that pain. Master Aren will help you. He's trying to find you now. Please hold on."

Drayden pulled air into his lungs and opened his good eye. "I've lost the Rrabbas and I've lost you. You surrendered to Tama to save me. He'll do horrible things to you. If I die, you have a chance to escape."

Tridia touched his battered face with the tips of her fingers. "I'm here because I chose to be. You matter to me. Not your bloodline. Not your future. Not some twisted vision of chaos or promise of peace. You, my foolish prince and my mate. Yes, I came to help you, but I'm giving up nothing without a fight. You have to get strong enough to fight back, too. We'll get out of here together. I won't leave without you and I can't move you in this condition."

"Together?" The word came as a plea from Drayden's lips.

"Together." Tridia affirmed. "We'll stay together. No more parting if I can prevent it."

Drayden smiled and heaved a deep sigh before drifting into unconsciousness. Tridia pressed her fingers to the pulse at his throat and waited for the slow rise of his chest to be sure he was alive. Ren Tama would pay for this. Somehow, in some life, she would make him suffer for every injury inflicted on Drayden's body and mind.

CHAPTER FORTY-FIVE

Tridia sat on the floor beside Drayden's bed for an hour, letting hatred seethe in her mind, before Ren Tama returned and opened the plasma shield. She jumped to her feet and vented her wrath before he'd crossed the cell.

"How dare you do this to a prisoner, one who's not even an enemy, and leave him without medical attention. No convention of war or conflict gives you the right to inflict this kind of torture on an innocent party."

"Control yourself, Commander. Kanu confirmed your story." Tama looked down at the unconscious Drayden and Tridia stopped short.

"Kanu?" she asked. "You told the Kanuan government you had the missing noble in your custody?"

"The empress herself was unavailable, but her attaché was most anxious to receive the boy and offered to send an envoy to fetch him immediately."

Tridia ran through scenario after scenario in her head. No one on Kanu would know anything about Drayden. The empress had held his existence in secrecy. With Zilisk dead, Tridia had no idea who might be posing as the empress's attaché. Or it could be a real attaché under Kel Anec control. Master Aren had said they couldn't turn to Kanu for help. He'd been right.

"You couldn't offer him up in this condition." Tridia glanced down at Drayden.

"I told them he wasn't actually in my custody, but I thought I knew where I could find him. I said I'd check my sources and contact them when I was sure."

"Giving you sufficient time to restore him to health."

Tama grabbed Tridia's shoulders and drew her close. "I could just

452

kill him and save us all the trouble."

"Then you'll lose any hope of coercing me." Tridia didn't flinch. "That remote activator will only get you so far before you have to kill me with it. You were right to use him as a bargaining chip. You and I were trained in the same system, Master Tama. I'd rather see him dead than used in this manner. I won't let myself be blackmailed for much longer. You desire my obedience, very well, here are my terms and they are not negotiable. He gets full medical attention and proper care. I get to see him for at least an hour every watch. You don't touch me until he's well enough to argue with you."

"*Your* terms, Commander? Not when I hold all the power. The prisoner doesn't design the prison."

"You want me obedient, subservient? Or maybe you want me to resist you to make the game more interesting," Tridia said. "I'm telling you my terms are the only means of achieving that end. If you hurt him more now, he'll die. Killing him isn't your goal and it won't get you what you want. My terms will get you to your true goal with a lot less effort on your part."

Tridia softened her voice and let her muscles relax in Tama's grip. "Would you rather have me like clay in your hands, or do you want to guard your throat from a knife every waking and sleeping moment?"

Tama drew her hard against his chest and shook her once. He lowered his lips to within an inch of her ear. "You've never been more wrong, Commander. It just so happens your terms coincide with my plans."

"Give me an oath you'll keep your word," Tridia said.

"Don't test me, Commander Odana. I've waited and watched over you for fifteen years. I'll wait one more week. Whatever his condition is then, he leaves and you stay."

Tridia did her best to hide her relief.

If we can stay out of Kel Anec hands for another week.

While they stood glaring at each other, an anti-grav carrier entered the room, followed by two human attendants in pale blue medic uniforms – one of them a fair haired girl of about sixteen. Tridia recognized Lera Cal at once and shook her head when the girl would have acknowledged her.

"Take the prisoner to the sick bay and make sure he remains under guard at all times. Severe punishment to the guard or medic who lets him leave without my direct orders."

Tama didn't wait for acknowledgement from the attendants. He left the room with Tridia in tow.

She limped along beside him until he ushered her into a spacious cabin with muted lighting and a pair of portals displaying a rapidly changing star field. The ship was underway.

"You'll find clothes in the dresser and the closet," Tama said. "Toiletries in the bathroom. Make yourself presentable. You'll dine with me in two hours. Don't try to leave, there will be guards outside your door and the vents are welded shut."

Tama left the room. The whine of the lock activating said he'd take no chances.

Tridia paced the room though each step sent pain through her leg. She had an ally. Lera had recognized her and kept silent. She'd watch over Drayden for Tridia's sake if not for the prince's own well-being. They had one week to nurse Drayden to health and find a means of escape. The consequence meant dealing with Ren Tama personally. Whatever he expected to receive from her was more than sex, of that she was certain. He could have his choice of women more accomplished than she, or virgins more beautiful. He'd been on Ceyon before the Chesan holocaust. What did he know about the Chesan mating experience? For that matter, what did she know? She'd only mentally bonded with Drayden, not mated with him. Or had Empress Dojene guessed correctly when she said Tridia's mother had infected Tama with a desire for power that could only be sated by a Chesan woman. Tridia swallowed hard at the thought.

She limped into the small bathroom and checked the mirror. Her eyes were red-rimmed and the bruise that darkened her cheek, gave it a sunken look. Her hair stuck out in wild disarray. Even on a battlefield she'd never looked so bad. No wonder Drayden thought Master Aren had beat her, or that Tama was willing to wait a week for her favors. Her fingers strayed to the collar at her neck. With enough time and the proper tools she might manage to get it off – or electrocute herself in the process – or blow her head off. Master Aren had told Deeca to get a standard control box. He repeated those words to Ren Tama. Any control box would work if she could get her hands on one. Cruisers kept good supply as standard issue in the armory.

The device's detonator weighed against her leg in her pocket. She'd have to hide it where it couldn't be found. Hierarchy procedures were to search every prisoner, their garments, and every place they contacted before the search. She'd been granted a lot of grace to not be stripped before Tama left her alone. Hiding places would be precious, but she'd think of something.

Options opened with each new piece of information, but everything revolved around Drayden's health. If she could get the collar off, she'd risk opening a portal, but she couldn't leave him and she couldn't take him in his present condition. If she collapsed in the process they'd both die. The better choice would be to use the collar as a bomb in some strategic place. But again, that would only work if Drayden could move under his own strength. Then there was her own injury to deal with. She had to see a medic, and soon. Wa'Ren's strike to her kidneys was already having an effect – even if she couldn't feel it.

Tridia spent the better part of an hour making contingency plans, before deciding to appease Ren Tama by making an effort with her appearance. She could stand a shower and a change of clothes that didn't smell of her own sweat or remind her of the recent battles. She found apparel of several types and sizes and tried to choose the least provocative of the lot.

After a shower and a quick change of clothes she brushed through her hair and studied the room. One access panel and two ventilation grates were the only breaks in the wall apart from two large portals. The access panel turned out to be part of the temperature controls and one of the ventilation ducts was too small for her to squeeze through. Nevertheless, she tested the grates, and found them welded shut just as Tama had said.

The tinkle of a bell warned her that someone was about to enter. She had just moved to the center of the room when the door swished open. Ren Tama stood there, dressed in black with a frown on his face. He entered without preamble and the door slid closed behind him. His eyes raked Tridia head to toe, but she didn't bother to lift her chin in defiance. Let him feast his eyes, as long as he kept his distance. She'd chosen the least provocative of the outfits, but its silky dark purple fabric clung to every small curve and changed hues when she moved.

"Come here."

Tama's harsh tone warned her this was not the time to provoke him. She moved to within arm's reach and waited with her hands at her sides. The red welts and scabs under the gold bands stood out on her wrists. Tama noticed them, but said nothing. He reached up to touch the collar.

"If I remove this, will I have to kill you?"

"Not as long as he's too injured to travel." Tridia's frankness seemed to surprise him.

"Not a way to advocate his healing." Tama clicked the button on the box and the collar loosened. "I suppose I will know when he is healed before you will."

Tridia remained motionless as he removed it and held it to the side.

"It goes back on when I decide," Tama said. "Any resistance will prove harmful to your young nobleman."

"As long as he's receiving medical attention and you keep your distance, I won't do anything to jeopardize his recovery. Break either of those agreements, Master Tama, and you might as well kill us both."

"Don't threaten, Commander. I'm not in the mood. You have

information I want that won't compromise your ward, but it may save all our lives."

"The Elstaar are coming after you." Tridia made a calculated guess and was rewarded by a surprised look from her captor.

"How did you know?" he asked.

"You told the Kanuan government you know where the young noble they want is hiding. An alien force most likely controls the empress's attaché and a portion of the Elstaar. The aliens want him for their own purposes. That's why Empress Dojene commissioned Master Aren to protect him. They won't stop until they've caught up with you and searched your ship, perhaps tortured you for the information on his hiding place. Those creatures control minds in several ways, Master Tama. Some of them revolting – all of them humiliating."

Ren Tama swore under his breath. "You've made your point, Commander. Keep your comments civil, at least until after dinner."

With his hand pressed against the small of her back, Tridia allowed Tama to guide her to a room that contained an elegant table set with candles. They dined in silence for most of the meal as Tama seemed lost in thought. She decided to break the silence herself.

"How is it that you're in command of a battle cruiser? You weren't commissioned to the fleet."

Tama eyed her with suspicion, but answered. "Like your master, Brenden Aren, I've ranked in more than one grid. I served with the Elstaar fleet for several years before I was reassigned to the Assassin's Grid. I worked with the engineers twice when injuries had me unable to serve elsewhere. I commanded a cruiser for two engagements during the Eleron revolt after the regular bridge crew was killed in a surprise attack. The White Level Master's rank affords me certain freedoms, but I also have rank in the fleet."

The Eleron revolt had been a bloody battle with the Hierarchy taking the heaviest losses in its history. For Tama to have taken part and survived brought renewed respect in her eyes. "The fleet part of your service record must be classified. It didn't come up during my research before the White Level Challenge."

"You won't find all of the information on every opponent in a computer bank, Commander." Tama sipped his wine before continuing. "This is an experimental ship with an experimental crew. I designed some of the features and volunteered to test it. Even if the Elstaar chase us, they may not be able to find us with what we've installed."

"The cloaking device?"

"You're well-informed, for a young woman who's had rank for less than two months. I won't bother to ask how you know, although *why* you know interests me."

"Every assassin needs to know how to hack a system, Master Tama. What we find when we hack could be pebbles or jewels," Tridia said.

"As we both know."

Tridia recalled the cloaked fighters that had escorted her and Master Aren from Odea. At the time she hadn't remembered the accidental discovery she'd made while researching Davik's whereabouts. The Hierarchy had taken the prototype to another level and installed it on a cruiser.

"The original spec required the cloak to block a scan beyond a thousand kilometers," Tama said. "We've refined the prototype to conceal a ship this size to beyond five hundred kilometers."

Tridia looked him in the eyes as he spoke. She had no need for coyness while talking shop. Her voice remained conversational when she spoke. "Impressive. What do you do if the Elstaar do find us?"

"Is there any way to combat the mind control?" Tama asked.

Tridia thought of the collar he'd taken from her neck. If it kept her thoughts in, it might keep the Kel Anec out. But the collar made her too ill to use her senses. She shivered at the thought of the feeders. At length she shook her head and answered.

"We've been lucky until now. The Sentinels have been there to help us. Their minds aren't vulnerable to control and they can remove the alien feeders."

"Sentinels are more machine than human."

"On the contrary, they're humanity in its most quintessential form. Their minds are pure, and their loyalty without question." Tridia defended the Sentinels, but sudden grief for the loss of Winniel's mate caused her voice to catch.

"You could say as much for an android."

"Be that as it may, the Sentinels saved us more than once, and sheer luck saw us through the rest of the time," Tridia said. "You're going to have to be clever if they catch up to us."

Tama dabbed his lips with his napkin then laid it on the table. A look came into his eyes that made Tridia sit back in her chair and lift her chin.

"Don't assume an attitude with me, Tridia." Tama smiled when he spoke her name. "I'll keep my word. We may need to fight side by side and I don't want thoughts of revenge clouding your tactical mind. Once we've dealt with the Elstaar and gotten rid of your noble young friend, we'll have our turn."

"I have to rely on your skills, as well, Master Tama. Even if I could leave with him now, I couldn't protect him on my own – not from an Elstaar cruiser." Tridia leaned forward, bracing her elbows and forearms on the table. "He must not be taken. The aliens who are after him would wreak havoc on the galaxy if they had him. We have to protect him, but if it appears he will be taken, you must destroy him – and me. Completely destroy, as in disintegrate our bodies. No DNA must remain."

Tama eyed her for a moment. "You're serious. You believe you must be obliterated."

"I know it, Master Tama. I've seen what the future is like otherwise."

"You've seen the future." Tama's eyes narrowed to slits. "There was once a prescient species in this galaxy, but they died out years ago. Could it be the boy is a Chesan survivor? How did that happen, I wonder? How is it that *you* came to see the future?"

Tama grabbed Tridia's arm in a vicelike grip and forced her to her knees at his side.

"The Chesan powers of seeing the future." Tama's eyes grew misty for a moment and his expression became one of near rapture. "I know my future, as well, Tridia. I've experienced the ecstasy of Chesan bonding. Your mother promised that I could experience it again if I saved you as a child. So, I saved you and watched over you. I've protected you from degradation in the training rooms and influenced the missions given to you when I could. I've kept you pure because that's what your mother said had to be done. Now you tell me you've seen the future and you're fawning over a Chesan nobleman. That means only one thing."

Tama's rapture switched to maniacal anger. His nostrils flared as he twisted Tridia's arm. He'd bonded with her mother and now he expected to do the same with her, but he'd wanted her pure and now he believed her tainted.

Her mother *had* infected Tama, just as Dojene had surmised. The young Hierarchy officer had fallen prey to a Chesan noblewoman's desperate attempt to save her child and her race. Drayden's life hung in the balance because Tama thought the prince had gotten to her first.

"It isn't what you think, Master Tama." Tridia didn't let fear into her voice. "Those plant creatures you had your Caroks destroy give off an aphrodisiac pollen when they go through their birthing process. He and I were both exposed. It did something to our minds. We both saw a vision of the future. There was no physical mating."

"You'd lie to protect him!" Tama shouted and gave Tridia's arm another twist.

"In a heartbeat!" Tridia shouted back. "My virginity is something you can have the medics confirm if you don't believe me."

Tama stood and dragged Tridia to her feet. "If you're lying to me, Commander Odana, you will both die, but not quickly."

In spite of the pain in her leg, Tridia jogged to keep up with Tama as he sailed down the halls to the sick bay. His orders to verify Tridia's words stunned the medics, but they took her into a room and had her lie on an examination table. An image of her reproductive organs hung above her abdomen and the medic sorted through it until he found the small piece of flesh he needed to see. Afterwards Tridia followed the medic to where Tama stood glaring down at Drayden's unconscious body.

"She is a virgin, Master Tama. There's no sign of sexual activity," The young medic said.

"That will be all." Tama looked at Tridia as if she'd just appeared beside him, then frowned. "You have no idea how close you came."

"Yes – I do." Tridia took a step closer to Tama. She spoke in a hushed voice. "I've made a deal with you, and you've confirmed your prize is still worth having. He's just an innocent caught in a power struggle he doesn't understand. I'm his guardian. That's all there is. Keep your side of the bargain and I'll keep mine. We'll fight together if it comes to that."

Tama raked her with his eyes again but didn't touch her. "You are persuasive, Commander. Just like your mother. The most remarkable woman I've ever known – or ever hope to. I'll keep my side of the bargain. You can see this fledgling of yours now. For one hour only. You will be observed and recorded. And you will wear the obedience collar."

"As you wish."

Tama snapped his fingers and one of the Caroks appeared with the collar. Tridia stood motionless as he fastened it around her neck. Her stomach sank as she heard the device click into place. Instead of stepping back, he let his hands linger on her shoulders and dropped his voice to a whisper when he spoke.

"The Chesan King's line produced the prescient seed in its firstborn son. There was a son at the time I bonded with your mother. His name was Drayden. Drayden Anjenay. He'd be about this age now. I just want you to know that I'm not a fool. This boy isn't some princeling under Kanu's protection. He's the Chesan prince, the son of the ruling house. He survived the Chesan genocide. From the setup I found on Xanaias it appears the nobility planned his survival, whereas you have me to thank for yours. If you'd bothered to share that when you came aboard, we might have been spared our approaching dilemma." Tama squeezed Tridia's shoulders and backed away.

Tridia moved to Drayden's side. Two guards and a medic stood on the other side of the bed. She reached out to touch him but stopped at the medic's instructions.

"He's not to be moved or disturbed. His injuries are critical. Jostling him around at this point could kill him. Master Tama, this man should have been brought to us days ago."

"It wasn't convenient. Be relieved he's here at all. As long as Commander Odana behaves herself I'm satisfied to leave him in your care. Just know that you could be healing a dead man."

The medic closed his lips against any further argument he might have made. Tridia laid her hand on the pillow beside Drayden's cheek.

"May I speak with him?"

"He can't hear you," the medic replied. "We've set his shoulder and his nose, given him pain medications, and started treatments on his internal injuries. We've set his broken bones, but until his lungs and kidneys heal we can't subject him to the mender."

Remembered pain shot through Tridia's body at the mention of the mender. In his current condition Drayden would never be able to handle that kind of pain.

"I'd still like to speak to him, if you don't mind." She leaned over Drayden's ear and placed her hand softly over his. "I'm here, Drayden. Remember what I told you. Get well."

Tridia stood at his side, brushed the hair away from his face, and asked for a warm cloth to wipe the blood from his mouth. The medic agreed and an attendant brought the cloth to her. Tridia reached for it without looking up, but the attendant didn't release it when she pulled at it. Tridia met Lera's stern gaze when she looked up. The girl let go of the cloth and glanced down at the Chesan prince.

"Is he a friend?" Lera spoke in an excellent bedside manner that gave no hint of prior knowledge of Tridia.

Tridia nodded as she wiped at the crusted blood, being careful not to press too hard. "We haven't known each other for very long. I'm supposed to protect him."

"Don't worry. He has a good medic and I'll be here most of the time to watch over him." The girl kept emotion from her voice.

"Thank you. That encourages me." Tridia managed a small smile and Lera shot her a conspiratorial one in returned.

Ren Tama's voice broke the quiet of the room. "Commander, do you intend to dawdle over him for a full hour?"

"No, Master Tama." She handed Lera Cal the cloth and turned her back to Drayden. "If he can't hear me, there's no purpose to my staying."

Tridia's leg collapsed as she moved away from the bed and Tama caught her before she fell.

"Medic, please examine Commander Odana's leg. She's been unable to walk without limping since I picked her up on Odea. Check the cut on her lip and any other complaints she has."

Tama lifted Tridia onto an examination table and stepped back as the medic slid the hem of her dress up to check her leg. Blood red bruises marked her thigh where the Marshal had squeezed the muscle. The medic reported minor muscle tears. Tridia mentioned the blow to her kidney and the medic made a further examination.

"This could be dangerous. Whoever did that intended to kill. You need rest – and I mean complete bed rest for at least two days. No fighting, sparring, or other activity." The medic glared at Tama before continuing. "You can walk back to your room, and we'll do treatments there. You'll be lightly sedated to keep you calm. Follow those instructions and you just might live."

He gave Tridia an injection and sent her away with Master Tama. Her eyelids drooped as she walked to her quarters. Tama walked beside her, not speaking and not touching her. The door didn't open automatically when she approached and she waited, swaying on her feet, for him to unlock the door.

"I thought you were exaggerating your injuries, Commander. My apologies for not getting you to sick bay sooner." Tama hesitated. "Did Aren do that to you?"

Tridia turned and blinked, trying to focus her vision. "Must be the hypo. I thought you called me Commander again. You just apologized."

"Don't goad me." Tama straightened his shoulders as he spoke. "Did Brenden Aren cause those injuries?"

"I'm sorry. I'm tired and drugged. It wasn't Master Aren. It was the Marshal of the Kennels and one of the inmates I sent there."

"The Marshal of the – How did he get his hands on you?"

"It's a really long story." Tridia swayed and sucked in a quick breath. "I have a favor to ask."

Tama's eyes narrowed. "Ask."

"If we engage the Elstaar – if there is a battle – I can't fight in the clothes you've so generously supplied. Is it possible to get a uniform without insignia or something less restrictive than the things in the closet and dresser?" Tridia waited, alternately blinking and stretching her eyes.

"I'll see what can be arranged."

Tridia nodded, but didn't move when he reached for her. One hand went to her neck, the other held the remote and she heard the click as the collar released.

"The guards will shoot you if you try anything at all. They will shoot to maim." Tama watched her face.

"Yes, sir." Tridia slurred the words. "I'll be on my best behavior."

He opened the door and waited as she entered. Tridia stepped through the entrance and turned to face him, forcing herself to breathe calmly and keep her gaze impassive.

"Get some rest. I'll see you in the next watch." Tama closed the door as Tridia stood there.

Someone had confiscated her soiled clothes in her absence. She needed to find something to sleep in that provided sufficient coverage from the surveillance cameras. The risqué clothing provided wouldn't cover much, but she decided being covered, however scantily, was better than complete exposure. To her surprise she found a cropped shirt and low-slung pants in the back of one of the drawers. The outfit left her entire midriff bare but covered pertinent areas.

She started to braid her hair, but fell asleep from the drugs before she'd half finished. Images of Drayden haunted her dreams. Every attempt to rescue him failed, leaving him dying or dead in a filthy cell, tormented by aliens. She woke with a start to the sound of the end-of-watch chimes. Rubbing her fingers across her eyes, she tried to tell herself they were only dreams, not visions. They lacked the clarity of her visions and the aliens tormenting Drayden looked nothing like the Caroks on the cruiser. The thought did little to alleviate her fear.

CHAPTER FORTY-SIX

The chime announced a visitor seconds before the door slid open. Tridia didn't bother to move. A female Ensign walked in carrying laundered clothes and shined boots, along with an unmarked uniform. Ren Tama entered on the woman's heels.

"Per the medic's instructions, you'll remain in bed today and tomorrow – all watches."

"You promised –"

"The boy is comatose and none the worse for the lack of your touch," Tama said. "I may let you see him tomorrow if you give me no grief. I'll have liquid food brought to you. The medic says even sitting up with this kind of injury could kill you. Stay down unless you need the facilities. If you do, call for Ensign Samos. She'll assist you. Those are orders, Commander. Obey them."

Tama left. Ensign Samos stayed long enough to help Tridia to the bathroom and give her a comlink to use if she needed assistance. Then she left and Tridia lay alone in the bed. The medic came in twice to massage her bare back with a machine to stimulate her kidneys. She catnapped most of the day, drank the broth and juices she received for meals, and called Ensign Samos when she needed the bathroom. Otherwise, she did nothing to break the monotony.

By the end of the second watch she felt less pain and was ready to move around. She would have done so, but the medic's warning and her own memories kept her bedridden. She'd once used the technique Wa'Ren had used on her. Her target had died in agony three days later.

Ensign Samos returned with the first watch chimes, all efficiency and not a shred of personality. Tridia wanted to drop her barrier just to see if the girl had a pulse, then realized she often behaved the same way herself. She let out a sigh of relief when Samos left.

Two more watches, a twenty-four hour day – and she'd return to Drayden. Lera showed up to administer another dose of medication, but she said nothing, and only once glanced over her shoulder toward the ceiling above the door. Tama was watching.

Tridia dozed again after Lera left and let the hours slide past unnoticed. When she awoke she turned onto her side as the chimes sounded for the second watch and stared at a computer monitor on the table. There'd been nothing on the table before her last nap. *Was there a computer attached to it?* If so, she'd only need a few minutes – No, Tama had probably sent it as a taunt to see if she would disobey him by getting out of bed. It was most likely connected to his personal monitor and would notify him the moment she touched it. She rolled onto her other side and faced the wall. An hour later the door chime sounded and Tama entered.

"They told me you were sleeping when they brought the monitor." He went straight to the screen and flicked it on.

Tridia lay on her back and looked toward the screen when he moved away. The monitor showed Drayden asleep in the sick bay.

"I stand by my promises, Commander," Tama said. "I gave my word you could see him for an hour each watch. You've been here for four watches. Gaze all you want for the next four hours. I'll send someone to retrieve the monitor afterward."

"Thank you, sir," Tridia said. "I will try to be as considerate in keeping my end of the bargain."

"I expect no less." Tama spoke over his shoulder as he left the room.

Tridia lay on her side watching Drayden for the entire time. Occasionally, Lera came into the frame, or the attending medic checked a pulse or pulled back Drayden's eyelids. None of them hurried or showed any anxiety. After four hours, two technicians entered Tridia's room and removed the monitor while an armed guard stood in the door. Tama had kept his word to the minute and Tridia wondered why he bothered to be so precise. What did he really expect from her, and why had her mother sent her to him?

The next watch Tama came into the room without Ensign Samos.

"Get dressed," he ordered.

Thus started what would become her normal day for the next three days. Tama waited in the main cabin while Tridia dressed in the bathroom. He snapped the obedience collar into place when she finished. They walked together to the sick bay to visit Drayden. He watched while she stroked his hair and spoke to his sleeping face. After the visit she walked with him to the training room where she did light weight training on her arms and torso, careful to place no stress on her injured leg. They ate breakfast at a separate table in the general dining hall then he took her back to her cabin where she rested until the noon meal. Guards delivered a tray of food to her door and she ate alone in her room. Three human guards accompanied her to the sick bay during the second watch and waited while she spoke to Drayden. One of the guards kept the remote control visible at all times, pressing the button to administer a small jolt only once when she hesitated to leave Drayden's side. They escorted her back to her cabin where she waited until she received instructions for the evening meal. She saw Tama in the mornings and for dinner. He insisted she wear non-uniform clothing each evening and he removed the obedience collar before dinner. After dinner he replaced the collar and they walked to the sick bay where Tama would again watch as she spoke to Drayden. The evening ended with Tama escorting her to her cabin and removing the collar.

On the third night she wore the same purple outfit she'd worn the first night. When Tama asked why, she told him everything else in the wardrobe was too risqué.

"Your modesty prevents?" he asked.

"Honor prevents." Tridia placed her napkin in her lap. "I won't be accused of teasing you when you've given your word to keep your distance."

"You couldn't if you tried," Tama said. "You look like her, talk like her, sometimes you move like her, but you aren't your mother."

His eyes took on a dreamy quality. Tridia frowned and Tama laughed.

"I do, however, appreciate the gesture," he said.

After dinner Tama walked her to the sick bay as usual. She lowered her barriers as she stood by Drayden's bed, hoping to get some sense of his condition. Ren Tama's confusion of thought hammered against her mind first, then Drayden caught her attention.

I'm awake. Drayden's words caressed her consciousness like a whisper in her ear.

Close your mind, Drayden. We're in danger of being exposed to the Kel Anec. Tridia's answer sounded harsh in her own mind, but Drayden persisted. Hadn't she just opened her mind?

I have to let you know I'm better. They've been keeping me drugged, but the young medic assigned to administer the dosage didn't give it to me today. She says the medical staff has been threatened to keep me sedated during your visits. I don't dare open my eyes.

I understand. Please don't take any chances. I will find a way to get us out of here. Do you think you could run if you had to? Tridia stroked his hair and examined the fading bruises. His cheeks looked pink beneath the bandages and the swelling in his eye had gone down.

Not yet. But it won't be long.

Don't give me any signals before you are sure you can. We may have to make a run for the storage bay or a hiding place. Now, please close your mind. I'll press my fingers into your palm when it's time to open it again. She demonstrated what she meant by pressing four fingers into the palm of his left hand. His fingers twitched in response and she hoped no one saw the reaction. *Keep still.*

Sorry. Involuntary reflex. One more thing? I've heard you every time. Our minds may be closed, but I can sense when you're near. Like the vision I saw of you in shackles. It came straight through my barriers.

Tridia hesitated to respond, but she had to say something. *I didn't see your capture, but I felt your pain. I wanted to come back to you, but I couldn't. We couldn't reach you fast enough to help. I should have taken you with me.*

No second guessing. We keep moving without looking back. Drayden let the thought settle for a moment then changed the subject. *You weren't really tortured?*

Not by Master Aren or anyone else in our group. We needed to create believable injuries so I could get back to the Hierarchy, but Master Aren was so gentle they weren't believed anyway. We were afraid of injuring you further. There was a fight later. Tridia recalled the four dead men in her wake without considering that Drayden would see them, too.

They meant to kill you. You had to protect yourself. I felt all of your injuries, too. I was already so far gone it didn't matter. If you were feeling all of my pain and yours, I don't know how you managed. This bond we've created may be keeping us alive by distributing the pain, but it makes the consequences of our actions something to consider. Don't hesitate if you need to fight for yourself. I can take whatever is necessary.

Close your mind, Drayden.

You can comfort and lie to me, but I can't reciprocate? Drayden's angry words slammed into Tridia like a sledgehammer. *Don't try to protect me from the truth, Tridia. Don't try to shut me out again. It hurts that you think I'm so weak. You were stronger than me on Zentel because I'd given you so much of my essence to strengthen you for our bonding and to survive the — to survive what came next. I know the Rrabbas are dead. You know it, too. Tama gave the order and those creatures obeyed. Don't try to shield me from the truth. I'm not a child.*

Alright! Tridia retaliated. She scowled, then caught Tama studying her face and relaxed. *They're probably gone, but I won't believe it until we find their bodies, which we may never have a chance to search for if you don't close your mind.*

Drayden's touch withdrew from her thoughts and Tridia almost whimpered as he left. He was angry and the sudden departure of his mind left an unexpected void in hers.

"I'm here Drayden." Tridia fought to control the tremor in her voice as she touched her fingers to his cheek. "Remember what I told you.

Get well."

Tama eyed her as she walked away from the bed. He kept his distance and his silence until they stood outside her door. "You say the same thing every time. I'm curious as to what it was you said to him and when you said it."

"The normal lies one says when trying to encourage someone to live." Tridia hoped the flippant reply would suffice. Tama didn't accept it.

"Be more specific, please," he insisted.

"In the cell, while we were waiting for you to return. I told him to hold on, get strong enough to escape, and I would take him away with me. He needed to think he could be free of your torture. I simply gave him something to believe." Tridia kept the explanation simple and straightforward to hide the depth of her commitment to the Chesan prince.

Tama reacted with violence. He shoved her against the wall and held her there with the heel of his hand pressing against her sternum.

"You won't leave with him. You'll no longer touch him. You won't get within ten feet of him."

"He's in a coma, Master Tama. What can I possibly do with an unconscious man? I've given you my word —"

"He's awake, Commander. I think you already know — if you truly are your mother's daughter. We've kept him drugged during your visits, but the medics tell me keeping him in that state could retard his recovery. I'm ready to be rid of him, though I haven't yet decided in what manner. My decision will rest on how we part company this evening."

Tridia's stomach churned. Without the collar she could escape from Tama, and possibly make it to the sick bay, but she couldn't carry Drayden to a ship, and she couldn't risk taking him through a portal yet.

"What do you expect from me, Master Tama? I may be my mother's daughter, but I was brought up without Chesan training. I know how to kill and destroy as a Blue Level Assassin Commander in the Odean Hierarchy. I don't know how to invoke any kind of Chesan rituals or give you powers I don't understand. I don't know what to do for you. I didn't even get the seduction training at Green Level because I was too young." Tridia's frustration seeped into her voice. "You know I'm inexperienced. Why would you want me of all the women you could have?"

Tama stood with his side to her, his arm stretched full length, and his weight against her sternum, cutting off her breath. She couldn't administer the *deathstrike* from that angle. She could try a kick to his knee, but if she missed he'd turn her position to his advantage.

"Your mother left explicit instructions on how to deal with you, and only by obeying her to the letter can you give me what I want."

"Then my mother was one sick woman." Tridia's mind raced. Her mother wouldn't have created a man like Tama simply to turn her daughter over to him. The woman had intended for Tridia to live and reach the peaceful side of the vision, not sate a sadist's twisted appetites.

Tama's face reddened and his dark eyes flashed. The turmoil of his thoughts folded into a singularity. "I've let your jibes against me go and let your suppositions run wild to keep you off balance. I won't allow you to ridicule the woman who risked everything to give you life!"

Tridia stared. "Let me go, Master Tama. Leave me alone in my cabin tonight. Don't make me go through with this without some sort of mental preparation."

The muscles in Tama's jaw tensed. "I can do that. And when I lock the door I'll go straight to the sick bay, place a blaster against the young prince's head and disintegrate his brain."

"No!" Tridia cried out without thinking and tried to force him to loosen the pressure on her chest.

"You show your hand, Commander. You're in love with this boy."

"You're wrong." Tridia's fingernails started to lengthen into claws again, and the fur sprouted on her hands and arms.

"I'm not," Tama said. "We can stand here and debate the matter all night for all I care, but if my guards don't hear from me in the next two minutes, they will kill your precious prince. So, if I were you, I'd get this Felinus transformation under control – now!"

"Contact them!" Tridia said, trying to calm her racing heart and stop the transformation that was already reshaping her teeth. "I won't resist you. I'm trying to reason with you."

"Reason with the wall, Commander. I'm tired of this game. I need you to be responsive tonight. No collar, no guards, no fights. Just you and me."

Tridia closed her eyes and wished she hadn't forced Drayden to close his mind. If she could communicate with him, make some plan –

Tridia. Drayden's presence took her by surprise and Tridia could have wept with relief.

Drayden, are there guards with you?

Yes, several and they look like they've got something nasty in mind.

They do. Whatever you do, don't anger them or make any sudden moves. If you die, I die.

All right. His thoughts seemed unsure.

Tridia let him into her mind completely then. She gave him what small hope she had to share then pushed him back.

Whatever you sense from me for the next couple of hours...

I understand. One day, I'll kill him for this. The thought came from Drayden loud and clear.

No, my pacifist prince. I will. Tridia shut her mind and lifted her chin. She drew in a few controlled breaths against the pain and the fur receded. Her claws became nails again and her teeth rounded. The effort left her weak and aching. Her teeth throbbed

"I will spend this night in any way you command, Master Tama. Call your guards and let me speak to the prince if he is awake. I want assurances he won't be harmed."

"You've already spoken to him, haven't you?"

Tridia didn't respond.

Tama backed away and let her stand free of the wall before he took her arm and led her to her cabin. He used the wall intercom to call the sick bay.

"Lieutenant Kieg, is the prisoner still alive?"

"Yes, Master." The guttural response from the Carok crackled into the room.

"He's to live tonight. See that no harm comes to him for the next four hours. I will contact you by end of watch. If you do not hear from me by then, kill him." Anger flashed again in Tama's eyes. "Is he awake?"

"Yes, Master."

"Let him speak." Tama backed away from the intercom and allowed Tridia to approach.

"Prince Drayden, are you well?" Tridia asked.

"I'm better for hearing the sound of your voice." Drayden's voice sounded weak compared with the strength of his thoughts.

"Do as they tell you. I hope to see you in the next watch."

"Rest well."

Tama silenced the intercom. With his eyes locked on Tridia's he stepped close and took her by the arm, forcing her to walk backwards. She walked on faith that the woman who'd molded her had planned for this contingency. Whatever her mother had instructed Ren Tama to do, Tridia hoped had more to do with the Chaos Vision than anything erotic.

"Sit." Tama said.

Tridia turned to see a chair behind her. She sat.

"Open your mouth." He pulled a vial of dark purple liquid from his jacket pocket.

Tridia sprang to her feet.

"What is that?" She eyed the vial. The enhancement drugs used by the assassins and covert agents of Odea produced uninhibited behavior in their recipients. Above all nights, she couldn't afford to lose control on this one.

"Something given to me by your mother." Tama caressed the vial with his thumb as he spoke. "This will induce the cycle you haven't grown into yet."

Tridia dared a glance into Tama's mind. Even though his thoughts and emotions had grated on her all evening, she hadn't intentionally sought information from him. Master Aren had warned her not to enter Tama's mind, and she'd heeded his warning – until now. She needed to know what he planned.

Tama's mind swirled in illusions and imaginings, but at the forefront was the memory of a woman who looked very much like Tridia, with dark hair and gray eyes. The woman's every movement was sensuous. Her touch sent tingles up his arm and stirred the core of his being. He hungered for her and she led him on, feeding him just enough to keep him restrained. She handed him a vial, told him to give it to the girl when she was older, old enough to understand her role, not still a child. The woman teased him and he responded with lust.

Tridia's mind became entwined with Tama's. His memory became her memory and blood rushed to her head, stirring emotions like the ones she'd experienced with Drayden under the influence of the pollen. Part of her realized the trap she'd caught herself in, another part wanted to relish the feelings that welled within her. She fought to disengage the memory and the sensations but found her body moving toward Tama. His surprise at her sudden change in behavior almost broke the bond between them, but Tridia couldn't get her traitorous body under control. She wrapped her arms around his neck, meshed her fingers in his hair, and pulled his mouth down to hers.

Tama pushed her away, but her emotions were bound to his memories and she couldn't stay away. He grabbed her arm when she came close and spun her around, holding her back against his chest with one arm. Tridia cried out and struggled to turn in his hold, but he held her in place as he brought the opened vial to her lips.

"Drink half of this." Tama panted.

Eager to please him as the woman in his memory had, Tridia allowed him to pour the liquid on her tongue. She held it in her mouth for a moment, then swallowed. As she stood with her back to his chest, her heart pounded in rhythm with his, his breathing became as ragged as hers, but he continued to hold her.

Tridia had given up hope of escaping Tama's thoughts when a hot flash started in her stomach, traveled up her throat, into her mouth. Blue energy snaked around her skin and became a cocoon of power encasing her body. It flung Tama backward against a wall. He melted to the floor. She stared at him without understanding. Her emotions stabilized as his mind became silent, but power pricked her skin. Surges of energy pulsed with her heartbeat. Comprehension blossomed in her mind.

The portal contained more than mists and flashes of light. It stored life. The essence of millions of lives comingled in the mists. Past, present, and future converged and changed in its vortex. As the drug opened her mind Tridia became aware of the enormity of power at her disposal. Her brief passes through the portals took their toll on her body and now she knew why. It was a place of diffused temporal energy where corporeal entities couldn't last. The time surges – the swirling mists – would tear away at anything bound in flesh and diffuse it throughout time.

Tridia let the energy course through her. Every cell called out for release from its mortal bondage and it took everything she had to hold herself together.

"Mother, what were you thinking?" she whispered. "To put so much power into the hands of one person – How can I handle this?"

She remembered her mother's voice in the mists. *Her mother's voice.* It hadn't been a vision or a dream. Her mother had spoken to her. The essence of the woman lingered in the portal. Tridia's hands shook as she formed a small circle using her index fingers and thumbs. She stared through the circle, seeing only the wall beyond it at first, then the space wavered and dissolved into a golden glow. A small portal opened between her hands. A face like her own, but older, appeared.

"You've come, Olana, my child." The face spoke in a voice Tridia remembered from her first visit to the mists.

An older memory called to her. A blinding flash of pain seared her eyes. The other barrier block. Tridia winced away the pain.

"I'm compelled to come." A strange calm settled in Tridia's mind and body. "My name is Tridia Odana now. The name you chose for me didn't survive my upbringing."

"Very well, Tridia. Ren Tama didn't wait the full eighteen years. Something desperate must have happened. Are you under attack? Are you injured?" There was genuine concern in her mother's thoughts.

"We're at risk, but not under attack as yet. I'm fine, but I may have injured him."

"I sense your anger, Tridia, but you mustn't kill him – and no, this has nothing to do with Chesan pacifism. You'll need him in your future. The Chesan race will need him. We haven't much time. The drug's power will wear off. It was only meant to bring you clarity so you could control your powers. They have been emerging, haven't they?"

"Yes," Tridia said.

"Have you discovered the Kel Anec threat? Have they attacked anywhere?"

"They've made covert attacks and quiet take-overs, but they're getting bolder."

"Let me give you my thoughts so you can understand the enormity of their position."

"I've closed my mind to protect Prince Drayden from what I feared would be my rape. We've mentally bonded. He's got to be worried about me. He won't understand what's happened."

"You've bonded with the prince? But you haven't mated?" The urgency in the question sent a shiver up Tridia's spine.

Tridia grimaced. "The Chaos Vision interrupted us before we mated. At present, I'm his protector. Ren Tama found him and beat him unconscious to find me. He used Drayden to blackmail me into submission."

"The path you walk now is a treacherous one. You must *not* mate with the prince before this war has ended. Steel yourself, Tridia. Any sexual union between you while you still have battles to face will assure the horrific side of chaos – especially now with your powers about to mature. You haven't lived the life I would have chosen for my daughter, but it is one that will stand you in good stead in the years ahead." Elise's face softened. "Open your mind, Tridia Odana, I can protect our prince from this painful knowledge and perhaps heal his body in the process."

Tridia dropped her barrier, opening her mind to receive her mother's thoughts. The touch of Elise's mind was gentle and familiar, but it invoked the barrier block's punishing pain. Information poured into her mind despite the agony. It came so fast she couldn't comprehend everything. Some pieces of history she recognized from Drayden's lessons, other things were new. Then finally the thing she waited for sprang into her mind and Tridia's eyes widened with wonder.

"It's that simple?" she asked.

"It may seem simple, but be wary. The energy required to perform even the smallest of these tasks could destroy you at this point. You must give your power time to mature. Recall and practice the skills I've described in this transfer. Most of what you've just learned will fade from your consciousness when the portal closes and you'll have to recall it as you mature. If the timeline remains intact, you should have a few years to do this. When you've mastered the techniques I've shown you, use the toy I gave you as a child. Ren has it. It's the final clue to take you to the tool you'll need to win this war. Use it wisely. The song I sang to you as an infant will open the toy. You've opened this small portal on your own for the first time and its energy sustains you – practically makes you invincible. Be careful, daughter, this power is addicting and debilitating. Use it with care only when necessary. *Only* with very small exposure until your powers mature. You'll be weaker than ever when you close this link. The weakness is the first stage. As your body grows accustomed to the energy, you will feel the effects less and less. Therein lies the danger. It will eat away at your body and mind if you absorb it too soon. You *will* lose your sanity. Slowly and in small stages. Hurry now, you and Drayden have been exposed too long."

"Are you – Mother, are you alive in the mists?"

"We'll discuss my presence another time. Now close this breach and rest your body. Let your prince know you're safe. He's worried. I must communicate with Ren."

The circle lost its golden glow and faded until Tridia found herself looking at the wall through the circle of her fingers. Power seeped from her body and she sank to the floor, her dress forming a purple heap of fabric around her. She looked down at herself. The blue energy ran off her skin in rivulets and drained toward Tama's body. Shivering, she pulled the covers from the bed to wrap around her shoulders.

Drayden? Even broadcasting the single word exhausted her.

I'm still here. Are you alright? Drayden asked the question but Tridia could tell he feared the answer.

I'm unharmed. What did you sense?

Silence hung in her mind for so long Tridia feared she or Drayden had fallen asleep. When he responded his thoughts were hesitant and tinged with sadness.

I felt your passion. It was savage.

That wasn't my passion. Tridia tried to hold her concentration, but it faltered. *It was his memories. A mistake in judgment on my part. Rest now. I'm safe.*

Tridia's connection with Drayden severed. She lacked the strength to concentrate. Her last coherent thought was that Ren Tama's hand moved toward her.

CHAPTER FORTY-SEVEN

Drayden lay with his eyes closed, confused by what had just happened. His connection with Tridia, so close even through their barriers, had pulled him into the heady emotions she'd experienced. Her absolute abandon had shocked him. Tridia had struggled against her passion and lost until Tama told her to drink something. She'd been so eager to please the beast that she'd taken it without hesitation. The emotional entrapment ended abruptly and a surge of power had shot through Drayden's body, mending broken bones and damaged organs. His pain ceased and his mind cleared. Whatever Tridia had experienced spilled its effects to him. Then the power and his strength faded, leaving him in his current state – whole, but too weak to open his eyes.

"Prince Drayden?" Lera whispered.

"Yes." Drayden's voice rasped in his ears.

"Master Tama has ordered that you be awake when he gets here. He's on his way."

"I'm conscious." Drayden forced his eyes open and blinked against the light.

"Can I do anything? He sounds really angry."

"Then don't get in his way. If he's angry he'll be looking for someone to hurt. You shouldn't be anywhere near me."

"Take these." She slipped a small packet into his hand. "It's medication. If they take you back to the cell they may not let us care for you. The red ones are pain killers, the blue are antibiotics, the yellow ones will make you sleep. If they – if you're cut, take the antibiotics. Take only one of any of them at a time in a standard day. They're very strong. There's six doses of each."

"Thank you," Drayden said. "Please go now."

Drayden slipped the packet into the hem of his shirt through an opening the girl had made the day before. They'd hidden his palmed drugs there. Her assistance had surprised him, but he'd followed all of her suggestions because he recognized her face from Tridia's memories – and from the Chaos Vision. Lera Cal was the second blonde queen in the peaceful vision. A queen for whom he'd felt no love or passion, but who sat on the Chesan throne, nonetheless.

Ren Tama stormed through the door. His disheveled appearance indicated that whatever had happened hadn't been gentle for him. Bloodshot eyes flashed at Lera. "Leave us."

She left without speaking and Drayden gave her time to get away before he raised his eyes to Tama. The master assassin's face glowered with fury contained by the finest of nets. Behind the barriers of his mind, Drayden pondered the cause of that fury. Tama had ignited Tridia's passion, but he hadn't received the explosive ending he'd expected. Even so, why direct anger at him?

Tama covered the distance that separated them in three steps and gathered the front on Drayden's shirt in one hand, pulling him to a sitting position.

"What is the connection between the two of you, Prince Drayden Anjenay?" Tama's demand caught Drayden off guard.

"What?" he asked.

"She's more than your bodyguard. More than a protector. I just spoke to her and she said your name in her sleep. She apologized to you. I want to know what has happened between the two of you." Tama's nostrils flared.

"I've known her all of three weeks, one of them I was unconscious." Drayden received a backhand slap for his answer. He stared into Tama's angry face and forced himself to remain still.

"You were together on that planet. What happened? Don't tell me she studied."

"Then should I make up something for you?" Another slap and Tama hauled Drayden to his feet. "Beat me all you want. It won't change the facts. She saved my life when a desert creature would have killed me. She nursed me through the night and we followed the Rrabbas to their birthing grounds. Under the effects of their pollen, our minds bonded. I kissed her – once. That's all she would allow. I took her to my bunker and she searched my archives like a woman obsessed. I begged her to take me with her when she left and she refused. That's the great romance you fear. A malfunctioning AI opened the door to the bunker, just as I said, and you brought me here and tortured me. The next time I saw her she was kneeling beside me in the cell, and she's been encouraging me to hold on and get well so she can fulfill her pledge to protect me. She's no more personally attached to me than she is to you. Tridia belongs to Brenden Aren. She's his slave. But she promised to protect me with her life."

The conviction in his voice had to make the lies sound true. If Tama ever found out the depth of his connection to Tridia, the assassin would kill one or both of them. Tama released him and Drayden leaned against the bed to keep from falling. Drayden remained motionless and silent as his captor prowled the room. When Tama stopped and glared at him, Drayden tried to stand erect.

"You're lying. That apology wasn't for letting you get injured. It was for wanting me. Shall I tell you about the abandon she released in my arms — or did you feel the emotions that claimed her?"

"If you feel the need to brag. My bodyguard's sensual pleasures aren't my concern. I respect myself too much to pursue a girl who doesn't want me. There will be other women. I am all that remains of a noble family and she has a responsibility for my safety. That's where our relationship ends." Drayden's abdomen tightened as he spoke. He had to make Tama believe his disinterest.

Tama crossed his arms over his chest.

"You're a smart man — if you can be believed. You're going back to your cell tonight. If Commander Odana insists on seeing you, she can look through the plasma field. In the meantime, you should get some rest, Your Highness, you look tired."

Drayden collapsed onto the bed as soon as Tama left. His face smarted from the blows, but Tama hadn't reinjured his jaw. Lera slipped into the room and helped him get under the thin cover.

"Are you injured again?" she asked.

Drayden shook his head. "That was gentle compared to his previous bursts of temper."

"His sentries are gone for now, but the cameras are still active so I suggest you not try to leave this room." The look in her eyes told Drayden that the girl's advice wasn't meant in the harsh tone she used.

"I doubt I could leave if I wanted to." Drayden managed a weak smile.

Strength returned to his body slowly. A few more hours and he'd be able to run if Tridia needed him to, and they could make good their escape. Tama had said she was sleeping. Drayden couldn't sense her mind or emotions. After the ordeal she'd been through he understood the need. But he couldn't sleep. His mind wouldn't rest.

"This is a large ship, isn't it?" he asked.

"Two thousand crewmen." Lera Cal tucked Drayden's sheet under the mattress as she spoke.

"I've been out of touch for a long time, but that sounds huge. Are there pilots among the crew? I've always wondered what it would be like to pilot a small craft, like a fighter or a shuttle."

"There's a full complement of fighters and twelve shuttles for ship to surface travel. Don't get any ideas. Those shuttles are too slow to make an escape and the fighters are in a separate hangar two floors up. I'm sure they wouldn't let you anywhere near them." Lera Cal winked conspiratorially.

"If you see Commander Odana, please tell her – Thank her for protecting me. I doubt he'll let me see her before they take me back to the cell tonight. I just hope I'm not asleep the next time she visits." Drayden adjusted his pillow. Lera Cal nodded. She understood his message. He needed to be conscious.

"If I see her, I'll tell her you showed signs of recovery. Now rest."

Drayden closed his eyes again and lay motionless for the cameras. He tried several times to reach out to Tridia without opening his mind, but had no success. He eventually drifted into a fitful sleep.

Several hours later, the sick bay lighting flashed red and four Carok guards ran into the room with weapons drawn.

"You come with us," the commander grunted.

"He's too weak to walk." Lera protested, following the guards into the room. One of them shoved her aside without slowing down.

Two more guards dragged Drayden to his feet and hustled him out the door. He struggled to gain his footing and managed to lope along with them as they forced him down the red-lit corridors. They passed the brig without slowing. Had Tama found some new way to torture him? The Caroks stopped at the docking bay and held him against the observation window. An unmarked black ship settled into the bay. Its hatch opened and four men clad in black armor descended the ramp. Tridia had dealt with men in black armor. They'd taken a Chesan survivor from the hospital ship, *Healer*. Fear inched up his spine like a cold hand.

"Commander Xiang. How nice of you to come so far out of your way to retrieve our guest," Tama said.

Drayden started at the sound of Tama's voice. He hadn't seen or heard the master assassin approach.

"The Kanuan monarchy is anxious for the prince's safety. They trust he has been well treated." Commander Xiang spoke through a tinny voice modulator.

"I have no wish to travel to Kanu." Drayden's objection drew everyone's attention. "I'm grateful to the Kanuan monarchy for their concern, but I wish to remain on this ship for the time being. No doubt Master Tama would deliver me there as a courtesy to the crown."

"Our apologies, Your Highness, but the prime minister was most insistent that we transport you to Kanu immediately." Xiang's tinny voice held no emotion.

"The Hierarchy has no wish to offend the Monarchy of Kanu," Tama stated. "The prince has not been well. As you can see, we've brought him here from his bed. We've cared for him to the best of our abilities in the sick bay, but perhaps it would be better to get him to proper facilities on Kanu. You might want to keep him sedated on the journey."

Drayden shot Tama a look of pure hate. "I doubt that will be necessary, Master Tama. I'm sure they have other means of dealing with my comforts. Is that not correct, Commander Xiang?"

"You will be well looked after, Your Highness. I'm sure you'll have no objections once we've left this ship."

"No doubt." Drayden stared at his reflection in Xiang's darkened visor.

He considered resisting, but with so many armed guards there wouldn't be a point. They didn't have to kill him to subdue him and the result would be the same. He'd end up on the black ship. Injuries to him would only hurt Tridia for no reason.

Tridia. He tried to rouse her consciousness. *They're taking me off the ship. They say to Kanu. Can you hear me?*

Drayden? You sound so far away. Tridia's sluggish thoughts reached him as he entered the docking bay surrounded by armored guards. He sighed audibly.

Tama's turned me over to soldiers dressed in black armor. The ship is black and unmarked.

Drayden, no! You've got to get away from them. The force of Tridia's thoughts hit him between the eyes and he winced.

It's no use, Tridia. Find me if you can. If it's too late when you reach me, destroy me. Don't let them use me – use us – the way we saw in the vision. Have no mercy just because it's my body they're using. I don't want to be a mindless drone.

I'll find you Drayden. Close your mind and keep it shut tight. I'll find you. Keep them out as long as you can.

Good-bye, my mate.

Drayden turned at the top of the ramp. Ren Tama stood on the bay floor, grim-faced and arms crossed. His mind had folded in on itself, unreadable and unreachable. Anger and hatred the like of which Drayden had never experienced boiled in his heart. With his mind fully opened he focused his thought energy like a javelin toward Tama's face. The master assassin's head jerked back before he slumped to the ground. The guards gathered around him.

Drayden closed his mind with his strongest barriers, turned, and walked into the black ship. He hadn't mastered the full energy block contained in Tridia's memories, but he could practice it behind his own shield. He'd have to perfect it quickly. His captors wouldn't take him to Kanu. Whatever waited on the ship would be more dangerous than anything Ren Tama could contemplate.

I won't give in to them, Tridia. Darkness closed around Drayden's mind as the ramp sealed behind him.

CHAPTER FORTY-EIGHT

The *Cera Gale,* carrying Brenden and Tran, dropped out of hyperspace just beyond the Hulac shield. Deeca and Winniel followed seconds later in the *Star Seeker.* A formation of six ships awaited them, black against the star field and nearly invisible to the eye. Brenden activated the *Cera Gale's* shield and waited for the black ships to make the next move.

"*Cera Gale,* come in." Deeca called on a secure channel.

"This is the *Cera Gale,*" Brenden answered.

"Winniel says these ships are Alanel's escort to Aga," Deeca said. "She asks if you would be present for the transfer of his body."

"I'll disembark at transfer platform three," Brenden said. "Tran can take the *Cera Gale* down from there. I'll accompany you afterward in the *Star Seeker.*"

Numerous small transfer platforms circled Hulac in stationary orbit. Too small to be considered docking stations, they allowed personnel to come from the planet's surface in the fruit tugs and board transport without polluting the atmosphere or risking contamination from alien vessels. All personnel transfers were performed by airlock. Brenden watched from the observation window as Tran eased the *Cera Gale* away and Deeca brought the *Star Seeker* alongside. After a few minutes Winniel guided the anti-gravity sled into the platform's receiving room. The Hierarchy attendants had wrapped Alanel's body in a pristine white cloth that shimmered as Winniel moved the sled into the light.

"I know there's nothing I could say to comfort you," Brenden said. He moved closer to the observation window to observe one of the black Sentinel ships replace the *Star Seeker* at the airlock. "While we have a moment alone, I want to thank you for everything you and Alanel have done. There was information transmitted to Elrel station that has been disseminated to the Guardians and the Sentinels, proving the Hierarchy was under attack from outside and within. It confirmed the intergalactic threat. Alanel didn't die in vain."

"No, he didn't," Winniel said. "But his mission, and mine, remains incomplete as long as Commander Odana and the Chesan prince are in danger. I will take the Chesan ship from here and meet with the Commander when she calls for me."

"She passed a plan to you before Tama took her away."

"Yes, Ambassador, and I cannot divulge her plan. Please don't ask for the details." Winniel caught Brenden's gaze. "I will commit Alanel's remains into the hands of my clan, then I'll leave. Few non-Sentinels have ever observed the ceremony you're about to see, but since you were present at Alanel's last breath, it's fitting you should be here to witness his rebirth."

"I am honored, Truthsayer, and I will do my best to honor him," Brenden said. He hadn't expected the tightening in his chest, and he set his jaw against any show of emotion.

Seven Sentinels came through the airlock. A J'Nai couple, Shanigan couple, and three Harioks – two male and one female. All knelt around Alanel's body without speaking. Brenden backed to the wall to be out of the way. Winniel stepped to Alanel's covered head and touched her hands to his hidden face as she'd done in the council room on Odea.

"Alanel, my mate, you have passed into memory where you will once again be reunited with our clans. You served well and with courage, be at peace in our thoughts." Winniel clasped hands with the Sentinels kneeling on either side of her, and they in turned joined hands with those beside them until they formed a circle around Alanel's corpse, heads bowed and eyes closed. They remained in that attitude for some minutes, until the Hariok male on Winniel's left stood and took her hand in his. She stood.

"Receive the life of the one who's gone before and awaken to me anew." Winniel touched the man's face as she had Alanel's. He closed his eyes and a look of supreme ecstasy crossed his features. A fierce light blazed in his eyes when he opened them again, focused only on Winniel.

"You have restored my life and my thoughts, Winniel. Receive me now as your mate. I am Ofein." The man pulled Winniel into his arms and engaged her in a passionate kiss.

The ceremony concluded, the other six Sentinels escorted Alanel's body through the airlock. Winniel didn't watch. Ofein kept her face tucked into the base of his neck and held her close. When the sound of the ship disengaging the airlock reached them, Winniel stepped away from Ofein and turned to Brenden.

"This is my mate, Ofein," she said. "Together we will finish the mission we've been given and honor the vows we've made."

"Ambassador," Ofein said. His voice sounded identical to Alanel's in Brenden's ears. "I thank you for the respect you showed Alanel and the courtesy you've granted Winniel. Alanel's memories are mine now, my mind was empty until he filled that void. I am not Alanel, please make the distinction."

"I will do my best, Ofein," Brenden said, not sure if there was a formal acknowledgment he should give. "Welcome to Hulac. My home will always be open to you."

***

Deeca joined Brenden and Tran outside the decontamination chamber on Hulac. Two medics hustled the unconscious Sonei toward the main house. Winniel and Ofein were already jogging toward the Chesan ship.

"Should we let them go?" she asked.

"Which one of you wants to step up to stop them?" Tran countered. "Did you see the look in her eyes? People are going to die and I don't want to be the first in line."

"What do we do now?" Deeca addressed her question to Brenden. "Any idea where Tama may have taken Tridia?"

"I can only speculate since I can't read Tama's thoughts," Brenden said. "His mind doesn't work like anyone else's."

"Winniel said the same thing," Deeca said. "She didn't talk much on the way here, apart from a few oaths to take Ren Tama apart if he dishonored the Commander. She did say Tama's mind was muddled. What does that mean?"

"Each person's thoughts are different, like their voices," Brenden explained, as they walked through the huttle orchard. "For instance, you, Deeca. Your emotions are strong and reading them is like looking through a telescope at the sun. I have to shield myself. I don't always see your thoughts clearly. Whereas Tran couldn't hide a thought in a forest but sensing his true emotions amid the false ones he always emits is exhausting."

Tran smiled. "I guess that's something I can hold dear, as you're shooting me in the back for this knowledge you've handed out so freely."

"Give it a rest, my friend," Brenden said. "Tama's thoughts are like looking at the back side of a tapestry. Things are skewed and tattered, thoughts appear broken and his emotions interweave with memory. Nothing makes sense unless you're on the inside looking out. Once you get inside that maelstrom, there's no breaking free. We were young officers on furlough in a tavern on some loose-cultured planet in free space. I made the mistake of getting inside his mind while we were playing cards. I was trapped there for two days sharing in every immoral act he could conjure – and thrilled to do so. I have a tattoo on my hip to commemorate the experience. I escaped only after he fell into an exhausted stupor. We almost missed our transport back to the ship. I never made the mistake of slipping into Tama's mind after that, although there have been times I've wanted to."

"Like this time," Deeca said.

"This is definitely one of them," Brenden confirmed. "Tran and I will make a few inquiries to our confidential sources to see if we can find Tama's ship. I need to speak with Robel. We'll leave tomorrow morning, so enjoy your time on the ground while you can."

***

Before Brenden, Deeca, and Tran left Hulac, the Controller issued orders for the Guardians to assemble at the Hierarchy border and wait for instructions. The instructions didn't include Brenden and Deeca, so they took the *Star Seeker* with Tran and combed free space at the edge of Odean territory, following up on every lead they could find for three days.

They took it in shifts to run the scanners and pilot the *Star Seeker*. Brenden and Tran sat in the cockpit. Brenden piloting, Tran scanning and monitoring the communications channels.

"Communication from the Embassy," Tran said. "Prince Drayden Anjenay is on his way to Kanu with a black guard escort. Master Ren Tama sends his compliments."

"Anything about Commander Odana?" Brenden asked.

"Nothing. That's the entire message." Tran removed the earpiece he'd been wearing.

Brenden swore. "Tama's still got her, and she would never have parted from Drayden if she had any way to prevent it. To Kanu of all places! Why would he send Drayden to Kanu?" Brenden sat in silence considering his options. Only one made any sense. "He's letting me know I now have the choice to chase Drayden or come after Commander Odana."

Deeca entered the cockpit as he spoke.

"We're going after Commander Odana?" she asked.

"No, we try to intercept the ship that's allegedly going to Kanu," Brenden replied. "Commander Odana is adept at caring for herself. If she's with Ren Tama she's not in immediate danger from the Kel Anec. Whatever Tama has planned for her won't impact the galaxy and she'll extract her pound of flesh for any unsavory actions he may take.

483

Besides, the Sentinels are looking for her.

"Prince Drayden, on the other hand, has no battle experience or intelligence about his captors. He could give the Kel Anec the means to the end they want. We have to save him or destroy him."

"May I remind you that this ship doesn't have the weaponry to take on a Fighter Hawk?" Deeca slid into the co-pilot's seat. She carried a plate of fruit that she munched between comments. "We couldn't engage in a fire fight anyway without risking the prince."

"I never said anything about engaging in a fire fight. We just need to find out where the ship is going."

Tran looked from one to the other of them. "Did I miss something? The message said Prince Drayden was being escorted to Kanu."

"Ren Tama may believe he is on the way to Kanu," Brenden said. "The Kel Anec operatives controlling Kanu are just that, operatives. Drayden is the noble piece in this game. They won't risk sending him to any place from which he might be rescued. They'll take him to their stronghold, and my instincts tell me that's Cystia."

"Send word to the embassy. Tell them to contact the Sentinels, it's urgent. We're going to need them if we have to go into the mine." Brenden stood in the small space and waited for Tran's communication.

The embassy response came within minutes.

"All Sentinels have vacated Aga. Only a handful remain to guard their compounds." Tran said. "No explanation."

"Do you sense anything from the Controller?" Brenden asked Deeca.

She shook her head. "Not since he called the Guardians to assemble at the border. It's as if he locked down the communications. There's only a skeleton staff in the Warren to hold security."

"Perfect." Brenden slid back into the pilot's seat and entered a new navigational heading. "We've played right into their hands."

"We're going without help?" Tran asked.

"We've made sure there is no one to help us. They've taken Drayden. Anza has only a handful of guards instead of an entire clan of Sentinels. The Kel have to know I'll go after Drayden, leaving Anza open. The Controller, possibly their greatest threat, is unprotected and weakened on a barren planet." Brenden engaged the engines at full speed.

"And Tridia?" Deeca turned in her seat just in time for the hyperdrive shift.

"Do you think anything in this galaxy could keep her from Drayden? She passed through a portal and got under the Chesan shield on his exile planet – two impossibilities. Escaping Tama will be child's play. She'll go to Drayden. Threaten him and she'll submit just as she did with

Tama. They'll take her without a fight. I was a fool to let her live!" Brenden slapped the arm of his chair in frustration. "The Kel Anec have out maneuvered us all along."

"Now that you know, is there any way to counter?" Deeca asked.

"There's a chance, but its infinitesimal. They predicted the outcome of every scenario, waited at the optimal junctions and made their moves with efficiency. The Commander has been the unknown factor. They didn't know she existed so they didn't plan for her. If they were linked to Frees B'Nay, they may believe she is dead. Our hope lies in the fact they don't know where she is or the full extent of her powers."

"Tama only mentioned Drayden in his communication," Tran said. "He still had Tridia under wraps at the time."

"He won't hold her long. She won't let him."

Brenden pulled the slender threads of his plan together. Deeca and Tran would object, but there were no other options. "Cystia is our target, but the two of you can't go to the planet's surface. Tran has no protection from the feeders and I can't remove them if they attach. With the Controller's silence, Deeca may also be at risk."

"I hope you aren't saying you're going to Cystia alone," Deeca said.

"No. I'll go to the planet with Prince Drayden."

A chorus of protests greeted his answer, as expected, and Brenden was grateful for the barriers that protected his mind from their anger. When the furor died down he launched into his explanation.

"I can protect my own mind for an indefinite period, and I doubt the Kel would allow the feeders to attach to Drayden or me unless we resist. If we resist passively, they'll just wait us out. I'm hoping the Commander will arrive before either of us submits."

"You just said she'd be no help. She'll give up if Drayden is threatened."

Brenden caught Deeca's glare in his peripheral vision, but he kept his eyes averted.

"If I'm there she'll have a harder time surrendering. It's our only option. We can't risk entering the mine without the Sentinels or the Controller. Our allies are engaged in a senseless battle that we orchestrated. The Hierarchy is imploding and the Guardians are at the border, but to help or conquer? The Sentinels have vanished. We've got the three most powerful forces in the galaxy out of position and vulnerable to a surprise attack."

"You realize if Tridia can't escape from Tama, you're handing yourself over to the monsters in that vision she conjured up," Tran said.

"I know," Brenden replied. "Someone has to get close enough to Drayden to destroy him if the Commander doesn't make it. I stand the best chance of that."

"Is it really that bad?" Tran asked. "You and Tridia are both committed to obliterating yourselves and this prince. Do you even know if it would help?"

"It's that bad," Brenden replied. "The vision was too clear. As long as Commander Odana is alive and sane, there's hope. If she falls, it would be best to destroy anyone the Kel Anec could use to reach their goals."

Deeca made no argument and Brenden chanced a glance in her direction. He sat upright in his seat and stared into Deeca's eyes. They'd taken on a distant look.

"What do you have to tell me about my induction?" Deeca raised her left forearm. Her eyes came into focus on Brenden. "Why was my training different from the other Guardians?"

Brenden turned to Tran. "Give us a few minutes here, will you?"

"Yeah, well, there's probably something really interesting going on in Deeca's cabin," Train said. "Why don't the two of you just go back and check it out? I can handle the ship for a while."

Brenden followed Deeca to her cabin. She shut the door and waited. Brenden had dreaded the day he'd hear those questions. They signaled a galaxy-changing event.

"The Controller sent me to watch over you the day of your induction. I'd had my own bands for less than three years at the time and I rebelled against the call to appear in the Warren. I never wanted to see that chamber again, but I went – I had no option.

"Two big Guardians bound and gagged me, then the Controller locked me behind a rock wall with only a slit to see through. The two Guardians stood in front of the wall so no one would get in the way. They wanted to make sure I had a clear view of the proceedings. They made me watch an entire class of candidates go through the induction torment. I was so disoriented I couldn't see clearly. All of the Guardian elect thought the ceremonies were finished. Everyone left except the two with me, then you came in with your eyes glazed. I knew you were in a trance, but I couldn't move to help you. You stood before the vat of gold and when your arms went out –" Brenden stopped and groped for the right words to describe what he'd witnessed. "The other candidates screamed when the molten gold wrapped around their wrists. The gold didn't wrap around your wrists, it encased your body. The Controller filtered your pain through me so the other Guardians wouldn't feel its intensity and think something had gone wrong. I nearly died from the agony of it.

"When I came to I was lying on the floor beside you. While I was out, the two Guardians covered you with the unguent and your flesh returned to cover the gold, except for the bands. They looked like any

Guardian bands, just wider, but I knew better. The Controller told me everything had been necessary, because you would be the future salvation of the Guardians. In the meantime, I was to be your personal Guardian, unseen and unknown. I resented the hell out of it until the day I touched your mind and saw the hopes and dreams you'd lost through no fault of your own."

Memories of that time flooded Brenden's thoughts. Deeca had hoped to marry and have children. She wanted nothing more than to live on the obscure planet where her father held a small kingdom and raise children in the traditions she'd known all her life. The Controller took those things away from her. Now the entity wanted Brenden to explain what happened. Behind his barriers, he couldn't sense Deeca's emotions. She'd have to share them on her own.

"I'd never touched a weapon in my life before that day. After my convalescence – which I couldn't remember – I woke up and knew how to use everything from swords to blasters. I knew how to kill and maim and injure." Deeca wiped angrily at the tears on her cheeks. "I realized I didn't feel the heat and cold the way I used to. I had physically become someone else and I could hear the Guardian's voices in my head. I heard the Gold's commands resonate through my body. You knew about this all along."

Brenden let the accusation hang in the air unanswered. He'd been as compelled to obedience as she.

"It's worse than that," he said, in a hoarse whisper. "After the Gold explained what had happened, the two Guardians helped me take you off-world where they left us in isolation to train. With so much sentient Gold in you, you were too vulnerable to be with any of the other Guardians. You'd have connected to every Guardian within the system before you could control those links. I had to nurse you back to health and train you."

"Why don't I recall any of this?" Deeca asked.

"Between the two of us, the Controller and I blocked those memories. I couldn't have done it on my own without leaving a painful trace."

"Unblock them," Deeca said.

"You don't want to see those memories, Deeca." Brenden's heart raced. With his entire being he wanted her to know what they'd shared. But having lived with the pain of denial for ten years, he couldn't be cruel enough to expose Deeca to something that could never be.

"Unlock them." Deeca's violet-blue eyes warmed. "As much as Tridia needed her memories, I need mine. It isn't fair for you to shoulder that burden alone."

Brenden took Deeca's face in his hands and lowered his forehead to hers.

"This may be uncomfortable," he whispered.

Deeca nodded.

He dropped the strongest barriers around his mind and touched her thoughts with all the gentleness he could manage, whispering words to conjure memory trails for him to follow to the place he'd hidden their past.

I'm sorry.

Like touching the latch on a spring-loaded lid, when Brenden released Deeca's memories they poured forth into her consciousness and his. Two weeks of utter agony flowed through her mind. Brenden fed her and cared for her needs while she lay in a frightened stupor. Another two weeks passed before she could stand on her own. He explained their situation and Deeca refused to believe it at first. After a few weeks she gave in and learned everything Brenden could teach her. The more he pushed her, the more she gave. They'd grown close – too close. Brenden left their cottage and camped in the wilderness to avoid the temptation they both endured, but her emotions drew him back, no longer willing to resist. They'd fallen into each other's arms like spirits possessed, and only came up for air when the Guardian transport arrived to take them away.

"There was no way we could be together once we left the planet," Brenden said. "You were the brightest Guardian to join the force in the centuries of their existence. I was a heretic deserter from the Hierarchy, barely acceptable in low-life company, but never with the Guardians. They would have always suspected and rejected you if they found out you were in love with me. You couldn't hide it from them once you joined their ranks. So, the Controller restrained you while I identified the memories and locked them away. We let you think you'd been recuperating in isolation all those months. It took me another two years to gain a reputable standing with the Alliance, but I could never break through to acceptance by the Guardians and by then you shared their contempt toward me."

"The Gold let that happen. Why didn't it send for us before we ever got so involved?"

"It tried. The ship the Controller sent ran into trouble crossing the Free Territories. It just got there too late," Brenden said. "Just as it's too late for us to change our paths now."

CHAPTER FORTY-NINE

"How am I supposed to be this savior?" Deeca asked. "What am I supposed to do?"

"I don't know." Brenden shook his head. "It could be anything from taking control of the Guardian Force to whatever fantasy you can conjure.

"The Controller's more than five thousand years old – transformed from a previous existence it doesn't recall. It doesn't know what form it'll take next, but it will cease to exist in its present form. It's trying to provide for the Guardians' continuation."

"That gave it the right to take my life away from me?" Deeca asked. "Twice?"

"No, it just gave it the means." Brenden looked at the thin gold bands on his wrists before he continued. "The Gold regretted the cost to you, and it's told me often it tried to find another way. Without this provision – whatever it will be – everyone wearing the bands will die when the Gold transforms. Their minds will comingle and they'll die insane, unable to function as individuals."

Deeca touched Brenden's wrist. "Is that your fate, as well?"

"I wear the bands. I could expect insanity at the very least."

"Tridia, too?"

"Have you ever seen bands like hers?" Deeca shook her head and Brenden continued. "They're not attached to her flesh. Her skin was raw and scarred, but the bands had come away the last time I saw her. They aren't imbedded the way ours are. I don't know what to make of it."

"Why me? There were hundreds of Guardians who would have volunteered for this duty."

"I asked the Controller once why it had chosen you. After the

Sharian incident, when you left the Guardians, I asked if it'd made a mistake in choosing you. It said no, if it hadn't chosen you, you would have died on your way back to your home world. Your future ended just beyond the buoy markers of Guardian space, and you could either become the Chosen of the Gold, or be murdered. The Controller chose to save you."

Deeca's shoulders slumped. "Tolen. Then his excitement to become a Guardian had been faked as well. He knew I'd come to see him before his induction. He found some way to sabotage the ship."

"The Controller never said who."

Brenden hit the intercom and spoke to Tran. "Unless there's a black ship bearing down on us with blasters and torpedoes firing, I don't want to hear a word out of you."

"Aye, skipper," Tran responded.

Brenden pulled Deeca into his arms. He held her close, kissed her hair, and offered her what strength he could give through his touch and with his thoughts. She wrapped her arms around him, content for the moment. Touching Deeca's thoughts meant exposing her to the possibility of his mental possession – or so Tridia had warned him. They were about to part, and Deeca had the Gold to protect her should he press the connection too far. He lowered the last of his barriers, and exposed Deeca's jealousy of his relationship with Tridia.

He laughed aloud and covered Deeca's lips with his, pulling back quickly as the honey-sweet taste of enzyme filled his mouth. He couldn't risk infecting her.

Commander Odana is a dangerous child. You're a desirable woman. Brenden couldn't keep the humor from his thoughts. *You have nothing to fear from that quarter.*

"I was afraid you'd see me as a freak," Deeca said.

"I'd be a fool to close my eyes to the woman you are." Brenden kissed Deeca's hair and hugged her close.

"Why aren't you kissing my lips, Brenden?" Deeca pulled back and looked into his eyes. The hurt in hers compelling a quick touch of their lips.

"Because I can't without infecting you with something we can't deal with right now," he said. "It's part of my Chesan physiology. A poisonous enzyme that could kill you if we don't –consummate the encounter."

He touched his lips to her brow to assure her his emotions were genuine. "For the past ten years I've watched you grow from an injured and confused girl to an amazing woman. I've seen you suffer beyond endurance and come back from the brink of oblivion. I've had to keep my distance, loving you the entire time. We may not survive the next few days, but I can promise you this, no matter what the Kel Anec might do to me, I'll never forget you or the way you feel in my arms right now."

Tran called on the intercom. Brenden ignored it for the moment.

"Thank you." Deeca spoke with her face hidden against his chest. "I needed this. I needed to know you care."

"Never doubt it." Brenden touched his lips to hers one last time, then pressed the intercom button.

"We've got company," Tran said. "Fighter Hawk class ship just came into sensor range."

"Don't engage and don't run. If they call for a halt, comply. I'll be there shortly."

"With all due respect, Ambassador, is this the time for – " Tran's words were cut short by Brenden's sharp reply.

"It's not what you're thinking, you degenerate-minded shape-shifter. I need a space suit, unless you want to face them on the ground."

"Sorry." Tran's voice held a chuckle.

"You're going outside the ship?" Deeca frowned.

"If they stop us and get close enough for me to walk, I'll leave the ship, but not before."

Brenden located the storage locker at the end of the short hall. Deeca followed at his heels.

"We don't have a tether long enough to span the distance between two drifting ships," Deeca said. "They're going to have to lock onto us somehow."

Once he found the suit and checked the seals Brenden turned to face Deeca. "I won't be tethered to the *Star Seeker*."

"Are you insane? You could end up floating forever out there."

"The Kel Anec can find me," Brenden said. "If they stop, they'll want me alive. If they don't stop, they aren't interested. If they come in shooting, we'll try to run. I'm betting they won't want to delay taking Drayden to their masters long enough to chase us."

"What if it's not the same ship? Just because it's a Fighter Hawk class, doesn't mean Drayden is aboard," Deeca said.

Brenden closed his eyes and opened his mind. He reached beyond the *Star Seeker* and her crew and into space. Tran's mind gave him the direction of the ship and he followed the line, stretching as far as his powers allowed. The ship appeared at the edge of his consciousness.

Several members of the crew wore no armor. The pilot of the Fighter Hawk studied his sensor readings and waited for instructions. Brenden sensed the man's consternation, but not much else. As the ships drew nearer to each other, more of the pilot's pressing thoughts became clear. He wanted to get the Chesan prince to home base. He didn't want a confrontation with an unknown ship but the masters insisted he force the Alliance ambassador to join him.

Brenden smiled and shared the humor with Deeca. "The pilot is afraid the ambassador in question is Brenden Aren. He thinks I could take over his ship if I went aboard."

"You could under normal circumstances, couldn't you?"

"Easier said than done. If I could impress the captain or one of the main crew members, maybe. I can't control a whole crew wearing armor shielding."

"Why go outside the ship?" Deeca's attempt at controlling her anxiety touched Brenden's heart.

"We can't let them attach an airlock to us. Once on board with weapons, they'd likely kill you and Tran and take me. If I'm outside, they have no reason to board. We'll make contact. If the Captain is worried, that plays in our favor. We can make a demand or two." Brenden winked and strode through the ship to the cockpit. "Hail them, Tran, on the Hierarchy's channel. Let's invite them to stop and chat."

Tran hailed the approaching ship. After a moment the Captain's curt response blared on the *Star Seeker's* speakers.

"State your business Alliance vessel. We're on a transport mission and have no time to waste with frivolity."

"Captain Eris, this is Ambassador Brenden Aren of the Odea-Hulac-Reyta embassy, lately retained to represent the Hierarchy in diplomatic relations within the Alliance territories. I wish to board your vessel."

Brenden grinned at the silence that ensued and the Captain's near stuttered reply.

"Ambassador Aren, as I've stated we're on a transport mission. If you board this ship you will remain with us for the duration of our journey. We'll be unable to stop again for you to disembark."

"Can't believe his good fortune." Brenden muted the channel and whispered to his companions. He opened the connection again and continued. "I'm willing to travel with you, Captain. The well-being of the monarch you're transporting concerns the Hierarchy as well as the Alliance. It's my intention to monitor the prince's health until he is released to his own people. I'd hate to see the Hierarchy blamed should anything happen to His Majesty."

"Very well, Ambassador. We'll dock with your ship and –"

"Your pardon, Captain." Brenden interrupted. "Our airlock is damaged. We have a suit but no tether. If you have a tether you could fire over to us I'll spacewalk the short distance to your ship."

"Remain in your present position. We'll send the tether within twenty standard."

"Thank you, Captain. I'll be waiting to receive it. *Star Seeker* out."

"Since when is the airlock damaged?" Tran asked.

"They can't chase you or turn to fire on you while I'm tethered to their hull. As soon as I've cleared enough distance, drop the ship and head for the nearest sling-sized planet. Get out of here as fast as you can. The *Star Seeker* is the only vessel that knows my whereabouts. If they destroy you – apart from making me very sad – they will be able to deny I ever boarded their ship. We lose any façade of threat and I conveniently vanish." Brenden looked from Deeca to Tran as he continued. "Do *not* follow that ship. I'll set a tracking beacon on its hull when I make contact. Report to the Sentinels and Guardians what I've done. Tell them I expect the ship to go to Cystia. They can make of that what they will. Come to Cystia if you can, but under no circumstances are you to land without hearing from me. There's no protection from the feeders and I won't risk you needlessly."

His companions nodded. Deeca's emotions buffeted the barrier he put in place, and Tran's thoughts ran the gamut of what he might do to assist. Both of them recognized a suicide mission, but they also hoped for his safe return. If they hoped for his return, they'd have trouble letting him go if the worst happened. He'd rather they not hope.

"I'll help you suit up." Deeca volunteered with a stone face.

"Go get the suit ready," Brenden said. "I need a few words with Tran."

Deeca left and Tran eyed Brenden warily. "Is this where I get it in the heart? Or the back?"

"Knock it off." Brenden scowled.

"What's the contingency plan?" Tran asked.

Brenden raised his eyebrows in surprise.

"So, I can still surprise you." Tran smiled. "How long have we worked together? That scowl shows itself when we're up against it and you're trying to devise a way out."

"Remember that your thoughts are clear as glass to me?"

"Yes, and hearing that was a little unnerving, considering some of the territory my thoughts have strayed into."

"I'm going to close my barriers – shut down my telepathy – while I give you these instructions," Brenden said. "I don't want to know what you're thinking as you hear them. Listen well and follow them to the letter. More than both our lives might depend on getting them right."

Tran watched Brenden's face intently. Brenden enforced enough of his barriers that the shifter's thoughts disappeared. "Okay."

"What? That's it?" Tran asked. "You don't turn blue or frown or give any indication when you switch this on and off?"

"None whatsoever," Brenden said. "Listen up. If I can read you that easily, another telepath can, too. You need to stay out of reach. If I'm compromised, you'll be in danger. I may be the brains behind Morgan Jacks, but it's you that makes the system work – all of it. From the embassy to the black market to the smuggling, you're the one with all of the information and the secret contacts. Without you, most of it unravels."

"I'm touched that you noticed," Tran grinned.

"I'm being serious." Brenden had to grin when Tran smiled. "Okay, fine. This is the bottom line. Commander Odana found a way to completely black out her memories. When I leave the ship, count me as lost. You know that drill."

"I knew what the drill was before you were a mind-reading freak." Tran stopped smiling. "I'm not so sure anymore."

"Stay with Deeca as long as she needs you and keep her safe if you can," Brenden said. "Once you part ways, disappear. Listen to the embassy channels and the underground sources, but don't make contact. If I'm alive, and you don't hear our code in the next six months standard, you stay disappeared. Don't come anywhere near me. Find Commander Odana, if she's alive, she's the only one who'll be able to undo what I'm about to do."

"Which is?" Tran asked.

"Erase you." Brenden let the statement hang. "If I don't remember you, they can't find you, and I'm less useful to them."

Tran's face fell. Brenden stood and placed a hand on the shifter's shoulder.

"Look at it this way," he said. "If I don't remember you, I can't kill you for all the forbidden knowledge you've gleaned in the past few weeks."

Tran served up a half-grin. "Right. Just a shifter on the run constantly looking over my shoulder in case you remembered something." He laughed. "This may actually have some paranoid possibilities."

"Send out a message to all of Jacks' contacts. Anyone wearing my face is unwelcome until you hear the code," Brenden said. "That includes Lolina and her troupe. They don't have to kill me, and they don't have to be gentle, just make sure I get nowhere near you. Move the *Elisia*. I don't want to know where you put it, just get it away from Elrel station, and take Mort H'Lar with it. He's an asset you can't afford to lose."

"Expense cap?" Tran asked.

"You have to ask?" Brenden countered. "There's no cap."

Tran grinned and turned back to the console, no doubt doing an excellent job of hiding his real emotions behind his search for the nearest sling planet and plotting a vector away from it.

***

Brenden entered Deeca's cabin, where she had the space suit ready. He put it on over his clothes. Deeca held the helmet as he secured the seals.

"Say it, Deeca. I refuse to read your mind at a time like this." Brenden took the helmet and tossed it on her bed. He dropped his barriers just enough to sense her emotions.

"We may never see each other again. We could both end up dead in this suicidal gambit. I just want you to know – I just – Thank you for all you've done, for all the things I never knew about. Thank you for being vigilant when I was being arrogant."

"They'll be here in a minute. Is there anything else?" Brenden tightened the seals on the gloves, paying careful attention to getting his fingers into the right spaces.

Deeca's face flamed and her anger kindled. "Damn you, Brenden Aren. I'm trying to tell you I love you. I want you to come back. I want us both to come back."

Brenden looked into her eyes and flashed a smile. "That's the spirit I was waiting for. I can't float off and leave you moping aboard this ship with Tran. He'll be merciless if that happens. I can't be worried about you behaving like a lovesick girl when we both need all our wits to stay alive and rescue Drayden. Now kiss me woman – but carefully."

Deeca stared open-mouthed at him, then gave a frustrated cry and threw her arms around his neck. She kissed his face, his neck, and any other bit of flesh she could reach. Finally, she touched her lips to his.

"I'll want more of that," Brenden said. "When we don't have to practice restraint."

"If there's any left to have, Morgan Jacks." Deeca lifted her chin.

Brenden gave an unintelligible reply in his pirate persona's gravelly voice. They both smiled, the tension between them dissolved. "We'd better survive this. I've waited too many years for this intimacy to be restored."

Deeca smiled. Brenden swallowed hard. He wanted her. The need to draw her memories into his screamed in his mind, just as Tridia had warned they might. Did he dare try now, with so little time and nothing but Tridia's and Drayden's experience to guide him?

Deeca sensed his hesitation and frowned.

"I need something more from you." Brenden held her at arm's length. "I need to touch your mind, to make your memories mine. I don't know how badly that would hurt you, or if it would at all."

Deeca shuddered. "It's what you were doing with her, on the planet. You were touching Tridia's mind."

"I was invading her mind," Brenden said. He had to confess the truth if he planned to expose the memory to Deeca. "It amounted to little more than a mental rape to make sure I got the truth from her. There were consequences to her actions. It was an unforgivable assault that may yet have a penalty. That's not the way I need to touch you. And I need to place part of my memories inside you."

Deeca searched his face. "If we don't do this, something bad will happen to you, won't it? I sense it."

"Yes. Another chance at insanity from what I'm told. I may be able to hold out for a while, maybe months, but if I start to slip while I'm on that ship —"

"Let's do it." Deeca cut him off. "There's no time for debate or explanation."

"You're sure?" Brenden asked.

"As sure as I've ever been about anything. You've been in my thoughts for years, this is just an extension to make it permanent."

Brenden touched his forehead to hers again and pulled back from her thoughts. *My name is Brenden Aren, will you share your memories with me?*

I am Deeca Varin. Yes, I will share my memories with you.

Brenden stepped into Deeca's memories, across feelings they'd already shared and actions they'd already taken. He lightly touched her childhood and her adolescence. It didn't take much to cement the bond between them, and he gasped when her memories became his. She tightened her arms around him.

Let me guide you into my memories. It shouldn't take much. Just say your name and hold on.

My name is Deeca Varin. Will you share your memories with me?

I am Brenden Aren. If you will have them, my memories are yours.

He pulled Deeca's consciousness into the depths of his memories but held back the full force of his presence. He showed her his parents, the strict training he'd undergone since childhood, and his betrayal into the Warren. Together they relived their time on the planet where Deeca recuperated. He exposed his short time with Tridia to end Deeca's worries, and finally he shared the feelings he held for her before leading her back to herself.

Brenden. The whisper of his name was a gentle touch on his thoughts.

They lingered only a moment before parting. Their bonding wasn't as intense as he'd sensed Tridia's had been with Drayden, but he wasn't the king's son, and Deeca wasn't Chesan nobility.

"We'll finish it when we meet again."

"Yes, we will," Deeca declared. She gave him a lingering kiss on the cheek.

"We'd better get to the airlock," Brenden said. "Just one more thing, once I leave the ship, only refer to Tran as the pilot. Don't mention him by name – to anyone."

Deeca frowned but agreed as she opened the door and preceded Brenden to the airlock. He pulled the helmet onto his head, shutting out the sounds of the ship and any other words Deeca might have said. He placed her memories inside a black vault and set them safely aside. Straightening his shoulders, he turned his back on her and walked into the tiny airlock. Four sturdy straps were fastened to the wall and he slid his hand through one of them, grasping the base for good measure. With the press of a button the room depressurized and the outer door opened. Suction pulled him toward the precipice of space. The vastness of the star field squeezed against his chest and held him breathless in its infinity. His hand tightened on the strap.

The Fighter Hawk drifted to a halt just beyond the *Star Seeker's* wings. A space-suited crewman stood in its airlock door with a tether line booster. The booster recoiled as the man fired the tether toward the hull opening. His aim was perfect and Brenden caught the tether with his free hand as it sailed into the airlock. A double clip and a tie line secured the tether to his suit. Drawing in one last deep breath he kicked away from the hatch, intentionally jumping upward instead of outward. The crewman would have to work at hauling him in rather than just catching him as he drifted over.

Get out of here now. Brenden projected his thoughts toward Deeca. The *Star Seeker* wasted no time in dropping beneath the Fighter Hawk and rolling into a dive toward the nearest solar system. It would be in hyperspace before the crewman could secure the airlock to allow a chase.

As he floated upward, Brenden thought of Tran, as Tran and only as Tran. Anything Mr. Tang did or said had to remain intact for the ruse to work. The friendship, the gambits, the humor, the schemes and dodges all gathered into a cabinet in Brenden's mind. Then he reached for darkness at the base of his greatest fear. Feeders awaited him there, but he shoved the cabinet into it and let it go.

Brenden frowned, trying to remember what he'd just been thinking. Was it something about Mr. Tang? Had he forgotten to give him some instruction? He shook his head. It probably wasn't important if he lost the thought so easily.

Only one thing remained. He had to be out of eyesight of the crewman when he made contact with the ship. The man made little effort to haul him in and let him drift upward to the end of his tether before there was a tug drawing him toward the open hatch. The black ship hung like an omen against the star field, blocking out the light and giving none of its own. As he drew nearer to the hatch, Brenden strained to find all he could from the Captain and the crewman tugging at his line.

The crewman wore no armor and his thoughts were open. He didn't like the idea of taking an Alliance ambassador on board, but he followed orders all the same. They'd tried to coerce the prisoner to opening his mind, but the man had no idea what that meant and thought perhaps their captive was being taken for telepathic study. Not all of the crew was under Kel Anec control.

Brenden drifted at ease in his weightlessness, assured the crewman intended to haul him aboard, but uneasy for the venture ahead. Every scenario counted on Tridia to either destroy or rescue them and she was beyond his control or his reach. He tried to contact Drayden, but the boy had his mind closed and never heard the call.

Brenden.

The contact of Deeca's thoughts in his mind startled him. He pulled on the tether. The crewman paused his hand-over-hand action to investigate the problem. Brenden waved him an apology and waited for Deeca's contact to continue.

The Controller has summoned me to the Warren. Can you hear me? His call was urgent. He's helping me reach out to you. Brenden?

Brenden's stomach twisted into knots. The Controller had waited until he and Deeca were separated to issue the summons. The entity had known Brenden would try to find a way for Deeca to not answer it.

I hear you. The Fighter Hawk loomed closer, just a few yards away now. *Be careful, my love. You'll be in my thoughts.*

Literally?

He smiled in spite of his trembling hands. *I have to shut down now. I'm almost in the ship. Deeca…*

Yes?

Her thoughts intruded on his hesitation. How could he not tell her what was about to happen to her?

You'll be fantastic.

Time ran out. He could see the crewman's face through his tinted visor. He closed his mind against thought or contact beyond the first five senses. Deeca could no longer reach him and he couldn't be tempted to open his mind to find her.

He laid a hand on the ship's exterior as his feet touched the airlock floor. The homing beacon, puttylike when not in contact with metal, would mold itself to the hull. It would release once the ship made atmosphere anywhere, and a signal would activate.

The hatch closed and pressurized air rushed into the lock. Sweat soaked his face as he removed the helmet even though he'd been in the coldness of space.

"Welcome aboard, Ambassador." The crewman's welcome was

formal. "I'm to escort you to Prince Drayden, and let you know the doctor hasn't met with him yet."

Brenden's muscles tightened. The message was a taunt. Drayden would only be safe until the doctor saw him. Did that mean they planned the same treatment for the prince they'd used on Anza? He had to stop those plans – by destroying the ship, if necessary.

CHAPTER FIFTY

Tridia prowled the cell and glared at the Carok guards gathered beyond the plasma shield. She'd awakened in her room with Drayden's message in her mind. It seemed a dream at the time, but when he put his barriers in place, breaking their connection, she went berserk. Tama hadn't locked the door when he left, or she might have transformed into her full Felinus form and broken through the wall to get out. As it was, she controlled the transformation enough to limit the change to just her claws. When she opened the door, she put down the two surprised Carok guards in the hall and made it all the way to sick bay before someone hit her legs with a stun blast. A human guard fastened the obedience collar around her neck while two more twisted her arms behind her back. Caroks swiped at her as the guards dragged her to the cell. The humans dumped her inside and activated the shield, more for her protection than to restrain her. She tried to drop her barriers once, but the accompanying vertigo had been worse than she experienced on Odea. Once the feeling returned to her legs she started pacing and hadn't stopped.

A group of five Caroks watched her from that moment, held back by three armed humans. No one made any attempt to communicate with her, and Ren Tama hadn't shown his face. It was all she could do to keep the Felinus rage at bay.

Tridia stopped pacing when Lera came to stand between the guards.

"Commander Odana," she said. "Ma'am, they've told me I can bring you a change of clothes and some food, if you'll just calm down. I can tend the scratches on your arms. Carok claws are filthy with bacteria. Those wounds could get infected if they aren't cleaned."

"Where is Ren Tama?" Tridia asked.

"He's in sick bay, Ma'am," Lera said. "He collapsed when the Elstaar

500

took Prince Drayden away."

Tridia's heart stopped. Drayden said there were men in black armor. "The Elstaar took the prince?"

"Yes, Ma'am. They said they were taking him to Kanu."

"You don't believe that." Tridia stared hard at Lera.

The girl stared back. "No, Ma'am. Kanu is an Alliance protectorate, pretty far across the border. The Core wouldn't let an Odean Fighter Hawk get that deep into their territory. There's no reason the Hierarchy would oblige a protectorate planet."

"Where have they taken him?" Tridia asked.

"I don't know, Ma'am. No one has mentioned any other destination."

Tridia resumed her pacing. Master Aren had destroyed the Starling base and its doctors. If the Kel Anec had been operating for as long as he suspected, they could have any number of bases anywhere in the galaxy. There was one place, however, they could easily secure while they did whatever they wanted to Drayden – Cystia. The Hierarchy defensive satellites would protect them from invasion. If anyone did get past the satellites, the feeders would attack whoever dared go into the tunnels. She had to get out of the cell.

"What's wrong with Master Tama?" Tridia asked.

"We're not sure what happened." Lera scowled as she relayed the information. "The guards who brought him in said he just collapsed, but he had a blunt trauma to his head and his left clavicle was broken. No one had touched him."

During her brief training with Empress Dojene on the hospital ship, Tridia had asked about the use of thought as a weapon. The empress had confirmed her suspicions.

You said I could have hurt you if I sent my thoughts too boldly. Can this ability also be used as a weapon?

Yes, this technique can be used as a limited weapon. But it must be used with care. Unless controlled carefully, it will kill the target. At the very least it could cause irreparable damage.

"Drayden," Tridia whispered.

"The prince was nowhere near Master Tama," Lera said.

Tridia clenched her fists. The practice of using thought energy as a weapon hadn't been taught in Drayden's lessons. He'd been taught no form of combat apart from the programs Master Aren left. Yet, Drayden used his thought energy to injure Tama, and he could only have known that was possible by accessing her memories. Through their bonding she'd given Drayden knowledge of many deadly techniques, but not a single shred of the discipline and self-control necessary to keep those things in check. He said he wasn't as weak as she thought him to be, and his emotions had overridden hers on Hulac when she confronted Dojene. Could his anger override her memories of caution? She had to get to him before he killed someone or was killed using a technique he couldn't control.

"Can you take me to sick bay? I need to see Master Tama." Tridia's voice showed no sign of how hard her heart pounded.

"That won't be necessary, Commander."

Tama stood behind Lera. A sling supported his left arm.

"Why did you give Prince Drayden to the Elstaar?" Tridia demanded. "You know they weren't envoys from Kanu."

"No, they were Elstaar, carrying enough fire power to disable this ship and take what they wanted," Tama said. "We couldn't fire on them without direct orders from the Supreme Commander. All of our communications went conveniently silent after they hailed us. I had no choice, to do otherwise would have caused a mutiny."

"We have to get him back," Tridia demanded. She kicked the plasma shield and a numbing jolt ran up her leg.

"You're behaving like a caged animal," Tama scolded. "It's beneath you. You spoke with your mother after you drank the elixir. She gave you instructions. She spoke to me as well. Should we have the rest of this conversation through a plasma shield or can you control yourself long enough to listen to what I have to say?"

"You have the means to ensure control of the situation." Tridia touched the collar around her neck.

Tama held up the control box. "You told me that I could control you for only so long with this thing before I had to kill you with it. Don't make me have to kill you, because I sincerely believe that you may be the only one who can get us out of this mess."

"You may be right," Tridia said. "I'll listen to what you have to say, but it'd better be something worthwhile."

"Take Commander Odana to the sick bay to have her wounds treated," Tama ordered the human guards. "Then escort her to her room so she can change clothes."

"If I may, sir," Lera said. "If you'll take the Commander straight to her room to change, I could meet her there with the medications she'll need."

Tama nodded and addressed the guards. "Take the Commander directly to her room. Stand guard outside. Let Apprentice Cal enter when she gets there, but no one else goes into that room without my permission."

Tridia followed the guards to her room. She washed the scratches on her arms, wincing as the water came into contact with her swollen flesh. The Caroks had scratched Drayden all over. Apart from broken bones and internal damage, his flesh had burned with infection even worse than hers. The door chime sounded, and Lera entered. The Apprentice applied antiseptics to the scratches and dressed the deepest of the wounds.

"That should take care of it, Ma'am." Lera put away the medications, then pulled a wrapped package from her kit. "You should eat this. You haven't had anything for hours and your face is sunken. I'm guessing the transformation of those claws cost you some nutrients."

"Thank you," Tridia said. She pulled on her shirt and sat down to put on her boots before accepting and devouring the food.

"Ma'am, I don't really know what's going on here, but I want to make sure you're not harmed." Lera said. "The Caroks are mumbling about Master Tama being weak where you're concerned. They wanted to kill you and the prince, but he kept them in check. They didn't like that. When you killed those two in the hall before you were captured in sick bay, they really complained. Said something about tasting your flesh."

"You realize that this room is bugged and you've seen the surveillance cameras in the corners there and there." Tridia pointed out the devices as she spoke.

"Yes, Ma'am." Lera nodded. "Master Tama should know what he's up against if he's going to protect you."

"If the Caroks hear that you've reported their behavior, you won't last long on this ship," Tridia said. Lera's eyes widened and she swallowed hard. Tridia shook her head. "You hadn't thought of that. It's a good thing you switched Grids."

Lera gave a sheepish smile. "I guess you're right."

"Stay close to me," Tridia said.

The door opened and Ren Tama entered.

"You're dismissed, Apprentice," he said.

Lera shouldered her bag and took a step toward the door.

"I'd like for her to stay." Tridia kept the anger out of her voice. "She has information you may want to hear before you leave this room. Will our discussion be monitored?"

"No, I'll disable the surveillance from here when necessary. Not before I'm sure you aren't going to attack," Tama said. "As I've already told you, I'm not a fool."

Tridia directed Lera to sit on the bed beside her.

"No games. No attacks," Tridia said.

"You don't mind if I take a few precautions, all the same." Tama sat in the only chair in the room and took the control box from his pocket. "What do you have to report, Apprentice?"

Tridia nodded and Lera repeated the story she'd told. When she finished Tama nodded.

"I was aware the Caroks would only follow me as long as I showed no weakness and gave in to their baser instincts. Did you know they eat their own fallen? They believe it increases their strength. They had a feast on the two you dispatched earlier."

Lera Cal paled. Tridia remained unmoved.

"I want Apprentice Cal with me at all times, Master Tama. She took care of Prince Drayden and she's gone out of her way to calm me down. I'd still be pacing the cell or tearing out your throat if not for her," Tridia said. "I can at least try to keep her alive in return."

"All right." Tama sat back and crossed his legs. "You've got a new shadow. Is she going to listen to the rest of our conversation?"

"I see no reason to withhold it from her. You said my mother spoke to you."

"Yes. She told me to make sure that you had only bonded mentally with the prince and that no other joining had occurred. Apparently, it matters exactly what you did. The portal had already closed, she sent the message through the residual energy. She was scared, Commander. Why it matters whether or not you've bedded this man eludes me, but she told me to kill you both if anything more than a simple mental bonding had happened. I questioned the prince, but he changed his story very little – apart from not claiming to be Davik Schie. I'd like to hear the same story from your lips, Commander. With the events exactly as he told it." Tama pulled a blaster from his belt. "Exactly."

Tridia scowled. The blaster setting showed maximum and it didn't hum. Tama had already primed it to kill. What had Drayden confessed?

"You already know that I haven't had sex with him, Master Tama. Your medic confirmed my virginity."

Tama leveled the blaster at Tridia's chest. "The exact story he told, if you please."

The only other thing that might matter was the depth of their bonding. Drayden would never have explained that. Tridia took a deep breath and raised her chin.

"I rescued Drayden from a monster called a skike on Zentel – Xanaias. He was badly injured, but the plant creatures he protected helped me get him to safety. I treated his wounds and waited. He woke up that night, delirious from a fever. When he passed out, I held him in my arms trying to keep him warm. He recovered and the next day we walked to the birthing grounds. The Rrabbas' pollen affected us. We bonded mentally. We kissed once, nothing more. He took me to his bunker where I accessed his computer banks for information. I found a message from my mother there. She told me to find you, although Drayden may not have shared that. We sparred once with battle staffs.

I'd just won our contest when the cruiser attacked the shield. I took his ship and left him in the bunker with strict orders not to open the door to anyone but the Sentinels or me. He told me the AI controlling the security malfunctioned and opened the door and you took him. Most likely not his *exact* words, but those are the events as they happened."

Tama lowered the blaster. "I heard what I needed to hear."

"Why did you let me think you wanted to rape me when all you wanted was to have me drink the elixir my mother gave you?"

"It kept you off balance and thinking you had a bargaining tool," Tama said. "I needed time to determine how connected you were to the prince, and to find out who he really was. He looks enough like Davik Schie to pass for him, but I know that Lieutenant Schie is part of an experiment on Cystia – if he's still alive."

"He's still alive," Tridia said. "How do you know him?"

"I know he applied for marriage privileges with you. Someone framed him to discredit him and take him out of the picture. I suspect Frees B'Nay, though I would have done something less drastic if he hadn't."

"You would have ruined an innocent man's career?" Tridia asked.

"If necessary. You had to remain pure," Tama said. "Again, I don't know why it matters, so don't ask."

Tridia swallowed her fury. Fighting with Tama wouldn't get her where she needed to be.

"I've got to get to Drayden."

"Not with the Caroks this unstable. You'll never make it out of this room without me. I need you here."

"Drayden must be rescued," Tridia demanded. "If they corrupt him, they corrupt everything."

"Even you can't fight them alone," Tama said. "Not if they're all you've claimed."

"I'll fight alone if I have to."

"Then you're a fool and I can't let you get away to be captured with him." Tama brought the blaster level again.

"I will go to him, or I will make sure they can't get what they want from him. If I die, he dies." It might not be true, but she'd take the chance.

"Just how will you see to that?" Tama asked.

"Two blue, one green, two red." Tridia drew a small black box from her pocket and held it up. Her thumb hovered over a red button. "I only have to push one more red. There's enough explosive in this collar to blast a hole in the side of the ship. If the blast doesn't kill you the vacuum will."

Tama waited. "Brenden Aren's doing, no doubt."

"He knows what I am, Master Tama," Tridia said. "He knows the carnage I could cause. He also knows that I'm the galaxy's best hope for peace – or he would have left me dead when he killed me on Odea. What neither of you seem to understand, though, is that my life doesn't matter to me. Only Drayden's freedom and Davik's release are of any significance. I'm going after Drayden, and once I've rescued him, I'll free Davik from his nightmare." Tridia leaned forward, her eyes cold, her voice low. "Release this collar now. If you don't, you and I will die right here, right now."

"Commander Odana," Lera said.

"I'm sorry, Apprentice." Tridia spoke without looking at her. "I should have sent you away. I had a feeling it would come to this."

"I'm with you, Commander, whatever you decide," Lera said. "But you might want to wait another ten seconds before you do anything drastic. Help is on the way."

Two short blaster bursts in the hall preceded an attack alarm. The intercom on the wall blared a warning.

"The Caroks have revolted. All hands to internal battle stations. Repeat, all hands to internal battle stations."

"How did you arrange that?" Tridia asked, risking a glance at Lera.

"I didn't," she answered. "I just had a couple of medics coming from sick bay."

"A mutiny?" Tama asked.

"An escape, sir," Lera Cal said.

"Release the collar, Tama. If we have to fight our way past the Caroks, I'm going to need my freedom," Tridia said.

"You can fight just as well with it on," Tama said.

"I won't ask again." Tridia held the black box forward and bent her thumb to press the button.

"Alright, Commander. For now."

Tama released the collar. Tridia pulled it from her neck and slid it toward the door just as the door swished open. Two medics backed into the room firing blasters into the hall. The door slid shut once they'd made their way inside.

"You made it!" Lera Cal exclaimed.

"Just barely," one of the men said. "The Caroks are shooting or shredding anything that moves. They're looking for Master Tama."

"I don't have time for this," Tridia said.

She made a circle with the thumb and forefinger of her left hand and focused her energy on the center. The circle wavered, then golden light burst through it. Tridia held a small sun in her hand. As she concentrated the brightness dimmed and the circle enlarged until it was big enough to walk through. Gray mists swirled inside the circle. Sweat broke out on Tridia's face as she concentrated. She pulled on the Chesan energy to strengthen and enlighten her. The lessons her mother had transferred became clear. Another portal opened inside the first, across the mists. A golden ship rested in a green mountain pasture beyond the second portal. Two Sentinels waited by its ramp.

"What's that?" Lera asked.

"Our escape route," Tridia said. "Get your stuff and run through to the second portal. I don't know if you can make it, but you stand a better chance there than facing the Caroks. Don't stop and don't slow down until you're all the way through."

"I can't leave you, Commander," Lera objected.

"I'll be right behind you," Tridia said. "I don't know how long I can keep the portals open, so I'd appreciate it if you'd hurry."

"Xander and Mel?" Lera Cal directed the question to the two men.

"I'll take my chances in the portal," one of them said.

"I'm with Mel," the other added.

"Then hurry!" Tridia shouted. The portal's energy flowing into her body might make her strong and smart, but she'd faint if the connection severed.

The three medics darted through the portal and ran without stopping through the mists. They collapsed on the grass once they exited on the far side. Winniel ran toward them.

"You next, Master Tama," Tridia said.

"What, you're not going to leave me here to face the circumstances?"

"I'd be just as happy to leave you here, but my mother said I need you alive."

"Can you open another one of those things into the engine room?" Tama asked.

"Are you insane?" Tridia asked. The portal wavered and she hurried to focus her thoughts to keep it open.

"I can make an escape from there," Tama said. "I can't leave the ship or the cloaking engine intact for the Caroks. The crew will already be evacuating to the escape pods, shuttles, and fighters. That was the drill should the Caroks ever revolt. A full third of the crew were Caroks. The human two-thirds stand no chance against them."

"Where do I look for the toy?" Tridia said.

"It's the crystal inside the toy that you need. I left an unfinished mission on record with the Hierarchy. The details you need are in the mission spec. The mission was to fall to you should I die before its completion."

"I can't return to the Hierarchy." Tridia glared at Tama.

"You won't need to," Tama said. "I'm sure Brenden Aren has

enough connections to obtain mission spec for you. It's an Assassin Grid mission."

Tridia closed her eyes and concentrated on a separate portal, then envisioned another one that opened into the engine room. Her breathing became rapid as she opened her eyes. Two portals hovered beside Ren Tama. He stared into the mists.

"Is it possible to bring them closer together?" he asked. "It won't do me much good to get to the engine room if I pass out once I'm there."

Tridia focused on the two portals. The engine room drew closer to the first opening. Tridia gasped.

"What's wrong?" Tama asked. He took a step toward Tridia, but she shook her head.

"Get going. This is a lot harder than it looks."

"Until next time, Commander." Tama jumped through the portal and entered the engine room in two steps.

He staggered when he passed through the second portal, but he didn't fall. Tridia let those portals snap shut. As she stepped into the portal on her side, the door swished open. Three Caroks raised their weapons, but Tridia closed the portal to the size of a dinner plate and their shots hit the wall. She pushed the red button before letting the portal close. A bright light flashed, but the blast didn't reach the mists.

Tridia waded through the mist as gray tendrils wrapped around her arms and legs. Blue energy covered her from the waist down as she slogged her way toward the distant opening. Any effort to pull the opening nearer failed and sapped her strength. How could the portal energize her when she stood outside, and drain her on the inside?

"No daughter, you mustn't leave now." Elise's voice cut through the gray. "You've absorbed too much energy. I told you to wait until you'd matured. You won't be able to resist opening it again too soon. The Kel Anec will track you by this. They'll enslave you once they find you. You've chosen the path of horror through the Chaos Vision."

"You're wrong." Tridia kept moving. "You don't know me and you don't know the decisions I'll make. You've set me on this path and a Hielos *tashan* won't keep me from it."

"Stop, Tridia!" Elise materialized, as a sparkling older version of Tridia. The mists swirled faster. "If you discharge this much energy you'll awaken the armada."

"If the armada isn't awake by now, they never will be," Tridia said. "The Kel Anec have been infesting the galaxy for twenty years."

"I can't let you do this." Elise raised her arms and the mists rose in a sheet around Tridia.

She stopped, unable to move another step. The mist hissed against the blue energy, tore at her clothing and picked at her flesh. She'd given up hope when a hand reached through the wall of mist and grabbed her arm. It pulled her through the veil and into the sunshine of a mountain pasture.

"Commander Odana?" Winniel asked, still holding her by the arm. A male Sentinel stood at her side. "It seemed you needed assistance."

"Your intervention was well-timed." Tridia panted. She held the portal in her palm and let its energy strengthen her as blue energy glowed around her injured flesh.

"Your ship is ready, Commander. We've received word that Ambassador Aren placed himself aboard a ship with Prince Drayden. They're bound for Cystia."

Tridia's stomach knotted at Winniel's words. Drayden hated Master Aren. The prince possessed the knowledge and willingness to kill. Even if they survived each other, the two of them together in Kel Anec control spelled disaster.

"I don't know what will happen when I close this link. I passed out for several hours the last time, and I've had a lot more power flowing through me this time."

"What are your instructions?" Winniel asked.

"Get me on the ship and put us on a heading to Cystia as fast as it will go. If I'm not awake by the time we get there, stay out of satellite range until I wake up. I'll give you the rest of the plan when we get there." Tridia breathed in the cold fresh air. "Winniel, if I die from this exposure, you've got to get to Prince Drayden and Master Aren. If they're compromised, destroy them both. Don't let the Kel Anec use them. Their invasion armada is huge, but it may still be in stasis, waiting for a signal. We have to make sure they never get it."

"Yes, Commander," Winniel said.

"There are things I can see and understand while I'm attached to the portal that I will lose when I let go," Tridia said. "Whatever I do when we've rescued Drayden and Master Aren, you have to let me do it. Don't try to stop me. I won't be able to explain then anymore than I can afford to explain now."

Tridia let her mind relax. The portal closed with an audible snap and the energy flow stopped just as abruptly.

"Commander Odana?" Lera sat upright on the grass, holding her head in her hands.

"Do whatever Winniel tells you," Tridia said.

She blinked a couple of times and fell into the male Sentinel's waiting arms.

CHAPTER FIFTY-ONE

Lera jumped to her feet and pressed her fingers against Tridia's neck to feel for a pulse. She breathed a huge sigh when she found one. Her plan to help Commander Odana escape had taken on new proportions with the revelation of the portal. What a convenient thing to have up one's sleeve – but the Commander appeared to suffer for its use.

"She's alive." The apprentice looked up into Winniel's face. The strange woman's etched beauty and obvious strength encouraged her, but the man's face looked grim. "I'm Medic Apprentice Lera Cal. I met Commander Odana on Odea."

"I am Winniel, First Truthsayer to the Hariok Clan of Sentinels, assigned by the Tribunal of the Core Alliance of Planets to watch over Commander Odana."

Lera's eyes widened. "A Sentinel? I've heard – "

"All that you've heard is true, Lera Cal." Ofein lifted Tridia's limp body and started toward the ship. "See to your friends. Commander Odana gave us instructions. We have a mission to complete."

Lera stood in stunned silence as the Sentinel carried Commander Odana to the ship. Sentinels were sworn enemies of the Hierarchy. What had the Commander done to have them assigned to watch over her? How was she allowed to give them orders? Lera hurried to check the pulses of her medic companions. Their beats were strong and the men came to shortly.

"Are we alive?" Mel asked, sitting up and holding his head.

"We're alive." Xander struggled to his feet and reached a hand down to help the disoriented Mel. "I'm not so sure I'd rush through another portal."

"Look alive, gentlemen. We've stepped into a flaming mess here." Lera shouldered her bag and started toward the ship. "Let's get these medicines stowed and look after the Commander. We'll be travelling with a Sentinel pilot."

"What?" The two men asked in chorus.

"Partnering with the Sentinels wasn't part of the plan," Mel grabbed his bag and hurried after Lera.

"You said we'd help Commander Odana escape and she'd get us off the ship and away from the Caroks. You said nothing about the Sentinels being involved with this," Xander chimed in, hustling to catch up.

"I told you there'd be no boredom with her." Lera smiled. Commander Odana's record had been worth every credit and favor she'd paid for it. "We're going after the Commander's mate and Ambassador Brenden Aren."

"The Brenden Aren?" Mel's voice jumped and octave.

"One and the same," Lera replied.

"We should have tried to reach an escape pod," Xander said.

The three of them boarded the golden ship and it took off before they made it to the lounge.

"My name is Ofein, mate to Winniel." The male Sentinel met them in the lounge. "Commander Odana is resting in the second room on the right. Attend to her needs."

Ofein left the medics staring after him. Lera regained her composure first and urged the men to follow her. They made no noise as they entered the darkened room. One small light illuminated Commander Odana as she lay uncovered on the bunk. Lera untucked the edge of the cover and folded it over her. A little exploration revealed the bathroom and the adjoining cabin, where they dropped their bags and sat on the bunks.

"Now what?" Mel asked in a whisper.

"We watch over the Commander and attend her needs. When she wakes up, she'll tell us what to do," Lera said.

"And if she doesn't wake up?" Xander asked.

"Then the Sentinels will deal with us in whatever way they deem fit," Lera said. "They dump us on a Hierarchy world or take us to the Core Alliance."

"You're awfully calm about this," Xander stated.

"Commander Odana wouldn't have sent us through that portal to be tortured or killed by the Sentinels," Lera explained. "They were waiting for her. She knew they were there. But she's going to wake up. Her mate —"

Lera paused to consider the word. *Mate.* The Commander had said she and the prince bonded mentally. What did that mean? Was Commander Odana a telepath?

"What about her mate?" Mel asked.

"Nothing," Lera said. "Let's just do what we can for her."

Just how much they could do remained to be seen. Xander and Mel made their way to the lounge. Lera returned to Tridia's room. She'd be there when the commander woke up.

CHAPTER FIFTY-TWO

Brenden sat on the floor of the cargo hold with his eyes closed. Prince Drayden sat across the hold, dressed only in infirmary pajamas with a thermal blanket draped about his shoulders. Neither man had spoken or made any attempt to communicate after their first formal greeting more than six hours before.

The prince had acknowledged Brenden with the same dignity the Chesan King had possessed, but his hostile glare warned he'd rather engage in combat than exchange civil greetings. The two of them had parted as friends when he'd left Drayden in the bunker. Had fifteen years of solitary Chesan brainwashing done this? Or had Tridia's memories shown too clearly what Brenden had done to her? The type of mental violation he'd committed brought the only death penalty in the Chesan legal system. Brenden wouldn't blame Drayden for wanting to enforce the penalty when the crime had been committed against his mate, but with so much at stake, they'd have to wait for a more appropriate time to deal with that issue.

The prince also appeared to be in perfect health. Winniel had said Ren Tama's chaotic thoughts revealed a young man beaten near to death. How could he have healed in a week? Either Drayden possessed remarkable powers of recuperation, or this wasn't the real prince. Had he walked into a trap?

Brenden opened his eyes at a noise from the hatch. Three armor-clad soldiers entered, two carrying weapons, one carrying a tray of food. The two with weapons stood at the door as the third soldier set the tray on the floor halfway across the hold. The Captain meant to take no chances with the likes of Brenden Aren.

"Ambassador, you and the prince will be taken individually to relieve yourselves since there are no facilities in this room." The food bearer spoke in the unmodified voice of a young man. "Your Majesty, if you'll accompany the guard?"

Drayden got to his feet and followed one of the soldiers out of the room. Brenden stretched his arms and started to stand. The guard at the door snapped his weapon up and the food-bearer took a step back.

"Sir, you'll please remain still until I tell you to rise."

"You could've pointed that out when you walked into the room, Sergeant, and saved us all a scare." Brenden eased his back against the wall. His legend had grown considerably since the last time he'd been around the troops.

"I'll try to be more specific in the future."

"Will we be in transit much longer?" Brenden asked.

An unmodified Fighter Hawk would take twenty-four hours to reach Cystia from where he came aboard. If he could get an answer, he could guage the crew's liberty to speak.

"I don't know, sir."

"I see. Would it be possible to speak with the Captain?"

"No, sir. I will convey any questions you might have and bring you the answers with your next rations."

"Thank you. My interest is the safety and well-being of His Majesty. I'd like to request Prince Drayden's release. I was told he wasn't well, but he seems fit enough. His – Our accommodations indicate that he is a prisoner, perhaps a hostage. If the latter is true, I'd like to negotiate his safe return."

"I'll inform the Captain, sir, and let you know."

Drayden entered the hold, crossed it, and returned to his place against the far wall.

The taut set of Drayden's shoulders and his clenched jaw indicated something had happened while he'd been away.

"Are you well, Your Majesty?" Brenden asked.

"I am well, Ambassador. Perhaps too well." Drayden glared up at the guard. "I don't need assistance to relieve myself, yet they insist upon watching."

Brenden stifled a laugh. "I'm sure their orders are strict and punishment swift if they fail to do as they're told. Otherwise they'd have no interest."

"His interest seemed keen enough when he examined my body parts."

Brenden sobered quickly and jumped to his feet. The guards snapped weapons to their shoulders. He spoke without moving, but his voice was hard.

"That isn't standard procedure. If the guard touched His Majesty in so familiar a manner, something other than security prompted him.

What is the meaning of such behavior?"

The sergeant stammered a response. "We – We were told to examine all visible flesh on the prince. We haven't asked him to submit to a strip search and the doctor hasn't approached him. The guard examined flesh as it became visible, sir. She was following orders."

"*She?*" Drayden's face reddened.

"Are there any other indignities to which you intend to subject him?" Brenden asked.

"Ambassador, you understand the Elstaar requirements for obedience to orders. What would you have us do, eject ourselves from the airlock?"

"Simply state your intentions, unless you've been told otherwise." Brenden turned to Drayden. "Stand up, Your Majesty, and disrobe."

"What?" Drayden's voice cracked with indignation.

"Would you rather they catch you off guard again? Disrobe and be done with it." Brenden used his best diplomat's voice.

"With a woman watching?"

"Well, she's already seen your most private parts, displaying the rest of your flesh is anti-climactic." A smile worked its way onto Brenden's lips.

Drayden glared, but he stood and disrobed, embarrassment and anger clear in each tense movement. The guards checked him thoroughly, then searched his clothing while he stood wrapped in the blanket.

"What are these?" the sergeant asked.

"Medication," Drayden said. "In case I was denied further medical treatment."

"If you need medical attention here, the doctor will see to it."

The guards confiscated the medication and returned Drayden's clothing. The prince redressed and sat down with his arms and legs crossed.

"Will that satisfy your doctor?" Brenden asked.

"If it doesn't, I will let you know, sir. Now if you will also disrobe?"

"Your security is lax, Sergeant. This should have taken place when I was brought aboard, not six hours into the trip. Your captain should be on report." Brenden removed his shirt as he spoke.

He tossed his clothing to the guards until he stood before them naked and acquiesced to a thorough search of the type he'd performed on numerous prisoners. He considered the lax security as he dressed and followed the guard to the ship's small head. Whoever was really running the ship knew without a physical examination that he carried no hidden weapons. One of the Kel Anec leaders must be on board, but the creature hadn't touched Drayden, whereas the doctors on Starling had treated Anza as an experimental subject. They had something else in store for the prince.

When he returned to the cargo hold, Brenden found Drayden sitting in the same position he'd assumed after his search. Although his indignation seemed to subside after he'd witnessed Brenden's equally thorough search, he'd relaxed his pose very little. The guards left and locked the hatch again.

"Why are they doing this?" Drayden asked.

"The strip search is standard procedure for prisoners," Brenden stated. "Catching you off guard like that was probably intended as a degradation – to show you they can do whatever they want with you. And to make a preliminary check of your breeding equipment."

"Breeding equipment?"

"They want your DNA, but they'll keep you for breeding. They want to rebuild the Chesan race. Why start from scratch if they have healthy specimens? They'll use you to start – along with Princess Anza if they get their hands on her again. They were making sure you're outwardly healthy."

"If I hadn't been?" Drayden asked.

"You'd still be a good source of DNA." Brenden opened a ration pack and sniffed it.

Drayden took a pack and opened it. He spoke quietly, without looking up, and the deadly calm in his voice sent a shiver up Brenden's spine.

"You mentally raped a young girl – a young girl who happens to be my mate. She went to you for help and I'll honor her wishes to work with you in any way I can to avert a holocaust." Drayden raised his eyes and locked his gaze on Brenden. "But be assured your crimes will *not* be forgotten."

"I did what I had to do," Brenden replied in a terse whisper. "Do the same when your time comes, but she is best not discussed in these circumstances."

"I've said what I needed to say." Drayden sniffed the rations he removed from the pack and spoke with no hint of his previous hostility. "Are these safe to eat?"

"As safe as anything we're likely to get. The seals weren't tampered with. If the food is drugged, it was done before it left Odea." Brenden bit into the food supplement and chewed before reaching for a water pack to wash it down. "Not my favorite flavor, but it should keep us alive."

"Is that our goal, then, to stay alive?" Drayden took the second water pack.

"For the present that's our only goal. We have a good assumption of what they want to do with you. I expect, since my Chesan blood isn't pure, they'll want me for my position and influence in the Hierarchy and the Core. They will try to possess me or compromise me in some way – and a quarter-Chesan is better than no Chesan if something happens to you."

"Slavery. Captivity. Mindless breeding. Not the life my parents envisioned when they locked me away fifteen years ago."

"No, they had something very different in mind." Brenden ate the last of his ration and crumpled the pack. "Did you use the tutorials I left for you?"

Drayden gave a dry laugh. "Every time I entered the projection rooms. I hated you for the injuries, but I kept at it. Then I got better. The training came in handy when I followed the Rrabbas away from the breeding ground. There were a lot of things we had to defend the village against. Life sometimes got hard on the escarpment."

"You didn't have to go with them."

Drayden's reaction didn't disappoint Brenden's expectations.

"They needed help, someone warm-blooded to stand the cold night watches. Someone long-lived to lead them back to the birthing grounds when their elders couldn't make the trip. I outlived generations of those creatures and each death – " Drayden stopped and Brenden waited. "It was difficult to watch them die and their numbers dwindle because of the shield changing their environment. So many died for my sake."

"Not just your sake, Your Highness. For the sake of an entire race. You're just the first vital part." Brenden got to his feet and offered his hand to Drayden. The prince took it and stood. "We need to exercise, if you're up to it."

"I think I can keep up," Drayden said. His voice hinted at sarcasm, but his glare had lessened in intensity.

"Follow my moves."

Brenden led Drayden through a series of complex stretches and katas to loosen their muscles. They continued into a partner kata, difficult and advanced. The prince performed the moves flawlessly. Drayden's kicks and punches came within a hair's breadth of contacting Brenden's face or body, testifying to the control he exerted. At least he'd be able to fight if they ever got the chance.

"How long can you keep your mind blocked?" Brenden's whispered question was barely audible above the sound of their steps and the rustle of their clothing.

"Indefinitely, I think. It's disorienting when I wake up, but I've never lost control." Drayden responded in a whisper.

"Can you shield someone else?"

"I've never tried."

"We may have reinforcements that need our protection, and we may need to bolster each other eventually." Brenden stopped at the end of his kata and pressed his hands palm down before him.

"I'll do what I can." Drayden spoke as he exhaled.

Both men returned to their places on the floor. Brenden's muscles tingled from the exertion, but he felt better for the movement and it was the only thing he could think of for cover sound. Now it was a waiting game to see how long they'd remain unmolested. Another sound from the hatch brought his attention back to the opening.

A slender man with white hair stood silhouetted in the doorway. He entered without speaking, walking slowly with his hands in the pockets of a long blue coat. When he turned, the light from the corridor exposed his face. For all the white hair, his face looked no older than Brenden's. The face belonged to the strange observer from the Public Hearing Room. His expression was curious.

"I am Dr. Rynoki."

"I am Ambassador Brenden Aren, of the Core Alliance of Planets. This is Prince Drayden Anjenay." Brenden observed the protocols, even though the Kel Anec-possessed man knew their names.

"Thank you for your courtesy, Ambassador. The guards tell me you've been most cooperative with their requests. My apologies for the intrusions, Your Highness. That should be the last of your indignities aboard this ship."

"I won't thank you. I'm sure you'll have plenty more in store for me when we reach our destination." Drayden spoke with venom in his voice.

"No doubt others have plans for both your body and your mind. I won't pretend that isn't the purpose of your presence here. I've come to make an offer of leniency for you."

"His Majesty will hear no offers that don't include his release," Brenden interjected.

"That could be arranged." Dr. Rynoki took a step toward the door then turned back. "We've had a sustained energy reading unlike any we've encountered since the Chesans fled our galaxy a thousand years ago. It came from the coordinates of the ship from which you were retrieved, Your Highness. A smaller reading of the same energy signature reached us from that ship shortly before you came aboard. We assumed the signature to be yours. Your body's been emitting low-level residue readings."

Brenden looked from Rynoki to Drayden and back. So Tridia had exposed Drayden to the portal. Why hadn't she used it to escape with him?

"I can't account for your readings, Doctor, any more than I can account for the color of my eyes. Some things simply are." Drayden relaxed his position.

Brenden tensed, ready in case the prince tried anything foolish. Without mental contact he couldn't warn the young man of the dangers of angering these people.

"We thought to return to the ship for the source of the energy, then we identified another reading from halfway across the galaxy, almost as strong, and pulsing in synchronization with the first. After a few minutes the energy source on the ship extinguished, as did all readings of that vessel. We assume the ship was destroyed. Almost immediately after we lost the vessel, the distant energy level diminished. It's dissipated at a constant rate and it's moving away from the original coordinates."

"Interesting. Will you be changing course to follow it?" Drayden asked.

Brenden smiled as the Kel Anec's mouth tightened at Drayden's words. Drayden had his father's knack for annoying the arrogant. Brenden had experienced that annoyance himself years before.

"There is no need. The signal is on a vector for our own destination. Whatever the source is, it will join us in a matter of days." A cynical smile replaced Rynoki's tightened lips. "The offer I make is this. Tell us what generates the energy signature, help us to contain it, and we'll give you freedom to come and go as you please. You'll be able to open your mind without fear of intrusion. If the source is potent enough, we may not need your other services, just your DNA samples, which we will take at any rate."

"Just that? Freedom to come and go?" Drayden asked.

"You will be tagged so we can trace you, should you refuse a call to return when required. You must agree, that's better than living in captivity with little more dignity than a lab specimen." Rynoki turned to Brenden. "Ambassador, would you not advise your young monarch that this is the best offer he will be given from us? He's had little experience with our kind. You, at least, have met my counterparts on Starling."

Brenden turned to Drayden. "He's right, Your Majesty. They won't make you a better offer. This species isn't concerned with the liberties of others. They'll take what they want from you, use your body, and force you to do their will mindlessly. The fact that he's even speaking with you says much about their desire to obtain a greater prize, using you in whatever way they can to obtain it."

Drayden stared at Brenden with disbelief in his eyes. He opened his mouth to speak but Brenden raised his hand to halt him.

"As the only counselor available to you at this time, Your Highness, I recommend that you listen to his words *and* his intent, then make your decision based on both." Brenden's electric-blue gaze held Drayden's as a smile appeared on the prince's face. Both men stood to face Rynoki.

"Thank you for your counsel, Ambassador." Drayden nodded in Brenden's direction. "Dr. Rynoki, your offer is no doubt generous in your own mind, but I cannot help you. I don't know the source of the energy, and even if I did, I would neither reveal it to you, nor assist you in its containment."

"We will take the information from you, Your Highness." The chill in Rynoki's voice sent warnings to Brenden's brain. "If not from you, then from the Ambassador, who is so much more vulnerable than he believes himself to be."

"You'll be disappointed. I don't know how the energy works, either, or what its source might be."

As he spoke, a strong mind wailed at his mental barriers, trying to get through to his thoughts. Only the Sentinels compared with the strength of that consciousness, then Brenden realized that two entities assaulted his mind – and one attacked from inside his barriers. He looked toward Drayden, but the prince seemed unaffected and scowled in response. Brenden tried to speak, but words wouldn't come. His hands remained frozen at his sides and his knees weakened.

Rynoki tilted his head to one side. "Your hidden enemy reveals itself, Ambassador. Your greatest fear tears at your mind even now. What did you unleash when you rescued Princess Anza? What was on the blade of the scalpel that sliced open your hand?"

A chill stole down Brenden's spine as moisture glistened above his lips. A dark presence rose from the depths of his subconscious. An energy-draining presence that threatened to consume him. He and the Sentinels hadn't rescued Anza from the malevolent presence of a Kel Anec possession, they'd released a feeder into his own mind to hibernate until summoned. He forced words from his paralyzed lips.

"This won't help you."

Brave words won't shield you, Ambassador. We've already broken through your defenses. Micro machines are even now replicating in your blood stream. Rynoki's words taunted Brenden's mind.

"You have been – what is the word your group has chosen to use?" Rynoki asked. "Ah, yes – you have been compromised."

A pounding started at his temples and pain seared behind his eyes as Brenden struggled to maintain the security of his mind. The internal invader didn't seem to want his mind just yet. It attacked him physically, weakening his body and siphoning off his resistance. Rynoki would take control of his mind as soon as the feeder took full control of his body.

Energy flowed into Brenden's failing barriers, offering relief in the shield it presented. He couldn't sense Drayden's thoughts, nor contact him to warn him of the catastrophe. He could only accept the prince's reinforcement to his failing barriers. The energy wouldn't sustain him, but it gave him enough time to safeguard the things he had to protect. In a hurried attempt to retain his identity, Brenden withdrew into himself, taking all knowledge of Tridia's power, the Chaos Vision, Deeca's identity and memories, the Controller's prescience, the knowledge of the Chesan survivors, the true identity of the Hulac workers, and the secret codes to open the shields of Hulac with him. The last thing he pulled into darkness was his identity as Morgan Jacks. Everything else he gave up to the invading presence. A dozen other personas revealed themselves to Rynoki's plundering mind. The structure and strength of the Core Alliance of Planets, the Sentinels, and the Hierarchy were laid bare for scrutiny, along with the plans to counteract the Kel Anec threat on Odea. Secrets poured from his mind into the cold Kel Anec operative. As Brenden's consciousness withdrew into darkness, Rynoki smiled.

CHAPTER FIFTY-THREE

Rynoki took a step nearer Brenden and Drayden placed a hand on the Ambassador's arm. He didn't understand the exchange of words between the two men, but Brenden needed help. He only ever shared energy with Tridia, and that was through their mental bonding. Doing it without dropping his barriers might not be possible, and the amount he could risk wouldn't restore Brenden's mental barrier if it had fallen, but it might give him room to think and halt Rynoki's advance.

Brenden shook away Drayden's hand. Rynoki kept his eyes riveted on Brenden, for a moment longer, whispered something about compromise, then smiled, as though he'd accomplished his goal.

"I don't have to press this issue now, Ambassador. We'll have plenty of time to get to know you intimately on Cystia. Until then." Rynoki inclined his head before leaving the cargo hold. The hatch slammed shut behind him and Brenden stared at the metal barrier.

"What just happened?" Drayden asked in a whisper, his hand poised to touch Brenden's arm again. "What did he mean by a hidden enemy? He said you'd been compromised."

"He attacked my mind with something I can't explain. He almost broke through my barriers. I won't have the strength to reject him on my own. Once we're on the planet, they'll separate us." Brenden gave Drayden's shoulder an appreciative squeeze, then paced the room. "I sensed part of their plan, but not enough to do us much good. They're more resourceful than we thought. Rynoki meant what he said, though. They won't compromise your mind if you'll work with them."

"I never believed he was insincere in his offer." Drayden took a step back, his eyes never leaving Brenden's face. "But I won't change my mind."

"They'll torture you. You'll eventually surrender everything you know in the end. You could save yourself a lot of pain."

Drayden stared in shocked surprise at Brenden's words. Not the words of an experienced diplomat or a soldier who'd been trained to deal with torture, but the words of a traitor. Drayden pulled on Tridia's memories for any suggestions on how to deal with the devastating turn of events. "How will I know if you're compromised?"

"You won't. The possession is subtle. Empress Dojene's men were normal until they turned on her. We could try to agree on some bit of information now and if I couldn't remember it later you'd have a clue. Even that isn't guaranteed if they take my memories. Once I fall asleep – or should we become separated – you'll have to treat me as an enemy. I'm sorry. I intended to be an ally. I'll hold my barrier in place as long as I can."

They studied each other in silence. The semi-darkness shadowed Brenden's brilliant blue eyes. Drayden's charcoal gray eyes remained hidden and wary. Losing the ambassador as an ally meant gaining a powerful and knowledgeable enemy. Since Brenden had accompanied him to his hiding place, did he also know the whereabouts of the other survivors? How much could his compromised mind betray? Had the ambassador been able to secure any of the information he held? If he had not, they had only one option.

"There is something we can do to stop this, isn't there?" Drayden clenched his fists as he spoke, but he held his voice steady.

"Yes." Brenden stopped pacing. "There is one final solution to this problem. We can keep them from reaching the planet."

"By destroying the ship."

"It won't be easy, Your Majesty. I can't save either of us if we succeed, and the conditions of our captivity will worsen if we fail."

"Stop with the titles. My name is Drayden. I let it go on this long because I had convinced myself I was jealous of you because of her." Drayden dropped the hint, knowing an uncompromised Brenden Aren would chasten him for it. "We're too far gone for jealousy now. I don't expect to be saved. If my body is emitting traceable energy, it should be completely destroyed, otherwise, they'll just find the remains."

Brenden's eyes held questions at Drayden's reference to Tridia. Not only did Brenden not chasten him, but he seemed to not know who Drayden referenced.

"We were told you were badly injured when you were on Ren Tama's ship. Near death. Did she help you recover?"

"The ship's medical staff were phenomenal. I don't know what they did, but my healing took place in record time." Drayden took another step away from Brenden. He stared for a moment longer, then sighed. "I think my efforts were too small and too late."

"Your suspicion would be well founded, if I hadn't just been plotting to destroy the ship with you."

"You're speaking in a normal voice and not a whisper. We worried about being overheard before, now we don't care? You didn't ask about my condition sooner. We've been here for hours."

"Now you're paranoid," Brenden said. "Are you going to help me destroy this ship or not?"

"I've seen at least ten armed guards at one time. There are another two or three command personnel and Dr. Rynoki. How do we destroy the ship with so many against us?"

"Every Hierarchy ship has a self-destruct mechanism that all but disintegrates the vessel. The switch is located on the bridge, but we'd never make it that far. However, we might make it to the self-destruct device. It's located in the armament locker, just down from the head. I didn't see a guard on that door when I was taken out."

"You believe you can get to it?" Drayden asked.

"Cause a disturbance at the next break. Make it loud enough to draw my escort back into this room. Even if you can only draw one of them away, I should be able to handle the other. I need two minutes to rig the device to explode," Brenden explained. "It may take another two for the explosion to occur. I'll remain in the locker to block the door."

"You're sure this will completely destroy our bodies?" Drayden's palms had started sweating.

"Yes. There won't be enough left to trace," Brenden said. "I can't hold the door and rig the device at the same time. I need the two minutes. If you have to open your mind, do it. It won't matter once the bomb detonates."

Drayden nodded in agreement, but he had no intention of compromising the only position he had left to defend. Brenden's true plan was to provide him a reason to lower his barriers. Drayden would play along – on the slim chance they could destroy the ship – but he held no belief that it would happen.

Once they'd agreed on the arrangement, Brenden sat and meditated in silence. Drayden kept his back to the bulkhead and a wary eye on his would-be ally. The hours crawled by. He spent his solitude thinking about Tridia, trying to recall the attacks she knew so well. If he could use a few of them, Brenden would have enough time to set the self-destruct. Tridia wouldn't be pleased that he'd draw on her skills, and the thought made him smile despite the circumstances.

When the guards appeared at the hatch again Drayden's heart pounded anew. His hands shook, but his steps remained sure. They took him out of the room and left him in privacy to do his business. Brenden nodded to him when he returned. Two guards accompanied

Brenden down the hall and Drayden waited a full minute before making his move. He wiped his palms on his thighs as he got to his feet. The sergeant ordered him to sit down again, but he continued to stand.

"How can you work for something as evil as the Kel Anec?" Drayden shouted so the guards in the corridor could hear him. "Don't you realize they plan to destroy all civilization as you know it? Can't you see what they're doing to your leaders? Haven't you questioned your strange orders?"

The sergeant again ordered him to return to his seat, but Drayden took two steps and landed a flying leap with both feet against the man's chest. The sergeant staggered back against the open door, as Drayden recovered his footing. One of Brenden's guards rushed back into the room, his weapon raised.

"Return to your seat, Prince Drayden, or we'll be forced to fire on you."

Drayden disregarded the order and spun to kick the weapon from the guard's hand. He made contact as the man fired. The energy blast hit the sergeant's armor, causing little, if any, damage. The second guard entered the room with his weapon primed.

"Stand down, Prince Drayden!"

Drayden halted, breathing heavily, more from nerves than exertion.

"Don't you understand who you're working for? What they'll do? How could you be so blind?" he shouted.

"This is your last warning. Both weapons will fire on you in ten seconds if you aren't seated on the floor."

"Fire on me? You make that sound like a bad thing. Set the power to maximum and fire away. It's more humane than anything they've got planned for me. We're only hours from their stronghold. I was supposed to be transported to Kanu to meet with their prime minister, but we aren't going there, are we? We're going to Cystia. I'm to be taken into the mines where the monsters live. I'll never come out of there alive. So, fire away."

Both guards raised their weapons at the end of his tirade and fired. Drayden flew backwards, his body numb from the stun blasts. All three guards advanced on him. They stretched him out and checked his pulse. One of them produced fabric restraints and bound his wrists and ankles. How long had it been? Did Brenden have enough time?

Drayden's ears rang and his vision blurred. Surely it had been two minutes. Did he have time to send a mental message to Tridia? It meant dropping his barriers, but what would it matter in another minute? Before he could release the barriers around his mind, Tridia's last urgings resounded in his memory.

I'll find you Drayden. Close your mind and keep it shut tight. I'll find you. Keep them out as long as you can.

Drayden reinforced the barriers around his mind. If he lived, she wouldn't find him helpless again.

"Where is Ambassador Aren?" the sergeant demanded.

"In the head, sir."

"Well, get him back in here, now!"

Two guards dashed out of sight and Drayden waited, trying to swallow the bitterness in his throat. There should have been an explosion by now. Brenden had failed. A tussle at the door proved his fears true as the guards shoved Brenden through the door, then hit him on the back of the head with the butt of a blaster. He fell face down at Drayden's side.

"He was in the armaments locker. The munitions officer is there now, defusing his efforts."

The sergeant pulled Brenden's arms behind him and secured them with another set of restraints, then did the same with his ankles.

"This is the legendary Brenden Aren?" he asked. "He almost pulled it off, but I expected something with a little more finesse from him."

The guards left, securing the door behind them. Drayden lay in the semi-darkness, waiting for the feeling – and the pain – to return to his body. He'd welcome anything to take his mind from their failed attempt.

Without warning, his mind reeled and he saw Tridia. She glowed with power and her eyes gleamed with a turquoise light. Her face held utter hatred, and her thoughts pounded against his barriers. Hatred, not for him, but for something she'd made herself believe about him. He'd helped her sell the lie to convince their enemies of her feelings. She raised her hand and sent a blue-white stream of energy directly toward him. Drayden flinched and found himself on the cargo hold floor again. Another vision of her future. Was she seeing him now? Did his numbness reach her? Thoughts of her consumed him as the door opened and Dr. Rynoki came in.

"You tried, and very nearly succeeded. You have forfeited all privilege, Your Highness. We'll let you keep your title so you can remember what you might have been, but you'll live closed away in your shell of consciousness for the rest of your very long natural life. By the time the ambassador wakes up and you are able to walk again, we'll be on Cystia. For the rest of this journey, contemplate all of the indignities and pain we can heap upon you, and I promise we will surpass your wildest imaginings."

"Never happen." Drayden forced the words from his mouth.

"Chesan dog!" Rynoki kicked Drayden in the side for emphasis.

Drayden felt nothing at the time, but there'd be an added hurt later. As Rynoki left, slamming the hatch, Drayden focused his mind on

Tridia's training again, and imagined all the ways he'd like to kill that particular Kel Anec himself. Rynoki would keep him alive for the torture value, even if he had no other purpose. That might keep him alive long enough for Tridia to find him.

It's all up to you now, my mate. The message wouldn't escape his barriers, but it comforted him to think it.

CHAPTER FIFTY-FOUR

Tridia sat frozen in the pilot's seat of the Chesan ship. She gripped the arms of the chair as though her life depended on not falling out of it.

"Commander?" Winniel asked.

"Drayden," Tridia whispered. She caught her breath and rubbed her ribs where a sharp pain had just stabbed. "He's alive. I just saw him standing in the mine on Cystia. Blue energy held him suspended in the air but he was surrounded by Kel Anec."

"He's on Cystia now? That's not possible. Our last coordinates on their ship —"

"No, it was a vision of the future," Tridia said. "He'll make it to Cystia alive, but something will happen to him there. What is the estimate for when they reach the planet?"

"At maximum speeds they should be another six to eight hours in flight." Winniel reported

"I saw *him*." Tridia glanced at Winniel. "This was not through his eyes, it was through mine."

"Then your plan is in jeopardy?" Winniel asked.

"If anything, it means it may work," Tridia said. "Have you made contact with your clan?"

"No, Commander. Communications are blacked out in our ships and it's too far for even our telepathy."

"Keep trying. If we fail it will be up to the Sentinels to finish the job." Tridia worked the monitors, pulling up and discarding numerous star charts as she spoke. Then she sat forward to study one of them. "Got it!"

"What have you got?" Ofein entered the cockpit.

His resemblance to Alanel had been unnerving in the beginning. But

528

the Sentinel clans were clones, each male and female identical to the others of their sex. Tridia had focused on Ofein when Winniel introduced him. He was younger than Alanel and lacked the minute habits Tridia had come to expect from him. Ofein possessed Alanel's memories but he had unique traits in the way he stood and the slight tilt of his head when he listened. Seeing him as Winniel's mate was difficult, even though Winniel seemed at ease.

"We'll be waiting for them when they get to Cystia. I've found a way to get us there," Tridia said.

"Impossible," Ofein argued. "At record hyperspeeds we'll need ten days to get there."

"Not with a Base Nine sling to fold space." Tridia pointed to the chart. "This is a heavy planet with a massive gravity well. It's posted against light craft travel and it has no atmosphere. Space is practically folding around it as it is."

"A ship this size would be unable to escape the planet's gravity. We'd need the thrust of a transport ship just to leave the system." Ofein studied the chart.

"Not if we're moving fast enough," Tridia said.

"This ship can't sustain the speeds that gravity well would produce. It will be torn to shreds before we send out a pulse to open the vortex." Winniel said.

Tridia looked around the cockpit and touched the console with her fingertips. "I've never seen or felt a ship like this. It's alive and sentient. Search your memories, Ofein, it's there. The Chesans built it at the height of their technology. We've already used its dimensional drive to create a wormhole in a smaller gravity well for a shorter distance. It won't fall apart. If it weakens, I'll strengthen it with Chesan energy."

"Could we not fly through a portal to the planet?" Ofein asked. "You've done so before."

Tridia shook her head.

"The amount of energy I'd need to bring the ship through would be too exhausting," she said. "The Guardian Controller supplied most of the power to move the ship through the portal the last time. Opening small portals on my own knocked me out for how long? This one would be much bigger and open longer. It won't do us much good to get there before them if I'm unconscious when the Kel Anec arrive. Besides, my plan will require all my energy reserves. We've got one shot to deal with the Kel. We can't afford failure."

"Why not open a portal to the prince and extract him?" Winniel asked.

"I'd be vulnerable holding the portal open. You'd have to go through to him, and we don't know what effect the mist would have on you – or what might be waiting on the other side. There's no telling what condition Drayden or Master Aren would be in. What if they're in stasis pods for the journey? How much time would we need to free them?" Tridia rubbed her side again. No, not in pods. Drayden, at least, was vulnerable to pain. "It would also leave the Kel Anec free to come after us again. We've got to stop them. We may need to use a portal to escape in the end. It's a gambit we can only use once."

The Sentinels made no other objection as Tridia went through the process of entering calculations and coordinates using the special holographic controls. She warned the medics to secure any loose items and strap in. The planet loomed into view a half-hour later. Its bulk filled the cockpit viewer before they neared the gravity field.

"We're about to enter the gravity well now," Winniel stated.

Tridia reached inside herself to touch the blue energy. It tingled at the edge of her consciousness, like the Sentinel connection, as if awaiting her attention. She'd use it to reinforce the outer hull of the ship. In addition to the Chesan energy, portal energy throbbed in her cells, changing her body as it seeped out, drawing bits of her resistance with it. The desire to open a new portal to draw more power beckoned, but she still had the power to resist it.

"Prepare to –" Tridia stopped as a faint presence touched her thoughts. "Controller?"

I saw this desperate plan many years ago. The words echoed weakly in Tridia's mind.

Will it work? Tridia kept her eyes on the instruments and listened to Winniel's navigational warnings while straining to hear the Controller.

The outcome is uncertain and depends on your skills. The Controller paused. *This ship was built from my sentient gold, a gift to the Chesan builders for this contingency, although* they *didn't know it. There is one moment, just before you reach the deepest point of the gravity well, where you must reinforce the stress points. Your senses and the ship will tell you when. I don't have the strength to help you beyond that.*

Can't I reinforce the points now?

No, the ship will absorb the energy too soon. You must wait until the last moment. Farewell, Tridia Odana.

"Controller?" Tridia called out, groping for contact.

"The entity has ceased communications, Commander." Winniel said. "I no longer sense its presence."

"Well, we were on our own before. At least now we know we have a chance."

The Controller had confirmed Tridia's discovery about the Chesan ship, it was a living thing and she could feed her will into it. The thin bracelets on her wrists glowed and burned. The ship reached out to her and its life force joined with hers. Adrenaline rushed through her veins as she fired the ship's engines and tilted the craft toward the planet. They'd fly as close as they could to sling through the dimensional fold from the deepest possible point of the well. She planned two orbits with decreasing spirals, slinging from the lowest point on the last orbit – if the ship held together.

Winniel read the increasing speeds as Ofein intoned the trajectories. One miscalculation now and the giant planet would be rained upon by bits of gold spaceship and body parts. Tridia reached out to sense the curve of space around the planet. With the portal energy pulsing in her cells, along with the changes and knowledge brought about her by exposure in the portal, she could sense the gravity well and the solar winds that buffeted the planet's surface. She'd taken both into account when she plotted their course using Drayden's mathematics. The crew's fear and their trust in her ability brushed against her thoughts. One of the medics heaved his last meal onto the floor, too afraid to be embarrassed.

The ship vibrated as Tridia steered it into the beginning of its second orbit, its systems no longer able to calculate the hyperspeed. She pressed her hand against the dimensional activator. Space folded around them as she forced the ship deeper into the gravity well and faster in its turn. The vibrations grew worse as she gunned the engines for all the reserves they possessed. The ship whined and for a moment she feared she'd led them all to their deaths, then the Chesan energy emerged, creating a blue aura around her body. Pain raced along her skin as she held the energy to the last second.

She discharged blue energy into the ship as it shot into the folding vortex. Power raced along fault lines and coated the ship in a thin blue shield. It reinforced the structure and bonded with the sentient metal. The ship held together as they floated into the vortex, but they weren't out of danger. No inertial shield had ever been designed for the kind of force that would pound their bodies when they exited the wormhole. The ship might hold, but its crew wouldn't necessarily live to tell of it.

Space bent and folded to accommodate the ship's passing toward the trajectory Tridia had calculated. In a matter of minutes, they'd traveled halfway across the galaxy and burst from the vortex. Lera cried out from the pressure. The male medic who hadn't vomited passed out. Winniel and Ofein remained immutable as stone. Tridia fought the controls to slow the ship without destroying what was left of the inertial shields. They objected as she banked around a solar system to counteract their forward speed. After three more loops and one orbit around a large sun, she slowed the ship into normal hyperspeed. When Winniel calculated their position, they'd overshot Cystia, but could make it back to the planet ahead of the Fighter Hawk without further dangerous experiments.

Tridia took a deep breath and sat back in her seat. She tapped the intercom and spoke.

"Is everyone alright back there?" Tridia only asked because the Lera needed a distraction.

The girl's shaky voice responded after a few moments. "Mel is dazed but conscious. Xander is out cold, but his pulse is strong. I'm on my feet."

Tridia gave a short laugh, her only concession to a release of nervous tension. Her hands shook and feeling left her face. The after-affects of the portal energy's drain hit with a vengeance. She had to get it under control before they reached the planet. There'd be no stopping to rest once she faced the Kel Anec.

"Take a seat until you aren't about to collapse. We'll fly at normal speeds for an hour or so then I'll come back and review the plan with everyone." Tridia nodded to Winniel – and passed out.

An hour later the Chesan ship hung motionless in space just out of scanner range of Cystia. Tridia sat in the lounge area with Winniel and the medics. She explained her plan to confront the Kel Anec just beyond the laser field – at the chasm. The image of Drayden flying toward that gaping hole haunted her, as did the vision she'd shared with Master Aren in which he died from a bolt of energy delivered by a glowing woman in a blue aura. In the vision, he believed he would die, but it wasn't certain he would. Could she control so much power without killing him and Drayden? Would she *need* to kill them to save them from a worse fate? There was too much at risk to make a mistake, but they had no other options if they hoped to rescue the men before the Kel Anec attached feeders or otherwise invaded their bodies.

"Commander, meaning no disrespect, Ma'am, but are you sure you can do this? What if one of those feeders attaches itself to you?" The pale, but conscious Xander held a cool compress to the back of his neck.

"I've repelled a feeder before, and I'll have the Sentinels there to help. The question is, can any of you fly this ship well enough to get it back to this location and wait for our signal to return?"

"I'm certified as a evac pilot, Commander. I don't know if that qualifies me to fly this thing." Mel volunteered with uncertainty in his voice, and hope in his thoughts.

"If you can handle the FH316 modified, you can fly this ship. It responds faster than anything you've ever flown, so you'll have to use a gentle touch, but the controls are similar." Tridia looked around at their faces. They had small insecurities, but no doubts about their responsibilities. "If you have no other questions, we'll head to the planet. Mel, join us on the bridge. You'll land and take the ship back up as soon as our feet touch the ground. Close the hatch after liftoff. I don't want you in the planet's atmosphere more than ten minutes, before *or* after the mission."

Mel swallowed hard and got to his feet to follow Tridia into the cockpit, but she sent him ahead with Winniel and drew Lera aside. Tridia took a chain with keys from her neck and handed them to the girl.

"Hold these in safekeeping for Prince Drayden," Tridia instructed. "The big one fits his cabin on this ship. I'm not sure about the other two, but he can find out on his own if I'm not here to help him. I don't know what kind of shape he'll be in, but I'm counting on you and your medics to take care of him if he needs you."

Lera took the keys and nodded. She wouldn't argue that Tridia would return to instruct the prince and look after him herself, but she held those thoughts tightly in her mind. She refused to believe Tridia would fail to return. Tridia conceded a small smile to the girl's unfailing devotion.

She returned to the bridge and instructed Mel on the ship's controls, lending him confidence when he seemed overwhelmed. After a few shaky maneuvers they were ready to make atmosphere. Tridia entered the coordinates for the mine's back opening, the small cave from which Winniel and Alanel had saved her. Winniel found the disengage codes for the defensive satellites in the mind of an idle guard in the security building on Cystia. She forced him to shut down the satellites, then left him and the entire security team out cold from her mental assault. With nothing barring their landing, Tridia and the Sentinels left the cockpit and made their way to the hatch.

Tridia blocked her energy signature on the way, grateful that she no longer had to be concerned about blocking the Sentinel's telepathy. Since the Chesan energy had discharged into the ship and the portal energy dispelled itself during the sling across the galaxy, the invaders couldn't track her by either unique emission. As long as they didn't cause a disruption, like triggering the laser field, the Kel Anec should be unaware of their presence. With Davik's help, they should make their target area before the captors escorted Brenden and Drayden too deep into the mine.

Mel landed the ship in a clearing a hundred yards from the opening. Tridia and the Sentinels jumped from the hatch and ran through the underbrush as the ship lifted off again. Tridia didn't look back, keeping her thoughts focused on the pressing matter of staying alive.

CHAPTER FIFTY-FIVE

They reached the opening unchallenged. Tridia dove through the horizontal slit and scurried toward the precipice she'd scaled blind. Her breath caught when she shined a light down the cliff face and the narrow steps of the crude stairs Davik had blasted. Apart from the stairs, handholds were few. How had she ever made the climb out?

Winniel and Ofein studied the stairs for a moment, then anchored rappelling lines farther along the cliff face so they would land on the far side of the abyss. They dropped ropes over the sides without seeming to notice the height. Tridia geared up but stepped back as a shapeless mass of flashing silver and gold lights in an indigo cloud rose from the abyss. The cloud took Davik's shape and its sparkling form hovered before her.

"I hoped you'd find us quickly," Tridia said.

"I wasn't far away and I detected movement where there should be none. Why have you come back? Who are your friends?" Davik spoke without touching her as he had before. His voice sounded deeper than she remembered it.

"My friends are Sentinels. We've come to destroy the Kel Anec, rescue some prisoners who are on their way here, and to keep my promise to you." Davik's energy brightened when Tridia identified the Sentinels. She rushed to reassure him. "They're friends. We need your help. Can you get us to the lakeside where you first found me? I need to reach the tunnel above it as quickly as possible."

"There isn't a direct route for a corporeal body, but you should be able to make it within two hours at a steady pace," Davik said. "A little longer if you have to stop."

"Do you know how many Kel Anec are here?" Tridia asked.

"Eight floaters, another eight possessing human technicians from

534

the Hierarchy lab. One of them took over Frees B'Nay, but he left and hasn't returned. There's about ten in Elstaar bodies, but they're outside the tunnel. There's only six feeders left. I've been thinning their ranks. The scientists no longer come into the tunnels. I think they're getting ready to close up shop. I may not have much time. There's been *a lot* of activity in the past couple of days."

"We should keep our conversations to a minimum," Ofein warned. "We don't want to give our enemies more ways to track us."

Everyone agreed, then Tridia stumbled and fell toward the cliff as the disorientation of millions of minds shattering their links to each other flooded her consciousness. Davik wrapped her in his sparkling blue shroud. Tridia clung to him for an anchor in the madness.

"Are you under attack, Commander?" Winniel whispered.

Tridia shook her head. She put an arm around Davik and held on as the fury whirled in her mind. The outpouring of thought mirrored the Guardian induction. An almost unrecognizable glimpse of Master Aren's consciousness raced across her mind. His thoughts were shallow and weak. Deeca's presence made no appearance in the maelstrom of thought. As the confusion subsided, the gold bracelets around Tridia's wrists went cold.

"The Guardian Controller is dead," she panted. "Only its demise would cause disruption in so many minds."

Tridia turned dazed eyes toward the Sentinels.

"Commander." Winniel's sharp tone brought Tridia back.

"We go forward." She extricated herself from Davik's hold.

"You're sure you're okay?" he asked.

Tridia nodded. She, Winniel, and Ofein attached green glow bulbs to their wrists and adjusted the light packs they wore. Tridia shook off the residue of her experience to survey the area around them. An eerie green glow illumined the cavern, broken by the sparkles from Davik's energy.

"We'll rappel down and follow Davik through the tunnel," Tridia said.

"I know how you hate heights." Davik lifted her in his arms and floated toward the edge. "Hold on and don't look down. I've got you."

Tridia buried her face in his shoulder and held on. Her stomach stayed at the top of the cliff, but Davik held her close and the descent took only a moment. She stood on shaky legs when he set her down.

"I'd be laughed out of the Challenge Grid if this fear ever became known," Tridia said. "You're my savior, yet again."

"It's quieter than rappelling." Davik lingered, holding Tridia's hand longer than necessary before going back for Winniel and Ofein. He brought them down together.

They all adjusted their packs again and stretched their legs once they were on solid ground.

"Try to set a pace that will get us there in two hours or less," Tridia said to Davik. "Don't slow unless we fall behind."

They ran for two hours, ducking stalactites, dodging stalagmites, and skipping rock-to-rock on broken floors. Tridia held both of her sides when they reached the ledge beside the underground lake. Her hands trembled as she moved her glow stick over the sandy floor. The glow illuminated her old backpack.

"I'm surprised the Kel Anec didn't take it, or shove it into the water," Tridia said.

"They didn't have an interest and I moved it to the side before the scientists came back," Davik said. "I intended to take it away for safekeeping, but never got around to it."

Tridia's knife lay on the ground. She pocketed it before kneeling to open the bulging pack. Inside she found rope, an anchor launcher, the reflective shields that had saved her life when the laser hit her from behind, dented, but intact. She pulled out the anchor launcher, anchors and rope and lay them aside. Then she pulled the cord with the DNA stasis pouch out of her shirt. She removed one of her DNA vials and held Winniel's gaze. They didn't speak. Winniel inclined her head a fraction of an inch before pocketing the vial.

Tridia placed a hand on Davik's sparkling shoulder. "Stay with them. They'll need your help if I fail, and they've been charged with fulfilling my obligation to you if I can't do it myself. You won't spend another day like this, I swear it."

"I knew you'd come back." Davik wrapped his arms around her and pulled her close, then held her at arm's length. Tridia shivered. "You're not well. Your heartbeat's erratic and your breathing's shallow. Running didn't do this to you."

"It's hard to explain, but you're right. I'm not well." Tridia touched Davik's cheek with a trembling hand. "That's why I need you to back me up. Whatever you do, stay below the entrance level and out of sight as long as you can manage until I call for you or Winniel tells you I'm dead."

"I can't let you do this on your own."

"I have to," Tridia said. "I'm the only one who can. If the Kel Anec suspect anyone else is involved it's all over."

"I can handle the Kel Anec – and their feeders," Davik said. "You don't have to go alone."

"I do," Tridia said. "They have prisoners on the way here. If they suspect anything, they won't let the ship land. The transport will leave and we'll have no way to track it."

Davik didn't reply at once. He dropped his hands to her waist and his sparkling eyes lingered on her face. Before he could speak, dark shapes drifted up the tunnel.

"Feeders!" Davik shouted. "They're sensing my energy. So many of them!"

More than a dozen feeders filled the tunnel. Davik stretched his shape until he became a shield between the feeders and Tridia. Flashes of energy shot from his shield, destroying one feeder after another. A tendril stretched from the back side of the shield and touched Tridia's cheek, then her ear.

I'll keep these things off your back, just be careful up there. And remember, I love you.

Tridia hurried to load the anchor launcher. The ceiling above the lake formed a bowl shape and the opening to the tunnel above was a break in its smooth line. Aiming at the highest point her length of rope would allow, Tridia fired. The anchor buried itself in the opposing rock overhang with a metallic thunk, hauling uncoiled lengths of rope behind it. Tridia turned to Ofein as she pulled on a pair of climbing gloves.

"A boost to get above the water?"

Winniel took one end of the rope and tugged to be sure the anchor had set, then held the end taut as Ofein knelt to take Tridia's boot in his hand. He launched her twelve feet along the length of the rope where she grabbed it and swung over the water. Her boots skimmed the surface as she clung to the line, then she started to climb. Her muscles screamed from the exertion. She slipped and struggled to grasp the rope with shaking hands, holding her position by wrapping the rope around her ankle. After a few heartbeats, she forced her hands to close around the rope. Three-quarters of the way up she had to pause to catch her breath. She glanced up to the anchor, then down at the water. The short climb should have taken no more than a minute, yet she had to steel herself to finish it.

The temptation to take strength from a portal gnawed at her resolve. Tridia made a small circle with the index finger and thumb of her right hand and looked through it. Just as the circle started to shimmer she snapped to the danger of what she'd contemplated. The Kel Anec would be on her in seconds if they sensed portal energy inside the mine. She flexed her fingers then wrapped them around the rope to continue the climb. Each grasp sapped a little more of her strength.

When she reached the top of the rope she coiled part of it around her ankle and pulled a second length from her small pack. She secured one end to the anchor imbedded in the rock, and the other to a second anchor, which she loaded into the anchor launcher on her belt. Aiming high enough for the anchor to lodge a foot below the top of the chasm,

Tridia pulled the trigger. The anchor made the same solid thunk as it embedded into the rock of the opposite wall.

The transition to the second rope would have been easy just a few days ago, but she barely managed to get a leg over it without falling. Hooking both legs over the rope she inched her way hand-over-hand across the chasm and up the other side. Two protrusions on that side of the chasm made the second half of her climb more difficult than the first, and Tridia's arms and legs quivered when she hauled herself over the rim. She lay on her side and stared over the edge.

The lake lay in darkness thirty feet below her. Shaking with the effort, she sat up and dropped a glow tube into the water as a signal she'd made it to the top. Tridia caught her breath and struggled to her feet. She paced the width of the tunnel and back to get rid of the spots before her eyes. The most difficult part lay ahead – a mental ordeal that would challenge her stability and take her to the brink of murder.

Just as she had built the consciousness for Nira Kayen, the Felinus Warrior, she had to build one for Tridia Odana, the victim. She had to convince the remaining Kel Anec she wanted to join them. Righteous anger for things that had happened to her, Drayden, and Davik wouldn't do. Only a burning rage in the depth of her being would be believed. She required an affront to herself to inspire the kind of hate she needed to fool the Kel Anec. Her heart broke at the thought those hateful deeds had to be perpetrated by Drayden, but there was no other way. She had to give him a new character she could hate – and she knew where to start.

As she paced, a face rose from her memory – Devereaux. Imposing Drayden's face on Devereaux's planned atrocities would get her part of the way there, but she had to *believe* she hated Drayden. She had to hide any respect and affection she felt for him. The Kel Anec would search her thoughts for subterfuge and she had to allow the search to convince them.

She had built Nira Kayen's consciousness by mixing truth and lie. The victim needed facts layered with falsehoods. She pulled up the memories of Devereaux's plans and laced them with the passion from Tama's memories. Then she recalled Drayden's sensual appearance under the influence of the Rrabbas pollen and the way he'd looked when he lowered his lips to hers. She cried as she made Drayden accountable for every injury and indignity. She placed herself and Drayden in a darkened room in the bunker. She hid Tama's existence to shield his memories and built her rage against Drayden, but it wasn't enough. She required *hate*. He had taken her, abused her, then ridiculed her when she would have appeased him on her own.

A new persona formed in Tridia's mind. The assassin stepped down.

The victim arose – a full consciousness sheathed in hate and vengeance. Tridia fed it memories of vile acts dredged from the dying thoughts of her despicable targets. Every disgusting act was perpetrated on her by a man wearing Drayden's face. And Brenden Aren looked on, encouraging the violence.

When she could contain the trauma no longer, she opened her mind and released her thoughts into the mine shafts.

A handful of feeders came first, hungry for the mental energy they sensed, but the Kel Anec floaters held them at bay as they approached from behind. Where Davik's energy twinkled silver and gold in a blue cloud, the Kel Anec energy forms flashed a malevolent black and green. The feeders swirled in shades of black and gray as their shapes morphed, straining toward her energy.

You've returned to us, exposing the Chesan telepathic powers. How did you get here without us sensing your presence?

"I've learned to protect myself." Tridia spoke aloud. "I came here to kill someone. Try to interfere and I'll destroy you, too."

You plan to destroy our greatest prize. We can't allow you to do that.

"You allow me nothing. Your *prize* is a disgusting creature hungry only for its own pleasure. Keep it and you'll find yourself years obtaining your goals. I can deliver them to you now."

"What game are you playing with us, demented child?" A man wearing a technician's garb asked. Five more walked up the tunnel and around her, to stand between her and the chasm.

A Kel Anec presence touched Tridia's mind. She gave it visions of a rape and abuse that never happened, then slammed the barriers in place.

"Keep away from me. I'll give you access to the power you want, but only after I've destroyed that man."

What do you know about the power we want?

In response, Tridia formed a circle with her hand and opened a small portal. Power flowed out and infused her cells, bringing strength back to exhausted limbs. The heady, reckless sense of power threatened to overwhelm her. Elise's warnings rang in her ears. Prolonged exposure to the power caused irreparable harm.

Stay focused. She shrank the portal to the width of her thumb. If she closed it completely she'd pass out and she couldn't afford that with the Kel Anec so close.

You will give us this energy source. The Kel Anec beings pulsated with lust for the power they sensed and Tridia struggled against her own greed for it. The possessed men took a step toward her. She could destroy these creatures with little effort now that she absorbed the portal's power, with the blue energy just below the surface, but she needed to wait for the entire advance force to gather.

"The energy source is my body and I will allow you to touch it only after I've destroyed that man."

We approve of your single-mindedness and your purpose. The Chesan prince is almost here. The ship is landing as we speak. Be warned, he has a protector – the Alliance Ambassador with whom you traveled accompanies him.

"Master Brenden Aren." Tridia spat the words. "He's just as degenerate as the so-called prince. Brenden Aren was my master. He sent me to Drayden Anjenay. As far as I'm concerned, he's just as guilty as the man who raped me."

The Kel Anec made no other comment nor did they attempt to touch her mind again. Tridia waited in the center of the tunnel, searching for the possessed Hierarchy personnel. Eight of them walked into view from the deactivated laser field. Half wore only Elstaar uniforms, the others wore the black armor.

Davik had said there were eighteen possessed men in all, ten soldiers and eight technicians. The other four eluded her until she searched beyond the mine. They had joined the landing party to escort the prisoners from the ship.

All accounted for. Brenden and Drayden's physical forms became clear, but they had closed their minds. They wouldn't know what she planned and their reactions could jeopardize the entire scenario. She'd have to deal with them first. She increased the size of the portal so it covered her palm and drank the energy into her body. Feelings of desperation alternated with exhilaration as she absorbed power until she became unsure which personality belonged to her. The icy presence of both Sentinels entered her mind. They moved within the turmoil of her consciousness and reinforced her faltering identity. They punched through the barrier and drew her back.

Remain strong, Commander. The Hariok Clan is with you.

Winniel's words stabilized her mind and Tridia recalled her plans. This contingency had been taken into account. In the middle of the Sentinel's calm, another truth crystalized. Truth Tridia hadn't understood in her mother's warning. The facts were there in the information her mother transferred, but Tridia couldn't access it in her memory without a link to the portal.

The splintering of the Chaos Vision came from the many choices that could lead to *either* destruction or peace. A Kel Anec jihad fueled by portal energy was one of many horrendous outcomes that could span multiple galaxies. The worst by far were the holocausts caused by the wielder of the Chesan blue energy. Those would originate in the insanity of one who used the portal too freely – as she had already done. In these holocausts, the Kel Anec did the bidding of the wielder, not the other way around. The wielder would take over intergalactic conquest where the vanquished Kel Anec left off, pulling on portal power and using the blue energy to repair its ravages to a corporeal body. All the while knowing of the danger, the wielder would do anything to access the healing power – even become a gateway to release it into this dimension. Tridia was the wielder in the twisted visions from Drayden's point of view, but she wasn't the only one who could use the Chesan energy. Davik had bonded with it and she'd poured it into Drayden's body to heal him. Davik had touched the portal when she'd exploded trying to get to Drayden, but the prince had used the portal for years. *Had they already corrupted their future?* So many things to consider in this desperate plan to buy the Chesan survivors and the galaxy some time. So many ways she could end up exploiting her own children and destroying the prince. *Would it be better to end it all here?*

Focus! Tridia gasped.

The chaos ended here only if she could control her mind and carry out her plan. Her own calm replaced the Sentinels' peace. Winniel and Ofein withdrew their presence.

Tridia's heart raced when the landing party came into view. The victim wanted to scream, the assassin held her in check. Drayden walked on his own. Two guards supported Master Aren between them. His arms were bound behind him and even at a distance the dazed look in his eyes made his face appear slack. The shattering of the Controller's influence had affected him, but more than that event had caused the vacancy in his eyes. No wonder she'd barely recognized him in the flood of consciousness. Tridia sent a tendril of blue energy to snake around Master Aren's body and connect with the gold bands on his wrists. The guards assisting him let him fall as the tendril exploded against the gold.

"Come back to me, Master Aren." *Wake up, Master. Remember who you are.* Tridia sent the thought along the energy stream as she spoke aloud for everyone else's benefit. "I want you in your right mind when I destroy you."

Brenden's eyes lost their glaze and he struggled to stand as Tridia fed the once-sentient gold bands with healing energy and severed his bonds. A second tendril knocked him backwards.

"What are you doing?" Drayden tried to reach Brenden's prone figure but guards held him back. "He's not well!"

"Let them be together." Tridia spoke in a voice made deep by portal power.

Obey her. The Kel Anec energy forms flashed brighter with the thrill of violence at hand. The guards stepped away.

"Send your human soldiers away," Tridia ordered. "This power may destroy their minds."

The Kel Anec gave the order and the unpossessed Elstaar soldiers from the ship hurried out of the tunnel. Drayden, his wrists bound in front of him, helped Brenden to his feet then stepped away. The two men looked at her with confusion on their faces. One from lack of comprehension, the other from lack of recognition.

"Bring them across the chasm. I want to look into their eyes."

The Kel Anec beings that had surrounded her drifted over the chasm and lifted the two men into the air.

"Stop." A white-haired man Tridia recognized from the Public Hearing Room stepped forward. "Why are we taking orders from this girl?"

She controls the energy. We've made a bargain. She will be allowed to destroy these men. In return, she stays with us. We get her body, the source of the power in this galaxy.

"Have you considered she may be trying to rescue them and not kill them?"

We've seen into her mind. Her hate is strong and her memories are clear. Prince Drayden raped her. Ambassador Aren gave her to him.

A stunned look crossed Drayden's face. Just as Tridia had been able to hear the Kel Anec through her barriers the first time, he heard their conversation now. His jaw clenched and his mouth set in a firm line. Brenden just stared across the chasm as if trying to recognize Tridia's face or read her mind. She wished she could accommodate his desire, but she didn't dare show him more compassion.

"Open your mind girl and let me sense these memories and emotions," Rynoki ordered.

"And allow you to control me before I've had my revenge? Not likely." Tridia glared at the white-haired man, daring him to make another demand.

Rynoki took a weapon from one of the guards and hurried to where Drayden hung suspended above the floor. He pulled Drayden to the floor and jammed the tip of the weapon behind his ear. "Open your mind or I will kill him now."

"You blackmail me with the death of a man I traveled across the galaxy to kill myself? Go ahead and kill him, but if you do, the energy will never be yours. I'll disintegrate his body and the samples you carry in your case. *Then I'll destroy you.*"

Tridia willed Rynoki to not call her bluff. She increased the size of the portal and its energy created a charged aura around her. A pale blue halo increased until it blocked the tunnel from floor to ceiling, hiding the portal behind it. The feeders went into a frenzy, trying to get to the power, but their masters restrained them.

The energy is pure. We've never experienced this level of output.

"Give him to me now." Tridia made the words a threat.

Release him, Rynoki!

Rynoki lowered the weapon but kept a restraining hand on Drayden's shoulder.

"Take the other one first. Let's see what type of destruction she has in mind. If her intent is true, then she can have this one."

CHAPTER FIFTY-SIX

Rynoki looked to his flashing companions and the possessed Elstaar soldiers for confirmation. They all agreed and four of the flashing Kel Anec carried Brenden across the chasm. He fell to his knees in front of Tridia. Before she could reach out to him, Rynoki held out his hand and a shimmering gray barrier formed around the ambassador. Any attempt to communicate with him would have to cross it. Tridia couldn't free him without Rynoki knowing. She'd have to kill him in order to save Drayden if she didn't come up with an alternative.

"You slithering serpent of a creature," she screamed. "You parade through your Core Alliance society like a paragon when your heart's viler than the abomination you sent me to. He violated my body and bent it to his will. You – you violated my mind. You stained every memory, contaminated any decent thought I had with your sick plans and manipulations. Why? So I could be handed to the first noble with whom you wished to curry favor? To act as your courier? Your pet? You branded my body." Tridia held up her arms to show the scars on her wrists and a blue-gold flash of energy reflected from the bracelets into Brenden's eyes. He winced as Rynoki's shimmering barrier flared and faltered. His blank stare became focused and he returned her angry glare with the first hint of recognition. Tridia pointed to Drayden. "Then you gave me to him."

"Stop complaining, whelp," Brenden shouted in response. "You were a Hierarchy slave when I took you in. Assassin is such an aristocratic way to describe that servitude. You took an oath of obedience to me of your own free will. I did nothing that exceeded my rights. Certainly nothing you didn't deserve. You're a slave. It's what you were born to be."

"Die!" Tridia gathered a bolt of energy and targeted Brenden's chest.

What remained of the barrier exploded with a bright burst of energy. The force of the impact flung Brenden to the edge of the chasm where he lay face down and motionless, one arm flung over the edge. The vision she'd shared with him had been fulfilled and she gasped. Was he dead? The victim cheered, the assassin swallowed her dread.

On the other side of the chasm, Rynoki fell to the ground holding his head. His body writhed. His mental barrier had absorbed the brunt of the bolt and transferred it to his body. Had it deflected enough to save Master Aren?

"Bring the other one," Tridia screeched. Portal energy coursed through her veins and mingled with the blue energy that fought to repair her body. Spittle gathered at the edge of her mouth.

The flashing Kel Anec carried Drayden across the chasm and dropped him at Tridia's feet, then hurried back to their comrades. Drayden stood and looked into her angry face. He carried no Kel Anec barriers, but his mind remained closed against her and his eyes glowed blue.

Tridia stared. Had their bonding changed Drayden into something beyond himself? She gathered her courage and focused the victim's rage.

"So innocent to look at. Who would believe what a black heart that pretty face conceals? To think I tried to save you, to keep you from the Elstaar. I thought you were someone worth protecting. Then you forced me into your bed when I would have gone willingly for the smallest show of tenderness from you."

"It's like the Ambassador said, you're a slave. A Chesan prince has a right to take a slave girl if he chooses. You should feel honored I would bother to notice you." Drayden raised his chin as he spoke. "Besides, if I'm the abomination that you claim, why were you writhing against me like a harlot? Why did you kiss me with such abandon? Why, if my presence is so unbearable to you, did you whimper for me to take you and give you release from your lust?"

Drayden's words stung Tridia to the heart. The accusation in his voice came from the anguish he'd felt over her behavior with Ren Tama. Her anger rekindled and she shouted back at him.

"You planted those seeds. What I felt was your lust."

"You came uninvited into my mind to receive those seeds. You wanted to be taken, I just obliged you, *slave*. If you don't want to be used, stop making yourself such an easy puppet."

Drayden's nostrils flared. Tridia's hands balled into fists. They both breathed heavily. Their anger convinced the Kel Anec of the depth of Tridia's hatred for Drayden. The creatures shivered in anticipation for the kill. The time had come to make her move.

"Puppet? You want to see a puppet, you insignificant waste of flesh?"

Tridia separated a thin sheet of energy from her aura and wrapped it around Drayden. His jaw clenched and he closed his fists. She severed the bonds at his wrists with a blade of energy, then raised his arms above his head.

"Dance for me, puppet." The energy string pulled and jerked Drayden in a macabre dance to the edge of the chasm. Tridia laughed maniacally as she released him beside Brenden's body. The victim's consciousness screamed for revenge. Her sanity hung by a thread.

"Come to this side of the chasm and stand beside me," she called to the Kel Anec. "If you're in the line of my rage you'll be disintegrated. Hurry!"

Sparks of energy shot toward the chasm. Drayden ducked and dodged to keep from being struck. One of the Elstaar soldiers moved to a switch on the wall to lower a bridge over the chasm, but Tridia wouldn't wait for the machinery to finish. She ordered the Kel Anec to carry their comrades. They complied, but left Rynoki's motionless body where it lay. They gathered beside her, bunched against the wall, skittish at the nearness of the blue aura.

"Prepare yourself, Prince Drayden, to see the extent of my loathing."

Drayden's fingers moved to Brenden's neck to feel for a pulse, then he looked up with fear in his eyes.

"Tridia, no! Don't do it." He rose to his knees as the plea left his lips.

Tridia shrank the aura just enough to bring it around the Kel Anec without touching them. Then, she pulled it in front of her, and enlarged it to again seal the tunnel. She'd created a barrier to separate her and the Kel Anec from Drayden and Brenden. She glared at the two of them, her chest heaving. Power gathered around her hands as she prepared to throw the killing bolts.

You must dismantle the victim! Winniel's voice shouted into her thoughts. *You must take her apart now, as you built her.*

Help me!

The Sentinel connection glowed in Tridia's mind, pointing out the falsehoods she'd planted to create the victim's consciousness. The victim fought harder than Nira Kayen's consciousness had. It demanded revenge for the wrongs committed against it, but Tridia took apart the falsehoods until only the memory of her plan remained. It had taken mere seconds once the Sentinels stabilized her mind, but it had seemed an eternity. Justified anger replaced the victim's false rage.

Behind Tridia yawned a portal that sealed the tunnel. She'd enlarged it and fed on its power after creating the aura. Without the aura blocking the portal, its energy formed a gray sheen on Tridia's skin and colored her vision with a turquoise tint. The portal tugged at her body. A vein burst in her temple and her eye ticked as reality dawned on the aliens beside her. She'd trapped them between the aura and the portal.

The corporeal Kel Anec shivered, and feeders flowed from their bodies. No wonder Davik's count had been wrong. Dozens of the creatures filled the space. Tridia placed a blue energy barrier between them and her. When no more feeders emerged, she opened a second portal inside the first and an artery throbbed in her neck. The second portal opened onto the corona of a yellow sun. Its intense light crossed the portal's mists and washed the menacing colors from the Kel Anec floaters. The feeders became translucent as they writhed in the radiant energy. In moments they all disappeared.

"You wanted to use this portal energy to travel to distant suns. This one isn't so distant, but you can go there if you choose," Tridia said.

The corporeal Kel Anec raised their Elstaar weapons while the energy forms mounted an attack against her mental barrier. Tridia destroyed the soldiers' weapons with strings of energy from the aura and kept enough energy between her and them to stave off their physical attacks. The attacks against her mental barrier amounted to nothing with the portal energy to feed her strength, but the demands of the power disintegrated her cells to the point that her corporeal form started to fade – even with the blue energy repairing it. Tridia pulled the aura backward, herding everyone toward the portal. Blue energy erupted from her body. It disintegrated the first soldier. The others inched away until they were on the threshold of the portal itself.

Tridia backed into the portal, keeping her eyes on the Kel Anec. Mists swirled around her legs in moist tentacles. When she pulled the aura against the portal, the Kel Anec crossed the threshold into the mists. They stood between Tridia and the flaming corona.

"Be absorbed by the mist, go into the corona, or be disintegrated by the aura." Spittle flew from Tridia's lips as she spoke. "Or walk into the darkness of nonexistence outside this corridor. Choose now, or I will tear you to shreds with this energy you so desired."

Tendrils of mist wove their way between the energy particles of the non-corporeal Kel Anec entities. The creatures made no sound and broadcast no thoughts, but they vibrated and flashed wildly before flinging themselves through the second portal into the sun's corona. The Kel Anec soldiers looked around with terror-filled eyes. Mists wrapped their bodies from ankles to waists. Their bodies disincorporated, just as Tridia's did, but they couldn't channel the blue energy to hold their forms together. In seconds they either ran into the sun or into the aura. None of them chanced the unknown darkness beyond the corridor.

When Tridia stood alone in the mists, she closed off the portal to the sun and shrank the one to the tunnel down to the size of a normal door. The aura shrank with it, holding her in and her friends out. Brenden sat up beside Drayden, a lost look on his face. The fear in Drayden's eyes turned toward hope and he struggled to come to her, but Brenden held him back.

Good. She needed a few moments to take care of a promise while she had enough conscious thought to do it.

"Davik?" Tridia had barely spoken the word when a shimmer of blue, gold, and silver rose from the chasm.

Davik's battle had drained his energy and diminished the light of his sparkling form. He floated toward Tridia, almost transparent. "They're all gone. There won't be any more this time."

"I promised to release you from this existence," Tridia said. "We both knew at the time that I intended to destroy your body. Would you return to it, if I could make you whole again?"

"For a chance to hold you with human arms, I'd gladly return to it," Davik said. "First, let me help you. You're exhausted. I can sense it through this shield."

"I'll be fine," Tridia replied. "If we don't do this now, I might not be able to try again for a while, and we need to leave here."

"Don't expend too much of yourself on this." Concern etched Davik's feature.

"I won't."

Tridia smiled tiredly and focused her thoughts. Energy shot from the portal and left the mine entrance. It blasted the doors of the command building and flung aside the few unfortunate soldiers who stood in the way. The lab doors blew apart beneath the irresistible force and the stasis capsule cracked open. Hoses and tubes severed and pulled away as healing blue energy enveloped Davik's inanimate body. All it needed was Davik's essence to come to life. Tridia held her consciousness together enough to speak.

"Your body's ready."

"I won't be long." Davik said.

His shimmer streaked from the tunnel. Tridia kept watch through the blue energy until Davik's consciousness united with his corporeal self. He would have run back into the mine, but she placed a thin shield of energy all around the lab. He raised his fist to beat against the unyielding shield.

No, Davik. Wait there for someone to retrieve you after the soldiers have been dealt with.

"What about you?" Davik shouted. "You need help!"

She didn't answer him and withdrew her presence, leaving behind enough energy to keep him contained until it was too late to interfere.

Drayden and Brenden concerned her more than anything at the moment. Brenden needed healing. The moment Rynoki's barrier disappeared, Brenden's mind became an open book. Two black voids clouded his thoughts. One of them was his own making, to hide his memories. The other was a feeder. She'd dazed the feeder in his body with the flash of power, and she'd planted false memories for it to react to, but the creature remained attached. With the feeder in a dormant state Brenden could function on his own, but it wouldn't stay dormant forever, and he'd be without whatever memories he'd hidden.

Blood rolled down Tridia's cheek from her eyes and her vision blurred. Despair rose from the mists like a predator and permeated her mind. How could she perform so delicate a removal without killing him?

"I don't have enough strength left."

"What are you saying?" Drayden would have run to the aura, but Brenden tightened his grip on the prince's arm. "We just helped you corner the Kel Anec so you could destroy yourself along with them? I played that disgusting game with you so you could leave me behind? Am I that distasteful to you?"

Tridia's heart broke at Drayden's anguish.

"No." Tears mingled with the blood sliding down her cheek. "You are good and noble. Everything a king should be. Handsome and desirable. But my mother took a terrible chance on the stability of my mind. Even now it's starting to unravel."

"Then come out and close the portal. Never open it again." Drayden struggled against Brenden's hold.

"I can't. I've absorbed too much energy. If I discharged it here, the resulting energy signature *would* awaken the armada and give them a beacon to follow for months. We won't catch them unaware again. There's no guarantee I'd be sane after the discharge. You'd be forever bonded to a madwoman who would use you and your children."

"She's addicted to the portal's power." Winniel's monotone voice cut through any objection Drayden might have made. "She wouldn't be able to resist opening a portal. The Sentinels wouldn't be able to stop her, neither could you."

The Sentinels climbed out of the chasm behind Brenden and Drayden, dripping water from their swim to reach the rope. Ofein stayed at the rim, but Winniel walked forward until she was only a few feet from the aura.

"We've contacted our clan, they're in near orbit. They agree the planet should be destroyed. We will deal with the Hierarchy."

"The uprising on Odea?" Tridia's head drooped forward and she jerked it upright. Just a few more answers and she could let go.

"Extinguished. Sentinels and Guardians identified and destroyed the alien-possessed soldiers around the planet some hours ago. The Guardians are in disarray. Their Controller's passing broke their cohesion while they were still on Odea. The Sentinel clans are enforcing a truce until someone with authority arrives to sort matters."

Tridia fought to hold onto her control a bit longer – she had to know. "Kanu and Aga, were the Sentinels able to purge the Kel Anec from those planets?"

"Yes. The cleansing was simultaneous to keep one faction from warning the other. If Ambassador Aren is correct, there are many more systems. Our war has just begun."

Tridia's mind wandered. She had to tell Winniel about something the Sentinels needed to know. It had been so critical, about one of the men she cared for. She frowned, then found a memory. "Davik is alive and well in the stasis chamber. You remember the instructions I gave you on the ship?"

Winniel inclined her head a fraction and moved closer to the aura.

Tridia held up her hand and bit her lip to keep from crying out. She looked down. Vines of mist wrapped her body up to her shoulders. Her mind wandered into the darkness. Voices floated through the air around her. She'd have followed them, but the sound of Drayden's voice brought her back.

"Stay, Tridia! Or take me with you! I can help you."

Drayden had ended up struggling in Winniel's grasp. His desperation tore at her heart. For a moment the sweet memory of the Chaos Vision's hopeful side touched her mind and she saw herself as his queen, laughing with their children many years in the future. Then the moment passed and the vision vanished. Her life force faded into the mist.

"Safe…for now." She forced the words from her lips. "No sacrifice. No…No sacrifice if there is another way. Back…back…"

She couldn't make him understand. Drayden's lips moved but his voice sounded far away and vague, indistinguishable from dozens of others echoing from the darkness. His frantic struggle to throw himself against the aura seemed to proceed in slow motion.

"Tridia." A voice in the darkness called her name. "Olana."

"Mother?" Tridia half-turned as she whispered the word. A force beyond the darkness compelled her to leave her friends behind.

Drayden slumped in Winniel's arms, then made one last desperate attempt to escape. He might have made it, had Ofein not caught his shoulders and held him back.

"Come, child, you torture our prince with your presence. Your training isn't complete."

"Yes." Tridia's thoughts melted into a dreamlike state. Her heart wrenched with a last look into Drayden's tear-filled eyes. Her numbed hands ached to reach out to him, hold him, and wipe away the tears, but she'd destroy him if she did. Instead, she steeled her mind for one final act of devotion. She withdrew her energy from the aura and let the portal close.

CHAPTER FIFTY-SEVEN

Drayden dropped to his knees. Tridia was gone. He stared blank-eyed into the empty tunnel as darkness filled his mind. She'd left him behind again. This time, he wouldn't let her go alone. He'd follow her into the void she'd chosen. He focused every thought and memory until a tiny portal opened in front of him. Pain gnawed at his body as the mist had gnawed at hers. Blue energy sheathed his skin, trying to repair damage that didn't exist. His consciousness raced to find her in the mist. He'd see through her eyes, or not at all. His body went limp in Ofein's grip. The tiny portal closed with a snap.

***

Brenden frowned at the scene before him, the Chesan prince glowing blue on the ground and the Sentinels trying to revive him. Drayden had raped and abused Tridia Odana, why now was he distraught at her passing? It made no sense.

You hid her from me! Rynoki's voice screamed into Brenden's mind and his body numbed. *It's gained you nothing. You've lost her as much as we have. Our original objective remains. We'll have access to the Chesan prince again through you.*

The voice laughed and Brenden shivered through his numbness. *The Chesan dogs wouldn't have protected this pup without leaving him subjects to rule. I will find them, too, and bring them to heel.*

Brenden tried to shake his head, but his body wouldn't respond. His energy and his will drained beyond his control. Fleeting glimpses of a dark presence taunted his memory and danced on the edge of recollection. Why couldn't he remember it? It had something to do with the Sentinels.

Don't despair, Ambassador. I'll restrain the creature until I'm ready for you

552

again. It will take only a little of your strength as it hibernates. I'll need time to rebuild the advance force and find the others. In the meantime, go about your affairs and forget our intrusion. Think that this girl freed you with her energy. The next time you won't have her to fight for you, and your many faces will hide my presence from anyone else who would.

Brenden regained control of his body with a start. His thoughts cleared and he turned to look across the chasm as he came to his knees. Only empty space lay in the direction of the tunnel entrance. Something should have been there. What was missing? What had happened? He sent tendrils of thought toward the chasm and the tunnel entrance. When had he dropped his mental barriers? He remembered nothing clearly from the time Rynoki entered the cargo hold on the ship. Rynoki, the white-haired man on the ship, what had happened to him? A white bolt of pain shot through his brain and he clamped down his mental barriers. Had something attacked him? He scanned the tunnel for the dark, amorphous shapes of the feeders. None appeared.

"We must leave this planet." Winniel's words drew his attention. He stood to face her. "We must destroy it. It was the Commander's last instruction."

"Get Drayden out of here." Brenden pointed toward the bridge that had snapped into place across the chasm. Why should he or the Sentinels care what his servant's last instruction had been? "Can you sense any other Kel Anec presence in this area?"

"No," Ofein said. "Davik Schie indicated these were all that remained on this planet."

"Then the faster we're away from here, the better."

"We'll alert the Sentinel crafts in orbit to send out alerts of gravitational shift when the planet is destroyed." Ofein, carrying Drayden on one shoulder, followed Winniel toward the entrance.

Brenden followed the trio across the bridge. Halfway across he looked down and strained to see anything rising from the chasm. Only darkness met his eyes.

"There are other Elstaar operatives at the mouth of the tunnel." Winniel's voice held no concern as she reported.

"You and Ofein secure the area. Make sure they don't activate the laser field. Give Drayden to me. We can't leave him alone in his state. Who knows what he'll do if he wakes up."

Ofein handed the unconscious Drayden over, then both Sentinels disappeared beyond the bend of the tunnel. Brenden hurried to get Drayden away from the chasm and himself away from the threat of feeders. The blue glow faded from the prince's skin the farther they moved from the chasm. Brenden pulled up his strongest barriers and prepared to use the energy block. It would take a few minutes to complete, but he'd feel safer behind it.

By the time he reached the entrance, the bodies of the remaining Elstaar littered the ground. Winniel's vengeance for Alanel's death wouldn't be sated unless she destroyed the entire Kel Anec race and all of their puppets. A chill ran up his spine at the thought. The female Sentinel appeared at his side as if from thin air, the breeze of her movement fanned his face before she stopped.

"The area is secure. Only Davik remains trapped behind Commander Odana's energy field. She instructed that we should take him with us."

"I'll go to him. We can put the prince on the bench in the security building until transport arrives."

"The Fighter Hawk in which you arrived is missing," Ofein said. "Some of the Elstaar may have escaped before the Commander finished in the mine."

"We'll have to count it as lost," Brenden said. "Tell your ships to be watchful and stop any Fighter Hawk they locate within the system, otherwise, let it go. Getting Drayden to safety is our first concern."

He and Winniel took Drayden into the control center and placed him on a cushioned bench in the lobby. Ofein made a quick tour of the building, then went out to scout the compound, leaving Winniel to keep watch over the prince.

Davik paced the stasis room as Brenden approached. Its door lay splintered on the floor and a transparent shield of energy shimmered across the blasted frame. Other than dripping with green liquid, Davik looked little worse for his imprisonment. He wore only a pair of loose fitting short pants, exposing the scars that laced his arms, legs, and torso – reminders of tubes, hoses, or other Hierarchy torture. He wiped at the liquid with a small cloth. The young man had a lot to come to grips with. Davik's slender frame stood taller than Brenden's as they faced each other through the shield.

"She's dead, isn't she?" Unshed tears darkened Davik's gray eyes. He ran a hand through his damp hair as he spoke. "The Sentinel wouldn't speak to me as he ran through, but I know Tridia is gone."

"Yes." Brenden didn't trust himself to utter more than the monosyllable response.

"She should have destroyed me, then. I thought she'd be here to help me with the transition back into flesh. I should have known. She wasn't well in the tunnel. If she would have let me help her." Davik chuffed and examined his hands, dropping the saturated cloth into the green puddle on the floor. "I wasn't afraid to try with her beside me. But my body is so much more confining than I expected. I'm not sure I can handle this alone. If I go back to the Hierarchy they'll turn me into that thing again. Which is worse?"

"You won't be alone, Lieutenant Schie. We won't turn you over to the Hierarchy and we won't abandon you. The Sentinels have orders from the Commander to take you with them. Once we destroy this planet the Hierarchy will write you off as dead and they'll never look for you again. No more experiments. We need to know everything you can tell us about the Kel Anec and their strategies."

Davik stared for a moment, then clenched his jaw before finding his tongue. "I recognize you from strategy class. Your pictures were in the texts. You're Master Brenden Aren. The Commander said – She said she was your property."

"Only when it suited her." Brenden gave a mirthless laugh. His dark and shallow memories showed Tridia as a headstrong young woman.

The energy field dissipated as they watched. When it disappeared altogether, Brenden extended his hand. "Come with us?"

Davik stared at Brenden's hand without grasping it. Emotions chased across his face. "I don't think I can stand to touch anyone right now, but I'll go with the Sentinels if that's what she wanted."

"She was explicit in the orders she gave to them." Brenden lowered his hand.

The golden Chesan ship settled onto the compound's main square in about the same place the Star Seeker had landed weeks before. Brenden greeted Lera with some surprise, then she introduced Mel and Xander as the three came down the ramp. They questioned him about Tridia and he gave them a condensed version of the events as he recalled them, leaving out the exact means of her death.

"She used that portal again, didn't she?" Lera asked.

"You know about the portal?" Brenden asked.

"Yes, sir. We traveled through it," the girl answered.

"Not that we'd ever want to do it again," Xander commented.

"Perhaps you'd better tell me what you know. Commander Odana never had the chance to fill me in." Brenden couldn't sense their thoughts through his barriers, but he needed to know how much Tridia had revealed to them.

"Is Prince Drayden here, sir?" Lera asked. "Commander Odana came to free him or to destroy him. So, is he here?" Lera's voice broke at the end.

Brenden fought the urge to dress the three of them down for not responding, but he was in no position to argue under the circumstances. His fragmented memory revealed that Lera's devotion to Commander Odana would supersede even a direct order from him. The obvious sorrow the three of them showed over the Commander's death sparked curiosity in him that softened his intended response. He'd get the information from them later in his own way.

"Prince Drayden is safe, but not well. Commander Odana's death affected him deeply."

Mel spoke up. "As Lera said, we're medics, sir. Well, Lera is still an Apprentice, but we should take the prince onto the ship immediately."

Brenden agreed and led them to the security building where Winniel, and now Davik, stood guard over Drayden's unconscious form. The medics' shock at seeing Davik, looking so much like Drayden, only wore off when Winniel introduced him as Tridia's friend from the Hierarchy. Davik helped Xander carry Drayden aboard the ship using the bench as a stretcher. Lera walked with them.

"Sir," Mel addressed Brenden with a frown as the others ascended the ramp. "Commander Odana gave us direct orders to not remain on the ground more than ten standard minutes."

"Then we'd better launch, hadn't we?"

"Yes, sir. But where do we go?"

"Hulac. Set a course for the planet Hulac."

Mel trotted up the ramp to prepare the ship for take-off. Before Brenden could follow, Ofein appeared at his elbow.

"Ambassador, Winniel and I will go with Prince Drayden and Davik Schie. The death of the Controller left the Guardian operatives unresponsive on Odea and they need someone to deal with the logistics. The Supreme Commander also appears affected. You've been requested to return to that planet to handle negotiations. A Sentinel ship will take you."

"Very well." Brenden's energy block snapped into place and Ofein stared.

"You're in no danger of feeders," the Sentinel said. "There's no need for such precautions."

"Please forgive my paranoia while I'm on this planet," Brenden said. "I'll be more at ease once I reach Odea."

Ofein nodded.

"Lieutenant Schie could do with your help. He's not very stable."

"We'll fulfill our obligations regarding Lieutenant Schie and Drayden Anjenay." Ofein tilted his head and scrutinized Brenden as he spoke. "Winniel shouldn't reach into other minds. Alanel's death, and now Commander Odana's, has had a grave impact on her."

"Be his counselors for now and watch over him on Hulac," Brenden said. "I'll join you when I can. Any word from your ships about the Fighter Hawk?"

Ofein's eyes became distant for a moment then focused on Brenden's face. "Our Clan destroyed the ship when it wouldn't halt, but the pilots say they detected no sentient thoughts or life forms aboard it."

"The crew could have been wearing that black armor. It's difficult to penetrate," Brenden said. "Please have your Clan continue to scan the planet. Regardless of what Lieutenant Schie reported, we can't take the chance any of the Kel Anec remain. If there are stragglers and they contact the armada, we'll be in this mess all over again."

"The Hariok Clan will see that it's done," Ofein said. He and Winniel hurried up the ramp.

Brenden got clear of the golden ship as it lifted into the air. He stood alone in the stillness. The laser cannons remained motionless, not even a breeze stirred the air. He turned to study the compound within the fenced-in area. No shadow moved. With his energy blocked, feeders couldn't attack him, but neither could he sense anything else that might. Instinct hammered a danger signal with no evidence to support it. Was he just being paranoid because of the sudden death of a girl he'd mistreated? A girl who'd saved his life and quite possibly the galaxy. A girl who everyone else had loved or respected. If she commanded such emotions in others, why were his memories of her so shallow? Brenden shook his head. He had an insurmountable task ahead of him to get the Guardians and Sentinels off Odea without a war breaking out. He couldn't afford to be looking over his shoulder for an invisible bogeyman. He needed to finish the job and get to Hulac to oversee Prince Drayden's care and settle Davik into a new life. Robel would fill in until he got there, and the Sentinels were more than capable of protecting everyone for the time being, but something unsettling niggled at Brenden's brain. Where was Mr. Tang when he needed him? He'd have to contact his embassy as soon as he had access to communications to get caught up on events.

A black Sentinel ship settled at the far end of the compound. Brenden made his way to it, every step dogged by a feeling of unease and the certainty that something had gone very wrong on Cystia.

EPILOGUE

The medical ship *Healer* circled the farthest solar system in its established route through the free territory and headed back toward Alliance space. Dr. Elenus stared into the monitor displaying Tridia Odana's DNA in proximity to that of a human. The chromosomes of the young assassin attacked the human helix and changed it, turning it into a replica of itself – except for personal characteristics such as gender, hair color, and eye color. The Felinus doctor had never seen anything like it. She used injections of Felinus DNA on rare occasions to promote healing. Even those transmutations had not been so aggressive or complete. They wore themselves out with time as the body repaired itself or with a rush of adrenaline through the system, but every humanoid sample she had tested with Tridia's DNA had remained stable after the change, no matter how much adrenaline she exposed it to afterward. Only the fact that the mutated human DNA did not cause similar mutations in subsequent exposure to normal humanoid genes kept the doctor from being truly terrified.

She had to contact Tridia to warn her of the dangers she carried in her DNA. An entirely new Chesan race could be built with simple injections made from the girl's blood. A race of people with all of the Chesan abilities and none of the Chesan training or morality could ravage and control the galaxy – or go insane from the sudden transition to telepathic powers. She could accept neither option. A quiet growl rumbled in her chest. She'd sent three vials of Tridia's DNA with the girl to stabilize her body. If Tridia hadn't used them, they needed to be secured, preferably destroyed.

***

Winniel sat in the pilot's seat of the Chesan ship. Lera Cal sat with the unconscious Prince Drayden, the other medics slept soundly in one of the spare cabins, and Davik sat alone in the lounge, his thoughts unsettled. All members of the crew accounted for. Ofein's hand rested on Winniel's shoulder as they waited for the connection to the Core Alliance Triad to complete.

A small screen displayed the empty chairs of the Public Hearing room. The Triad members filed in and took their places.

"You have a report for us, Truthsayer?" Judge Ericol asked.

"We do," Winniel said. "Commander Tridia Odana, formerly of the Odean Hierarchy, did not commit the crimes she denied. Nor did she merit punishment for any act against the Sentinels. Her amnesty record should be complete and without condition."

"It's good to hear we made the right decision," Bertol said.

Winniel's face remained impassive. Bertol had been anxious to condemn Tridia at her hearing.

"Will you return to Aga now?" Judge Conna asked.

"No," Winniel replied. "My mate and I have other duties that will keep us from Aga for some time."

"The Sentinel compounds remain empty," Ericol said. "We've mustered the military to protect the planet in your prolonged absence."

"A wise decision," Winniel said. "With the Guardians incapacitated and the Sentinels otherwise occupied, Aga is in a vulnerable position. Enough members of each clan remain on the planet to cleanse the government of hostile control, but there are not enough to protect the entire planet from invasion."

"We'll make sure the word is spread throughout the Core Alliance." Ericol frowned.

"Is Commander Odana available?" Conna asked.

"I'm afraid Commander Odana was a casualty in our confrontation with the Kel Anec advance force on Cystia," Winniel replied. "Her efforts alone gave us the victory."

"I'm sorry," Conna said. "We owe her an apology and a great debt."

Winniel gave a curt nod. "Ofein and I will not contact you again unless a situation arises that demands it. And you will not be able to contact us. This is our last communication."

Winniel cut the connection before Bertol could make a speech. She caressed a small vial in her hand.

"Will you use it?" Ofein asked.

Winniel smiled up at him. "That remains to be seen. Our instructions don't end with caring for these two Chesan males."

"The person giving us those instructions hasn't made an appearance in years. Are you sure they're still valid? We no longer sense the Commander through our connection."

"Arenel had no doubt," Winniel said. "Commander Odana never saw the rest of the visions her mother left. We were assured that she would see all of them if this timestream is to remain intact. If the Commander is alive, she can't open the vault in her mind without our assistance. But if she's dead…

Winniel caressed the vial again before returning it to her pocket, then brushed her fingers over the leather bracelet on her wrist.

Ofein squeezed her shoulder. "Then it would seem we haven't seen the last of her – one way or another."